1993 Guide to Literary Agents
& Art/Photo Reps

1 9 9 3

Guide to

Literary

Agents &

Art/Photo

Reps

Edited by Roseann Shaughnessy

Writer's
Digest
Books

Cincinnati, Ohio

Distributed in Canada by McGraw-Hill,
300 Water Street,
Whitby Ontario L1N 9B6.
Distributed in Australia by Kirby Books, Private
Bag No. 19, P.O. Alexandria NSW2015.
Distributed in New Zealand by David Bateman
Ltd. P.O. Box 100-242 North Shore Mail Centre
Auckland 10 New Zealand.

Managing Editor, Market Books Department:
Constance J. Achabal; Supervisory Editor: Mark
Garvey

International Standard Serial Number
ISSN 1055-6087
International Standard Book Number
0-89879-558-3

Cover illustration by David Tillinghast

Contents

Art/Photo Reps

Resources

Indexes

From the Editor

Welcome to the 1993 *Guide to Literary Agents & Art/Photo Reps*. This, our second edition, provides writers, artists and photographers seeking representation with a wealth of new and updated information. Whether you are looking for an agent or rep for the first time, or are looking to make a change from your existing one, the *Guide* will help you make an informed decision.

Specifically, we have included several comprehensive articles on career strategies, contract negotiation, and the increasing importance of the role of agents from the perspectives of both editors and agents. We have also updated listings from the first edition, and incorporated new ones to provide you with more possibilities for representation.

Literary agents

As mentioned in the first edition of the *Guide*, the literary agent is often the stable force in a writer's career. With the pervasive flux of the publishing industry, and with writers frequently orphaned after corporate mergers, restructurings, and shutdowns, an agent can serve as a writer's most important ally. Pat Matson Knapp explores this issue in her article, Why Work with an Agent?

And while agents can act as professional buffers for writers, it is essential that writers arm themselves with as much knowledge of the publishing industry as possible. They should understand the basic principles of copyright and contract negotiation before they sign on with a publisher. For this reason, we have included Understanding Rights, by agent B.J. Doyen and Negotiating a Sale, by agent Malaga Baldi. You will also find articles by agents Ethan Ellenberg and Eileen Fallon discussing specific strategies used by their clients to build successful writing careers.

Art/photo reps

Unlike new writers looking for literary agents, those who seek representation in the areas of fine or commercial art or photography are usually established in their fields. They seek representation to help them expand their client lists and handle paperwork. For more information on working with reps, see Finding and Working with Art and Photo Reps, by rep Barbara Gordon.

We have attempted to include as much information as possible on the promotional materials you will need before approaching a rep. And in the listings we've given the specifics on the types of advertising and promotional material preferred by each of the reps listed.

In addition . . .

The *Guide* features two additional sections: Script Agents and Fine Art Reps. Screenwriter and editor of *Hollywood Scriptwriter*, Kerry Cox wrote Finding and Working with a Script Agent to lead off the section of agents who are primarily interested in handling scripts. The Fine Arts Section is provided for artists seeking assistance in finding galleries and other outlets for their work.

Much of the other material in this book comes as a result of our experience with publishing other annual directories. For example, we've found category indexes to be most helpful in identifying appropriate listings for our readers with specific needs. The Literary Agents and Script Agents sections are indexed by fiction and nonfiction subjects, while the Art/Photo Reps and Fine Art Reps sections are indexed geographically by state. Many of the agents and reps listed are also interested in handling work in other categories and these are cross-referenced in the Additional list at the end of each section. Listings are ranked by levels of openness to submissions and there is a Glossary and a list of resources helpful to writers, illustrators and photographers.

We are pleased with the number of new and existing listings and the quality of information in this second edition. We will continue to update, augment and improve this information with each edition. Your suggestions, comments and concerns are appreciated and carefully considered as we develop each new edition of the *Guide to Literary Agents & Art/Photo Reps*. I invite you to keep me apprised of what information you need and what questions you'd like answered. I look forward to hearing from you and wish you the best of luck as you seek representation for your work.

Roseann Shaughnessy

How to Use Your Guide to Literary Agents & Art/Photo Reps

Your goal as a writer or artist seeking representation is to find the agent or rep most suited to selling the type of material you produce. Individual agents and reps are as unique as individual writers and artists. Each generally works within specific genres and/or subject areas; each has a particular level of experience and expertise; each is seeking a client with similar aspirations and objectives. The *Guide* is designed to provide you with the information you will need in locating the most appropriate agent or rep for your work. By carefully reading the upfront articles and researching the markets, you can target representation and move toward achieving your goals.

Where to begin?

The book is divided into two areas: feature articles and listings. The articles provide you with various perspectives on the author/agent and artist/rep relationship, as well as information on contract negotiation, copyright and other business information. The listings serve as profiles of individual agencies seeking new clients, including their specific needs and policies.

The listings are grouped into chapters corresponding to specific types of agents and reps. Each chapter begins with an introduction on how to approach that type of agent, followed by an explanation of the ranking system we use to designate each agency's openness to submissions.

Literary and script agents

Perhaps the most important question to consider before beginning your search for an agent is, "Am I willing to pay a fee to have my work considered by an agent?"

Fee-charging agents charge a fee to writers for various services (e.g., reading, critiquing, editing, evaluation, consultation, marketing, etc.), in addition to a commission on sales. Since they are being compensated for additional services, they are generally more receptive to handling the work of new writers. However, reading and other fees can be extremely high, and payment of them rarely ensures that an agent will agree to take you on as a client. Your best bet is to to develop your novel, nonfiction book or script to the point at which it is salable enough to attract a nonfee-charging agent. If you do choose to approach a fee-charging agent, be sure to research the agency carefully, requesting references and sample critiques.

Nonfee-charging agents earn income from commissions made on the sale of manuscripts. Their focus is selling books, and they do not edit manuscripts or promote books that have already been published. Nonfee-charging agents tend to be highly selective, and prefer to work with established writers and experts in specific fields. While most will accept queries from new writers, many are not looking for new clients. Be sure to check the listing carefully to determine an agent's current needs.

Having made the decision to go with either a fee- or nonfee-charging agent, you can refer directly to the appropriate listing section. While both nonfee and fee-charging script agents are grouped in one section, listings for fee-charging script agents are clearly indicated with an open box (□)symbol.

We have included a number of special indexes in the back of the book to expedite your search. The Subject Index is divided into sections for nonfee-charging and fee-charging literary agents and script agents. Each section in the index is then divided by nonfiction and fiction subject categories. Because certain agencies did not want to restrict themselves to specific subjects, we have listed them in the subject heading "open" in both nonfiction and fiction.

Art/photo reps

Commercial art and photography and fine art reps can be located in the Art/Photo Reps section of the book. Reps handle various types of visual art, including photography, illustration, graphic design and fine art. Most do not charge additional expenses beyond those incurred preparing your portfolio. Some require payment for special portfolios or advertising materials. A few charge monthly retainers to cover marketing expenses. We have designated these listings with a filled-in box (■) symbol.

Reps have been indexed geographically by state and province in the back of the book. There is also an Agents and Reps Index to help you locate individual reps who may be employed by large agencies.

Targeting agents and reps

You've identified the type of agent or rep you wish to submit work to. The next step is to research within each section to find the individual agencies that will be most interested in your work.

First check the number code after each listing to determine how receptive the agency is to receiving submissions. Most users of the *Guide to Literary Agents & Art/Photo Reps* should check three items within the listing: types of work the agency handles; agency's terms, including commission and contract information; and preferred method of submission, found under "Will Handle" for agents and "How to Contact" for reps.

Your writing or art will not be appropriate for submission to all agencies. As mentioned earlier, most agents and reps have very specific interests and needs, and are not likely to consider submissions outside of their realm. Consider only those agents whose interests correspond with your type of work. Then study the terms of those agencies to determine whether their commission and contract policies (if applicable) are acceptable to you. Recent sales information can also be helpful to you, as it clues you in to the quality of work and caliber of clients the agent deals with.

When you are confident that you have targeted the best agent or rep for your work, submit it according to the procedures outlined in the listing. For more specific information on approaching agents and reps, see Finding and Working with Literary Agents, Finding and Working with Script Agents and Finding and Working with Art/Photo Reps at the start of each respective section.

Taking Stock: Are You Ready for an Agent?

by Rod Pennington

The most frequently asked question whenever writers gather is, "Do you have an agent?" The better question might be, "Are you ready for an agent and do you really need one?" Many aspiring writers make the mistake of looking for an agent before they have anything to sell. Agents are brokers and their commodity is the written word. Unless you are an established writer with a track record of producing marketable books or scripts, you will need to have a completed project in hand before you will get the attention of an agent.

Agents are not super humans who will solve all of a writer's problems with one phone call to the right editor. In fact, an agent cannot sell anything you couldn't sell yourself if you were willing to do the leg work. Agents will look after your interests and usually squeeze enough extra out of a publisher so that they more than earn their fee. However, the best agent in the world cannot sell a badly flawed manuscript.

What agents will handle

Few agents handle poetry or short stories so if those are your markets then you probably don't need, nor could you find, representation. Category fiction, such as romance novels, westerns, science fiction and so on, is fairly open to newcomers. The rates of compensation do not vary much in category fiction for beginning writers and an agent, while able to open a few doors and move your manuscript to the top of the stack, probably isn't going to get you a better deal than you could get for yourself. Nonfiction is usually written by an expert in a field who is known to agents and publishers before he even begins writing. This type of writer is often approached directly by publishers and has little trouble finding representation if the project is large enough. Celebrities and their "close personal friends" have little trouble finding someone to represent them. If you are the disgruntled ex-mistress of a New York crime boss who wants to tell all, the agents will find you.

So, what is left? Novels and screenplays. Most book publishers are located in New York and most screenplays are sold in Hollywood. It would logically follow that if you have a literary work you will want a New York agent and if you are trying to sell a screenplay you will want a California agent. New York agents can sell screenplays and California agents can sell books and many bigger agencies have offices on both coasts. In the age of fax machines and overnight mail, however, an agent does not have to live near either of the major markets. But, since this agent is out of the "loop" of day-to-day activity, they will have to be well-connected or deal with a specialized market to be effective.

It is not the job of an agent to fix plot problems, correct the spelling or tie up your dangling participles.

*Author of five novels and more than 300 articles and short stories, **Rod Pennington** has a screenplay in production. He is a Writer's Digest School instructor and teaches writing in adult education classes. He originally developed his Agent Acquisition Checklist for use in the classroom.*

Before approaching an agent

Your work must be professional and polished and you must have the right attitude toward a career in writing before you embark on the task of securing an agent. Answering the questions on page 7 will help you determine where you stand on these matters.

First, your work must be in the proper format; *The Writer's Digest Guide to Manuscript Formats*, by Dian Dincin Buchman and Seli Groves, is a good place to look and there are many other excellent books on the subject. A manuscript or script which is not in the proper format will wave a red flag to an editor that he is not dealing with a "pro." The copy which you present for review must be clean with dark type. Don't cost yourself a contract because you were too lazy to change a typewriter ribbon. If you use a computer, avoid dot matrix printers, use a letter quality printer. Do not use justified margins, the added spacing can lead to typesetting errors and can be annoying to read.

Before you approach an agent, you must be confident that you are writing at a professional, marketable level. Do your homework. Read what's being published or produced in your field. Be honest with yourself: Is your work as good as or better than what's currently on the market?

Writing can be a brutal career path. Editors make decisions based on what they feel their readers will want to read and occasionally reject otherwise excellent projects simply because they are not what they currently need. Are you mentally prepared to accept the inevitable rejections and understand that a rejection is a professional decision and not a personal rebuff?

Do you have the self-confidence to compete with other experienced writers? Do you know in your heart that this is the best possible writing which you are capable of producing at this time?

Selecting an agent

Perhaps the most important thing you will ever write is the query letter you use to solicit an agent. The only thing an agent will have to judge you by is your query. In about 500 words you must sell your project and, more importantly, yourself. Your query must be professional and compelling if you want to tickle the fancy of a top agent. Don't exaggerate or make false claims such as, "a sure best seller" or "I'm the next Tom Clancy." False bravado will make the eyes of most agents glaze over. In crisp, concise language explain your project, give a brief description of your skills and experiences, and ALWAYS enclose a self-addressed, stamped envelope.

The selection of the right agent can be tricky. The more you know about a potential agent the greater the likelihood there will be a fruitful relationship. If you are writing a novel, is the agent you plan to query a member of the Association of Authors' Representatives (AAR)? If you plan to sell more than one screenplay, your agent must have signed the Writers Guild of America Artists Managers' Basic Agreement. All of these organizations provide lists of agents who have agreed to abide by the groups' codes of ethics and standards. See Resources for contact information for AAR and the Writers Guild.

Agents are frequent speakers at writers' conferences and this offers an excellent opportunity to meet them face-to-face and see if there is a possible match. If you "network" with other writers you often can get an introduction to an agent. An excellent source of agent referrals is from editors whom you respect; they will refer you to someone they are comfortable working with.

Agent Acquisition Checklist

My Manuscript or Screenplay

Answer the following questions: Yes (Y), No (N), Uncertain (U)

☐ I have a completed manuscript or screenplay.

☐ I am writing at a professional level.

☐ I have the self-confidence in my work to compete with other experienced writers.

☐ I realize that rejection letters are inevitable but I am prepared to accept them and continue writing.

If you answered all of these questions "YES," then proceed to the next section. If you answered any of these questions "No" or "Uncertain" then go back to working on your manuscript or screenplay. You are not ready for an agent.

Manuscript or Screenplay Checklist

☐ My manuscript or screenplay is in the proper format.

☐ ALL spelling, typographical and grammatical errors have been corrected.

☐ This is the best possible writing I am capable of producing at this time.

My Plan of Action

☐ I have prepared a professional quality query letter to send to prospective agents.

☐ I have prepared a list of potential agents who are experienced in my area of interest.

☐ I know if my prospective agent charges a reading fee.

☐ I am aware of my prospective agent's commission structure.

Choosing the Right Agent

☐ After an agent has expressed a willingness to represent me, we will discuss my career goals before any contracts are signed.

© 1991 Rod Pennington

Know what you want

What type of relationship are you looking for from your agent? Are you an able business person who is good at sales and likes to have control over every phase of your work? Do you only need an agent to be sure that you are getting the best possible deal? Do you want to turn the entire business side of your career over to your agent so that you can get back to your writing? Do you want your agent to just be the middle-man and not comment on your work or do you want a nurturing sounding board? Or, are you somewhere in between?

Before you sign on with an agent you should discuss your career goals and needs. It is not necessary to jump into a relationship with the first agent who bats his eyes in your direction. Ask a few questions first!

Has the agent successfully represented a project in your field of interest? What is the agent's commission structure? Does the agent charge a reading fee? What items will be charged to you—photocopies, long distance phone calls, courier serivces, etc.—and what will be paid by the agent?

Is the agent sensitive to your needs? Is the agent interested in your writing goals for the next year, five years, 20 years? Will the agent help you in planning your "next move?"

Working with an agent is like a marriage; some last a lifetime, some end in an ugly divorce. If you approach the relationship with a professional attitude you will increase your chances for success.

Why Work with an Agent?

by Pat Matson Knapp

Not long ago, the editor was a writer's best friend — his talent scout, guidance counselor, mentor and champion. Discovering and nurturing new talent was an important editorial role, and the editor was perhaps the single most powerful influence in a writer's career. But the growth and consolidation of the publishing industry in recent years have resulted in some dramatic changes, not the least of which has been major streamlining of editorial staffs.

The bottom line for aspiring writers? There are fewer front-line editors to review an increasing number of manuscripts. After mergers, takeovers and wholesale reorganization of some publishing houses, those editors who still have jobs are often overworked, juggling editorial responsibilities with sales, marketing and administrative duties. In short, they no longer have the time to scout and develop new writing talent.

At the same time, the competition to publish is at an all-time high. According to statistics in the 1992 edition of Bowker's *Annual Library and Book Trade Almanac*, an estimated 45,829 titles were published in the United States in 1991. But even more astonishing, those in the publishing industry project that for every book published, 100 go unpublished. Many of these are relegated to the bottom of slush piles, waiting for the one-in-thousand chance that an editor will read them and recognize their potential.

Where does this leave the legions of writers trying to find publishers for their manuscripts? In the hands of literary agents, whose numbers have swelled to more than 1,000 in the U.S. and Canada and whose clout in the industry has increased dramatically in the past two decades. In fact, the number of agents in the U.S. and Canada has increased by more than 20 percent in just the past three years.

Editors on the front lines of the publishing industry agree that writers trying to break into book publishing will find it more difficult to succeed without the representation of a literary agent. The reasons? First, because of heavy workloads, editors rely on agents to "make the first cut" in evaluating new work. Second, the financial dynamics of the industry demand that writers have an advocate to protect their financial and career interests. Finally, the volatility of the industry, with editors frequently changing jobs and leaving unpublished books in the works, requires a thread of continuity that only agents can provide.

The role of an agent

Literary agents have taken on many of the roles traditionally filled by editors. Agents often serve as their clients' editors, marketers, business representatives and career managers. As editors, they may evaluate and refine manuscripts to make them more attractive to potential publishers. They also often help authors brainstorm and develop book ideas. As marketers, their first and most obvious role is to find the best publisher for their client. Once this has been achieved, they are often actively involved in publicity and advertising to promote the book. As business representatives, they not only negotiate lucrative ad-

Pat Matson Knapp is a Cincinnati-based journalist and writer and frequent contributor to HOW and The Artist's Magazine.

vances and other contract terms for first serial rights, they also look after writers' best interests in the sale of foreign and subsidiary rights. They also serve as administrators of the publishing contract, monitoring the payment of advances and royalties and serving as administrative watchdogs for their clients.

Unlocking the doors

Perhaps the best reason for a writer to obtain representation for his or her work is that the doors of many publishing houses are no longer open to unagented writers. Many publishers have policies against accepting unsolicited manuscripts, warning that over-the transom submissions will either be discarded or returned unopened. While publishers don't often follow through on this threat, the odds of being published out of the "slush pile" are low.

"They're almost nil, frankly," according to Rick Kot, associate editor-in-chief at Harper-Collins. "There's always a story every few years of one that gets accepted, but it's very rare." Kot says that, although HarperCollins has a policy against accepting unsolicited manuscripts, everything gets read—eventually. But almost 100 percent of the approximately 400 titles published by the house each year are agented.

"I have published from the slush pile," says Doug Stumpf, executive editor for Villard Books (Random House), "but not often. We strongly discourage unagented material." At Villard, as at many other publishing houses, the slush pile is the venue of assistant editors.

Stumpf says that while agents have an obvious incentive to sell a manuscript for their clients, they are also objective. Good agents will rarely submit low quality manuscripts to editors, because doing so would damage their credibility. "It's easier to deal with someone who is a little objective," notes Stumpf. He says he still occasionally receives telephone calls from aspiring writers who want to talk at length about their manuscripts. "It would be really nice if I had time to talk to them," explains Stumpf, "but to be honest, I don't, and the phone calls (from writers) can be a pain. Agents are more professional than that. They know better."

Lee Goerner, publisher at Atheneum, an imprint of Macmillan, tells of a rare success story for an unagented writer. A few years ago, Atheneum received a letter from a Missouri woman who wrote that she was a book editor for a national news service, was aware that Atheneum liked to publish books about women as well as biographies, and wondered if they would be interested in her biography of Olivia Langdon Clemens (Mrs. Mark Twain). "Well, we were interested, and we just published it," says Goerner.

But, he admits, "that's certainly not typical." Atheneum receives 10,000 submissions each year, and while almost all are read, they are first shuffled through the system. The few writers who do get published without representation are those who, according to HarperCollins' Kot, know the business and have done their homework; they know only to query those publishers whose interests are similar to their manuscript. Successful unagented writers, he adds, usually have established track records as freelance writers. Goerner's Missouri author is a rare case in point.

If a submission comes from an agent, on the other hand, it receives more immediate attention. "If the manuscript comes with a recommendation from an agent, it's more like a passkey for the writer," Atheneum's Goerner notes. "We know that the quality of books coming from agents is going to be much higher."

"Filtering" agents

In the wake of publishing mergers, acquisitions, reorganizations and subsequent editorial streamlining, agents have assumed a more significant role in reading and evaluating the work of new writers. Unable to keep up with the tide of manuscripts flowing into their offices, many editors rely on recommendations from trusted agents as near-guarantees of quality.

"Editors are so overwhelmed with the amount of work they have to do, they count on agents to do a cut in terms of the quality of the material coming in," says Stumpf of Villard Books. "If a manuscript comes from an agent we've worked with and know . . . we know it's of at least a certain minimal level of quality. Agents also know editors, and they know what we like."

"It's pretty simple," says Goerner. "Agents are part of a refining process. By the time a manuscript has gone through an agent, I know the quality must be pretty good, especially if I know the agent and have worked with him or her before. Agents have an idea of what my tastes are. The bottom line is I don't have to read everything the agent reads."

Kot (HarperCollins) adds, "If you receive something from an agent you have the sense that it has been prejudged to some degree, and if you trust the agent's taste you know that it's already past the first step in the process."

The business side

An obvious advantage of having representation is agents' inside knowledge of the publishing industry and their ability to find a publisher, then negotiate the most beneficial contracts for their clients. Many agents are former editors or publishing house executives, and have years of experience in the industry, not to mention valuable contacts and daily communication with the people who could publish their clients' manuscripts. Many are also skilled in marketing and promotion. Basically, agents hold down the business fort, allowing their clients to concentrate on what they do best: write.

A skilled agent recognizes a marketable manuscript, refines it if necessary to make it more salable, then approaches the editor or editors whom, through experience, he knows will be most interested in it, according to Kot (HarperCollins). Because agents know the publishing industry, they can determine which publishing house and editor are right for the writer. Matching the manuscript to an individual editor's taste is key to the process, and the agent's credibility with editors is critical, he adds. "If you have a good relationship with the agent and you like the agent's taste and the agent knows your taste, of course you'll pay more attention to something he or she sends in."

The money side of publishing, adds Kot, is one of the primary reasons for literary agents' prominence, because writers rely on them to negotiate the best contracts. "There were always powerful agents in this business, but now that money has become the outstanding issue, writers want agents to look after their best interests. Obviously, agents know best how to market books to the publishers through auctions or whatever," he notes. In the past several years agents have wrangled record-high advances from publishers, not only for proven authors, but for first-time writers perceived to be highly marketable. "Basically agents are business people, and most writers aren't," says Villard's Doug Stumpf. "They can get the writer more money up front and negotiate the contract to benefit the writer in other ways."

But an agent's job is not over once the deal has been made. Kot (HarperCollins) says that, while he never hears from some agents after the contract has been signed, the best agents continue to watch out for their clients' interests throughout the life of the contract, monitoring the payment of advances and royalties and ensuring that the letter of the contract is carried out. "A good agents will always stay on the case with an author and an editor to make sure everything is being done and that a publishing house is doing what it has promised," he says. "The best agents will not only get good first serial sales, they'll work on the movie part of it and also keep editors on their toes. Ideally, the agent and the editor should work hand in hand."

The agent as ally

Perhaps most important, agents are a valuable ally and a constant guiding force for writers in an industry fraught by high turnover in the editorial ranks. Today, it is rare for an editor to stay with one publishing house for his or her entire career. When editors leave a firm, they also leave projects midway in the publication process and unpublished books (and their authors) without an inhouse contact. With so many editors switching from one publishing house to another, it is not uncommon for a book to be handled by several different editors during the course of its publication.

In this unstable environment, agents are their clients' ballast and anchors, says Kot, guiding them through virtually every step of the publishing process and protecting their interests throughout. "Agents have essentially become the only constant in a writer's career," he notes.

Is an agent for everyone?

Writers who concentrate on magazine articles, short stories or poetry will have a difficult time finding an agent to represent their work. Major magazines generally solicit their own pieces, and work for regional and "little" magazines is best submitted to editors directly. Short stories and poetry can be submitted directly to literary journals; book publishers will generally consider publishing poetry and short story collections from only the most renowned authors. Commissions from the sale of magazine articles, short stories, inspirational pieces, or poetry would most likely be so low that the agent would have little incentive to sell them.

For writers whose goal is to publish books, however, finding literary representation is often considered advisable. "It's much more the rule than the exception for people now to have agents," says Kot (HarperCollins). The exceptions, he says, are writers who live in New York and can potentially have regular contact with publishers, and writers with experience in representing their own work. Successful unagented writers, he says, "have tended to be fairly established in the magazine business and essentially know their way around how publishing works."

For beginning writers of category or "genre" fiction, such as romance novels, science fiction and westerns, an agent can be helpful in getting the attention of a publisher, but will probably have less latitude in negotiating compensation, say editors. Children's books, historically a less popular form for agents, are becoming more attractive as publishers pay increasingly higher advances for them. Juvenile and young adult literature is a growing field and has also become more popular with agents in recent years.

While they emphasize the importance of agents to a book author's success, editors also advise writers to begin establishing their careers long before obtaining representation. Developing a reputation as a magazine or newspaper writer is an excellent way to gain experience and publishing contacts. Writers with a body of published magazine and/or newspaper work will be in a better position to approach agents and, ultimately, publishers.

"When a writer approaches the point that he or she wants to publish a book, an agent can only help," says Stumpf (Villard). "The bottom line is that we're (editors) just harder to get to now. It helps to have someone who knows the business and knows what editors are looking for."

When Should You Put Yourself in an Agent's Hands?

by Dean R. Koontz

The incomparable Frank Sinatra once said, "Hell hath no fury like a hustler with a literary agent." Elitist intellectuals may grimace and inquire why I would quote a saloon crooner in matters literary. Well, in addition to being the greatest singer of pop songs this country has ever produced, Francis Albert Sinatra is street-smart, profoundly so, and street-smart is something every writer must be if he is to survive on publishers' turf. As regards literary agents, I could offer a quote from Alfred A. Knopf, the famous and prestigious publisher, in place of that crooner's wisecrack. "Trust your publishers," Knopf said, "and he can't fail to treat you generously." Now, if you have any street smarts whatsoever, you will have no difficulty determining which of those two quotations contains the most truth and wisdom.

Marvin Josephson, the agent, said, "The relationship of an agent to a publisher is that of a knife to a throat." Josephson might have overstated the case a bit, but if Sinatra had to choose a companion to accompany him on a long walk through a bad neighborhood at night, I have no doubt that he would prefer Josephson to Knopf.

I have had several knives protecting my interests during my career. I have been with my current knife for nine years, and I expect the association to last much longer, in part because this blade is sharper than the others that were previously brandished in my behalf.

I did not, however, begin my career with a knife. Unassisted, I sold three novels. Although an agent is eventually of great value if one is going to have a well-managed career, I recommend that every writer start by marketing himself, for he will learn invaluable lessons about the depth of the publishing river, the coldness of the water, and the treachery of the currents, by wading in alone.

When I have spoken at writers conferences, I have been dismayed by how many new writers are *obsessed* with getting an agent. Often, they are frantic to line up representation even though they have not yet finished a book. From their point of view, a literary agent is a sorcerer, someone who has the magic, the proper spells, and who never fails to place what he markets, regardless of its quality. This is, of course, not true. An agent can only sell what is publishable, and if the agent can sell it, so can the writer. Agents perform many invaluable functions and can be the writer's shield against the world, making it possible for him to produce more and better books. But agents cannot work magic, and it is a serious mistake for new writers to expend as much energy searching for representation as they expend creating their books.

Knife guys

New writers frequently operate under the misapprehension that putting a Dudley Moore suit on Orson Welles is easier than an unagented writer selling a book. On the contrary: Though some houses do not accept unsolicited manuscripts, most do, even though the economics of reading over-the-transom material is crazy. If one in five hundred unsolic-

Dean R. Koontz *is a bestselling author of suspense novels, including* Hideaway, Cold Fire, The Bad Place, *and* Midnight *(all Putnam).* Dragon Tears *was published by Putnam in January 1993.*

ited books is publishable, bleary-eyed first readers are jubilant, and their employers continue to consider them worth their paychecks. No self-respecting efficiency expert would argue in favor of the slush-pile system, but most publishers continue to read everything — or at least a few pages of everything sent to them. Why? Because they are hungry for product, *starving*, and the competition for good writers is so fierce that no source of potential bestsellers can be overlooked.

Some writers function well for years without an agent, and some never acquire one. Isaac Asimov, author of more than three hundred books, has never used an agent. Although he did not begin to reach the bestseller lists until he had written at least two hundred eighty of those volumes, he was not starving in the meantime. For years, Irving Wallace had no book agent, relying upon a knowledgeable attorney to vet his contracts. Joseph Wambaugh, the Los Angeles police detective who first wrote novels as a sideline and now is a fulltime freelancer, has no agent. Perhaps skill with a .357 magnum is even more persuasive than a knife.

If you are writing only short stories or articles, you virtually have to represent yourself — in the beginning, anyway — for you will not be of interest to most agents; handling lots of short manuscripts that are sold for small fees is not cost-effective. Until you have a book in print from a major publisher — or a letter in hand from an editor expressing the desire to acquire one of your books — the chances are very small that you will be able to get a first- or even second-rate agent. About the only other way an unpublished writer can acquire a *good* agent is through the persuasive intervention of a writer-friend who is a successful client of the firm; thereafter, until you actually *do* sell something, you will always be "the *schlemazl* who's a friend of Joe's," a pity case. Otherwise, those who would take you on as a client when you are unpublished are very often crooked or incompetent or both.

(Perhaps I should not be quite so declarative. Good and honest agents are always looking for new clients, and most of them will read a businesslike query letter and the first fifty pages of a manuscript, but in this article I am dealing with the *best* way to get the *best* agent.)

Nameless and aimless

To the new writer struggling to break in, even a third-rate agent can seem attractive. Better a bent, dull-bladed knife than no knife at all. Right? Wrong. There are people out there, claiming the ability to make new writers rich and famous, who can do far more harm than good.

Consider "Mr. Nameless," a guy who constantly acquires new writers for his list and who might be a big-league agent if he spent as much time and energy representing his authors as he devotes to bilking them. He once had — and may still have — a neat scam that worked like this:

1. Upon signing up a new client with a finished project, Mr. Nameless eventually finds a home for the book at a legitimate paperback house, which we will call Humongous Books, where he tentatively accepts an offer for, say, $5,000.

2. He does not pass this good news along to the author.

3. Instead, he phones his client and says, "I love your book, but it just isn't publishable in its current state. I've shown it to several editors and got turndowns. However, there is this company, Dreck Salvaging, Incorporated, that specializes in taking almost-publishable books and transforming them into salable properties. They cut, paste, polish, do a general all-around editing job, and then try to sell the revised version. They take a big risk with a

marginal script like yours because they might never sell it, so of course their advances are small. And they don't pay royalties. Now, if there were *any* hope of selling this book as it stands, I'd hammer on doors and talk my head off for ten years until I found a home for it. But I'm convinced the only deal we'll obtain is the one from Dreck Salvaging. The price is $1,000 for all rights, not a lot of money but *real* money, and at least it's a start for you."

4. Sometimes the client says, "Well, gee, why don't you tell me what's wrong with the script, and I'll do the rewriting myself rather than give away all rights to Dreck Salvaging." In which case, Mr. Nameless says, "You're too close to the book, too fond of it to be able to chop it apart and reassemble it with the necessary objectivity. Besides, before you can learn how to revise a book properly, you've got to know how to write one pretty solidly in the first place, and you're still learning *that*. Listen, you have such tremendous raw potential that I don't want you wasting more time on this minor book. No matter how much you improve it, we can't get much dough for it. Better to start another project than waste energy on this dog."

5. The client, admittedly tantalized by getting even just $1,000 for his work, starry-eyed at the prospect of seeing his name on a book, usually agrees to the Dreck deal.

6. Mr. Nameless then sells the novel to Dreck for $1,000, takes a $100 commission, and forwards a check to the client for $900.

7. An employee of Dreck spends one day on the script, changing descriptions, cutting some, adding a little, but doing nothing to improve upon or particularly detract from the original story. The only reason for making any changes at all is to allay the suspicions of the author, who will eventually read the finished book to see how his prose was "cleaned up."

8. Mr. Nameless takes the altered but unimproved script back to the paperback house that made the original offer and, as agent for Dreck Salvaging, sells it for the $5,000 offer. The key to the scam is that Dreck Salvaging is a paper company, totally owned by Mr. Nameless, who pockets $4,100, plus all rights and future royalties, while the hapless author takes home $900.

Nameless fleeces some authors once or twice, others more often, before telling them that they are at last good enough to sell straight to a publisher without Dreck's assistance. Most never learn they have been taken, and even if they discover the truth, it is difficult to prove the "editorial assistance" provided by Dreck Salvaging was not, in fact, essential to the sale of the book. Nameless's deception of the client is conducted on the phone, never in letters, so the content and tone of those conversations cannot be independently verified.

Over the years I have heard about this scam from three editors in different publishing houses. Each thought the practice was scandalous, and each felt sorry for the victimized writers, *but none ever hinted about these improprieties to the authors being cheated*. Startling? Shocking? Wait — there's worse. Of the three, two dealt with Nameless and Dreck Salvaging on a regular basis! Why? For one thing, they lived in the same city as Nameless, worked in the same industry, went to the same restaurants and parties; therefore, keeping peace with him took priority over defending the rights of authors who lived elsewhere and who moved in different social circles. More important, editors dealt with Nameless and Dreck because they needed product, lots of it, to fill their monthly lists, and Nameless was a reliable source of bottom-of-the-list books that could be bought cheaply. Understandably, even the best editors put writers third on any list of priorities: 1) they look out for themselves, primarily (and rightfully) concerned first about their own careers; 2) they protect the interests of the publishers who employ them; 3) they do what they can for their authors. Mr. Sinatra would be embarrassed for you if you expected more than that.

Some new writers will feel that paying Mr. Nameless's price might be worthwhile if that made it possible to get books in print, establish a track record, and then use that record to obtain a better agent, but they are mistaken. What I said earlier is dismayingly true: A couple of years with a lousy agent can do more harm than good. Mr. Nameless's authors are tainted by association with him. Because he is a third-rate agent, the good agents in the industry consider his writers third-rate, as well. Some *are* bad writers, but some are not, yet, regardless of their abilities, they might find it a bit difficult to get a reputable agent to consider them seriously when they are ready to leave the Nameless stable. Furthermore, because Nameless deals almost exclusively with the least powerful editors at the bottom of the ladder, his clients' books are usually released as "fillers," to plug gaps in the lower half of the publisher's list, and they receive no advertising budgets or publicity. Therefore, if you *do* get a better agent after a few years with Nameless, your credits will work *against* you; influential editors will look at your published titles, will see a string of unheard-of books that sold modestly at best, and will probably decide that you do not have what it takes to reach a wide audience. Then you will have to spend years trying to prove that you are better than they think you are.

The lesson is clear: Do not worry about getting an agent until you have first written a publishable book *that an editor wants to buy*. After all, creating the product must come before selling it. Obsessive concern about getting an agent can lead you to make rash judgments that you will later regret. The best way to find a *good* agent is to have one recommended to you by an editor who likes your work and wants to pay for it; that editor might not be able to place you with the top literary rep in the best agency in town, but he will surely steer you away from the crooks and the incompetents.

Rights and wrongs

Once you have a good agent, your worries are not necessarily over. Even a good agent may not be the *right* one for you. For example:

I was once represented by an intelligent and amusing and honest and altogether charming person I will call Mr. Formidable. I liked him immensely, and I always had a good time in his company. He had a well-deserved reputation as a shrewd and aggressive bargainer, and he had done very well by several clients. For a time we worked together without friction, and Mr. Formidable wrangled higher advances for me than I had gotten before. Then, one day while my wife and I were lunching with him in an extremely expensive restaurant that served overrated food, I wondered aloud why my most recent novel, which had seemed perfectly suited for the movies, had received no offers whatsoever for film rights—and I got a shock that almost made me faint face-first into my unpalatable spring-vegetable soup.

"Oh," he said, "we had an offer for an outright sale at $100,000, but we turned it down."

For a moment I was speechless while I watched him consume scallops in a curdled sauce. Finally I said, "We turned it down?"

And my wife, in an uncharacteristically squeaky voice that sounded like a Mickey Mouse impression, said, "Why did we turn it down?"

Formidable explained that the man who made the offer was a fine producer but a poor director, and unfortunately he wanted to buy my novel with the intention of both producing and directing a film based on it. "He'd screw it up," Mr. Formidable said. "It'd be a bad film. We'll sell the rights to someone else, with a better chance of getting a good picture made, and that'll be more helpful to your career."

I had such respect and affection for Mr. Formidable that I took a deep breath, calmed myself, and managed to make myself believe that he knew best.

Weeks dragged by without another film offer turning up, and in fact none ever did, but it was not Mr. Formidable's autocratic rejection of 100K that finally drove me to seek new representation. I was able to forgive him that transgression because I convinced myself that he knew best in the long run. Oh, I was *young* then! However, subsequent to that never-to-be-forgotten luncheon conversation, I sent Formidable an outline for a more ambitious book than any I had yet attempted — and he refused to handle it. He told me that it was not the kind of thing that I could do, and he said that even if I *could* do it, the market would not be receptive to a novel of that sort. Unmarketable, he said. He wanted me to stick with the shorter, less-complex books that I had been doing and that he had been able to place with ease. *That* was what made me go elsewhere. An agent can offer guidance and market suggestions, but he must not be the absolute determiner of what stories his client will tell. He must encourage his client to grow, to try new ideas that challenge the client's talents. If an agent will not trust a client's artistic instincts, if he will not sell what the *client* wants to write, he is the wrong representative for that particular author.

Firing Mr. Formidable was one of the most painful things I have ever had to do, for I felt a special bond of friendship with him that I had reason to believe he felt as well. I know he was hurt by my departure, and his unconcealed pain made me feel even worse. But I found new representation, and that supposedly unmarketable outline was sold for the largest advance I had yet received. When the book was published, it went through seven printings and one million copies, appearing on several bestseller lists, with royalties mounting well into six figures. That novel was a turning point in my career, and it taught me a vital lesson that freed me from a lot of hampering illusions: In essence — even a *good* agent is not always the right agent.

Rights and wrongs, part II

You will know that you have found both a good representative *and* the right one when: 1) he always answers or returns your phone calls promptly (assuming that you do not call every day); 2) he appreciates the strengths of your writing but forthrightly notes your weaknesses; 3) he will explain his marketing intentions for a project in detail and will give real weight to your objections if you have any; 4) he urges you to be artistically ambitious, to write better and more complex books every time out of the gate; 5) he will risk antagonizing and even alienating a publisher to obtain something that is rightfully yours, such as long-overdue royalties or a revised accounting of what appears to be grossly under-reported sales; 6) he talks with you about long-term goals specifically rather than generally and does not try to load you up with too much quick-buck work to grab nice commissions in the short run; 7) he never turns down *or accepts* a deal without discussing everything with you; 8) you can have harsh words with him, forcefully express your dissatisfactions, and not damage your relationship with him; 9) he laughs at the same things you do.

Number nine is more important than it may seem. Publishers can be encouraging and honorable, but some of them can also be demanding, obstinate, inconstant, imperious, and sometimes even crooked and spiteful and consciously cruel. More writers fail than succeed; some go a little loony from the pressure and disappointment and uncertainty of a free-lancer's existence, many become horribly bitter, and most have difficulty keeping body and soul together. If you care passionately about your writing, the freelancer's life can be a heartbreaker. Even if you are a survivor, even if your hard work ultimately pays off big, there are many times when sanity is saved and perspective restored by having an agent who is also a friend and who shares your world view, so the two of you can make jokes about the insanity of the publishing madhouse and try to lighten the dark moments with comradely laughter of the sort that helps soldiers survive battlefields and trenches.

You will know that you have the *wrong* agent if, among other things I have already discussed: 1) you do *not* laugh at the same things; 2) he does not promptly return your calls; 3) he does not read and report on your manuscripts within two weeks of receipt; 4) he is not open with you when you ask him about his marketing intentions for a project; 5) he professes to love everything you write; 6) he dislikes most everything you write; 7) he tries to steer you into writing in whatever genre is currently hot, without regard for your interests and style; 8) he is unwilling to show you a client list. (If he is any good at all, there should be several authors on his list whose names you recognize. In fact, there should be at least one client on the list who has made the major bestseller lists, preferably more than one.); 9) he wants to charge you a whole series of reading fees.

(It may be valuable to pay a reading fee for editorial and market suggestions, *but only once or twice*. The best agencies do not charge those fees. Agents who charge for reading scripts are often readers first, agents only secondarily, generating most of their income from fees rather than actually making sales and earning commissions. In those cases where the fee-reading income *is* the minor part of the business, the agent will seldom review your manuscript himself; he will be busy selling the work of successful clients, so he will hire people to read your stuff and write reports, to which he will sign his name. You are not his *client* if you are paying him to read your work; in a genuine agent-*client* relationship, the agent receives no compensation other than commissions from work that he sells.)

Finally, he is the wrong agent if the majority of deals he makes for you and for his other clients are with book packagers rather than directly with publishers. An agent who works almost exclusively in that fashion is more likely to be on the lookout for finder's fees and subpackaging fees. Those bites of the pie, taken in addition to his standard commission, come out of the author's piece.

Take heart: There are at least as many good agents as bad, and the vast majority of them, both the good ones and the bad ones, are honest. Incompetent representation is usually the worst problem a writer will have with an agent, and when you have finally found Mr.—or Mrs. or Miss or Ms.—Right, your life will be made infinitely easier. That perfect representative will relieve you of many business worries, will act as buffer between you and your publisher in order to preserve both your dignity and sanity, and will be a diplomat when antagonism develops between you and your editor. He will know which editors and houses will best suit a particular writer's talent and temperament. He will know what your work is worth and will be able to get the top dollar for it. He will do battle to see that your books are advertised, that they receive publicity, and that they are placed as close to the top of the publisher's monthly list as possible, rather than in the middle or at the bottom where the salespeople will not pay attention to them. Such exemplary agents deserve more attention than they receive from literary historians, for they give their authors the peace of mind, confidence, financial security and encouragement that make it possible for good books to be written.

The good fight

With the ideal agent, a writer gets more pleasure from each success than he might otherwise have felt, more joy from each triumph, for he has a fellow soldier in the trenches with whom to share the shining moments. Shared joy is always more satisfying than that experienced in solitude. If the new writer is patient, if he realizes that all new writers begin without agents and that most place their first books on their own, if he lets go of his many illusions about the magical power of an agent, if he relies solely on his hard work to gain him a publisher and *then* an agent, if he fully understands that writing is a craft — and an art — but not a racket, if he accepts that there are no shortcuts to the top, he will one day find first-rate representation. He will experience the intense pleasure of winning against all odds, with a business associate at his side who is also a friend, a reliable ally, and a paladin who fights the good fight to clear the barbarians and deadfalls out of the artist's path.

Building a Career

by Ethan Ellenberg

The career vs. the big deal

The big deal. Every author dreams of it. So does every agent. Whether you read your local newspaper, *Publishers Weekly* or any number of magazines that cover publishing and writing, you're sure to find news about the latest big deal almost every week. And I'll bet it makes your mouth water. It may also make your stomach sick as you think of the injustice of it all, the stupidity of publishers, and how there won't be any money left to pay your advance.

I'm going to tell you all about my big deal, but before I do, I'm going to talk about something even more important, because it was the key to my big deal: it's called a "career." Now "career" may not sound quite as awesome as "the big deal," but if you're serious about your writing, it's more important, it's more likely and it's the surest way to eventually get your big deal. Let me reveal something else. The sweetest big deal for publishers is with an author whose career they've helped build and whose "backlist" of previously published titles is being published by the house. In the age of computerized sales information, your previously published titles will follow you everywhere, and a record of success will be the most valuable asset you have.

I first spoke to Mark Berent in the fall of 1986. I was just beginning my career as an agent and I had learned that Bantam Books was looking for a number of military writers to author books in a nonfiction series they were planning. Mark's name was given to me by a mutual friend who was then editing a military magazine. Mark was editing a military magazine himself, *Asian Defense Journal*. I told him about the Bantam series and tried to recruit him to write for it, with me as his agent. He responded with a handsome package of book ideas and sample articles. Included in the package was an article that had been published in *Air Force Magazine* in 1970, when Mark was finishing his third tour as a combat pilot in Vietnam. The article was called "Night Flight on the Ho Chi Minh Trail."

It was a wonderful little piece. It put you in the cockpit in the inky darkness, above the karst-topped mountains that crawl up the spine of Vietnam. I read it and immediately thought Mark would make a great novelist of military fiction. I called him right away and told him so. He confessed to having a book idea or two, but said he had never been able to do anything about it. He tentatively agreed to try to pull something together and send it to me and we left it at that.

I didn't see any material from Mark for almost a year, though I called him every month or two to let him know I was still interested. Finally I received a proposal for a three-book Vietnam war series and almost 70 pages of text.

It was great stuff. The opening scene had fighter pilot Court Bannister babying his shot-up jet in a crash landing on his home airfield. The characters were great; the action was great; I loved everything about it. You can check me on this by picking up *Rolling Thunder* at your bookstore.

Ethan Ellenberg, *former Associate Contracts Manager of Bantam and Contracts Manager of Berkley/Jove, established his own literary agency eight years ago. The New York-based agency represents 75 clients and specializes in commercial fiction of all types and children's books.*

Now I had enough to work with to launch Mark's career. This was at the end of the summer of 1987, and techno thrillers were enjoying a strong showing after the successes of Tom Clancy and Stephen Coonts. I thought Mark's initial chapters were strong enough to command a hardcover deal. I knew that the three-book series format was more suited to paperback. Hardcover publishers tend to see their books as a more substantial investment and like to publish an author's first book and see how it does before buying others. Paperback houses that mainly publish genre fiction are more attuned to continuity publishing and are more likely to commit to more than one book. A three-book hardcover deal is a big commitment, but I thought Mark's samples were worthy of it. I approached a dozen top hardcover publishers and promptly collected 12 rejections.

It was not a pleasant experience. I pride myself on my ability to judge fiction. I knew Mark was something special. I knew the publishers were wrong. I second guessed myself relentlessly about having allowed Mark to use the series format, thinking that our request for a three-book hardcover deal alone may have prejudiced my client's chances. Mark and I discussed the situation. He was very supportive. He confessed he wasn't sure he was ever hardcover calibre to begin with. We moved to step two of our marketing strategy. A few days after collecting my last hardcover rejection I submitted the series to ten paperback publishers.

I was very anxious. A week went by and I wondered why the phone didn't ring. Another week passed and I received my first rejection letter. It was a positive letter, from an editor who shared my enthusiasm for military fiction and nonfiction and claimed to be turning it down only because he couldn't commit to three books. I sweated a few more days. Then one afternoon the phone rang. It was Roger Cooper, editor-in-chief of Berkley.

After a few minutes of chitchat, Roger got to the point. Berkley liked the Berent trilogy and they were interested in knowing my price. I expressed confidence that Berkley wouldn't be the only house interested and I'd be able to auction the property. I suggested it could go for anywhere from $25,000 to $75,000 per book. Roger was confident he could get something just as good for $5,000 a book. The lines had been drawn.

I managed to set up an auction; three houses participated and happily for everyone involved, Berkley came away with the series with a final bid of $25,000 per book. It was the least I thought the series was worth originally, but Mark and I were happy with the results. It was with a good house that was beginning to specialize in military fiction, it was with a very talented and enthusiastic editor, and the three-book deal was a major commitment. Mark would have a real chance to build an audience in the marketplace. It wasn't the "big deal," but it was a career maker.

More good news was still to come. Mark finished the first book two months early and I critiqued and edited it before we sent it on to Ed Breslin, his editor at Berkley. I still believed Mark belonged in hardcover. Ed did too; he had already been laying the groundwork with Berkley's sister company, Putnam, to see if they would take it on. A few weeks after delivering the final manuscript, Ed told me we had made the cut. *Rolling Thunder* was going to be a Putnam hardcover and Mark had a new editor, Neil Nyren. In fact, all three books had been moved over to the Putnam side. I felt vindicated.

Rolling Thunder did modestly well as a hardcover. Rights were sold in Japan and England. It got some good reviews, including selection in the *New York Times'* best books of the year, one of only ten or so thrillers to be chosen, taking its place next to books by Le Carre and others. The first printing of the paperback was 600,000 copies and it made the *Publishers Weekly* bestseller list as a candidate.

As Mark completed the final two books on the initial contract, Neil Nyren and I negotiated what was to become my "big deal." We settled on $400,000 for Mark's fourth and fifth books in the "series," advances I think any agent and author would be proud to receive. *Eagle Station*, the fourth book, was published in hardcover in June of 1992 and *Storm Flight* is scheduled for hardcover publication in June of 1993.

Thinking "career"

I think Mark's story illustrates important lessons. Don't fixate on the big deal. It's just not likely or important enough in the grand scheme of being a working writer. You've got to think career.

To develop your writing skills, I recommend reading avidly, with an emphasis on the kind of book you want to write. Study the genre and your favorite books. Join a writer's critique group or a writer's workshop at a local university. You have to expose your work, get expert criticism and use it. You have to work hard. I know that's a truism, but too many writers underestimate the need to work through all the initial mistakes until their voice surfaces and their skills come together.

Get a good agent. I know how hard that is. My office receives more than 100 new pieces of mail every week. I still look at every piece of mail, because I have taken writers out of the "slush" and on to a career. I'm not the only one. Most agents dream of finding that great new writer. Increase your chances by writing a great one-page letter that's focused and knowledgable. Describe the book you have to sell and make clear what genre it fits. Follow that with just a paragraph of relevant credits or credentials. I prefer the first three chapters and a synopsis, and always include a self-addressed stamped envelope.

When you've managed to interest an agent, make certain she's enthusiastic and responsive. She must return your phone calls and answer your letters. She must answer your questions. She should have some proven expertise in the business aspects of publishing and a client list that includes published authors. I feel that editorial help is the most valuable service a good agent can provide. Find out if your prospective agent provides such help. I do not recommend agents who charge reading fees or fees for editorial work except in very special circumstances.

Plan to have a career as a published author. Be prepared to start small, with a modest book that commands a modest advance. Think about what you will write after your first book is published and how and in what direction you hope to grow. If I had to sum it up in one cut phrase I'd say big deals grow out of small deals. So get a small deal. The big ones will follow.

How Agents and Editors Create Books

by Eileen Fallon

What's the bane of the life of the literary agent? (*What*, you ask, *it's not all glamour*?) The fellow party guest, or doctor, or cab driver, or candlestick maker who, on hearing of your line of work, says, "You know, if any of your clients ever needs an idea, I've got lots of them. In fact, if I just had the time, I'd write this book myself . . . ."

Indeed.

Well, I'm sure you can guess an agent's general reaction to such an announcement. We assure our potential idea giver that no, in fact, the clients don't need ideas, that coming up with ideas is, actually, a very big part of the writer's job.

Yet when *The Guide to Literary Agents & Art/Photo Reps* asked me to write an article about project creation on the part of agents, I thought about how often both agents and book editors generate ideas and then look for suitable writers to execute them.

Where ideas come from

. . . from editors

In a number of publishing houses, editors are strongly encouraged to generate book projects. Where do their ideas come from? The most obvious and the most frequently used sources are newspapers, television news programs and magazines (the latter is the place agents and editors turn to most frequently to find writers for nonfiction projects, but more on that a bit further on). The more dynamic the editor, the wider the net is cast. Someone actively creating projects doesn't turn solely to local papers and periodicals in the quest for marketable ideas, but subscribes to major papers from across the country and to a number of regional (and, nowadays, even international) magazines.

And some of the not-so-obvious places? Well, for those editors interested in the sciences, there are the medical and scientific journals, for those seeking to develop history books, the scholarly journals in that field, and so on. Editors also attend the professional conferences of groups as diverse as psychologists, professors of English and cutting edge musicians.

As we all saw from the recent success of the humor book *All I Need to Know I Learned from My Cat*, books are often inspired by the success of earlier books. An editor's use of this time-honored inspiration led to the first project I ever created. One day I was having lunch with an editor of practical nonfiction. She'd had a great deal of success with a trade paperback that gave women all the basic information they would need about the nine months of their pregnancy. Written by an obstetrician teamed with a professional nonfiction writer, it was now being ordered by thousands of obstetricians every month. To avoid dealing with the same basic questions every expectant mother asks, doctors would give the

Eileen Fallon was an agent for Lowenstein Associates for eight years before establishing her own agency, The Fallon Literary Agency, in 1990. The agency handles a range of fiction and nonfiction and is building a reputation in the field for handling mainstream fiction, mystery and romance fiction.

book to a patient on her first visit, ask her to read it, and then ask if she had any further questions.

So pleased was the editor with the book's outstanding performance, she was eager to think of another such medical situation, one in which patients would necessarily work with a doctor over a period of time.

The idea came to me immediately. "Heart attack," I said. We looked at each other, and knew we had a winner on our hands.

Since the editor had no specific writer or doctor in mind for the project, I decided to propose the idea to a writer with a degree in biology who had yet to write a book in this subject area, but had frequently written health pieces for magazines. Then I obtained the name of a prominent cardiologist at one of New York's major hospitals; he agreed to co-write the book. In a project like this the credentials of the expert in his field are of more importance to the potential publisher than those of the writer who collaborates with the expert, although it's best if the writer has done some magazine work in the field.

Through a circuitous route (with which I'm sure all published authors are familiar), *The Heart Attack Recovery Handbook* ended up being published by a different major New York house than the one for which my lunch partner worked. But, it was my first created project . . . and I was hooked.

. . . from agents

Agents tend to do more project generating than editors, and use the same sources. However, as generally self-employed entrepreneurs, agents don't have to convince an editor-in-chief to have the house foot the bill for a trip to a distant conference. If an agent suspects that at least one good book will come out of such a journey, she or he will just go for it. Also, though many agents spend long hours working with authors to shape both nonfiction proposals and novels before submitting them to editors for consideration, the job of the agent does not involve the same amount of time spent editing as that of the editor. Agents therefore frequently have more time to create projects than editors do.

An important source of book ideas by agents is their own (or an editor's) personal interests or needs. One book that came from both my experience and that of an editor was *Recovering from a Stroke* (HarperPaperbacks). I had sold a limited series of books to Harper called *Recovering from . . .* , each of which would focus on the process of recovering from an illness or operation. (And guess what book previously mentioned in this article was the inspiration for the series?) Stroke was not one of the initially pitched topics. However, after the series proposal was written, the mother of one of my friends, the father of another, as well as the husband of a client, all suffered strokes. And before I could tell the acquiring editor that I thought stroke recovery should be the topic of one of the books, she asked me if we could include the topic—it seems that her own father had suffered a stroke in recent years.

. . . from authors

As with the creation of *The Heart Attack Recovery Handbook*, conversations between book professionals often lead to the development of successful projects. I had one such conversation at the Kansas breakfast table of a client who's a nonfiction writer while I was in that state for a writer's conference.

Andrea Warren had just completed her work as co-writer of one of the books in the *Recovering from . . .* series. We were discussing her next project (or, what we *thought* was going to be her next project when we began the conversation), a business writing book for the general public based on seminars the writer gave across the country for major corporations. As conversations tend to do, however, ours took a turn to even more immediate concerns. Alarmed that her high school-age step-daughter was becoming sexually active, Andrea had spoken to other mothers of teens and found that this topic was their number one concern. As a writer, she had naturally looked to her local bookstore for help—only to find nothing suitable there.

That was the start of *Everybody's Doing It: How to Survive Your Teenagers' Sex Life, and Help Them Survive It, Too* (Viking, April 1993) by Andrea Warren and her husband Jay Wiedenkeller.

Idea to sale—putting the proposal together

I was especially pleased with the sale of the proposal for *Everybody's Doing It*; the authors had worked very hard to produce what I considered a selling proposal.

However, it wasn't only seeing the writers' toil rewarded that made me so happy to finalize the deal for this book; we had negotiated the problem of *credentials*. What was the problem? The client had co-authored a book in the health field (she had been teamed with a leading oncologist to write *Recovering from Breast Cancer* for HarperPaperbacks), *and* she was the mother of two teenage daughters. She was daily confronting the issue of teen sexuality, but as a lay person, not as an expert in the field with a wide range of experience, such as a psychologist whose practice includes a number of parents and teens attempting to deal with the issue.

The truth is, my first instinct had been to team Andrea with just such an expert, someone with the right initials behind his or her name, an established practice in this field and perhaps a few articles published in professional journals. Maybe we'd really get lucky and find all that, along with an affiliation with a major university or other prestigious institution *and* a "mediagenic" face and personality.

But Andrea didn't want just one expert's view. She wanted to investigate the issue from a number of angles and explore various experts' approaches, not just present one professional's findings and recommendations. Our key to establishing her credentials lay in the word "investigate." The writer held a master's degree in journalism, and had for a number of years pursued a very successful freelance writing career, which included writing parenting articles for *Good Housekeeping*. And remember she did have one co-authoring credit of a book in the health field. We were therefore able to make a good case for her having the right credentials to do the book.

As you can see from the development of *Everybody's Doing It*, writers must have certain credentials to be chosen by an agent or editor to do a book. In almost all cases, these will include clippings, samples of newspaper and/or magazine articles they've written. It's not agents who help writers gain these credentials; writers themselves must land those assignments long before they begin looking for agents, who tend primarily to handle books rather than articles. Magazine articles, more so than newspaper articles, bring you to the attention of agents and editors.

So how do you go about getting magazine assignments? The following stories of three writers, all of whom built their professional bios writing for magazines and are now successful nonfiction collaborators, will help you think about steps you may want to take as you build your own writing career.

Establishing credentials—three writers' stories

Cheryl Solimini graduated from Syracuse University with a newspaper journalism degree. Between editorial stints at major magazines such as *Country Living, Woman's World* and *Family Circle*, Cheryl began to place freelance health-related articles in similar magazines. She was writing a fitness column for *New Woman* when I phoned her editor looking for a health writer to be teamed with a doctor on a book for a major publisher. Cheryl has done two such books with me, and I've just put her in touch with yet another doctor with a book idea. Living in New York can be a great help in developing a career like Cheryl's. Getting to know editors in that way is wonderful; Cheryl thinks she may have written *one* query letter in her entire career. But what if you can't get to New York?

The path of Diana Tonnessen's career, though similar in some ways to Cheryl's, began outside New York, at Whittle Communications. From there she moved to *Health* magazine as a senior editor. Like Cheryl, she began writing for her editorial contacts. In writing articles, Diana generally interviewed experts on the topics she was covering. That experience, combined with what she had learned from speaking to other professional writers, made her realize that publishers take your work more seriously when you're teamed with an expert in the area you're writing about. Eventually two agents showed interest in working with Diana; she chose one and began her book-writing career. In each of her books, she is teamed with a respected MD.

We've seen two writers, one in New York and one not, use the magazine editorial route to establish both contacts *and* a portfolio of clippings. Has any writer ever developed a career outside of New York on the strength of query letters alone?

Author Gary Ferguson started writing magazine articles part-time in 1978 while working as a naturalist for the U.S. Park Service in the West. He began querying small regional magazines about nature and travel pieces—an area in which he was credentialed due to his Park Service work. He used those clips from the smaller magazines as a springboard to larger ones. And talk about query letters! In order to place the 40 articles he wanted to sell each year, he sent out over 200 letters annually, finding that about one in every six attempts was successful. It took about three years for Gary to get his query letter routine down pat. He would open his query with the first paragraph of the proposed article, then tell the editor what the article would cover, the names of experts he would interview, specs (to impress on the editor that he was very familiar with the particular magazine and its requirements), what he'd written before, and he'd include two or three appropriate clips. In order not to dwell too much on rejections; he would revise the query and send it out immediately to the next name on his list as soon as he got a negative response.

Gary warns that trying to build a freelance writing career is very tough. But he eventually built up enough clippings to join the ASJA (the American Association of Journalists and Authors), a professional society with stringent admissions requirements. It was through the ASJA that he got the name of the agency in which I worked. I sold his first book-length work, *Walks of California* to Prentice Hall Press in the mid-80s; he went on to write three more travel books in the *Walks of . . .* series, and his first armchair travel book, *Wild Heart*, was published by Simon & Schuster in 1993. When Gary works outside his area of expertise, however, he does so in collaboration with an expert. His current project of that nature is for a book on rituals for HarperSanFrancisco, written with a psychologist he himself located by reading professional journals on the subject of ritual.

Though their paths to writing books—indeed, to being courted by agents and *asked* to write books—were somewhat different, these three writers shared certain qualities in addition to their skill as writers. The *focused* their efforts, establishing themselves in particular subject areas and expanding those areas slowly and conscientiously. They also built networks of professional contacts which all culminated in their being welcomed onto the lists of agents who could do the most for them at a particular stage of their careers.

Understanding Rights

by B.J. Doyen

Many authors are so glad to get a contract offer that they sign over their rights without understanding what they are doing. Like marriage, your relationship with your publisher should be regarded as permanent; unlike marriage, it is hard, if not impossible, to get a "divorce" from your publisher once you realize you've made a poor deal.

Both parties bring something to the relationship. The author gives the publisher the exclusive rights to print and sell his or her book, and the publisher gives the author an advance and promises to pay him more in the form of royalties once the upfront cash has been earned back.

Defining your rights

Reprint rights, book club rights and revised editions almost always go with the deal. A writer who insists on retaining these rights may jeopardize the sale as the publisher may be counting on income from these sources when calculating the potential profitability of your book.

Reprint rights

Reprint rights is a broad term that can mean hardcover, trade paperback and/or mass market paperback rights. If sales take off, the latter can be quite lucrative. For example: George Burns' nonfiction bestseller, *Gracie: A Love Story*, was published in hardcover and then in trade paperback before mass market paperback rights were sold for over $600,000.

In theory, a book coming out in any one of these formats can be reprinted into any other—but in reality, it would be unusual for a paperback book to be reprinted as a hardcover. We've had clients receive a simultaneous hard/soft deal, where the book is published in both hardcover and trade paperback from the first printing. A common procedure is printing first in hardcover or trade paperback and then in mass market paperback. Many books start out as mass market paperbacks, never to be published in the other formats.

Your agent will consider how appealing your book might be to each market, evaluating the way to get the best deal. If a book is of interest to publishers in both hard and soft cover, it will usually come out first in hardcover with the paperback edition (particularly mass market paperbacks) coming out months or years later so that hardcover sales are maximized before the cheaper form is available. This works well when the hardcover publisher also does the paperback, but when paperback rights are licensed to another publisher, the hardcover house will want a split of the author's royalties.

Book club rights

Book club rights sales can generate a tidy sum. Your publisher can offer your book to the club "as is" at a discount or it can license a book club "reprint" edition. The publisher

B.J. Doyen *is president of Doyen Literary Services, Inc., an agency serving 50 authors. She has written many instructional materials for writers, including an audiotape series endorsed by James Michener. On weekends, B.J. presents intensive* Write to $ell® *seminars with her business partner and husband, Robert H. Doyen.*

should seek out appropriate book club markets as soon as possible because they increase the public's awareness of your book and stimulate retail sales.

Revised edition rights

Somewhere between 10 to 20 percent of the books published in the U.S. are revised or updated editions. If the author makes a few changes to keep the text current, the book is republished as an "update." If at least 30 percent of the text is new material and the book has been republished with a new cover, a new ISBN and new promotion, the book is called a "revised edition." Each update or revision should bring the author another advance; our client, Barbara Brabec gets paid for each new edition of her book, *Homemade Money*.

Updates and revisions extend the life of the book and increase the author's—and the publisher's—profits. The person responsible for the text changes should be the author, but if the publisher requests a revision and the author refuses or is unable to do it, most contracts give the publisher the right to have another writer do the revision, charging the costs of preparing that revision against the original author's earnings.

The publisher may negotiate to retain and exercise excerpt rights in the U.S. and abroad, serial rights, one-time rights, simultaneous rights and syndication rights. Your agent will most likely reserve these rights for you if you are already well-published in major periodicals and have good contacts for your work.

If the publisher retains these rights, it's to your benefit not to be too stingy with the royalty splits (as long as the publisher will indeed aggressively pursue these sales) because the publisher must have a fair profit as an incentive. The splits are negotiable—but the author shouldn't give the publisher more than 50 percent.

If you are offering your work to these markets as a primary sale (that is, not as subsidiary rights to a book contract), be certain you've reserved control of your other rights for possible future use. Why? Your article may later be developed into a film, book or play—as in the case of Budd Schulberg. Based on his newspaper article series, he wrote a screenplay, *On the Waterfront*, that went on to win eight Oscars for best film in 1954. Then he wrote *Waterfront*, the novel, and *On the Waterfront*, the theatrical play, with Stanley Silverman which debuted at the Cleveland Playhouse in 1988.

Excerpt rights

Excerpt (or serial) rights (allowing passages selected from your book or sometimes the entire text, to be printed in magazines, newspapers or newsletters) should be pursued vigorously because of the tremendous publicity this generates for the book.

At one time, sales of these rights would bring the author more money than from book publication. Serial sales can still be quite lucrative, especially if they involve a celebrity. (For example, *Woman's Day* paid $200,000 for Rose Kennedy's autobiography, *Times to Remember*.) But even if little or no money is forthcoming, my more savvy clients mine their nonfiction books heavily for excerpts, getting in print as extensively as possible—because this sells lots of books.

You should try to suggest ideas for excerpts to the rights director at your publishing house, or to your agent if she's handling these sales. Be specific. If you think your chapter three checklist could be lifted and made into an article titled "How Do I Know If I'm Happy in Love?" which looks just right for *Redbook*, suggest it.

Serial rights

These excerpts can be marketed to American periodicals, or you can offer them abroad, in which case you'd be selling the foreign serial rights. The excerpt can come out either before publication (first serial rights) or after publication (second serial rights).

First North American serial rights are purchased by periodicals which are distributed in both the United States and Canada for simultaneous first appearances of the excerpt in each country. Serial rights can be sold on a nonexclusive basis, that is, excerpts from different parts of the book to different buyers. First Serial Rights sales could involve exclusive rights to the entire book or just to a part of it.

Obviously, you can sell the right to be the first to publish the excerpt only once; this should go to the buyer most likely to pay the highest dollar and give you the best exposure. After that, it could be sold as second serial rights, one-time rights or perhaps as simultaneous rights, probably to periodicals without overlapping circulation; these rights can also bring in good money. For example: after First Serial Rights for Judith Krantz's *Till We Meet Again* went to *Cosmopolitan*, Second Serial Rights for the novel went to *Redbook* for $25,000.

Syndication rights

Newspapers regularly buy and print material they've received from syndicates, which are agencies specializing in these sales. The syndicate is granted exclusive rights to sell your pieces all over the world in first publication and in reprint. Syndicates simultaneously offer their material to many buyers, usually guaranteeing the buyer exclusivity in a particular geographic area.

Books that are to be excerpted in several continuing installments or as columns might be picked up by a syndicate. The value of syndication rights should be more than what the author would get for First Serial sales to one publication. The syndicate takes 50 percent of the earnings. If the author has granted the publisher the right to license syndication, the remaining 50 percent would be split between the author and the publisher as agreed in the publishing contract. If the agent has retained these rights, she can approach a syndicate on the author's behalf. Another option for the author is to self-syndicate.

When selling excerpt rights, it's important to understand what the benefits are to each party in these agreements. We've already mentioned that the author gets good money and, even more important, publicity for his book.

The publication that purchases First Serial Rights gets to "scoop" your book to the world, thus capitalizing on any prepublication publicity your book has generated. The excerpt will require less editing, and it may cost the publication less to buy these rights than it would to commission a freelance writer to do a major piece.

Even though they've lost some of the "scoop" value, Second Serial Rights are attractive because they're cheaper than First Serial Rights. The publication still benefits from the book's publicity and promotion, and the manuscript has already been edited and proofread—a savings in editors' time and energy.

To maximize the effect of the publicity of your book, try to time the publication of excerpts to coincide with your book's availability in bookstores. Keep in mind that the First Serial appearance *must* occur prior to the book's publication date.

Foreign rights

Foreign sales and translations don't always go with the sale of the book. Foreign sales can involve selling the American edition abroad "as is" (in Canada, for example) or it can mean selling the rights to publish another edition in English or translations into other languages. Here again, sales are handled by the publisher or agent, depending on whether these rights were part of the publisher's contract. It is desirable to go with the publisher if they have staff whose only job is to handle these rights, or if they have an international foreign rights department. When the agent has reserved these rights for the author and arranges the sale, the author then gets all of the money instead of giving the publisher a split.

The license for the publication of foreign editions is usually granted for a particular period of time, usually a number of years. When the license expires, it can be renewed by your publisher or agent in your behalf.

Film rights

Publishers feel entitled to a share of your film rights because they believe their publication of your book greatly enhances the chances of the sale; this despite the fact the publisher will be benefitting directly from increased book sales once the movie is out.

Publishers also buy novelization rights to screenplays, which can then go on to become bestsellers; *Return of the Jedi, Ghostbusters* and *Rocky* are examples. Either way, book into movie or movie into book, the tie-in enhances the sales in each media.

With the decline of the networks' power and the proliferation of cable companies and independent producers, more and more original movies are being made expressly for TV. This requires a supply of material—good news to the writer. But you should realize that film sales from books are still a long shot.

Theatrical films (to be released in movie theaters) are the longest shot of all, since roughly 80 or 100 movies are made yearly, and many of these come from original screenplays, not derived from book material. Of those books optioned, dismally few get produced as movies, even among those on the best-seller lists.

The very best time to market film rights is after the book is sold but prior to its publication—that's when it's hottest to the movie people. After publication, it loses its appeal unless the book goes onto best-sellerdom or receives great reviews, which greatly enhances interest.

Film rights sales start out as an option. The author is paid a certain amount of cash in return for allowing the movie people a certain amount of time to line up the movie's production. Usually the time frame is for six to twelve months and the cash starts in the higher five figures on up, but I know of at least one four-figure deal, and one option purchased with no cash at all. (This is a bad deal for the author. If the option falls through the author will have nothing in return for withdrawing his property from the other film markets.)

At the end of the option's term it can be renewed, in which case you should receive more money, or it expires, and you are free to sell the option to someone else. If "picked up" (that is, purchased), your option has been sold for the already-agreed-upon additional amount of money.

If you're an author with clout, you might be able to swing a percentage of the movie's profits as part of your deal. Usually, however, it's in your best interest to go for as much upfront money as possible.

Two other ways you can benefit from your movie sales are Film Sequel Rights, where a second movie is based on your book, and Remake Rights, where the movie is rewritten and reshot with a different cast. Then there are Television and Cable Film Rights, TV Specials, TV Series based on your work, and Videotapes for direct sale or rental to the consumer.

Film rights sales should be handled by someone who specializes in this area and has access to the industry. If your literary agent doesn't handle this herself, she will probably have a West Coast affiliate who does.

Electronic media rights

Publishers are including clauses to cover rights you may not even think of. Some of these, like computer and other electronic media rights, may seem worthless when you are selling your book, but may prove to be quite valuable in our high-tech future.

Educational software, computer games and interactive novels for use on home computers, CD-ROM (which will soon be used for home instruction and entertainment), and electronic databases which would be accessed through computer services like CompuServe, are some rights that may be commonly exercised in the future.

Other rights

Other subsidiary rights like filmstrips/AV materials, audio recordings, large type editions and Braille editions for the blind may or may not go along with the book sale. Although budget cuts have forced educational institutions to limit spending in the area of filmstrips/AV materials, it's still a market possibility. If you think your book could profitably be made into filmstrips or other AV materials (like microfiche, microfilm or transparencies) for sale to institutions, organizations or even the general public, discuss this with your agent or publisher. These rights will probably not bring in a lot of money, and with the availability of videoplayers, the markets for filmstrips and transparencies are shrinking.

Audio rights for books on tape, records or compact discs is a growing market more publishers are pursuing. These rights, to the entire book or to excerpts, can be sold separately. They can be divided and sold as direct mail-order rights or as retail rights. These rights can be exercised to sell combination book-tape packages.

Large print editions are appreciated by people with limited vision. Bowker has a directory of these that will help you get a sense of how attractive your book might be to this specialized market. The money isn't terrific, but the markets for these books are increasing as our population ages.

Braille editions and other editions for the physically handicapped are rights usually given away in the copyright application, and I recommend allowing the publisher to grant the right for copies to be made by the Library of Congress' Division for the Blind and Physically Handicapped, with no recompense to the author so long as the publisher also receives no recompense.

Protecting your rights

Allowing your work to be published without a copyright notice can be like allowing squatters to build themselves permanent dwellings on your land. As in real estate, where someone using your property, even without your knowledge, might set a legal precedent for them to continue to do so, so can the author lose or compromise his literary rights by not properly protecting them. And you cannot sell what you do not own.

Copyrights

Although under the Copyright Law of 1978 you do have ownership of your literary material from the time you create it, protecting these rights requires that you be conscientious about filing for copyrights. The copyright should be in the author's name (although it will be the publisher's job to register it) and the copyright notice must appear in the proper form in the published work.

Permissions

If someone wants to use an excerpt of your copyrighted work in his book, he must get permission from you (or your publisher) in writing. Usually, this involves a payment, even if it's just a token amount.

Material that can be used by anyone without permission is said to have entered the Public Domain. It can include material for which copyright protection has not been provided, and material for which the copyright has expired or not been renewed. (The latter applies only to books published before Jan. 1, 1978. Copyright for books published after that date automatically extends to 50 years after the author's death.)

Reversions

Selling the "rights" to use your literary material is separate from selling the actual "ownership" of the material. You are not really selling your property, you are selling the rights to use your property for a period of time. Your agent will see to it that your literary contract will have provisions for your rights to revert back to you.

The publisher should supply the author's agent (or the author) with copies of the licenses entered on the author's behalf, but unfortunately, this is not standard procedure. Even if your publishing contract is later terminated, these licenses remain in force for the time period specified in the license agreement, and the publisher and author each still receive their respective share of the profits.

If you sell the copyright, you lose ownership—at least for 35 years, after which time you may get the property back. But most material has lost its market appeal by then, and who knows if you'll be around to benefit from it anyway?

Work-for-hire

Selling your writing as a work-for-hire is not a good idea, since all rights, as well as the copyright, go to the publisher, usually for one flat sum. Your name won't likely appear anywhere on the published piece, and your work can be altered or used in any manner the buyer pleases. You will not get royalties (the exception being in the case of textbooks), you will not get recognition for your work, nor will you even necessarily know how your material has been used. Think carefully before selling your rights this way.

An author must understand that his literary properties involve a myriad of rights and each right should be given knowledgable consideration when any sale is made. Not only should you understand what rights you are selling, you also should know how you and your publisher will share the earnings from the rights you grant to them—all of which will be spelled out in the publisher's contract.

It's desirable to pursue every possible subsidiary right. Not only does this translate into more earnings for the author, but it greatly enhances the sale of the published book. If the publisher has no interest in pursuing certain rights, these should be retained and marketed by your agent.

Negotiating a Sale

by Malaga Baldi

What is a successful negotiation?

As a literary agent, I must keep several goals in mind when negotiating a sale. Because I am my author's advocate, his or her needs come first. A successful negotiation:

- results in the best contract terms for my author
- spells out specifics so that later controversy is avoided
- has terms that allow all of us (author, agent and publisher) to profit from the book's publication, even if it is not a bestseller

What is a successful book?

The majority of writers I represent are "first-timers"—writers who have never been published before. First books, whether fiction or nonfiction, are hard to sell. A conventionally "successful" book gets many favorable reviews, makes the *New York Times Book Review* bestseller list, and sells so well that author, publisher and agent are happy. This narrow definition allows for very few successes.

My definition of a successful book is simply one that has "earned out." For example, if I sold a first novel for $10,000 (the advance against royalties paid to the author through me), I would be pleased if the book earned out the advance after one to two years. To earn out means that the publisher does not lose money on the deal. Once a book has earned out, the author begins to receive royalties every six to eight months for additional books sold.

Negotiating contract points

Here are some of the specific contract terms I pay close attention to, on the author's behalf, when negotiating a sale.

Advance

An advance is actually a payment of royalties *in advance* of a book's publication. It's a lump sum meant to provide some income for the author as he writes the book. When the book eventually is published, the publisher will pay itself back the amount of the advance from the author's royalty account before distributing any further royalties to the author. Sadly, the amount of time a first-time author has spent on a book has little to do with the size of the advance offered. Topical, timely and commercial subjects can attract a very high advance. If more than one publisher is interested in the book, the agent encourages competitive bidding. This could be an event planned to take place on one day (an auction), or it could take place over a longer period, as different publishers express interest and make offers. Usually it is in the author's best interest for me to get the highest advance possible.

A large advance usually indicates that the publisher is behind the book. The converse is not necessarily true. Small publishers often cannot pay the large advances that make the

Malaga Baldi is president of Malaga Baldi Literary Agency. She specializes in literary novels and nonfiction books.

business and entertainment page headlines. However, a small, independent publisher may put more time and energy into promoting a book than a large, busy publisher will. Because attention and promotion are so important to a book, the choice of publisher sometimes weighs more heavily than dollars. To get paid a lot of money by a big publisher for a book that dies due to lack of promotion can be a terrible blow to an author's career.

The advance proposed by an editor comes from a careful estimation of the profit and loss (P&L) profile. A P&L is the publisher's best guess as to how much money a book will make. The equation involves production costs, distribution expenses, and an estimate of projected sales. With a P&L in hand, the publisher has a good guess as to the amount of royalties a book may earn for its author. With *that* information the publisher can decide upon a reasonable advance against those royalties.

Royalties

These are often standard clauses. For example, on hardcover contracts the first 5,000 copies sold will draw a 10% (of the list price) royalty rate, up to 10,000 copies at 12.5%, and 15% thereafter. Paperback royalties run lower (6-8%), and the sales figures at which royalties escalate are negotiable.

Liabilities and indemnity

This is insurance the publisher will use to back up the author in the event of a lawsuit. This is especially important in a book that involves nonfictional characters. I argue for the publisher to provide maximal coverage.

Consultation on jacket, title and design of the book

The publisher has the ultimate say on these points, but I negotiate for author input. The publisher can make these decisions quickly, and if a consultation clause is not included in the contract, the publisher may bypass the author completely.

Permissions

If a book is an anthology of various works or is highly illustrated, one must obtain permission to use each contribution. This process takes a lot of time (tracking down who has rights, negotiating costs, organizing responses). I negotiate for the publisher to take on as much responsibility as possible.

Publicity and promotion

It is hard to get a budget for publicity for an author's first book. It becomes easier to negotiate for subsequent books. A marketing program will help any book. Readings, book tours, postcards, advertisements and review copies are all components of publicity and promotion.

Subsidiary rights

Depending on the international appeal of the book, many publishers will want to keep world or world English language rights as opposed to U.S./Canada only. Also open to discussion are first serial and dramatic rights. First serial rights are more easily exploited with nonfiction works. The appearance of a piece in a magazine is good early publicity for a book. Whether it is best for the agent or publisher to handle various rights depends on the experience and interest of each party.

Option clause

This gives the publisher the right to get the first look at the author's next book. If the publisher feels very strongly about keeping this right, I will argue to keep the amount of time they are allowed to consider—and the amount of material they need to make a decision—to a minimum.

Signing on the dotted line

Every author and publisher prioritizes these contract points, as well as those not mentioned, in a different order. After a publisher offers a contract I work through it, making comments, suggestions, deletions, alterations and insertions. Contracts vary from house to house. I often refer to favorite bits and pieces from previous contracts I have negotiated. The Author's Guild and the National Writers Union publish useful contract guidelines with specific explanations and examples.

Most editors will bend over backward to negotiate a contract an author and agent are comfortable with, but there is always a moment during a contract negotiation when the publisher and editor will not budge on a specific issue. It is good to know when to stop pushing, so that good will is preserved between editor, author and agent. There is a long and important relationship ahead from the time a book is sold to the day it appears on bookstore shelves. Hopefully there are also many years of royalties in the future.

Finding and Working with Literary Agents

by Robin Gee

The articles included in this book cover a number of very important aspects of the author/ agent relationship, including how agents work, what to look for in an agent, when to know you are ready for an agent and how to know if you and your agent are working well together. We're pleased also to offer almost 400 detailed listings of literary agents and script agents. Yet, with all this information, it's still possible to overlook some of the more basic requirements of working with an agent.

We've included this section to make sure these fundamentals are covered. Written especially for those of you looking for an agent for the first time, the information provided here will help you with querying an agent, preparing and presenting your work to an agent, and knowing what you can and cannot expect from your agent. Authors who may be considering changing agents will also find this material helpful.

Thinking about getting an agent

If you've just completed a manuscript or have been sending out your work directly to publishers for awhile without success, you may be thinking of getting an agent. Before you start to query agents, however, you must first have a clear idea of what you want and of what you expect your agent to accomplish.

Many agents complain of writers who expect too much; it's important to note what agents do not do. Agents are not teachers. They may give advice or recommend changes based on their experience and what they know about the market, but no agent is able or willing to try to sell an unsalable manuscript. Before contacting any agent, you must be certain your work is of publishable quality.

For the most part, agents do not handle short pieces such as magazine articles, poetry or short stories. A few agents will handle short work if they also handle a writer's book-length material, more as a friendly gesture than for profit. The reason is agents' commissions on short work are just too small to make handling such material profitable.

In general you don't need an agent to sell very specialized or experimental work or to sell work to a small or specialized publisher. Most agents work with the big, commercial publishers and look for books with wide appeal, although there are exceptions.

Simply put, an agent's job is to sell your work, help you maximize your earnings from your work, help keep track of your earnings and, thus, advance your career. It is often said agents are one part salesperson, one part business partner.

If you have a book-length manuscript you feel is publishable, and would like someone to manage the marketing of your work, an agent can help. Agents can open doors to publishers who do not take unagented manuscripts. They can put an unsolicited manuscript on an editor's desk that on its own might lie buried under the "slush" pile in the outer office.

Robin Gee is former editor of Guide to Literary Agents & Art/Photo Reps, *editor of* Novel & Short Story Writer's Market *and a regular contributor to* The Artist's Magazine.

Looking for an agent

Yet finding the right agent can be almost as hard as finding the right publisher. It's important to put just as much effort into your search. Start by reading all you can about the agent/author process. The articles and introductions in this book were chosen to help answer some of the most frequently asked questions writers have about agents. We've also included within the Resources section a list of books on agents.

Most agents find clients in one of two ways—direct contact or through referrals. One way to make direct contact is to send a query or a proposal package to the agent. Agents list in directories such as this book to let writers know how to get in touch with them. Examine the listings included in this book and check the Subject Indexes (located before the Listings Index at the back of the book) to find an agent who handles the type of work you write.

Another way to make direct contact with an agent is to meet one at a writers' conference. Often conferences will invite agents to participate in a panel, give a speech and be the "resident agent" for the conference. Although most agents would not appreciate your just "stopping by" their office for a chat, agents set aside time at conferences to do just that. Writers can sign up to talk with an agent. Some agents will look at material writers send in before the conference, but many just want to meet writers and talk generally about their work. If interested, the agent will ask the writer to send a query and samples after the conference is over.

Many agents find referrals very helpful. A recommendation from an editor, another agent or one of the agent's other clients tells the agent someone else thinks your work is worth considering. Even if you do not know any big-name authors or editors, you can make helpful contacts with them at conferences, readings and any place writers gather. Ask around. Some experienced writers are more than happy to share information and contacts.

Approaching an agent

Most agents will accept unsolicited queries. Many will also look at outlines and sample chapters. Few are interested in seeing unsolicited manuscripts, but those who handle fiction may be more willing to do so. Agents, for the most part, are slow in responding to queries, so they understand the writer's need to contact several at one time. When sending a manuscript, however, it is best to send it to one agent at a time.

This should go without saying, but submitting to an agent requires the same professional approach you would use when approaching a publisher. Work must be clean, typed, double-spaced and relatively free of cross-outs and typos. If you are sending a computer printout copy, make sure it is printed on at least a near-letter quality printer and the type is dark and easy-to-read. Always include a self-addressed, stamped envelope large enough to return your material. To save money, many writers do not want their outlines or manuscripts returned—they just send a self-addressed, stamped envelope or postcard for a reply.

Queries to agents should be brief (one-page) and to-the-point. The first paragraph should quickly state your purpose—you are looking for representation. In the second paragraph you might mention why you are querying this agent and whether you were referred to them by someone. If you chose that agent because of their interest in books like yours, be sure to mention this—in other words, show you have done a little research and are informed about this agent's business.

In the next paragraph or two describe the project. Include the type of book or script it is and the proposed audience. If your book fits into a genre or specific category, be sure to mention this. For example, if you have written a private eye detective novel, a cookbook

WILL I. DREW
122 22nd Drive
Louisville, Colorado 80077
Telephone: (303)555-5432

Ms. Mary Miller
The Wilbert Will Agency
1776 No. Houston Street
New York, NY 10077

Dear Ms. Miller:

I have a manuscript I propose to submit for publication some time soon. I do not have an agent at this time, and would like to discuss the possibility of your representing me.

I was referred to you by Dudley Jenkins, one of your clients, who told me of your interest in how-to-books.

I have prepared an outline and two chapters for a book I call, Time-and Trouble-Savers at Home. This book contains 50 time-and energy-saving tips and techniques that would be of interest to homemakers, nursing home managers, hoteliers, health spa managers and others.

I teach home economics at Johnson High School in Louisville. I also teach courses in time and motion studies for corporate clients.

I have had two articles on home care published in Homelife Magazine. I can provide you with copies.

Please let me know if you would like me to send you the outline and chapters for my book. I look forward to hearing from you.

Sincerely,

Will I Drew

This agent query is concise and direct. The writer mentions a referral from one of the agent's clients, while in the same sentence he demonstrates a knowledge of the type of work the agent handles. He follows with a one-paragraph description of the project, his credentials and background and publishing credits. This sample is from the Writer's Digest Guide to Manuscript Formats, copyright © 1987, Dian Dincin Buchman & Seli Groves. Used with permission of Writer's Digest Books.

or a movie-of-the-week, be sure to say so. This saves the agent (and yourself) time. You may also want to mention approximate length and any special features.

Follow this with a very short paragraph of personal information. Include some publication credits, if you have any, especially other published books or scripts. For nonfiction, list your professional credentials or experience related to the project. For fiction, you may want to relate something personal that lends credibility to your story. For example, if your novel is about a dentist and you are a dentist, by all means mention this. If it takes place in Mexico City and you once lived there, you want to mention this too. The rule of thumb is to include only that information directly related to your project or what lends credibility.

Close your query with an offer to send either an outline, sample chapters or the complete manuscript. Some agents ask for an outline and/or sample chapters with the query, while some want queries only and will ask for more, if interested. Within this section we've included a sample agent query from *Guide to Manuscript Formats*. This book is also a good source for standard formats for just about any type of material, including scripts, novels, outlines, proposals and cover letters. Script and screen writers will also want to see the article by Kerry Cox on working with script agents featured at the beginning of the Script Agents section.

Making an informed decision

Unfortunately, in most states, agents are not required to have a license or formal training. Basically anyone who can afford a phone can call themselves an agent, but there are ways to determine if an agent is legitimate, recognized in the publishing industry and has enough professional experience and potential to sell your work.

Remember you are entering a business agreement. You have the right to ask for references or other information that will help you determine if the agent is the right one for you. Some agents freely give out client names, recent sales or editorial references. Others feel it is an invasion of their client's privacy, but you should ask.

Do some checking by talking to other writers about their experiences with agents. Several writers' clubs have information on agents on file and share this by written request or through their club newsletters.

While some very reputable agents are not affiliated with any agent group, those who do belong to a professional organization are required to maintain certain standards. Agents who are members of the Association of Authors' Representatives (AAR) or signatories of the Writers Guild of America East or West have met certain qualifications and have agreed to a code of ethics. We have listed these affiliations within the listings.

Here's a list of questions you may wish to ask a potential agent. Much of this material is contained in the listings in this book, but it's always good to check if there have been any policy changes.

● How soon do you report on queries? On manuscripts?

● Do you charge a reading fee or a critique fee? If so, how much? If a critique is involved, who will do it? What kind of feedback will I receive? Is the fee nonrefundable? Or will it be credited toward my expenses or refunded, if I become a client?

● Do you offer a written contract? If so, how long is it binding? What projects will it cover? Will (or must) it cover all of my writing?

● What is your commission on domestic, foreign, dramatic and other rights? Will I be responsible for certain expenses? If so, which ones and will they be deducted from earnings, billed directly or paid by an initial deposit?

● How can our agreement be terminated? After termination, what will happen to work already sold, current submissions, etc.?

● Will I receive regular status reports? How often can I expect to receive this information? Will I receive all information or good news only? Copies of editors' letters?

● Which subsidiary rights do you market directly? Which are marketed through subagents? Which are handled by the publisher?

● Do you offer editorial support? How much?

● Do you offer other services such as tax/legal consultation, manuscript typing, book promotion? Which cost extra and which would be covered by the commission?

How agencies make money

The primary way agents make money is by taking a commission on work sold. This is usually a 10 to 20 percent commission taken from a writer's advance and royalties. Most agents charge a slightly higher commission on the sale of foreign rights or other special rights, because they may have to split some of the money with a foreign or specialized agent.

The agents listed in our Nonfee-charging Agents section and many of those listed in the Script Agents section make almost all of their money from commissions earned on sales. Most, however, do deduct some expenses from an author's earnings in addition to the commission. These expenses may include postage costs, long-distance calls, extensive photocopying or express mail fees. Be sure you know exactly what expenses you might be charged before signing an agreement with an agency. Ask your agent to give you prior notification of any large or unusual expenses.

Many agents also charge reading or critique fees. In our book we've put these literary agents into the Fee-charging Agents section. Some script agents also charge for reading and/or critiquing and they are marked with an open box symbol (□) in the Script Agent section.

Reading fees are intended to be used as payment for an outside person to read and report on a manuscript. This saves the agent time and effort. Reading fees can range from $25-$50 on up to $300-$400. Quite often the fee is nonrefundable. Reading fees almost never obligate the agent to agree to represent you, but some agents will refund the fee, if they decide to take you as a client. Others will refund the fee after they sell your work or will credit your account. Some agents also include a report or even a critique with the fee. Before you pay any fees, make sure you have a clear understanding of what the fee will cover.

Many agents also offer critique or editorial services. The fees for these services vary widely as do the quality and extent of the critiques. It's important to ask for a fee schedule and to check the credentials of agents offering these services. Remember, too, while many agents have some editing and writing background, most are unable or unwilling to rewrite entire manuscripts.

Agents may also offer a variety of other services including consultation, publicity and ghostwriting. A few agents are also lawyers and may be available for legal consultation or representation. Keep in mind, however, that if an agent's income is mostly generated by additional services, there is less incentive to sell your book for a commission.

What agencies do

In order to sell your work, an agent must keep up with the market. Agents must maintain constant contact with editors and publishers. They must study the market and know what publishers want. This sounds easier than it really is. Publishing companies are being bought out at a dizzying rate these days and editors change jobs frequently. Until recently, agents near New York (for publishing) and the West Coast (for film) had an advantage of being close to the market. Today, proximity, while still helpful, is less important thanks to modern office technology—faxes, computers, special phone services, etc.

An agent's job is to get the most money or the best deal for your work. Agents try to help you hold onto your rights so that you can maximize your profits from one piece of work. Depending on your work and the market, an agent may submit your work to various publishers and wait for the best offer. Agents also conduct "auctions" in which publishers are invited to bid for the work at a set time. Work is then sold to the highest bidder.

The agent will represent you in contract negotiations. The final decision is ultimately yours, but the agent will advise you on how to get the best deal, what rights to sell and what rights to try to keep. Once you've sold the work, the agent may continue to try to sell additional rights or options to other publishers, movie or television producers, book clubs, audio or video producers, etc.

Agents also keep track of your business. Some agents will give you periodic reports about the status of your work. This may include a list of publishers contacted and copies of publishers' letters. Some only report on good news, while others will send you copies of reject letters as well. After the sale, the agent will keep records of your income. Publishers will send the money to the agent for you. Once the agent has deducted the commission and expenses (if any), a check will be forwarded to you.

You can also call on your agent to handle disputes or problems that come up while you are working with an editor or publisher. The agent will check your royalty statements and will ask for an audit, if needed.

Some additional information

For more information on working with agents, see the articles written by agents or other writing professionals in the Literary Agents section. Check also the introductions to each section. These cover material directly related to the entries contained within a section and will help you understand more about each type of agent listed.

At the end of the Literary Agents: Nonfee-charging and the Literary Agents: Fee-charging section introductions you will find sample listings. These samples describe each item included in the listing in detail. We explain why each piece of information is important and how it can help you make an informed decision.

We've also included a number of indexes. The Subject Index for each section contains a list of subjects in both nonfiction and fiction. Agencies who have specified interest in handling particular types of material are listed within each subject section. The Agents and Reps Index lists the names of agents and their agency affiliation. This index will be most helpful to writers who have heard or read about a good agent, but do not know the agency for which the agent works.

Listing Policy and Complaint Procedure

Listings in Guide to Literary Agents & Art/Photo Reps *are compiled from detailed questionnaires, phone interviews and information provided by agents and representatives. The industry is volatile and agencies change addresses, needs and policies frequently. We rely on our readers for information on their dealings with agents and changes in policies or fees that are different from what has been reported to the editor. Write to us if you have new information, questions about agents or if you have any problems dealing with the agencies listed or suggestions on how to improve our listings.*

Listings are published free of charge and are not *advertisements. Although the information is as accurate as possible, the listings are* not *endorsed or guaranteed by the editor or publisher of* Guide to Literary Agents & Art/Photo Reps. *If you feel you have not been treated fairly by an agent or representative listed in* Guide to Literary Agents & Art/Photo Reps, *we advise you to take the following steps:*

● *First try to contact the listing. Sometimes one phone call or a letter can quickly clear up the matter.*
● *Document all your correspondence with the listing. When you write to us with a complaint, we will ask for the name of your manuscript or type of artwork, the date of your first contact with the agency and the nature of your subsequent correspondence.*
● *We will write to the agency and ask them to resolve the problem. We will then enter your letter into our files.*
● *The number, frequency and severity of complaints will be considered in our decision whether or not to delete the listing from our upcoming edition.*

Guide to Literary Agents & Art/Photo Reps *reserves the right to exclude any listing for any reason.*

Key to Symbols and Abbreviations

‡*A listing new to this edition.*
**Agents who charge fees to previously unpublished writers only*
□*Script agents who charge reading or other fees*
■*Art/photo representatives who charge a one-time or monthly fee for handling, marketing or other services in addition to commission and advertising costs*
ms/mss—manuscript/manuscripts
SASE—self-addressed, stamped envelope
SAE—self-addressed envelope
FAX—a communications system used to transmit documents over telephone lines.
AAR—Association of Authors' Representatives (merger of ILAA and SAR)
SPAR—Society of Photographers and Artists Representatives
WGA (East or West)—Writers Guild of America (East or West divisions)
See the Glossary for definitions of words and expressions used throughout the book.

Literary Agents: Nonfee-charging

In this section you will find literary agents who do not charge reading fees or other fees for services such as critiquing, editing or marketing. These agents derive from 98 to 100 percent of their business from commissions made on the sale of their clients' work.

One advantage to working with this type of literary agent is, of course, you do not have to pay a fee before you sell your work. Another important advantage is the agent has a built-in incentive to selling your work—if these agents do not sell, they do not make money. They are not involved in making money in other ways such as editing manuscripts or promoting published books. They devote all their time to selling. Their job is to know the market and establish valuable contacts in the field.

A disadvantage may be that these agents are very selective. Many prefer to work with established authors, celebrities or those who have professional expertise in a particular field. Almost all will look at queries from new writers, but they are looking for outstanding talent and the competition is keen.

To save time and money, check the listing or query first to find out if the agent you are interested in is open to new clients. A few ask to see outlines or sample chapters with queries, but send them only if they are requested within the listing. Always include a self-addressed, stamped envelope or postcard for reply. Agents tend to take a long time looking at queries, so you may want to send queries to more than one agent. When sending a requested manuscript, however, it is best to let one agent at a time consider the piece.

Commissions range from 10 to 20 percent for domestic sales and usually slightly higher for foreign or dramatic sales. The additional commission is used to pay a foreign agent or a subagent.

Many of the agents in this section charge for expenses in addition to taking a commission. Expenses can include foreign postage, fax charges, long-distance phone calls, messenger services, express mail and photocopying. Most of the agents listed only charge for what they consider extraordinary expenses. Make sure you have a clear understanding of what these "extraordinary" expenses might be before signing an agency agreement. Most agents will agree to discuss these expenses as they come up and negotiate with their clients on payment.

While most agents take expenses from the money made on sales, a few agents included in this section charge a low (no more than $50) one-time-only expense fee. Sometimes these are called "marketing" fees. These are fees charged every client to cover general expenses. Agents charging more than $50 were included in the Literary Agents: Fee-charging section.

To help you with your search for an agent, we've included a number of special indexes in the back of this book. The Subject Index is divided into sections for nonfee-charging and fee-charging literary agents and script agents. Each of these sections in the index is then divided by nonfiction and fiction subject categories. If you have written a romance novel and you are interested in nonfee-charging agents, turn to the fiction subjects listed in that section of the Subject Index. You will find a subject heading for romance and then the names of agencies interested in this type of work. Some agencies did not want to restrict themselves to specific subjects. They have been grouped in the subject heading "open" in both nonfiction and fiction.

We've included the Agents and Reps Index as well. Often you will read about an agent, but since that agent is an employee of a large agency, you may not be able to find that person's business phone or address. Agencies were asked to give the names of agents on their staffs. Then the names were listed in alphabetical order along with the name of their agency. Find the name of the person you would like to contact and then check the agency listing. You will find the page number for the agency's listing in the Listings Index.

Some art representatives, especially those interested in humor (cartoons and comics) and children's books, are also looking for writers. If the agency is primarily an art representative, but is also interested in writers, we've included them in a list (Additional Nonfee-charging Agents) in this section. For example, if ABC Art Reps, Inc. primarily handles the work of artists, but is also interested in writers who can draw, it is in the Additional Nonfee-charging Agents list. The company's complete listing, however, appears in the Commercial Art/Photo Reps section.

Many of the literary agents in this section are also interested in scripts and vice versa. If the agency's primary function is selling scripts, but it is interested in seeing some book manuscripts, we've also included them in Additional Nonfee-charging Agents. Their complete listings, however, appear in the Script Agent section.

For more information on approaching agents and the specifics of our listings, please see 1) How to Use Your Guide to Literary Agents & Art/Photo Reps and 2) Finding and Working with Literary Agents. See also the various articles at the beginning of this book for the answers to a wide variety of questions concerning the author/agent relationship.

We've ranked the agencies listed in this section according to their openness to submissions. Below is our ranking system:

I Newer agency actively seeking clients.
II Agency seeking both new and established writers.
III Agency prefers to work with established writers, mostly obtains new clients through referrals.
IV Agency handling only certain types of work or work by writers under certain circumstances.
V Agency not currently seeking new clients. (If an agency chose this designation, only the address is given.) We have included mention of agencies rated V only to let you know they are not open to new clients at this time. In addition to those ranked V, we have included a few well-known agencies' names who have declined listings. *Unless you have a strong recommendation from someone respected in the field, our advice is to approach only those agents ranked I-IV.*

‡A.M.C. LITERARY AGENCY (II, IV), 234 Fifth Ave., New York NY 10001. (212)673-9551. Fax: (212) 779-3493. Contact: Alexandra Chalusiak. Estab. 1989. Represents 7 clients. 90% of clients are new/ previously unpublished writers. Specializes in nonfiction; fiction (murder/mystery). Currently handles: 90% nonfiction books; 10% novels.
Handles: Nonfiction books, novels. Will consider these nonfiction areas: biography/autobiography, child guidance/parenting, current affairs, history, military/war, true crime/investigative, women's issues/women's studies. Will consider these fiction areas: action/adventure, detective/police/crime, mystery/suspense, psychic/supernatural, thriller/espionage. Query with outline and 3 sample chapters for fiction; query with outline/proposal for nonfiction. Will report in 2 weeks on queries; 1 month on mss.
Terms: Agent receives 15% commission on domestic sales; 10% on foreign sales. Offers written contract. "Usually one year with option for automatic renewal."
Writers' Conferences: Attends ABA conference, New Orleans.
Tips: Obtains new clients through *Literary Marketplace* and personal pursuit of clients. "1. Please specify if you want materials returned with reply. 2. *Always* double-space submissions. 3. Fiction should be *at least* 350 double-spaced pages. 4. Stay away from esoteric and bizarre subject matter."

ACTON, DYSTEL, LEONE & JAFFE, INC. (II), (formerly Acton and Dystel, Inc.), 928 Broadway, New York NY 10010. (212)473-1700. Fax: (212)505-0278. Contact: M. Perkins. Estab. 1976. Member of AAR. Represents 200 clients. 30% of clients are new/previously unpublished writers. Specializes in commercial nonfiction and fiction; some category fiction; some literary fiction. Currently handles: 50% nonfiction books; 50% novels.

Handles: Nonfiction books, novels. Will consider these nonfiction areas: animals; biography/autobiography; business; child guidance/parenting; cooking/food/nutrition; current affairs; ethnic/cultural interests; gay/lesbian issues; government/politics/law; health/medicine; history; military/war; money/finance/economics; music/dance/theater/film; nature/environment; psychology; true crime/investigative; science/technology; self-help/personal improvement; sports; women's issues/women's studies. Will consider these fiction areas: action/adventure; contemporary issues; detective/police/crime; ethnic; family saga; glitz; historical; literary; mainstream; mystery/suspense; romance; sports; thriller/espionage. Query. Will report in 2 weeks on queries; 1 month on fiction mss and 3 weeks on nonfiction mss.

Terms: Agent receives 15% on domestic sales; 19% on foreign sales. Offers a written contract. Charges for photocopying and Federal Express.

Tips: Obtains new clients through recommendations from others.

AGENCY CHICAGO (I), P.O. Box 11200, Chicago IL 60611. Contact: Ernest Santucci. Estab. 1990. Represents 4 clients. 50% of clients are new/previously unpublished writers. Specializes in ghost writing. Currently handles: 40% nonfiction books; 20% scholarly books; 10% novels; 10% movie scripts; 20% TV scripts.

Handles: Nonfiction books, movie and TV scripts, sports books. Will consider these nonfiction areas: animals; art/architecture/design; ethnic/cultural interests; music/dance/theater/film; sports. Will consider these fiction areas: detective/police/crime; erotica; experimental; humor/satire; regional. Send outline/proposal and SASE. Will report in 1 month on queries and mss.

Terms: Agent receives 10-15% commission on domestic sales; 15% on foreign sales. Offers a written contract, binding for 1 year.

Writers' Conferences: Attends Midwest Writers Conference; International Writers and Translators Conference.

Tips: Obtains new clients through recommendations. "Do not send dot matrix printed manuscripts. Manuscripts should have a clean professional look, with correct grammar and punctuation."

AGENTS INC. FOR MEDICAL AND MENTAL HEALTH PROFESSIONALS (II), P.O. Box 4956, Fresno CA 93744-4956. (209)226-0761. Fax: (209)226-0761 (press asterisk). Director: Sydney H. Harriet, Ph.D. Estab. 1987. Member of APA. Represents 20 clients. 45% of clients are new/previously unpublished writers. Specializes in "writers who have education and experience in the medical and mental health professions. It is helpful if the writer is licensed, but not necessary. Prior book publication not necessary." Currently handles: 85% nonfiction books; 5% scholarly books; 5% textbooks; 3% novels; 2% syndicated material.

Handles: Nonfiction books, textbooks, scholarly books, novels, syndicated material. Will consider these nonfiction areas: child guidance/parenting; nutrition; health/medicine; psychology; science/technology; self-help/personal improvement; sociology; sports; sports medicine/psychology; mind-body healing; how-to; reference. Will consider these fiction areas: contemporary issues; literary; "fiction focused toward health professions." Query with vita. Will report in 2 weeks on queries; 1 month on mss.

Recent Sales: *Not Getting Any Better,* by Joseph Wolpe, M.D. and Tom Giles, Psy.D. (Avery); *Juicing For Good Health,* by Maureen Keane, (Pocket Books).

Terms: Agent receives 15% commission on domestic sales; 20% on foreign sales. Offers a written contract, binding for 3-9 months. "After contract with a publisher is signed, office expenses are negotiated."

 The double dagger before a listing indicates the listing is new in this edition.

Writers' Conferences: Attends writers' conferences in California. "Plans are being made to present marketing workshops at nationwide medical and mental health conferences."
Tips: "45% of our clients are referred. The rest are obtained from writers using this guide. Our specialty has been to help writers with their manuscripts. If the idea is unique, but the writing needs work, that's where we have done our best work. We rarely receive a manuscript that's immediately contracted by a publisher. Unfortunately, we cannot respond to queries or proposals without receiving a return envelope and sufficient postage."

THE JOSEPH S. AJLOUNY AGENCY (II), 29205 Greening Blvd., Farmington Hills MI 48334. (313)932-0090. Fax: (313)932-8763. Contact: Joe Ajlouny. Estab. 1987. Member of WGA. "Represents humor and comedy writers, humorous illustrators, cartoonists." Member agents: Joe Ajlouny (original humor, how-to); Elena Pantel (music, popular culture); Lisa McDonald (general nonfiction).
Handles: "In addition to humor and titles concerning American popular culture, we will consider general nonfiction in the areas of 'how-to' books, history, health, cookbooks, self-help, social commentary, criticism, travel, biography and memoirs." Query first with SASE. Reports in 2-4 weeks.
Recent Sales: *How the Animals Do It*, by Larry Feign (Barricade Books); *101 Things Not to Say During Sex*, by Potnicki & Rumsey (Warner Books); *In Their Prime*, by Stewart Francke (Simon & Schuster).
Terms: Agent receives 15% commission on domestic sales. Charges for postage, photocopying and phone expenses.
Tips: Obtains new clients "typically from referrals and by some advertising and public relations projects. We also frequently speak at seminars for writers on the process of being published. Just make sure your project is marketable and professionally prepared. We see too much material that is limited in scope and appeal. It helps immeasurably to have credentials in the field or topic being written about."

LEE ALLAN AGENCY (II), P.O. Box 18617, Milwaukee WI 53218. (414)357-7708. Fax: (Call for number). Contact: Lee Matthias. Estab. 1983. Member of WGA. Represents 25 clients. 50% of clients are new/previously unpublished writers. Specializes in suspense fiction. Currently handles: 15% nonfiction books; 75% novels; 5% movie scripts; 5% TV scripts. Member agents: Lee A. Matthias (all types of genre fiction and screenplays, nonfiction); Andrea Knickerbocker (fantasy and science fiction, juvenile fiction, nonfiction); C.J. Bobke (all types); Joanne Erickson (all types); Chris Hill (fantasy).
Handles: Nonfiction books, juvenile books, novels, movie scripts. Will consider these nonfiction areas: biography/autobiography; business; child guidance/parenting; computers/electronics; cooking/food/nutrition; current affairs; government/politics/law; health/medicine; history; juvenile nonfiction; military/war; money/finance/economics; music/dance/theater/film; nature/environment; psychology; true crime/investigative; science/technology; self-help/personal improvement; sports. Will consider these fiction areas: action/adventure; detective/police/crime; fantasy; historical; humor/satire; juvenile; literary; mainstream; mystery/suspense; psychic/supernatural; romance (contemporary, historical); science fiction; thriller/espionage; westerns/frontier; young adult. Query. Will report in 2-3 weeks on queries; 6 weeks-3 months on mss.
Recent Sales: Untitled episode, *Star Trek: Deep Space 9*, by Sally Caves (Paramount TV); *The Quests of Winter*, by John Deakins (Roc Fantasy); *Destiny Betrayed: JFK, Cuba And The Garrison Case*, by James Dieugenio (Sheridan Square Press).
Terms: Agent receives 15% commission on domestic sales; 25% on foreign sales. Offers a written contract. Charges for "occasional shipping/mailing costs; photocopying; international telephone calls and/or excessive long-distance telephone calls."
Writers' Conferences: Attends World Fantasy Conference, and others.
Tips: Obtains new clients through "recommendations and solicitations, mainly." If interested in agency representation, "read agency listings carefully and query the most compatible. Always query by letter with SASE or IRC with envelope. A very brief, straightforward letter (1-2 pages, maximum) introducing yourself, describing or summarizing your material will suffice. Avoid patronizing or "cute" approaches. We *do not reply* to queries *without* SASE. Do not expect an agent to sell a manuscript which you know is not a likely sale if nonagented. Agents are not magicians; they serve best to find better and more of the likeliest publishers or producers. And they really do their work after an offer by way of negotiating contracts, selling subsidiary rights, administrating the account(s), advising the writer with objectivity, and acting as the buffer between writer and editor."

JAMES ALLEN, LITERARY AGENCY (III), P.O. Box 278, Milford PA 18337. Estab. 1974. Member of WGA. Represents 40 clients. 10% of clients are new/previously unpublished writers. "I handle all kinds of genre fiction (except westerns) and specialize in science fiction and fantasy." Currently handles: 2% nonfiction books; 8% juvenile books; 90% novels.
Handles: Novels. Will consider these fiction areas: detective/police/crime; fantasy; historical; mainstream; mystery/suspense; romance (historical, regency); science fiction. Query. Will respond in 1 week on queries; 2 months on mss. "I prefer first contact to be a query letter with 2-3 page plot synopsis and SASE with a response time of 1 week. If my interest is piqued, I then ask for the first 4 chapters, response time again 1 week. If I'm impressed by the writing, I then ask for the balance of the ms, response time about 2 months."
Recent Sales: *They Followed The Plume*, by Robert J. Trout (Stackpole); fantasy trilogy (as yet untitled), by Tara K. Harper (Del Rey); *Perfect* and *Promises*, by Jane Renick (HarperCollins).
Terms: Agent receives 10% on domestic print sales; 20% on film sales; 20% on foreign sales. Offers a written contract, binding for 3 years "automatically renewed. No reading fees or other up-front charges. I reserve the right to charge for extraordinary expenses. I do not bill the author, but deduct the charges from incoming earnings."
Tips: *First time at book length need not apply*— "*only* taking on authors who have the foundations of their writing careers in place and can use help in building the rest. A cogent, to-the-point query letter is necessary, laying out the author's track record and giving a brief blurb for the book. The response to a mere 'I have written a novel, will you look at it?' is universally 'NO!' "

LINDA ALLEN LITERARY AGENCY (II), Suite 5, 1949 Green St., San Francisco CA 94123. (415)921-6437. Contact: Linda Allen. Estab. 1982. Represents 35-40 clients. Specializes in "good books and nice people."
Handles: Nonfiction, novels (adult and juvenile). Will consider all nonfiction and fiction areas except picture books. Query. Will report in 2-3 weeks on queries.
Terms: Agent receives 15% commission. Charges for photocopying.
Tips: Obtains new clients "by referral mostly."

MARCIA AMSTERDAM AGENCY (II), 41 W. 82 St., New York NY 10024. (212)873-4945. Contact: Marcia Amsterdam. Estab. 1969. Signatory of WGA.
Handles: Novels, movie and TV scripts. Will consider these fiction areas: action/adventure; glitz; historical; humor; mainstream; mystery/suspense; romance (contemporary, historical); science fiction; thriller/espionage; westerns/frontier; young adult; horror. Send outline plus first 3 sample chapters and SASE. Will report in 1 month on queries.
Recent Sales: *White Night*, by William Lovejoy (Zebra); *Moonkeeper*, by Patricia Rowe (Warner); *The Tiger Orchard*, by Joyce Sweeney (Delacorte).
Terms: Agent receives 15% commission on domestic sales; 20% on foreign sales. Offers a written contract, binding for 1 year, "renewable." Charges for "cable, legal fees (chargeable only when agreed to), foreign postage."
Tips: "We are always looking for interesting literary voices."

BART ANDREWS & ASSOCIATES INC. (III), Suite 100, 7510 Sunset Blvd., Los Angeles CA 90046. (213)851-8158. Contact: Bart Andrews. Estab. 1982. Represents 25 clients. 25% of clients are new/ previously unpublished authors. Specializes in nonfiction only, and in the general category of entertainment (movies, TV, biographies, autobiographies). Currently handles: 100% nonfiction books.
Handles: Nonfiction books. Will consider these nonfiction areas: biography/autobiography; music/ dance/theater/film; TV. Query. Will report in 1 week on queries; 1 month on mss.
Terms: Agent receives 15% on domestic sales; 15% on foreign sales (after sub-agent takes his 10%). Offers a written contract, "binding on a project-by-project basis." Author/client is charged for all photocopying, mailing, phone calls, postage, etc.
Writers' Conferences: Frequently lectures at UCLA in Los Angeles.
Tips: "Recommendations from existing clients or professionals are best, although I find a lot of new clients by seeking them out myself. I rarely find a new client through the mails. Spend time writing a query letter. Sell yourself like a product. The bottom line is writing ability, and then the idea itself. It takes a lot to convince me. I've seen it all! I hear from too many first-time authors who don't do their homework. They're trying to get a book published and they haven't the faintest idea what is required of them. There are plenty of good books on the subject and, in my opinion, it's their responsibility— not mine—to educate themselves before they try to find an agent to represent their work. When I ask an author to see a manuscript or even a partial manuscript, I really must be convinced I want to read

it—based on a strong query letter—because I have no intention of wasting my time reading just for the fun of it."

APPLESEEDS MANAGEMENT (II), Suite 302, 300 E. 30th St., San Bernardino CA 92404. (909)882-1667. For screenplays and teleplays only, send to Suite 560, 1870 N. Vermont, Hollywood CA 90027. Executive Manager: S. James Foiles. Estab. 1988. Member of WGA, licensed by state of California. Represents 25 clients. 40% of clients are new/previously unpublished writers. Specializes in action/adventure, fantasy, horror/occult, mystery and science fiction novels; also in nonfiction, true crime, biography, health/medicine and self-help; also in materials that could be adapted from book to screen; and in screenplays and teleplays. "We're not accepting unsolicited screenplays and teleplays at this time." Currently handles: 25% nonfiction books; 40% novels; 20% movie scripts; 15% teleplays (movie of the week).
Handles: Nonfiction books, novels, movie and TV scripts (no episodic), teleplays (MOW). Will consider these nonfiction areas: biography/autobiography; business; health/medicine; money/finance/economics; music/dance/theater/film; psychology; true crime/investigative; self-help/personal improvement; general nonfiction. Will consider these fiction areas: action/adventure; detective/police/crime; fantasy; historical; humor/satire; mainstream; mystery/suspense; psychic/supernatural; science fiction; thriller/espionage; occult, horror novels. Query. Will report in 2 weeks on queries; 2 months on mss.
Terms: Agent receives 10-15% commission on domestic sales; 20% on foreign sales. Offers a written contract, binding for 1-7 years.
Tips: "In your query, please describe your intended target audience and distinguish your book/script from similar works."

THE AXELROD AGENCY (III), 66 Church St., Lenox MA 01240. (413)637-2000. Fax: (413)637-4725. Estab. 1983. Member of AAR. Represents 30 clients. Specializes in commercial fiction and nonfiction. Currently handles: 50% nonfiction books; 50% fiction.
Handles: Will consider these nonfiction areas: art; business; computers; government/politics/law; health/medicine; history; money/finance/economics; music/dance/theater/film; nature/environment; science/technology. Will consider these fiction areas: cartoon/comic; detective/police/crime; family saga; historical; literary; mainstream; mystery/suspense; picture book; romance; thriller/espionage. Query. Will report in 10 days on queries; 2-3 weeks on mss.
Terms: Agent receives 10% commission on domestic sales; 20% on foreign sales. Charges for photocopying.
Writers' Conferences: Attends Romance Writers of America conferences.
Tips: Obtains new clients through referrals.

JULIAN BACH LITERARY AGENCY (II), 22 E. 71 St., New York NY 10021. (212)772-8900. Fax: (212)772-2617. Contact: Julian Bach. Estab. 1956. Member of AAR. Represents 300 clients. Currently handles: 50% nonfiction books, 50% novels. Member agents: Julian Bach; Trish Lande.
Handles: Nonfiction books, novels. Will consider these nonfiction areas: anthropology/archaeology; biography/autobiography; business; cooking/food/nutrition; current affairs; government/politics; history; language/literature/criticism; military/war; music/dance/theater/film; nature/environment; new age/metaphysics; psychology; true crime/investigative; self-help/personal improvement; sports; women's issues/women's studies. Will consider these fiction areas: detective/police/crime; feminist; literary; mainstream; religious/inspirational. Query.
Terms: No information provided. Written contract.

MALAGA BALDI LITERARY AGENCY (II), P.O. Box 591, Radio City Station, New York NY 10101. (212)222-1221. Contact: Malaga Baldi. Estab. 1985. Represents 40-50 clients. 80% of clients are new/previously unpublished writers. Specializes in quality literary fiction and nonfiction. Currently handles: 60% nonfiction books; 30% novels; 5% novellas; 5% short story collections.
Handles: Nonfiction books, novels, novellas, short story collections. Will consider any well-written nonfiction, but do *not* send child guidance, crafts, juvenile nonfiction, new age/metaphysics, religious/inspirational or sports material. Will consider any well-written fiction, but do *not* send confessional, family saga, fantasy, glitz, juvenile, picture book, psychic/supernatural, religious/inspirational, romance, science fiction, western or young adult. Query, but "prefers entire manuscript for fiction." Will report within minimum of 10 weeks. "Please enclose self-addressed jiffy bag with submission and self-addressed postcard for acknowledgement of receipt of manuscript."

Recent Sales: *Small Beer: A Handbook to the 19th Century English Novel*, by Daniel Pool (Simon & Schuster); *Minus Time*, a novel by Catherine Bush (Hyperion); *Scissors, Paper, Rock*, by Fenton Johnson (Pocket Books).
Terms: Agent receives 15% commission on domestic sales; 20% on foreign sales. Offers a written contract. Charges "initial $50 fee to cover photocopying expenses. If the manuscript is lengthy, I prefer the author to cover expense of photocopying."
Tips: "From the day I agree to represent the author, my role is to serve as his or her advocate in contract negotiations and publicity efforts. Along the way, I wear many different hats. To one author I may serve as a nudge, to another a confidante, and to many simply as a supportive friend. I am also a critic, researcher, legal expert, messenger, diplomat, listener, counselor and source of publishing information and gossip. I work with writers on developing a presentable submission and make myself available during all aspects of a book's publication."

BALKIN AGENCY, INC. (III), P.O. Box 222, Amherst MA 01004. (413)548-9835. Fax: (413)548-9836. President: R. Balkin. Estab. 1972. Member of AAR. Represents 50 clients. 10% of clients are new/ previously unpublished writers. Specializes in adult nonfiction. Currently handles: 85% nonfiction books; 5% scholarly books; 10% textbooks.
Handles: Nonfiction books, textbooks, scholarly books. Will consider these nonfiction areas: animals; anthropology/archaeology; biography; child guidance/parenting; current affairs; health/medicine; history; language/literature/criticism; music/dance/theater/film; nature/environment; pop culture; true crime/investigative; science/technology; sociology; translations, travel. Query with outline/proposal. Will report in 2 weeks on queries; 3 weeks on mss.
Terms: Agent receives 15% on domestic sales; 20% on foreign sales. Offers a written contract, binding for 1 year. Charges for photocopying, trans-Atlantic long-distance calls or faxes, and express mail.
Tips: Obtains new clients through referrals. "I do not take on books described as bestsellers or potential bestsellers."

‡**THE BANK STREET LITERARY AGENCY (II)**, 155 Bank St., New York NY 10014. Contact: Julia Ward. Currently handles: 60% nonfiction books, 40% novels.
Handles: Nonfiction books and novels. Query. Will report in 2 weeks on queries.
Terms: Agent receives 10% commission on domestic sales; 10% on foreign sales.
Tips: "Send a letter telling us your situation. The letter serves as a writing sample. We form an impression based on it."

VIRGINIA BARBER LITERARY AGENCY, INC., 353 W. 21st St., New York NY 10011. Prefers not to share information.

LORETTA BARRETT BOOKS INC. (II), 101 5th Ave., New York NY 10003. (212)242-3420. Fax: (212)727-0280. President: Loretta A. Barrett. Associate: Morgan Barnes. Estab. 1990. Member of AAR. Represents 40 clients. Specializes in general interest books. Currently handles: 40% fiction; 60% nonfiction.
Handles: Will consider all areas of nonfiction and fiction. Query first, then send partial ms and a synopsis. Will report in 4-6 weeks on queries and mss.
Terms: Agent receives 15% commission on domestic sales; 20% on foreign sales. Offers a written contract. Charges for "all professional expenses."

HELEN BARRETT LITERARY AGENCY (II), 175 W. 13th St., New York NY 10011. (212)645-7430. Contact: Helen Barrett. Estab. 1988. ("After 14 years as a literary agent at William Morris, where I handled many bestsellers, I went on my own.") Currently handles: 40% nonfiction books; 60% novels.
Handles: Nonfiction books, novels (hardcover). Will consider these nonfiction areas: anthropology/ archaeology; biography/autobiography; current affairs; government/politics/law; history; interior design/decorating; true crime/investigative; self-help/personal improvement; women's issues/women's studies. Will consider these fiction areas: action/adventure; confessional; contemporary issues; detective/police/crime; family saga; historical; mainstream; mystery/suspense; romance; thriller/espionage. Query first with SASE. Will report in 3 weeks on queries; 1 month on mss.
Terms: Agent receives 15% commission on domestic sales; 20% on foreign sales.
Tips: Obtains new clients mainly through recommendations. "Must have been previously published. No new writers being accepted at this time. Be straightforward in the query. Do not hype. Tell enough in a bio to give a good picture of your background that would relate to material to be submitted, education, publishing history, etc."

‡**GENE BARTCZAK ASSOCIATES INC. (II)**, Box 751, North Bellmore NY 11710. (516)781-6230. Fax: "available on request only." Vice President: Sue Bartczak. Estab. 1980. Represents 10 clients. 100% of clients are new/previously unpublished writers. Currently handles; 40% nonfiction books; 20% juvenile books; 40% novels.
Handles: Nonfiction books, juvenile books. "No picture books." Will consider these nonfiction areas: biography/autobiography, juvenile nonfiction, women's issues/women's studies. Will consider these fiction areas: contemporary issues, juvenile (no picture books). Query. Must have SASE. Will report in 2 weeks on queries; 4-6 weeks on mss.
Recent Sales: *Mr. Stumpguss* and *The 3rd Grade's Skinny Pig* by Kathleen Duey (Avon Books).
Terms: Agent receives 15% commission on domestic sales; 20% on foreign sales. Offers written contract, binding for 1 year; then automatic renewal for 1 year terms unless given 90 days prior written notice to terminate by either party.
Tips: Obtains new clients through recommendations and agency listings. "Be sure to include SASE with any material sent to an agent if you expect to get an answer. If you want the material you sent returned to you, be sure that your SASE has enough postage to take care of that."

DAVID BLACK LITERARY AGENCY, INC. (II), 220 5th Ave., New York NY 10001. (212)689-5154. Fax: (212)684-2606. Associate: Lev Fruchter. Estab. 1990. Member of AAR. Represents 150 clients. Specializes in sports, politics, novels. Currently handles: 80% nonfiction; 20% novels.
Handles: Nonfiction books, novels. Will consider these nonfiction areas: politics, sports. Query with outline. Reports in 1 month on queries.
Recent Sales: *Bo*, by Glenn "Bo" Schembechler and Mitch Albom (Warner); *If I Had a Hammer*, by Henry Aaron and Lonnie Wheeler (HarperCollins); *Birdsong Ascending*, by Sam Harrison (HBJ); *There Are No Children Here*, by Alex Kotlowitz.
Terms: Agent receives 15% commission. Charges for photocopying manuscripts and for books purchased for sale of foreign rights.

REID BOATES LITERARY AGENCY (II), P.O. Box 328, 274 Cooks Crossroad, Pittstown NJ 08867. (908)730-8523. Fax: (908)730-8931. Contact: Reid Boates. Estab. 1985. Represents 45 clients. 15% of clients are new/previously unpublished writers. Specializes in general fiction and nonfiction, investigative journalism/current affairs; bios and autobiographies; serious self-help; literary humor; issue-oriented business; popular science; "no category fiction." Currently handles: 85% nonfiction books; 15% novels; "very rarely accept short story collections."
Handles: Nonfiction books, novels. Will consider these nonfiction areas: animals; anthropology/archaeology; art/architecture/design; biography/autobiography; business; child guidance/parenting; current affairs; ethnic/cultural interests; government/politics/law; health/medicine; history; language/literature/criticism; nature/environment; psychology; true crime/investigative; science/technology; self-help/personal improvement; sports; women's issues/women's studies. Will consider these fiction areas: contemporary issues; crime; family saga; mainstream; mystery/suspense; thriller/espionage. Query. Will report in 2 weeks on queries; 6 weeks on mss.
Terms: Agent receives 15% commission on domestic sales; 20% on foreign sales. Offers a written contract, binding "until terminated by either party." Charges for photocopying costs above $50.
Tips: Obtain new clients through recommendations from others.

ALISON M. BOND LTD., 171 W. 79th St., New York NY 10024. Prefers not to share information.

GEORGES BORCHARDT INC. (III), 136 E. 57th St., New York NY 10022. (212)753-5785. Fax: (212)838-6518. Estab. 1967. Member of AAR. Represents 200+ clients. 10% of clients are new/previously unpublished writers. Specializes in literary fiction and outstanding nonfiction. Currently handles: 60% nonfiction books; 1% juvenile books; 37% novels; 1% novellas; 1% poetry books. Member agents: Denise Shannon; Cindy Klein; Alexandra Harding.
Handles: Nonfiction books, novels. Will consider these nonfiction areas: anthropology/archaeology; biography/autobiography; current affairs; history; women's issues/women's studies. Will consider these fiction areas: literary. "Must be recommended by someone we know." Will report in 1 week on queries; 3-4 weeks on mss.
Recent Sales: Has sold fiction book by T. Coraghessan Boyle (Viking); nonfiction book by Tracy Kidder (Houghton Mifflin); and *A New Collection of Poems*, by John Ashbery (Knopf).
Terms: Agent receives 10% on domestic sales; 15% British sales; 20% on foreign sales (translation). Offers a written contract. "We charge cost of (outside) photocopying and shipping mss or books overseas."

Tips: Obtains new clients through recommendations from others.

THE BARBARA BOVA LITERARY AGENCY (II), 207 Sedgwick Rd., West Hartford CT 06107. (203)521-5915. Estab. 1974. Represents 20 clients. Specializes in nonfiction science. Currently handles: 50% nonfiction books; 50% novels.
Handles: Will consider these nonfiction areas: science/technology; social sciences. Will consider these fiction areas: contemporary issues; mainstream; mystery/suspense. Query with SASE. Will report in 1 month on queries.
Terms: Agent receives 10% commission on domestic sales.
Tips: Obtains new clients through recommendations from others.

BRANDENBURGH & ASSOCIATES LITERARY AGENCY (III), 24555 Corte Jaramillo, Murrieta CA 92562. (909)698-5200. Owner: Don Brandenburgh. Estab. 1986. Represents 30 clients. "We prefer previously published authors, but will evaluate submissions on their own merits." Works with a small number of new/unpublished authors. Specializes in adult nonfiction for the religious market; limited fiction for religious market, and limited nonfiction for the general market. Currently handles: 70% nonfiction books; 20% novels; 10% textbooks.
Handles: Nonfiction books, novels and textbooks. Query with outline. Reports in 2 weeks on queries.
Recent Sales: *One Prince*, by Bill Hand (Thomas Nelson)); *If Only You Would Change . . .*, by Mark Luciano and ChristopherMerris (Thomas Nelson); *Search For Meaning*, by Thomas Naylor, Magdalena Naylor, William Willimon and William Sachs (Abingdon Press).
Terms: Agent receives 10% commission on domestic sales; 20% on dramatic sales; 20% on foreign sales. Charges a $35 mailing/materials fee with signed agency agreement.

THE JOAN BRANDT AGENCY (II), 52 South Prado N.E., Atlanta GA 30309. (404)881-0023. Fax: (404)888-9217. Contact: Joan Brandt. Estab. 1990. Represents 100 clients. Also handles movie rights for other agents.
Handles: Novels, nonfiction books, scripts. Will consider these fiction areas: contemporary issues; detective/police/crime; literary; mainstream; mystery/suspense; thriller/espionage; "also will consider popular, topical nonfiction." Query with SAE. Will report in 2 weeks on queries.
Terms: Agent receives 15% commission on domestic sales, 20% on foreign sales (co-agents in all major marketplaces). Charges for photocopying and long-distance postage.
Tips: Obtains new clients through recommendations from others and over-the-transom submissions.

BRANDT & BRANDT LITERARY AGENTS INC. (III), 1501 Broadway, New York NY 10036. Contact: Carl Brandt, Gail Hochman, Charles Schlcssiger. Estab. 1913. Member of AAR. Represents 200 clients.
Handles: Nonfiction books, scholarly books, juvenile books, novels, novellas, short story collections. Will consider these nonfiction areas: agriculture/horticulture; animals; anthropology/archaeology; art/architecture/design; biography/autobiography; business; child guidance/parenting; cooking/food/nutrition; crafts/hobbies; current affairs; ethnic/cultural interests; gay/lesbian issues; government/politics/law; health/medicine; history; interior design/decorating; juvenile nonfiction; language/literature/criticism; military/war; money/finance/economics; music/dance/theater/film; nature/environment; psychology; true crime/investigative; science/technology; self-help/personal improvement; sociology; sports; women's issues/women's studies. Will consider these fiction areas: action/adventure; contemporary issues; detective/police/crime; erotica; ethnic; experimental; family saga; feminist; gay; historical; humor/satire; lesbian; literary; mainstream; mystery/suspense; psychic/supernatural; regional; romance; science fiction; sports; thriller/espionage; westerns/frontier; young adult. Query. Will report in 2-4 weeks on queries.
Terms: Agent receives 10% commission on domestic sales; 20% on foreign sales. Charges for "manuscript duplication or other special expenses agreed to in advance."
Tips: Obtains new clients through recommendations from others or "upon occasion, a really good letter. Write a letter which will give the agent a sense of you as a professional writer, your long-term interests as well as a short description of the work at hand."

MARIE BROWN ASSOCIATES INC. (II,III), Rm. 902, 625 Broadway, New York NY 10012. (212)533-5534. Fax: (212)533-0849. Contact: Marie Brown. Estab. 1984. Represents 100 clients. Specializes in multicultural African-American writers. Currently handles: 50% nonfiction books; 25% juvenile books; 25% other.

Handles: Will consider these nonfiction areas: art; biography; business; child guidance/parenting; cooking/food/nutrition; ethnic/cultural interests; gay/lesbian issues; history; juvenile nonfiction; money/finance/economics; music/dance/theater/film; new age; photography; psychology; religious/inspirational; self-help/personal improvement; sociology; women's issues/women's studies. Will consider these fiction areas: contemporary issues; ethnic; family saga; feminist; gay; historical; humor/satire; juvenile; literary; mainstream; mystery/suspense; picture book; regional; science fiction. Query with SASE. Will report in 8-10 weeks on queries.
Terms: Agent receives 15% commission on domestic sales; 25% on foreign sales. Offers a written contract.
Tips: Obtains new clients through recommendations from others.

ANDREA BROWN LITERARY AGENCY, INC. (III,IV), P.O. Box 429, El Granada CA 94018-0429. (415)726-1783. Contact: Andrea Brown. Estab. 1981. Member of AAR, WNBA. 25% of clients are new/previously unpublished writers. Specializes in "all kinds of juveniles—illustrators and authors." Currently handles: 99% juvenile books, 1% novels.
Handles: Juvenile books. Will consider these nonfiction areas: animals; juvenile nonfiction; science/technology. Will consider these fiction areas: juvenile; picture book; young adult. Query. Will report in 2 weeks on queries; 2 months on mss.
Recent Sales: *Sunset Island Series*, by Cherie Bennett (Berkley); *How to Find Buried Treasure*, by James Doem (Houghton Mifflin); *Principal From the Black Lagoon*, by Mike Thaler (Scholastic).
Terms: Agent receives 15% commission on domestic sales; 20% on foreign sales.
Writers' Conferences: Attends Jack London Writers Conference; UCLA Writer's Workshop Conference and various SCBW conferences.

CURTIS BROWN LTD. (II), 10 Astor Pl., New York NY 10003. (212)473-5400. Member of AAR. Queries: Laura J. Blake. Chairman & CEO: Perry Knowlton. President: Peter L. Ginsberg. Member agents: Emilie Jacobson, Irene Skolnick, Emma Sweeney, Clyde Taylor, Maureen Walters, Timothy Knowlton (film screenplays and plays), Laura J. Blake, Virginia Knowlton, Marilyn Marlowe, Jess Taylor (audio rights), Jeannine Edmunds (film screenplays and plays).
Handles: Nonfiction books, juvenile books, novels, novellas, short story collections, poetry books, movie and TV scripts, stage plays. All categories of nonfiction and fiction considered. Query. Will report in 3 weeks on queries; 3-5 weeks on mss "only if requested."
Terms: Agent receives 15% on domestic sales; 20% on foreign sales. Offers a written contract. Charges for photocopying, some postage, "but only with prior approval of author."
Tips: Obtains new clients through recommendations from others, solicitation, at conferences and query letters.

KNOX BURGER ASSOCIATES LTD., 39½ Washington Square South, New York NY 10012. Prefers not to share information.

JANE BUTLER, ART AND LITERARY AGENT (II, III), P.O. Box 33, Metamoras PA 18336. Estab. 1981. "Prefers published credits, but all queries are welcome; no SASE, no reply." Specializes in fiction. Currently handles: 15% nonfiction books; 80% novels; 5% juvenile books.
Handles: Nonfiction books and novels. Will consider these fiction areas: science fiction, fantasy, romantic fantasy, romantic suspense, historical fantasy, dark fantasy, Y.A. and children's fiction, some horror.
Recent Sales: *Lord of the Two Lands*, by Judith Tarr (Tor Books); *Forests of the Night*, by S. Andrew Swan (Daw Books); *The Castle of the Silver Wheel*, by Teresa Edgerton (Berkley Books).
Terms: Agent receives 10% commission on domestic sales; 15% on dramatic sales; 20% on foreign sales.

SHEREE BYKOFSKY ASSOCIATES (IV), Suite 11-D, Box WD, 211 E. 51st St., New York NY 10022. Estab. 1984. Represents "a limited number of" clients. Specializes in popular reference nonfiction. Currently handles: 80% nonfiction; 20% fiction.
Handles: Nonfiction books. Will consider all nonfiction areas. Query with SASE. "No unsolicited manuscripts. No phone calls." Will report in 1 month on queries.
Terms: Agent receives 15% commission on domestic sales; 15% on foreign sales. Offers a written contract, binding for 1 year "usually." Charges for postage, photocopying and fax.
Tips: Obtains new clients through recommendations from others. "Read the agent listing carefully and comply with guidelines."

CANTRELL-COLAS INC., LITERARY AGENCY (II), 229 E. 79th St., New York NY 10021. (212)737-8503. Contact: Maryanne C. Colas. Estab. 1980. Represents 80 clients. Currently handles: 50% nonfiction books; 25% juvenile books; 25% mainstream.

Handles: Will consider these nonfiction areas: anthropology; art; biography; child guidance/parenting; cooking/food/nutrition; current affairs; ethnic/cultural interests; government/politics/law; health/medicine; history; juvenile nonfiction; language/literature/criticism; military/war; money/finance/economics; nature/environment; new age/metaphysics; psychology; true crime/investigative; science/technology; self-help/personal improvement; sociology; women's issues/women's studies. Will consider these fiction areas: contemporary issues; detective/police/crime; ethnic; experimental; family saga; feminist; historical; humor/satire; juvenile; literary; mainstream; mystery/suspense; psychic/supernatural; science fiction; thriller/espionage; young adult. Query with SASE and outline plus 2 sample chapters, and "something about author also." Will report in 2 months on queries.

Recent Sales: *Well and Truly*, by Evelyn Wilde-Mayerson (NAL); *Roosevelt and DeGaulle*, by Raoul Aglion (McMillan/The Free Press); *White Hare's Horses*, by Penina Spinka (Atheneum).

Terms: Agent receives 15% commission on domestic sales; commission varies on foreign sales. Offers a written contract. Charges for foreign postage and photocopying.

Tips: Obtains new clients through recommendations from others. "Make sure your manuscript is in excellent condition both grammatically and cosmetically. In other words, check for spelling, typing errors and legibility."

MARIA CARVAINIS AGENCY, INC. (II), Suite 15F, 235 West End Ave., New York NY 10023. (212)580-1559. Fax: (212)877-3486. Contact: Maria Carvainis. Estab. 1977. Member of AAR, WGA, Authors Guild. Represents 50 clients. 10% of clients are new/previously unpublished writers. Currently handles: 25% nonfiction books; 15% juvenile books; 55% novels; 5% poetry books.

Handles: Nonfiction books, scholarly books, novels, poetry books. Will consider these nonfiction areas: biography/autobiography; business; current affairs; government/politics/law; health/medicine; history; military/war; money/finance/economics; psychology; true crime/investigative; women's issues/women's studies; popular science. Will consider these fiction areas: action/adventure; detective/police/crime; family saga; fantasy; glitz; historical; humor/satire; juvenile; literary; mainstream; mystery/suspense; romance; thriller/espionage; westerns/frontier; young adult. Query first w/SASE. Will report in 2-3 weeks on queries; 3 months on mss.

Recent Sales: *The Competitive Edge*, by Fran Tarkenton and Joseph H. Boyett (Dutton/Plume); *French Silk*, by Sandra Brown (Warner); *Splendor*, by Catherine Hart (Avon).

Terms: Agent receives 15% commission on domestic sales; 20% on foreign sales. Offers a written contract, binding for 2 years "on a book-by-book basis." Charges for foreign postage and bulk copying.

Tips: "75% of new clients derived from recommendations or conferences. 25% of new clients derived from letters of query."

‡SJ CLARK LITERARY AGENCY (IV), 56 Glenwood, Hercules CA 94547. Fax: (510)236-1052. Contact: Sue Clark. Estab. 1982. Represents 10 clients. 100% of clients are new/previously unpublished writers. Specializes in mysteries/suspense, children's books. Currently handles: 25% juvenile books; 75% novels.

Handles: Juvenile books and novels. Will consider these nonfiction areas: new age/metaphysics. Will consider these fiction areas: detective/police/crime; juvenile; mystery/suspense; psychic/supernatural; thriller/espionage; young adult. Query with entire ms. Will report in 1 month on queries; 2 months on mss.

Terms: Agent receives 20% commission on domestic sales. Offers written contract.

Tips: Obtains new clients by word of mouth.

CONNIE CLAUSEN ASSOCIATES (II), #16H, 250 E. 87th St., New York NY 10128. (212)427-6135. Fax: (212)996-7111. Contact: Connie Clausen. Estab. 1976. 10% of clients are new/previously unpublished writers. Specializes in true crime, autobiography, biography, health, women's issues, psychology, celebrity, beauty-fashion, how-to, financial. Currently handles: 100% nonfiction books (in New York). Member Agent: Amy Fastenberg.

Handles: Nonfiction books. Will consider these nonfiction areas: biography/autobiography; business; cooking/food/nutrition; current affairs; ethnic/cultural interests; gay/lesbian issues; health/medicine; money/finance/economics; music/dance/theater/film; nature/environment; psychology; true crime/investigative; self-help/personal improvement; women's issues/women's studies. Send outline/proposal. Will report in 3 weeks on queries; 4-6 weeks on mss.

Recent Sales: *The Invisible Woman: How Gender Bias Affects Your Health*, by Eileen Nechas and Denise Foley (Simon & Schuster); *Italian Chic*, by Susan Sommers; *Confessions of a CPA: The Book the IRS Wishes Had Never Been Written*, by Martin Kaplan, CPA, and Naomi Wei.

Terms: Agent receives 15% commission on domestic sales; 20% on foreign sales. Offers a written contract, terms vary. Charges for office expenses.

Tips: Obtains new clients through referrals by other clients, publishers, magazine editors and *Writer's Digest*. "Always include SASE. Go to the library and read a book or two on publishing and proposal writing."

‡DIANE CLEAVER INC. (III), 55 Fifth Ave., New York NY 10003. (212)206-5606. Fax: (212)463-8718. Estab. 1979. Member of AAR. Currently handles: 60% nonfiction books; 40% novels.

Handles: Nonfiction books and novels. Generally open to most nonfiction areas. Will consider these fiction areas: mainstream; mystery/suspense; thriller/espionage. Query. Will report in 1 or 2 weeks on queries.

Terms: Agent receives 15% commission on domestic sales; 19% on foreign sales. Charges for photocopying of books on foreign submission.

Tips: Obtains new clients through recommendations from others.

RUTH COHEN, INC. LITERARY AGENCY (II), P.O. Box 7626, Menlo Park CA 94025. (415)854-2054. Contact: Ruth Cohen or associates. Estab. 1982. Member of AAR, Authors Guild, SCBW. Represents 75 clients. 20% of clients are new/previously unpublished writers. Specializes in "quality writing in juvenile fiction; mysteries; regency and historical romances, adult women's fiction." Currently handles: 15% nonfiction books; 40% juvenile books; 45% novels.

Handles: Juvenile books, adult novels. Will consider these nonfiction areas: ethnic/cultural interests; juvenile nonfiction; true crime/investigative; women's issues/women's studies. Will consider these fiction areas: detective/police; ethnic; family saga; historical; juvenile; literary; mainstream; mystery/suspense; romance; young adult. Send outline plus 2 sample chapters plus SASE. Will report in 1 month on queries. NO UNSOLICITED MSS.

Terms: Agent receives 15% commission on domestic sales; 20% on foreign sales, "if a foreign agent is involved." Offers a written contract, binding for 1 year "continuing to next." Charges for foreign postage and photocopying for submissions.

Tips: Obtains new clients through recommendations from others. "A good writer cares about the words he/she uses – so do I. Also, if no SASE is included, material will not be read."

HY COHEN LITERARY AGENCY LTD. (II), #1400, 111 W. 57th St., New York NY 10019. (212)757-5237. Contact: Hy Cohen. "Mail ms to P.O. Box 743, Upper Montclair NJ 07043." Estab. 1975. Represents 25 clients. 50% of clients are new/previously unpublished writers. Currently handles: 20% nonfiction books; 5% juvenile books; 75% novels.

Handles: Nonfiction books, novels. All categories of nonfiction and fiction considered. Send 100 pages with SASE. Will report in about 2 weeks (on 100-page submission).

Recent Sales: *Crazymaker*, by Thomas O'Donnell (HarperCollins); *Gunmen*, by Gary Friedman (Wm. Morrow); *Bittersweet Country*, by Elaine Long (St. Martin's).

Terms: Agent receives 10% commission.

Tips: Obtains new clients through recommendations from others and unsolicited submissions. "Send double-spaced, legible scripts and SASE. Good writing helps."

‡COLE AND LUBENOW: BOOKS (II), 1645 Terrace Way, Santa Rosa CA 95404. (707)571-8344. Contact: Jerry Lubenow. Estab. 1990. Represents 27 clients. 80% of clients are new/previously unpublished writers. Currently handles: 80% nonfiction books; 20% novels. "Both Tom Cole and Jerry Lubenow deal with full range of fiction and nonfiction."

Handles: Nonfiction books and novels. Will consider these nonfiction areas: animals; art/architecture/design; biography/autobiography; business; child guidance/parenting; cooking/food/nutrition; current affairs; government/politics/law; history; language/literature/criticism; money/finance/economics; music/dance/theater/film; nature/environment; psychology; religious/inspirational; science/technology; self-help/personal improvement and sports. Will consider these fiction areas: literary and science fiction. Query with outline plus 2 sample chapters. Will report in 2 weeks on queries; 1 month on mss.

Recent Sales: *Dangerous Craziness*, by E. Jean Carroll (Dutton); *Sutures*, by Chris Sanford (Soho); *When Computers Take Over*, by Gene Rochlin (Free Press).
Terms: Agent receives 15% commission on domestic sales; 30% on foreign sales. Offers written contract, binding for 3 years (unilaterally with 90 days notice). Charges for mailing and copying. 100% of business derived from commissions on ms sales.
Tips: Obtains new clients "almost entirely by referral; some through listings. It's all in the writing; hyping an agent is like offering Ross Perot a loan."

COLLIER ASSOCIATES (III), 2000 Flat Run Rd., Seaman OH 45679. (513)764-1234. Contact: Oscar Collier. Estab. 1976. Member of AAR. Represents 75+ clients. 10% of clients are new/previously unpublished writers. Specializes in "adult fiction and nonfiction books only." Currently handles: 50% nonfiction books; 50% novels. Member agents: Oscar Collier (category fiction, nonfiction); Carol Cartaino (how-to and self-help nonfiction). "This is a small agency that rarely takes on new clients because of the many authors it represents already."
Handles: Nonfiction, novels. Query with SASE. Will report in 6-8 weeks on queries; 3-4 months "or longer" on mss.
Recent Sales: *The Glass Cockpit*, by Robert P. Davis (St. Martin's Press); *Dancing With the Wheel*, by Sun Bear, Wabun Wind and Crysalis Mulligan (Prentice-Hall); *Renegade's Angel*, by Phoebe Fitzjames (Zebra Books).
Terms: Agent receives 10-15% commission on domestic sales; 20% on foreign sales. Offers a written contract "sometimes." Charges for photocopying and express mail, "if requested, with author's consent, and for copies of author's published books used for rights sales."
Tips: Obtains new clients through recommendations from others. "Send biographical information with query; must have SASE. Don't telephone. Read my books *How to Write and Sell Your First Novel* and *How to Write and Sell Your First Nonfiction Book*."

‡FRANCES COLLIN LITERARY AGENT, (III), Suite 1403, 110 West 40th St., New York NY 10018. (212)840-8664. Contact: Betty-Anne Crawford. Estab. 1948. Member of AAR. Represents 90 clients. 30% of clients are new/previously unpublished writers. Currently handles 48% nonfiction books; 1% textbooks; 50% novels; 1% poetry books.
Handles: Nonfiction books, novels. Will consider these nonfiction areas: anthropology/archaeology; biography/autiobiography; business; health/medicine; history; nature/environment; true crime/investigative. Will consider these fiction areas: detective/police/crime; ethnic; family saga; fantasy; historical; literary; mainstream; mystery/suspense; psychic/supernatural; regional; romance (historical); science fiction. Query. Will report in 1 week on queries; 6-8 weeks on mss.
Terms: Agent receives 15% commission on domestic sales; 20% on foreign sales. Offers written contract. Charges for overseas postage for books mailed to foreign agents; photocopying of manuscripts, books, proposals; copyright registration fees; registered mail fees; pass along cost of any books purchased.
Tips: Obtains new clients through recommendations from others.

COLUMBIA LITERARY ASSOCIATES, INC. (II,IV), 7902 Nottingham Way, Ellicott City MD 21043. (410)465-1595. Contact: Linda Hayes, Kathryn Jenson. Estab. 1980. Member of AAR. Represents 40+ clients. 10% of clients are new/previously unpublished writers. Specializes in women's fiction (mainstream/genre), commercial nonfiction, especially cookbooks. Currently handles: 40% nonfiction books; 60% novels.
Handles: Nonfiction books, novels. Will consider these nonfiction areas: business; parenting; cooking/food/nutrition; health/medicine; self-help/personal improvement. Will consider these fiction areas: mainstream; fast-paced mystery/suspense; romance; thrillers. Will report in 2-4 weeks on queries; 4-8 weeks on mss, "rejections faster."
Recent Sales: *Sister Act* and *Dark Side of Harmony*, by Chassie West (Harper Paperbacks); *Dream Desserts*, by Nancy Baggett (Stewart, Tabori & Chang); *Forty-Three Light Street Series, Books 7-8-9*, by Rebecca York (Harlequin Intrigue).

Check the Literary and Script Agents Subject Index to find the agents who indicate an interest in your nonfiction or fiction subject area.

Terms: Agent receives 15% commission on domestic sales. Offers single- or multiple-book written contract, binding for 6 months terms. "Standard expenses are billed against book income (e.g., books for subrights exploitation, tolls, UPS)."
Writers' Conferences: Attends Romance Writers of America and International Association of Culinary Professionals conferences.
Tips: Obtains new clients through referrals and mail. "For fiction, send a query letter with author credits, narrative synopsis, first few chapters, manuscript word count and submission history (publishers/agents); self-addressed, stamped mailer mandatory for response/ms return. Same for nonfiction, plus note audience, how project is different and better than competition. Please note that we do *not* handle: sf/fantasy, military books, poetry, short stories or screenplays."

DON CONGDON ASSOCIATES INC. (III), Suite 625, 156 5th Ave., New York NY 10010. (212)645-1229. Fax: (212)727-2688. Contact: Don Congdon, Michael Congdon, Susan Ramer. Estab. 1983. Member of AAR. Represents 100+ clients. Currently handles: 50% fiction; 50% nonfiction books.
Handles: Nonfiction books, novels. Will consider all nonfiction and fiction areas, especially literary fiction. Query. "If interested, we ask for sample chapters and outline." Will report in 3-4 weeks on manuscript.
Terms: Agent receives 10% on domestic sales.
Tips: Obtains new clients through referrals from other authors. "Writing a query letter is a must."

BONNIE R. CROWN INTERNATIONAL LITERATURE AND ARTS AGENCY (IV), 50 E. 10th St., New York NY 10003. (212)475-1999. Contact: Bonnie Crown. Estab. 1976. Represents 8-11 clients. 100% of clients are previously published writers. Specializes in cross-cultural and translations of literary works, American writers influenced by one or more Asian culture. Currently handles: 10% nonfiction books; 70% fiction, 20% poetry (translations only).
Handles: Nonfiction books, novels. Will consider these nonfiction areas: animals; ethnic/cultural interests; nature/environment; translations; women's issues/women's studies. Will consider these fiction areas: ethnic; family saga; historical; literary. Query with SASE. Will report in 1 week on queries.
Terms: Agent receives 15% commission on domestic sales; 20% on foreign sales. Charges for processing, usually $25, on submission of ms.
Tips: Obtains new clients through "referrals through other authors and listings in reference works. If interested in agency representation, send brief query with SASE."

RICHARD CURTIS ASSOCIATES, INC. (III), 171 E. 74th St., New York NY 10021. (212)772-7363. Fax: (212)772-7393. Contact: Richard Curtis. Estab. 1969. Member of AAR. Represents 150 clients. 5% of clients are new/previously unpublished writers. Specializes in genre paperback fiction such as science fiction, women's romance, horror, fantasy, action-adventure. Currently handles: 9% nonfiction books; 1% juvenile books; 90% novels. Member agents: Roberta Cohen, Richard Henshaw.
Handles: Nonfiction books, novels. Will consider these nonfiction areas: biography/autobiography; business; child guidance/parenting; history; military/war; money/finance/economics; music/dance/theater/film; true crime/investigative; science/technology; self-help/personal improvement; sports. Will consider these fiction areas: action/adventure; detective/police/crime; family saga; fantasy; feminist; historical; mainstream; mystery/suspense; romance; science fiction; thriller/espionage; westerns/frontier. Query. Will report in 1 week on queries.
Recent Sales: Three historical romance novels by Susan Wiggs (HarperCollins); two horror novels by Dan Simmons (The Putnam Group); ten Western novels by Terry C. Johnston (Bantam).
Terms: Agent receives 15% commission on domestic sales; 20% on foreign sales. Charges for photocopying, express, fax, international postage, book orders.
Tips: Obtains new clients through recommendations from others.

THE CURTIS BRUCE AGENCY (II), Suite A, 3015 Evergeen Dr., Plover WI 54467-9479. Fax: (715)345-2630. President: Bruce W. Zabel. Contact: Curtis H.C. Lundgren. Estab. 1990. Represents approximately 50 clients. 10% of clients are new/previously unpublished writers. Writer must have some published work (no vanity presses or self-published titles) and either a finished novel or proposed nonfiction book. Specializes in novels, commercial fiction of all genres, mainstream fiction and nonfiction. Special interest in *bildungsroman*. Currently handles: 65% fiction; 20% nonfiction; 15% juvenile books.
Handles: Novels, nonfiction and juvenile books. Will consider these nonfiction areas: autobiography/biography; child guidance/parenting; religious/inspirational; self-help/personal improvement. Interested in most all commercial fiction. Will to look—at no charge—at queries with brief synopsis. Send

query with resume, synopsis, sample chapter and return postage labeled shipper. Will report in 2-3 weeks on queries; 12-18 weeks on mss.

Recent Sales: *Portofino*, by Frank Schaeffer (Macmillan); *Pendragon IV*, by Stephen R. Lawhead (Avon Books).

Terms: Agent receives 10% commission on domestic fiction; 15% on nonfiction sales; 15% on dramatic sales; and 20% on foreign sales. Offers a written contract. Charges for photocopying, purchase of books for subrights sales, cables, fax, overnight airfreight, U.S.P.S. postage, U.P.S. Less than 3% of income derived from the following services: Marketability evaluation service available on request with costs to author ranging from $100-200. More in-depth critique service also available with costs to author ranging from $300-500.

Tips: "Obtains most new clients by referral. Tell about yourself briefly: your accomplishments and your experiences. Be sure to include your publishing history (even if it is scant) in your resume. Don't phone query. We have contacts in U.K. and enjoy working with British authors and publishers."

DARHANSOFF & VERRILL LITERARY AGENTS (II), 1220 Park Ave., New York NY 10128. (212)534-2479. Fax: (212)996-1601. Estab. 1975. Member of AAR. Represents 100 clients. 10% of clients are new/previously unpublished writers. Specializes in literary fiction. Currently handles: 25% nonfiction books; 60% novels; 15% short story collections. Member agents: Liz Darhansoff; Charles Verrill; Leigh Feldman.

Handles: Nonfiction books, novels, short story collections. Will consider these nonfiction areas: anthropology/archaeology; biography/autobiography; current affairs; health/medicine; history; language/literature/criticism; nature/environment; science/technology. Will consider literary and thriller fiction. Query letter only. Will report in 2 weeks on queries.

Tips: Obtains new clients through recommendations from others.

ELAINE DAVIE LITERARY AGENCY (II), Village Gate Square, 274 N. Goodman St., Rochester NY 14607. (716)442-0830. President: Elaine Davie. Estab. 1986. Represents 70 clients. 30% of clients are new/unpublished writers. Works with a small number of new/unpublished authors. Specializes in adult fiction and nonfiction, particularly books by and for women and genre/fiction. Currently handles: 30% nonfiction; 60% novels; 10% juvenile books.

Handles: Nonfiction books, novels (no short stories, children's books or poetry). Will consider these nonfiction areas: self-help, true crime, women's issues. Will consider these fiction areas: genre fiction, history, horror, mystery, romance, western. Query with outline or synopsis and brief description. Reports in 2 weeks on queries.

Recent Sales: *The Ruby*, by Christina Skye (Dell); *Guardian Spirit*, by Marcia Evanick (Bantam); *Private Scandals* (Bantam).

Terms: Agent receives 15% commission on domestic sales; 20% on dramatic sales; 20% on foreign sales.

Tips: "Our agency specializes in books by and for women. We pride ourselves on our prompt responses to queries and that we never charge a fee of any kind."

THE LOIS DE LA HABA AGENCY INC. (II), 142 Bank St., New York NY 10014. (212)929-4838. Fax: (212)924-3885. Contact: Lois de la Haba. Estab. 1978. Represents 100 clients. Currently handles: 65% nonfiction books; 25% juvenile books; 15% novels.

Handles: Nonfiction books, juvenile books, novels. Will consider these nonfiction areas: agriculture/horticulture; animals; anthropology/archaeology; art/architecture/design; biography/autobiography; health/medicine; history; juvenile nonfiction; psychology/healing; science/technology. Will consider these fiction areas: contemporary issues; experimental; historical; juvenile; literary; mainstream; mystery/suspense; picture book; psychic/supernatural; science fiction; sports; thriller/espionage; westerns/frontier; young adult. Send outline/proposal plus 2 sample chapters. SASE. Will report in 3-4 weeks on queries.

Recent Sales: *More Wealth Without Risk*, by Charles J. Givens (Simon & Schuster); *Through Time into Healing*, by Brian L. Weiss, M.D. (Simon and Schuster).

Terms: Agent receives 15% commission on domestic sales; 20% on foreign sales. Offers a written contract. Charges for "out-of-pocket expenses."

Tips: Obtains new clients through recommendations from others.

ANITA DIAMANT, THE WRITER'S WORKSHOP, INC. (II), 310 Madison Ave., New York NY 10017. (212)687-1122. Contact: Anita Diamant. Estab. 1917. Member of AAR. Represents 120 clients. 25% of clients are new/previously unpublished writers. Currently handles: 20% nonfiction books; 80% novels. Member agents: Robin Rue (fiction and nonfiction).
Handles: Nonfiction books, young adults, novels. Will consider these nonfiction areas: animals; art/architecture/design; biography/autobiography; business; child guidance/parenting; cooking/food/nutrition; crafts/hobbies; current affairs; government/politics/law; health/medicine; history; juvenile nonfiction; money/finance/economics; nature/environment; new age/metaphysics; psychology; religious/inspirational; true crime/investigative; science/technology; self-help/personal improvement; sports; women's issues/women's studies. Will consider these fiction areas: action/adventure; contemporary issues; detective/police/crime; experimental; family saga; feminist; gay; historical; juvenile; literary; mainstream; mystery/suspense; psychic/supernatural; religious/inspiration; romance; thriller/espionage; westerns/frontier; young adult. Query. Will report "at once" on queries; 3 weeks on mss.
Recent Sales: *Twilight's Child*, by V.C. Andrews (Pocket Books); *The India Exhibition*, by Richard Conroy (St. Martin's); *Miracle of Language*, by Richard Lederer (Pocket).
Terms: Agent receives 15% on domestic sales; 20% on foreign sales. Offers a written contract.
Writers' Conferences: Attends the Romance Writers of American Annual Conference and the A.B.A.
Tips: Obtains new clients through "recommendations from publishers and clients, appearances at writers' conferences, and through readers of my written articles."

DIAMOND LITERARY AGENCY, INC. (III), 3063 S. Kearney St., Denver CO 80222. (303)759-0291. Contact: Carol Atwell. President: Pat Dalton. Estab. 1982. Represents 20 clients. 10% of clients are new/previously unpublished writers. Specializes in romance, romantic suspense, women's fiction, thrillers, mysteries. Currently handles: 25% nonfiction books; 70% novels; 3% movie scripts; 2% TV scripts.
Handles: Nonfiction books, novels, scripts. Will consider these nonfiction areas: animals; biography/autobiography; business; child guidance/parenting; computers/electronics; cooking/food/nutrition; crafts/hobbies; current affairs; ethnic/cultural interests; health/medicine; history; military/war; money/finance/economics; music/dance/theater/film; nature/environment; photography; psychology; religious/inspirational; true crime/investigative; science/technology; self-help/personal improvement; sociology; women's issues/women's studies. Will consider these fiction areas: action/adventure; contemporary issues; detective/police/crime; erotica; ethnic; family saga; feminist; glitz; historical; humor/satire; mainstream; mystery/suspense; religious/inspiration; romance; thriller/espionage. Will report in 1 month on mss (partials).
Recent Sales: *Home Fires*, by Sharon Brondos (Harlequin); *Moriah's Mutiny*, by Elizabeth Beverly (Silhouette); *Full Steam*, by Cassia Miles (Meteor).
Terms: Agent receives 10-15% commission on domestic sales; 20% on foreign sales. Offers a written contract, binding for two years "unless author is well established." Charges a "$15 submission fee for writers who have not previously published/sold the same type of project." Charges for express and foreign postage. "Writers provide the necessary photostat copies."
Tips: Obtains new clients through "referrals from writers, or someone's submitting salable material. We represent only clients who are professionals in writing quality, presentation, conduct and attitudes—whether published or unpublished. Send an SASE for agency information and submission procedures. People who are not yet clients should not telephone. We consider query letters a waste of time—most of all the writer's, secondly the agent's. Submit approximately first 50 pages and complete synopsis for books, or full scripts, along with SASE and standard-sized audiocassette tape for possible agent comments. Nonclients who haven't sold the SAME TYPE of book or script within five years must include a $15 submission fee by money order or cashier's check. Material not accompanied by SASE is not returned. We are not encouraging submissions from unpublished writers at this time."

SANDRA DIJKSTRA LITERARY AGENCY (II), #515, 1155 Camino del Mar, Del Mar CA 92014. (619)755-3115. Contact: Katherine Saideman. Estab. 1981. Member of Authors Guild, PENN West, Poets and Editors, Mystery Writers of America, AAR. Represents 80-100 clients. 60% of clients are new/previously unpublished writers. "We specialize in a number of fields." Currently handles: 50% nonfiction books; 5% juvenile books; 45% novels. Member agents: Sandra Dijkstra, president (adult nonfiction, literary and mainstream fiction, selected children's projects, mysteries and thrillers); Katherine Saideman associate agent (adult nonfiction, mystery and thrillers, literary and mainstream fiction, science fiction/fantasy, horror and historical/sagas).

Handles: Nonfiction books, novels, some juvenile books. Will consider these nonfiction areas: art/architecture/design; biography/autobiography; business; child guidance/parenting; cooking/food/nutrition; current affairs; ethnic/cultural interests; government/politics; health/medicine; history; lit studies (trade only); military/war (trade only); money/finance/economics; music/dance/theater/film; nature/environment; new age/metaphysics; psychology; true crime/investigative; science/technology; self-help/personal improvement; sociology; sports; translations; women's issues/women's studies. Will consider these fiction areas: contemporary issues; detective/police/crime; ethnic; family saga; fantasy; feminist; glitz; historical; humor/satire; juvenile; literary; mainstream; mystery/suspense; picture book; romance (historical); science fiction; sports; thriller/espionage; young adult; horror. "Send query letter with SASE first. Response period for submissions is 1-6 weeks.
Recent Sales: *The Man Question*, by Susan Faludi.
Terms: Agent receives 15% commission on domestic sales; 20% on foreign sales. Offers a written contract, 2-year term. Charges "an expense fee to cover domestic costs so that we can spend time selling books instead of accounting expenses. We also charge for the photocopying of the full manuscript or nonfiction proposal and for foreign postage."
Writers' Conferences: "Attends Squaw Valley, Santa Barbara, Asilomar, Southern California Writers Conference, Rocky Mt. Fiction Writers, "to name a few. We also speak regularly for writers groups such as PENN West and the Independent Writers Association."
Tips: Obtains new clients "primarily through referrals/recommendations, but also through queries and conferences and often by solicitation. Be professional and learn the standard procedures for submitting your work. Give full biographical information on yourself, especially for a nonfiction project. Always include SAE with correct return postage for your own protection of your work. Call if you don't hear within a reasonable period of time. Be a regular patron of bookstores and learn what kind of books are being published. Check out your local library and bookstores—you'll find lots of books on writing and the publishing industry that will help you! At conferences, ask published writers about their agents. Don't believe the myth that an agent has to be in New York to be successful—we've already disproved it!"

THE JONATHAN DOLGER AGENCY (II), Suite 9B, 49 E. 96th St., New York NY 10128. (212)427-1853. President: Jonathan Dolger. Contact: Carol Ann Dearnaley. Estab. 1980. Member of AAR. Represents 70 clients. 25% of clients are new/unpublished writers. Writer must have been previously published if submitting fiction. Prefers to work with published/established authors; works with a small number of new/unpublished writers. Specializes in adult trade fiction and nonfiction, and illustrated books.
Handles: Nonfiction books, novels and illustrated books. Query with outline and SASE.
Terms: Agent receives 15% commission on domestic sales; 10% on dramatic sales; 25-30% on foreign sales. Charges for "standard expenses."

DONADIO & ASHWORTH INC. LITERARY REPRESENTATIVES, 231 W. 22nd St., New York NY 10011. Prefers not to share information.

THOMAS C. DONLAN (II, IV), 143 E. 43rd St., New York NY 10017. (212)697-1629. Agent: Thomas C. Donlan. Estab. 1983. Represents 12 clients. "Our agency limits itself to philosophy and theology, mainly, but not exclusively Roman Catholic. No special requirements of earlier publication." Prefers to work with published/established authors. Specializes in philosophical and theological writings, including translations. Currently handles: 2% magazine articles; 90% nonfiction books; 8% textbooks.
Handles: Nonfiction books, textbooks. Will consider these nonfiction areas: philosophy, theology, translations. Query with outline. Reports in 2 weeks on queries. *Absolutely no unsolicited mss.*
Terms: Agent receives 10% commission on domestic sales; 6% on foreign sales.

*DOYEN LITERARY SERVICES, INC. (II), 19005 660th St., Newell IA 50568-7613. (712)272-3300. President: B.J. Doyen. Associate: Susan Harvey. Estab. 1988. Member of NWC, RWA, HWA, SCBA, SFWA. Represents 50 clients. 20% of clients are new/previously unpublished writers. Specializes in all genre and mainstream fiction and nonfiction mainly for adults (some children's). Currently handles: 40% nonfiction books; 5% juvenile books; 50% novels; 1% poetry books; 2% movie scripts; 2% TV scripts.
Handles: Nonfiction books, juvenile books, novels. Will consider most nonfiction areas. No gay/lesbian issues, religious/inspirational, sports or translations. Will consider these fiction areas: action/adventure; contemporary issues; detective/police/crime; ethnic; experimental; family saga; fantasy; glitz; historical; humor/satire; juvenile; mainstream; mystery/suspense; picture book; psychic/supernatural;

romance; science fiction; thriller/espionage; westerns/frontier; young adult. Query first with SASE. Will report in 1-2 weeks on queries; 6-8 weeks on mss.

Terms: Agent receives 15% commission on domestic sales; 20% commission on foreign sales. Offers a written contract, binding for 1 year.

Tips: "Many writers come to us from referrals, but we also get quite a few who initially approach us with query letters. Do *not* use phone queries unless you are successfully published, a celebrity or have an extremely hot, timely idea that can't wait. Send us a sparkling query letter with SASE. It is best if you do not collect editorial rejections prior to seeking an agent, but if you do, be up-front and honest about it. Do not submit your manuscript to more than one agent at a time—querying first can save you (and us) much time. We're open to established or beginning writers—just send us a terrific manuscript!"

ROBERT DUCAS (II), 350 Hudson St., New York NY 10014. (212)924-8120. Fax: (212)924-8079. Contact: R. Ducas. Estab. 1981. Represents 55 clients. 15% of clients are new/previously unpublished writers. Specializes in nonfiction, journalistic exposé, biography, history. Currently handles: 70% nonfiction books; 1% scholarly books; 28% novels; 1% novellas.

Handles: Nonfiction books, novels, novellas. Will consider these nonfiction areas: animals; biography/autobiography; business; current affairs; gay/lesbian issues; government/politics/law; health/medicine; history; military/war; money/finance/economics; nature/environment; true crime/investigative; science/technology; sports. Will consider these fiction areas: action/adventure; contemporary issues; detective/police/crime; family saga; feminist; gay; historical; humor/satire; lesbian; literary; mainstream; mystery/suspense; sports; thriller/espionage; westerns/frontier. Send outline/proposal. Will report in 2 weeks on queries; 1 month on mss.

Terms: Agent receives 12½% commission on domestic sales; 20% on foreign sales. Charges for photocopying and postage. "I also charge for messengers and overseas couriers to subagents."

Tips: Obtains new clients through recommendations.

DUPREE/MILLER AND ASSOCIATES INC. LITERARY (II), Suite 3, 5518 Dyer St., Dallas TX 75206. (214)692-1388. Fax: (214)987-9654. Contact: Jan Miller. Estab. 1984. Represents 120+ clients. 20% of clients are new/previously unpublished writers. Specializes in commercial fiction and nonfiction. Currently handles: 50% nonfiction books; 35% novels. Member agents: Jan Miller; Davis Smith; Sunita Batra; Dean Williamson; Michael Broussard.

Handles: Nonfiction books, scholarly books, novels, movie scripts, syndicated material. Will consider all nonfiction areas. Will consider these fiction areas: action/adventure; cartoon/comic; contemporary issues; detective/police/crime; family saga; feminist; gay; glitz; historical; humor/satire; literary; mainstream; mystery/suspense; psychic/supernatural; romance (contemporary, historical); science fiction; sports; thriller/espionage; westerns/frontier. Send outline plus 3 sample chapters. Will report in 1 week on queries; 8-12 weeks on mss.

Terms: Agent receives 15% commission on domestic sales. Offers a written contract, binding for "no set amount of time. The contract can be cancelled by either agent or client, effective 30 days after cancellation." Charges $20 processing fee and Federal Express charges.

Writers' Conferences: "Will be attending many national conventions. Also have lectures at colleges across nation."

Tips: Obtains new client through conferences, lectures, clients and "very frequently through publisher's referrals." If interested in agency representation "it is vital to have the material in the proper working format. As agents' policies differ it is important to follow their guidelines. The best advice I can give is to work on establishing a strong proposal that provides sample chapters, an overall synopsis (fairly detailed) and some bio information on yourself. Do not send your proposal in pieces; it should be complete upon submission. Remember you are trying to sell your work and it should be in its best condition."

‡EDUCATIONAL DESIGN SERVICES, INC. (II, IV), P.O. Box 253, Wantagh NY 11793. (718)539-4107 or (516)221-0995. President: Bertram L. Linder. Vice President: Edwin Selzer. Estab. 1979. Represents 17 clients. 70% of clients are new/previously unpublished writers. Specializes in textual material for educational market. Currently handles: 100% textbooks.

Handles: Textbooks, scholarly books. Will consider these nonfiction areas: anthropology/archaeology; business; child guidance/parenting; current affairs; ethnic/cultural interests; government/politics/law; history; juvenile nonfiction; language/literature/criticism; military/war; money/finance/economics; science/technology; sociology; women's issues/women's studies. Query with outline/proposal or outline plus 1-2 sample chapters. Will report in 1 month on queries; 4-6 weeks on mss.

Recent Sales: *New York in U.S. History* (Amsco); *Nueva Historia de Los Estados Unidos* (Minerva Books).
Terms: Agent receives 15% commission on domestic sales; 25% on foreign sales. Offers written contract. Charges for photocopying.
Tips: Obtains new clients through recommendations, conferences, queries.

VICKI EISENBERG LITERARY AGENCY (II), 929 Fernwood, Richardson TX 75080. (214)918-9593. Fax: (214)521-8454. Contact: Vicki Eisenberg. Estab. 1985. Represents 30 clients. Currently handles: 60% nonfiction books; 40% novels.
Handles: Will consider all nonfiction areas. Will consider mainstream and mystery/suspense fiction. Query with SASE. Will report in 6 weeks on queries.
Terms: Agent receives 15% commission on domestic sales. Offers a written contract.
Tips: Obtains new clients through referrals from other agencies and authors.

PETER ELEK ASSOCIATES (II, IV), Box 223, Canal Street Station, New York NY 10013. (212)431-9368. Fax: (212)966-5768. Contact: Michelle Roberts. Estab. 1979. Represents 20 clients. 5% of clients are new/previously unpublished writers. Specializes in children's books—picture books, adult nonfiction and juvenile art. Currently handles: 30% juvenile books.
Handles: Juvenile books (fiction, nonfiction, picture books). Will consider juvenile nonfiction. Will consider these fiction areas: juvenile, picture books. Query with outline/proposal. Reports in 2 weeks on queries; 3 weeks on mss.
Recent Sales: *Mothering the New Mother*, by Sally Placksin (Newmarket); *The Lost Ships of Guadalcanal*, by Robert D. Ballard (Warner); *Into the Mummy's Tomb*, by Christopher Reeve (Scholastic).
Terms: Agent receives 15% commission on domestic sales; 20% commission on foreign sales. If required, charges for photocopying, typing, courier charges.
Tips: Obtains new clients through recommendations and studying consumer and trade magazines. "No work returned unless appropriate packing and postage is remitted."

ETHAN ELLENBERG LITERARY AGENCY (II), #5-E, 548 Broadway, New York NY 10012. (212)431-4554. Fax: (212)941-4652. Contact: Ethan Ellenberg. Estab. 1983. Represents 65 clients. 35% of clients are new/previously unpublished writers. Specializes in commercial and literary fiction, including first novels, thrillers, mysteries, science fiction, fantasy and horror, all categories of romance fiction, quality nonfiction, including biography, history, health, business and popular science. Currently handles: 25% nonfiction books; 75% novels.
Handles: Nonfiction books, novels. Will consider these nonfiction areas: biography/autobiography; business; child guidance/parenting; cooking/food/nutrition; crafts/hobbies; current affairs; government/politics/law; health/medicine; history; juvenile nonfiction; military/war; money/finance/economics; nature/environment; new age/metaphysics; psychology; religious/inspirational; true crime/investigative; science/technology; self-help/personal improvement; sports. Will consider these fiction areas: action; cartoon/comic; detective/police/crime; family saga; fantasy; glitz; historical; humor/satire; juvenile; literary; mainstream; mystery/suspense; picture book; romance; science fiction; sports; thriller/espionage; westerns/frontier; young adult. Send outline plus 3 sample chapters. Will report in 10 days on queries; 3-4 weeks on mss.
Recent Sales: Two untitled picture books, by Catherine Hepworth (Putnam); untitled novel, by Clay Reynolds (Dutton); *Cassandra Prophecy*, by Charles Wilson (Carroll & Graf); *Deadly Force, Last American Heroes, Fighting Man*, by Charles Sasser (Pocket).
Terms: Agent receives 15% on domestic sales; 10% on foreign sales. Offers a written contract, "flexible." Charges for "direct expenses only: photocopying, postage."
Writers' Conferences: Speaks at Vassar Conference on Children's Publishing, attends a number of other RWA conferences.
Tips: "I obtain clients by client and editor recommendation, active recruitment from magazines, newspapers, etc. and my unsoliciteds. I very seriously consider all new material and have done very well through unsolicited manuscripts. Write a good, clear letter, with a succinct description of your book. Show that you understand the basics and don't make outrageous claims for your book. Make sure you only submit your best material and that it's prepared professionally—perfectly typed with good margins. Find out what any prospective agent will do for you, make sure you have some rapport. Don't be fooled by big names or phony pitches—what will the agent do for you. Good agents are busy, don't waste their time, but don't be afraid to find out what's going on. Besides my professionalism, my greatest skills are editorial—helping novelists develop. We give ample editorial advice for no charge to clients the agency takes."

NICHOLAS ELLISON, INC. (II), 55 5th Ave., 15th Floor, New York NY 10003. (212)206-6050. Affiliated with Sanford J. Greenburger Associates. Contact: Elizabeth Ziemska. Estab. 1983. Represents 70 clients. Currently handles: 25% nonfiction books; 75% novels.
Handles: Nonfiction, novels. Will consider most nonfiction areas. No biography, gay/lesbian issues or self-help. Will consider these fiction areas: literary; mainstream. Query with SASE. Reporting time varies on queries.
Recent Sales: *The General's Daughter*, by Nelson De Mille (Warner Books); *Tygers of Wrath*, by Philip Rosenberg (St. Martin's Press); *Typhoon*, by Mark Joseph (Simon & Schuster).
Terms: Agent receives 15% commission on domestic sales; 20% commission on foreign sales.
Tips: Usually obtains new clients from word-of-mouth referrals.

ANN ELMO AGENCY INC. (III), 60 E. 42nd St., New York NY 10165. (212)661-2880, 2881, 2883. Contact: Ann Elmo or Lettie Lee. Estab. 1961. Member of AAR, MWA, Authors Guild.
Handles: Nonfiction, novels. Will consider these nonfiction areas: cooking/food/nutrition; juvenile nonfiction; women's issues. Will consider these fiction areas: historical; romance. Query with outline/proposal. Will report in 4-6 weeks "average" on queries.
Terms: Agent receives 15% commission on domestic sales; 20% on foreign sales. Offers a written contract (standard AAR contract).
Tips: Obtains new clients through referrals. "Send properly prepared manuscript. A readable manuscript is the best recommendation. Double space."

‡EMBERS LITERARY AGENCY (I), R.R. 3, Box 173, Spencer IN 47460. Contact: Kenni Miller. Estab. 1992. Represents 3 clients. 67% of clients are new/previously unpublished authors. Currently handles: 20% scholarly books; 20% juvenile books; 20% novels; 40% short story collections. Member agents: Kenni Miller (romance, religion and juvenile).
Handles: Nonfiction books, scholarly books, juvenile books, novels, novellas, short story collections. Will consider all areas of nonfiction. Will consider these fiction areas: action/adventure; fantasy; juvenile; literary; mainstream; mystery/suspense; picture book; religious/inspiration; romance (contemporary, gothic, historical, regency); science fiction; western frontier; young adult. Send entire ms. Will report in 2 weeks on queries; 2-4 weeks on mss.
Terms: Agent receives 10% commission on domestic sales; 15% on foreign sales. Offers a written contract. Charges mailing and processing fee, depending on length of book (not to exceed $50). "This fee is reimbursed to author on sale of book."
Tips: Obtains new clients through ads run in college newspapers. "Don't be offended by constructive criticism. Be grateful for it."

FELICIA ETH LITERARY REPRESENTATION (II), Suite 350, 555 Bryant St., Palo Alto CA 94301. (415)375-1276. Contact: Felicia Eth. Estab. 1988. Member of AAR. Represents 25-30 clients. Eager to work with new/unpublished writers; "for nonfiction, established expertise is certainly a plus, as is magazine publication—though not a prerequisite. Specializes in provocative, intelligent, thoughtful nonfiction on a wide array of subjects which are commercial and high-quality fiction; preferably mainstream and contemporary. I am highly selective, but also highly dedicated to those projects I represent." Currently handles: 75% nonfiction, 25% novels.
Handles: Nonfiction books, novels. Query with outline. Reports in 3 weeks on queries; 1 month on proposals and sample pages.
Recent Sales: *How To Be The Father You Wish Your Father Had Been*, by Jerrold Shapiro Ph.D. (Dell/Delacorte); *Sex And Power On The Playing Fields*, by Mariah Burton Nelson (Harcort Brace, Jovanovich)); *Kill The Cowboy: A Battle of Mythology In The West*, by Sherman Russell (Addison-Wesley).
Terms: Agent receives 15% commission on domestic sales; 20% on dramatic sales; 20% on foreign sales. Charges for photocopying, fax, Federal Express service—extraordinary expenses.

Agents ranked I and II are most open to both established and new writers. Agents ranked III are open to established writers with publishing-industry references.

THE FALLON LITERARY AGENCY (III), Suite 13B, 301 W. 53rd St., New York NY 10019. (212)399-1369. Fax: (212)315-3823. Contact: Eileen Fallon. Estab. 1990. Member of AAR. Represents 40 clients. 20% of clients are new/previously unpublished writers. Specializes in mainstream and literary fiction, romance, mystery and nonfiction. Currently handles: 20% nonfiction books; 80% novels.
Handles: Nonfiction, novels. Will consider these nonfiction areas: biography/autobiography; health/medicine; history; language/literature/criticism; natural history; psychology; self help/personal improvement; women's issues/women's studies. Will consider these fiction areas: literary; mainstream, mystery/suspense; romance. Query first. "I *must* see a query letter and agree to have the material sent before I will consider the material—no over-the-transom partials or manuscripts." Will report in 2 weeks on queries; usually 2 months on ms.
Terms: Agent receives 15% commission on domestic sales; 20% on foreign sales. Does not usually offer a written contract, unless requested. Charges for photocopying.
Tips: Usually obtains new clients through referrals from editors or sometimes other agents. "Target your material—send it only to an agent who handles the kind of project you've written."

JOHN FARQUHARSON LTD., 250 W. 57th St., New York NY 10107. Prefers not to share information.

MARJE FIELDS-RITA SCOTT INC. (II), #1205, 165 W. 46th, New York NY 10036. (212)764-5740. Member of AAR. Represents 40 clients. 20% of clients are new/previously unpublished writers. Specializes in fiction and nonfiction. Currently handles: 5% nonfiction books; 10% juvenile books; 75% novels; 10% stage plays.
Handles: Nonfiction books, novels. Will consider these nonfiction areas: biography/autobiography; cooking/food/nutrition; gay/lesbian issues; health/medicine; true crime/investigative; self-help/personal improvement; sports. Will consider these fiction areas: action/adventure; confessional; detective/police/crime; family saga; gay; historical; literary; mainstream; mystery/suspense; historical romance; sports; thriller/espionage; westerns/frontier; young adult. Query. Will report in 1 week on queries; 2 weeks on mss.
Recent Sales: *Sweet Deal,* by John Westermann (Soho Press); *Live Free or Die,* by Ernest Hebert (Viking); *Summer Girl,* by Deborah Moulton (Dial); *Hearts of Glass,* by Nicole Jeffords (Crown).
Terms: Agent receives 15% on domestic sales; 20% on foreign sales. Offers a written contract, binding for 1 year.
Tips: Obtains new cilents through referrals and queries.

FOGELMAN PUBLISHING INTERESTS INC. (I), Suite 241, 5050 Quorum, Dallas TX 75240. (214)980-6975. Fax: (214)980-6978. Contact: Evan Fogelman or Linda Diehl. Estab. 1990. Represents 50-60 clients. Specializes in contemporary women's fiction and nonfiction, contemporary women's issues. Currently handles: 30% nonfiction books; 70% novels.
Handles: Will consider these nonfiction areas: biography; business; parenting; nutrition; current affairs; government/politics/law; money/finance/economics; true crime; self-help/personal improvement; women's issues/women's studies; gardening. Will consider these fiction areas: romance; mainstream; contemporary; historical. Query with SASE. Will report in 6 weeks on queries. Unsolicited mss not accepted.
Terms: Agent receives 15% commission on domestic sales; varying on foreign sales.
Writers' Conferences: St. Louis, Chicago, Phoenix, Houston, Kansas City, Wisconsin, 2nd Miami RWA, National RWA, various multi-genre conferences.
Tips: Obtains new clients through referrals, through writers conferences and through solicited submissions. "If you have any questions, call. All books can't be treated alike."

CANDICE FUHRMAN LITERARY AGENCY, (II), Box F, Forest Knolls, Forest Knolls CA 94933. (415)488-0161. Fax: (415)488-4335. Contact: Candice Fuhrman. Estab. 1987. Represents 45 clients. 80% of clients are new/previously unpublished writers. 95% nonfiction books; 5% novels.
Handles: Nonfiction books, novels. Will consider these nonfiction areas: animals; anthropology/archaeology; art/architecture/design; biography/autobiography; business; child guidance/parenting; cooking/food/nutrition; crafts/hobbies; current affairs; ethnic/cultural interests; health/medicine; history; interior design/decorating; language/literature/criticism; money/finance/economics; music/dance/theater/film; nature/environment; new age/metaphysics; psychology; religious/inspirational; true crime/investigative; science/technology; self-help/personal improvement; sociology; sports; women's issues/women's studies; recovery. Will consider these fiction areas: literary, mainstream. Send outline plus 1 sample chapter. Will report in 1 month on queries.

Terms: Agent receives 15% commission on domestic sales; 20% on foreign sales. Offers a written contract, binding for 6 months to 1 year. Charges postage and photocopying.

Tips: Obtains new clients through recommendations and solicitation. "Please do not call. Send succinct query and well-thought-out proposal. Check out your idea with *Subject Books in Print* and look at the competition to see how your book is different. (This is for nonfiction, of course)."

JAY GARON-BROOKE ASSOC. INC. (II), Suite 80, 101 W. 55th St., New York NY 10019. (212)581-8300. Contact: Nancy Coffey or Jay Garon. Estab. 1952. Member of AAR, WGA. Represents 80 clients. 10% of clients are new/previously unpublished writers. Specializes in mainstream fiction and nonfiction. Currently handles: 15% nonfiction books; 75% novels; 5% movie scripts; 2% stage plays; 3% TV scripts.

Handles: Nonfiction books, novels, movie and TV scripts, stage plays. Will consider these nonfiction areas: biography/autobiography; child guidance/parenting; gay/lesbian issues; health/medicine; history; military/war; music/dance/theater/film; psychology; true crime/investigative; self-help/personal improvement. Will consider these fiction areas: action/adventure; contemporary issues; detective/police/crime; family saga; fantasy; gay; glitz; historical; literary; mainstream; mystery/suspense; romance; science fiction. Query. Will report in 3 weeks on queries; 5-8 weeks on mss.

Recent Sales: *The Pelican Brief,* by John Grisham (Doubleday-Dell); *A Time to Kill,* by John Grisham (Dell); *Under Contract,* by Cherokee Paul McDonald (Donald I. Fine Inc.).

Terms: Agent receives 15% on domestic sales; 30% on foreign sales. Offers a written contract, binding for 3-5 years. Charges for "photocopying if author does not provide copies."

Tips: Obtains new clients through referrals and from queries. "Send query letter first giving the essence of the manuscript and a personal or career bio with SASE."

MAX GARTENBERG, LITERARY AGENT (II,III), Suite 1700, 521 5th Ave., New York NY 10175. (212)860-8451. Fax: (201)535-5033. Contact: Max Gartenberg. Estab. 1954. Represents 30 clients. 5% of clients are new writers. Currently handles: 90% nonfiction books; 10% novels.

Handles: Nonfiction books, novels. Will consider these nonfiction areas: agriculture/horticulture; animals; art/architecture/design; biography/autobiography; child guidance/parenting; current affairs; health/medicine; history; military/war; money/finance/economics; music/dance/theater/film; nature/environment; psychology; true crime/investigative; science/technology; self-help/personal improvement; sports; women's issues/women's studies. Will consider mainstream and mystery/suspense fiction. Query. Will report in 2 weeks on queries; 6 weeks on mss.

Recent Sales: *Notes from New Zealand,* by Edward Kanze (Henry Holt & Co.); *Eco/Nomics,* by William Ashworth (Houghton Mifflin); *Arthritis: What Exercises Work,* by Dava Sobel and Arthur C. Klein (St. Martin's Press).

Terms: Agent receives 10% on domestic sales; 15% on foreign sales. Offers a written contract.

Tips: Obtains new clients "primarily, by recommendations from others, but often enough by following up on good query letters. Take pains in drafting your query letter. It makes the important first impression an agent has of you. Without going on at great length, be specific about what you have to offer and include a few relevant facts about yourself. The most exasperating letter an agent receives is the one which reads, 'I have just completed a novel. If you would like to read the manuscript, please let me know. A SASE is enclosed for your convenience.'"

RONALD GOLDFARB & ASSOCIATES (II), (formerly Goldfarb, Kaufman & O'Toole), 918-16 St., NW, Washington DC 20006. (202)466-3030. Fax: (202)293-3187. Contact: Ronald Goldfarb. Estab. 1966. Represents "hundreds" of clients. "Minority" of clients are new/previously unpublished writers. Specializes in nonfiction, "books with TV tie-ins." Currently handles: 80% nonfiction books; 1% scholarly books; 1% textbooks; 1% juvenile books; 10% novels; 1% novellas; 1% poetry books; 1% short story collections; 1% movie scripts; 1% stage plays; 1% TV scripts; 1% syndicated material. Member agents: Ronald Goldfarb, Joshua Kaufman, Nina Graybill.

> *Agents who specialize in a specific subject area such as children's books or in handling the work of certain writers such as Southwestern writers are ranked IV.*

Handles: Nonfiction books, textbooks, scholarly books, juvenile books, novels, novellas, short story collections, poetry books, movie and TV scripts, stage plays, syndicated material. Will consider all nonfiction and fiction areas. Send outline plus 1 or 2 sample chapters. Will report in 1 week on queries; within a month on mss.
Writers' Conferences: Attends Washington Independent Writers Conference; Medical Writers Conference.
Tips: Obtains new clients mostly through recommendations from others. "We are a law firm which can help writers with related problems, Freedom of Information Act requests, libel, copyright, contracts, etc. We are published writers."

GOODMAN ASSOCIATES (III), 500 West End Ave., New York NY 10024. Contact: Elise Simon Goodman. Estab. 1976. Member of AAR (Arnold Goodman is former president of ILAA). Represents 100 clients. "Presently accepting new clients on a very selective basis."
Handles: Nonfiction, novels. Will consider most adult nonfiction and fiction areas. No "poetry, articles, individual stories, children's or YA material." Query with SASE. Will report in 10 days on queries; 1 month on mss.
Terms: Agent receives 15% commission on domestic sales; 20% on foreign sales. Charges for certain expenses: faxes, toll calls, overseas postage, photocopying, book purchases.

IRENE GOODMAN LITERARY AGENCY (II), 17th Floor, 521 5th Ave., New York NY 10175. (212)682-1978. Contact: Irene Goodman, president. Estab. 1978. Member of AAR. Represents 45 clients. 10% of clients are new/unpublished writers. Works with a small number of new/unpublished authors. Specializes in women's fiction, popular nonfiction, reference and genre fiction. Currently handles: 20% nonfiction books; 80% novels.
Handles: Novels and nonfiction books. Will consider these nonfiction areas: popular and reference. Will consider these fiction areas: historical romance, romance, mainstream, mystery, genre fiction. Query only (no unsolicited mss). Reports in 6 weeks. "No reply without SASE."
Terms: Agent receives 15% commission on domestic sales; 20% on foreign sales.

CHARLOTTE GORDON AGENCY (II), 235 E. 22nd St., New York NY 10010. (212)679-5363. Contact: Charlotte Gordon. Estab. 1986. Represents 30 clients. 20% of clients are new/unpublished writers. "I'll work with writers whose work is interesting to me. Specializes in books (not magazine material, except for my writers, and then only in special situations). My taste is eclectic." Currently handles: 40% nonfiction; 40% novels; 20% juvenile.
Handles: Nonfiction books, novels and juveniles (fiction and nonfiction). Must query first, enclosing first chapter of book in addition to letter. Does not read unsolicited manuscripts. Reports in 2 weeks on queries.
Terms: Agent receives 15% commission on domestic sales; 10% on dramatic sales; 10% on foreign sales. Charges writers for photocopying manuscripts.

GOTHAM ART & LITERARY AGENCY INC. (II), Suite 10H, 1133 Broadway, New York NY 10010. (212)989-2737. Fax: (212)633-1004. Contact: Anne Elisabeth Suter. Estab. 1983. Currently handles: 10% nonfiction books; 45% juvenile books; 45% novels.
Handles: Will consider all nonfiction areas. Will consider juvenile, literary and mainstream fiction. Query with SASE. Reports in 2 weeks on queries.
Recent Sales: *Ripley Under Water*, by Patricia Highsmith (Knopf); *Follow the Dream: Story of Christopher Columbus*, by Peter Sis (Knopf); *Heidi*, by Tomi Ungerer (Delacorte).
Terms: Agent receives 15% commission on domestic sales; 20% on foreign sales. Offers written contract "on demand." If postage expenses get excessive, will discuss with author.
Writers' Conferences: Attends book fairs in Frankfort and Bologna (International Children Book Fair).

JOEL GOTLER METROPOLITAN TALENT AGENCY, (III), (formerly Joel Gotler Inc.), 9320 Wilshire Blvd., Beverly Hills CA 90212. (310)247-5580. Fax: (310)247-5599. Contact: Joel Gotler. Represents 50 clients. Specializes in selling movies and TV rights from books.
Handles: Nonfiction and novels. Will consider these nonfiction areas: biography/autobiography; history; film; true crime/investigative. Will consider these fiction areas: action/adventure; contemporary issue; detective/police/crime; ethnic; family saga; fantasy; historical; humor/satire; literary; mainstream; mystery/suspense; science fiction; thriller/espionage. Query with SASE and outline plus 2 sample chapters. Will report in 1 month on queries.

Terms: Agent receives 15% commission on domestic book; 10% on film.
Tips: Obtains news clients through recommendations from others.

STANFORD J. GREENBURGER ASSOCIATES (II), 55 Fifth Ave., New York NY 10003. (212)206-5600. Fax: (212)463-8718. Contact: Heide Lange. Estab. 1945. Member of AAR. Represents 500 clients. Member agents: Heide Lange, Faith Hamlin, Beth Vesel, Diane Cleaver.
Handles: Nonfiction books, novels. Will consider all nonfiction areas. Will consider these fiction areas: action/adventure; contemporary issues, detective/police/crime; ethnic; family saga; feminist; gay; glitz; historical; humor/satire; juvenile; lesbian; literary; mainstream; mystery/suspense; picture books; psychic/supernatural; regional; sports; thriller/espionage. Query first. Will report in 1-2 weeks on queries; 1-2 months on mss.
Terms: Agent receives 15% commission on domestic sales; 19% on foreign sales. Charges for photocopying, books for foreign and subsidiary rights submissions.

MAIA GREGORY ASSOCIATES (II), 311 E. 72nd St., New York NY 10021. (212)288-0310. Contact: Maia Gregory. Estab. 1978. Represents 10-12 clients. Currently handles: 95% nonfiction books.
Handles: Will consider these nonfiction areas: art; history; language; music/dance/theater/film; religious. Will consider literary fiction. Query with SASE and outline plus 1 sample chapter. Will report in 2 weeks on queries.
Terms: Agent receives 10% commission on domestic sales; varies on foreign sales.
Tips: Obtains new clients through recommendations and queries.

‡LEW GRIMES LITERARY AGENCY (II), Suite 800, 250 W. 54 St., New York NY 10019-5586. (212)974-9505. Fax: (212)974-9525. Contact: Lew Grimes. Estab. 1991. 50% of clients are new/previously unpublished writers. Currently handles: 40% nonfiction books; 5% scholarly books; 1% textbooks; 50% novels; 2% poetry books; 2% movie scripts.
Handles: Nonfiction books and novels. Query. Will report in 3-4 weeks on queries; 3 months on mss.
Terms: Agent receives 15% commission on domestic sales; 20% on foreign sales. Offers written contract. Charges $15 postage and handling for return of ms. "Expenses are reimbursed for unpublished authors and for non-commercial projects."
Tips: Obtains new clients through referral and by query. "Provide brief query and resume showing publishing history clearly. Always put phone number and address on correspondence and enclose SASE."

MAXINE GROFFSKY LITERARY AGENCY, 2 Fifth Ave., New York NY 10011. Prefers not to share information.

THE CHARLOTTE GUSAY LITERARY AGENCY (II, IV), 10532 Blythe, Los Angeles CA 90064. (213)559-0831. Fax: (213)559-2639. Contact: Charlotte Gusay. Estab. 1988. Represents 20 clients. 50% of clients are new/previously unpublished writers. Specializes in fiction, nonfiction, children's with illustrations. "Percentage breakdown of the manuscripts different at different times."
Handles: Nonfiction books, scholarly books, juvenile books, novels, movie scripts. Will consider all nonfiction and fiction areas. No science fiction or horror. Query. Reports in 2-4 weeks on queries; 6-8 weeks on mss.
Recent Sales: *Holy Women, Healers & Pipe Carriers*, by Mark St. Pierre and Tilda Long Soldier (Touchstone/Simon & Schuster); *Dropoff* and *Big Fish*, by Ken Grissom (St. Martins); *Dead Languages*, by David Shields (Knopf).
Terms: Agent receives 15% commission on domestic sales; 10% on dramatic sales. Charges for "some basic costs for printing, photocopying and mailing may be later assessed, usually agreed upon between author and agent."
Tips: Usually obtains new clients through recommendations.

Agents ranked I-IV are actively seeking new clients. Those ranked V or those who prefer not to be listed have been included to inform you they are not currently looking for new clients.

THE MITCHELL J. HAMILBURG AGENCY (II), Suite 312, 292 S. La Cienega Blvd., Beverly Hills CA 90211. (213)657-1501. Contact: Michael Hamilburg. Estab. 1960. Member of WGA. Represents 40 clients. Currently handles: 75% nonfiction books; 25% novels.
Handles: Nonfiction, novels. Will consider all nonfiction areas and most fiction areas. No romance. Send outline plus 2 sample chapters. Reports in 3-4 weeks on mss.
Recent Sales: *A Biography of the Leakey Family*, by Virginia Marrell (Simon & Schuster); *A Biography of Agnes De Mille*, by Carol Easton (Little, Brown).
Terms: Agent receives 10-15% on domestic sales.
Tips: Usually obtains new clients through recommendations from others, at conferences or personal search. "Good luck! Keep writing!"

JOHN HAWKINS & ASSOCIATES, INC. (II), 71 W. 23rd St., New York NY 10010. (212)807-7040. Fax: (212)807-9555. Contact: John Hawkins, William Reiss, Sharon Friedman. Estab. 1893. Member of AAR. Represents 100+ clients. 5-10% of clients are new/previously unpublished writers. Currently handles: 40% nonfiction books; 20% juvenile books; 40% novels.
Handles: Nonfiction books, juvenile books, novels. Will consider all nonfiction areas except computers/electronics; religion/inspirational; translations. Will consider all fiction areas except confessional; erotica; fantasy; romance. Query with outline/proposal. Will report in 1 month on queries.
Terms: Agent receives 15% on domestic sales; 20% on foreign sales. Charges for photocopying.
Tips: Obtains new clients through recommendations from others.

THE JEFF HERMAN AGENCY INC. (II), #501C, 500 Greenwich St., New York NY 10013. (212)941-0540. Contact: Jeffrey H. Herman. Estab. 1985. Member of AAR. Represents 150 clients. 20% of clients are new/previously unpublished writers. Specializes in adult nonfiction. Currently handles: 85% nonfiction books; 5% scholarly books; 5% textbooks; 5% novels.
Handles: Nonfiction books, textbooks, scholarly books. Will consider all nonfiction areas. Query. Will report in 2 weeks on queries; 1 month on mss.
Recent Sales: *The Insider's Guide to Book Editors, Publishers, and Literary Agents* (St. Martin's Press); *Nonfiction Book Proposals that Sold! and Why* (John Wiley); *The Tom Hopkins Guide To Selling* (Warner).
Terms: Agent receives 15% commission on domestic sales. Offers a written contract.
Tips: Obtains new clients through referrals and over the transom.

SUSAN HERNER RIGHTS AGENCY (II), P.O. Box 303, Scarsdale NY 10583. (914)725-8967. Contact: Susan Herner or Sue Yuen. Estab. 1987. Represents 50 clients. 25% of clients are new/unpublished writers. Eager to work with new/unpublished writers. Currently handles: 60% nonfiction books; 40% novels.
Handles: Nonfiction books and novels. Will consider these fiction areas: literary, romance, science fiction, mystery, thriller, horror, mainstream (genre). Query with outline and sample chapters. Reports in 1 month on queries.
Recent Sales: *Finding Each Other*, by Mary and Don Kelly (Simon & Schuster); *Something's Cooking*, by Joanne Pence (Harper); *The Stream*, by J. J. Fraxedas (St. Martin's Press).
Terms: Agent receives 15% commission on domestic sales; 20% on dramatic sales; 20% on foreign sales. Charges for extraordinary postage, handling and photocopying. "Agency has two divisions: one represents writers on a commission-only basis; the other represents the rights for small publishers and packagers who do not have in-house subsidiary rights representation. Percentage of income derived from each division is currently 70-30."

FREDERICK HILL ASSOCIATES, 1325 B, N. Olive Dr., West Hollywood CA 90069. (415)921-2910. Fax: (213)650-4093. Contact: Bonnie Nadell. Estab. 1979. Represents 100 clients. 50% of clients are new/unpublished writers. Specializes in general nonfiction, fiction, young adult fiction.
Handles: Nonfiction books and novels.
Terms: Agent receives 15% commission on domestic sales; 15% on dramatic sales; 20% on foreign sales. Charges for overseas airmail (books, proofs only).

HOLUB & ASSOCIATES (II), 24 Old Colony Rd., North Stonington CT 06359. (203)535-0689. Contact: William Holub. Estab. 1967. Specializes in Roman Catholic publications. Currently handles: 100% nonfiction books.

Handles: Nonfiction books. Will consider these nonfiction areas: biography; religious/inspirational; theology. Query with SASE and outline plus 2 sample chapters.
Terms: Agent receives 15% commission on domestic sales. Charges for postage and photocopying.
Tips: Obtains new clients through recommendations from others.

HULL HOUSE LITERARY AGENCY (II), 240 E. 82nd St., New York NY 10028. (212)988-0725. Fax: (212)794-8758. President: David Stewart Hull. Associate: Lydia Mortimer. Estab. 1987. Represents 38 clients. 15% of clients are new/previously unpublished writers. Specializes in military and general history, true crime, mystery fiction, general commercial fiction. Currently handles: 60% nonfiction books; 40% novels. Member agents: David Stewart Hull (history, biography, military books, true crime, mystery fiction, commercial fiction by published authors); Lydia Mortimer (new fiction by unpublished writers, nonfiction of general nature including women's studies).
Handles: Nonfiction books, novels. Will consider these nonfiction areas: anthropology/archaeology; art/architecture/design; biography/autobiography; business; current affairs; ethnic/cultural interests; government/politics/law; history; military/war; money/finance/economics; music/dance/theater/film; true crime/investigative; sociology. Will consider these fiction areas: detective/police/crime; literary; mainstream; mystery/suspense. Query with SASE. Will report in 1 week on queries; 1 month on mss.
Terms: Agent receives 15% commission on domestic sales; 20% on foreign sales, "split with foreign agent." Written contract is optional, "at mutual agreement between author and agency." Charges for photocopying, express mail, extensive overseas telephone expenses.
Tips: Obtains new clients through "referrals from clients, listings in various standard publications such as *LMP*, this directory, etc. If interested in agency representation, send a single-page letter outlining your project, always accompanied by a SASE. If nonfiction, sample chapter(s) are often valuable. A record of past publications is a big plus."

INTERNATIONAL CREATIVE MANAGEMENT, 40 W. 57th St., New York NY 10019. Prefers not to share information.

INTERNATIONAL PUBLISHER ASSOCIATES INC. (II), 746 W. Shore, Sparta NJ 07871. (201)729-9321. Contact: Joseph De Rogatis. Estab. 1983. Represents 15 clients. Currently handles: 100% nonfiction books.
Handles: Will consider all nonfiction areas. Will consider mainstream fiction "mostly." Query with SASE. Will report in 3 weeks on queries.
Recent Sales: *The Childrens Medicine Chest*, by John Cuppola (Doubleday).
Terms: Agent receives 15% commission on domestic sales; 20% on foreign sales. Offers a written contract, binding for life of book. Charges for postage and photocopying.
Tips: Obtains new clients through word of mouth.

J DE S ASSOCIATES INC. (II), 9 Shagbark Rd., Wilson Point, South Norwalk CT 06854. (203)838-7571. Contact: Jacques de Spoelberch. Estab. 1975. Represents 50 clients. Currently handles: 50% nonfiction books; 50% novels.
Handles: Nonfiction books, novels. Will consider these nonfiction areas: biography/autobiography; business; current affairs; ethnic/cultural interests; government/politics/law; health/medicine; history; military/war; new age; self-help/personal improvement; sociology; sports; translations. Will consider these fiction areas: detective/police/crime; historical; juvenile; literary; mainstream; mystery/suspense; westerns/frontier; young adult; new age. Query with SASE. Will report in 2 months on queries.
Terms: Agent receives 15% commission on domestic sales; 20% on foreign sales. Charges for foreign postage and photocopying.
Tips: Obtains new clients through recommendations from others, authors and other clients.

MELANIE JACKSON AGENCY, Suite 1119, 250 W. 57th St., New York NY 10107. Prefers not to share information.

JANKLOW & NESBIT ASSOCIATES, 598 Madison Ave., New York NY 10022. Prefers not to share information.

SHARON JARVIS & CO., INC. (III), 260 Willard Ave., Staten Island NY 10314. (718)720-2120. Contact: Sharon Jarvis, Joan Winston. Estab. 1984. Member of AAR. Represents 85 clients. 20% of clients are new/previously unpublished writers. Specializes in genre fiction, popular nonfiction. Currently handles: 25% nonfiction books; 75% novels.

Handles: Nonfiction books, "genre fiction." Will consider these nonfiction areas: agriculture/horticulture; biography/autobiography; business; crafts/hobbies; health/medicine; military/war; money/finance/economics; nature/environment; new age/metaphysics; psychology; true crime/investigative; science/technology; self-help/personal improvement. Will consider these fiction areas: action/adventure; detective/police/crime; fantasy; glitz; historical; mainstream; mystery/suspense; psychic/supernatural; romance; science fiction; thriller/espionage. Does not accept any children's books. Query only with SASE. Will report in 2 weeks on queries.
Recent Sales: *Encyclopedia Fantastica*, by Kurland & Marano (Prentice Hall); *Moonfire*, by Elizabeth Lane (Silhouette); *Blood Brothers*, by T. Lucien Wright (Zebra).
Terms: Agent receives 15% commission on domestic sales; 10% on foreign sales. Offers a written contract, binding for 1 year. Charges for special services such as overnight mail.
Tips: Obtains new clients through recommendations from publishing professionals and at conferences.

JET LITERARY ASSOCIATES, INC. (III), 124 E. 84th St., New York NY 10028. (212)879-2578. President: James Trupin. Estab. 1976. Represents 85 clients. 5% of clients are new/unpublished writers. Writers must have published articles or books. Prefers to work with published/established authors. Specializes in nonfiction. Currently handles: 50% nonfiction books; 50% novels.
Handles: Nonfiction books and novels. Does not read unsolicited mss. Reports in 2 weeks on queries; 1 month on mss.
Recent Sales: *Deep Thoughts*, by Jack Handey (Berkley); *Everything I Learned In Life I Learned From Elvis*, by Jeff Rovin (Harper); *When Did Wild Poodles Roam The Earth? And Other Imponderables*, by David Feldman (Harper).
Terms: Agent receives 15% commission on domestic sales; 15% on dramatic sales; 25% on foreign sales. Charges for international phone and postage expenses.

LLOYD JONES LITERARY AGENCY (II), 4301 Hidden Creek, Arlington TX 76016. (817)483-5103. Fax: (817)483-8791. Contact: Lloyd Jones. Estab. 1988. Represents 32 clients. 40% of clients are new/previously unpublished writers. Currently handles: 60% nonfiction books; 10% juvenile books; 30% novels. Member agent: Sheree Sutton (new writers).
Handles: Nonfiction books. Will consider these nonfiction areas: business; current affairs; ethnic/cultural interests; health/medicine; juvenile nonfiction; money/finance/economics; psychology; true crime/investigative; self-help/personal improvement; sports; women's issues/women's studies. Send synopsis. Will report in 2 weeks on queries; 6-8 weeks on mss.
Terms: Agent receives 15% commission on domestic sales; 15% on foreign sales. Offers a written contract "for project only."
Tips: Obtains new clients through recommendations from publishers and writers. "Include a bio on writing projects, and define the target market for the proposed book."

THE KARPFINGER AGENCY (II), Suite 2800, 500 5th Ave., New York NY 10110. Prefers not to share information.

‡KC COMMUNICATIONS (I), Suite 201, 11512 N. Poema Pl., Chatsworth CA 91311. (818)998-7265. Fax: same. Contact: K.C. Nichols. Estab. 1991. Represents 16 clients. 80% of clients are new/previously unpublished authors. "We specialize in books for and by women." Currently handles: 20% nonfiction books, 80% novels. Member agents: K.C. Nichols (fiction, Native American stories, historical romance); Julie Steele (nonfiction, music/art/photo books); Rhonda Nichols (nonfiction, women's biographies).
Handles: Nonfiction books, novels, movie scripts, syndicated material. Will consider these nonfiction areas: biography/autobiography; history; music/dance/theater/film; photography; Native American history/issues. Will consider these fiction areas: family saga; historical; literary; mainstream; mystery/suspense; romance (gothic, historical); westerns/frontier. Send query with outline plus 5 sample chapters. Reports in 3 weeks on queries; 2 months on mss.
Terms: Agent receives 15% commission on domestic sales; 20% on foreign sales. Offers a written contract, binding for one year. ("We will represent without a contract.")
Tips: Obtains new clients through referrals.

LOUISE B. KETZ AGENCY (II), Suite 4B, 1485 1st Ave., New York NY 10021. (212)535-9259. Contact: Louise B. Ketz. Estab. 1983. Represents 16 clients. 15% of clients are new/previously unpublished writers. Specializes in science, business, sports, history and reference. Currently handles: 100% nonfiction books.

Handles: Nonfiction books. Will consider these nonfiction areas: anthropology/archaeology; biography/autobiography; business; current affairs; history; military/war; money/finance/economics; true crime/investigative; science/technology; sports. Send outline plus 2 sample chapters. Will report in 4-6 weeks on queries and mss.
Terms: Agent receives 10-15% commission on domestic sales; 10% on foreign sales. Offers a written contract.
Tips: Obtains new clients through recommendations, idea development.

VIRGINIA KIDD, LITERARY AGENT (V), Box 278, Milford PA 18337. Agency not currently seeking new clients.

KIDDE, HOYT & PICARD (III), 335 E. 51st St., New York NY 10022. (212)755-9461. Contact: Katharine Kidde. Estab. 1980. Member of AAR. Represents 50 clients. Specializes in mainstream fiction. Currently handles: 12% nonfiction books; 5% juvenile books; 80% novels; 2% novellas; 1% poetry books.
Handles: Nonfiction books, novels. Will consider these nonfiction areas: animals; biography; gay/lesbian issues; photography; psychology; religious/inspirational; self-help; women's issues. Will consider these fiction areas: detective/police/crime; feminist; gay; humor/satire; lesbian; literary; mainstream; mystery/suspense; romance; thrillers. Query. Will report in a few weeks on queries; 3-4 weeks on mss.
Terms: Agent receives 10% on domestic sales; 10% on foreign sales. Charges for photocopying.
Tips: Obtains new clients through recommendations from others, "former authors from when I was an editor at NAL, Harcourt, etc.; listings in *LMP*, writers guides."

KIRCHOFF/WOHLBERG, INC., AUTHORS' REPRESENTATION DIVISION (II), 866 United Nations Plaza, #525, New York NY 10017. (212)644-2020. Fax: (212)223-4387. Director of Operations: John R. Whitman. Estab. 1930's. Member of Association of American Publishers, Society of Illustrators, SPAR, Bookbuilders of Boston, New York Bookbinders' Guild, AIGA. Represent 30 authors. 33% of clients are new/previously unpublished writers. Specializes in juvenile and young adult trade books and textbooks. Currently handles: 5% nonfiction books; 80% juvenile books; 5% novels; 5% novellas; 5% young adult. Member agent: Elizabeth Pulitzer-Voges (juvenile and young adult authors).
Handles: "We are interested in any original projects of quality that are appropriate to the juvenile and young adult trade book markets. Send either a query or a query that includes an outline and a sample; SASE required." Will report in 1 month on queries; 6 weeks on mss. Please send queries to the attention of: Liza Pulitzer-Voges
Recent Sales: *Moon Rope*, by Lois Ehlert (HBJ); *The Dear One*, by Jacqueline Woodson (Delacorte Press); *The Bridge Book*, by Polly Carter (Simon & Schuster); *Baby Wiggle Mobiles*, by Lizi Boyd (Workman); *Nightsongs*, by Anne Miranda (Bradbury).
Terms: Agent receives standard commission "depends upon whether it is an author only, illustrator only, or an author/illustrator book." Offers a written contract, binding for not less than six months.
Tips: "Usually obtains new clients through recommendations from authors, illustrators and editors. Kirchoff/Wohlberg has been in business for over 50 years."

HARVEY KLINGER, INC. (III), 301 W. 53 St., New York NY 10019. (212)581-7068. Fax: (212)315-3823. Contact: Harvey Klinger. Estab. 1977. Represents 100 clients. 25% of clients are new/previously unpublished writers. Specializes in "big, mainstream contemporary fiction and nonfiction." Currently handles: 50% nonfiction books; 50% novels.
Handles: Nonfiction books, novels. Will consider these nonfiction areas: biography/autobiography; cooking/food/nutrition; health/medicine; psychology; true crime/investigative; science/technology; self-help/personal improvement; sports; women's issues/women's studies. Will consider these fiction areas: action/adventure; detective/police/crime; family saga; glitz; literary; mainstream; mystery/suspense; romance (contemporary); thriller/espionage. Query. Will report in 2 weeks on queries; 6-8 weeks on mss.
Recent Sales: *Are You the One for Me*, by Barbara DeAngelis (Delacorte); *Virgins of Paradise*, by Barbara Wood (Random House); *The King is Dead*, by Sarah Shankmans (Pocket).
Terms: Agent receives 15% commission on domestic sales; 25% on foreign sales. Offers a written contract. Charges for photocopying manuscripts, overseas postage for manuscripts.
Tips: Obtains new clients through recommendations from others.

BARBARA S. KOUTS, LITERARY AGENT (II), P.O. Box 558, Bellport NY 11713. (516)286-1278. Contact: Barbara Kouts. Estab. 1980. Member of AAR. Represent 50 clients. 25% of clients are new/previously unpublished writers. Specializes in adult fiction and nonfiction and children's books. Currently handles: 20% nonfiction books; 40% juvenile books; 40% novels.
Handles: Nonfiction books, juvenile books, novels. Will consider these nonfiction areas: biography/autobiography; business; child guidance/parenting; current affairs; ethnic/cultural interests; health/medicine; history; juvenile nonfiction; music/dance/theater/film; nature/environment; psychology; self-help/personal improvement; women's issues/women's studies. Will consider these fiction areas: contemporary issues; family saga; feminist; historical; juvenile; literary; mainstream; mystery/suspense; picture book; romance (gothic, historical); young adult. Query. Will report in 2-3 days on queries; 4-6 weeks on mss.
Terms: Agent receives 10% commission on domestic sales; 20% on foreign sales. Charges for photocopying.
Tips: Obtains new clients through recommendations from others, solicitation, at conferences, etc. "Write, do not call. Be professional in your writing."

LUCY KROLL AGENCY (II,III), 390 W. End Ave., New York NY 10024. (212)877-0627. Fax: (212)769-2832. Agent: Barbara Hogenson. Member of SAR and WGA East and West. Represents 60 clients. 5% of clients are new/unpublished writers. Specializes in nonfiction, screenplays, plays. Currently handles: 45% nonfiction books; 15% novels; 15% movie scripts; 25% stage plays.
Handles: Nonfiction, movie and TV scripts, stage plays. Query with outline and SASE. Does not read unsolicited manuscripts. Reports in 1 month.
Terms: Agent receives 10% commission on domestic sales; 10% on dramatic sales; 20% on foreign sales.

EDITE KROLL LITERARY AGENCY (II), 12 Grayhurst Park, Portland ME 04102. (207)773-4922. Fax: (207)773-3936. Contact: Edite Kroll. Estab. 1981. Represents 40 clients. Currently handles: 60% adult books; 40% juvenile books.
Handles: Nonfiction, juvenile books, humor, novels. Will consider these nonfiction areas: social and political issues (especially feminist); current affairs. Will consider these fiction areas: contemporary issues; feminist; literary; mainstream; mystery/suspense; juvenile; picture books by author/artists. Query with SASE. For nonfiction, send outline/proposal. For fiction, send outline plus 1 sample chapter or dummy. Reports in 2 weeks on queries; 6 weeks on mss.

PETER LAMPACK AGENCY, INC. (II), Suite 2015, 551 5th Ave., New York NY 10017. (212)687-9106. Fax: (212)687-9109. Contact: Peter Lampack. Estab. 1977. Represents 50 clients. 10% of clients are new/previously unpublished writers. Specializes in commercial fiction, male-oriented action/adventure, contemporary relationships, distinguished literary fiction, nonfiction by a recognized expert in a given field. Currently handles: 15% nonfiction books; 80% novels; 5% movie scripts. Member agents: Peter Lampack (psychological suspense, action/adventure, literary fiction, nonfiction, contemporary relationships); Anthony Gardner (international thrillers, important nonfiction, humor); Sandra Blanton (contemporary relationships, psychological thrillers, mysteries).
Handles: Nonfiction books, novels, movie scripts. Will consider these nonfiction areas: biography/autobiography; business; current affairs; government/politics/law; health/medicine; history; money/finance/economics; true crime/investigative. Will consider these fiction areas: action/adventure; cartoon/comic; contemporary relationships; detective/police/crime; family saga; glitz; historical; literary; mystery/suspense; thriller/espionage. Query. Will report in 2 weeks on queries; 1 month on mss.

The publishing field is constantly changing! If you're still using this book and it is 1994 or later, buy the newest edition of Guide to Literary Agents & Art/Photo Reps *at your favorite bookstore or order directly from* Writer's Digest Books.

Recent Sales: *Sahara*, by Clive Cussler (Simon & Schuster); *Just Killing Time*, by Derek Van Arman (NAL); *The House on the Hill*, by Judith Kelman (Bantam Books).
Terms: Agent receives 15% commission on domestic sales; 20% on foreign sales. Offers a written contract, binding for 1-3 years. "Writer is required to furnish copies of his/her work for submission purposes."
Tips: Obtains new clients from referrals made by clients. "Submit only your best work for consideration. Have a very specific agenda of goals you wish your prospective agent to accomplish for you. Provide the agent with a comprehensive statement of your credentials — educational and professional."

THE ROBERT LANTZ-JOY HARRIS LITERARY AGENCY (II), 888 7th Ave., New York NY 10106. (212)262-8177. Fax: (212)262-8707. Contact: Joy Harris. Member of AAR. Represents 150 clients. Currently handles: 30% nonfiction books; 70% novels.
Handles: Will consider "adult-type books, not juvenile." Will consider all fiction areas except fantasy; juvenile; science fiction; westerns/frontier. Query with SASE and outline/proposal. Will report in 1-2 months on queries.
Terms: Agent receives 15% commission on domestic sales; 20% on foreign sales. Offers a written contract. Charges for extra expenses.
Tips: Obtains new clients through recommendations from clients and editors. "No unsolicited manuscripts, just query letters."

MICHAEL LARSEN/ELIZABETH POMADA LITERARY AGENTS (II), 1029 Jones St., San Francisco CA 94109. (415)673-0939. Contact: Mike Larsen or Elizabeth Pomada. Estab. 1972. Member of AAR. Represents 100 clients. 50-55% of clients are new/unpublished writers. Eager to work with new/unpublished writers. "We have very diverse tastes and do not specialize. We look for fresh voices with new ideas. We handle literary, commercial, and genre fiction, and the full range of nonfiction books." Currently handles: 60% nonfiction books; 40% novels.
Handles: Adult nonfiction books and novels. Query with the first 30 pages and synopsis of completed novel. Reports in 2 months on queries. For nonfiction, call first. "Always include SASE. Send SASE for brochure."
Recent Sales: *Days of Blood & Fire*, by Katharine Kerr (Bantam/Spectra); *Guerilla Marketing's Golden Rules*, by Jay Conrad Levinson (Houghton Mifflin); *Lost Star: The Search for Amelia Earheart*, by Randall Brink (Norton).
Terms: Agent receives 15% commission on domestic sales; 15% on dramatic sales; 20% on foreign sales. May charge writer for printing, postage for multiple submissions, foreign mail, foreign phone calls, galleys, books, and legal fees.

M. SUE LASBURY LITERARY AGENCY (I), 4861 Ocean Blvd., San Diego CA 92109. (619)483-7170. Fax: (619)483-1853. Contact: Sue Lasbury or John Cochran, Associate. Estab. 1990. Represents 15 clients. 40% of clients are new/previously unpublished writers. "We focus primarily, but not exclusively, on West Coast authors who want to write for the general trade book market." Currently handles: 80% nonfiction books; 20% novels. Member agents: M. Sue Lasbury; John C. Cochran.
Handles: Will consider these nonfiction areas: business; current affairs; government/politics/law; health/medicine; history; money/finance/economics; Native Americans; nature/environment; popular culture; psychology; true crime/investigative; popular science; self-help/personal improvement; sociology; women's issues. Will consider these fiction areas: contemporary issues; detective/police/crime; literary; mainstream; mystery/suspense. Query. Will report in 3 weeks on queries; 6 weeks on mss.
Terms: Agent receives 15% commission on domestic sales; 20% on foreign sales. Offers a written author/agent agreement which can be cancelled by author at any time. Charges for photocopying and shipping.
Writers' Conferences: Attends Pacific Northwest Writers Conference, California Writers Club Conference at Asilomar, Southwest Writers Conference and Pasadena City College conference.
Tips: Obtains new clients through recommendations from others. "I travel to meet with potential clients all over the West. Sometimes I seek out authors, they are recommended to me, or they contact me directly. Nonfiction authors should have a strong background related to their book idea. They should carefully research the market and be prepared to do a thoughtful proposal and at least one or two sample chapters. For first time authors, a novel should be completed before seeking an agent."

LEVANT & WALES, LITERARY AGENCY, INC. (IV), 108 Hayes St., Seattle WA 98109. (206)284-7114. Fax: (206)286-1025. Agents: Elizabeth Wales and Dan Levant. Estab. 1988. Member of Pacific Northwest Writers' Conference, Book Publishers' Northwest. Represents 40 clients. "We are inter-

ested in published and not yet published writers." Prefers writers from the Pacific Northwest. Specializes in nonfiction and mainstream fiction. Currently handles: 75% nonfiction books; 25% novels.
Handles: Nonfiction books and novels. Will consider these nonfiction areas: business, gardening, health, lifestyle, nature, popular culture, psychology, science — open to creative or serious treatments of almost any nonfiction subject. Will consider these fiction areas: mainstream (no genre fiction). Query first. Reports in 3 weeks on queries; 6 weeks on mss.
Recent Sales: *Women and Doctors*, by John M. Smith M.D. (Atlantic Monthly Press); *In The Company Of My Sisters: Black Women and Self-Esteem*, by Julia Boyd (Dutton); *Customer Service The Nordstrom Way*, by McCarthy and Spector (Wiley).
Terms: Agent receives 15% commission on domestic sales. We make all our income from commissions. We offer editorial help for some of our clients and help some clients with the development of a proposal, but we do not charge for these services. We do charge, after a sale, for express mail, ms photocopying costs, foreign postage and outside USA telephone costs.

ELLEN LEVINE LITERARY AGENCY, INC. (II, III), Suite 1801, 15 E. 26th St., New York NY 10010. (212)889-0620. Fax: (212)725-4501. Contact: Ellen Levine, Diana Finch, Anne Dubuisson. Member of AAR. "My two younger colleagues at the agency (Anne Dubuisson and Diana Finch) are seeking both new and established writers. I prefer to work with established writers, mostly through referrals." Estab. 1980. Member of AAR, secretary of AAR. Represents over 100 clients. 20% of clients are new/previously unpublished writers. Specializes in literary fiction, women's fiction/thrillers, women's issues, books by journalists, current affairs, science, contemporary culture, biographies. Currently handles: 45% nonfiction books; 8% juvenile books; 45% novels; 2% short story collections.
Handles: Nonfiction books, textbooks, juvenile books, novels, short story collections. Query. Will report in 2-3 weeks on queries, if SASE provided; 4-6 weeks on mss, if submission requested.
Terms: Agent receives 15% commission on domestic sales; 20% on foreign sales. Charges for overseas postage, photocopying, messenger fees, overseas telephone and fax, books ordered for use in rights submissions.
Tips: Obtains new clients through recommendations from others.

ROBERT LEWIS, 65 E. 96th St., New York NY 10128. Agency not currently seeking new clients. Published writers may query.

‡THE LIEBERMAN AGENCY (II), 1515 Middle Country Rd., Centereach NY 11720. (516)451-8995. Contact: Richard Branson. Estab. 1989. Member of WGA. Represents 150 clients. 60% of clients are new/previously unpublished writers. "We specialize in helping new writers become established authors." Currently handles: 40% nonfiction books, 15% novels, 5% poetry books, 7% short story collections, 30% movie scripts, 3% TV scripts. Member agents: Richard Branson (Director of New Client Services); Roger Berstein (screenplays, TV/movie); Mary P. Getty (novels, short story collections, poetry); Foster Clark (nonfiction).
Handles: Nonfiction books, juvenile books, novels, short story collections, poetry books, movie scripts. Will consider all areas of nonfiction. Will consider all areas of fiction except erotica. Send outline/proposal or outline plus 2-3 sample chapters. Reports in one week on queries; 2-3 weeks on mss.
Terms: Agent receives 10% commission on domestic sales; 10% on foreign. Offers a written contract, binding for two years. Offers a criticism service at no extra charge. "Critiques are done inhouse. Types of critiques vary; some are more in-depth than others." Charges for postage, copying and long distance phone calls.
Tips: Obtains 90% of clients through recommendations; 5% at conferences; 5% from listings.

RAY LINCOLN LITERARY AGENCY (II), Suite 107-B, Elkins Park House, 7900 Old York Rd., Elkins Park PA 19117. (215)635-0827. Contact: Mrs. Ray Lincoln. Estab. 1974. Represents 34 clients. 35% of clients are new/previously unpublished writers. Specializes in biography, nature, the sciences, fiction in both adult and children's categories. Currently handles: 30% nonfiction books, 20% juvenile books, 50% novels.
Handles: Nonfiction books, scholarly books, juvenile books, novels. Will consider these nonfiction areas: horticulture; animals; anthropology/archaeology; art/architecture/design; biography/autobiography; business; child guidance/parenting; cooking/food/nutrition; crafts/hobbies; current affairs; ethnic/cultural interests; gay/lesbian issues; government/politics/law; health/medicine; history; interior design/decorating; juvenile nonfiction; language/literature/criticism; money/finance/economics; music/dance/theater/film; nature/environment; psychology; science/technology; self-help/personal improvement; sociology; sports; women's issues/women's studies. Will consider these fiction areas: action/

adventure; contemporary issues; detective/police/crime; ethnic; family saga; fantasy; feminist; gay; historical; humor/satire; juvenile; lesbian; literary; mainstream; mystery/suspense; psychic/supernatural; regional; romance (contemporary, gothic, historical); science fiction; sports; thriller/espionage; young adult. Query "first, then send outline plus 2 sample chapters with SASE. I send for balance of ms if it is a likely project." Will report in 2 weeks on queries; 1 month on mss.

Recent Sales: A biography by Willard S. Randall (Henry Holt); a young adult novella by Jerry Spinelli (Simon & Schuster); a new novel by Jeanne Larsen (Holt).

Terms: Agent receives commission 15% on domestic sales; 20% on foreign sales. Offers a written contract, binding "but with notice, may be cancelled. Charges only for overseas telephone calls. I request authors to do manuscript photocopying themselves. No other expenses."

Tips: Obtains new clients usually from recommendations. "I always look for polished writing style, fresh points of view and professional attitudes."

WENDY LIPKIND AGENCY (II), 165 E 66th St., New York NY 10021. (212)628-9653. Fax: (212)628-2693. Contact: Wendy Lipkind. Estab. 1977. Member of AAR. Represents 60 clients. Specializes in adult nonfiction. Currently handles: 80% nonfiction books; 20% novels.

Handles: Nonfiction, novels. Will consider these nonfiction areas: biography; current affairs; health/medicine; history; science; social history. Will consider mainstream and mystery/suspense fiction. No mass market originals. For nonfiction query with outline/proposal. For fiction query with SASE only. Reports in 1 month on queries.

Terms: Agent receives 15% commission on domestic sales; 20% on foreign sales. Sometimes offers a written contract. Charges for foreign postage and messenger service.

Tips: Usually obtains new clients through recommendations from others. "Send intelligent query letter first. Let me know if you sent to other agents."

LITERARY AND CREATIVE ARTISTS AGENCY (III), 3539 Albemarle St. NW, Washington DC 20008. (202)362-4688. President: Muriel Nellis. Associate: Jane Roberts. Estab. 1982. Member of Authors Guild and associate member of American Bar Association. Represents over 40 clients. "While we prefer published writers, it is not required if the proposed work has great merit." Requires exclusive review of material; no simultaneous submissions. Currently handles: 65% nonfiction books; 20% novels; 5% juvenile books; 5% movie scripts; 5% cookbooks and other one-shots.

Handles: Nonfiction books, novels, theatrical and TV scripts. Will consider these nonfiction areas: business, cooking, health, how-to, human drama, lifestyle, memoir, philosophy, politics. Query with outline, bio and SASE. Does not read unsolicited mss. Reports in 2 weeks on queries.

Recent Sales: *Unconditional Life*, by Dr. D. Chopra (Bantam); *Daring the Dream*, by M. Jackson (Doubleday); *Prayer, Healing and Medicine*, by Dr. L. Dossey (Harper San Francisco); *Untitled Short Story Collection*, by J. Heyner (Knopf); *The Ayurvedic Woman*, by Drs. M. Brown, V. Butler and N. Lonsdorf (Tarcher/Putnam).

Terms: Agent receives 15% commission on domestic sales; 20% on dramatic sales; 25% on foreign sales. Charges for long-distance phone and fax, photocopying and shipping.

‡THE LITERARY BRIDGE (I, II), Box 250 Alamo C.C., Alamo TX 78516. (512)702-4873. Contact: Genero or Rhobie Capshaw. Estab. 1992. Member of RGV Writers Guild. Represents 15-20 clients. 50% of clients are new/previously unpublished writers. "We specialize in helping authors turn a good idea and good writing into a marketable manuscript." Currently handles: 60% nonfiction books; 40% novels. Member agents: Genero Capshaw, Rhobie Capshaw.

Handles: Nonfiction books, novels, how-to and self-help. Will consider these nonfiction areas: animals; anthropology; biography/autobiography; business; government/politics/law; health/medicine; history; juvenile nonfiction; money/finance/economics; nature/environment; new age/metaphysics; psychology; true crime/investigative; self-help/personal improvement; sports; women's issues/women's studies. Will consider these fiction areas: action/adventure; confessional; contemporary issues; detective/police/crime; family saga; fantasy; feminist; glitz; historical; humor/satire; mainstream; mystery/suspense; psychic/supernatural; regional; romance: contemporary, historical; science fiction; sports; thriller/espionage; westerns/frontier; young adult. Query with 3 sample chapters. Will report in 1-2 weeks on queries; 4-6 weeks on mss.

Terms: Agent receives 10-15% commission on domestic sales; 15-20% on foreign sales; 20% on dramatic sales. Offers written contract for 1 year. "The handling fee includes phone, photocopying and postage and is refunded upon the sale of the manuscript by this agency." 95% of business is derived from commissions on manuscript sales.

Tips: Obtains new clients through solicitation and conferences. "We bridge the gap between writers who know their genre or category and publishers who want quality work."

THE LITERARY GROUP (II), #7A, 153 E. 32nd St., New York NY 10016. (212)779-9214. Fax: (212)779-9238. Contact: Frank Weimann. Estab. 1985. Represents 45 clients. 75% of clients are new/previously unpublished writers. Specializes in nonfiction (true crime; biography; sports; how-to). Currently handles: 80% nonfiction books; 20% novels.
Handles: Nonfiction books, novels. Will consider these nonfiction areas: animals; biography/autobiography; business; child guidance/parenting; current affairs; gay/lesbian issues; health/medicine; history; music/dance/theater/film; nature/environment; psychology; true crime/investigative; self-help/personal improvement; sociology; sports; women's issues/women's studies. Will consider these fiction areas: action/adventure; detective/police/crime; humor/satire; mystery/suspense; sports; thriller/espionage. Query with outline plus 3 sample chapters. Will report in 1 week on queries; 1 month on mss.
Recent Sales: *Back from Tuichi,* by Yossi Ghinsberg (Random House); *Marilyn, The Kennedys and Me,* by Fred Otash (New American Library).
Terms: Agent receives 15% commission on domestic sales; 20% on foreign sales. Offers a written contract, which "can be cancelled after 30 days."
Writers' Conferences: Attends Florida Suncoast Writers Conference; Southwest Writers Conference; Palm Springs Writers Group.
Tips: Obtains new clients through referrals, writers conferences, query letters.

STERLING LORD LITERISTIC, INC. (III), One Madison Ave., New York NY 10010. (212)696-2800. Fax: (212)686-6976. Contact: Peter Matson. Estab. 1952. Member of AAR, WGA. Represents 500+ clients. Specializes in "mainstream nonfiction and fiction." Currently handles: 50% nonfiction books, 50% novels. Member agents: Peter Matson, Sterling Lord; Jody Hotchkiss (film scripts); Elizabeth Kaplan; Phillipa Brophy; Stuart Krichevsky; Elizabeth Grossman.
Handles: Nonfiction books, novels. Will consider "mainstream nonfiction and fiction." Query. Will report in 1 month on mss.
Terms: Agent receives 15% commission on domestic sales; 20% on foreign sales. Offers a written contract. Charges for photocopying.
Tips: Obtains new clients through recommendations from others.

LOS ANGELES LITERARY ASSOCIATES (II), 6324 Tahoe Dr., Los Angeles CA 90068. (213)464-6444. Contact: Andrew Ettinger. Estab. 1984. Specializes in nonfiction books. Currently handles: 70% nonfiction books; 30% novels.
Handles: Nonfiction and novels. Will consider these nonfiction areas: biography; business; history; money/finance/economics; self-help/personal improvement; inspirational. Will consider these fiction areas: contemporary issues; mainstream; thriller/espionage. Query with SASE and outline/proposal. Reports in 1 month on queries.
Terms: Agent receives 10-15% commission on domestic sales; varies on foreign sales.
Writers' Conferences: Attends Santa Barbara Writers Conference.
Tips: Usually obtains new clients by word of mouth and referrals. "Do your grass roots market research, in bookstores and the library. It's important not to forget about your libraries because they'll give you a depth of knowledge that can't be found in cruising a typical bookstore."

NANCY LOVE LITERARY AGENCY (III), 250 E. 65th St., New York NY 10021. (212)980-3499. Fax: (212)308-6405. Contact: Nancy Love. Estab. 1984. Member of AAR. Represents 60 clients. Specializes in adult nonfiction. Currently handles: 90% nonfiction books; 10% novels.
Handles: Nonfiction books, novels. Will consider these nonfiction areas: biography/autobiography; business; child guidance/parenting; cooking/food/nutrition; current affairs; ethnic/cultural interests; government/politics/law; health/medicine; history; money/finance/economics; nature/environment; psychology; true crime/investigative; science/technology; self-help/personal improvement; sociology; women's issues/women's studies. Will consider these fiction areas: action/adventure; contemporary issues; detective/police/crime; ethnic; literary; mainstream; mystery/suspense; thriller/espionage. "For nonfiction, send a proposal, chapter summary and sample chapter. For fiction, send the first 40-50 pages plus summary of the rest (will consider only *completed* novels)." Will report in 2 weeks on queries; 3 weeks on mss.
Recent Sales: *The Children's National Medical Center A-Z: Guide to Your Child's Behavior,* by Mrazek, Garrison and Elliott (Putnam); *Sexual Energy Ecstasy,* by Ellen and David Ramsdale (Bantam); *The Last Investigation,* by Gaeton Fonzi (Thunder's Mouth Press).

Terms: Agent receives 15% commission on domestic sales; 20% on foreign sales. Offers a written contract. Charge for photocopying, "if it runs over $20."

Tips: Obtains new clients through recommendations and solicitation. "Many also come through the Writer's Union, where I have a number of clients and a very high rating. I prefer a call to a query letter. That cuts out a step and allows me to express my preference for an exclusive and to discuss the author's credentials. I can also tell a writer that I won't return material without a SASE."

LOWENSTEIN ASSOCIATES, INC. (II), #601, 121 W. 27th St., New York NY 10001. (212)206-1630. President: Barbara Lowenstein. Agents: Norman Kurz and Nancy Yost. Estab. 1976. Member of AAR. Represents 120 clients. 15% of clients are new/unpublished writers. Specializes in nonfiction— especially science and medical-topic books for the general public—general fiction. Currently handles: 2% magazine articles; 55% nonfiction books; 43% novels.

Handles: Nonfiction books and novels. Will consider these nonfiction areas: medicine, science. Will consider these fiction areas: romance (historical, contemporary) and "bigger women's fiction," mainstream. Query. Will not accept unsolicited mss.

Terms: Agent receives 15% commission on domestic sales; 15% on dramatic sales; 20% on foreign sales. Charges for photocopying, foreign postage and messenger expenses.

‡LYCEUM CREATIVE PROPERTIES, INC. (I, II), P.O. Box 12370, San Antonio TX 78212. (210)732-0200. President: Guy Robin Custer. Estab. 1992. Member of WGA. Represents 11 clients. 70% of clients are new/previously unpublished writers. Currently handles: 20% nonfiction books; 5% scholarly books, 40% novels; 25% movie scripts; 5% stage plays; 5% TV scripts. Member agents: Guy Robin Custer (novels, nonfiction, some screenplays); Dave Roy (novels, screenplays, stage plays); Geoff Osborne (nonfiction, screenplays, stage plays); Caspar Jasso (translations, ethnic/cultural).

Handles: Nonfiction books, textbooks, scholarly books, juvenile books, novels, novellas, movie scripts, stage plays, features for television (no episodics). Will consider these nonfiction areas: anthropology/archaeology; art/architecture/design; biography/autobiography; business; child guidance/parenting; computers/electronics; cooking/food/nutrition; current affairs; ethnic/cultural interests; gay/lesbian issues; government/politics/law; history; juvenile nonfiction; language/literature/criticism; music/dance/theater/film; nature/environment; new age/metaphysics; psychology; true crime/investigative; sociology; translations; travel; exposé. Will consider these fiction areas: action/adventure; cartoon/comic; contemporary issues; detective/police/crime; erotica; ethnic; experimental; fantasy; feminist; gay; historical; humor/satire; juvenile; lesbian; literary; mainstream; mystery/suspense; picture book; psychic/supernatural; romance (gothic, historical); science fiction; thriller/espionage; westerns/frontier; political satire. Query. Will report in 2 weeks on queries; 6-8 weeks on mss.

Terms: Agent receives 10% commission on domestic sales; 20% on foreign sales. Offers written contract, binding for 6 months to 2 years. "Free editorial support is available to our signed clients." Writer offsets expenses for long distance tolls, postage, photocopying and any unusual expenses, all agreed upon in advance.

Writers' Conferences: Attends Brown Symposium held at Southwestern University in Georgetown, Texas in February 1993.

Tips: Obtains new clients through well-written queries and referrals. "Always include SASE with your letter of query. All our agents will consider a new writer. We'd rather not read first drafts or unfinished work. Please, no phone queries."

MARGRET MCBRIDE LITERARY AGENCY (II), Suite 225, 4350 Executive Dr., San Diego CA 92121. (619)457-0550. Fax: (619)457-2315. Contact: Winifred Golden or Susan Travis. Estab. 1980. Member of AAR. Represents 25 clients. 10% of clients are new/unpublished writers. Specializes in mainstream fiction and nonfiction.

Handles: Publishing, audio, video film rights. Query with synopsis or outline. Does not read unsolicited mss. Reports in 6 weeks on queries. "We are looking for two more novelists to complete our client list."

Recent Sales: *Rain Of Gold*, by Victor Villasenor (Arte Publico/Dell); *The Egoscue Method*, by Pete Egoscue with Roger Gittines (HarperCollins); *Yes or No*, by Spencer Johnson, M.D. (HarperCollins); *Coffee Will Make You Black*, by April Sinclair (Hyperion).

Terms: Agent receives 15% commission on domestic sales; 10% on dramatic sales; 25% on foreign sales.

DONALD MACCAMPBELL INC. (III), 12 E. 41st St., New York NY 10017. (212)683-5580. Editor: Maureen Moran. Estab. 1940. Represents 50 clients. "The agency does not handle unpublished writers." Specializes in women's book-length fiction in all categories. Currently handles: 100% novels.
Handles: Novels. Query; does not read unsolicited mss. Reports in 1 week on queries.
Recent Sales: *Sins of the Children*, by Emilie Richards (Dell); *Alpine Adventure*, by Mary Daheim (Ballentine); *Playhouse Wench*, by Margaret Porter (NAL).
Terms: Agent receives 10% commission on domestic sales; 20% on foreign sales.

ANITA D. MCCLELLAN ASSOCIATES (III), 50 Stearns St., Cambridge MA 02138. (617)864-3448. Estab. 1988. Member of AAR & Barton Literary Agents' Association. 25% of clients are new/previously unpublished writers. Specializes in general book-length trade fiction and nonfiction.
Handles: Query with SASE only. "No certified mail, no telephone queries, no unsolicited manuscripts." Will report in 3 weeks on queries.
Terms: Agent receives 15% commission on domestic sales; 20% on foreign sales. Charges for photocopying, postage, copies of galleys and books, fax and telephone.
Writers' Conferences: Attends International Feminist Book Fair; National Writers Union Conference.

GINA MACCOBY LITERARY AGENCY (II), Suite 1010, 1123 Broadway, New York NY 10010. (212)627-9210. Contact: Gina Maccoby. Estab. 1986. Represents 30 clients. Currently handles: 33% nonfiction books; 33% juvenile books; 33% novels.
Handles: Nonfiction, juvenile books, novels. Will consider these nonfiction areas: biography; current affairs; ethnic/cultural interests; juvenile nonfiction; dance/theater/film; women's issues/women's studies. Will consider these fiction areas: literary; juvenile; mainstream; mystery/suspense; thriller/espionage; young adult. Query with SASE. Reports in 4-6 weeks.
Terms: Agent receives 10% commission on domestic sales; 20-25% on foreign sales. May recover certain costs such as airmail postage to Europe or Japan or legal fees.
Tips: Usually obtains new clients through recommendations from own clients.

RICHARD P. MCDONOUGH, LITERARY AGENT (II), P.O. Box 1950, Boston MA 02130. (617)522-6388. Contact: Richard P. McDonough. Estab. 1986. Represents 30 clients. 50% of clients are new/unpublished writers. Works with unpublished and published writers "whose work I think has merit and requires a committed advocate." Specializes in nonfiction for general contract and fiction. Currently handles: 80% nonfiction books; 10% novels.
Handles: Nonfiction books, novels. Query with outline and SASE or send 3 chapters and SASE. Reports in 2 weeks on queries; 5 weeks on mss.
Recent Sales: *Parents Who Love Reading, Kids Who Don't*, by M. Leonhardt (Crown); *We Will Gather at the River*, by M.R. Montgomery (Simon & Schuster).
Terms: Agent receives 15% commission on domestic sales; 15% on dramatic sales; 15% on foreign sales. Charges for photocopying, phone beyond 300 miles; postage for sold work only.

HELEN MCGRATH (III), 1406 Idaho Ct., Concord CA 94521. (415)672-6211. Contact: Helen McGrath. Estab. 1977. Currently handles: 50% nonfiction books; 50% novels.
Handles: Nonfiction and novels. Will consider these nonfiction areas: biography; business; current affairs; health/medicine; history; military/war; psychology; self-help/personal improvement; sports; women's issues/women's studies; how-to. Will consider these fiction areas: contemporary issues; detective/police/crime; family saga; literary; mainstream; mystery/suspense; psychic/supernatural; science fiction; sports; thriller/espionage; westerns/frontier. Query with SASE and proposal. No unsolicited mss. Reports in 6-8 weeks on queries.
Terms: Agent receives 15% commission on domestic sales. Sometimes offers a written contract. Charges for photocopying.
Tips: Usually obtains new clients through recommendations from others.

CAROL MANN AGENCY (II,III), 55 5th Ave., New York NY 10003. (212)206-5635. Fax: (212)463-8718. Contact: Carol Mann. Estab. 1977. Member of AAR. Represents 100+ clients. 25% of clients are new/previously unpublished writers. Specializes in current affairs; self-help; psychology; parenting; history. Currently handles: 80% nonfiction books; 15% scholarly books; 5% novels. Member agent: Victoria Sanders (contemporary, fiction and nonfiction.).

Handles: Nonfiction books. Will consider these nonfiction areas: anthropology/archaeology; art/architecture/design; biography/autobiography; business; child guidance/parenting; current affairs; ethnic/cultural interests; government/politics/law; health/medicine; history; interior design/decorating; money/finance/economics; psychology; true crime/investigative; self-help/personal improvement; sociology; women's issues/women's studies. Will consider literary fiction. Query with outline/proposal. Will report in 3 weeks on queries.
Recent Sales: *Leviathan*, by Paul Auster (Viking/Penguin); *Breaking Blue*, by Tim Egan (Knopf); *Family Affairs*, by Andy Hoffman (Pocket).
Terms: Agent receives 15% commission on domestic sales; 20% on foreign sales. Offers a written contract, binding for 1 year.

MARCH TENTH, INC. (III), 4 Myrtle St., Haworth NJ 07641. (201)387-6551. Fax: (201)387-6552. President: Sandra Choron. Estab. 1982. Represents 40 clients. 5% of clients are new/unpublished writers. "Writers must have professional expertise in the field in which they are writing." Prefers to work with published/established writers. Currently handles: 100% nonfiction books.
Handles: Nonfiction books. Query. Does not read unsolicited mss. Reports in 1 month.
Recent Sales: *The Hollywood Lawyers*, by Emily Couric (St. Martin's Press); *Louie Louie: A Social History Of The Song*, by Dave Marsh (Hyperion); *The Book of College Lists*, by Steven Antonoff (Ballantine).
Terms: Agent receives 15% commission on domestic sales; 20% on dramatic sales; 20% on foreign sales. Charges writers for postage, photocopying and overseas phone expenses.

BARBARA MARKOWITZ LITERARY AGENCY (II), 117 N. Mansfield Ave., Los Angeles CA 90036. (213)939-5927. Literary Agent/President: Barbara Markowitz. Estab. 1980. Represents 14 clients. Works with a small number of new/unpublished authors. Specializes in mid-level and young adult only; adult trade fiction and nonfiction. Currently handles: 25% nonfiction books; 25% novels; 50% juvenile books.
Handles: Nonfiction books, novels and juvenile books. Query with outline. SASE required for return of any material. Reports in 3 weeks.
Recent Sales: *Jimmy Spoon and the Pony Express*, by K. Gregory (Scholastic); *No Big Deal*, by Ellen Jaffe McClain (Lodestar); *Sexual Strategies: How Females Choose Their Mates*, by Mary Batten (Tarcher).
Terms: Agent receives 15% commission on domestic sales; 15% on dramatic sales; 15% on foreign sales. Charges writers for mailing, postage.

ELAINE MARKSON LITERARY AGENCY (II), 44 Greenwich Ave., New York NY 10011. (212)243-8480. Estab. 1972. Member of AAR. Represents 200 clients. 10% of clients are new/unpublished writers. Specializes in literary fiction, commercial fiction and trade nonfiction. Currently handles: 30% nonfiction books; 40% novels; 20% juvenile books; 5% movie scripts. Member Agents: Geri Thomas; Sally Wofford; Karin Beisch; Lisa Callamaro (screenplays only); Joanna Cole (children's and young adults only).
Handles: Novels and nonfiction books. Query with outline (must include SASE). SASE is required for the return of any material.
Terms: Agent receives 15% commission on domestic sales; 10% on dramatic sales; 20% on foreign sales. Charges for postage, photocopying, foreign mailing, faxing, long-distance telephone and other special expenses.

‡MILDRED MARMUR ASSOCIATES LTD. (II), Suite 607, 310 Madison Ave., New York NY 10017. (212)949-6055. Fax: (212)687-6894. Contact: Mildred Marmur, Naomi H. Wittes. Estab. 1987. Member of AAR. Represents 45 clients. 30% of clients are new/previously unpublished writers. Specializes in serious nonfiction, literary fiction, juveniles, illustrators. Currently handles: 60% nonfiction books;

If you're looking for a particular agent, check the Agents and Reps Index to find at which agency the agent works. Then look up the listing for that agency in the appropriate section.

15% juvenile books; 25% novels. Member agents: Mildred Marmur—submissions to book publishers; Naomi Wittes—subsidiary rights for books under contract.

Handles: Nonfiction books, novels. Will consider these nonfiction areas: biography/autobiography; business; cooking/food/nutrition; current affairs; ethnic/cultural interests; government/politics/law; health/medicine; history; juvenile nonfiction; military war; money/finance/economics; music/dance/ theater/film; nature/environment; religious/inspirational; true crime/investigative; science/technology; sports; women's issues/women's studies. Will consider these fiction areas: contemporary issues; detective/police/crime; family saga; feminist; juvenile; literary; mainstream; mystery/suspense; thriller/espionage; young adult. Query with SASE. Will report in 2 weeks on queries; 4-6 weeks on ms.

Recent Sales: *Forms of Shelter*, by Angela Davis-Gardner (Ticknor & Fields); *Bread in Half the Time*, by Linda Eckhardt and Diana Butts (Crown); *Battle Lines*, by Jim Lederman (Holt).

Terms: Agent receives 15% commission on domestic sales; 20% on foreign sales. Sometimes offers written contract (book-by-book). 100% of business derived from commissions on manuscript sales.

Tips: Obtains new clients through recommendations from other clients. "Browse in a bookstore or library and look at the acknowledgments in books similar to yours. If an author of a nonfiction book in your general area thanks his or her agent, send your ms to that person and point out the link. If you can't figure out who the agent is, try phoning the publisher. At least you'll have a more targeted person. Also, agents are more receptive to written submissions than to pitches over the phone."

THE MARTELL AGENCY (III), 555 5th Ave., New York NY 10017. (212)692-9770. Contact: Paul Plunkett or Alice Fried Martell. Estab. 1984. Represents 75 clients. Currently handles: 65% nonfiction books; 35% novels.

Handles: Nonfiction and novels. Will consider all nonfiction areas. Will consider most fiction areas. No science fiction or poetry. Query with SASE and outline plus 2 sample chapters. If interested, will report in 3 weeks on queries.

Terms: Agent receives 15% on domestic sales; 20% on foreign sales. Offers a written contract, binding for 1 year. Charges for foreign postage, photocopying.

Tips: Usually obtains new clients by recommendations from agents and editors.

HAROLD MATSON CO. INC., 276 Fifth Ave., New York NY 10001. Prefers not to share information.

GREG MERHIGE-MERDON MARKETING/PROMO CO. INC. (II), Suite 203, 1080 E. Indiantown Rd., Jupiter FL 33477. (407)747-9951. Fax: (407)747-6516. Contact: Greg Merhige. Estab. 1989. Member of WGA and Actors Guild. Represents 20 clients. 90% of clients are new/previously unpublished writers. Currently handles: 5% nonfiction books; 40% juvenile books; 5% novels; 5% novellas; 15% movie scripts; 5% stage plays; 20% TV scripts. Member: Cheryl McCarthy, Account Executive.

Handles: Nonfiction books, juvenile books, novels, novellas, short story collections, poetry books, movie and TV scripts, stage plays. Will consider these nonfiction areas: animals; art/architecture/ design; biography/autobiography; child guidance/parenting; cooking/food/nutrition; ethnic/cultural interests; juvenile nonfiction; military/war; music/dance/theater/film; photography; true crime/investigative; self-help/personal improvement; sociology; sports; women's issues/women's studies. Will consider these fiction areas: action/adventure; cartoon/comic; confessional; detective/police/crime; ethnic; family saga; fantasy; feminist; humor/satire; juvenile; literary; mainstream; mystery/suspense; picture book; psychic/supernatural; regional; religious/inspiration; romance; science fiction; sports; thriller/espionage; westerns/frontier; young adult. Send entire ms plus outline. Will report in 12 days on queries; 45 days on mss.

Recent Sales: *Happy Birthday Hector*, by Laura Kingston (Golden Books); *My Soul to Keep*, by Jim Black (screenplay sold to producer John Hardy).

Terms: Agent receives 10% commission on domestic sales; 15% on foreign sales. Offers a written contract, binding for 1 or 1½ years. Charges expenses on special situations.

Tips: Obtains new clients through recommendations from others. "Listen to your agent. Do not try to make your own deal."

✝ **The double dagger before a listing indicates the listing is new in this edition.**

MGA AGENCY INC. (II), Suite 510, 10 St. Mary St., Toronto, ON M4Y 1P9 Canada. (416)964-3302. Fax: (416)975-9209. Contact: Carol Bonnett, Lesley Harrison or Linda McKnight. Estab. 1989. Represents approximately 200 clients. Currently handles: 50% nonfiction books; 40% fiction, 10% juvenile books.
Handles: Nonfiction, novels. Will consider all nonfiction areas. Will consider these fiction areas: juvenile; mystery/suspense; picture book; romance; science fiction; young adult. Query with résumé and SASE. Reports in 4-6 weeks on queries.
Recent Sales: *A Song For Arbonne*, by Guy Gauniel Kay (Crown); *You Never Know*, by Isabel Huggan (Viking).
Terms: Agent receives 15% commission on domestic sales; 20% on foreign sales. Offers a written contract. Charges for postage, photocopying, fax.
Tips: Usually obtains new clients through recommendations from others, and at conferences.

‡ROBERTA D. MILLER ASSOCIATES (I), 42 E. 12th St., New York NY 10003. Contact: Roberta D. Miller. Estab. 1991. Represents 4 clients. 75% of clients are new/previously unpublished writers. Specializes in literary fiction, young adult. Currently handles 25% juvenile books; 75% novels. Member agents: Elisabeth Whelan (young adult).
Handles: Nonfiction books, juvenile books, novels. Will consider these nonfiction areas: art/architecture/design; biography/autobiography; current affairs; ethnic/cultural interests; language/literature/criticism. Will consider these fiction areas: cartoon/comic; contemporary issues; detective/police/crime; humor/satire; literary; mainstream; young adult. Query with outline/proposal or outline plus 1 sample chapter. Will report in 1 week on queries; 1 month on mss.
Terms: Agent receives 15% commission on domestic sales; 25% on foreign sales. Offers a written contract. Charges for photocopying, international postage, fax charges. 100% of business derived from commissions on manuscript sales.
Tips: Obtains new clients from recommendations, agent listings, editors.

MOORE LITERARY AGENCY, 4 Dove St., Newburyport MA 01950. (508)465-9015. Fax: (508)465-8817. Contact: Claudette Moore. Estab. 1989. 20% of clients are new/previously unpublished writers. Specializes in trade computer books. Currently handles: 100% computer-related books.
Handles: Computer books only. Send outline/proposal. Will report in 3 weeks on queries.
Recent Sales: *Van Wolverton's Guide to Windows*, by Van Wolverton and Michael Boom (Random House).
Terms: Agent receives 15% commission on all sales. Offers a written contract, varies book by book.
Tips: Obtains new clients through recommendations/referrals and conferences.

WILLIAM MORRIS AGENCY (III), 1350 Avenue of the Americas, New York NY 10019. (212)586-5100. Estab. 1898. Member of AAR. Works with a small number of new/unpublished authors. Specializes in novels and nonfiction.
Handles: Nonfiction books and novels. Query only. Reports in 6 weeks.
Terms: Agent receives 10% commission on domestic sales; 10% on dramatic sales; 20% on foreign sales.

HENRY MORRISON, INC. (II), P.O. Box 235, Bedford Hills NY 10507. Prefers not to share information.

MULTIMEDIA PRODUCT DEVELOPMENT, INC. (III), Suite 724, 410 S. Michigan Ave., Chicago IL 60605. (312)922-3063. Fax: (312)922-1905. President: Jane Jordan Browne. Estab. 1971. Member of AAR, ASJA-MWA; SCBW. Represents 100 clients. 5% of clients are new/previously unpublished writers. "Generalists." Currently handles: 60% nonfiction books; 5% juvenile books; 35% novels.
Handles: Nonfiction books, novels. Will consider these nonfiction areas: biography/autobiography; business; cooking/food/nutrition; current affairs; health/medicine; money/finance; nature; true crime/investigative; science. Will consider these fiction areas: detective/police/crime; family saga; glitz; historical; mainstream; mystery/suspense; romance (contemporary, western historical, regency); thriller/espionage. Query "by mail with SASE required. We answer queries with SASE's same or next day, 4-6 weeks on mss."
Recent Sales: *Stanwyck: A Biography*, by Axel Madsen (HarperCollins); *The Dictionary of Film Quotations*, by Melinda Corey and George Ochoa (Crown); *50 Essential Things To Do When The Doctor Says, "It's Cancer,"* by Greg Anderson (NAL).

Terms: Agent receives 15% commission on domestic sales; 20% on foreign sales. Offers a written contract, binding for 2 years. Charges for photocopying, overseas postage, faxes, phone calls.
Tips: Obtains new clients through "referrals, queries by professional, marketable authors. If interested in agency representation, be well informed."

JEAN V. NAGGAR LITERARY AGENCY (III), 1E, 216 E. 75th St., New York NY 10021. (212)794-1082. Contact: Jean Naggar. Estab. 1978. Member of AAR. Represents 100 clients. 20% of clients are new/previously unpublished writers. Currently handles: 30% nonfiction books; 5% scholarly books; 15% juvenile books; 40% novels; 5% short story collections. Member agent: Teresa Cavanaugh. Agent-at-large: Anne Engel (nonfiction).
Handles: Nonfiction books, juvenile books, novels. Will consider these nonfiction areas: biography/autobiography; business; child guidance/parenting; cooking/food/nutrition; current affairs; gay/lesbian issues; government/politics/law; health/medicine; history; interior design/decorating; juvenile nonfiction; money/finance/economics; music/dance/theater/film; new age/metaphysics; psychology; religious/inspirational; true crime/investigative; self-help/personal improvement; sociology; women's issues/women's studies. "We would, of course, consider a query regarding an exceptional mainstream manuscript touching on any area." Will consider these fiction areas: action/adventure; contemporary issues; detective/police/crime; ethnic; family saga; fantasy; feminist; gay; glitz; historical; juvenile; lesbian; literary; mainstream; mystery/suspense; picture book; psychic/supernatural; regional; science fiction; thriller/espionage; young adult. Query. Will report in 24 hours on queries; 2 months on mss.
Recent Sales: *Sister Water*, by Nancy Willard (Knopf); *Gone, But Not Forgotten*, by Philip Margolis; *Critical Care*, by Richard Dooling (Morrow).
Terms: Agent receives 15% commission on domestic sales; 20% on foreign sales. Offers a written contract. Charges for overseas mailing; messenger services; book purchases; long-distance telephone; photocopying. "These are deductible from royalties received."
Writers' Conferences: Has attended Willamette Writers Conference; Bread Loaf, Pacific Northwest, Southwest and many others.
Tips: Obtains new clients through "recommendations from publishers, editors, clients and others, and from writers' conferences, as well as from query letters. Use a professional presentation."

RUTH NATHAN (II), 80 5th Ave., Rm. 706, New York NY 10011. (212)675-6063. Fax: (212)691-1561. Estab. 1980. Member of AAR. Represents 12 clients. 10% of clients are new/previously unpublished writers. Specializes in art, decorative arts, fine art; theater; film; show business. Currently handles: 90% nonfiction books; 10% novels.
Handles: Nonfiction books and novels. Will consider these nonfiction areas: art/architecture/design; biography/autobiography; theater/film. Query. Will report in 2 weeks on queries; 1 month on mss.
Recent Sales: *OK Oklahoma*, by Max Wilk (Grove Weidenfeld); *My Posse Don't Do Homework*, by Lou Anne Johnson (St. Martin's).
Terms: Agent receives 15% commission on domestic sales; 20% on foreign sales. Charges for office expenses, postage, photocopying, etc.
Tips: "Read carefully what my requirements are before wasting your time and mine."

NEW ENGLAND PUBLISHING ASSOCIATES, INC. (II), P.O. Box 5, Chester CT 06412. (203)345-4976 and (203)345-READ. Fax: (203)345-3660. Contact: Elizabeth Frost Knappman or Edward W. Knappman. Estab. 1983. Member of AAR. Represents over 100 clients. 25% of clients are new/previously unpublished writers. Specializes in adult nonfiction books of serious purpose. Currently handles: 100% nonfiction books.
Handles: Nonfiction books. Will consider these nonfiction areas: biography/autobiography; business; child guidance/parenting; government/politics/law; health/medicine; history; language/literature/criticism; military/war; money/finance/economics; nature/environment; psychology; true crime/investigative; science/technology; self-help/personal improvement; sociology; women's issues/women's studies. Send outline/proposal or "phone us to describe your book." Will report in 2 weeks on queries; 3-4 weeks on mss.
Recent Sales: *Dimwits Dictionary*, by Robert Fiske (Writers Digest); *500 Great Books by Women*, by dr. Erica Bauermeister, et. al. (Viking-Penguin); *The Human Odyssey: Companion to the Hall of Biology and Human Evolution, American Museum of Natural History*, by Dr. Ian Tattersoll, Curator (Prentice-Hall).

Terms: Agent receives 15% commission on domestic sales; 20% foreign sales (split with overseas agent). Offers a written contract, binding for 6 months.

Tips: Obtains new clients through recommendations from other clients or editors; calls from writers who see our listing in *LMP*, etc., personal contacts. "Never give up. There is usually a publisher who will see the value in your work if you are persistent. Try to specialize in one area until your reputation is built up. Really analyze your competition. Remember that publishing at heart will always be a craft, so try to have another source of income besides books."

REGULA NOETZLI LITERARY AGENCY (II), 444 E. 85th St., New York NY 10028. (212)628-1537. Fax: (212)744-3145. Contact: Regula Noetzli. Estab. 1989. Represents 35 clients. 85% of clients are new/ previously unpublished writers. Specializes in psychology, popular science, history, biographies, literary fiction, mysteries. Currently handles: 80% nonfiction books, 20% novels.

Handles: Nonfiction books, novels. Will consider these nonfiction areas: animals; anthropology/archaeology; biography/autobiography; child guidance/parenting; current affairs; ethnic/cultural interests; health/medicine; history; money/finance/economics; nature/environment; new age/metaphysics; psychology; true crime/investigative; science/technology; self-help/personal improvement; sociology; sports; women's issues/women's studies. Will consider these fiction areas: contemporary issues; detective/police/crime; ethnic; family saga; feminist; historical; humor/satire; literary; mainstream; mystery/suspense; psychic/supernatural; sports; thriller/espionage. Send outline/proposal for nonfiction and outline plus sample chapters for fiction. Will report in 2 weeks on queries; 1 month on mss.

Terms: Agent receives 15% commission on domestic sales; 20% on foreign sales. "If I submit multiple copies, I ask authors to provide copies."

THE BETSY NOLAN LITERARY AGENCY (II), Suite 9 West, 50 W. 29th St., New York NY 10001. (212)779-0700. Fax: (212)689-0376. President: Betsy Nolan. Agents: Donald Lehr and Carla Glasser. Estab. 1980. Member of AAR. Represents 100 clients. !0% of clients are new/unpublished writers. Works with a small number of new/unpublished authors. Currently handles: 80% nonfiction books; 20% novels.

Handles: Nonfiction books and novels. Query with outline. Reports in 2 weeks on queries; 2 months on mss.

Terms: Agent receives 15% commission on domestic sales; 20% on foreign sales.

THE NORMA-LEWIS AGENCY (II), 521 5th Ave., New York NY 10175. (212)751-4955. Contact: Norma Liebert. Estab. 1980. 50% of clients are new/previously unpublished writers. Specializes in juvenile books (pre-school-high school). Currently handles: 60% juvenile books; 40% adult books.

Handles: Juvenile and adult nonfiction and fiction, movie and tv scripts, radio scripts, stage plays. Query first.

Terms: Agent receives 15% commission on domestic sales; 20% on foreign sales.

HAROLD OBER ASSOCIATES (III), 425 Madison Ave., New York NY 10017. (212)759-8600. Fax: (212)759-9428. Estab. 1929. Member of AAR. Represents 250 clients. 15% of clients are new/previously unpublished writers. Currently handles: 35% nonfiction books, 15% juvenile books, 50% novels. Member agents: Claire Smith; Phyllis Westberg; Peter Shepherd; Henry Dunow.

Handles: Nonfiction books, juvenile books, novels. Will consider all nonfiction and fiction subjects. Query letters *only*. Will report in 1 week on queries; 2-3 weeks on mss.

Terms: Agent receives 10-15% commission on domestic sales; 15-20% on foreign sales. Charges for photocopying for multiple submissions.

Tips: Obtains new clients through recommendations from others.

THE ODENWALD CONNECTION (II), Suite 1296, 3010 LBJ Freeway, Dallas TX 75234. (214)221-5793. Fax: (224)221-1081. Contact: Sylvia Odenwald. Estab. 1984. Represents 25 clients. Specializes in business and how-to books. Currently handles: 100% nonfiction books.

Handles: Nonfiction. Will consider these nonfiction areas: business; current affairs; self-help/personal improvement. Query with SASE and outline/proposal. Reports in 1 month on queries.

Terms: Agent receives 15% on domestic sales; 20% on foreign sales.

Writers' Conferences: Attends the American Society for Training and Development Conference.

Tips: Usually obtains new clients through referrals from other clients and publishers.

THE OTTE COMPANY (II), 9 Goden St., Belmont MA 02178. (617)484-8505. Contact: Jane H. Otte or L. David Otte. Estab. 1973. Represents 35 clients. 33% of clients are new/unpublished writers. Works with a small number of new/unpublished authors. Specializes in quality adult trade books. Currently handles: 40% nonfiction books; 60% novels.
Handles: Nonfiction books and novels. "Does not handle poetry, juvenile or 'by-the-number' romance." Query. Reports in 1 week on queries; 1 month on mss.
Terms: Agent receives 15% commission on domestic sales; 7½% on dramatic sales; 10% on foreign sales plus 10% to foreign agent. Charges for photocopying, overseas phone and postage expenses.

THE RICHARD PARKS AGENCY (III), 5th Floor, 138 E. 16th St., New York NY 10003. (212)254-9067. Fax: (212)777-4694. Contact: Richard Parks. Estab. 1988. Member of AAR. Currently handles: 50% nonfiction books; 5% young adult books; 40% novels; 5% short story collections.
Handles: Nonfiction books, novels. Will consider these nonfiction areas: horticulture; animals; anthropology/archaeology; art/architecture/design; biography/autobiography; business; child guidance/parenting; cooking/food/nutrition; crafts/hobbies; current affairs; ethnic/cultural interests; gay/lesbian issues; government/politics; health/medicine; history; language/literature/criticism; military/war; money/finance/economics; music/dance/theater/film; nature/environment; psychology; true crime/investigative; science/technology; self-help/personal improvement; sociology; women's issues/women's studies. Will consider these fiction areas: action/adventure; contemporary issues; detective/police/crime; family saga; gay; glitz; historical; lesbian; literary; mainstream; mystery/suspense; psychic/supernatural; thriller/espionage; westerns/frontier; young adult. Query with SASE. "We will not accept any unsolicited material." Will report in 2 weeks on queries.
Terms: Agent receives 15% commission on domestic sales; 20% on foreign sales. Charges for photocopying or any unusual expense incurred at the writer's request.
Tips: Obtains new clients through recommendations and referrals.

KATHI J. PATON LITERARY AGENCY (II), 19 W. 55th St., New York NY 10019-4907. (212)265-6586. Fax: available (call first). Contact: Kathi Paton. Estab. 1987. Specializes in adult nonfiction. Currently handles: 65% nonfiction books; 35% fiction.
Handles: Nonfiction, novels, short story collections. Will consider these nonfiction areas: business; sociology; psychology; women's issues/women's studies; how-to. Will consider these fiction areas: literary; mainstream; short stories. For nonfiction, send proposal, sample chapter and SASE. For fiction, send first 40 pages and plot summary or 3 short stories.
Recent Sales: *Total Customer Service*, by Bro Uttal (HarperCollins); *The Myth of the Bad Mother*, by Jane Swigart (Doubleday); *The Rat Becomes Light*, by Donald Secreast (HarperCollins).
Terms: Agent receives 15% commission on domestic sales; 20% on foreign sales. Offers written contract. Length of time binding is on a per-book basis. Charges for photocopying.
Writers' Conferences: Attends International Womens Writing Guild panels and the Pacific Northwest Writers Conference.
Tips: Usually obtains new clients through recommendations from other clients. "Write well."

RODNEY PELTER (II), 129 E. 61st St., New York NY 10021. (212)838-3432. Contact: Rodney Pelter. Estab. 1978. Represents 10-12 clients. Currently handles: 25% nonfiction books; 75% novels.
Handles: Nonfiction books and novels. Will consider all nonfiction areas. Will consider most fiction areas. No juvenile, romance or science fiction. For nonfiction, query with SASE. For fiction, send outline and 50-75 pages with SASE. Reports in 1-3 months.
Terms: Agent receives 15% on domestic sales; 20% on foreign sales. Offers a written contract. Charges for foreign postage, photocopying.
Tips: Usually obtains new clients through recommendations from others.

L. PERKINS ASSOCIATES (IV), 5800 Arlington Ave., Riverdale NY 10471. (212)543-5344. Fax: (212)543-5355. Contact: Lori Perkins. Estab. 1990. Member of AAR, HWA. Represents 50 clients. 10% of clients are new/previously unpublished writers. Specializes in horror, dark thrillers, literary fiction, pop culture. Currently handles: 35% nonfiction books; 65% novels.
Handles: Nonfiction books, novels. Will consider these nonfiction areas: art/architecture/design; current affairs; ethnic/cultural interests; music/dance/theater/film; "subjects that fall under pop culture – TV, music, art, books and authors, film, etc." Will consider these fiction areas: adventure; cartoon; detective/police/crime; ethnic; literary; mainstream; mystery/suspense; psychic/supernatural; thriller. Query with SASE. Will report immediately on queries "with SASE"; 6-10 weeks on mss.

Terms: Agent receives 15% commission on domestic sales; 20% on foreign sales. Offers a written contract "if requested." Charges for photocopying.
Writers' Conferences: Attends Horror Writers of America Conference; World Fantasy Conference; Necon and Lunacon.
Tips: Obtains new clients through recommendations from others, solicitation, at conferences, etc. "Sometimes I come up with book ideas and find authors (*Coupon Queen*, for example). Be professional. Read *Publishers Weekly* and genre-related magazines. Join writers' organizations. Go to conferences. Know your market."

PERKINS' LITERARY AGENCY (V), P.O. Box 48, Childs MD 21916. Agent not currently seeking new clients.

JAMES PETER ASSOCIATES, INC. (III,IV), P.O. Box 772, Tenafly NJ 07670. (201)568-0760. Fax: (201)568-2959. Contact: Bert Holtje. Estab. 1971. Member of AAR. Represents 56 clients. 5% of clients are new/previously unpublished writers. Specializes in nonfiction (history, politics, psychology, health, popular culture, business, biography, reference). Currently handles: 100% nonfiction books.
Handles: Nonfiction books. Will consider these nonfiction areas: anthropology/archaeology; art/architecture/design; biography/autobiography; business; crafts/hobbies; current affairs; ethnic/cultural interests; government/politics/law; health/medicine; history; interior design/decorating; military/war; money/finance/economics; psychology; self-help/personal improvement. Send outline/proposal and SASE. Will report in 3-4 weeks on queries.
Recent Sales: *The War Between the Spies*, by Alan Axelrod (Atlantic Monthly Press/Morgan Entrekin Books); *The Beckoning Darkness: An Encyclopedia of Unusual Experiences*, by Leonard George, Ph.D. (Facts On File).
Terms: Agent receives 15% commission on domestic sales; 20% on foreign sales. Offers a written contract; "separate contracts written for each project." Charges for photocopying.
Tips: Obtains new clients through "recommendations from other clients and publishing house editors. I read widely in areas which interest me and contact people who write articles on subjects which could be books. Be an expert in an interesting field, and be able to write well on the subject. Be flexible."

ALISON J. PICARD LITERARY AGENT (II), P.O. Box 2000, Cotuit MA 02635. (508)420-6163. Fax: (508)420-0762. Contact: Alison Picard. Assistant: Janet Burke. Estab. 1985. Represents 60 clients. 25% of clients are new/previously unpublished writers. "Most interested in nonfiction at this time, especially self-help/recovery, pop psychology, how-to, business and current affairs." Currently handles: 40% nonfiction books; 30% juvenile books; 30% novels.
Handles: Will consider these nonfiction areas: any general trade. Will consider these fiction areas: any except science fiction/fantasy. Query with SASE. Send written query first. No phone/fax queries. Will report in 1 week on queries; 1 month on mss.
Recent Sales: *Nightmare*, by S.K. Epperson (Donald I. Fine Inc.); *Peace of Mind*, by Amy Dean (Bantam Books); *The Nature Almanac*, by Alison Smith (Crown Publishers).
Terms: Agent receives 15% commission on domestic sales; 15% on foreign sales.
Writers' Conferences: Attends Cape Cod Writer's Conference.
Tips: Obtains new clients through recommendations.

AARON M. PRIEST LITERARY AGENCY (II), 708 Third Ave., New York NY 10017. (212)818-0344. Contact: Aaron Priest, Molly Friedrich or Laurie Liss. Currently handles: 50% nonfiction books; 50% fiction.
Handles: Fiction and nonfiction books. Query only (must be accompanied by SASE). Unsolicited mss will be returned unread.
Recent Sales: *Disappearing Acts*, by Terry McMillan; *Ordinary Love and Good Will*, by Jane Smiley; *Longing for Darkness*, by China Galland.
Terms: Agent receives 15% commission on domestic sales. Charges for photocopying and foreign postage expenses.

PRINTED TREE, INC. (II), 2357 Trail Dr., Evansville IN 47711. (812)476-9015. Contact: Jo Frohbieter-Mueller. Estab. 1983. Represents 29 clients. 80% of clients are new/previously unpublished writers. Specializes in selling serious nonfiction and textbooks. Currently handles: 50% nonfiction books; 50% textbooks.

Handles: Nonfiction books, textbooks. Send outline/proposal and SASE. Will report within 3 weeks on proposal/outline.
Recent Sales: *Conducting Choral Excellence* (Longwood).
Terms: Agent receives 15% commission on domestic sales; 20% on foreign sales. Offers a written contract. Charges for mailing, phone calls, photocopying and other out-of-pocket expenses.
Tips: Obtains new clients through recommendations, listings. "Along with an outline/proposal, include a list of similar books on the market and identify your targeted readers."

SUSAN ANN PROTTER LITERARY AGENT (II), Suite 1408, 110 W. 40th St., New York NY 10018. (212)840-0480. Contact: Susan Protter. Estab. 1971. Member of AAR. Represents 50 clients. 10% of clients are new/unpublished writers. Writer must have book-length project or manuscript that is ready to be sold. Works with a small number of new/unpublished authors. Currently handles: 5% magazine articles; 45% nonfiction books; 50% novels.
Handles: Nonfiction books and novels. Will consider these nonfiction areas: general nonfiction, health, biography, medicine, psychology, science. Will consider these fiction areas: mystery; science fiction, thrillers. Query with outline. "Must include SASE." Reports in 2 weeks on queries; 6 weeks on solicited mss. "Please do not call; mail queries only."
Recent Sales: *Iapetus*, by William S. Kirby (Ace); *Peteys*, by Terry Bisson (TOR); *The Hacker and the Ants*, by Rudy Rucker (Morrow/Avonova); *Touches the Stars* and *Dreamcatcher*, by Lynn Armistead McKee (Diamond/Berkley).
Terms: Agent receives 15% commission on domestic sales; 15% on TV, film and dramatic sales; 25% on foreign sales. Charges for long distance, photocopying, messenger, express mail and airmail expenses.
Tips: "Please send neat and professionally organized queries. Make sure to include an SASE or we cannot reply. We receive up to 100 queries a week and read them in the order they arrive. We usually reply within two weeks to any query. Do not call. If you are sending a multiple query, make sure to note that in your letter."

ROBERTA PRYOR, INC. (II), 24 W. 55th St., New York NY 10019. (212)245-0420. President: Roberta Pryor. Estab. 1985. Member of AAR. Represents 50 clients. Prefers to work with published/established authors; works with a small number of new/unpublished writers. Specializes in serious nonfiction and (tends toward) literary fiction. Special interest in natural history and good cookbooks. Currently handles: 10% magazine fiction; 40% nonfiction books; 40% novels; 10% textbooks; 10% juvenile books.
Handles: Nonfiction books, novels, textbooks, juvenile books. Query. SASE required for any correspondence. Reports in 10 weeks on queries.
Recent Sales: *Pacific Street*, by Cecilia Holland (Houghton Mifflin); *The Boy Who Never Grew Up*, by David Handler (Doubleday/Bantam); *Latinos*, by Earl Shorris (W.W. Norton); *Frontiers*, by Noel Mostert (Knopf); Untitled book on the Media and Gulf War, by Mark Crispin Miller (Poseiden/Simon and Schuster).
Terms: Charges 15% commission on domestic sales; 15% on dramatic sales; 20% on foreign sales. Charges for photocopying, Federal Express service sometimes.
Writer's Conferences: Attends Antioch Writers Conference.

PUDDINGSTONE LITERARY AGENCY (II), Affiliate of SBC Enterprises Inc. (formerly SBC Enterprises, Inc.), 11 Mabro Dr., Denville NJ 07834-9607. (201)366-3622. Contact: Alec Bernard and Eugenia Cohen. Estab. 1979. Represents 25 clients. 80% of clients are new/previously unpublished writers. Currently handles: 10% nonfiction books; 70% novels; 20% movie scripts.
Handles: Nonfiction books, novels, movie scripts. Query first with SASE. Will report immediately on queries; 1 month on mss "that are requested by us."
Terms: Agent receives 10-15% sliding scale (decreasing) on domestic sales; 20% on foreign sales. Offers a written contract, binding for 1 year with renewals.
Tips: Obtains new clients through referrals and listings.

QUICKSILVER BOOKS-LITERARY AGENTS (II), 50 Wilson St., Hartsdale NY 10530. (914)946-8748. Contact: Bob Silverstein. Estab. 1973 as packager; 1987 as literary agency. Represents 50+ clients. 50% of clients are new/previously unpublished writers. Specializes in literary and commercial mainstream fiction and nonfiction (especially psychology, new age, holistic healing, consciousness, ecology, environment, spirituality). Currently handles: 75% nonfiction books; 25% novels.

Handles: Nonfiction books, novels. Will consider these nonfiction areas: anthropology/archaeology; biography; business; child guidance/parenting; cooking/food/nutrition; health/medicine; literature; nature/environment; new age/metaphysics; psychology; inspirational; true crime/investigative; self-help/personal improvement. Will consider these fiction areas: contemporary issues; literary; mainstream. Query, always include SASE. Will report in 2 weeks or sooner on queries; 1 month or sooner on mss.
Recent Sales: *Jackie Gleason: The Intimate Portrait of The Great One*, by W.J. Weatherby (Pharos); *Act of Treason: The Role of J. Edgar Hoover in the Assassination of President Kennedy*, by Mark North (Carroll & Graf); *The Lover's Tarot*, by Robert Mueller, Signetthols and Sandra Thomson (Avon Books).
Terms: Agent receives 15% commission on domestic sales; 20% on foreign sales. Offers a written contract, "only if requested. It is open ended, unless author requests time frame." Charges for postage. Authors are expected to supply SASE for return of manuscripts and for query letter responses.
Writers' Conferences: Attends National Writers Union Conference.
Tips: Obtains new clients through recommendations, listings in sourcebooks, solicitations, workshop participation.

‡CHARLOTTE CECIL RAYMOND, LITERARY AGENT (III), 32 Bradlee Rd., Marblehead MA 01945. Contact: Charlotte Cecil Raymond. Estab. 1983. Represents 25 clients. 25% of clients are new/previously unpublished writers. Currently handles 70% nonfiction books; 10% juvenile books; 20% novels.
Handles: Nonfiction books, juvenile books and novels. Biography; child guidance/parenting; current affairs; ethnic/cultural interests; gay/lesbian issues; politics; health/medicine; history; juvenile nonfiction; money/finance/economics; nature/environment; psychology; true crime/investigative; sociology; translations; women's issues/women's studies. Will consider these fiction areas: contemporary issues; ethnic; feminist; gay; lesbian; literary; mainstream; regional; thriller/espionage; young adult. Query with outline/proposal. Will report in 1 week on queries; 6 weeks on mss.
Terms: Agent receives 15% commission on domestic sales; 20% on foreign sales. 100% of business derived from commissions on ms sales.

HELEN REES LITERARY AGENCY (II, III), 308 Commonwealth Ave., Boston MA 02116. (617)262-2401. Fax: (617)262-2401. Contact: Joan Mazmamian. Estab. 1981. Member of AAR. Represents 50 clients. 50% of clients are new/previously unpublished writers. Specializes in general nonfiction, health, business, world politics, autobiographies, psychology, women's issues. Currently handles: 60% nonfiction books; 30% novels; 10% syndicated material.
Handles: Nonfiction books, novels. Will consider these nonfiction areas: biography/autobiography; business; current affairs; ethnic/cultural interests; government/politics/law; health/medicine; history; new age/metaphysics; psychology; religious/inspirational; true crime/investigative; science/technology; self-help/personal improvement; sociology; sports; women's issues/women's studies. Will consider these fiction areas: contemporary issues; detective/police/crime; family saga; feminist; glitz; historical; humor/satire; mainstream; mystery/suspense; sports; thriller/espionage. Query with outline plus 2 sample chapters. Will report in 1 week on queries; 3 weeks on mss.
Recent Sales: *Bankruptcy 1995*, by Harry Figgie, Jr. (Little, Brown); *Re-Engineering the Corporation*, by Michael Hammer and James Champy (HarperCollins); *The Dork of Cork*, by Chel Raymo (Warner Books).
Terms: Agent receives 15% commission on domestic sales; 20% on foreign sales.
Tips: Obtains new clients through recommendations from others, solicitation, at conferences, etc.

RHODES LITERARY AGENCY (II), 140 West End Ave., New York NY 10023. (212)580-1300. Estab. 1971. Member of AAR.
Handles: Nonfiction books, novels (a limited number), juvenile books. Query with outline. Include SASE. Reports in 2 weeks on queries.
Terms: Agent receives 15% commission on domestic sales; 20% on foreign sales.

RIVERSIDE LITERARY AGENCY (I, II), #132, 2673 Broadway, New York NY 10025. (212)666-0622. Fax: (212)749-0858. Contact: Susan Lee Cohen. Estab. 1991. Represents 30 clients. 20% of clients are new/previously unpublished writers. Currently handles: 65% nonfiction books; 30% novels; 5% short story collections.
Handles: Nonfiction books, novels, short story collections. Will consider these nonfiction areas: animals; biography/autobiography; business; child guidance/parenting; cooking/food/nutrition; gay/lesbian issues; health/medicine; history; language/literature/criticism; military/war; money/finance/economics; music/dance/theater/film; nature/environment; new age/metaphysics; psychology; true crime/

investigative; science/technology; self-help/personal improvement; women's issues/women's studies. Will consider these fiction areas: contemporary issues; detective/police/crime; ethnic; fantasy; feminist; gay; glitz; historical; lesbian; literary; mainstream; mystery/suspense; psychic/supernatural; science fiction; thriller/espionage. Query. Reports in 1 week on queries; 3 weeks on mss.

Terms: Agent receives 15% commission on domestic sales; 20% on foreign sales. Offers written contract, binding until terminated by either party. Will charge extraordinary expenses (photocopying, foreign postage) to the author's account.

Tips: Usually obtains new clients through recommendations.

THE ROBBINS OFFICE, INC. (II), 866 2nd Ave., New York NY 10017. (212)223-0720. Fax: (212)223-2535. Contact: Kathy P. Robbins, Elizabeth Mackey. Specializes in selling mainstream nonfiction, commercial and literary fiction.

Handles: Nonfiction books, novels and magazine articles for book writers under contract. Does not read unsolicited mss.

Terms: Agent receives 15% commission on all domestic, dramatic and foreign sales. Bills back specific expenses incurred in doing business for a client.

ROCK LITERARY AGENCY (II), P.O. Box 625, Newport RI 02840. (401)849-4442. Fax: (401)849-3440. Contact: Andrew T. Rock. Estab. 1984. Represents 26 clients. Specializes in recreation, health, politics and business. Currently handles: 90% nonfiction books; 10% fiction (package and projects).

Handles: Nonfiction books. Will consider these nonfiction areas: business; health; money/finance/economics; recreation. Will consider "only general, adult" fiction areas. Query with SASE. Reports in 10 days on queries.

Terms: Agent receives 15% commission on domestic sales; 20% on foreign sales. Offers written contract.

Tips: Usually obtains new clients through recommendations from others, and "I go out and get people I want to represent."

IRENE ROGERS, LITERARY REPRESENTATIVE (III), Suite 600, 9454 Wilshire Blvd., Beverly Hills CA 90212. (213)837-3511. Estab. 1977. Currently represents 10 clients. 10% of clients are new/previously unpublished authors. "Not presently accepting new clients, but this changes from month to month." Currently handles: 50% nonfiction, 50% novels.

Handles: Nonfiction and novels. Query. Responds to queries in 6-8 weeks.

Terms: Agent receives 10% commission on domestic sales; 5% on foreign sales.

‡ROSE LITERARY AGENCY (II), Suite 302, 688 Ave. of the Americas, New York NY 10010. (212)242-7702. Fax: (212)242-8947. Contact: Mitchell Rose. Estab. 1986. Represents 60 clients. 25% of clients are new/previously unpublished writers. "We have a broad list, but do have a few areas in which we specialize: film, exposé, history, politics, psychology, nutrition and innovative literary fiction." Currently handles: 80% nonfiction books; 15% novels; 5% short story collections.

Handles: Nonfiction books, novels, short story collections. Will consider these nonfiction areas: anthropology/archaeology; art/architecture/design; biography/autobiography; business; child guidance/parenting; cooking/food/nutrition; current affairs; ethnic/cultural interests; gay/lesbian issues; government/politics/law; health/medicine; history; language/literature/criticism; military/war; money/finance/economics; music/dance/theater/film; nature/environment; psychology; true crime/investigative; science/technology; self-help/personal improvement; sociology; sports; women's issues/women's studies. Will consider these fiction areas: contemporary issues; ethnic; feminist; gay; humor/satire; literary; thriller/espionage. Query. Will report in 2 weeks on queries; 1 month on mss.

Recent Sales: *Lawrence of Arabia*, by Morris and Raskin (Doubleday); *Kennedy as President*, by Gerald Strober (HarperCollins); *Healing Through Nutrition*, by Melvyn Werbach (HarperCollins); *Consumer's Guide to Today's Health Care*, by Stephen Isaacs and Ava Swartz (Houghton Mifflin).

Terms: Agent receives 15% commission on domestic sales; 20% on foreign sales. Offers written contract. "For projects and authors that show promise, we offer extensive editorial feedback at no charge. Critiques are written by myself and staff project developers." Charges fees "but only for very high volume photocopying. Any expense would be approved by the client before it is incurred."

Tips: Obtains new clients mostly through recommendations of existing clients and from editors. "We have taken on several clients whose initial contacts were through query letters."

JEAN ROSENTHAL LITERARY AGENCY (III), 28 E. 11th St., New York NY 10003. (212)677-4248.
Contact: Jean Rosenthal. Estab. 1980. Specializes in "co-productions and series of titles." Currently
handles: 60% nonfiction books; 20% juvenile books.
Handles: Nonfiction books, juvenile books. Will consider these nonfiction areas: animals; anthropol-
ogy/archaeology; art/architecture/design; biography; child guidance/parenting; health/medicine; history. Will consider these fiction areas: mystery/suspense. Query with outline/proposal. Will report in
1 month on queries.
Recent Sales: A five-volume *Encyclopedia of Mammals*, by Bernhard Grzimek (McGraw Hill); *CD
Rom Program* (McGraw Hill London); Pre-school juvenile series to Checkerboard Press.
Terms: Agent receives 15% commission on domestic sales; 25% on foreign sales. Offers a written
contract, binding for "6 months as agent, in perpetuity for sales. I charge postage, fax, telephone and
ask that an advance of $50 is sent to me as a draw against expenses if I take on a client."
Tips: Obtains new clients "any way they come. Write a tight proposal, enclose a SASE and indicate
if query is being simultaneously sent to lots of agents. Put telephone number on query letter."

‡THE ROTH LITERARY AGENCY (II, III), No. 2, 106 Rockview St., Boston MA 02130. (617)522-3213.
Fax: (617)522-3213. Contact: Shelley E. Roth. Member of Boston Literary Agents Association. Currently handles: 50% fiction; 50% nonfiction books.
Handles: Nonfiction books, novels, movie scripts. Will consider these nonfiction areas: biography/
autobiography; business; nutrition; current affairs; gardening; parenting; ethnic/cultural interests; gov-
ernment/politics/law; health/medicine; history; language/literature/criticism; music/dance/theater/
film; nature/ environment; photography; psychology; true crime/investigative; self-help/personal improvement; sociology; women's issues/women's studies; pop culture. Will consider these fiction areas:
contemporary issues; ethnic; family saga; feminist; historical; humor/satire; literary; mainstream; mys-
tery/suspense; thriller/espionage. (Fiction) Query with first 50 pp. of ms and proposal consisting of
overview of ms, submission history of ms, author bio and SASE. (Nonfiction) Query, annotated table
of contents, author bio, submission history of ms, 3 chapters, a survey of competition and SASE.
Terms: Agent receives 15% commission on domestic sales; 20% on foreign sales. Offers written
contract. "Some expenses are charged to the writer, as mutually agreed." 100% of business is derived
from commission on manuscript sales.
Writers' Conferences: Attends Mystery Writers of America (Edgar Awards) and various other con-
ferences/workshops throughout the year.
Tips: Obtains new clients through recommendations from others, solicitation and at conferences. "The
more writers know their market and audience, and the more they've familiarized themselves with the
publishing process, the better. This knowledge, plus knowing the competition, is crucial for the new
nonfiction writer. Let agents know how you were referred to them, and if you've published before.
The concept as well as the execution of the ms must both be excellent, or at least have the potential
to be so. Quality writing, a professional attitude, and a sense of humor (you need one in this industry)
are important. Credentials and writing credits are a plus."

JANE ROTROSEN AGENCY (II), 318 E. 51st St., New York NY 10022. (212)593-4330. Estab. 1974.
Member of AAR. Represents 100 clients. Works with published and unpublished writers. Specializes
in trade fiction and nonfiction. Currently handles: 40% nonfiction books; 60% novels.
Handles: Nonfiction books, novels and juvenile books. Query with "short" outline. Reports in 2 weeks.
Terms: Receives 15% commission on domestic sales; 15% on dramatic sales; 20% on foreign sales.
Charges writers for photocopying, long-distance/transoceanic telephone, telegraph, Telex, messenger
service and foreign postage.

PESHA RUBINSTEIN, LITERARY AGENCY, INC. (II), #1D, 37 Overlook Terrace, New York NY 10033.
(212)781-7845. Contact: Pesha Rubinstein. Estab. 1990. Member of AAR. Represents 35 clients. 80%
of clients are new/previously unpublished writers. Specializes in romance and children's (juvenile and
young adult) books. Currently handles: 20% juvenile books; 80% novels.
Handles: Genre fiction, juvenile books and picture book illustration. Will consider these nonfiction
areas: juvenile nonfiction; nature/environment; true crime/investigative; translations. Will consider
these fiction areas: cartoon/comic; detective/police/crime; glitz; historical; juvenile; mystery/suspense;
picture book; romance; young adult. "No science fiction." Send outline plus 3 sample chapters with
SASE. Will report in 2 weeks on queries; 6 weeks on mss.
Recent Sales: 3 untitled historical romances, by Penelope Neri (Zebra Books); *Captain Of My Heart*,
by Danelle Harmon (Avon); *Double Vision*, by Sheryl Lynn (Harlequin); 1 young adult ethnic novel
by Sara Gogol (Lerner); illustrations by Tatsuro Kiuchi (Simon & Schuster).

Terms: Agent receives 15% commission on domestic sales; 20% on foreign sales. Offers a written contract. Charges for photocopying. No collect calls.
Tips: "I advertise with writers' groups, with *Romantic Times*, the RWA and SCBW. For children's book illustrators, I go to galleries, keep an eye on magazine ads. Keep the query letter and synopsis short. The work speaks for itself better than any description can. Never send originals. A phone call after 1 month is acceptable. Always include SASE covering return of the entire package with the material."

SANDUM & ASSOCIATES (II), 144 E. 84th St., New York NY 10028. (212)737-2011. Fax number by request. President: Howard E. Sandum. Estab. 1987. Represents 35 clients. 20% of clients are new/unpublished writers. Specializes in general nonfiction—all categories of adult books; commercial and literary fiction. Currently handles: 60% nonfiction books; 40% novels.
Handles: Nonfiction books and novels. Query with outline. Do not send full ms unless requested. Include SASE. Reports in 2 weeks on queries.
Terms: Agent receives 15% commission. Agent fee adjustable on dramatic and foreign sales. Charges writers for photocopying, air express, long-distance telephone.

SCHAFFNER AGENCY, INC. (II), 6625 N. Casas Adobes Rd., Tucson AZ 85704. (602)797-8000. Fax: (602)797-8271. Contact: Timothy Schaffner or Jennifer Powers. Estab. 1948. Represents approximately 40 clients. Specializes in literary fiction and nonfiction, nature and ecology issues, Southwestern and Latin American writers, American popular culture and music.
Handles: Nonfiction books, novels. Will consider these nonfiction areas: biography/autobiography; nature/environment; conservation issues. Will consider these fiction areas: feminist, literary. Query with SASE. Will report within 4-6 weeks on queries.
Recent Sales: *Charles Keating Biography*, by Charles Bowden (Random House).
Terms: Agent receives 15% commission on domestic sales; 20% on foreign sales. Offers written contract, if requested. Charges $15 to cover postage costs.
Tips: "Query first and keep initial presentations concise. Always include SASE."

HAROLD SCHMIDT LITERARY AGENCY (II), Suite 1005, 668 Greenwich St., New York NY 10014. (212)727-7473. Fax: (212)807-6025. Contact: Harold Schmidt. Estab. 1983. Member AAR. Represents 30 clients. 20% of clients are new/previously unpublished writers. Currently handles: 45% nonfiction books; 5% scholarly books; 50% novels.
Handles: Nonfiction books, scholarly books, novels, short story collections. Will consider these nonfiction areas: anthropology/archaeology; art/architecture/design; biography/autobiography; business; current affairs; ethnic/cultural interests; gay/lesbian issues; government/politics/law; health/medicine; history; language/literature/criticism; military/war; money/finance/economics; music/dance/theater/film; nature/environment; new age/metaphysics; psychology; true crime/investigative; science/technology; self-help/personal improvement; sociology; translations; women's issues/women's studies. Will consider these fiction areas: action/adventure; contemporary issues; detective/police/crime; ethnic; family saga; feminist; gay; glitz; historical; lesbian; literary; mainstream; mystery/suspense; psychic/supernatural; science fiction; thriller/espionage; westerns/frontier; horror. Query. Will report within 2 weeks on queries; 4-6 weeks on mss.
Terms: Agent receives 15% commission on domestic sales; 20% commission on foreign sales. Offers a written contract "on occasion—time frame always subject to consultation with author." Charges for "larger than incidental photocopying, long distance telephone calls and faxes, manuscript submission postage costs."
Tips: Obtains new clients through recommendations from others and solicitation. "I cannot stress enough how important it is for the new writer to present a clear, concise and professionally presented query letter."

LAURENS R. SCHWARTZ AGENCY (II), Suite 15D, 5 E. 22nd St., New York NY 10010-5315. (212)228-2614. Contact: Laurens R. Schwartz. Estab. 1984. Represents 100 clients. Primarily nonfiction, some adult and juvenile fiction. Within nonfiction, half of authors have doctoral and post-doctoral degress and write for both the academic and crossover (education and trade) markets; other half are general trade (astrology through Zen) and professional/business (real estate, finances, teleconferencing, graphics, etc). Also works with celebrities. Adult fiction: contemporary; fantasy; literary/mainstream. Juvenile: illustrated; series. Currently handles: 60% nonfiction books; 40% fiction (adult and juvenile).

Handles: Everything described above, plus ancillaries (from screenplays to calendars). Does movie tie-in novelizations. "Do not like receiving mass mailings sent to all agents. Be selective—do your homework. Do not send *everything* you have ever written. Choose *one* work and promote that. *Always* include an SASE. *Never* send your only copy. *Always* include a background sheet on yourself and a *one*-page synopsis of the work (too many summaries end up being as long as the work)." No longer handle screenplays except as tied in to a book, or unless we solicit the screenwriter directly. Does not read unsolicited mss. Reports in 1 month.
Terms: Agent receives 15% commission on domestic sales; up to 25% on foreign sales. "No fees except for photocopying, and that fee is avoided by an author providing necessary copies or, in certain instances, transferring files on diskette—must be IBM compatible." Where necessary to bring a project into publishable form, editorial work and some rewriting provided as part of service. Works with authors on long-term career goals and promotion.

LYNN SELIGMAN, LITERARY AGENT (II), 400 Highland Ave., Upper Montclair NJ 07043. (201)783-3631. Contact: Lynn Seligman. Estab. 1985. Represents 32 clients. 15% of clients are new/previously unpublished writers. Currently handles: 75% nonfiction books; 15% novels; 10% photography books.
Handles: Nonfiction books; novels; photography books. Will consider these nonfiction areas: anthropology/archaeology; art/architecture/design; biography/autobiography; business; child guidance/parenting; cooking/food/nutrition; current affairs; ethnic/cultural interests; government/politics/law; health/medicine; history; interior design/decorating; language/literature/criticism; money/finance/economics; music/dance/theater/film; nature/environment; psychology; true crime/investigative; science/technology; self-help/personal improvement; sociology; translations; women's issues/women's studies. Will consider these fiction areas: contemporary issues; detective/police/crime; ethnic; fantasy; feminist; historical; humor/satire; literary; mainstream; mystery/suspense. Query with letter or outline/proposal plus 1 sample chapter with SASE. Will report in 2 weeks on queries; 1-2 months on mss.
Recent Sales: *Strange Devices of the Sun and Moon*, by Lisa Goldstein (TOR); *When Parents Disagree*, by Dr. Ron Laffel with Roberta Israeloff (Morrow); *The Victorian Collectibles Book*, by Carol McD. Wallace (Abrams).
Terms: Agent receives 15% commission on domestic sales; 25% on foreign sales. Charges for photocopying, unusual postage or telephone expenses (checking first with the author), Express Mail.
Writers' Conferences: Attends Dorothy Canfield Fisher Conference.
Tips: Obtains new clients usually from other writers or from editors.

‡THE SEYMOUR AGENCY (I), 7 Rensselaer Ave., P.O. Box 376, Heuvelton NY 13654. (315)344-7223. Contact: Mike Seymour/Mary Sue Seymour. Estab. 1992. Member of Romance Writers of America. 100% of clients are new/previously unpublished writers. Specializes in women's fiction, especially romantic, general young adult. Currently handles: 100% novels. Member agents: Mary Sue Seymour (women's fiction, young adult); Mike Seymour (all areas).
Handles: Juvenile books, novels. Will consider these fiction areas: juvenile; romance (contemporary, gothic, historical, regency); young adult. Query with 3 sample chapters and synopsis. Will report in 1 month on queries; 6 weeks on mss.
Terms: Agent receives 15% commission on domestic sales; 15% on foreign sales. Offers written contract, binding for 1 year. Offers criticism service. $25 for 1st 50 pp.; $100 for remainder of ms. "We provide a general critique—line-to-line editing on first 50 pps. only. Postage fees refundable when/if ms sells." 99% of business derived from commissions on ms sales.
Tips: Obtains new clients through recommendations from others. "I am looking for writers (published or unpublished) with *completed* young adult or romantic novels. I look for great dialogue and unusual storylines. Send query, synopsis and 3 chapters with SASE."

CHARLOTTE SHEEDY LITERARY AGENCY, INC. (II), 41 King St., New York NY 10014. Prefers not to share information.

THE SHEPARD AGENCY (II), Suite 3, Pawling Savings Bank Bldg., Southeast Plaza, Brewster NY 10509. (914)279-2900 or (914)279-3236. Fax: (914)279-3239. Contact: Jean or Lance Shepard. Specializes in "some fiction; nonfiction: business, biography, homemaking; inspirational; self-help." Currently handles: 75% nonfiction books; 5% juvenile books; 20% novels.
Handles: Nonfiction books, scholarly books, novels. Will consider these nonfiction areas: agriculture; horticulture; animals; biography/autobiography; business; child guidance/parenting; computers/electronics; cooking/food/nutrition; crafts/hobbies; current affairs; government/politics/law; health/medicine; history; interior design/decorating; juvenile nonfiction; language/literature/criticism; money/fi-

nance/economics; music/dance/theater/film; nature/environment; psychology; religious/inspirational; self-help/personal improvement; sociology; sports; women's issues/women's studies. Will consider these fiction areas: contemporary issues; family saga; historical; humor/satire; literary; regional; sports; thriller/espionage. Query with outline, sample chapters plus SASE. Will report in 1 month on queries; 2 months on mss.
Terms: Agent receives 10% on domestic sales. Offers written contract. Charges for extraordinary postage, photocopying and long-distance phone calls.
Tips: Obtains new clients through referrals and listings in various directories for writers and publishers. "Provide info on those publishers who have already been contacted, seen work, accepted or rejected same. Provide complete bio and marketing info."

BOBBE SIEGEL LITERARY AGENCY (II), 41 W. 83rd St., New York NY 10024. (212)877-4985. Fax: (212)877-4985. Contact: Bobbe Siegel. Estab. 1975. Represents 60 clients. 30% of clients are new/previously unpublished writers. Currently handles: 65% nonfiction books; 35% novels.
Handles: Nonfiction books, novels. Will consider these nonfiction areas: archaeology; biography/autobiography; child guidance/parenting; nutrition; ethnic; health/medicine; history; literature; music/dance/theater/film; nature/environment; psychology; inspirational; true crime/investigative; self-help/personal improvement; sports; women's issues. Will consider these fiction areas: action/adventure; contemporary issues; detective/police/crime; family saga; fantasy; feminist; glitz; historical; literary; mainstream; mystery/suspense; psychic/supernatural; romance (historical); science fiction; thriller/espionage. Query. Will report in 2 weeks on queries; 2 months on mss.
Recent Sales: *The Famous Dar Murder Mystery* and *The Famous Rotary Club Mystery*, by Graham Landrum (St. Martin's Press); *Jade Lady Burning*, by Martin Limon (Soho Press).
Terms: Agent receives 15% on domestic sales; 20% on foreign sales. Offers a written contract. Charges for photocopying; long-distance or overseas telephone calls or fax messages; airmail postage, both foreign and domestic.
Writers' Conferences: Attends Santa Barbara Writers Conference.
Tips: Obtains new clients through "word of mouth; editors' and authors' recommendations; through conferences and from people who see my name in publications. Write clear and neat letters of inquiry; always remember to include SASE. Never use dot matrix. In your letter never tell the agent why your book is great. Letters should be spaced and paragraphed so they are easy to read and should not be more than 2 pages."

SIERRA LITERARY AGENCY (II), P.O. Box 1090, Janesville CA 96114. (916)253-3250. Contact: Mary Barr. Estab. 1988. Eager to work with new/unpublished writers. Specializes in contemporary women's novels, mainstream fiction and nonfiction, self-help, self-esteem books.
Handles: Fiction, nonfiction books and novels. Query with outline or entire ms. Reports in 2 weeks on queries; 6 weeks on mss.
Terms: Agent receives 10% commission on domestic sales; 15% on dramatic sales; 20% on foreign sales. Charges writers for photocopying, phone and overseas postage.

EVELYN SINGER LITERARY AGENCY INC. (III), P.O. Box 594, White Plains NY 10602. (914)631-5160/1147. Contact: Evelyn Singer. Estab. 1951. Represents 45 clients. 25% of clients are new/previously unpublished writers. Specializes in nonfiction (adult/juvenile, adult suspense).
Handles: Nonfiction books, juvenile books, novels. Will consider these nonfiction areas: anthropology/archaeology; biography; business; child guidance; computers/electronics; current affairs; government/politics/law; health/medicine; juvenile nonfiction; money/finance/economics; science/technology; self-help/personal improvement. Will consider these fiction areas: contemporary issues; detective/police/crime; historical; mystery/suspense; thriller/espionage. Query. Will report in 2 weeks on queries; 6-8 weeks on mss. "SASE must be enclosed for reply or return of manuscript."
Terms: Agent receives 15% on domestic sales; 20% on foreign sales. Offers a written contract, binding for 3 years. Charges for long-distance phone calls, overseas postage ("authorized expenses only").
Tips: Obtains new clients through recommendations. "I am accepting writers who have earned at least $20,000 from freelance writing. SASE must accompany all queries and material for reply and or return of ms."

VALERIE SMITH, LITERARY AGENT (III), 1746 Rt. 44/55, Modena NY 12548. (914)883-5848. Contact: Valerie Smith. Estab. 1978. Represents 30 clients. 1% of clients are new/previously unpublished writers. Specializes in science fiction and fantasy. Currently handles: 2% nonfiction books; 96% novels; 1% novellas; 1% short story collections.

Handles: Novels. Will consider these fiction areas: fantasy; literary; mainstream; science fiction; young adult. Query. Will report in 2 weeks on queries; 2 months on mss.
Terms: Agent receives 15% on domestic sales; 20% on foreign sales. Offers a written contract. Charges for "extraordinary expenses by mutual consent."
Tips: Obtains new clients through recommendations from other clients, various respected contacts.

MICHAEL SNELL LITERARY AGENCY (II), Box 655, Truro MA 02666. (508)349-3718. Contact: Michael Snell. Estab. 1980. Represents 200 clients. 25% of clients are new/previously unpublished authors. Specializes in all types of business and computer books, from low-level how-to to professional and reference. Currently handles: 90% nonfiction books, 10% novels. Member agents: Michael Snell (nonfiction); Patricia Smith (fiction and children's books).
Handles: Nonfiction books, textbooks, scholarly books, juvenile books. Open to all nonfiction categories. Will consider these fiction areas: literary; mystery/suspense; thriller/espionage. Query with SASE. Will report in 1 week on queries; 2 weeks on mss.
Recent Sales: *The Brothers,* by David James Duncan (Doubleday); *The Strategy Game,* by Craig Hickman (McGraw-Hill); *The Genius of Sitting Bull,* by Emmett Murphy (Prentice-Hall); *Kids' Answers to Life's Big Questions,* by Bob Adams; *Color Publishing on the Mac and PC,* by Kim and Sunny Baker (Random House).
Terms: Agent receives 15% on domestic sales; 15% on foreign sales.
Tips: Obtains new clients through unsolicited manuscripts, word-of-mouth, *LMP* and *Writer's Market.* "Send a half- to a full-page query. We offer a booklet, 'How to Write a Book Proposal,' available on request with SASE."

ELYSE SOMMER, INC. (II), P.O. Box E, 110-34 73rd Rd., Forest Hills NY 11375. (718)263-2668. President: Elyse Sommer. Estab. 1952. Member of AAR. Represents 20 clients. Works with a small number of new/unpublished authors. Specializes in nonfiction: reference books, dictionaries, popular culture. Currently handles: 90% nonfiction books; 5% novels; 5% juvenile.
Handles: Novels (some mystery but no sci-fi), juvenile books (no pre-school). Query with outline. Reports in 2 weeks on queries.
Recent Sales: The Panel Digest (annuals), Kids' World Almanac Books, Metaphors Dictionary, several biographies, *Falser Than a Weeping Crocodile.*
Terms: Agent receives 15% commission on domestic sales (when advance is under 20,000, 10% over); 20% on dramatic sales; 20% on foreign sales. Charges for photocopying, long distance, express mail, extraordinary expenses.

DAVID M. SPATT, ESQ. (II), P.O. Box 19, Saunderstown RI 02874. (401)789-5686. Contact: David M. Spatt. Estab. 1989. 33% of clients are new/previously unpublished writers. Specializes in mostly novel-length fiction in science fiction, fantasy and horror genres. Currently handles: 5% nonfiction books; 95% novels.
Handles: Will consider these fiction areas: erotica; fantasy; psychic/supernatural; science fiction; illustrated fiction; horror. Send outline plus 2 sample chapters. Will report in 1 month on queries; 2 months on mss.
Terms: Agent receives 15% on domestic sales; 15% on foreign sales. Offers a written contract, binding for at least 1 year. "Certain office expenses related directly to the marketing of a writer's ms may be charged, but such would be spelled out in any written contract."
Tips: Obtains new clients through recommendations from others. "This is an arts/entertainment law practice which also acts as a literary agent on behalf of a small number of writers who are past clients, as well as promising new writers. Advice? Always deal with agents and others in written contracts, which you read and understand before signing. Get it right the first time, and you probably won't get burnt later."

F. JOSEPH SPIELER (V), 13th Floor, Room 135, 154 W. 57th St., New York NY 10019. (212)757-4439. Fax: (212)333-2019. Contact: Joe Spieler or Lisa Ross. Estab. 1981. Represents 47 clients. 2% of clients are new/previously unpublished writers.

Agents who specialize in a specific subject area such as children's books or in handling the work of certain writers such as Southwestern writers are ranked IV.

Handles: Nonfiction books, novels. Will consider these nonfiction areas: biography/autobiography; business; child guidance/parenting; cooking/food/nutrition; current affairs; ethnic/cultural interests; gay/lesbian issues; government/politics/law; history; money/finance/economics; sociology; women's issues/women's studies. Will consider these fiction areas: ethnic; family saga; feminist; gay; humor/satire; lesbian; literary; mainstream. Query. Will report in 1-2 weeks on queries; 3-5 weeks on manuscripts.
Terms: Agent receives 15% commission on domestic sales. Charges for long distance phone/fax, photocopying, postage.
Tips: Obtains new clients through recommendations and *Literary Marketplace* listing.

PHILIP G. SPITZER LITERARY AGENCY (III), 788 9th Ave., New York NY 10019. (212)265-6003. Fax: (212)765-0953. Contact: Philip Spitzer. Estab. 1969. Member of AAR. Represents 60 clients. 10% of clients are new/previously unpublished writers. Specializes in mystery/suspense, literary fiction, sports, general nonfiction (not how-to). Currently handles: 50% nonfiction books; 45% novels; 5% short story collections.
Handles: Nonfiction books, novels. Will consider these nonfiction areas: biography/autobiography; business; current affairs; ethnic/cultural interests; government/politics/law; health/medicine; history; military/war; music/dance/theater/film; nature/environment; psychology; true crime/investigative; sociology; sports. Will consider these fiction areas: contemporary issues; detective/police/crime; literary; mainstream; mystery/suspense; sports. Send outline plus 1 sample chapter and SASE. Reports in 1 week on queries; 6 weeks on mss.
Terms: Agent receives 15% commission on domestic sales; 20% on foreign sales. Charge for photocopying.
Tips: Usually obtains new clients on referral.

NANCY STAUFFER ASSOCIATES (II, III), Suite 1007, 156 Fifth Ave., New York NY 10010. (212)229-9027. Fax: (212)229-9018. Contact: Nancy Stauffer. Estab. 1989. Member of PEN Center USA West. Represents 50 clients. 10% of clients are new/previously unpublished writers. Currently handles: 65% nonfiction books; 35% novels.
Handles: Nonfiction books, novels, novellas, short story collections. Will consider these nonfiction areas: biography/autobiography; current affairs; ethnic/cultural interests; language/literature/criticism; music/dance/theater/film; nature/environment; self-help/personal improvement; sociology; sports; translations; women's issues/women's studies; popular culture. Will consider these fiction areas: contemporary issues; literary; mainstream; regional. Query with outline or sample chapter and SASE. Will report in 3 weeks on queries; 1 month on mss.
Recent Sales: *I Wish I'd Said That*, by Linda McCallister, Ph.D. (John Wiley & Sons); *Seven Centuries of English Cooking*, by Maxime de la Falaise (Grove Press).
Terms: Agent receives 15% commission on domestic sales; 20% on foreign sales. Offers a written contract. Charges for "long-distance telephone and fax; messenger and express delivery; photocopying."
Writers' Conferences: "I teach a seminar at the UCLA Extension Writers' Program titled 'Getting Published: A One Day Tour Through the World of New York Publishing' and participate in writers conferences around the country."
Tips: Obtains new clients primarily through referrals from existing clients.

LYLE STEELE & CO., LTD. (II), Suite 6, 511 E. 73rd St., New York NY 10021. (212)288-2981. Contact: Lyle Steele. Estab. 1985. Member of WGA. Represents 125 clients. 20% of clients are new/previously unpublished writers. "In nonfiction we are particularly interested in current events, unique personal stories, biography and autobiography, popular business, true crime, health, parenting, personal growth and psychological self-help. In fiction we are interested in good mysteries not of the hard-boiled type, horror and occult of all types, thrillers and historical novels. We are also open to quality fiction." Currently handles: 70% nonfiction books; 30% novels. Member agent: Jim Kepler (Chicago, nonfiction).
Handles: Nonfiction books, novels. Will consider these nonfiction areas: anthropology/archaeology; biography/autobiography; business; child guidance/parenting; cooking/food/nutrition; current affairs; ethnic/cultural interests; gay/lesbian issues; government/politics/law; health/medicine; history; money/finance/economics; nature/environment; new age/metaphysics; psychology; true crime/investigative; science/technology; self-help/personal improvement; sociology; sports. Will consider these fiction areas: detective/police/crime; family saga; gay; historical; lesbian; literary; mystery/suspense; psychic/supernatural; thriller/espionage; horror. Send outline plus 2 sample chapters. Will report in 10 days on queries; 2 weeks on mss.

Terms: Agent receives 10% commission on domestic sales. Offers a written contract, binding for 1 year.

Tips: Obtains new clients through recommendations and solicitations. "Our goal is to represent books that provide readers with solid information they can use to improve and change their personal and professional lives. In addition, we take the long view of an author's career. A successful writing career is built step by step, and our goal is to provide the long-term professional management required to achieve it. Be prepared to send your material quickly once an agent has responded. Frequently, we'll have room to take on only a few new clients and a slow response may mean the openings will be filled by the time your material arrives."

GLORIA STERN LITERARY AGENCY (II,III,IV), 15E, 1230 Park Ave., New York NY 10128. (212)289-7698. Contact: Gloria Stern. Estab. 1976. Member of AAR. Represents 35 clients. 20% of clients are new/previously unpublished writers. Specializes in history, biography, women's studies, child guidance, parenting, business, cookbooks, health, cooking, finance, true crime, sociology. Currently handles: 80% nonfiction books; 5% scholarly books; 15% novels.

Handles: Nonfiction books, scholarly books, juvenile books, novels. Will consider these nonfiction areas: anthropology/archaeology; art/architecture/design; biography/autobiography; business; child guidance/parenting; cooking/food/nutrition; current affairs; ethnic/cultural interests; government/politics/law; health/medicine; history; young adult nonfiction; language/literature/criticism; money/finance/economics; psychology; true crime/investigative; science/technology; self-help/personal improvement; sociology; sports; women's issues/women's studies. Will consider these fiction areas: contemporary issues; detective/police/crime; ethnic; experimental; family saga; fantasy; feminist; literary; mainstream; mystery/suspense; romance (contemporary); thriller/espionage; young adult. Query with outline plus 2 sample chapters with SASE. Will report in 1 week on queries; 1 month on mss.

Terms: Agent receives 15% on domestic sales; 20% on foreign sales (shared). Offers a written contract, binding for 60 days.

Tips: Obtain new clients through editors, previous clients, listings. "I prefer fiction authors that have some published work such as short stories in either commercial or literary magazines or come recommended by an editor or writer. I need a short outline of less than a page, 1 or 2 chapters and SASE. For nonfiction, I need credentials, an outline, competitive books and 1 or 2 chapters and SASE. No unsolicited mss."

‡LARRY STERNIG LITERARY AGENCY (V), 742 Robertson St., Milwaukee WI 53213. Agency not currently seeking new clients.

‡ROSLYN TARG LITERARY AGENCY, INC. (III), 105 W. 13th St., New York NY 10011. (212)206-9390. Fax: (212)989-6233. Contact: William Clark, Robert Simpson, Roslyn Targ. Estab. 1962. Member of AAR. Represents 100 clients. 30% of clients are new/previously unpublished writers. Currently handles: 40% nonfiction books; 5% scholarly books; 10% juvenile books; 40% novels; 5% short story collections.

Handles: Nonfiction books, scholarly books, juvenile books, novels, novellas, short story collections. self-help, genre fiction. Will consider these nonfiction areas: anthropology/archaeology; art/architecture/design; biography/autobiography; business; child guidance/parenting; cooking/food/nutrition; current affairs; ethnic/cultural interests; health/medicine; history; juvenile nonfiction; language/literature/criticism; money/finance economics; music/dance/theater/film; nature/environment; true crime/investigative; science/technology; self-help/personal improvement; translations. Will consider these fiction areas: action/adventure; detective/police/crime; ethnic; experimental; family saga; feminist; gay; glitz; historical; humor/satire; juvenile; literary; mainstream; mystery/suspense; romance (contemporary, gothic, historical, regency); thriller/espionage; young adult. Query with outline/proposal, curriculum vitae. Will report in 1 week (no ms without queries first).

Recent Sales: *The Continual Pilgrimage: American Writers in Paris 1944-1960*, by Christopher Sawyer-Laucanno (Grove); *Love's Blood*, by Clark Howard (Crown); *The Weeds & The Weather*, by Mary Stolz (Morrow).

Terms: Agent receives 10-15% commission on domestic sales; 20% on foreign sales. Charges standard agency fees (bank charges, long distance fax, postage, photocopying, shipping of books, etc.).

Tips: Obtains new clients through recommendations, solicitation, queries. "This agency reads on an exclusive basis only."

PATRICIA TEAL LITERARY AGENCY (III), 2036 Vista Del Rosa, Fullerton CA 92631. (714)738-8333. Contact: Patricia Teal. Estab. 1978. Member of AAR, RWA, The Authors Guild and Western Writers of America. Represents 50 clients. 10% of clients are new/previously unpublished writers. Specializes in category fiction and commercial, how-to and self-help nonfiction. Currently handles: 10% nonfiction books, 90% novels.
Handles: Nonfiction books, novels. Will consider these nonfiction areas: biography/autobiography; child guidance/parenting; health/medicine; psychology; true crime/investigative; self-help/personal improvement; women's issues. Will consider these fiction areas: glitz; mainstream (published authors only); mystery/suspense; romance. Query. Will report in 10 days on queries; 6 weeks on mss.
Recent Sales: *By Her Own Design*, by June Triglia (New American Library); *Come Spring*, by Jill Marie Landis (Berkeley/Jove).
Terms: Agent receives 10-15% on domestic sales; 20% on foreign sales. Offers written contract, binding for 1 year. Charges for postage, photocopying.
Writers' Conferences: Attends several Romance Writers of America conferences, Asilomar (California Writers Club) and Bouchercon.
Tips: Usually obtains new clients through recommendations from others or at conferences. "Attend writing classes and writers' conferences to learn your craft before submitting to agents. Include SASE with all correspondence."

VAN DER LEUN & ASSOCIATES (II), 464 Mill Hill Dr., Southport CT 06490. (203)259-4897. Contact: Patricia Van der Leun. Estab. 1984. Represents 30 clients. 50% of clients are new/previously unpublished authors. Specializes in fiction, science, biography. Currently handles: 50% nonfiction books; 40% novels; 10% short story collections.
Handles: Nonfiction books, novels, short story collections. "Any nonfiction subject OK." Will consider these fiction areas: cartoon/comic; contemporary issues; ethnic; historical; literary; mainstream. Query. Will report in 2 weeks on queries; 1 month on mss.
Recent Sales: *Goatwalking*, by Jim Corbett (Viking-Penguin); *Catching the Light*, by Arthur Zajonc (Bantam); *Uh-Oh*, by Robert Fulghum (Villard).
Terms: Agent receives 15% on domestic sales; 25% on foreign sales. Offers written contract.
Tips: "We are interested in high-quality, serious writers only."

‡ERIKA WAIN AGENCY (II), #102, 1418 N. Highland, Hollywood CA 90028. (213)460-4224. Contact: Erika Wain. Estab. 1979. Member of WGA, SAG-AFTRA Authors Guild. 50% of clients are new/previously unpublished writers. Currently handles 5% juvenile books; 80% movie scripts; 15% TV scripts.
Handles: Juvenile books, movie scripts, TV scripts. Will consider these nonfiction areas: animals; military/war; true crime/investigative; science/technology; women's issues/women's studies. Will consider these fiction areas: action/adventure; detective/police/crime; family saga; fantasy; feminist; humor/satire; juvenile; mystery/suspense; science fiction; thriller/espionage. Query. Will report immediately if interested on queries and ms.
Terms: Agent receives 10% commission on domestic sales. Offers written contract.
Tips: Obtains new clients through recommendation from others, solicitation.

MARY JACK WALD ASSOCIATES, INC. (III), 111 E. 14th St., New York NY 10003. (212)254-7842. Contact: Danis Sher. Estab. 1985. Member of Authors' Guild, SCBW. Represents 60 clients. 10% of clients are new/previously unpublished writers. Specializes in literary works, juvenile, TV/film scripts. Currently handles: 10% nonfiction books; 50% juvenile books; 20% novels; 5% novellas; 5% short story collections; 5% movie scripts; 5% TV scripts. Member agents: Danis Sher; Lem Lloyd.
Handles: Nonfiction books, juvenile books, novels, novellas, short story collections, movie and TV scripts. Will consider these nonfiction areas: biography/autobiography; current affairs; ethnic/cultural interests; health/medicine; history; juvenile nonfiction; language/literature/criticism; military/war; money/finance/economics; music/dance/theater/film; nature/environment; photography; true crime/investigative; science/technology; self-help/personal improvement; sociology; sports; translations. Will consider these fiction areas: action/adventure; contemporary issues; detective/police/crime; ethnic; experimental; family saga; fantasy; feminist; gay; glitz; historical; humor/satire; juvenile; literary; mainstream; mystery/suspense; picture book; psychic/supernatural; romance (gothic, historical, regency); science fiction; sports; thriller; westerns/frontier; young adult. Query. Will report in 1 month on queries; 2 months on mss.

Recent Sales: *Hey Cowboy, Wanna Get Lucky?*, by Baxter Black (Crown Publishers, Inc.); *Bloodroots*, by Richie Tankerslay Cusick (Pocket Books Inc.); *Realtime, Shadowtime*, by John Peel (Simon & Schuster).
Terms: Agent receives 15% commission on domestic sales; 15-30% on foreign sales. Offers a written contract, binding for 1 year.
Tips: Obtains new clients through recommendations from others. "Send a query letter with brief description and credits, if any. If we are interested, we'll request 50 pages. If that interests us, we'll request entire ms, which should be double-spaced. SASE should be enclosed."

‡**BESS WALLACE LITERARY AGENCY (II)**, P.O. Box 972, Duchesne UT 84021. (801)738-2317. Contact: Bess D. Wallace. Estab. 1978. Represents 13 clients. 90% of clients are new/previously unpublished writers. Currently handles 90% nonfiction books; 5% scholarly books; 5% textbooks. Specialty criminal psychology.
Handles: Nonfiction books, textbooks, scholarly books. Will consider these nonfiction areas: agriculture/horticulture; animals; anthropology/archaeology; current affairs; government/politics/law; history; juvenile nonfiction; military/war; psychology; true crime/investigative. Will consider this fiction area: romance. Query with outline/proposal. Will report in 3 weeks on queries; 6 weeks on mss.
Terms: Agent receives 15% commission on domestic sales; 10% commission on foreign sales. Offers written contract if author wishes it, binding for 2 years. Offers criticism service. "Usually $75 for any size ms." Letter which explains errors in plot, sentence stucture etc. by Bess D. Wallace. Other fees charged only if requested to edit and/or retype. $1.50 per page to edit; $2 per page to edit and re-type. 80% of business derived from commission on ms sales. 20% derived from reading fees or criticism services. Payment of criticism fee does not ensure representation.
Tips: Obtains new clients through *LMP*, etc. Send query first or call.

JOHN A. WARE LITERARY AGENCY (II), 392 Central Park West, New York NY 10025. (212)866-4733. Fax: (212)866-4734. Contact: John Ware. Estab. 1978. Represents 60 clients. 40% of clients are new/ previously unpublished writers. Currently handles: 75% nonfiction books; 25% novels.
Handles: Nonfiction books, novels. Will consider these nonfiction areas: anthropology; biography/ autobiography (memoirs); current affairs; investigative journalism, history (including oral history, Americana and folklore), psychology and health (academic credentials required); science; sports, 'bird's eye' views of phenomena. Will consider these fiction areas: accessible literate noncategory fiction; mystery/suspense; thriller/espionage. Query with outline first, include SASE. Will report in 2 weeks on queries.
Recent Sales: *Punished By Rewards*, by Alfie Kohn (Houghton Mifflin); *Gay In The Workplace*, by Brian McNaught (St. Martin's); *The Invisible Worm*, by Jennifer Johnston (Carroll & Graf).
Terms: Agent receives 15% commission on domestic sales; 15% on dramatic sales; 20% on foreign sales. Charges for messenger service, photocopying, extraordinary expenses.
Tips: "Writers must have appropriate credentials for authorship of proposal (nonfiction) or manuscript (fiction); no publishing track record required. Open to good writing and interesting ideas by new or veteran writers."

HARRIET WASSERMAN LITERARY AGENCY (III), 137 E. 36th St., New York NY 10016. (212)689-3257. Contact: Harriet Wasserman. Member of AAR. Specializes in foreign, Great Britain fiction.
Handles: Nonfiction books, novels. Will consider "mostly fiction (novels)." Query only. No unsolicited material.
Terms: Information not provided.

WATKINS LOOMIS AGENCY, INC. (II), Suite 530, 150 E. 35th St., New York NY 10016. (212)532-0080. Contact: Nicole Aragi. Estab. 1908. Represents 85 clients. Specializes in literary fiction, London/ UK translations.
Handles: Nonfiction books, novels. Will consider these nonfiction areas: art/architecture/design; history; science/technology; translations; journalism. Will consider these fiction areas: contemporary issues; literary; mainstream; mystery/suspense; science fiction. Query with SASE. Will report within 3 weeks on queries.
Terms: Agent receives 10% commission on domestic sales; 20% on foreign sales.

WECKSLER-INCOMCO (III), 170 W. End Ave., New York NY 10023. (212)787-2239. Fax: (212)496-7035. Contact: Sally Wecksler. Estab. 1970. Represents 15 clients. 10% of clients are new/previously unpublishcd writers. Specializes in nonfiction with illustrations (photos and art). Currently handles: 70% nonfiction books, 30% novels. Member agent: Joann Amparan.

Handles: Nonfiction books, novels. Will consider these nonfiction areas: anthropology/archaeology; art/architecture design; biography/autobiography; business; current affairs; history; music/dance/theater/film; nature/environment; photography. Will consider these fiction areas: historical; literary; thriller/espionage. Query with outline plus 3 sample chapters. Will report in 6 weeks-2 months on queries; 3 months on mss.
Terms: Agent receives 12-15% commission on domestic sales; 20% on foreign sales. Offers a written contract, binding for 3 years.
Tips: Obtains new clients through recommendations from others.

THE WENDY WEIL AGENCY, INC. (V), Suite 1300, 232 Madison Ave., New York NY 10016. Agency not currently seeking new clients.

CHERRY WEINER LITERARY AGENCY (III), 28 Kipling Way, Manalapan NJ 07726. (908)446-2096. Contact: Cherry Weiner. Estab. 1977. Represents 40+ clients. 10% of clients are new/previously unpublished writers. Specializes in science fiction, fantasy, westerns, all the genre romances. Currently handles: 2-3% nonfiction books; 97% novels.
Handles: Nonfiction books, novels. Will consider self-help/improvement and sociology nonfiction. Will consider these fiction areas: action/adventure; contemporary issues; detective/police/crime; family saga; fantasy; glitz; historical; mainstream; mystery/suspense; psychic/supernatural; romance; science fiction; thriller/espionage; westerns/frontier. Query. Will report in 1 week on queries; 6-8 weeks on mss.
Terms: Agent receives 15% on domestic sales; 15% on foreign sales. Offers a written contract. Charges for extra copies of manuscripts "but would prefer author do it"; 1st class postage for author's copies of books; Express Mail for important document/manuscripts.
Writers' Conferences: Attends Western Writers Convention; Golden Triangle; Fantasy Convention.
Tips: "Meet agents and publishers at conferences. Establish a relationship, then get in touch with them reminding them of meetings and conference."

THE WEINGEL-FIDEL AGENCY (III), #21E, 310 E. 46th St., New York NY 10017. (212)599-2959. Contact: Loretta Fidel. Estab. 1989. Represents 35 clients. 25% of clients are new/previously unpublished writers. Specializes in commercial and literary fiction and nonfiction. Currently handles: 50% nonfiction books; 50% novels.
Handles: Nonfiction books, novels. Will consider these nonfiction areas: anthropology/archaeology; art/architecture/design; biography/autobiography; health/medicine; music/dance/theater/film; psychology; true crime/investigative; science; sociology; women's issues/women's studies. Will consider these fiction areas: contemporary issues; detective/police/crime; literary; mainstream; mystery/suspense; thriller/espionage. Query with cover letter, résumé and SASE. Will report in 2 weeks on queries; do not send manuscript.
Recent Sales: *A Safe Place*, by Lorenzo Carcaterra (Villard Books); *Thing of Beauty*, by Stephen Fried (Pocket Books); *Altared States*, by Jennie Nash (Crown Publishers).
Terms: Agent receives 15% on domestic sales; 20% on foreign sales. Offers a written contract, binding for 1 year automatic renewal. Bill back to clients all reasonable expenses such as UPS, Federal Express, photocopying, etc.
Tips: Obtains new clients through referrals. "Be forthcoming about prior representation and previous submissions to publishers."

‡WESTCHESTER LITERARY AGENCY, INC. (II), Suite 4-I, 50 E. Hartsdale Ave., Hartsdale NY 10530. (914)428-8897. Fax: (914)949-8406. Contact: Neil G. McCluskey. Estab. 1991. Represents 41 clients. 40% of clients are new/previously unpublished writers. Specializes in trade mss and proposals from quality writers with an academic or school background. Currently handles 50% nonfiction books; 3% juvenile books; 30% novels; 10% novellas; 2% movie scripts; 2% stage plays; 3% TV scripts.
Handles: Nonfiction books, juvenile books, novels, novellas, short story collections, movie scripts, TV scripts. Will consider these nonfiction areas: biography/autobiography; business; child guidance/parenting; government/politics/law; history; juvenile nonfiction; language/literature/criticism; military/war; music/dance/theater/film; nature/environment; photography; psychology; religious/inspirational; true crime/investigative; self-help/personal improvement. Will consider these fiction areas: action/adventure; contemporary/issues; detective/police/crime; family saga; fantasy; historical; humor/satire; juvenile; literary; mainstream; mystery/suspense; religious/inspiration; romance (contemporary, gothic, historical, regency); thriller/espionage; westerns/frontier; young adult. Query with outline/proposal. Will report in 2 weeks on queries; 2 months on mss.

Recent Sales: *Your Corner of the Universe*, by Andrea Campbell (Bob Adams Publishers); *The Kall Index*, by Wm. J. Slattery (Libraries Unlimited); *Your Bathroom Buddy*, by Leon Frechette (TAB-McGraw Hill).
Terms: Agent receives 15% commission on domestic sales; 20% on foreign sales. Offers written contract, binding for one year and renewable. Charges for photocopying and postage unless supplied by writer.
Tips: Obtains new clients through LMP, story in WD, recommendations from others, grapevine.

RHODA WEYR AGENCY (II, III), 151 Bergen St., Brooklyn NY 11217. (718)522-0480. President: Rhoda A. Weyr. Estab. 1983. Member of AAR. Prefers to work with published/established authors; works with a small number of new/unpublished authors. Specializes in general nonfiction and fiction.
Handles: Nonfiction books and novels. Query with outline and sample chapters with SASE.
Terms: Agent receives 15% commission on domestic sales; 20% on foreign sales.

‡WIESER & WIESER, INC. (III), 118 E. 25th St., 7 Fl., New York NY 10010. (212)260-0860. Fax: (212)505-7186. Contact: Olga Wieser. Estab. 1975. 30% of clients are new/previously unpublished writers. Specializes in mainstream fiction and nonfiction. Currently handles 50% nonfiction books; 50% novels. Member agents: Larry Gershel (true crime, business and mysteries); Jake Elwell (history, contemporary and sports); George Wieser (contemporary fiction, thrillers and current affairs); Olga Wieser (psychology, fiction, historicals, translations and literary fiction).
Handles: Nonfiction books, novels. Will consider these nonfiction areas: business; cooking/food/nutrition; current affairs; health/medicine; history; money/finance/economics; nature/environment; psychology; true crime/investigative; translations. Will consider these fiction areas: contemporary issues; detective/police/crime; family saga; historical; literary; mainstream; mystery/suspense; romance (contemporary, historical, regency); thriller/espionage. Query with outline/proposal. Will report in 1 week on queries; 1 month on mss.
Terms: Agent receives 15% commission on domestic sales; 20% on foreign sales. Offers written contract. Offers criticism. "No charge to our clients or potential clients." Charges for duplicating of ms and overseas mailing of ms or promotional material.
Tips: Obtains new clients through author's recommendations and industry professionals.

‡GARY S. WOHL LITERARY AGENCY (II,III), One Fifth Ave., New York NY 10003. (212)254-9126. Estab. 1983. Represents 16 clients. 10% of clients are new/previously unpublished writers. Specializes in textbooks; ESL/bilingual books; how-to books. Currently handles: 30% nonfiction books; 50% textbooks; 10% movie scripts; 10% TV scripts.
Handles: Nonfiction books, textbooks, movie scripts, TV scripts. Will consider these nonfiction areas: business; cooking/food/nutrition; crafts/hobbies; sports. Will consider these fiction areas: humor/satire; mystery/suspense; romance; sports. Query with outline/proposal. Will reports within 2 weeks on mss.
Terms: Agent receives 15% commission on domestic sales; 15% on foreign sales. Offers written contract. 100% of business derived from commissions on ms sales.

RUTH WRESCHNER, AUTHORS' REPRESENTATIVE (II, III), 10 W. 74th St., New York NY 10023. (212)877-2605. Fax: (212)595-5843. Agent. Ruth Wreschner. Estab. 1981. Represents 60 clients. 70% of clients are new/unpublished writers. "In fiction, if a client is not published yet, I prefer writers who have written for magazines; in nonfiction, a person well qualified in his field is acceptable. Prefers to work with published/established authors; works with new/unpublished authors. I will always pay attention to a writer referred by another client." Specializes in popular medicine, health, how-to books and fiction (no pornography, screenplays or dramatic plays). Currently handles: 5% magazine articles; 80% nonfiction books; 10% novels; 5% textbooks; 5% juvenile books.
Handles: Adult and young adult fiction, nonfiction, textbooks, magazine articles (only if appropriate for commercial magazines). Particularly interested in mainstream and mystery fiction. Query with outline. Reports in 2 weeks on queries.
Recent Sales: *The Joslin Diabetes Center Healthcare Book*, Joslin Diabetes Center (Simon & Schuster); *Writing Irresistable Cover Letters*, by Stanley Wynett (Writers Digest); *Sick And Tired Of Feeling Sick And Tired*, by Paul Donoghue, Ph.D. and Mary Siegel, Ph.D. (W.W. Norton).
Terms: Agent receives 15% commission on domestic sales; 20% on foreign sales. Charges for photocopying expenses. "Once a book is placed, I will retain some money from the second advance to cover airmail postage of books, long-distance calls, etc. on foreign sales. I may consider charging for reviewing contracts in future. In that case I will charge $50/hour plus long-distance calls, if any."

rejected 1990 ̄

X

WRITERS HOUSE (III), 21 W. 26th St., New York NY 10010. (212)685-2400. Fax: (212)685-1781. Contact: Albert Zuckerman. Estab. 1974. Member of AAR. Represents 280 clients. 50% of clients were new/unpublished writers. Specializes in all types of popular fiction and nonfiction. No scholarly, professional, poetry and no screenplays. Currently handles: 25% nonfiction books; 35% juvenile books; 40% novels. Member agents: Albert Zuckerman (major novels, thrillers, women's fiction, important nonfiction); Amy Berkower (major juvenile authors, women's fiction, art and decorating, cookbooks, psychology); Merrillee Heifetz (science fiction and fantasy, popular culture, literary fiction); Susan Cohen (juvenile and young adult fiction and nonfiction, Judaism, women's issues); Susan Ginsberg (serious and popular fiction, true crime, narrative nonfiction, personality books, cookbooks).
Handles: Nonfiction books, juvenile books, novels. Will consider these nonfiction areas: animals; art/architecture/design; biography/autobiography; business; child guidance/parenting; cooking/food/nutrition; health/medicine; history; interior design/decorating; juvenile nonfiction; military/war; money/finance/economics; music/dance/theater/film; nature/environment; psychology; true crime/investigative; science/technology; self-help/personal improvement; women's issues/women's studies. Will consider any fiction area. "Quality is everything." Query. Will report in 1 month on queries.
Terms: Agent receives 15% on domestic sales; 20% on foreign sales; 10% on juvenile and young adult books. Offers a written contract, binding for 1 year.
Tips: Obtain new clients through recommendations from others. "Do not send manuscripts. Write a compelling letter. If you do, we'll ask to see your work."

WRITERS' PRODUCTIONS (II), P.O. Box 630, Westport CT 06881. (203)227-8199. Contact: David L. Meth. Estab. 1982. Represents 25 clients. Specializes in literary-quality fiction and nonfiction, with a special interest in Asia. Currently handles: 40% nonfiction books, 60% novels.
Handles: Nonfiction books, novels. "Literary quality fiction." Send outline plus 2 or 3 sample chapters (30-50 pages). Will report in 1 week on queries; 1 month on mss.
Recent Sales: *Night of the Milky Way Railway*, by Miyazawa Kenji (M.E. Sharpe); *Children of the Paper Crane*, by Masamoto Nasu (M.E. Sharpe); *Jinsei Annai: Letters to the Advice Column*, by John and Asako McKinsing (M.E. Sharpe); *Trial by Fire*, by Kathleen Barnes (Thunder's Mouth).
Terms: Agent receives 15% on domestic sales; 20-25% on foreign sales. Offers a written contract. Charges for electronic transmissions, long-distance calls, express or overnight mail, courier service, etc.
Tips: Obtain new clients through word of mouth. "Send only your best, most professionally prepared work. Do not send it before it is ready. We must have SASE for all correspondence and return of manuscripts. No telephone calls, please."

WRITERS' REPRESENTATIVES, INC. (II), 25 W. 19th St., New York NY 10011-4202. (212)620-9009. Contact: Glen Hartley or Lynn Chu. Estab. 1985. Represents 40 clients. 25% of clients are new/previously unpublished writers. Currently handles: 90% nonfiction books; 10% novels.
Handles: Nonfiction books, novels. Will consider literary fiction. "Nonfiction submissions should include book proposal, detailed table of contents and sample chapter(s). For fiction submissions send sample chapters—not synopses. All submissions should include author biography, publication list and, if available, reviews. SASE required." Does not accept unsolicited material. Will report in 2-3 weeks on queries; 4-6 weeks on mss.
Recent Sales: *Signs of the Times*, by David Lehman (Poseidon Press); *The Making of a Cop*, by Harvey Rachlin (Pocket Books); *Black Hills/White Justice*, by Edward Lazarus (HarperCollins).
Terms: Agent receives 15% commission on domestic sales; 20% on foreign sales. "We charge for out-of-house photocopying as well as messengers, courier services (e.g., Federal Express), etc."
Tips: Obtains new clients "mostly on the basis of recommendations from others. Always include SASE that will ensure a response from the agent and the return of material submitted."

SUSAN ZECKENDORF ASSOC. INC. (II), 171 W. 57th St., New York NY 10019. (212)245-2928. Contact: Susan Zeckendorf. Estab. 1979. Member of AAR. Represents 35 clients. 25% of clients are new/previously unpublished writers. Currently handles: 50% nonfiction books; 50% fiction.
Handles: Nonfiction books, novels, short story collections. Will consider these nonfiction areas: art/architecture/design; biography/autobiography; business; child guidance/parenting; health/medicine; history; music/dance/theater/film; psychology; true crime/investigative; science/technology; sociology; women's issues/women's studies. Will consider these fiction areas: action/adventure; contemporary issues; detective/police/crime; ethnic; family saga; glitz; historical; literary; mainstream; mystery/suspense; romance (contemporary, gothic, historical); thriller/espionage. Query. Will report in 10 days on queries; 2-3 weeks mss.

Recent Sales: *The Palace Affair*, by Una-Mary Parker (New American Library); *Street Lights: Illumina-tions on the Urban Black Experience—Anthology* (Viking); *The True Life Story of Isabel Roundtree* (August House).
Terms: Agent receives 15% commission on domestic sales; 20% on foreign sales. Charges for photocopying, messenger services.
Writers' Conferences: Attends Central Valley Writers Conference and the Tucson Publishers Association Conference.
Tips: Obtains new clients through recommendations, listings in writer's manuals.

Additional Nonfee-charging Agents

The following nonfee-charging agencies have full listings in other sections of this book. These agencies have indicated that they are *primarily* interested in handling the work of scriptwriters, artists or photographers, but are also interested in book manuscripts. After reading the listing (you can find the page number in the Listings Index), send them a query to obtain more information on their needs and manuscript submissions policies.

Allied Artists
All-Star Talent Agency
Amato Agency, Michael
Beal Agency, The Mary
Cinema Talent International
Circle of Confusion Ltd.
Comedy Ink
Diskant & Associates
Farber Literary Agency Inc.

Kohner, Inc., Paul
Leone Agency, Inc., The Adele
Merrill Ltd., Helen
Montgomery-West Literary
    Agency
Panda Talent
Raintree Agency
Scagnetti Talent & Literary
    Agency, Jack

Scribe Agency
Steele & Associates, Ellen
    Lively
Swanson Inc., H.N.
Total Acting Experience, A
Wright Representatives, Inc.,
    Ann

Nonfee-charging Agents/'92-'93 changes

The following agencies appeared in the last (1992) edition of *Guide to Literary Agents & Art/Photo Reps* but are absent from the 1993 edition. These agencies failed to respond to our request for an update of their listing, or were left out for the reasons indicated in parentheses following the agency name.

Dominick Abel Literary
    Agency, Inc. (removed per
    request)
Authors and Artists Group,
    Inc. (removed per request)
Blassingame, McCauley &
    Wood (removed for one
    year per request)
Harry Bloom
Jane Buchanan Literary
    Agency (unable to contact)
Howard Buck Agency
Martha Casselman Literary
    Agent
Faith Childs Literary Agency
    (removed per request)
Julia Cooopersmith Literary
    Agency (overwhelmed by
    submissions)
The Doe Coover Agency
Janet Dight Literary Agency
    (removed per request)
Robert Eisenbach Inc. (removed per request)
Joseph Elder Agency (removed
    per request)

Evans and Associates
Florence Feiler Literary
    Agency (unable to contact)
Flaming Star Literary Enterprises (unable to contact)
The Fox Chase Agency Inc.
    (overwhelmed by submissions)
John L. Hochmann Books ((removed for one year per request)
Berenice Hoffman Literary
    Agency
Leon Jones Agency (complaints)
The Lazear Agency Incorporated (removed per request)
The Ned Leavitt Agency, Inc.
    (overwhelmed by submissions)
Lescher & Lescher
James Levine Communications
Robert Lewis
Living Faith Literary Agency
    (complaints)
Gerard McCauley (removed

    for one year per request)
Janet Wilkins Manus Literary
    Agency (removed per request)
Toni Mendez Inc. (removed
    per request)
Martha Millard Literary
    Agency (overwhelmed by
    submissions
Charles Neighbors, Inc.
Ray E. Nugent Literary Agency
    (removed per request)
Fifi Oscard Associates (unable
    to contact)
John K. Payne Literary Agency,
    Inc. (unable to contact)
John R. Riina Literary Agency
Schlessinger-Van Dyck Agency
Charlotte Sheedy Literary
    Agency, Inc.
2M Communications Ltd. (unable to contact)
Wingra Woods Press/Agenting
    Division

Literary Agents:
Fee-charging

Over the years the cost of marketing manuscripts to publishers has soared. Postage, long-distance telephone charges, travel expenses, legal fees, salaries and freelance wages continue to rise. At the same time more publishers are looking to agents to screen incoming manuscripts and more writers are turning to agents for editorial advice as well as marketing help. To remain competitive, some agents have hired outside readers and editors and are charging fees to help cover the costs. Others are supplementing their income from commissions with fees from other services such as editing, consulting and publicizing books.

All the literary agents included in this section charge a fee to writers in addition to a commission on sales. The commissions from sales of work are the same as those taken by agents who do not charge fees. For domestic sales, the average commission is 10 to 15 percent and for foreign or dramatic sales, it's slightly higher—10 to 20 percent. The additional commission is usually charged to help pay a foreign agent or subagent.

If an agent charges a one-time fee to cover expenses such as postage or long-distance calls and that fee is more than $50, we've included that agency in this section. Agents who charge less than $50 for expenses and do not charge for other services have been included in the Literary Agents: Nonfee-charging section.

Several agencies only charge fees to previously unpublished writers. We've indicated these agencies by placing an asterisk (*) at the beginning of the listing. If you have local or small press publication credits only, some of these agencies will consider you "unpublished" and may charge the fee. If you are not sure if your publishing credits will be acceptable, you may want to check with the agency before sending material.

One problem with grouping fee-charging agents together is the wide variety of fees and the differences in terminology used to describe these fees from agency to agency. Some charge for reading a manuscript, some for reading and evaluation. Others will read manuscripts for free but charge for critiquing or editing. A few offer consultation for a fee and still others offer typing services.

Be sure to ask for a fee schedule and to ask questions about fees. It's important for writers to have a clear understanding of what the fees cover, how they will be charged and what they can expect for their money. Here's a list of some of the terms used and how each is generally defined:

● Reading fees—This is a fee charged for reading a manuscript. Most agents do not charge to look at queries alone. For many agents, the fee is used to pay an outside reader to sift through the unsolicited manuscripts. It is generally a one-time, nonrefundable fee, but some agents will return the money if they agree to take you on as a client.

● Evaluation fees—Sometimes a reading fee will include a written evaluation, but many agents charge for evaluations separately. The evaluation may be a one-paragraph report on the marketability of the manuscript or a full, several page evaluation covering marketability, flaws and strengths.

● Critiquing service—Although some agents use the terms critique and evaluation interchangeably, a critiquing service is usually a more extensive report with suggestions on ways to improve the manuscript. Many agents offer critiques as a separate service and have a standard fee scale. Fees may be based on the extent of the service—from a one-page overview to complete line-by-line commentary. Some agents charge fees based on a per-page or word-length basis.

● Editing service—While we do not list businesses whose primary source of income is providing editing services, we do list agencies who also offer some editing. Many do not make the distinction between critiques and edits, but we define editing services as critiques that also include detailed suggestions on how to improve the work and reduce weaknesses in the piece. As with critiques, editing services may be charged on an extent basis, a per-page basis or on a word-length basis.

● Marketing fees—These fees are usually one-time fees. They are used to offset the costs of handling your work. They usually cover a variety of expenses and may include initial reading or evaluation. Sometimes these fees are refunded after the manuscript is sold.

● Consultation service—Some agents will charge an hourly rate to act as a marketing consultant. This service is usually offered to writers who are not clients and who just want advice on marketing or on a publisher's contract. A few agents are also lawyers and may offer legal advice for an hourly rate.

● Other services—Depending on an agent's background or abilities, the agent may offer a variety of other services to writers including typing, copyediting, proofreading and even book publicity.

Payment of a reading or other fee hardly ever ensures that an agent will agree to take you on as a client. Ask for references or sample critiques, so you have a good idea what you will receive for your money.

Because they are charging for the additional service, fee-charging agents tend to be more open to reading and handling the work of new writers. If you feel you need more than sales help and would not mind paying for an evaluation or critique from a professional, then the agents listed in this section may interest you. We cannot stress enough, however, the importance of researching these agencies. Do not hesitate to ask any questions you feel will help you to make your decision. (A list of possible questions and other important information on agents appears in Finding and Working with Literary Agents starting on page 36.)

To help you with your search for an agent, we've included a number of special indexes in the back of this book. The Subject Index is divided into sections for fee-charging and nonfee-charging literary agents and script agents. Each of these sections in the index is then divided by nonfiction and fiction subject categories. If you have written a book on psychology and you would consider a fee-charging agent, turn to the nonfiction subjects listed in that section of the Subject Index. You will find a subject heading for psychology followed by the names of agencies interested in this type of work. Some agencies did not want to restrict themselves to specific subjects. We've grouped them in the heading "open" in the nonfiction and fiction categories.

We've included an Agents and Reps Index as well. Often you will read about an agent, but since that agent is an employee of a large agency, you may not be able to find that person's business address or phone number. We've asked agencies to give us the names of agents on their staffs. Then we've listed the names in alphabetical order along with the name of their agency. Find the name of the person you would like to contact and then check the listing for that agency. You will find the page number for the agency's listing in the Listings Index at the end of the book.

Some art representatives, especially those interested in humor (cartoons and comics) and children's books, are also looking for writers. If the agency is primarily an art representative, but also interested in writers and that agency charges a reading or submission fee, we've included it in Additional Fee-charging Agents at the end of the listings in this section.

For example if ABC Art Reps, Inc. handles the work of artists, but may be interested in writers who can draw, they would be mentioned in the list, but their complete listing will appear in the Commercial Art/Photo Reps section.

Many of the literary agents listed in this section are also interested in scripts and vice versa. If the agency's primary function is selling scripts, but is interested in seeing some book manuscripts and charges a reading fee, we've also included them in Additional Fee-charging Agents. Their complete listings, however, appear in the Script Agent section.

For more information on approaching agents and the specifics of our listings, please see Finding and Working with Literary Agents. See also the various articles included at the beginning of this book for the answers to a wide variety of questions concerning the author/agent relationship.

We've ranked the agencies listed in this section according to their openness to submissions. Below is our ranking system:

I   Newer agency actively seeking clients.
II Agency seeking both new and established writers.
III Agency prefers to work with established writers, mostly obtains new clients through referrals.
IV Agency handling only certain types of work or work by writers under certain circumstances.
V   Agency not currently seeking new clients. (If an agency chose this designation, only the address is given). We have included mention of agencies rated V only to let you know they are not open to new clients at this time. In addition to those ranked V, we have included a few well-known agencies' names who have declined listings. *Unless you have a strong recommendation from someone well respected in the field, our advice is to approach only those agents ranked I-IV.*

‡A & R BURKE CORPORATION (II), P.O. Box 11794, Ft. Lauderdale FL 33339-1794. (305)525-0531. Fax: (305)761-1952. Contact: Anna Mae Burke or Robert Burke. Corporation formed 1977, expanded to non-insider writers in 1991. Represents 15 clients. 60% of clients are new/previously unpublished writers. In addition to adult and young adult fiction, the agency handles technical books, textbooks and computer software among its nonfiction specialties. Currently handles: 5% nonfiction books; 5% scholarly books; 5% textbooks; 10% juvenile books; 60% novels; 15% computer. Member agents: Anna Mae Burke (fiction: adult and young readers, nonfiction: technical); Robert Burke (nonfiction, technical and computer software).
Handles: Nonfiction books, textbooks, scholarly books, juvenile books, novels. Will consider these nonfiction areas: art/architecture/design; biography/autobiography; business; computers/electronics; current affairs; psychology; government/politics/law; history; juvenile nonfiction; language/literature/criticism; military/war; money/finance/economics; music/dance/theater/film; true crime/investigative; science/technology; self-help/personal improvement; sociology; sports; women's issues/women's studies. Will consider these fiction areas: action/adventure; contemporary issues; detective/police/crime; ethnic; family saga; fantasy; feminist; historical; humor/satire; juvenile; literary; mainstream; mystery/suspense; picture book; romance (contemporary, gothic, historical, regency); science fiction; sports; thriller/espionage; young adult; computer software. Query with outline plus 2 sample chapters. Will report in 2 weeks on queries; 1 month on mss.
Terms: Agent receives 15% commission on domestic sales; 20% on foreign sales. Offers written contract, binding for 1 year.
Fees: Charges $35 reading fee. "The fee is charged to new writers and waived for published writers, and sometimes for those who have made a contact at a writer's meeting and have discussed the work with us and have been encouraged to send a ms." Offers criticism service. 85% of business derived from commissions of ms sales; 15% derived from reading fees or criticism service.

Writer's Conferences: North Carolina Writers Conference, Mystery Writers of America (FL chapter), Florida Freelance Writers Conference.
Tips: "We are always conscious of seeking new clients and may meet one almost anywhere. While we prefer material to be from a published author, unpublished authors have a chance with us. Anna Mae Burke is an attorney and reviews contracts from that perspective at no additional charge to the writer."

ACACIA HOUSE PUBLISHING SERVICES LTD. (II, III), 51 Acacia Rd., Toronto Ontario M4S 2K6 Canada. (416)484-8356. Fax: (416)484-8356. Contact: Frances Hanna. Estab. 1985. Represents 30 clients. "I prefer that writers be previously published, with at least a few articles to their credit. Strongest consideration will be given to those with, say, three or more published books. However, I *would* take on an unpublished writer of outstanding talent." Works with a small number of new/ unpublished authors. Specializes in contemporary fiction: literary or commercial (no horror, occult or science fiction); nonfiction: all categories but business/economics—in the trade, not textbook area; children's: a few picture books; young adult, mainly fiction. Currently handles: 35% nonfiction books; 35% novels; 30% juvenile books.
Handles: Nonfiction books, novels and juvenile books. Query with outline. Does not read unsolicited manuscripts. Reports in 3 weeks on queries.
Recent Sales: *Dear M. . . . ,* by Jack Pollock (McClelland & Stewart & Bloomsbury—UK); *The Daycare Handbook*, by Judy Rasminsky and Barbara Kaiser (Little, Brown—Canada); *Mayhem* (U.S. title, *Mirage* and *Carousel*, first two titles of a mystery series by J. Robert Janes (Constable—UK; Donald I. Fine—USA); *The Alice Factor*, by Robert Janes (Stoddart—Canada; Avon—USA).
Terms: Agent receives 15% commission on domestic sales; 15% on dramatic sales; and 30% on foreign sales.
Fees: Charges a reading fee on manuscripts over 200 pages (typed, double-spaced) in length; waives reading fee when representing the writer. 4% of income derived from reading fees. Charges $200/200 pages. If a critique is wanted on a ms under 200 pages in length, then the charge is the same as the reading fee for a longer ms (which incorporates a critique). 5% of income derived from criticism fees. Critique includes "two- to three-page overall evaluation which will contain any specific points that are thought important enough to detail. Marketing advice is not usually included, since most mss evaluated in this way are not considered to be publishable." Charges writers for photocopying, courier, postage, telephone/fax "if these are excessive."

‡ACKERMAN LITERARY SERVICES (I), P.O. Box 1611, Tybee Island GA 31328. (912)786-6174. Contact: Sharon Ackerman. Estab. 1992. Represents 2 clients. 100% of new clients are new/previously unpublished authors. Currently handles: 100% novels. Member agents: Jodi Geriale, Christine Hopkins.
Handles: Novels, novellas, short story collections, magazine short stories. Will consider these nonfiction areas: crafts/hobbies; true crime/investigative. Will consider these fiction areas: confessional; detective/police/crime; family saga; glitz; historical; mainstream; mystery/suspense; psychic/supernatural; romance (contemporary, gothic); thriller/espionage. Query with entire ms. Reports in 1 week on queries; 1 month on mss.
Terms: Agent receives 10% commission on domestic sales; 15% on foreign sales.
Fees: Does not charge a reading fee. Charges criticism fee of $50, refundable upon sale of manuscript. "I prefer to make notations on manuscripts, in addition to a 2-3 pg. report on marketability, characterization, plot, style, etc. We work with the author on correcting weak points." Charges for postage, photocopying, telephone, etc. "We also offer a manuscript typing service for $2/pg."
Writer's Conferences: Attended Romance Writers of America Conference, Savannah GA.
Tips: Obtains new clients through advertising and recommendations. "Manuscripts should have a professional look, correct grammar, no typing errors. We want new writers to know we're here to help. We're interested in long-term career goals. Know the market you're writing for. Don't give up. Make a commitment to writing."

 The double dagger before a listing indicates the listing is new in this edition.

‡THE AHEARN AGENCY, INC. (I), 2021 Pine St., New Orleans LA 70118. (504)861-8395. Contact: Pamela G. Ahearn. Estab. 1992. Member of Romance Writers of America. Represents 15 clients. 33% of clients are new/previously unpublished writers. Specializes in historical romance; also very interested in mysteries and suspense fiction. Currently handles 10% nonfiction books; 20% juvenile books; 70% novels. Member agents: Pamela G. Ahearn (historical romance).
Handles: Nonfiction books, juvenile books, novels, short story collections (if stories previously published), young adult (no picture books). Will consider these nonfiction areas: animals; biography; business; child guidance/parenting; current affairs; ethnic/cultural interests; gay/lesbian issues; health/medicine; history; juvenile nonfiction; music/dance/theater/film; true crime/investigative; self-help/personal improvement; women's issues/women's studies. Will consider these fiction areas: action/adventure; contemporary issues; detective/police/crime; ethnic; family saga; fantasy; feminist; gay; glitz; historical; humor/satire; juvenile; lesbian; literary; mainstream; mystery/suspense; psychic/supernatural; regional; romance (contemporary, gothic, historical, regency); science fiction; thriller/espionage; westerns/frontier; young adult. Query. Will report in 2-3 weeks on queries; 6-8 weeks on mss.
Recent Sales: *Dark Heavens* by Meagan McKinney (Dell); 2 untitled historicals, by Rexanne Becnel (Dell); *The HIV Test: What You Need to Know to Make an Informed Decision*, by Marc Vargo (Pocket); *New Orleans in the 20s*, by Mary Lou Widmer (Pelican).
Terms: Agent receives 15% commission on domestic sales; 20% on foreign sales. Offers written contract, binding for 1 year; renewable by mutual consent.
Fees: "I charge a reading fee to previously unpublished authors, based on length of material. Fees range from $125-400. Fee is non-refundable. Offers criticism service. When authors pay a reading fee, they receive a 3-5 single-spaced-page critique of their work, addressing writing quality and marketability." Critiques written by Pamela G. Ahearn. Charges for photocopying. 90% of business derived from commissions; 10% derived from reading fees or criticism services. Payment of reading or criticism fees does not ensure representation.
Writers' Conferences: Attends Midwest Writers Workshop, Moonlight & Magnolias and RWA National conference.
Tips: Obtains new clients, "usually through listings such as this one and client recommendations. Sometimes at conferences. Be professional! Always send in exactly what an agent/editor asks for, no more, no less. Keep query letters brief and to the point, giving your writing credentials and a very brief summary of your book. If one agent rejects you, keep trying—there are a lot of us out there!"

*FAREL T. ALDEN–LITERARY SERVICE (I), 407 Peach St., Washington IL 61571-1929. (309)745-5411. Contact: Farel T. Alden. Estab. 1990. Represents 22 clients. 50% of clients are new/previously unpublished writers. Currently handles: 70% novels; 10% nonfiction books; 20% juvenile books. Member agents: Farel T. Alden (action/adventure, mystery/suspense, historical, scripts, nonfiction); Joan Reynolds (consultant, fiction and nonfiction); Doris Cerea (consultant).
Handles: Nonfiction books, juvenile books, novels. Will consider these nonfiction areas: animals; history; juvenile nonfiction; new age/metaphysics; true crime/investigative; self-help/personal improvement. Will consider these fiction areas: action/adventure; detective/police/crime; family saga; fantasy; historical; humor/satire; juvenile; mainstream; mystery/suspense; picture book; psychic/supernatural; romance; science fiction; thriller/espionage; westerns/frontier. Query first. Will report in 3-4 weeks on queries; 2-3 months on mss.
Terms: Agent receives 15% commission on domestic sales; 20% on foreign sales. Offers a written contract, "which can be cancelled with 60 days notice. We use a standard contract compiled by an attorney specializing in the literary field."
Fees: Does not charge a reading fee. Offers criticism service: "If the writer wishes a critique, he/she may request one. The charge is $1 per double-spaced, manuscript page. We also prefer to make notations on manuscripts in addition to the formal critique. We do them ourselves. They are detailed. We find one of the major problems is an inadequate knowledge of grammar and punctuation! We show the corrections directly on manuscript." Charges for postage, photocopying, telephone. Also offers a manuscript typing service if the writer has a need. Cost starts at $1.25/page (double-spaced). 60% of business is derived from commissions on ms sales; 40% derived from reading fees or criticism service. "We expect to derive most of our income from sales commissions. The critiquing is a service offered our clients." Payment of a criticism fee does not ensure representation.
Tips: Obtains new clients through recommendations from others. "All our clients to date have come through recommendations. Our agency does not send a publisher a manuscript that is not properly formatted, correctly spelled and properly punctuated. If the writer is not a good typist and lacks in the foregoing areas, we suggest hiring someone to do it; either us or someone locally. Naturally, our emphasis is on content, but appearance is important in a presentation package for a publisher."

JOSEPH ANTHONY AGENCY (II), 15 Locust Ct. Rd., Mays Landing NJ 08330. (609)625-7608. Contact: Joseph Anthony. Estab. 1964. Member of WGA. Represents 30 clients. 80% of clients are new/previously unpublished writers. "Specializes in general fiction and nonfiction. Always interested in screenplays." Currently handles: 5% juvenile books; 80% novellas; 5% short story collections; 2% stage plays; 10% TV scripts. Member agent: Lena Fortunato.
Handles: Nonfiction and juvenile books, novels, movie and TV scripts. Will consider these nonfiction areas: health/medicine; military/war; psychology; true crime/investigative; science/technology; self-help/personal improvement. Will consider these fiction areas: action/adventure; confessional; detective/police/crime; erotica; fantasy; mystery/suspense; psychic/supernatural; romance (gothic, historical, regency); science fiction; thriller/espionage; young adult. Query, SASE required. Will report in 2 weeks on queries; 1 month on mss.
Terms: Agent receives 15% commission on domestic sales; 20% on foreign sales.
Fees: Charges $85 reading fee for novels up to 100,000 words. "Fees are returned after a sale of $3,000 or more." Charges for postage and photocopying up to 3 copies. 10% of business is derived from commissions on ms sales; 90% is derived from reading fees or criticism service (because I work with new writers). Payment of criticism fee does not ensure representation.
Tips: Obtains new clients through recommendations from others, solicitation. "If your script is salable, I will try to sell it to the best possible markets. I will cover sales of additional rights through the world. If your material is unsalable as it stands but can be rewritten and repaired, I will tell you why it has been turned down. After you have rewritten your script, you may return it for a second reading without *any additional fee*. But . . . if it is completely unsalable in our evaluation for the markets, I will tell you why it has been turned down again and give you specific advice on how to avoid these errors in your future material. I do not write, edit or blue pencil your script. I am an *agent* and an agent is out to sell a script."

‡ARGONAUT LITERARY AGENCY (I), P.O. Box 8446, Clearwater FL 34618. (813)442-2511. Contact: R.R. Reed. Estab. 1992. Represents 3 clients. 66% of clients are new/previously unpublished authors. Currently handles: 30% nonfiction books; 20% scholarly books; 50% novels.
Handles: Nonfiction books, novels. Will consider these nonfiction areas: biography/autobiography; current affairs; history; military/war; money/finance/economics; true crime/investigative; sports. Will handle these fiction areas: action/adventure; confessional; contemporary issues; detective/police/crime; historical; humor/satire; mystery/suspense; sports; thriller/espionage; westerns/frontier. Query. Reports in 1 month on queries; 3 months on mss.
Terms: Agent receives 10% commission on domestic sales; 15% on foreign sales. Offers a written contract, binding for 2 years.
Fees: Charges a $35 reading fee. Offers a criticism service for $100. Payment of criticism fee ensures agency representation.

*AUTHOR AID ASSOCIATES (II), 340 E. 52nd St., New York NY 10022. (212)758-4213; 980-9179. Editorial Director: Arthur Orrmont. Estab. 1967. Represents 150 clients. Specializes in aviation, war, biography, novels, autobiography. Currently handles: 5% magazine fiction; 35% nonfiction books; 38% novels; 5% juvenile books; 5% movie scripts; 2% stage plays; 5% poetry and 5% other. Member agent: Leonie Rosenstiel, vice president "is a musicologist and authority on New Age subjects and nutrition."
Handles: Magazine fiction, nonfiction books, novels, juvenile books, movie scripts, stage plays, TV scripts and poetry collections. Query with outline. "Short queries answered by return mail." Reports within 6 weeks on mss.
Terms: Agent receives 15% commission on domestic sales; 15% on dramatic sales; 20% on foreign sales.
Fees: Charges a reading fee to new authors, refundable from commission on sale. Charges for cable, photocopying and messenger express. Offers a consultation service through which writers not represented can get advice on a contract. 85% of income from sales of writers' work; 15% of income derived from reading fees.
Tips: Publishers of *Literary Agents of North America*.

‡AUTHOR AUTHOR LITERARY AGENCY (I, II), P.O. Box 34051, 1200-37 St. S.W., Calgary, Alberta T3C 3W2 Canada. (403)242-0226. Fax: (403)242-0226. President: Joan Rickard. Estab. 1992. Member oF Calgary Writers' Assoc., Writers' Guild of Alberta and Canadian Authors' Assoc. Represents 12 clients. 75% of clients are new/previously unpublished writers. Currently handles 15% nonfiction books; 5% scholarly books; 5% textbooks; 25% juvenile books; 25% novels; 15% novellas; 10% short story collections.

Handles: Nonfiction books, textbooks, scholarly books, juvenile book, novels, novellas, short story collections. Will consider these nonfiction areas: biography/autobiography; business; child guidance/parenting; gay/lesbian issues; language/literature; new age/metaphysics; psychology; religious/inspirational; true crime/investigative; self-help/personal improvement; sociology; women's issues/women's studies. Will consider these fiction areas: confessional; contemporary issues; detective/police/crime; erotica; feminist; gay; juvenile; lesbian; literary; mainstream; mystery/suspense; psychic/supernatural; romance (contemporary, gothic, historical, regency); science fiction; thriller/espionage; young adult. Query or send entire ms or outline/proposal, or outline plus 3 sample chapters. Will report in 2 weeks on queries; 1 month on mss.
Terms: Agent receives 15% commission on domestic sales; 20% on foreign sales. Offers written contract, binding for 1 year.
Fees: Charges $100 reading fee for first 10,000 words plus $5/1,000 additional words. Novels of over 80,000 words: Flat rate of $450. Criticism service: Reading, editing, evaluating and handling services included within basic fee. Charges for postage, photocopying and long distance calls to promote sales. Payment of reading or criticism fee does not ensure representation.
Tips: Obtains new clients through recommendations and advertisements. "We accept no poetry or screenplays."

THE AUTHORS AND ARTISTS RESOURCE CENTER/TARC LITERARY AGENCY (II), P.O. Box 64785, Tucson AZ 85728-1785. (602)325-4733. Contact: Martha R. Gores. Estab. 1984. Represents 30 clients. Specializes in mainstream adult fiction and nonfiction books. Currently handles: 80% nonfiction books; 20% novels.
Handles: Nonfiction books, novels. Will consider all nonfiction areas except essays, autobiography (unless celebrity) and journals. "Especially interested in how-to or self-help books by professionals; parenting books by psychologists or M.D.s." Query with outline. Does not read unsolicited manuscripts. Reports in 2 months if SASE.
Recent Sales: *The Good Sex Book*, by Sherry Sedgwich (Compcare); *Late Connections*, by Mary McConnell (Harbinger House).
Terms: Agent receives 15% commission on domestic sales; 20% on dramatic sales; 20% on foreign sales.
Fees: Does not charge a reading fee. Charges a criticism fee "only if it is requested by the author." No set fee. "Each critique tailored to the individual needs of the writer. We hire working editors who are employed by book publishers to do critiquing, editing, etc." Charges writers for mailing, photocopying, faxing, telephone calls.
Tips: "We do ghosting for professional people. In order to do ghosting, you must be published by a professional, reputable publisher. To be considered, send a business card with your résumé."

‡AUTHORS' LITERARY AGENCY (I), 1707 Donley Dr., P.O. Box 184, Euless TX 76039-0184. (817)267-1078. Fax: (214)594-6413. Contact: Dick Smith. Estab. 1992. Represents 7 clients. 90% of clients are new/previously unpublished writers. Currently handles: 5% nonfiction books; 95% novels.
Handles: Nonfiction books, textbooks, novels. Will consider these nonfiction areas: biography/autobiography; business; child guideance/parenting; computers/electronics; cooking/food/nutrition; current affairs; government/politics/law; health/medicine; history; interior design/decorating; juvenile nonfiction; military/war; money/finance/economics; music/dance/theater/film; nature/environment; true crime/investigative; self-help/personal improvement; women's issues/women's studies. Will consider these fiction areas: action/adventure; contemporary issues; detective/police/crime; literary; mainstream; mystery/suspense; thriller/espionage; young adult. Query first always. Unsolicited ms will be returned unread. Will report in 1 month on queries; 2 months on mss.
Recent Sales: *By The Book*, by Susan Mary Malone (Baskerville Publ. Ltd.); *Bound*, by Chris Manno (Baskerville Publ. Ltd.).
Terms: Agent receives 15% commission on domestic sales; 10% on foreign sales. Offers written contract, binding until cancelled by either party.
Fees: Charges for extraordinary expenses for copying or postage not to exceed $200 per year. 100% of business derived from commissions of ms sales.
Writers' Conferences: Attends Golden Triangle Writers Conference held in Beaumont TX in October; and DFW Writers' Workshop Symposium held in Euless TX each year.
Tips: Obtains new clients through recommendations, networking at conferences. "Join a read-and-critique group similar to the DFW Writers' Workshop. Participate actively and apply critique to your work. Query first. Enclose SASE with all submissions. Work submitted without SASE will neither be considered nor returned."

*AUTHORS' MARKETING SERVICES LTD. (II), 217 Degrassi St., Toronto, Ontario M4M 2K8 Canada. (416)463-7200. Fax: (416)469-4494. Contact: Larry Hoffman. Estab. 1978. Represents 17 clients. 25% of clients are new/previously unpublished writers. Specializes in thrillers, romance, parenting and self-help. Currently handles: 65% nonfiction books; 10% juvenile books; 20% novels; 5% other.
Handles: Nonfiction books and novels. Will consider these nonfiction areas: biography/autobiography; business; child guidance/parenting; current affairs; military/war; true crime/investigative. Will consider these fiction areas: action/adventure; detective/police/crime; mystery/suspense; romance; thriller/espionage. Query. Will report in 1 week on queries; 1-2 months on mss.
Recent Sales: *Strong Eye*, by Dennis Jones (D.I. Fine); *Goodhearted Women and Honky Tonk Angels*, by Catherine Saxberg (Zebra); *University of Toronto/Faculty of Medicine Effective Health Management Guide*, by Dr. June V. Engel (Key-Porter); *Making Canada Work*, by Professor John Crispo (Random House).
Terms: Agent receives 15% commission on domestic sales; 20% on foreign sales. Offers a written contract, binding for 6-9 months to complete first sale.
Fees: Charges $275 reading fee. "A reading/evaluation fee of $275 applies only to unpublished authors, and the fee must accompany the completed manuscript. Criticism service is included in the reading fee. The critique averages 3-4 pages in length, and discusses strengths and weaknesses of the execution, as well as advice aimed at eliminating weaknesses." 95% of business is derived from commissions on ms sales; 5% is derived from reading fees or criticism service. Payment of a criticism fee does not ensure representation.
Tips: Obtains new clients through recommendations from other writers and publishers, occasional solicitation. "Never submit first drafts. Prepare the manuscript as cleanly and as perfect, in the writer's opinion, as possible."

‡MAXIMILIAN BECKER (II), 115 E. 82nd St., New York NY 10028. (212)988-3887. President: Maximilian Becker. Associate: Aleta Daley. Estab. 1950. Works with a small number of new/unpublished authors.
Handles: Nonfiction books, novels and stage plays. Query. Does not accept unsolicited mss. Reports in 2 weeks on queries; 3 weeks on mss.
Recent Sales: *Goering*, by David Irving (William Morrow); *Enigma*, by David Kahn (Houghton Mifflin); and *Cecile*, by Jamine Boissard (Little Brown).
Terms: Agent receives 15% commission on domestic sales; 20% on foreign sales.
Fees: Does not charge a reading fee. Charges a criticism fee "if detailed criticism is requested. Writers receive a detailed criticism with suggestions—five to ten pages. No criticism is given if manuscript is hopeless."

*MEREDITH BERNSTEIN LITERARY AGENCY (II), Suite 503 A, 2112 Broadway, New York NY 10023. (212)799-1007. Fax: (212)799-1145. Contact: Meredith Bernstein. Estab. 1981. Member of AAR. Represents approximately 75 clients. 20% of clients are new/previously unpublished writers. Does not specialize; "very eclectic." Currently handles: 50% nonfiction books; 50% fiction. Member agents: Elizabeth Cavanaugh and Patrick Lo Brutto.
Handles: Fiction and nonfiction books. Query first.
Terms: Agent receives 15% commission on domestic sales; 20% on foreign sales.
Fees: Charges reading fee of up to $100 for unpublished writers only. Charges a $75 disbursement fee per year. 98% of business is derived from commissions on ms sales; 2% is derived from reading or criticism services. Payment of criticism fees does not ensure agency representation.
Tips: Obtains new clients through recommendations from others, solicitation, at conferences; own ideas developed and packaged.

‡THE BLAKE GROUP LITERARY AGENCY (II, III), Suite 600, One Turtle Creek Village, Dallas TX 75219. (214)520-8562. Director/Agent: Ms. Lee B. Halff. Estab. 1979. Member of Texas Publishers Association (TPA) and Texas Booksellers Association (TBA). Represents 45 clients. Works with published/established authors; works with a small number of new/unpublished authors. Currently

An asterisk indicates those agents who only charge fees to new or previously unpublished writers or to writers only under certain conditions.

handles: 11% fiction; 30% nonfiction books; 43% novels; 2% textbooks; 9% juvenile books; 2% poetry; 3% science fiction.
Handles: Nonfiction books, novels, textbooks and juvenile books. Query; send synopsis 2 sample chapters. Reports within 3 months. Pre-stamped return mailer must accompany submissions or they will not be read.
Recent Sales: *Captured Corregidor: Diary of an American P.O.W. in WWII*, by John M. Wright, Jr. (McFarland & Co); *Modern Languages for Musicians*, by Julie Yarbrough (Pendragon Press); and *Weight Loss for Super Wellness*, by Ted L. Edwards Jr.
Terms: Agent receives 10% commission on domestic sales; 15% on dramatic sales; 20% on foreign sales.

BRADY LITERARY MANAGEMENT (III), 267 Dudley Rd., Bedford MA 01730. Did not respond.

‡THE BRINK LITERARY AGENCY (II), (formerly The Erikson Literary Agency), 4498 Foothill Rd., Carpinteria CA 93013. (805)684-9655. Contact: Jude Barvin. Estab. 1988. Represents 24 clients. Currently handles: 25% nonfiction books; 50% novels; 25% movie scripts.
Handles: Will consider these nonfiction areas: anthropology, sociology, general. Will consider all fiction areas. Query with SASE.
Recent Sales: *Elvis My Brother*, by Billy Stanley (St. Martins Press).
Terms: Agent receives 15% commissions on domestic sales; 20% on foreign sales. Offers a written contract, binding for 1 year.
Fees: Charges a reading fee of $125 for novel manuscript; $100 for screenplays. Criticism service: money deducted from agency expenses or commissions. Charges for office expenses, postage, photocopying.
Writers' Conferences: Attends Santa Barbara Writers Conference.
Tips: Obtains new clients through recommendations from others, queries, mail.

RUTH HAGY BROD LITERARY AGENCY (III), 15 Park Ave., New York NY 10016. (212)683-3232. Fax: (212)269-0313. President: A.T. Brod. Estab. 1975. Represents 10 clients. 10-15% of clients are new/unpublished authors. Prefers to work with published/established authors. Specializes in trade books. Currently handles: 95% nonfiction books; 5% novels.
Handles: Nonfiction books. Query or send entire manuscript. Reports in 5 weeks on queries; 2 months on mss.
Terms: Agent receives 15% commission on domestic sales; 20% on foreign sales.
Fees: Charges a reading fee; waives reading fee when representing writer. 5% of income derived from reading fees. Charges a criticism fee. 5% of income derived from criticism fees.

PEMA BROWNE LTD. (II), Pine Rd., HCR Box 104B, Neversink NY 12765. (914)985-2936. Fax: (914)985-7635. Contact: Perry Browne or Pema Browne. Estab. 1966. Member of WGA and Society of Children's Book Writers. Represents 34 clients. Handles any commercial fiction or nonfiction and juvenile. Currently handles: 25% nonfiction books; 25% juvenile books; 45% novels; 5% movie scripts.
Handles: Nonfiction books, textbooks, scholarly books, juvenile books, novels. Will consider these nonfiction areas: anthropology/archaeology; art/architecture/design; biography/autobiography; business; child guidance/parenting; cooking/food/nutrition; government/politics/law; health/medicine; juvenile nonfiction; military/war; nature/environment; new age/metaphysics; psychology; religious/inspirational; true crime/investigative; science/technology; self-help/personal improvement; sports; women's issues/women's studies. Will consider these fiction areas: action/adventure, contemporary issues; detective/police/crime; feminist; glitz; historical; humor/satire; juvenile; literary; mainstream; mystery/suspense; picture book; psychic/supernatural; religious/inspiration; romance; science fiction; thriller/espionage; young adult. Query with SASE. Will report in 1 week on queries; 2 weeks on mss.
Recent Sales: *Get the Job You Want—30 Ways in 30 Days*, by Gary T. Grappo (Putnam).
Terms: Agent receives 15% commission on domestic sales; 15% on foreign sales.
Fees: Charges reading fee. "Reading fee is nonrefundable inasmuch as we hire an outside editor/reader for a review of manuscript. A copy is sent to the author." Criticism service: $170 for ms up to 80,000 words; $215 for up to 100,000 words; $260 for up to 125,000 words. Outside editor/reader reports as to plot, character development, writing style, etc. 98% of business is derived from commissions on ms sales; 2% is derived from reading fees or criticism services. Payment of a criticism fee does not ensure representation.

Tips: Obtains new clients through "editors, authors, *LMP, Writer's Digest* and as a result of longevity! If writing romance, be sure to receive guidelines from various romance publishers. In nonfiction, one must have credentials to lend credence to a proposal. Make sure of margins, double-space and use heavy-weight type."

THE CATALOG™ LITERARY AGENCY (II), P.O. Box 2964, Vancouver WA 98668. (206)694-8531. Contact: Douglas Storey. Estab. 1986. Represents 31 clients. 50% of clients are new/previously unpublished writers. Specializes in business, health, psychology, money, science, how-to, self-help, technology, women's interest. Currently handles: 50% nonfiction books; 20% juvenile books; 30% novels.
Handles: Nonfiction books, textbooks, juvenile books, novels. Will consider these nonfiction areas: agriculture/horticulture; business; child guidance/parenting; computers/electronics; crafts/hobbies; health/medicine; juvenile nonfiction; money/finance/economics; nature/environment; psychology; science/technology; self-help/personal improvement; women's issues/women's studies. Will consider these fiction areas: juvenile and mainstream. Query. Will report in 2 weeks on queries; 3 weeks on mss.
Terms: Agent receives 15% on domestic sales; 20% on foreign sales. Offers a written contract, binding for about 9 months.
Fees: Does not charge a reading fee. Charges an up-front handling fee from $85-250 that covers photocopying, telephone and postage expense.

CHADD-STEVENS LITERARY AGENCY (I), 926 Spur Trail, Granbury TX 76049. (817)579-1405. Contact: L.F.Jordan. Estab. 1991. Represents 10 clients. Specializes in working with previously unpublished authors.
Handles: Novels, novellas, short story collections. Will consider these fiction areas: action/adventure; erotica; young adult; experimental; fantasy; mystery/suspense; psychic/supernatural; horror. Send entire ms or 3 sample chapters with SASE. Will report within 6 weeks on mss.
Terms: Agent receives 10% commission on domestic sales; 15% on foreign sales. Offers written contract, binding for 3 months.
Fees: Does not charge a reading fee. Charges a $35 handling fee for entire ms only. Charges for expenses. Payment of handling fee does not ensure agency representation.
Writers' Conferences: Attends several regional (Texas and Southwest) writers' conferences.
Tips: "I'm interested in working with people who have been turned down by other agents and publishers. I'm interested in first-time novelists—there's a market for your work if it's good. Don't give up. I think there is a world of good unpublished fiction out there and I'd like to see it."

LINDA CHESTER LITERARY AGENCY (II), 265 Coast, LaJolla CA 92037. (619)454-3966. Fax: (619)454-7338. Contact: Linda Chester. Estab. 1978. Represents 60 clients. 25% of clients are new/previously unpublished writers. Specializes in quality fiction and nonfiction. Currently handles: 70% nonfiction books; 30% novels. Member agents: Laurie Fox (associate agent).
Handles: Nonfiction books, novels, especially literary fiction. Will consider these nonfiction areas: art/architecture; biography/autobiography; business; child guidance/parenting; current affairs; health/medicine; history; literature; money/finance/economics; performing arts; environment; psychology; true crime/investigative; women's issues. Will consider these fiction areas: contemporary issues; ethnic; feminist; literary; mainstream; mystery/suspense. Query first, then send outline/proposal. Will report in 2 weeks on queries; 3 weeks on mss.
Recent Sales: *She's Come Undone*, by Wally Comb (Pocket Books); *Two Halves of New Haven*, by Martin Schecter (Crown Publishers Inc.); *Juggernaut: The Germaning of Business*, by Philip Glouchevitch (Simon & Schuster); *Investing From the Heart: A Guide to Socially Responsible Investment*, by Jack Brill and Alan Reder (Crown).
Terms: Agent receives 15% commission on domestic sales; 30% on foreign sales. Offers a written contract, binding for 1 year.
Fees: Does not charge a reading fee. Criticism service: $350 for manuscripts up to 400 pages. Consists of a 3-5 page critique/evaluation of manuscripts in terms of presentation, marketability, writing quality, voice, plot, characterization, style, etc. In-house professional editors write the critiques. Charges for photocopying of manuscript and other office expenses. 95% of business is derived from commissions on ms sales; 5% is derived from criticism services. Payment of a criticism fee does not ensure representation.
Writers' Conferences: Attends Santa Barbara Writers' Conference.
Tips: Obtains new clients through recommendations from others and solicitation.

COLBY: LITERARY AGENCY (I), 2864-20 Jefferson Ave., Yuba City CA 95993. (916)674-3378. Contact: Pat Colby. Estab. 1990. Represents 11 clients. 100% of clients are new/previously unpublished writers. Specializes in fiction — mystery and comedy. Currently handles: 100% novels. Member agent: Richard Colby.
Handles: Novels, novellas, short story collections. Will consider these fiction areas: cartoon/comic; detective/police/crime; humor/satire; mystery/suspense; sports; thriller/espionage; westerns/frontier. Query or send entire ms. Will report within 1 week on queries; 1 month on mss.
Terms: Agent receives 12% commission on domestic sales; 15% commission on foreign sales. Offers a written contract, binding for 1 year.
Fees: Charges a reading fee. Charges $125 for up to 100,000 words, prorated if more than 100,000. Fee is nonrefundable. Offers criticism service, but this is covered by reading fee. Criticisms are done by Pat Colby or Richard Colby. Charges for photocopying and postage. Payment of reading or criticism fees does not ensure agency representation.

CONNOR LITERARY AGENCY (III, IV), 640 W. 153rd St., New York NY 10031. (212)491-5233. Fax: (212)491-5233. Contact: Marlene K. Connor. Estab. 1985. Represents 25 clients. 30% of clients are new/previously unpublished writers. Specializes in popular fiction and nonfiction. Currently handles: 50% nonfiction books; 50% novels.
Handles: Nonfiction books, novels, children's books (especially with a minority slant). Will consider these nonfiction areas: child guidance/parenting; cooking/food/nutrition; crafts/hobbies; current affairs; ethnic/cultural interests; health/medicine; money/finance/economics; photography; true crime/investigative; self-help/personal improvement; sports. Will consider these fiction areas: contemporary issues; ethnic; glitz; humor/satire; literary; mystery/suspense; picture book; sports. Query with outline/proposal. Will report in 4 weeks on queries; 4-6 weeks on mss.
Recent Sales: *Miss America*, by Ann-Marie Bivans (Master-Media); *Simplicity's Home Decorating Book*, by Simplicity Pattern Company (Prentice-Hall); *Doll Eyes*, by Randy Russell (Bantam Books).
Terms: Agent receives 15% commission on domestic sales; 25% on foreign sales. Offers a written contract, binding for 1 year.
Fees: Charges a reading fee. "Fee depends on length: $75-125. Deductible from commissions; reader's reports provided for all manuscripts read with fees charged." Charges for general expenses — messenger, photocopying, postage. "Less than $100 in most cases. Deducted from commissions and explained." 99% of business derived from commissions on ms sales; 1% is derived from reading fees or criticism services.
Writers' Conferences: Attends Heart of America Writer's Conference and Howard University Publishing Conference.
Tips: Obtains new clients through queries, recommendations, conferences, grapevine, etc. "Seeking previously published writers with good sales records."

‡BRUCE COOK AGENCY (I), P.O. Box 75995, St. Paul MN 55175-0995. (612)487-9355. Proprietor: Elizabeth Young. Estab. 1992. Member of The Loft (writer's organization). 50% of clients are new/previously unpublished writers. Subject areas include romance, mystery, science fiction, juvenile and religion. Currently handles: 20% nonfiction books; 10% scholarly books; textbooks; 30% novels; 10% short story collections; 10% movie scripts; 10% TV scripts. Member agents: Elizabeth Young (13 years of experience with two other agencies).
Handles: Nonfiction books, textbooks, scholarly books, juvenile books, novels, short story collections, movie scripts, stage plays, TV scripts. Will consider these nonfiction areas: biography/autobiography; business; child guidance/parenting; cooking/food/nutrition; health/medicine; history; juvenile nonfiction; language/literature/criticism; music/dance/theater/film; nature/environment; psychology; religious/inspirational; self-help/personal improvement; sociology. Will consider these fiction areas: action/adventure; cartoon/comic; family saga; fantasy; historical; humor/satire; juvenile; literary; mystery/suspense; regional; religious/inspiration; science fiction; thriller/espionage; young adult. Query with 1-page outline. Will report in 2 weeks on queries; 1-2 months on mss.
Terms: Agent receives 15% commission on domestic sales; 25% on foreign sales. Offers written contract.
Fees: Reading fee for a published author is minimal. Evaluation by qualified professionals based on number of pages to be reviewed and primarily for new authors. Critiques are 5-10 pages long and done by Elizabeth Young. Charges for out-of-pocket expenses incurred in marketing the ms are charged to the client. Services for marketing are on a contingency basis." 60% of business is derived from commissions on ms sales; 40% is derived from reading fees or criticism services. Payment of fees does not ensure representation, must be made in advance of service rendered, and is nonrefundable.

Writers' Conferences: Attends Minneapolis Writers Workshop held in Minneapolis MN in August, Association of PEN Women held in St. Paul MN in October.
Tips: Obtains new clients through referrals, networking and advertising. "Make a point of meeting your agent in person. Insist on regular communication. Your ms should be legible, typed, double-spaced and with pages marked. Be open to suggestions for improving your ms."

*BILL COOPER ASSOC., INC. (II), Suite 411, 224 W. 49th St., New York NY 10019. (212)307-1100. Contact: William Cooper. Estab. 1964. Represents 10 clients. 10% of clients are new/unpublished writers. Prefers to work with published/established authors; works with a small number of new/unpublished authors. Specializes in contemporary fiction. Currently handles: 90% novels; 10% movie scripts.
Handles: Novels and movie scripts. Reports in 2 weeks on queries and mss. No unsolicited submissions.
Terms: Agent receives 15% commission on domestic sales; 15% on dramatic sales; 20% on foreign sales.
Fees: May charge a reading fee for unpublished authors. Payment of a reading or criticism fee does not ensure representation.

*CREATIVE CONCEPTS LITERARY AGENCY (II), P.O. Box 10261, Harrisburg PA 17105-0261. (717)432-5054. Contact: Michele Glance Sewach. Estab. 1987. Represents 12 clients. 50% of clients are new/previously unpublished writers. Specializes in self-help books, how-to books, travel guides and career books. Currently handles: 60% nonfiction books; 2% scholarly books; 2% textbooks; 5% juvenile books; 20% novels; 2% short story collections; 5% movie scripts; 2% TV scripts; 2% syndicated material.
Handles: Nonfiction books, textbooks, scholarly books, juvenile books, novels, novellas, short story collections, movie scripts, TV scripts. Will consider these nonfiction areas: animals; biography/autobiography; business; child guidance/parenting; computers/electronics; cooking/food/nutrition; crafts/hobbies; current affairs; ethnic/cultural interests; government/politics/law; health/medicine; interior design/decorating; juvenile nonfiction; language/literature/criticism; military/war; money/finance/economics; nature/environment; psychology; science/technology; self-help/personal improvement; sociology; women's issues/women's studies; gardening; journalism/writing; career books; travel guides. Will consider these fiction areas: action/adventure; contemporary issues; detective/police/crime; family saga; glitz; historical; literary; mainstream; mystery/suspense; religious/inspirational; romance; science fiction; thriller/espionage; young adult. Query. Will report "promptly" on queries and mss.
Recent Sales: *A Change of Heart* by Willie Watkins (Colonial Press).
Terms: Agent receives 10% commission on domestic sales; 10% on foreign sales. Offers a written contract.
Fees: Does not charge a reading fee. "We charge a *critiquing* fee of $145, refundable upon author's first book sale. There is no fee for authors who have already had a book published in the same area. Critiques are 2-5 typed pages addressing marketability, writing style, etc. Critiques are done by the agency director or agency editors. Other expenses are individually negotiated when the contract is written between the agency and author." 90% of business is derived from commissions on ms sales; 10% is derived from reading fees or criticism services. Payment of criticism fee does not ensure representation.
Tips: Obtains new clients through "over-the-transom queries and recommendations from publishers and writers. Writers should include information on their writing credits and background that will convince agents they are well qualified to write their book."

DORESE AGENCY LTD. (III), 37965 Palo Verde Dr., Cathedral City CA 92234. (619)321-1115. Fax: (619)321-1049. Contact: Alyss Barlow Dorese. Estab. 1977. Represents 30 clients. Currently handles: 65% nonfiction books; 35% novels.
Handles: Will consider these nonfiction areas: art; biography/autobiography; business; child guidance/parenting; cooking/food/nutrition; crafts/hobbies; current affairs; gay/lesbian issues; government/politics/law; health/medicine; history; interior design/decorating; language/literature/criticism; military/war; money/finance/economics; music/dance/theater/film; new age/metaphysics; photography; psy-

Check the Literary and Script Agents Subject Index to find the agents who indicate an interest in your nonfiction or fiction subject area.

chology; true crime/investigative; self-help/personal improvement; sociology; sports; women's issues/women's studies. Will consider these fiction areas: action/adventure; contemporary issues; detective/police/crime; ethnic; family saga; feminist; gay; glitz; historical; lesbian; literary; mainstream; mystery/suspense; psychic/supernatural; regional; inspirational; sports; young adult. Send outline/proposal and SASE. Will report in 6 weeks on queries.

Terms: Agent receives 15% commission on domestic sales; 20% on foreign sales. Offers a written contract, binding for 2 years.

Fees: Does not charge a reading fee. Offers criticism service. Criticism service depends on length of book.

Tips: Obtains new clients through referrals from past clients. "Don't say, 'I've written The Great American Novel.' It's an immediate turnoff."

‡**DYKEMAN ASSOCIATES INC. (III),** 4115 Rawlins, Dallas TX 65219. (214)528-2991. Fax: (214)528-0241. Contact: Alice Dykeman. Estab. 1988. 20% of clients are new/previously unpublished writers. Currently handles: 20% novels; 20% business and other; 60% TV scripts.

Handles: Novels, short story collections, movie scripts, TV scripts. Will consider these nonfiction areas: biography/autobiography; business; money/finance/economics; religious/inspirational. Will consider these fiction areas: action/adventure; contemporary issues; detective/police/crime; fantasy; mystery/suspense; religious/inspiration; science fiction; thriller/espionage. Query with outline/proposal or outline plus 3 sample chapters. Will report in 1 week on queries; 1 month on mss.

Terms: Agent receives 15% commission on domestic sales; 15% on foreign sales. Offers written contract.

Fees: Charges $250 reading fee. Criticism service is included in reading fee. Critiques are written by readers and reviewed by Alice Dykeman. Charges for postage, copies, long distance phone calls. Payment of criticism fees does not ensure representation.

Tips: Obtains new clients through listings in directories and word of mouth.

EXECUTIVE EXCELLENCE, 1 East Center, Provo UT 84606. (801)375-4014. Fax: (801)377-5960. President: Ken Shelton. Agent: Roger Terry. Estab. 1984. Represents 25 clients. Specializes in nonfiction trade books/management and personal development—books with a special focus such as ethics in business, managerial effectiveness, organizational productivity. Currently handles: 100% nonfiction.

Handles: Nonfiction books, magazine articles.

Recent Sales: *The Networker,* by Wayne Baker (McGraw-Hill); *Beyond Counterfeit Leadership,* by Ken Shelton (Berrett-Koehler); *Luck is a Four-Letter Word,* by Emil Salvini (Bob Adams); *12 Natural Laws of Time and Life Management,* by Hyrum Smith (Warner).

Terms: Agent receives 15% commission on domestic sales. 90% of business is derived from commissions on ms sales; 10% is derived from reading fees or criticism services.

Fees: "We charge a $1 per page ($150 minimum) critical reading and review fee. Waives reading fee if we represent the writer. A $500 deposit is made by the author at the time of signing a contract to cover expenses (calls, mail, etc.)"

*FRIEDA FISHBEIN LTD. (II), 2556 Hubbard St., Brooklyn NY 11235. (212)247-4398. Contact: Janice Fishbein. Estab. 1928. Represents 30 clients. 50% of clients are new/previously unpublished writers. Currently handles: 10% nonfiction books; 5% young adult; 60% novels; 10% movie scripts; 10% stage plays; 5% TV scripts. Member agents: Heidi Carlson; Douglas Michael.

Handles: Nonfiction books, young adult books, novels, movie scripts, stage plays, TV scripts ("not geared to a series"). Will consider these nonfiction areas: animals; biography/autobiography; cooking/food/nutrition; current affairs; juvenile nonfiction; military/war; nature/environment; true crime/investigative; self-help/personal improvement; women's issues/women's studies. Will consider these fiction areas: action/adventure; contemporary issues; detective/police/crime; family saga; fantasy; feminist; historical; humor/satire; mainstream; mystery/suspense; romance (contemporary, historical, regency); science fiction; thriller/espionage; young adult. Query letter a must before sending ms or fees. Will report in 2-3 weeks on queries; 4-6 weeks on mss accepted for evaluation.

Recent Sales: *Incident in Iraq,* by Herbert L. Fisher (Avon); *Fat is Not a 4 Letter Word,* by Roy Schroder (Chronamed); *Double Cross,* screenplay (Pathe/MGM).

Terms: Agent receives 10% commission on domestic sales; 15% on foreign sales. Offers a written contract, binding for 30 days, cancelable by either party, except for properties being marketed or already sold.

Fees: Charges $75 reading fee first 50,000 words, $1 per 1,000 words thereafter for new authors; $75 for plays, TV, screenplays. Criticism service offered together with reading fee. Offers "an overall critique. Sometimes specific staff readers may refer to associates for no charge for additional readings if warranted." 60% of business is derived from commissions on ms sales; 40% is derived from reading fees or criticism services. Payment of a criticism fee does not ensure representation.

Tips: Obtains new clients through recommendations from others. "*Always* submit a query letter first with an SASE. Manuscripts should be done in large type, double-spaced and one and one-half-inch margins, clean copy and edited for typos, etc."

*JOYCE A. FLAHERTY, LITERARY AGENT (II, III), 816 Lynda Ct., St. Louis MO 63122. (314)966-3057. Contact: Joyce or John Flaherty. Estab. 1980. Member of AAR, RWA, MWA, WWA. Represents 65 clients. 15% of clients are new/previously unpublished writers. Currently handles: 30% nonfiction books; 70% novels.

Handles: Nonfiction books, novels. Will consider these nonfiction areas: animals; biography/autobiography; business; child guidance/parenting; cooking/food/nutrition; crafts/hobbies; health/medicine; history; military/war; money; nature/environment; psychology; true crime/investigative; self-help/personal improvement; sports; women's issues/women's studies; Americana. Will consider these fiction areas: action/adventure; contemporary issues; crime; family saga; feminist; historical; literary; mainstream; mystery/suspense; psychic/supernatural; romance; thriller/espionage; frontier; military/aviation/war; and women's fiction. Send outline plus 1 sample chapter and SASE. No unsolicited manuscripts. Will report in 6 weeks on queries; 2-3 months on mss unless otherwise agreed on.

Recent Sales: *American Coverlet Series*, by Coleen L. Johnston (St. Martin's Press); *Filo Fantastic*, by Mary H. Crownover (Taylor Publishing Co.); *The Fortune Trilogy*, by Judith E. French (Avon Books).

Terms: Agent receives 15% commission on domestic sales; 25-30% on foreign sales.

Fees: Charges $50 marketing fee for new clients unless currently published book authors.

Writers' Conferences: Attends Romance Writers of America; Missouri Romance Writers Conference; Love Designers Writers' Club; Western Writers of America Conference; Moonlight and Magnolias; Heartland Writers Guild Conference; Romantic Times Conference.

Tips: Obtains new clients through recommendations from editors and clients, writers conferences and from queries. "Be concise in a letter or by phone and well focused. Always include an SASE as well as your phone number. If you want an agent to return your call, leave word to call you collect if you're not currently the agent's client. If a query is a multiple submission, be sure to say so and mail them all at the same time so that everyone has the same chance. Know something about the agent beforehand so that you're not wasting each other's time. Be specific about word length of project and when it will be completed if not completed at the time of contact. Be brief!"

‡FLANNERY, WHITE AND STONE (II), Suite 404, 180 Cook St., Denver CO 80206. (303)399-2264. Fax: (303)399-3006. Contact: Constance Solowiejo. Estab. 1987. Represents 45 clients. 60% of clients are new/previously unpublished writers. Specializes in mainstream and literary fiction, juvenile, unique nonfiction, business and medical books. Currently handles: 40% nonfiction books; 20% juvenile books; 40% fiction. Member agents: Kendall Bohannon (mainstream and literary fiction, juvenile); Constance Solowiej (mainstream and literary fiction, nonfiction, business); Robert FitzGerald (business, medical, humor).

Handles: Nonfiction and juvenile books; novels; short story collections. Will consider these nonfiction areas: business; child guidance/parenting; current affairs; ethnic/cultural interests; gay/lesbian issues; government/politics/law; health/medicine; juvenile nonfiction; money/finance/economics; music/dance/theater/film; nature/environment; psychology; self-help/personal improvement; sociology; sports; women's issues/women's studies. Will consider these fiction areas: action/adventure; contemporary issues; ethnic; experimental; family saga; feminist; gay; historical; humor/satire; juvenile; lesbian; literary; mainstream; mystery/suspense; picture book; psychic/supernatural; regional; romance (contemporary, historical); science fiction; thriller/espionage; young adult. Send outline/proposal plus 2 sample chapters. Will report in 2 weeks on queries; 6 weeks on mss.

Recent Sales: *The Kind of Light That Shines on Texas*, by Reginald McKnight (Little, Brown & Co.); *West of the Divide*, by Tim Carrier (Fulcrum).

Terms: Agent receives 15% on domestic sales; 20% on foreign sales. Offers written contract.

Fees: "Due to the overwhelming number of mss we receive, FW&S now charges a reading/critique fee for completed mss by new/unpublished authors; $100/100,000 words. The fee includes a 3-5 page, line-by-line and overall evaluation report. Charges for photocopying unless author provides copies." 70% of business is derived from commissions; 30% from critiques. Payment of a criticism fee does not ensure representation.

Tips: "Make your nonfiction proposals professional and publisher-ready; let your fiction speak for itself."

JOAN FOLLENDORE LITERARY AGENCY (II), 1286 Miraleste, San Luis Obispo CA 93401. (805)545-9297. Fax: (805)545-9297. Contact: Joan Follendore, adult nonfiction; L. J. Knightstep, adult fiction; Sandra Uchitel, children's books. Estab. 1988. Member of Book Publicists of Southern California; American Booksellers Assoc. Represents 60 clients. 75% of clients are new/previously unpublished writers. Currently handles: 45% nonfiction books; 5% scholarly books; 25% juvenile books; 20% novels; 2% poetry books; 3% short story collections.
Handles: Fiction/nonfiction books, textbooks, scholarly books, juvenile books, picture books, short story collections. Will consider all areas, except scripts for stage or screen. Query first. Will report in 1 week on queries.
Recent Sales: *Breastfeeding Your Baby*, by Carl Jones (Macmillan); *How to Hypnotize Yourself & Others*, by Dr. Rachel Copelan (HarperCollins); *Endangered Animals of the Rainforest*, by Sandra Uchitel (Price/Stern/Sloan); *How To Sell The Tough Buyer* (Bob Adams, Inc.).
Terms: Agent receives 15% on domestic sales; 20% on foreign sales. Offers a written contract.
Fees: "No fee to authors who've been published in the prior few years by a major house. Other authors are charged a reading fee and our editing service is offered. For nonfiction, we completely edit the proposal/outline and sample chapter; for fiction and children's, we need the entire manuscript. Editing includes book formats, questions, comments, suggestions for expansion, cutting and pasting, etc." Also offers other services: proofreading, rewriting, proposal development, authors' public relations, etc. 65% of business is derived from commissions on ms sales; 35% is derived from reading or editing fees. Payment of fees does not ensure representation unless "revisions meet our standards."
Tips: Obtains new clients through recommendations from others and personal contacts at literary functions. "Study and make your query as perfect and professional as you possibly can."

FORTHWRITE LITERARY AGENCY (II), P.O. Box 922101, Sylmar CA 91392. (818)365-3400. Fax: (818)362-3443. Contact: Wendy L. Zhorne. Estab. 1989. Represents 40 clients. 33% of clients are new/previously unpublished writers. Specializes in fiction, nonfiction and juvenile, "but not limited to those categories. Currently handles: 40% nonfiction books; 20% juvenile books; 40% novels.
Handles: Nonfiction, juvenile fiction and nonfiction, including picture books. Will consider these nonfiction areas: agriculture; animals; anthropology; art; biography; business; child guidance; cooking; crafts; health; history; interior design; juvenile nonfiction; economics; theater/film; environment; photography; psychology; inspirational; technology; personal improvement; sociology; women's studies. Will consider these fiction areas: action; family saga; historical; juvenile; literary; mainstream; mystery/suspense; picture book; romance (historical); young adult. Query. Will report in 3-4 weeks on queries; 4-6 weeks on ms. "No unsolicited manuscripts!"
Recent Sales: *Witch Doctor's Handbook* (Barricade/Lyle Stuart); *Mystic Cures* (Sterling); *Juvenile historical fiction series* (8 books) (Capstone Press); *Civilize Your Puppy* (Barron's); *Children's Craft Ideas* (Baker Book House).
Terms: Agent receives 15% on domestic sales; 20% on foreign sales. Offers a written contract, which is binding for 1 year.
Fees: Charges $65 reading/critique fee "for all materials requested, unless writer has previous serious credits related to topic (same field/genre); $25 for juvenile under 5,000 words. In extreme circumstances we will critique an exemplary manuscript line by line to aid in improvement so we can represent the writer. Our reading fee includes an overview of major strengths/weaknesses, such as dialogue, plot, flow, characterization for fiction; structure, subject organization, readability, for nonfiction and the 'why' of acceptance or rejection by us. All writers provide copies of their material to us."
Writers' Conferences: Attends London Book Fair, many California conferences and regularly lectures at local colleges and universities on finding an agent or how to write more effectively.
Tips: Obtains new clients through advertising, referrals, conferences, recommendations by producers, chambers of commerce, satisfied auithors etc. "Please check your material, including query, for spelling and typing errors before sending. If you are worried whether your material will arrive, send it certified; don't search area codes for agent's home number; always send a SASE with everything.

Agents ranked I and II are most open to both established and new writers. Agents ranked III are open to established writers with publishing-industry references.

Never tell an agent, 'All my friends loved it.' Know your subject, genre and competition."

GLADDEN UNLIMITED (II), Box 7912, San Diego CA 92167. (619)224-5051. Agent Contact: Carolan Gladden. Estab. 1987. Member of WGA. Represents 20 clients. 95% of clients are new/previously unpublished writers. Currently handles: 20% nonfiction; 70% novels; 10% movie scripts.
Handles: Novels and nonfiction. Will consider these nonfiction areas: celebrity biography; how-to; self-help; business. Will consider these fiction areas: action/adventure, fantasy, horror, mainstream, science fiction, thriller. "No romance or children's." Query. Responds in 2 weeks on queries; 2 months on mss.
Terms: Agent's commission: 15% on domestic sales; 10% on film sales; 20% on foreign sales.
Fees: Does not charge a reading fee. Charges evaluation fee: $100 (refundable on placement of project) is charged for diagnostic marketability evaluation. Offers 6-8 pages of specific recommendations to turn the project into a salable commodity. "We also include a copy of our handy guide 'The Writer's Simple, Straightforward, Common Sense Rules of Marketability.' Also offers range of editorial services and is dedicated to helping new authors achieve publication."

GLENMARK LITERARY AGENCY (I), 5041 Byrne Rd., Oregon WI 53575. (608)255-1812. Contact: Glenn Schaeffer. Estab. 1990. Represents 6 clients. Currently handles: 50% nonfiction books; 50% novels.
Handles: Nonfiction books, novels. Will consider all mainstream nonfiction and fiction areas. Query first. Will report in 1 week on queries; 2 weeks on mss.
Terms: Agent receives 15% commission on domestic sales; 15% commission on foreign sales. Offers a written contract, binding for 1 year.
Fees: Charges a $50 reading fee. "The charge is for first-time offerings only. When we receive a query, we tell the client we will thoroughly review the manuscript for $50. If we like the manuscript and decide to represent the writer, the money is refunded. Offers criticism, but it is covered by the reading fee. We try to cover all aspects of the writing—presentation, use of language, characterization, plot, dialogue, subject matter and more. My wife, who has a Ph.D. in English literature, and I both review. Outside of the one-time charge, there are no other charges or fees." 50% of business is derived from reading fees. "Eventually, as we mature, we hope 100% of income will come from sales."
Tips: "Generally, writers hear about us through the grapevine . . . discover that there is indeed a literary agency that has time for them, will respond to queries . . . We try to make it clear that writing on a professional level is not easy. It takes a great deal of thought, research, time and effort. A writer can't expect the world to accept, with open arms, anything they decide to write. The subject must appeal to the public. Then they must polish and perfect their manuscript if it is going to make it in today's competitive market."

LUCIANNE S. GOLDBERG LITERARY AGENTS, INC. (II), Suite 6-A, 2255 W. 84th St., New York NY 10024. (212)799-1260. Editorial Director: Sandrine Olm. Estab. 1974. Represents 65 clients. 10% of clients are new/unpublished writers. "Any author we decide to represent must have a good idea, a good presentation of that idea and writing skill to compete with the market. Representation depends solely on the execution of the work whether writer is published or unpublished." Specializes in nonfiction works, "but will review a limited number of novels." Currently handles: 75% nonfiction books; 25% novels.
Handles: Nonfiction books and novels. Query with outline. Reports in 2 weeks on queries; 3 weeks on mss. "If our agency does not respond within 1 month to your request to become a client, you may submit requests elsewhere."
Recent Sales: *Senatorial Privilege*, by Leo Damore (Delacorte-Dell); *Who's Who in Hollywood*, by David Ragan (Facts on File); and *Nina's Journey*, by Nina Markovna (Regnery-Gateway).
Terms: Agent receives 15% commission on domestic sales; 25% on dramatic sales; 25% on foreign sales.
Fees: Charges reading fee on unsolicited mss: $150/full-length ms. Criticism is included in reading fee. 1% of income derived from reading fees. "Our critiques run 3-4 pages, single-spaced. They deal with the overall evaluation of the work. Three agents within the organization read and then confer. Marketing advice is included." Payment of fee does not ensure the agency will represent a writer. Charges for phone expenses, cable fees, photocopying and messenger service after the work is sold. 80% of income derived from commission on ms sales.

LARNEY GOODKIND (II), (Div. of Representing the Arts) (IV), 180 E. 79th St., New York NY 10021. (212)249-3185. Contact: Larney Goodkind. Estab. 1949. Have sponsored concert artists. Represents artists. Currently handles: 60% nonfiction books; 40% novels.
Handles: Will consider all nonfiction and fiction areas. Query with SASE. Will report in 2-4 weeks on queries.
Terms: Agent receives 10% commission on domestic sales.
Fees: Charges $100 reading fee for novels. "A set amount is returnable to writer in royalties." Offers a criticism service.
Tips: Obtains new clients through "people who know about me."

THE HAMERSFIELD AGENCY (I,II), Rt. 2, Box 48, Marianna FL 32446. (904)526-7631. Senior Partner: J.P.R. Ducat. Estab. 1990. Represents 78 clients. 80% of clients are new/previously unpublished writers. Specializes in English and French nonfiction, children's/juvenile literature, photo-travel books and quality photo-journal "table top" books. Currently handles: 70% nonfiction books; 10% photo/travel books; 2% photo-journal books; 18% juvenile books.
Handles: Nonfiction books, novels, juvenile books, photo/travel/journal books. No poetry, lyrics, "absolutely no TV, movie scripts or pornography." Query with outline or send entire ms (if prior arrangement is made). SASE required. Will report within 4-6 weeks on queries.
Terms: Agent receives 15% commission on domestic sales; 20% on foreign sales.
Fees: No reading fee for first reading. Charges a reading fee for a second reading/criticism for new writers. "Reading fee may be waved at our discretion." Charges $150 for 200 pages, $250 for 350 pages, typed, double-spaced mss. Offers critique service and ghostwriting. Charges $75 per hour for contract reviewing. Charges for expenses. 70% of business is derived from commissions on ms sales; 30% from reading fees or criticism service. Payment of fees does not ensure agency representation.
Tips: "Our interest is in a good writer whether he is a new writer or one who has a book previously published—our purpose is to market and promote our client onto the 'bestsellers' list.' "

‡ANDREW HAMILTON'S LITERARY AGENCY (II), 23811 Chagrin Blvd., LL42, Beachwood OH 44122. (216)831-7523. Fax: (216)831-7564. Contact: Andrew Hamilton. Estab. 1991. Represents 12 clients. 60% of clients are new/previously unpublished writers. Currently handles: 50% nonfiction books; 2% scholarly books; 3% juvenile books; 20% novels; 5% poetry books; 20% magazine articles.
Handles: Nonfiction books, juvenile books, novels, novellas. Will consider these nonfiction areas: animals; biography/autobiography; business; child guidance/parenting; cooking/food/nutrition; current affairs; ethnic/cultural interests; government/politics/law; health/medicine; history; juvenile nonfiction; money/finance/economics; music/dance/theater/film; psychology; religious/inspirational; true crime/investigative; self-help/personal improvement; sociology; sports; women's issues/women's studies; minority concerns; pop music. Will consider these fiction areas: action/adventure; cartoon/comic; confessional; contemporary issues; detective/police/crime; erotica; ethnic; family saga; humor/satire; juvenile; mystery/suspense; psychic/supernatural; religious/inspiration; romance (contemporary); sports; thriller/espionage; westerns/frontier; young adult. Send entire ms or send outline plus 3 sample chapters. Will report in 1 week on queries; 3 weeks on mss.
Recent Sales: *How to Select Competent, Cost Effective Legal Counsel*, by Philip J. Hermann (Business Publishing).
Terms: Agent receives 15% commission on domestic sales; 20% on foreign sales. Offers written contract.
Fees: "Reading fees are for new authors and are nonrefundable. My reading fee is $50 for 60,000 words or less and $75 for ms over 60,000 words. I charge a yearly marketing fee of $150 for mss and $75 for magazine articles." 70% of business derived from commissions on ms sales; 30% from reading fees or criticism services.
Tips: Obtains new clients through recommendations, solicitation and writing seminars. "Be patient: the wheels turn slowly in the publishing world."

Agents who specialize in a specific subject area such as children's books or in handling the work of certain writers such as Southwestern writers are ranked IV.

‡MARISA HANDARIS, LITERARY AGENCY (I), 706 S. Superior St., Albion MI 49224. (517)629-4919. Directors: Marisa Handaris, Mellie Hanke. Estab. 1992. Represents 5 clients. 75% of clients are new/previously unpublished writers. Currently handles 100% novels. Specialty: historical novels.
Handles: Novels. Will consider these fiction areas: detective/police/crime; historical; mystery; romance (historical); westerns. Will report in 6 weeks on mss.
Terms: Agent receives 10% commission on domestic sales; 15% on foreign sales.
Fees: Charges reading fee of $100 for up to 100,000 words; $125 for over 100,000 words. Offers criticism service. Marisa Handaris writes critiques. Charges for photocopying only. Payment of criticism fee does not ensure representation.

HEACOCK LITERARY AGENCY, INC., Suite #14, 1523 6th St., Santa Monica CA 90401. (213)393-6227. Contact: Jim or Rosalie Heacock. Estab. 1978. Member of AAR, Association of Talent Agents, Writers Guild of America. Represents 60 clients. 30% of clients are new/previously unpublished writers. Currently handles: 85% nonfiction books; 5% juvenile books; 5% novels; 5% movie scripts. Member agents: Jim Heacock (business expertise, parenting, psychology, sports, health, nutrition); Rosalie Heacock (psychology, philosophy, women's studies, alternative health).
Handles: Nonfiction books, movie scripts. Will consider these areas of nonfiction: health, nutrition, exercise, sports, psychology, new science and new age, crafts, women's studies, business expertise, pregnancy and parenting, alternative health concepts, contemporary celebrity biographies, a very limited selection of the top children's book authors. Query with sample chapters. Will report in 2 weeks on queries; 2 months on mss.
Recent Sales: *The Save Your Business Book*, by John Goldhammer, CPA (Macmillan Publishing); *Silly Sally*, by Audery Wood (Harcourt Brace Jovanovich); *Beyond the Hero*, by Allen Chinnen, M.D. (Jeremy P. Tarcher); *The Art of Creative Thinking*, by Wilferd Peterson (Hay House); *Nontoxic Baby Care Secrets*, by Louis M. Pottkotter, M.D. (Contemporary Books).
Terms: Agent receives 15% commission on domestic sales; 25% on foreign sales, "if foreign agent used; if sold directly, it is 15%." Offers a written contract, which is binding for 1 year.
Fees: Does not charge a reading fee. "We provide consultant services to authors who need assistance in negotiating their contracts. Charge is $125/hour and no commission charges (10% of our business). Charges for actual expense for telephone, postage, packing, photocopying. We provide copies of each publisher submission letter and the publisher's response." 90% of business is derived from commission on ms sales.
Writers' Conferences: Attends Santa Barbara City College Annual Writer's Workshop; Pasadena City College Writer's Forum; UCLA Symposiums on Writing Nonfiction Books.
Tips: Obtains new clients through "referrals from present clients and industry sources as well as mail queries. Take time to write an informative query letter expressing your book idea, the market for it, your qualifications to write the book, the 'hook' that would make a potential reader buy the book. Always enclose SASE, compare your book to others on similar subjects and show how it is original."

INDEPENDENT PUBLISHING AGENCY (I), Box 176, Southport CT 06490. (203)268-4878. Contact: Henry Berry. Estab. 1990. Represents 25 clients. 30% of clients are new/previously unpublished writers. Especially interested in topical nonfiction (historical, political, social topics) and literary fiction. Currently handles: 50% nonfiction books; 10% juvenile books; 20% novels; 20% short story collections.
Handles: Nonfiction books, juvenile books, novels, short story collections. Will consider these nonfiction areas: anthropology/archaeology; art/architecture/design; biography/autobiography; business; child guidance/parenting; cooking/food/nutrition; crafts/hobbies; current affairs; ethnic/cultural interests; government/politics/law; history; juvenile nonfiction; language/literature/criticism; military/war; money/finance/economics; music/dance/theater/film; nature/environment; photography; psychology; religious; true crime/investigative; science/technology; self-help/personal improvement; sociology; sports; women's issues/women's studies. Will consider these fiction areas: action/adventure; cartoon/comic; confessional; contemporary issues; crime; erotica; ethnic; experimental; fantasy; feminist; historical; humor/satire; juvenile; literary; mainstream; mystery/suspense; picture book; psychic/supernatural; thriller/espionage; young adult. Will consider outline/proposal but prefers synopsis outline plus 2 sample chapters. Reports in 2 weeks on queries; 4-6 weeks on mss.
Terms: Agent receives 15% commission on domestic sales; 20% on foreign sales. Offers "agreement that spells out author-agent relationship."
Fees: Does not charge a reading fee. Offers a criticism service if requested. Charges average $1/page, with $50 minimum for poetry and stories; $100 minimum for novels and nonfiction. Written critique averages 3 pages—includes critique of the material, suggestions on how to make it marketable and advice on marketing it. Charges for postage, photocopying and U.P.S. mailing, legal fees (if necessary).

All expenses over $25 cleared with client. 90% of business is derived from commissions on ms sales; 10% derived from reading fees or criticism services.
Tips: Usually obtains new clients through referrals from clients, notices in writer's publications. Looks for "proposal or chapters professionally presented, with clarification of the distinctiveness of the project and grasp of intended readership."

*GARY F. IORIO, ESQ. (I,II), 3530-47 Long Beach Rd., Oceanside NY 11572. (516)536-5152. Contact: Gary Iorio. Estab. 1990. Represents less than 10 clients. Currently handles 10% nonfiction books; 40% novels; 10% short story collections; 40% movie scripts.
Handles: Nonfiction books, novels, novellas, short story collections, movie scripts, stage plays, TV scripts (includes scripts and treatments for TV documentaries). Will consider these nonfiction areas: biography/autobiography; business; government/politics/law; history; military/war; money/finance/economics; true crime/investigative; sociology; sports. Will consider these fiction areas: action/adventure; contemporary issues; detective/police/crime; erotica; experimental; fantasy; historical; literary; mainstream; mystery/suspense; science fiction; sports; thriller/espionage; westerns/frontier. Query with outline plus 3 sample chapters. Will report in 3 weeks on queries; 3 months on mss.
Terms: Agent receives 15% commission on domestic sales; 20% on foreign sales. Offers a written contract.
Fees: Charges a reading fee only for short story collections. Fee schedule will be negotiated in writing in response to a query. "I will critique short stories and/or collections myself for the reading fee. There are no other reading fees charged for other materials." Charges for postage, photocopying and charges directly related to the marketing of the writer's work. 95% of business is derived from commissions on ms sales; 5% from reading or critique fees. Payment of the reading fee ensures agency representation, "because reading/criticism fee is part of the contract of representation."
Tips: "I am an attorney who also graduated from the Iowa Writers' Workshop in 1976. I have obtained all my clients to date from either my law practice or from Iowa associates."

‡CAROLYN JENKS AGENCY (II), 205 Walden St., Cambridge MA 02140. (617)876-6927. Contact: Carolyn Jenks. Estab. 1966. Represents 45 clients. Currently handles: 25% nonfiction books; 75% fiction.
Handles: Nonfiction books and novels. Will consider all nonfiction and fiction areas. Query with SASE.
Terms: Agent receives 15% commission on domestic sales. Offers written contract, binding for 3 years.
Fees: Charges $60 reading fee but no critique of novel. "May offer suggestions or resources for editorial help."
Tips: Usually obtains new clients through referrals. "I prefer projects that have a potential film or TV sale. I was the agent who first introduced Avery Corman ("Kramer vs Kramer"); Joan Micklin Silver (who later directed Hester Street); and Spike Lee's father."

*JLM LITERARY AGENTS (III), Suite L, 17221 E. 17th St., Santa Ana CA 92701. (714)547-4870. Fax: (714)840-5660. Contact: Judy Semler. Estab. 1985. Represents 35 clients. 30% of clients are new/previously unpublished writers. Agency is "generalist with an affinity for high-quality, self-help psychology and mystery/suspense." Currently handles: 90% nonfiction books; 10% novels.
Handles: Nonfiction books, novels. Will consider these nonfiction areas: biography/autobiography; current affairs; nature/environment; psychology; religious/inspirational; true crime/investigative; self-help/personal improvement; sociology; women's issues/women's studies. Will consider these fiction areas: glitz; mystery/suspense; psychic/supernatural; contemporary romance. Send an outline with 2 sample chapters for nonfiction, query with 3 chapters for fiction—except for mystery/suspense, send entire ms. Will report in 1 month on queries; 8-10 weeks on mss.

Agents ranked I-IV are actively seeking new clients. Those ranked V or those who prefer not to be listed have been included to inform you they are not currently looking for new clients.

Recent Sales: *Interrupted Lives: Women Experiencing Breast Cancer*, by Kathy Latour (Morrow); *The Shame Trap*, by Christine Evans (Ballentine).

Terms: Agent receives 15% commission on domestic sales; 10% on foreign sales plus 15% to subagent. Offers a written contract, binding for 1 year.

Fees: Does not charge a reading fee. Does not do critiques, but will refer to freelancers. Charges $150 marketing fee for unpublished authors or to authors changing genres. Charges for routine office expenses associated with the marketing. 100% of business is derived from commissions on manuscript sales.

Tips: "Most of my clients are referred to me by other clients or editors. If you want to be successful, learn all you can about proper submission and invest in the equipment or service to make your project *look* dazzling. Computers are available to everyone and the competition looks good. You must at least match that to even get noticed."

LARRY KALTMAN LITERARY AGENCY (II), 1301 S. Scott St., Arlington VA 22204. (703)920-3771. Contact: Larry Kaltman. Estab. 1984. Represents 15 clients. 75% of clients are new/previously unpublished writers. Currently handles: 10% nonfiction books; 75% novels; 10% novellas; 5% short story collections.

Handles: Nonfiction books, novels, novellas, short story collections. Will consider these nonfiction areas: health/medicine; science/technology; self-help/personal improvement; sports. Will consider these fiction areas: action/adventure; confessional; contemporary issues; detective/police/crime; erotica; ethnic; humor/satire; literary; mainstream; mystery/suspense; romance (contemporary); sports; thriller/espionage; young adult. Query. Will report in 1 week on queries; 2 weeks on mss.

Recent Sales: *A Well-Behaved Little Boy*, by Tom Smith (STARbooks Press); *The Presidential Watering Hole*, by Carolyn Caldwell (Atrocity); *A Year of Favor*, by Julia MacDonnell (Morrow).

Terms: Agent receives 15% commission on domestic sales; 25% on foreign sales. Offers a written contract, binding for 1 year.

Fees: Charges a reading fee "for all unsolicited manuscripts; for up to 300 pages, the fee is $250. For each additional page the charge is 50¢/page. The criticism and reading services are indistinguishable. Author receives an approximately 1,500-word report commenting on writing quality, structure and organization and estimate of marketability. I write all critiques." Charges for postage, mailing envelopes and long-distance phone calls.

Writers' Conferences: Attends Washington Independent Writers Spring Conference.

Tips: Obtains new clients through query letters, solicitation. "Plots, synopses and outlines have very little effect. A sample of the writing is the most significant factor. I also sponsor the Washington Prize for Fiction, an annual competition for unpublished works." Awards: $2,000 (1st prize), $1,000 (2nd prize), $500 (3rd prize).

*J. KELLOCK & ASSOCIATES LTD. (II), 11017 80th Ave., Edmonton, Alberta T6G 0R2 Canada. (403)433-0274. Contact: Joanne Kellock. Estab. 1981. Member of Writer's Guild of Alberta. Represents 50 clients. 10% of clients are new/previously unpublished writers. "I do very well with all works for children; adult fiction (all genre and literary); serious nonfiction." Currently handles: 20% nonfiction books; 5% scholarly books; 50% juvenile books; 25% novels.

Handles: Nonfiction, scholarly and juvenile books and novels. Will consider these nonfiction areas: animals; anthropology/archaeology; art/architecture/design; biography/autobiography; business; child guidance/parenting; cooking/food/nutrition; current affairs; government/politics/law; health/medicine; history; juvenile nonfiction; language/literature/criticism; money/finance/economics; music/dance/theater/film; nature/environment; new age/metaphysics; true crime/investigative; self-help/personal improvement; sports; women's issues/women's studies. Will consider these fiction areas: action/adventure; contemporary issues; detective/police/crime; ethnic; experimental; family saga; fantasy; feminist; glitz; historical; humor/satire; juvenile; literary; mainstream; mystery/suspense; picture book; psychic/supernatural; romance; science fiction; sports; thriller/espionage; westerns/frontier; young adult; horror. Query with outline plus 3 sample chapters. Will report in 6 weeks on queries; 3 months on mss.

Recent Sales: *Trail Of The Black Moon*, by Frank Pesando (New American Library); *Hunters Of The Dark Hills* and *The Gift/Picture Book*, by Aliana Brodmann-Menkes (Simon & Schuster); *A Parent's Guide To Children's Allergies*, by Jackie Webber (Prentice-Hall/Canada).

Terms: Agent receives 15% commission on domestic sales (English language); 20% on foreign sales. Offers a written contract, binding for 3 years.

Fees: Charges $85 reading fee. "Fee under no circumstances is refundable. *New writers only are charged.* $75 (U.S.) to read three chapters plus brief synopsis of any work; $60 for children's picture book material. If style is working with subject, the balance is read free of charge. Criticism is also provided for the fee. If style is not working with the subject, I explain why not; if talent is obvious, I explain how to make the manuscript work. I either do critiques myself or my reader does them. Critiques concern themselves with use of language, theme, plotting—all the usual. Return postage is always required. I cannot mail to the U.S. with U.S. postage so always enclose a self-addressed envelope, plus either international postage or cash. Canadian postage is more expensive, so double the amount for either international or cash. I do not return on-spec long-distance calls, if the writer chooses to telephone, please request that I return the call collect. However, a query letter is much more appropriate." 75% of business is derived from commissions on ms sales; 25% is derived from reading fees or criticism service. Payment of criticism fee does not ensure representation.

Tips: Obtains new clients through recommendations from others. "Do not send first drafts. Always double space. Very brief outlines and synopsis are more likely to be read first. For the picture book writer, the toughest sale to make in the business, please study the market before putting pen to paper. All works written for children must fit into the proper age groups regarding length of story, vocabulary level. For writers of the genre novel, read hundreds of books in the genre you've chosen to write, first. In other words, know your competition. Follow the rules of the genre exactly. For writers of science fiction/fantasy and the mystery, it is important a new writer has many more than one such book in him/her. Publishers are not willing today to buy single books in most areas of genre. Publishers who buy Sci/Fi/Fantasy usually want a two/three book deal at the beginning."

*NATASHA KERN LITERARY AGENCY (II), P.O. Box 2908, Portland OR 97208-2908. (503)297-6190. Contact: Natasha Kern. Estab. 1986. Member of AAR. Specializes in literary and commercial fiction and nonfiction.

Handles: Nonfiction books, novels. Will consider these nonfiction areas: biography/autobiography; business; child guidance/parenting; cooking/food/nutrition; current affairs; health/medicine; psychology; science/technology; self-help/personal improvement; women's issues/women's studies. Will consider these fiction areas: action/adventure; historical; mainstream; mystery/suspense; romance; thriller/espionage; westerns/frontier; young adult. "Send a detailed, one-page query with an SASE, including the submission history, writing credits and information about how complete the project is. For fiction, send a two- or three-page synopsis, a one-paragraph precis in addition to the first three chapters. Also send a blurb about the author and information about the length of the manuscript. For category fiction, a 5-10-page synopsis should be sent with the chapters. For children's books, send the entire manuscript if it is a picture book. Do not send illustrations." Will report in 5-6 weeks on queries.

Recent Sales: *Spandau Phoenix*, by Greg Iles (Penguin USA).

Terms: Agent receives 15% commission on domestic sales; 20% on foreign sales.

Fees: Charges $45 reading fee for new authors. "When your work is sold, your fee will be credited to your account."

Writers' Conference: Attends RWA National Conference; Santa Barbara Writer's Conference; Golden Triangle Writer's Conference.

‡KEYSER LITERARY AGENCY (II), 663 Hollywood Ave., Salt Lake City UT 84105. "We communicate only by U.S. mail, UPS or Fax." Fax: (801)487-9254. Contact: John O. Keyser. Estab. 1987. Represents 35 clients. 50% of clients are new/unpublished writers. Specializes in "adult mss written by Ph.D's, or college graduates at any level. Also highly specialized in religious Christian texts, New Age and science fiction." Currently handles 27% nonfiction books; 12% scholarly books; 5% textbooks; 12% juvenile books; 27% novels; 5% novellas; 10% short story collections; 2% TV scripts. Member agents: John O. Keyser (40 yrs. experience teaching at university level and has written religious and scientific texts); Grace R. Keyser (women authors and women's studies).

Handles: Nonfiction books; textbooks; scholarly books; juvenile books; novels; short story collections; TV scripts. Will consider these nonfiction areas: biography/autobiography; current affairs; ethnic/cultural interests; politics; history; language/literature/criticism; new age/metaphysics; psychology; religious/inspirational; science/technology; sociology; women's issues/women's studies. Will consider these fiction areas: action/adventure; contemporary issues; ethnic; experimental; family saga; fantasy; feminist; historical; humor/satire; literary; mainstream; psychic/supernatural; regional; religious/inspiration; historical romance; science fiction with hard science; westerns/frontier; medieval. Send entire ms. Will report in 1 week on queries; 1 month on mss. "After 30 days on query—look for another agent."

Recent Sales: *Merlin, Wizard of the Dark Ages*, by Norman L. Koch (Winston/Derek).
Terms: Agent receives 15% commission on domestic sales; 20% on foreign sales. Offers written contract, "two-year initial term unless terminated by either party with 30 day written notice."
Fees: Charges for editing service—$5 per hour per ms for correcting spelling, syntax, mechanics of ms and overall structure and content. Critique includes "honest overall appraisal with regard to quality and content, in consultation with the author to determine if needed." Submission fee for presenting ms to publisher ranging from $25-40 depending on size of ms. 25% of business derived from commissions on ms sales; 75% derived from reading fees or criticism services. Criticism fee ensures representation "after editing by agency."
Tips: Obtains new clients by literary agency listing in various publications. "Agency wants mss written by adults only—no juvenile clients. Also, we are highly knowledgeable about literary awards, as well as literary prizes and contests which we keep up on and continually study. We welcome established/published writers who seek an improved human writer/agent relationship and also unpublished authors who believe in quality. We *do* read unsolicited mss. Definitely *no lesbian, gay, or porno mss*. We want to engender strong author-agent relationship. We also solicit writers who are producing 'series' books. We are in touch with such publishers and book creators—a popular trend today."

‡**LAW OFFICES OF ROBERT L. FENTON PC**, #390, 31800 Northwestern Hwy., Farmington Hills MI 48334. (313)855-8780. Fax: (313)855-3302. Contact: Robert L. Fenton. Estab. 1960. Represents 25 clients. 25% of clients are new/previously unpublished writers. Currently handles: 20% nonfiction books; 50% novels; 15% movie scripts; 15% TV scripts.
Handles: Nonfiction books, novels, movie and TV scripts. Will consider these nonfiction areas: biography/autobiography; business; child guidance/parenting; current affairs; government/politics/law; military/war; money/finance/economics; music/dance/theater/film; religious/inspirational; true crime/investigative; self-help/personal improvement; sports; women's issues/women's studies. Will consider these fiction areas: action/adventure; contemporary issues; detective/police/crime; glitz; humor/satire; mystery/suspense; romance; science fiction; sports; thriller/espionage; westerns/frontier. Send 3 or 4 sample chapters (approximately 75 pages). Will report in 2 weeks on queries.
Recent Sales: *Black Tie Only*, by Julia Fenton (Contemporary Books); *Clash of Eagles*, by Leo Rutman (Fawcett); *Blue Orchids*, by Julia Fenton (Berkley).
Terms: Agent receives 15% on domestic sales. Offers a written contract, binding for 1 year.
Fees: Charges a reading fee. "To waive reading fee, author must have been published at least three times by a mainline New York publishing house." Criticism service: $350. Charges for office expenses, postage, photocopying, etc. 75% of business is derived from commissions on ms sales; 25% derived from reading fees or criticism service. Payment of a criticism fee does not ensure representation.
Tips: Obtains new clients through recommendations from others, individual inquiry.

‡**LEE SHORE AGENCY (II)**, 440 Friday Rd., The Sterling Building, Pittsburgh PA 15209. (412)821-0440. Fax: (412)821-6099. Owner: Cynthia Sterling. Estab. 1988. Represents 46 clients. 50% of clients are new/unpublished writers "who have a strong desire to publish and a serious and professional approach to their work." We prefer to handle self-help, how-to, textbooks, quality mainstream fiction, military and genre. Please do not send children's or poetry. Currently handles: 20% self-help, 20% New Age, 50% novels, 10% young adult.
Handles: Young adult, nonfiction and mass market fiction. Query with outline. Reports on query in 1 week; 6 weeks on mss.
Recent Sales: *A Cross Burns Brightly: The Mel Blount Story*, screenplay, (The Landsburg Company); *Within Hollering Distance*, by Jane Farrell (Decje Novine); *Spirits in Exile*, by Diana Kwiatkowski Rubin (Decje Novine).
Terms: Agent receives 15% commission on domestic sales; 15% on dramatic sales; 20% on foreign sales.
Fees: Charges a reading fee for proposal and first 100-150 pages; 10% of income derived from reading fees. No additional reading fee once the balance of manuscript is requested. Charges for standard expenses.

LIGHTHOUSE LITERARY AGENCY (II), P.O. Box 2105, Winter Park FL 32740. (407)831-3813. Contact: Sandra Kangas. Estab. 1988. Member of WIF, Authors Guild, ABA. Represents 50 clients. 54% of clients are new/previously unpublished writers. Specializes in fiction and nonfiction adult books. Currently handles: 27% nonfiction books; 15% juvenile books; 37% novels; 3% novellas; 3% poetry books; 4% short story collections; 10% movie scripts; 1% humor.

Handles: Nonfiction, juvenile books, novels, novellas, short story collections, poetry books, movie scripts. Will consider these nonfiction areas: agriculture/horticulture; animals; anthropology/archaeology; art/architecture/design; biography/autobiography; business; child guidance/parenting; computers/electronics; cooking/food/nutrition; crafts/hobbies; current affairs; ethnic/cultural interest; health/medicine; history; interior design/decorating; juvenile nonfiction; military/war; money/finance/economics; music/dance/theater/film; nature/environment; photography; psychology; self-help/personal improvement; sports; women's issues/women's studies. Will consider these fiction areas: action/adventure; cartoon/comic; contemporary issues; detective/police/crime; ethnic; experimental; family saga; feminist; historical; humor/satire; juvenile; literary; mainstream; mystery/suspense; picture book; regional; science fiction; sports; thriller/espionage; westerns/frontier; young adult. Query with outline plus 3 or more sample chapters for nonfiction or entire ms for fiction. Will report in 2 weeks on queries; 2 months on mss.
Terms: Agent receives 15% commission on domestic sales; 20% on foreign sales. Offers a written contract.
Fees: Charges $60 reading fee. "Waived for recent/trade published authors. Fee is applied toward marketing expenses if author is accepted as client. Criticism service: $1 per manuscript page, minimum $200. Longer works may be discounted. Critiques are done by writers who have been published in the field they are asked to judge. Charges small marketing fee. Covers all normal marketing expenses such as phone, postage, domestic fax. No charge for currently, trade-published authors." 82% of business is derived from commissions on ms sales; 18% derived from reading fees or criticism services. Critique fee does not ensure representation. "If author rewrites the work, we agree to read it again at no charge, no guarantee."
Tips: Obtains new clients through professional organizations, recommendations from clients and editors. "Send a short query or cover letter with brief description of the project. Mention qualifications and experience. Say what made you decide to write it, why there's a need for it, what your book will have that others don't. Always enclose a stamped return mailer. Even if the work is accepted, we might have to return it for changes."

‡**LITERARY REPRESENTATION SOUTH (I),** P.O. Box 715, Charleston SC 29402. (803)763-2214. Fax: (803)556-4622. Contact: Lee Sexton. Estab. 1992. Represents 20 clients. 30% of clients are new/previously unpublished writers. Specializes in sci-fi fantasy; romance (historical and contemporary); mystery; action adventure. Currently handles 20% nonfiction books; 10% juvenile books; 60% novels; 10% scripts.
Handles: Nonfiction books, novels, short story collections, movie scripts, TV scripts. Will consider all nonfiction and fiction areas. Fiction: query with 3 sample chapters or 50 pages, published clips. Nonfiction: query/outline/proposal, state specific market and qualifications. Will report in 1 month on queries; 3 months on mss.
Terms: Agent receives 15% commission on domestic sales; 20% on foreign and dramatic sales.
Fees: Charges reading fee. "We read at no charge sample chapters which accompany a chapter by chapter synopsis for authors already published. A nominal fee of $25 is charged to evaluate the work of writers who have not been published by a mainstream book publisher or national/regional magazine. Fee is refundable upon the sale of ms." Charges for postage, photocopying, cables, long distance calls, messengers and purchases of books for subsidiary promotions. 80% of business derived from commissions on ms sales; 20% from reading fees or criticism services. Payment of criticism fee does not ensure representation.
Tips: Obtains new clients through recommendations from others, conferences, workshops, magazine advertisements. "Have manuscript in the final draft before querying this agency. Do not send entire manuscript. We will request full manuscript if we are interested."

‡**LITERARY/BUSINESS ASSOCIATES (II),** Suite 3, 2000 North Ivar, Hollywood CA 90068. (213)465-2630. Contact: Shelley Gross. Estab. 1980. Represents 5 clients. 90% of clients are new/previously unpublished writers. Specializes in pop psychology, philosophy, mysticism, Eastern religion, self-help, business, health, philosophy, contemporary novels. ("No fantasy or SF.") Currently handles: 40% nonfiction; 60% fiction (novels).
Recent Sales: A rock music reference book (Simon & Schuster); a novel (Avon); an anthology (Bantam).
Terms: Agent receives 15% commission on domestic sales; 20% on foreign sales. Offers a written contract, binding for 6 months.
Fees: Does not charge a reading fee. Charges $85 critique fee for manuscripts up to 300 pages, $10 each additional 50 pages. "Critique fees are 100% refundable if a sale is made." Critique consists of "detailed analysis of manuscript in terms of structure, style, characterizations, etc. and marketing

potential, plus free guidesheets for fiction or nonfiction." Charges $60 marketing fee. 50% of business is derived from commission on ms sales; 50% is derived from criticism services. Payment of a criticism fee does not ensure agency representation.
Tips: Obtains new clients through recommendations from others, solicitation.

‡MARCH MEDIA INC., Suite 256, 7003 Chadwick Dr., Brentwood TN 37027. (615)370-3148. Fax: (615)370-3148. Contact: Etta Wilson. Estab. 1989. Represents 20 clients. Specializes in juvenile authors and illustrators. Currently handles: 30% nonfiction books; 70% juvenile books.
Handles: Will consider juvenile nonfiction and fiction. Send entire ms with SASE. Will report in 1 month on ms.
Terms: Agent receives 12% commission on domestic sales, "depends on whether they are author or author/illustrator." Offers a written contract, binding for 5 years.
Fees: Does not charge a reading fee. Offers criticism service: $25 per chapter; picture book hourly rated.
Tips: Obtains new clients through contacts from having been editor. "The agent is helpful in 2 ways: 1) specific knowledge about publisher's current needs; 2) reviews and negotiates contract."

‡THE DENISE MARCIL LITERARY AGENCY (II), 685 West End Ave., New York NY 10025. (212)932-3110. Contact: Denise Marcil. Estab. 1977. Member of AAR. Represents 100 clients. 40% of clients are new/previously unpublished authors. Specializes in women's commercial fiction, how-to, self-help and business books. Currently handles: 30% nonfiction books; 70% novels.
Handles: Nonfiction books and novels. Will consider these nonfiction areas: design; business; child guidance/parenting; nutrition; health/medicine; interior design/decorating; money/finance/economics; music/dance/theater/film; nature/environment; psychology; true crime/investigative; self-help/personal improvement; women's issues/women's studies. Will consider these fiction areas: family saga; historical; romance (contemporary, historical, regency). Query with SASE *only*! Will report in 2-3 weeks on queries; "we do not read unsolicited mss."
Recent Sales: *Pulling Ahead of the Pack: The Fine Art of Motivating Everyone*; by Saul Gellerman (Dutton); *The Baby Book*, by William Sears, M.D. and Martha Sears, R.N. (Little Brown); *Song of the Wolf*, by Rosanne Bittner (Bantam).
Terms: Agent receives 15% commission on domestic sales; 20% on foreign sales. Offers a written contract, binding for 2 years.
Fees: Charges $45 reading fee for 3 chapters and outline "that we request only." Charges $100 per year for postage, photocopying, long-distance calls, etc. 99.9% of business is derived from commissions on ms sales; .1% is derived from reading fees and criticism.
Writers' Conferences: Attends University of Texas Conference at Dallas.
Tips: Obtains new clients through recommendations from other authors and "35% of my list is from query letters! Only send a one-page query letter. I read them all and ask for plenty of material. I find many of my clients this way and *always* send SASE."

*THE EVAN MARSHALL AGENCY (III), Suite 216, 22 S. Park St., Montclair NJ 07042. (201)744-1661. Fax: (201)744-6312. Contact: Evan Marshall. Estab. 1987. Member of AAR and Romance Writers of America. Currently handles: 48% nonfiction books; 48% novels; 2% movie scripts; 2% TV scripts.
Handles: Nonfiction books; novels; movie scripts. Will consider these nonfiction areas: biography/autobiography; business; child guidance/parenting; cooking/food/nutrition; current affairs; government/politics/law; health/medicine; history; interior design/decorating; money/finance/economics; music/dance/theater/film; new age/metaphysics; psychology; true crime/investigative; self-help/personal improvement. Will consider these fiction areas: action/adventure; contemporary issues; detective/police/crime; family saga; glitz; historical; mainstream; mystery/suspense; psychic/supernatural; romance; thriller/espionage. Query. Will report in 1 week on queries; 2 months on mss.
Terms: Agent receives 15% on domestic sales; 20% on foreign sales. Offers written contract.
Fees: Charges a fee to consider for representation material by *writers who have not sold a book or script*: "Send SASE for fee schedule. There is no fee if referred by a client or an editor or if you are already published in the genre of your submission."

 The double dagger before a listing indicates the listing is new in this edition.

Tips: Obtains many new clients through referrals from clients and editors.

*SCOTT MEREDITH, INC. (II), 845 3rd Ave., New York NY 10022. (212)245-5500. Fax: (212)755-2972. Vice President and Editorial Director: Jack Scovil. Estab. 1946. Represents 2,000 clients. 10% of clients are new/unpublished writers. "We'll represent on a straight commission basis writers who've sold one or more recent books to major publishers, or several (three or four) magazine pieces to major magazines, or a screenplay or teleplay to a major producer. We're a very large agency (staff of 51) and handle all types of material except individual cartoons or drawings, though we will handle collections of these as well." Currently handles 5% magazine articles; 5% magazine fiction; 23% nonfiction books; 23% novels; 5% textbooks; 10% juvenile books; 5% movie scripts; 2% radio scripts; 2% stage plays; 5% TV scripts; 5% syndicated material; 5% poetry.
Handles: Magazine articles, magazine fiction, nonfiction books, novels, textbooks, juvenile books, movie scripts, radio scripts, stage plays, TV scripts, syndicated material and poetry. Query with outline or entire manuscript. Reports in 2 weeks.
Recent Sales: *Murder at the Kennedy Center*, by Margaret Truman (Random House); *Rendezvous with Rama II*, by Arthur C. Clarke (Bantam Books); *Stand Up!*, by Roseanne Barr (Harper & Row).
Terms: Agent receives 10% commission on domestic sales; 10% on dramatic sales; 20% on foreign sales.
Fees: Charges "a single fee which covers multiple readers, revision assistance or critique as needed. When a script is returned as irreparably unsalable, the accompanying letter of explanation will usually run 2 single-spaced pages minimum on short stories or articles, or from 4-10 single-spaced pages on book-length manuscripts, teleplays or screenplays. All reports are done by agents on full-time staff. No marketing advice is included, since, if it's salable, we'll market and sell it ourselves." 90% of business is derived from commission on ms sales; 10% is derived from fees.

*MEWS BOOKS LTD., 20 Bluewater Hill, Westport CT 06880. (203)227-1836. Fax: (203)227-1144. Contact: Sidney B. Kramer. Estab. 1972. Represents 35 clients. Prefers to work with published/established authors; works with small number of new/unpublished authors "producing professional work." Specializes in juvenile (pre-school through young adult), cookery, self-help, adult nonfiction and fiction, technical and medical. Currently handles 20% nonfiction; 20% novels; 50% juvenile books; 10% miscellaneous. Member agents: Fran Pollak (assistant).
Handles: Nonfiction books, novels, juvenile books, character merchandising and video use of illustrated published books. Will read unsolicited queries which include a precis, outline, character description and a few pages of writing sample and author's bio.
Terms: Agent receives 10% commission for published, 15% for unpublished authors; 20% foreign sales.
Fees: Does not charge a reading fee. "If material is accepted, agency asks for $350 circulation fee (4-5 publishers), which will be applied against commissions (waived for published authors)." Charges for photocopying, postage expenses, telephone calls and other direct costs.
Tips: "Principle agent is an attorney and former publisher. Offers consultation service through which writers can get advice on a contract or on publishing problems."

‡*DAVID H. MORGAN LITERARY AGENCY, INC. (II), P.O. Box 14810, Richmond VA 23221. (804)672-2740. Contact: David Morgan or Katherine Morgan. Estab. 1987. Represents 25-30 clients. Currently handles: 70% nonfiction; 30% novels.
Handles: Nonfiction, novels. Will consider all nonfiction and fiction areas. Query with SASE. Will report in 1 week on queries.
Recent Sales: *The Love Your Heart Guide for the 1990s*, by Lee Belshin (Contemporary); *Prophecies & Predictions: Everyone's Guide to the Coming Changes*, by Moira Timms Valentine.
Terms: Agent receives 15% commission on domestic sales; 20% on foreign sales. Offers a written contract.
Fees: Charges a fee to unpublished authors. "Please query for details." Charges for postage, photocopying. 95% of business is derived from commissions on ms sales; 5% is derived from reading or criticism fees.
Tips: Obtains new clients through recommendations from others.

*BK NELSON LITERARY AGENCY & LECTURE BUREAU (II, III), 84 Woodland Rd., Pleasantville NY 10570. (914)741-1322. Fax: (914)741-1324. Contact: Bonita Nelson, John Benson or Charles Romine. Estab. 1980. Represents 52 clients. 45% of clients are new/previously unpublished writers. Specializes in business/self-help/how-to/computer books. Currently handles: 50% nonfiction books; 5% scholarly books; 5% textbooks; 20% novels; 5% movie scripts; 10% TV scripts; 5% stage plays. Member agents: Bonita Nelson (business books); John Benson (Director of Lecture Bureau); Charles Romine (novels and television scripts); Dave Donnelly (videos).

Handles: Nonfiction books, textbooks, scholarly books; novels; movie scripts; stage plays; TV scripts. Will consider these nonfiction areas: animals; anthropology/archaeology; biography/autobiography; business; child guidance/parenting; computers/electronics; cooking/food/nutrition; crafts/hobbies; current affairs; health/medicine; military/war; money/finance/economics; music/dance/theater/film; nature/environment; psychology; religious/inspirational; true cime/investigative; science/technology; self-help/personal improvement; sociology; sports; women's issues/women's studies. Will consider these fiction areas: action/adventure; contemporary issues; family saga; feminist; literary; mainstream; mystery/suspense; romance; sports; thriller/espionage. Query. Will report in 1 week on queries; 2-3 weeks on ms.

Recent Sales: *Keeping Clients Satisfied*, by Robert W. Bly (Simon & Schuster); *How To Sell A House, Co-op Or Condo*, by Amy Bly (Consumer Books); *Secrets Of Successful Speakers*, by Lillet Walters (McGraw-Hill).

Terms: Agent receives 15% on domestic sales; 10% on foreign sales. Offers a written contract, exclusive for 6 months.

Fees: Charges $325 reading fee for *new writers' material only*. "It is not refundable. We usually charge for the first reading only. The reason for charging in addition to time/expense is to determine if the writer is salable and thus a potential client."

Tips: Obtains new clients through referrals and reputation with editors. "We handle the business aspect of the literary and lecture fields. We handle careers as well as individual book projects. If the author has the ability to write and we are harmonious, success is certain to follow with us handling the selling/business."

NEW AGE WORLD SERVICES (II, IV), 62091 Valley View Circle, Joshua Tree CA 92252. (619)366-2833. Owner: Victoria Vandertuin. Estab. 1957. Member of New Age Publishing, Academy of Science Fiction, Fantasy & Horror Films and Retailing Alliance and the Institute of Mentalphysics. Represents 35 clients. 100% of clients are new/unpublished writers. Eager to work with new/unpublished writers. Specializes in all New Age fields: occult, astrology, metaphysical, yoga, U.F.O., ancient continents, para sciences, mystical, magical, beauty, political and all New Age categories in fiction and nonfiction. Writer's guidelines for #10 SASE with four first-class stamps. Currently handles 40% nonfiction books; 30% novels; 10% poetry.

Handles: Nonfiction books, novels and poetry. Query with outline or entire manuscript. Reports in 6-8 weeks.

Terms: Receives 15% commission on domestic sales; 20% on foreign sales.

Fees: Charges reading fee of $150 for 300-page, typed, double-spaced ms; reading fee waived if representing writer. Charges criticism fee of $135 for new writers (300-page ms.); 10% of income derived from criticism fees. "I personally read all manuscripts for critique or evaluation, which is typed, double-spaced with about 4 or more pages, depending on the manuscript and the service for the manuscript the author requests. If requested, marketing advice is included. We charge a representation fee if we represent the author's manuscript." Charges writer for editorial readings, compiling of query letter and synopsis, printing of same, compiling lists and mailings.

‡NEW WRITERS LITERARY PROJECT (II), Suite 277, 2809 Bird Ave., Miami FL 33133. (305)460-2254. Fax: (305)374-4754. Contact: Robert S. Catz. Estab. 1987. Represents 20 clients. 85% of clients are new/previously unpublished writers. "We specialize in new, unpublished authors." Currently handles: 70% nonfiction books; 30% novels. Member agents: Robert S. Catz, Susan R. Chalker.

Handles: Nonfiction books and novels. Will consider all areas of nonfiction. Will consider all areas of fiction. Send outline/proposal or outline plus 3 sample chapters and SASE. Will report in 3 weeks on queries; 7 weeks on mss.

An asterisk indicates those agents who only charge fees to new or previously unpublished writers or to writers only under certain conditions.

Recent Sales: *Power & Greed* by Friedman & Schwarz (Franklin-Watts); *The Thomas Rimmer Story*, by Rimmer & Morris (William Morrow).
Terms: Agent receives 15% commission on domestic sales; 20% on foreign sales. Offers written contract.
Fees: Charges reading fee. (New writers only. Fee off-set against advances and/or royalties.) 85% of business derived from commission on ms sales; 15% from reading fees or criticism services.
Tips: Obtains new clients through recommendations from others, solicitation, at conferences, etc. "A well-written, thoughtful book proposal is most helpful!"

‡**NEW WRITING AGENCY (I, II)**, Box 1812, Amherst NY 14226-1812. Estab. 1991. Presently represents few clients. 90% of clients are new/previously unpublished writers. Specializes in "nurturing and representation of new writers." Currently handles: 20% nonfiction books; 60% novels; 5% novellas; 5% poetry books; 5% short story collections; 5% other. Member agents: Richard Lynch (literary, short story, poetry); Sam Meade (science fiction, western, action/adventure); Mason Deitz.
Handles: Nonfiction books, scholarly books, novels, novellas, short story collections, poetry books, movie scripts, stage plays. Considers all areas of fiction and nonfiction. Will report in 1 week on queries; 2-3 weeks on mss. Send SASE.
Terms: Agent receives 12.5% commission on domestic sales; 17.5% on foreign sales and sub agents." Offers written contract, binding for 1 year (options).
Fees: Charges $35 for unsolicited manuscripts. Criticism service: $1/page reading/critique. "Varies for line by line edit based on sample (free to those seeking service). Also have workshops by mail. All critiques are done inhouse. At least 3 pages of single space written critique addresses content, form, writing problems, successes, and offers suggestions. (All submissions considered for representation— free re-reading for exceptional and promising manuscripts). Fees at our cost for postage, photocopying, etc., but only with consent of the writer." Payment of reading or criticism fees does not ensure representation.
Tips: "We often obtain clients from workshop or reading/critiquing service as we work to achieve proper standards in the writing. We accept only exceptional work for representation, but are willing to work with those who can take our criticism and use it in improving a text. Criticism is based on our knowledge of the market, and our replies to writers reflect marketability."

*****NORTHEAST LITERARY AGENCY (II)**, 69 Broadway, Concord NH 03301. (603)225-9162. Contact: Victor A. Levine. Estab. 1973. Represents 11 clients. 35% of clients are new/previously unpublished writers. Specializes in popular fiction, children's picture books. Currently handles 50% nonfiction books; 50% novels.
Handles: Novels, nonfiction books, juvenile books, short story collections, poetry books, movie and TV scripts. Will consider all nonfiction subjects. Will consider all fiction, especially mystery and suspense, contemporary romance and science fiction. Query. Will report in 5 days on queries; 10 days on mss.
Recent Sales: *Christmas Babies*, by Keane & Black (Pocket Books); *Spelling For Adults*, by Dixon (St. Martin's).
Terms: Agent receives 15% commission on domestic sales; 25% on foreign sales. Offers a written contract cancellable on 3-months' notice.
Fees: Charges a reading fee to unpublished writers, "refundable following a sale." Criticism service: costs depend on type of criticism and whether conducted by mail or in a seminar or workshop setting. Charges for extraordinary expenses, such as express mail, long-distance phone calls, extensive photocopying but not for marketing or ordinary office expenses.
Writers' Conferences: Underwrites Wells Writer's Workshop, which meets twice yearly in Wells Maine.
Tips: Obtains new clients through classes, workshops, conferences, advertising in *Writer's Digest*, referrals. "Please be very specific about writing background, published credits and current project(s)." Always include SASE.

NORTHWEST LITERARY SERVICES (II), 9-2845 Bellendean Rd. RR1, Shawnigan Lake, British Columbia V0R 2W0 Canada. (604)743-8236. Contact: Brent Laughren. Estab. 1986. Represents 20 clients. 75% of clients are new/previously unpublished writers. Specializes in working with new writers. Currently handles: 25% nonfiction books; 5% juvenile books; 55% novels; 10% short story collections; 2% movie scripts; 1% stage plays; 2% TV scripts.
Handles: Nonfiction books; juvenile books; novels; movie scripts; stage plays; TV scripts. Will consider these nonfiction areas: agriculture/horticulture; animals; art/architecture/design; biography/autobiography; child guidance/parenting; cooking/food/nutrition; crafts/hobbies; health/medicine; history; juve-

nile nonfiction; language/literature/criticism; music/dance/theater/film; nature/environment; new age/ metaphysics; photography; true crime/investigative; self-help/personal improvement; sports; translations; women's issues/women's studies. Will consider these fiction areas: action/adventure; confessional; contemporary issues; detective/police/crime; erotica; ethnic; experimental; family saga; fantasy; feminist; historical; humor/satire; juvenile; literary; mainstream; mystery/suspense; picture book; psychic/supernatural; regional; romance; science fiction; sports; thriller/espionage; westerns/frontier; young adult. Query with outline/proposal. Will report in 1 month on queries; 2 months on mss.
Terms: Agent receives 15% on domestic sales; 20% on foreign sales. Offers a written contract.
Fees: Does not charge a reading fee. Charges criticism fee: $100 for book outline and sample chapters up to 20,000 words. Charges 75¢-$1/page for copyediting and content editing; $1/page for proofreading; $10-20/page for research. "Other related editorial services available at negotiated rates. Critiques are 2-3 page overall evaluations, with suggestions. All fees, if charged are authorized by the writer in advance." 95% of business is derived from commissions on ms sales; 5% is derived from reading fees or criticism service. Payment of criticism fee doesn't ensure representation.
Tips: Obtains new clients through recommendations. "Northwest Literary Services is particularly interested in the development and marketing of new and unpublished writers, though not exclusively, since this can be a long-term project without monetary reward. We are also interested in literary fiction, though again not exclusively."

*OCEANIC PRESS (II), Seaview Business Park, 1030 Calle Cordillera, Unit #106, San Clemente CA 92673. (714)498-7227. Fax: (714)498-2162. Contact: Peter Carbone. Estab. 1956. Represents 25 clients. 15% of clients are new/previously unpublished writers. Specializes in celebrity interviews. Currently handles: 20% nonfiction books; 20% novels; 60% syndicated material. Member agent: Katherine Singer (child development, family relations).
Handles: Nonfiction books, novels, syndicated material, biographies. Will consider these nonfiction areas: biography/autobiography; business; child guidance/parenting; computers/electronics; health/ medicine; money/finance/economics; music/dance/theater/film; new age/metaphysics; psychology; true crime/investigative; science/technology; self-help/personal improvement; sports; women's issues/ women's studies; movies. Will consider these fiction areas: detective/police/crime; erotica; experimental; family saga; mainstream; mystery/suspense; psychic/supernatural; romance (contemporary, gothic, regency); science fiction; sports; thriller/espionage; westerns/frontier; young adult. Send outline/proposal and list of published work. Will report in 1 month on queries; 6 weeks on mss.
Terms: Agent receives 15% commission on domestic sales; 20% on foreign sales; "50% syndication only if wanted." Offers a written contract, binding for 1 year.
Fees: Charges a $250 reading fee to new writers only. Criticism service is included in reading fee. Criticism done by professional readers. 98% of business is derived from commissions on ms sales; 2% is derived from reading fees or criticism service. Payment of a criticism fee ensures representation.
Tips: Obtains new clients through recommendations. Do "good writing and good research. Study the market."

OCEANIC PRESS SERVICE, Seaview Business Park, 1030 Calle Cordillera, Unit #106, San Clemente CA 92672. (714)498-7227. Fax: (714)498-2162. Manager: Helen J. Lee. Estab. 1940. Represents 100 clients. Prefers to work with published/established authors; will work with a small number of new/ unpublished authors. Specializes in selling features of worldwide interest; romance books, mysteries, biographies, nonfiction of timeless subjects, reprints of out-of-print titles. Currently handles: 20% nonfiction books; 30% novels; 10% juvenile books; 40% syndicated material.
Handles: Magazine articles, nonfiction books, novels, juvenile books, syndicated material. Will read— at no charge—unsolicited queries and outlines. Reports in 2 weeks on queries.
Terms: Agent receives 15% commission on domestic sales; 20% on foreign sales.
Fees: Charges reading fee: $350/350 pages. Reading fee includes detailed critique. "We have authors who published many books of their own to do the reading and give a very thorough critique." 2% of income derived from reading fees.

‡ANDREA OLESHA AGENCY (I, II), P.O. Box 243, Wood Village OR 97060. (503)667-9039. Contact: Andrea Olesha. Estab. 1992. Member of Willamette Writer's. Represents 2 clients. 100% of clients are new/previously unpublished writers. Specializes in nonfiction. Currently handles: 50% nonfiction books; 50% fiction.
Handles: Nonfiction books, juvenile books, novels. Will consider these nonfiction areas: cooking/food/ nutrition; ethnic/cultural interests; gay/lesbian issues; interior design/decorating; language/literature/ criticism; music/dance/theater/film; nature/environment; self-help/personal improvement; women's is-

sues/women's studies. Will consider these fiction areas: action/adventure; contemporary issues; ethnic; experimental; family saga; fantasy; feminist; gay; glitz; humor/satire; juvenile; lesbian; literary; mainstream; mystery/suspense; psychic/supernatural; regional; religious/inspiration; science fiction; young adult. Query with sample chapters. Will report in 2 months on queries; 1 month on mss. "I do not return any material without an SASE."

Terms: Agent receives 10% commission on domestic sales; 15% on foreign sales. Offers written contract, binding for 1 year.

Fees: Charges reading fee "to new authors, refundable upon sale." Charges for postage.

Writers' Conferences: Attends Willamette Writers Conference held in Portland OR in August.

Tips: Obtains new clients through advertising and listings in literary circles. "We have the contacts."

THE PANETTIERI AGENCY (II), 142 Marcella Rd., Hampton VA 23666. (804)825-1708. Contact: Eugenia Panettieri. Estab. 1988. Member of Romance Writers of America and Horror Writers. Represents 40 clients. 20% of clients are new/previously unpublished writers. Specializes in fiction of substantial commercial value; larger women's fiction, suspense. "However, we do handle almost all types of projects." Currently handles: 10% nonfiction books; 10% juvenile books; 80% novels. Member agents: Eugenia Panettieri (women's fiction, mystery, romances, thrillers, horror); Cynthia Richey (historical and contemporary romances).

Handles: Juvenile books, novels and nonfiction books. Will consider these nonfiction areas: child guidance/parenting; health/medicine; psychology; true crime/investigative; self-help/personal improvement; women's issues/women's studies. Will consider these fiction areas: action/adventure; detective/police/crime; family saga; glitz; historical; juvenile; mainstream; mystery/suspense; psychology; true crime/investigative; self-help/personal improvement; women's issues/women's studies. Query with outline plus 3 sample chapters. Will report in 2 weeks on queries; 1 month on mss.

Recent Sales: *Traitor's Kiss*, by Joy Tucker (Avon); *Shadow Whispers*, by Wendy Haley (Zebra); *Golden Chances*, by Rebeca Lee (Berkley Homespun).

Terms: Agent receives 10% commission on domestic sales; 20% on foreign sales. Offers a written contract, binding for 1 year.

Fees: Charges a reading fee; will waive fee for published authors. $25 for partial ms and outline, no more than 75 pages; $50 for complete mss of no more than 65,000 words; $75 for complete mss of no more than 85,000 words; $100 for mss between 85-150,000 words. "Writers receive a written analysis of their work, 1-3 single-spaced pages in length, commenting on the major elements of the book and the project's salability. It is done by office agents only." 90% of business is derived from commissions on ms sales; 10% is derived from reading fees. Payment of reading fee does not ensure representation. "We offer representation based on the project's salability only. A reading fee does insure an unbiased, well-detailed evaluation of the project, with suggestions for revisions."

Writers Conferences: Romance Writers of America, Romantic Times Convention.

Tips: "Most of our clients come from normal submissions, either solicited or over-the-transom. Some are through recommendations from existing clients, but a recommendation isn't necessary to merit a thorough consideration. Because most agencies, including this one, get an enormous number of queries, we place a lot of emphasis on a quick, to-the-point cover letter or query. Show us that you've studied your market, where you think your project fits in, and whether it is complete or still 'in the works.' If your cover letter or query seems unfocused or rambles, we tend to believe the project may be the same way. First impressions can be very important! Also, don't try to overwhelm the agent with too much material. Send in a partial, at first, if you're coming in unsolicited. Often we read those first (they're less intimidating than a huge box!). Don't sweat the synopsis too much. If your chapters are great, that's what really counts. Just be sure the synopsis accurately describes the plot without loose ends or breaks. Be professional. Please don't try to 'bully' an agent to show her how much you know about the industry. An agent loves a considerate, well-mannered client, and will return your respect with her enthusiasm for you as well as your work!"

PEGASUS INTERNATIONAL, INC., LITERARY & FILM AGENTS (II), P.O. Box 5470, Winter Park FL 32793-5470. (407)831-1008. Director: Gene Lovitz. Contact: Carole Morling. Estab. 1987. Represents 300 clients. 85% of clients are new/previously unpublished writers. Specializes in "literary assistance to unpublished authors." Currently handles: 15% nonfiction books; 5% scholarly books; 5% textbooks; 5% juvenile books; 25% novels; 30% movie scripts; 10% TV scripts; 5% cookbooks. Member agents: Carole Morling (novels, creative writing, line-editing, styling and trade presentation); Gene Lovitz (biography, crime, law, health, business, film/TV, photography, firearms).

Handles: Nonfiction books, textbooks, scholarly books, juvenile books, novels, short story collections, movie scripts, TV scripts, video. Will consider these nonfiction areas: animals; anthropology/archaeology; art/architecture/design; biography/autobiography; business; child guidance/parenting; computers/electronics; cooking/food/nutrition; crafts/hobbies; current affairs; ethnic/cultural interests; government/politics/law; health/medicine; history; juvenile nonfiction; military/war; money/finance/economics; nature/environment; new age/metaphysics; photography; psychology; religious/inspirational; true crime/investigative; science/technology; self-help/personal improvement; sociology; sports; translations. Will consider these fiction areas: action/adventure; confessional; contemporary issues; detective/police/crime; erotica; ethnic; experimental; family saga; fantasy; historical; humor/satire; juvenile; literary; mainstream; mystery/suspense; picture book; psychic/supernatural; religious/inspiration; romance; science fiction; sports; thriller/espionage; westerns/frontier; young adult; horror; new age fiction. Query with outline/proposal plus 2 sample chapters. "Also call." Will report immediately on queries; 6 weeks on mss ("depending on length; it could take a little longer").
Terms: Agent receives 10% commission on domestic sales; 15% on foreign sales. Offers a written contract "at client's request," binding for 6 months to 1 year.
Fees: Charges a $200 reading fee for up to 400 double-spaced pages. "Lower fees for pamphlets, chapbooks, etc. Fees refundable upon publication. Installments acceptable. Fees apply to all clients. We have one fee only, which is all-inclusive of reading, critique, marketing and line-by-line editing. There are no hidden costs. We pay postage, phone calls, etc. to publishers. Critiques are done by our senior editor and staff. Outside content reports are often used with technical and/or nonfiction manuscripts. Critiques are delivered on an individual basis by phone or mail." 85% of business is derived from commissions on ms sales; 15% is derived from reading fees or criticism services. Payment of a criticism fee ensures representation.
Tips: Obtains new clients through queries, client referrals and publisher(s) recommendations. "Phone calls and/or written queries are equally welcomed. (Prompt global RSVP by phone.) We will read—at no charge—unsolicited queries and outlines accompanied by SASE. We do not read unsolicited manuscripts. Unpublished authors needing editorial help are welcomed. Manuscripts with high film potential need not be submitted in screenplay form, whereby we will endeavor to place with filmmakers and publishers alike at no additional fee. Once an author becomes a client, we will work as long as necessary to edit and market the material. We consider our clients as family, and work with them on a friendly one-to-one basis (usually by phone). Beginning authors should remember: 'There is no such thing as a dumb question, only unasked questions.' "

‡**WILLIAM PELL AGENCY (II),** Suite 8D, 300 E. 40th St., New York NY 10016. (212)490-2845. Contact: William Pell. Estab. 1990. Represents 6 clients. 95% of clients are new/previously unpublished writers.
Handles: Novels. Will consider this nonfiction area: photography. Will consider these fiction areas: detective/police/crime; humor/satire; thriller/espionage. Query with 2 sample chapters. Will report in 1 month on queries; 3 months on mss.
Recent Sales: *Endangered Beasties,* by Derek Pell (Dover Publishing).
Terms: Agent receives 15% commission on domestic sales; 20% on foreign sales. Offers written contract, binding for 1 year.
Fees: Charges reading fee of $100 for new writers. 90% of business is derived from commission on ms sales; 10% is derived from reading fees or criticism services. Payment of criticism fees does not ensure representation.

PENMARIN BOOKS (II), Suite L, 2171 E. Francisco Blvd., San Rafael CA 94901. (415)457-7746. Fax: (415)454-0426. President: Hal Lockwood. Editorial Director: John Painter. Estab. 1987. Represents 20 clients. 80% of clients are new/unpublished writers. "No previous publication is necessary. We do expect authoritative credentials in terms of history, politics, science and the like." Handles general trade nonfiction and illustrated books, as well as fiction.
Handles: Nonfiction books, query with outline. For fiction books, query with outline and sample chapters. Will read submissions at no charge, but may charge a criticism fee or service charge for work performed after the initial reading. Reports in 2 weeks on queries; 1 month on mss.
Recent Sales: *Kids Ending Hunger: What Can We Do?,* by Tracy and Sage Howard (Andrews & McMeel); *The American Dream Car,* by Michael Yazzolino (Motorbooks).
Terms: Agent receives 15% commission on domestic sales; 15% on dramatic sales; 15% on foreign sales.
Fees: "We normally do not provide extensive criticism as part of our reading but, for a fee, will prepare guidance for editorial development. Charges $200/300 pages. Our editorial director writes critiques. These may be 2-10 pages long. They usually include an overall evaluation and then analysis and recommendations about specific sections, organization or style."

PETERSON ASSOCIATES LITERARY AGENCY (I,II), 1651 W. Foothill Blvd. #F-335, Upland CA 91786. (714)949-0166. Contact: Lawerence Peterson, Ph.D. Estab. 1990. Represents 20 clients. 75% of clients are new/previously unpublished writers. Currently handles: 50% nonfiction books; 10% textbooks; 30% novels; 10% poetry books.
Handles: Nonfiction books, novels, poetry books. Will consider these nonfiction areas: anthropology/archaeology; business; new age/metaphysics; psychology; science/technology; self-help/personal improvement. Will consider these fiction areas: action/adventure; erotica; fantasy; humor/satire; mainstream; psychic/supernatural; science fiction; thriller/espionage. Query or send entire manuscript. Will report in 2 weeks on queries; 1 month on mss.
Terms: Agent receives 15% commission on domestic sales; 20% on foreign sales. Offers a written contract.
Fees: Charges a reading fee, refundable upon sale of work. Offers a criticism service. "Fees contingent upon amount of work and complexity of material—i.e., if research is required . . . Comprehensive writing critiques done by Lawerence Peterson." Charges for postage, photocopying, phone calls. Payment of reading or criticism fees does not ensure agency representation.
Tips: Obtains new clients through referrals and advertising.

ARTHUR PINE ASSOCIATES, INC. (III), 250 W. 57th St., New York NY 10019. (212)265-7330. Estab. 1966. Represents 100 clients. 25% of clients are new/previously unpublished writers. Specializes in fiction and nonfiction. Currently handles: 75% nonfiction; 25% novels.
Handles: Nonfiction books, novels. Will consider these nonfiction areas: business; current affairs; money/finance/economics; psychology. Will consider these fiction areas: action/adventure; detective/police/crime; family saga; literary; thriller/espionage. Send outline proposal. Will report in 3 weeks on queries. "All correspondence must be accompanied by a SASE. Will not read manuscripts before receiving a letter of inquiry."
Recent Sales: *Sunday Nights at Seven*, by Joan Benny (Warner); *The Power in You*, by Wally Amos (Donald I. Fine); *Geek Love*, by Katherine Dunne (Knopf/Warner).
Terms: Agency receives 15% commission on domestic sales; 25% on foreign sales. Offers a written contract, which varies from book to book.
Fees: Charges a reading fee based on number of words in the manuscript. Offers a criticism service. 98% of business is derived from commissions on ms sales; 2% is derived from reading fees or criticism service. Payment of a criticism fee does not ensure representation.
Tips: Obtain new clients through recommendations from others.

PMA LITERARY AND FILM MANAGEMENT, INC., (formerly The Peter Miller Agency, Inc.), Suite 501, 220 W. 19th St., New York NY 10011. (212)929-1222. Fax: (212)206-0238. President: Peter Miller. Associate Agents: Jennifer Robinson, Anthony Schneider. Estab. 1975. Represents 80 clients. 50% of clients are new/unpublished writers. Specializes in commercial fiction and nonfiction, thrillers, true crime and "fiction with *real* motion picture and television potential." Writer's guidelines for 5 × 8½ SASE and 2 first class stamps. Currently handles 50% fiction; 25% nonfiction; 25% screenplays.
Recent Sales: *Tramp Star*, by Steven Yount (Ballantine Books); *Fall of the House of Windsor*, by Nigel Blundell and Sarah Blackhall.
Handles: Fiction, nonfiction and film scripts. Will consider these nonfiction areas: history, science, biographies. Will consider these fiction areas: thrillers, adventure, suspense, horror and women's issues. Query with outline and/or sample chapters. Reports in 1 week on queries; 2-4 weeks on mss.
Terms: Agent receives 15% commission on domestic sales; 20-25% on foreign sales.
Fees: Does not charge a reading fee. Paid reading evaluation service available upon request. The evaluation, usually 4-7 pages in length, gives a detailed analysis of literary craft and commercial potential as well as further recommendations for improving the work. Charges for photocopying expenses.

JULIE POPKIN (II), #204, 15340 Albright St., Pacific Palisades CA 90272. (310)459-2834. Fax: (310)459-4128. Estab. 1989. Represents 16 clients. 33% of clients are new/unpublished writers. Specializes in selling book-length mss including fiction — all genres — and nonfiction. Especially interested in social issues. Currently handles 50% nonfiction books, 50% novels and some scripts.
Recent Sales: *Moments of Light*, by Fred Chappell (New South); *Speak out for Age*, by Grace Goldin (Third Age Press) (poetry); *Chapter and Verse*, by Joel Barr (Peregrine Smith).
Handles: Nonfiction books and novels. Will consider these nonfiction areas: how-to; self-help; history; art. Will consider these fiction areas: mainstream; literary; romance; science fiction; mystery; juvenile. Reports in 1 month on queries; 2 months on mss.

Terms: Agent receives 15% commission on domestic sales; 10% on dramatic sales; 20% on foreign sales.

Fees: Does not charge a reading fee, but may charge a criticism fee or service charge for work performed after the initial reading. Charges writers for photocopying, extraordinary mailing fees.

*SIDNEY E. PORCELAIN (II,III), 414 Leisure Loop, Milford PA 18337-9568. (717)296-6420. Manager: Sidney Porcelain. Estab. 1952. Represents 20 clients. 50% of clients are new/unpublished writers. Prefers to work with published/established authors; works with a small number of new/unpublished authors. Specializes in fiction (novels, mysteries and suspense) and nonfiction (celebrity and exposé). Currently handles: 2% magazine articles; 5% magazine fiction; 5% nonfiction books; 50% novels; 5% juvenile books; 2% movie scripts; 1% TV scripts; 30% "comments for new writers."

Handles: Magazine articles, magazine fiction, nonfiction books, novels, juvenile books. Query with outline or entire ms. Reports in 2 weeks on queries; 3 weeks on mss.

Terms: Agent receives 10% commission on domestic sales; 10% on dramatic sales; 10% on foreign sales.

Fees: Does not charge a reading fee. Offers a criticism service to new writers. 50% of income derived from commission on ms sales.

‡QCORP LITERARY AGENCY (I), P.O. Box 8, Hillsboro OR 97123-0008. (800)775-6038. Contact: William C. Brown. Estab. 1990. Represents 8 clients. 60% of clients are new/previously unpublished writers. Currently handles: 38% nonfiction books; 55% novels; 7% juvenile books. Member agent: William C. Brown.

Handles: Nonfiction books, textbooks, scholarly books, juvenile books, novels, novellas, short story collections, poetry books, movie and TV scripts, stage plays. Will consider these nonfiction areas: anthropology/archaeology; biography/autobiography; business; computers/electronics; current affairs; gay/lesbian issues; government/politics/law; history; military/war; nature/environment; new age/metaphysics; psychology; religious/inspirational; true crime/investigative; science/technology; sociology; women's issues/women's studies; physics; astronomy. "Will consider all areas of fiction, excluding cartoon/comic and picture books." Query through critique service. Reports in 2 weeks on queries; 1 month on mss.

Terms: Agent receives 10% commission on domestic sales; 20% on foreign sales. Offers written contract, binding for 6 months, automatically renewed unless cancelled by author.

Fees: Offers critique service. "No charges are made to agency authors if no sales are procured. If sales are generated, then charges are itemized and collected from proceeds up to a limit of $200, after which all expenses are absorbed by Agency." 33% of business derived from commissions on ms sales; 66% from reading fees or critique services.

Tips: Obtains new clients through recommendations from others and from critique service. "New authors should use our critique service and its free, no obligation first chapter critique to introduce themselves. Call or write for details. Our critique service is serious business, line by line and comprehensive. Established writers should call or send resume. Of interest to established writers: we often deal directly with foreign publishers. We are admittedly new but very attentive and vigorous."

D. RADLEY-REGAN & ASSOCIATES (II), P.O. Box 243, Jamestown NC 27282-0243. (919)454-5040. President and Editor: D. Radley-Regan. Estab. 1987. Eager to work with new/unpublished writers. Specializes in fiction, nonfiction, mystery, thriller. Currently handles 10% nonfiction books; 40% novels; 25% movie scripts; 25% TV scripts.

Handles: Nonfiction books, novels, movie and TV scripts. Query. Reports in 6 weeks on queries; 3-4 months on mss.

Terms: Agent receives 25% commission on domestic sales; 25% on dramatic sales; 25% on foreign sales.

Fees: Charges reading fee for full mss. Writer receives overall evaluation, marketing advice and agency service. 10% of income derived from commission on mss sales. Payment of criticism fee does not ensure that writer will be represented.

‡RHODES LITERARY AGENCY (II), P.O. Box 89133, Honolulu HI 96830-9133. (808)947-4689. Director: Fred C. Pugarelli. Agent: Ms. Angela Pugarelli. Estab. 1971. Represents 40 clients. 99% of clients are new/previously unpublished writers. Specializes in novels and screenplays. Currently handles 10% nonfiction books, 70% novels, 20% movie scripts.

Handles: Nonfiction books, textbooks, scholarly books, juvenile books, novels, novellas, short story collections, poetry books, movie scripts, stage plays, TV scripts, syndicated material. Will consider all fiction and nonfiction areas. Query or send entire ms, outline/proposal or send outline plus sample chapters. Will report in 2-4 weeks on queries; 1-2 months on mss.

Recent Sales: "No sales during past year, but over the years we have sold over 100 short stories, articles and poems to *Travel & Leisure, Mature Years, The Diners' Club Magazine* (now *Signature*), *Millionaire Magazine, The Saint Mystery Magazine, The Saint Mystery Library, 77 Sunset Strip, Men's Digest, Rascal, Opinion, Hyacinths and Biscuits* and other national periodicals."

Terms: Agent receives 15% commissions on domestic sales; 20% on foreign sales.

Fees: Charges $145 reading fee for books up to 45,000 words; $155 for books over 45,000 words; $145 for screenplays. Charges for photocopying and some unusual office expenses. 10% of business is derived from commissions on ms sales; 90% is derived from reading fees or criticism services.

Tips: Obtains new clients through listing in various market guides and recommendations. "Send a one or two-page query first with a SASE."

RIGHTS UNLIMITED (II), Suite 2D, 101 W. 55th St., New York NY 10019. (212)246-0900. Fax: (212)246-2114. Agent: B. Kurman. Estab. 1984. Represents 57 clients. Works with a small number of new/unpublished authors. Specializes in fiction and nonfiction. Currently handles 35% novels; 50% textbooks; 15% movie scripts.

Handles: Nonfiction books, novels and juvenile books. Query or send entire manuscript. Reports in 2 weeks on queries; 1 month on manuscripts.

Terms: Agent receives 15% commission on domestic sales; 15% on dramatic sales; 20% on foreign sales.

Fees: Does not charge a reading fee, but may charge a criticism fee or service charge for work performed after the initial reading.

SHERRY ROBB LITERARY PROPERTIES (III), #102, 17250 Beverly Blvd., Los Angeles CA 90036. (213)965-8780. Fax: (213)965-8784. Contact: Sherry Robb. Estab. 1982. Member of AAR. Represents 60 clients. 20% of clients are new/previously unpublished writers. Currently handles: 30% nonfiction books; 40% novels; 10% movie scripts; 20% TV scripts. Member agents: Jim Pinkston (nonfiction); Sherry Robb (TV scripts/sit com).

Handles: Novels, movie and TV scripts. Will consider these nonfiction areas: biography/autobiography; true crime/investigative. Will consider these nonfiction areas: glitz; literary; mainstream; mystery/suspense. Send outline plus 3 sample chapters. Will report in 2 weeks on queries; 2 months on mss.

Recent Sales: *Star Trek: The Technical Manual* (Pocket Books); *The James Bond Encyclopedia* (Contemporary Books); *The Godmother* (Simon & Schuster).

Terms: Agent receives 15% on domestic sales; 15% on foreign sales. Offers a written contract, binding for one year.

Fees: Does not charge a reading fee. Offers criticism service: $2 per page. "We use two editors who line edit manuscripts and give a 10-page critique at least." Charges for postage and photocopying. Payment of a criticism fee does not ensure representation.

Tips: Obtains new clients through recommendations.

RICHARD H. ROFFMAN ASSOCIATES (III), Suite 6A, 697 West End Ave., New York NY 10025. (212)749-3647/3648. President: Richard H. Roffman. Estab. 1967. 70% of clients are new/unpublished writers. Prefers to work with published/established writers. Specializes in nonfiction primarily. Currently handles: 10% magazine articles; 5% magazine fiction; 5% textbooks; 5% juvenile books; 5% radio scripts; 5% movie scripts; 5% TV scripts; 5% syndicated material; 5% poetry; 50% other.

If you're looking for a particular agent, check the Agents and Reps Index to find at which agency the agent works. Then look up the listing for that agency in the appropriate section.

Handles: Nonfiction books. Query only. Does not read unsolicited mss. Reports in 2 weeks. "SASE if written answer requested, please."
Terms: Agent receives 10% commission on domestic sales; 10% on dramatic sales; 10% on foreign sales.
Fees: "We do not read material (for a fee) actually, only on special occasions. We prefer to refer to other people specializing in that." 10% of income derived from reading fees. "We suggest a moderate monthly retainer." Charges for mailings, phone calls, photocopying and messenger service. Offers consultation service through which writers can get advice on a contract. "I am also an attorney at law."

‡RUSSELL-SIMENAUER LITERARY AGENCY INC. (II). 14 Capron Lane, Upper Montclair NJ 07043. (201)746-0539. Fax: (201)746-0754. Contact: Jacqueline Simenauer or Margaret Russell. Estab. 1990. Member of Author's Guild, Authors League, National Association Science Writers. Represents 35 clients. 75% of clients are new/previously unpublished writers. Specializes in psychiatry/psychology, self-help, how-to, human sexuality. Currently handles 77% nonfiction books, 5% juvenile books, 10% novels, 3% movie scripts, 5% TV scripts. Member agents: Jacqueline Simenauer, (manuscript/outline critiques); Margaret Russell, (restructuring, editing, rewriting, ghosting, ms appraisal).
Handles: Nonfiction books, juvenile books, novels, movie scripts, TV scripts. Will consider these nonfiction areas: child guidance/parenting; health/medicine; juvenile nonfiction; money/finance/economics; psychology; religious/inspirational; true crime/investigative; self-help/personal improvement; sociology; women's issues/women's studies; human sexuality; psychiatry. Will consider these fiction areas: detective/police/crime; family saga; feminist; juvenile; mainstream; mystery/suspense; psychic/supernatural; romance (contemporary); thriller/espionage. Query with outline/proposal. Will report in 2-3 weeks on queries; 3-4 weeks on mss.
Terms: Agent receives 15% commission on domestic sales; 25% on foreign sales.
Fees: There is no charge for reading an outline/proposal which will consist of a critique of editorial content and analysis of effectiveness. If a client, however, wants a complete manuscript critique, the fee is $1.25/page. Criticism service involves analysis of originality of ideas (marketability), effectiveness, organization of information and writing. There are no fees for published writers. Charges for postage, photocopying, phone, fax, if sale is made. 90% of business is derived from commissions on ms sales; 10% is derived from reading fees or criticism services.
Tips: Obtains new clients through recommendations from others; advertising in various journals, newsletters, etc. and professional conferences.

*THE SUSAN SCHULMAN LITERARY AGENCY, INC., 454 W. 44th St., New York NY 10036. (212)713-1633/4/5. Fax: (212)586-8830. President: Susan Schulman. Estab. 1978. Member of AAR. 10-15% of clients are new/unpublished writers. Prefers to work with published/established authors; works with a small number of new/unpublished authors. Currently handles: 50% nonfiction books; 40% novels; 10% stage plays.
Handles: Nonfiction, fiction and plays, especially genre fiction such as mysteries. Query with outline. Reports in 2 weeks on queries; 6 weeks on mss. SASE required.
Recent Sales: *Beauty*, by Brian D'Amato (Delacorte); *Sorrowheart*, by M.K. Lorens (Bantam Doubleday Dell); *Red Bride*, by Christopher Fowler(Rock at Penguin USA).
Terms: Agent receives 15% commission on domestic sales; 10-20% on dramatic sales; and 7½-10% on foreign sales (plus 7½-10% to co-agent).
Fees: Charges a $50 reading fee if detailed analysis requested; fee will be waived if representing the writer. Less than 1% of income derived from reading fees. Charges for foreign mail, special messenger or delivery services.

*SEBASTIAN LITERARY AGENCY (III), Suite 708, 333 Kearny St., San Francisco CA 94108. (415)391-2331. Fax: (415)391-2377. Owner Agent: Laurie Harper. Assoc.: Jan Johnson. Estab. 1985. Represents approximately 50 clients. Specializes in psychology, sociology and business. Currently handles: 75% nonfiction books; 25% fiction (novels).
Handles: Nonfiction books, novels. "No children's or YA." Will consider these nonfiction areas: anthropology/archaeology; art/architecture/design; biography/autobiography; business; child guidance/parenting; computers/electronics; current affairs; ethnic/cultural interests; government/politics/law; health/medicine; history; military/war; money/finance/economics; nature/environment; psychology; true crime/investigative; science/technology; self-help/personal improvement; sociology; sports; women's issues/women's studies. Will consider these fiction areas: contemporary issues; detective/police/crime; ethnic; family saga; gay; glitz; historical; literary; mainstream; mystery/suspense; thriller/

espionage; westerns/frontier. Query with outline plus 3 sample chapters and author bio. Will report in 3 weeks on queries; 4-6 weeks on mss.

Recent Sales: *The Book of BE Attitudes*, by Bob Baumann (Putnam/Perigee); *Making Love Stay*, by Peggy and James Vaughan (Lowell House/RGA); *Malkah and Her Children*, by Marjorie Edelson (Ballantine).

Terms: Agent receives 15% commission on domestic sales; 20% on foreign sales. Offers a written contract.

Fees: Charges a $100 annual administration fee for clients and charges for photocopies of manuscript for submission to publisher. No reading fees.

Tips: Obtains new clients through "referrals from authors and editors, some at conferences and some from unsolicited queries from around the country. If interested in agency representation, for *fiction*, "know the category that your novel belongs in, according to market study, and be sure that you have made it conforming to that category. Too many novels fall in-between categories, and are unsalable as a result. For *nonfiction*, it is important to convey more than the facts and statistics about the subject of your book—you need to convey its *relevance* to us, and your fascination or enthusiasm for it."

‡SHOESTRING PRESS (I), Box 1223, Main Post Office, Edmonton, Alberta T5J 2M4 Canada. Contact: Carolyn. Estab. 1991. Represents 5 clients. 40% of clients are new/previously unpublished writers. Currently handles 30% nonfiction books; 50% scholarly books; 20% novellas.

Handles: Nonfiction books, scholarly books, novels, novellas, poetry books. Will consider these nonfiction areas: biography/autobiography; government/politics/law; history; military/war; new age/metaphysics; religious/inspirational; science/technology. Will consider these fiction areas: action/adventure; literary; science fiction; espionage; westerns. Query or send entire ms, outline/proposal. Include SASE. Will report in 3 months on mss.

Terms: Offer written contract, binding for 2-5 years.

Fees: Fees are "very situational. We get a lot of junk." Charges for postage, photocopying, "but depends on client." 90% of business is derived from commissions on ms sales; 10% is derived from reading fees or criticism services.

Tips: Obtains new business through recommendations from others. "We respond slowly."

SINGER MEDIA CORPORATION (III), Seaview Business Park, 1030 Calle Cordillera, Unit #106, San Clemente CA 92672. (714)498-7227. Fax: (714)498-2162. Contact: Kurt Singer. Estab. 1940. Represents 100+ clients for books, features, cartoons. 15% of clients are new/previously unpublished writers. Specializes in romance, business, self-help, dictionaries, quiz books, cartoons, interviews. Currently handles: 25% nonfiction books; 35% novels; 40% syndicated material. Member agents: Helen J. Lee (general novels); Barbara Nalaer (romance titles); Kurt Singer (business books); Katherine Han (self-help); Peter Carbone (Asia department).

Handles: Nonfiction books, syndicated material, business titles, cartoons. Will consider these nonfiction areas: biography/autobiography; business; child guidance/parenting; computers/electronics; health/medicine; money/finance/economics; psychology; true crime/investigative; self-help/personal improvement; translations; women's issues/women's studies; cartoons; dictionaries; juvenile activities; interviews with celebrities. Will consider these fiction areas: cartoon/comic; detective/police/crime; erotica; fantasy; glitz; mystery/suspense; picture book; psychic/supernatural; romance (contemporary); science fiction; thriller/espionage; westerns/frontier; teenage romance. Query. Give writing credits. Will report in 3 weeks on queries; 4-6 weeks on mss.

Terms: Agent receives 15% commission on domestic sales; 20% on foreign sales.

Fees: Charges $350 reading fee "only to unpublished writers. Criticism service is part of our reading fee. Our readers are published authors or ghostwriters." 97% of business is derived from commissions on manuscript and book sales; 3% is derived from reading fees or criticism service. Payment of a criticism fee ensures representation "unless it is not salable to the commercial market."

Writers' Conference: Attends Romance Writers of America.

Tips: "We have been in business for 52 years and are known. If interested in agency representation, books are not written, but rewritten and rewritten. Syndication is done on a worldwide basis, and must be of global interest. Hollywood's winning formula is God/inspiration, sex and action. Try to get reprints of books overseas and in the USA if out of print."

‡SOUTHERN LITERARY AGENCY (III), 2323 Augusta Dr., #14, Houston TX 77057. (713)780-9443. Contact: Michael Doran. Estab. 1980. Member of WGA. Represents 58 clients. 20% of clients are new/previously unpublished writers. "We are most interested in popular financial, professional and technical books." Currently handles 70% nonfiction books; 20% novels; 10% movie scripts. Member

agents: Michael Doran (nonfiction); Patricia Coleman (mainstream novels, some nonfiction).
Handles: Nonfiction books, novels, movie scripts. Will consider these nonfiction areas: anthropology/archaeology; biography/autobiography; business; child guidance/parenting; health/medicine; history; money/finance/economics; psychology; self-help/personal improvement. Will consider these fiction areas: action/adventure; detective/police/crime; humor/satire; mainstream; mystery/suspense; thriller/espionage. Telephone query. Will report in 3-4 weeks on mss.
Recent Sales: *Fresh Start*, by John Ventura (Dearborn); *How to Repair Any Small Engine*, by Paul Dempsey (TAB); *Ms. Ima and the Hogg Family*, by Gwen Neeley (Hendricks-Long).
Terms: Agent receives 15% commission on domestic sales; 20% on foreign sales. Offers written contract.
Fees: "There is a $200 fee on unpublished new novelists, returnable if their manuscript is publishable and we do the selling of it. Refund on first royalties. Offers multi-page critique on manuscripts which can be made marketable; one page remarks and suggestions for writing improvements otherwise. Charges cost-per on extraordinary costs, pre-agreed." 90% of business derived from commissions on ms sales; 10% from reading fees or criticism services.
Writers' Conferences: ABA; Texas and other Southern regional.
Tips: Obtains new clients through conferences, yellow pages—mainly referrals. "Learn about the book business through conferences and reading before contacting the agent."

*SOUTHERN WRITERS (II), Suite 1020, 228 St. Charles Ave., New Orleans LA 70130. (504)525-6390. Fax: (504)524-7349. Contact: Emilie Griffin. Estab. 1979. Member of Romance Writers of America. Represents 30 clients. 40% of clients are new/previously unpublished writers. Specializes in fiction/nonfiction based in the Deep South; romance (both historical and contemporary). Currently handles: 30% nonfiction books; 10% juvenile books; 60% novels.
Handles: Nonfiction books, juvenile books, ("young adult and young readers, not children's picture books"), novels. Will consider these nonfiction areas: biography; business; child guidance/parenting; current affairs; gay/lesbian issues; health/medicine; history; juvenile nonfiction; money/finance/economics; music/dance/theater/film; psychology; religious/inspirational; true crime/investigative; self-help/personal improvement; women's issues/women's studies. Will consider these fiction areas: action/adventure; contemporary issues; detective/police/crime; family saga; fantasy; feminist; gay; glitz; historical; humor/satire; juvenile; lesbian; literary; mainstream; mystery/suspense; psychic/supernatural; regional; religious/inspiration; romance; science fiction; thriller/espionage; westerns/frontier; young adult. Query. Will report in 2-3 weeks on queries; 6-8 weeks on mss.
Recent Sales: *Lions and Lace*, by Meagan McKinney (Dell); *Deadly Currents* and *Fatal Ingredients*, by Caroline Burnes (Harlequin Intrigue); *Second Son*, by Kate Moore (Avon).
Terms: Agent receives 15% commission on domestic sales; 20% on foreign sales. Offers a written contract, binding for 1 year.
Fees: Charges a reading fee of up to $450 for 200,000-word ms. "Reading fees are charged to unpublished authors, and to authors writing in areas other than those of previous publication (i.e., nonfiction authors writing fiction). Fee is nonrefundable. We offer criticism at a fee slightly higher than our reading fees. Authors who pay a reading fee or criticism fee receive a 3-5 page, single-spaced letter, explaining what we feel the problems of their books are from both a qualitative and marketing standpoint. We charge for postage on an author's first book only if it is sold. On subsequent books there's no charge." 75% of business is derived from commissions on ms sales. 25% is derived from reading fees or criticism services. Payment of a criticism fee does not ensure representation.
Writers' Conferences: Attends Romance Writers of America Conference; Gulf Coast Writers Association; New Orleans Writer's Conference.
Tips: Obtains new clients through solicitation at conferences and most frequently through recommendations from others. "You should query an agent first, and only send what he/she asks to see. If asked to send 3 chapters, make sure they're the first 3, not the ones you consider to be the strongest. Your manuscript should be in complete form and polished before you contact an agent. It should be double-

---

The publishing field is constantly changing! If you're still using this book and it is 1994 or later, buy the newest edition of Guide to Literary Agents & Art/Photo Reps *at your favorite bookstore or order directly from Writer's Digest Books.*

spaced on 8½×11 white bond paper, unbound. Make your query letter brief and to the point, listing publishing credentials, writer's groups and organizations you may belong to, awards, etc. Do *not* make it cute, outlandish or hostile!"

‡STATE OF THE ART LTD. (II), Suite 200, 1625 S. Broadway, Denver CO 80210. (303)722-7177. Fax: (303)722-7191. Contact: Bruce Fleenor. Estab. 1983. Represents 10 clients. Currently handles: 50% nonfiction books, 50% novels.
Handles: Nonfiction and novels. Will consider these nonfiction areas: art; new age/metaphysics; self-help/personal improvement; women's studies; also open to other areas. Will consider these fiction areas: contemporary issues; feminist; mystery/suspense; science fiction. Query with SASE first. If they respond, send 3 sample chapters. Reports in 1 week on queries.
Terms: Agent receives 10% and up commission on domestic sales. Offers written contract, binding for 2 years.
Fees: Charges a reading fee. Charges $75 minimum; over 100 pages, $30/hour. Offers criticism service.
Tips: Usually obtains new clients from directory listings. "Do some research. Find out what professional presentation is like."

MICHAEL STEINBERG LITERARY AGENCY (III), P.O. Box 274, Glencoe IL 60027. (708)835-8881. Contact: Michael Steinberg. Estab. 1980. Represents 27 clients. 5% of clients are new/previously unpublished writers. Specializes in business and general nonfiction, mysteries, science fiction. Currently handles: 75% nonfiction books; 25% novels.
Handles: Nonfiction books; novels. Will consider these nonfiction areas: biography; business; child guidance; computer; current affairs; ethnic/cultural interests; government/politics/law; history; money/finance/economics; nature/environment; psychology; self-help/personal improvement. Will consider these fiction areas: action/adventure; contemporary issues; detective/police/crime; erotica; mainstream; mystery/suspense; science fiction; thriller/espionage. Query for guidelines. Will report in 2 weeks on queries; 6 weeks on mss.
Terms: Agent receives 15% on domestic sales; 15-20% on foreign sales. Offers a written contract, which is binding, "but at will."
Fees: Charges $75 reading fee for outline and chapters 1-3; $200 for a full ms to 100,000 words. Offers a criticism service, which is part of the reading fee. Charges actual phone and postage, which is billed back quarterly. 95% of business is derived from commissions on ms sales; 5% is derived from reading fees or criticism services.
Tips: Obtains new clients through unsolicited inquiries and referrals from editors and authors. "We do not solicit new clients. Do not send unsolicited material. Write for guidelines and include SASE. Do not send generically addressed, photocopied query letters."

*MARIANNE STRONG (III), 65 E. 96th St., New York NY 10128. (212)249-1000. Fax: (212)831-3241. Contact: Marianne Strong, Tonia Shoumatoff. Estab. 1978. Represents 10 clients.
Handles: Nonfiction books, novels, movie and TV scripts. Will consider these nonfiction areas: current affairs; interior design/decorating; money/finance/economics; true crime/investigative. Will consider these fiction areas: confessional; detective/police/crime; family saga; romance; thriller/espionage. Send outline plus 3 sample chapters. Will report "quickly."
Terms: Agent receives 15% commission on domestic sales; 15% on foreign sales. Offers a written contract, binding for the life of book or play "assuming it is sold."
Fees: Charges a reading fee for new writers only, "fee refundable when manuscript sold." Offers a criticism service.
Tips: Obtains new clients through recommendations from others.

*MARK SULLIVAN ASSOCIATES (II), Suite 1700, 521 Fifth Ave., New York NY 10175. (212)682-5844. Fax: (212)315-3860. Contact: Mark Sullivan. Estab. 1989. 50% of clients are new/previously unpublished writers. Currently handles: 20% nonfiction books; 5% textbooks; 60% novels; 5% poetry books; 10% movie scripts. Specializes in science fiction, women's romance, detective/mystery/spy, but handles all genres.
Handles: Nonfiction books, textbooks, scholarly books, novels, novellas, short story collections, poetry books, movie scripts. Will consider these nonfiction areas: anthropology/archaeology; biography/autobiography; business; cooking/food/nutrition; crafts/hobbies; current affairs; health/medicine; interior design/decorating; language/literature/criticism; military/war; money/finance/economics; music/dance/theater/film; nature/environment; new age/metaphysics; photography; psychology; religious/inspirational; science/technology; sports. Will consider all fiction areas. Query or send query with 3 sample

chapters and outline. Will report in 2 weeks on queries; 3-4 weeks on mss.
Terms: Agent receives 10-15% commission on domestic sales; 20% on foreign sales. Offers a written contract.
Fees: Charges $85 reading fee for new writers whose work is chosen from among queries and sample chapters submitted. Critique is provided with reading fee. Charges for photocopying and long-distance telephone calls. 90% of business is derived from commissions on ms sales; 10% of business is derived from reading fees or criticism services. Payment of fees does not ensure agency representation. "However, the firm's offer to read an entire manuscript is a reflection of our strong interest."
Tips: Obtains new clients through "advertising, reputation, recommendations, conferences. Quality of presentation of query letter, sample chapters and manuscript is important. Completed manuscripts are preferred to works in progress."

‡DAWSON TAYLOR LITERARY AGENCY (II), 4722 Holly Lake Dr., Lake Worth FL 33463. (407)965-4150. Contact: Dawson Taylor, Attorney at Law. Estab. 1974. Represents 21 clients. 80% of clients are new/previously unpublished writers. Specializes in nonfiction, fiction, sports, military history. Currently handles: 80% nonfiction; 5% scholarly books; 15% novels.
Handles: Nonfiction books, textbooks, scholarly books, novels, nonfiction on sports, especially golf. Query with outline. Will report in 5 days on queries; 10 days on mss.
Recent Sales: *The Man Who Killed Boys*, by C. Linedecker (St. Martins).
Terms: Agent receives 15% or 20% commission "depending upon editorial help." Offers written contract. Indefinite, but cancellable on 60 days notice by either party.
Fees: "Reading fees are subject to negotiation, usually $100 for normal length manuscript . . . more for lengthy ones. (Includes critique and sample editing.) Criticism service subject to negotiation . . . from $100. Critiques are on style and content, include editing of ms, and are written by myself." 90% of business is derived from commissions on ms sales; 10% is derived from reading fees or criticism services. Payment of reading or criticism fees does not ensure representation.
Tips: Obtains new clients through "recommendations from publishers and authors who are presently in my stable."

TIGER MOON ENTERPRISES (I), 1890 St. James Rd., Cambria CA 93428. (805)927-3920. Contact: Terry Kennedy or Mark James Miller. Estab. 1991. Represents 13 clients. 50% of clients are new/previously unpublished writers. "We prefer books written by successful entrepreneurs, teaching their skills to others. Children's books which teach the five human values of love, truth, peace, nonviolence and righteous living also interest us." Currently handles: 40% novels; 20% poetry books; 40% short story collections (10% of these are new age). Member agents: Terry Kennedy (business, how-to, children's); Mark Miller (fiction, history, investigative research).
Handles: Nonfiction books, scholarly books, juvenile books, novels, novellas, short story collections, poetry books and work that is "spiritually uplifting, life-guiding." Will consider these nonfiction areas: cooking; crafts; health/medicine; history; juvenile nonfiction; military/war; money; music; nature; new age; religious; self-help. Will consider these fiction areas: contemporary issues; family saga; historical; literary; psychic; regional; religious. Query with a 10-page sample and SASE. Will report "immediately" on queries; in 2 weeks on mss.
Recent Sales: *Frontage Road*, by Frank Sisti (Tiger Moon Press); *Voices of the Boat People*, by Mark James Miller (Golden West College).
Terms: Agent receives 15% commission on domestic sales; 15% on foreign sales. Offers a written contract, duration varies.
Fees: Charges a reading fee. Offers four service options: manuscript reading service for $1.50/page. Provides 750-word critique; copyediting service for $3/page; rewriting package for $4.50/page. Provides publication-ready copy with major mechanical and technical reconstruction; total book packaging. Cost estimates on request. Critiques are written by agents. "We agent a manuscript for a specific fee, custom designed for each client. We offer book packaging services to clients who do not want to wait for mainstream publishing houses to back them." 50% of business derived from ms sales; 50% is derived from reading or criticism (or other) fees. Payment of a criticism fee does not ensure agency representation.
Tips: "We have been in the writing business for 14 years. We have many personal contacts. We have a huge mailing list to draw from, but we are always interested in new contacts. If you are the type of person who really believes in your work, we are interested in doing business with you. We are not equipped to build up your self esteem as a writer. Believe that what you have written is going to be of genuine interest to many readers, send us a professional package and we'll be attentive to your proposal."

*JEANNE TOOMEY ASSOCIATES (II), 95 Belden St., Falls Village CT 06031. (203)824-0831/5469. Fax: (203)824-5460. Contact: Jeanne Toomey. Estab. 1985. Represents 10 clients. 50% of clients are new/previously unpublished writers. Specializes in "nonfiction; biographies of famous men and women; history with a flair—murder and detection. No children's books, no poetry, no Harlequin-type romances." Currently handles: 45% nonfiction books; 20% novels; 35% movie scripts.
Handles: Nonfiction books, novels, short story collections, movie scripts. Will consider these nonfiction areas: agriculture/horticulture; animals; anthropology/archaeology; art/architecture/design; biography/autobiography; government/politics/law; history; interior design/decorating; money/finance/economics; nature/environment; true crime/investigative. Will consider these fiction areas: detective/police/crime; psychic/supernatural; thriller/espionage. Send outline plus 3 sample chapters. Will report in 1 month.
Terms: Agent receives 15% commission on domestic sales.
Fees: Charges $100 reading fee for unpublished authors; no fee for published authors. "The $100 covers marketing fee, office expenses, postage, photocopying. We absorb those costs in the case of published authors."

PHYLLIS TORNETTA AGENCY (II), Box 423, Croton-on-Hudson NY 10521. (914)737-3464. President: Phyllis Tornetta. Estab. 1979. Represents 22 clients. 35% of clients are new/unpublished writers. Specializes in romance, contemporary, mystery. Currently handles: 90% novels and 10% juvenile.
Handles: Novels and juvenile. Query with outline. Does not read unsolicited mss. Reports in 1 month.
Recent Sales: *Intimate Strangers*, by S. Hoover (Harlequin); *Accused* (Silhouette) and *Ride Eagle* (Worldwide).
Terms: Agent receives 15% commission on domestic sales and 20% on foreign sales.
Fees: Charges a reading fee "for full manuscripts." Charges $75/300 pages.

*SUSAN P. URSTADT INC. WRITERS AND ARTISTS AGENCY (II), P.O. Box 1676, New Canaan CT 06840. (203)966-6111. Contact: Susan Urstadt. Estab. 1975. Member of AAR. Represents 45 clients. 10% of clients are new/previously unpublished authors. Specializes in illustrated books, popular reference, art, antiques, decorative arts, gardening, travel, horses, armchair cookbooks, business, self-help, crafts, hobbies, collectibles. Currently handles: 95% nonfiction books.
Handles: Nonfiction books. Will consider these nonfiction areas: agriculture/horticulture; animals; anthropology/archaeology; art/architecture/design; biography/autobiography; business; child guidance/parenting; cooking/food/nutrition; crafts/hobbies; current affairs; health/medicine; interior design/decorating; military/war; money/finance/economics; music/dance/theater/film; nature/environment; photography; self-help/personal improvement; sports. "No unsolicited fiction please." Send outline plus 2 sample chapters, SASE and short author bio. Will report in 3 weeks on queries.
Recent Sales: *History of American Folk Art*, by Elizabeth Stillinger (Henry Holt); *History of American Wildflowers*, by Tim Coffey (Facts on File); *Southern Christmas Traditions*, by Emyl Jenkins (Crown).
Terms: Agent receives 15% commission on domestic sales; 20% on foreign sales. Offers written contract.
Fees: Charges $275 "start-up" fee *for new authors* (only for authors who are accepted as clients). 95% of business is derived from commissions on ms sales.
Tips: Obtains new clients through recommendations from others. "We are interested in building a writer's career through the long term and only want dedicated writers with special knowledge, which they share in a professional way."

*THE GERRY B. WALLERSTEIN AGENCY (II), Suite 12, 2315 Powell Ave., Erie PA 16506. (814)833-5511. Contact: Ms. Gerry B. Wallerstein. Estab. 1984. Member of The Authors Guild, Inc. and Society of Professional Journalists. Represents 40 clients. 25% of clients are new/previously unpublished writers. Specializes in nonfiction books and "personalized help for new novelists." Currently handles: 52% nonfiction books; 2% scholarly books; 2% juvenile books; 35% novels; 2% short story collections; 2% TV scripts; 2% short material. (Note: Juvenile books, scripts and short material marketed for *clients only!*)
Handles: Nonfiction books, scholarly trade books, novels, short story collections. Will consider all nonfiction areas provided book is for general trade ("no textbooks"). Will consider these fiction areas: action/adventure; contemporary issues; detective/police/crime; family saga; glitz; historical; humor/satire; literary; mainstream; mystery/suspense; romance; thriller/espionage; westerns/frontier; young adult. To query, send entire manuscript for fiction; a proposal (including 3 chapters) for nonfiction books. "No manuscripts are reviewed until writer has received my brochure." Will report in 1 week on queries; 2 months on mss.

Recent Sales: *Satanic Cult Witch Hunt*, by Jeffrey S. Victor (Open Court Publishing Co.); *European Cars Never Built*, by Gregory Janicki (Sterling Publishing Co., Inc.); *Divine Origin*, by Susan Teklits (Harper Paperbacks/HarperCollins).
Terms: Agent receives 15% on domestic sales; 20% on foreign sales. Offers a written contract, which "can be cancelled by either party, with 60 days' notice of termination."
Fees: "To justify my investment of time, effort and expertise in working with newer or beginning writers, I charge a reading/critique fee based on length of manuscript, for example: $350 for each manuscript of 105,000 to 125,000 words." Critique included as part of reading fee. "Reports are 1-2 pages for proposals and short material; 2-4 pages for full-length mss; done by agent." Charges clients $20/month postage/telephone fee; and if required, manuscript photocopying or typing, copyright fees, cables, attorney fees (if approved by author), travel expense (if approved by author). 50% of business is derived from commissions on ms sales; 50% is derived from reading fees and critique services. Payment of a critique fee does not ensure representation.
Writers' Conferences: Westminster College Conference; Midwest Writers' Conference; National Writers' Uplink.
Tips: Obtains new clients through recommendations; listings in directories; referrals from clients and publishers/editors. "A query letter that tells me something about the writer and his/her work is more likely to get a personal response."

WATERSIDE PRODUCTIONS, INC. (II), 2191 San Elijo Ave., Cardiff-by-the-Sea CA 92007. (619)632-9190. Fax: (619)632-9295. President: Bill Gladstone. Estab. 1982. Member of AAR. Represents 200 clients. 20% of clients are new/previously unpublished writers. Currently handles: 80% nonfiction, 20% novels. Member agents: Bill Gladstone (trade computer titles, business); Julie Castiglia (women's issues, serious nonfiction, fiction); Matthew Wagner (trade computer titles, nonfiction, screenplays).
Handles: Nonfiction books, novels. Will consider these nonfiction areas: anthropology/archaeology; art/architecture/design; biography/autobiography; business; child guidance/parenting; computers/electronics; ethnic/cultural interests; health/medicine; money/finance/economics; music/dance/theater/film; nature/environment; new age/metaphysics; psychology; true crime/investigative; sociology; sports; women's issues/women's studies. Will consider these fiction areas: action/adventure; contemporary issues; detective/police/crime; glitz; literary; mainstream; mystery/suspense; romance; thriller/espionage. Query with outline/proposal. Will report in 2 weeks on queries; 6-8 weeks on mss.
Recent Sales: *The Second Nine Months*, by Jacqueline Shannon (Contemporary); *Building Relationships with Adult Children*, by Karen O'Connor (Thomas Nelson); *Task Force*, by Mike Dunn (Avon).
Terms: Agent receives 15% commission on domestic sales; 25% on foreign sales. Offers a written contract.
Fees: Does not charge a reading fee. Offers a criticism service. Charges $50 an hour. Agents write critiques. Charges for photocopying and other unusual expenses. 99.9% of business is derived from commissions on ms sales; .1% derived from reading fees or criticism services.
Tips: Usually obtains new clients through recommendations from others. "Be professional. The more professional a submission, the more seriously it's viewed. Beginning writers should go to a writers workshop and learn how a presentation should be made."

*SANDRA WATT & ASSOCIATES (II), Suite 4053, 8033 Sunset Blvd., Hollywood CA 90046. (213)653-2339. Contact: David A. South. Estab. 1977. Member of WGA, SAG, AFTRA. Represents 55 clients. 15% of clients are new/previously unpublished writers. Specializes in scripts: film noir, romantic comedies; books: women's fiction, mystery, commercial nonfiction. Currently handles: 40% nonfiction books, 35% novels, 25% movie scripts. Member agents: Sandra Watt (scripts, nonfiction, novels); David A. South (scripts).
Handles: Nonfiction books, novels, movie scripts. Will consider these nonfiction areas: animals; anthropology/archaeology; new age/metaphysics; true crime/investigative; self-help/personal improvement; sports; women's issues/women's studies. Will consider these fiction areas: detective/police/crime; glitz; mainstream; mystery/suspense; thriller/espionage. Query. Will report in 1 week on queries; 2 months on mss.
Recent Sales: *Borrowed Lives*, by Laramie Dunaway (Warner); *Doing Good: The Dictionary of the Ethical and Moral Universe*, by Raymond Obstfeld (Morrow); *Cyberpunk*, executive producer Freddi Fields (Universal); *The Romantic Imperative*, by Jay Russell (Tarcher).

Terms: Agent receives 15% commission on domestic sales; 25% on foreign sales. Offers written contract, binding for 1 year.
Fees: Does not charge reading fee. Charges a one-time nonrefundable marketing fee of $100 *for unpublished authors*.
Tips: Obtains new clients through recommendations from others, referrals and "from wonderful query letters. Don't forget the SASE!"

WEST COAST LITERARY ASSOCIATES (II), Suite 151, 7960-B Soquel Dr., Aptos CA 95003. (408)685-9548. Fax: (408)662-0755. Contact: Acquisitions Editor. Estab. 1986. Member of Authors League of America. Represents 80 clients. 50% of clients are new/previously unpublished clients. Currently handles: 30% nonfiction books; 70% novels.
Handles: Nonfiction books, novels. Will consider these nonfiction areas: biography/autobiography; current affairs; ethnic/cultural interests; government/politics/law; history; language/literature/criticism; music/dance/theater/film; nature/environment; psychology; true crime/investigative; women's issues/women's studies. Will consider these fiction areas: action/adventure; contemporary issues; detective/police/crime; experimental; historical; literary; mainstream; mystery/suspense; regional; contemporary and historical romance; science fiction; thriller/espionage; westerns/frontier. Query first. Will report in 2 weeks on queries; 1 month on mss.
Terms: Agent receives 10% commission on domestic sales; 20% commission on foreign sales. Offers a written contract, binding for 6 months.
Recent Sales: *High Roller*, by Jan Welles (New Horizon Press); *Carnival of Saints*, by George Herman (Ballantine); *The Ballad of Rocky Ruiz*, by Manuel Ramos (St. Martin's).
Fees: Does not charge a reading fee. Charges an agency marketing and materials fee between $75 and $95, depending on genre and length. Fees are refunded in full upon sale of the property.
Tips: "Query with SASE for submission guidelines before sending material."

THE WILSHIRE LITERARY AGENCY (I), Suite 705, 8484 Wilshire Blvd., Beverly Hills CA 90211. (310)652-3967. Contact: Carol McCleary. Estab. 1990. Specializes in mystery novels. Currently handles: 100% novels.
Handles: Novels. Will consider these fiction areas: action/adventure; detective/police/crime; literary; mainstream; mystery/suspense. Send outline plus 3 sample chapters. Will report in 1 month on queries and mss.
Terms: Agent receives 15% commission on domestic sales; 15% on foreign sales. Offers a written contract.
Fees: Does not charge reading fee. Offers criticism service: $2 per page. "We use two freelance editors for line editing and 10-15-page critique." Charges for postage and photocopying; "only fee charged." 98% of business is derived from commission on ms sales; 2% is derived from reading fees and criticism services. Payment of criticism does not ensure representation.
Tips: Obtains new clients through recommendations from others.

*STEPHEN WRIGHT AUTHORS' REPRESENTATIVE (III), P.O. Box 1341, F.D.R. Station, New York NY 10150-1341. (212)213-4382. Authors' Representative: Stephen Wright. Estab. 1984. Prefers to work with published/established authors. Works with a small number of new/unpublished authors. Specializes in fiction, nonfiction and screenplays. Currently handles: 20% nonfiction, 60% novels, 10% movie scripts, 10% TV scripts.
Handles: Nonfiction books, novels, young adult and juvenile books, movie scripts, radio scripts, stage plays, TV scripts, syndicated material. Query first; do *not* send ms. Include SASE with query. Reports in 3 weeks on queries.
Terms: Agent receives 10-15% commission on domestic sales; 10-15% on dramatic sales; 15-20% on foreign sales.
Fees: "When the writer is a beginner or has had no prior sales in the medium for which he or she is writing, we charge a reading criticism fee; does not waive fee when representing the writer. Charges $600/300 pages; or $100/50 pages (double-spaced). We simply do not 'read' a ms, but give the writer an in-depth criticism. If we like what we read, we would represent the writer. Or if the writer revises ms to meet our professional standards and we believe there is a market for said ms, we would also represent the writer. We tell the writer whether we believe his/her work is marketable. I normally provide the critiques."

*WRITER'S CONSULTING GROUP (II, III), P.O. Box 492, Burbank CA 91503. (818)841-9294. Director: Jim Barmeier. Estab. 1983. Represents 10 clients. "We prefer to work with established writers unless the author has an unusual true story." Currently handles: 40% nonfiction books; 20% novels; 40% movie scripts.
Handles: True stories for which the author has the right; nonfiction books; how-to; health; true crime; business; true stories about unusual women; novels (women's, mainstream, contemporary thrillers); movie scripts (romantic comedies, stories about women). Query or send proposal. Include SASE. Reports in 1 month on queries; 3 months on mss.
Recent Sales: "We have helped writers sell everything from episodes for children's TV shows ('Smurfs') to movie-of-the-week options (including the Craig Smith espionage story)."
Terms: "We will explain our terms to clients when they wish to sign. We receive a 10% commission on domestic sales."
Fees: Sometimes charges reading fee. "Additionally, we offer ghostwriting and editorial services, as well as book publicity services for authors. Mr. Barmeier is a graduate of Stanford University's Master's Degree in Creative Writing Program."
Tips: "We are looking for good women's stories that could be turned into a movie-of-the-week."

TOM ZELASKY LITERARY AGENCY (II), 3138 Parkridge Crescent, Chamblee (Atlanta) GA 30341. (404)458-0391. Contact: Tom Zelasky. Estab. 1986. Represents 5 clients. 60% of clients are new/previously unpublished writers. Specializes in detectives and westerns, Vietnam, others (depending on quality and marketability). Currently handles: 10% nonfiction books; 10% juvenile books; 80% novels.
Handles: Nonfiction books, juvenile books, novels, novellas, short story collections, movie scripts, stage plays, westerns, detectives. Will consider these nonfiction areas: biography/autobiography; current affairs; government/politics; juvenile nonfiction; military/war; true crime/investigative; self-help/personal improvement; women's issues/women's studies. Will consider these fiction areas: confessional; contemporary issues; detective/police/crime; family saga; feminist; historical; juvenile; literary; mainstream; mystery/suspense; romance (contemporary); science fiction; thriller/espionage; westerns/frontier; young adult. Query first, then send entire ms with synopsis. Will report in 1-2 weeks on queries; 2-3 months on mss.
Terms: Agent receives 10-15% commission on domestic sales; 20-25% on foreign sales. Offers a written contract, binding for 1 year and "renewed automatically by 30 days after end of year."
Fees: "A reading fee of $100 is charged. The reading fee is for reviewing and reading a manuscript. A one-page critique is sent if the manuscript is rejected by the agency. My readers and I write the critique, which covers basic writing concerns, the physical format presentation of the manuscript and especially the technique. Postage and photocopying is deducted from the reading fee or after the royalty commission is earned." 50% of business is derived from commissions on ms sales; 50% is derived from reading fees and criticism services. Payment of a reading fee ensures representation, if ms is acceptable.
Writers' Conferences: Attends the Florida Suncoast Writers' Conference, Tennessee Mountain Writers Conference, Council Authors' and Journalists' Conference, South Eastern Writers Conference and other conferences. "I don't attend these conferences every year, but use the scatter theory."
Tips: Obtains new clients through query letters, phone queries, conferences, directories, "publishers from everywhere. Know the mechanics and techniques of the art of writing. Practice and produce. Don't rely on past laurels. Use writing knowledge at all facets of writing. Go where the writing is done to acquaint oneself about the writing/publishing profession. And, set a daily pattern of writing as a laboring job, 8 hours or what hours preferable, depending upon a job-for-living necessity. You will be successful in the long run but it may take years, decades. Who knows?"

Additional Fee-charging Agents

The following fee-charging agencies have full listings in other sections of this book. These agencies have indicated they are *primarily* interested in handling the work of scriptwriters, artists or photographers, but are also interested in book manuscripts. After reading the listing (you can find the page number in the Listings Index), send them a query to obtain more information on their needs and manuscript submission policies.

Eth Literary Representation, Felicia
Executive Excellence
American Play Co., Inc.
Berzon Agency, The Marian

Cameron Agency, The Marshall
Earth Tracks Agency
Film And Fiction Agency, The
Hilton Literary Agency, Alice

Lee Literary Agency, L. Harry
Pacific Design Studio
Raintree Agency
Talent Bank Agency, The

Fee-charging Agents/'92-'93 changes

The following agencies appeared in the last (1992) edition of *Guide to Literary Agents & Art/Photo Reps* but are absent from the 1993 edition. These agencies failed to respond to our request for an update of their listing, or were left out for the reasons indicated in parentheses following the agency name.

About Books Inc. (removed per request)
Maxwell Aley Associates of Aspen (removed per request)
Brady Literary Management

(unable to contact)
Warren Cook Literary Agency (unable to contact)
Dorothy Deering Literary Agency (complaints)

Gelles-Cole Literary Agency
Doris Francis Kuller Associates (unable to contact)
Literary Marketing Consultants
Stacy Ann Scott, Synergy Creative Agency (unable to contact)

Script Agents

Finding and Working with Script Agents

by Kerry Cox

As editor and publisher of a newsletter targeted solely at aspiring and professional script-writers, I've talked to dozens of agents and hundreds of writers, all embroiled in a daily search for each other. Each wants what the other has to offer: The agent needs material to sell and the writer needs someone to sell material. Seems like it should be a piece of cake to find the right match and start making money, right?

Of course, the reality is that it's not easy at all. The reason? According to writers, it's "They don't recognize my talent; they read my stuff and send it back." Talk to an agent, though, and the story you'll hear is, "Ninety-five percent of what I receive is garbage. When I find a truly talented writer, I fall all over myself to sign that writer right away!"

So there's the clue. If you, the writer, want to attract and land an agent, you have to concentrate your efforts not on finding the agent, but on writing top-notch scripts. The simple fact is, if you can write an outstanding script, you can find an outstanding agent.

Now, there are some basic rules to follow in bringing that script to the agent's attention. But before we go into that, let's answer the question that's probably uppermost in your mind as you begin your Agent Quest.

Do I really need an agent?

Nope. If you want, you can approach production companies on your own, and try to convince them to let you submit your script with a release form. The smaller companies will probably let you do that. The larger ones, studios included, might possibly let you do it too, although it's becoming less and less likely. Television producers will almost invariably ignore, if not prohibit, unagented submissions.

So, if you really want to give your script the best shot possible, yes, you should very, very seriously consider getting an agent. For one thing, production companies and studios are plagued by "nuisance" lawsuits, where a writer claims that his or her script has been stolen. To protect themselves from these legal hassles, producers have come to rely on agents to provide a kind of safety screen and keep things on a professional level.

Additionally, producers have no time to wade through the oceans of scripts that get sent to Hollywood every day by prospective writers. They rely on the agent to handle that,

Kerry Cox *is a scriptwriter with over two dozen television credits with Aaron Spelling Productions, The Disney Channel and others. He has had a play produced in New York, written a feature film on assignment, and co-authored* Successful Scriptwriting, *by Writer's Digest Books. He is the editor and publisher of* The Hollywood Scriptwriter.

and perform a quality control function in weeding out the bad and circulating only the worthwhile scripts.

All right, so you need an agent to submit your script for you. Is that all an agent does?

What they do

In an interview with *The Hollywood Scriptwriter*, one agent refers to her function as a "yenta" for writers. "My job is to introduce writers to producers, and hope they'll build a business relationship. I find work for my writers, and negotiate the deals for them." An agent will act, on any given day, as a negotiator, mediator, trouble-shooter, critic, advisor and salesperson. And most of them do all of this for the standard ten percent off the top.

Let's talk a minute about commissions and fees, because script agents differ somewhat from their "literary" counterparts in this regard. First, there's the matter of reading fees. The Writers Guild of America specifically prohibits signatory agents from charging reading fees. Period. Now, there is no rule that says that an agent has to be a Guild-signatory, but this goes back to the question of respectability and credibility; producers are more likely to seriously consider material sent by recognized professionals, and *all* the top agencies (and the vast majority of mid-size and small agencies, for that matter) are Guild-signatory agencies.

On the other hand, there is no rule that prohibits an agency from offering a critique service, and there are a number of agencies that do so. Be careful, however, of agencies who will (for a fee) "develop" your work until it is ready for representation — most likely this "development" will go on a mighty long time, and be quite expensive.

Finally, a script agent customarily gets ten percent of the "deal." For example, if you were hired to write a single television episode, your agent would be entitled to ten percent of the writing fee. It is not mandatory to pay an agent's commission on residuals (money you get for reruns of the episode), although some writers choose to do so.

In case where an agent has had to cut another agent in on the deal, such as a foreign sale, the writer might have to pay a 15% commission. In all cases, the commission is well worth the time, trouble, and expense a good agent puts forth in marketing your work.

What they don't do

An agent can't guarantee you will have a successful career. They are not the end — they are the means to an end. Keep in mind that once you have an agent, you are still the one who is responsible for your career, and will be expected to write, and try to make professional contacts, and write some more.

An agent won't necessarily represent everything you write. If you turn in something they honestly feel they can't sell, they will explain to you that the work is not up to your usual standards, and feel it would be harmful to your reputation to send it out. If you insist, they will either send it to a few friends in the business for an objective opinion, or they will refuse to put it on the market. Obviously, at that point you have a decision to make.

An agent won't give you a daily update on how your material is doing. There simply isn't enough time. The best thing to do is check in with your agent about once every two weeks.

Unless your agent is also a lawyer, he or she cannot represent you in court. Generally speaking, an agent provides no legal protection or resources, although most have a working relationship with at least one entertainment attorney and can recommend one when necessary.

An agent's job is to sell your work, and/or find you writing work. That's all.

So how do I get one?

A successful agent once told us, "An agent doesn't like to be 'got' any more than anyone else." Instead, she likened the process to something more akin to a "romance," where there is a courtship period and eventual commitment.

The courtship begins with you, the writer, taking the initiative. If you have a friend or acquaintance who has an agent and might be willing to recommend your work, that's the best way to go. If you have attended a seminar or workshop in which an agent was a guest speaker or panelist, and you are able to make some personal contact, that's another good avenue.

If, however, you're coming in from the cold, like the majority of writers are, your approach needs to begin with a query letter. This letter isn't all that different from the query letters you may have sent to magazines or book publishers in the past, and the goals are the same: a) demonstrate to the agent that you are a relatively sane, competent professional who understands the craft; and b) pique the agent's personal and professional interest enough to request a look at your work.

When you write your query letter, consider the fact that the agent will probably get about a dozen others that day, along with an assortment of scripts, business mail, and the junk mail we all get. Your job is to make your letter practically jump out of that pile, excite the reader and encourage a fast response.

Start by making sure the letter and even the envelope you mail it in are professional in appearance. Get some decent letterhead. It doesn't have to be fancy, but it should look like you take your writing career seriously. Listings for agents in directories such as this usually give contact names. If not, call an agency, and talk to the receptionist, a secretary, or even an agent, and get the name of someone specific to whom you can address the letter. Addressing the letter to, "Dear Sir/Madam," just doesn't cut it.

Third step: plan the letter. You don't want it to take up more than one page if at all possible. Leave out any information that isn't absolutely necessary. Avoid hardsell, glittering claims about the abundance of money your script will make the agent, or the sheer genius you demonstrated in crafting this masterpiece. Instead, you'll want to include two things: a) Your credentials, if any (and not just writing credentials. For instance, if your script is a detective drama, and you're a detective, by all means mention that fact); b) A brief summary of your script—"brief" meaning no more than a paragraph or two.

Some other items that might be important would be related to the type of script you've written. If it's an historical drama, for instance, you might note that you have spent x number of years researching the period, especially if your story is based upon true events. You might also want to mention that you have written a number of other spec scripts, too (assuming you have—and you should), which shows the agent that you are not sending out your first effort, but have been earnestly working at this a while.

When summarizing your story in the letter, you may feel reluctant to tell the whole tale, and give away the ending. There are no rules about this. A good generalization would be to craft your query letter in such a way that it leaves the agent wanting more—whether wanting to find out the ending, or find out how you managed to create the ending you've described.

Once you've written the letter, be sure to include a SASE for response, send it off to as many agents as you'd like, and get to work on your next script.

What if they say yes?

Writers are so preconditioned for—and often experienced with—failure, that a positive response tends to induce sudden euphoria and a subsequent lack of judgment.

If an agent expresses an interest in seeing your material, stop and think for a moment. First, is your script already being considered by another agent, one who responded more promptly? If so, it's generally considered poor etiquette to circulate your script to more than one prospective agent at a time (although it's not necessarily an uncommon practice).

Second, are you absolutely sure your script is ready to be seen? This could represent a very important moment in your career, and you don't want to blow it by being overeager. Even though you were positive it was ready when you sent out the query letter, take an hour or so and read the script one more time, keeping as objective a frame of mind as possible. If any part of it feels weak to you, or bothers you in some way—if you even find a typo or two—don't sent it out until it's *perfect*.

Assuming you send the script and the agent likes it, several things might happen. You might be asked, "What else have you got?" This is pretty common, and usually means that your script showed some real writing talent, but the agent doesn't feel quite ready to invest the time and effort necessary to develop a new client without first determining if you are a "One-Script Wonder." An agent is interested not only in selling your first script, but wants to know that you have long-term potential as well. This is a very crucial stage of the "romance," and this next point can't be stressed enough: *Don't send another script if it's not just as good as the first one*. Presumably, you have already sent what you consider to be your best work; but it should have been a tough call, because you weren't sure if your second one was really your best. If you have a second script that's good, send it. If you don't, tell the agent you're working on one, and will be happy to submit it once you're finished. If you panic, and send one of your earlier scripts that isn't quite as good, but it's all you've got—you'll lose your chance with that agent, who will probably send both scripts back to you, most likely with one of those highly personal form rejection letters.

Now, let's say the agent calls, and wants to represent you. In fact, she wants you to sign a one-year, or even (less common) a two-year contract. Do you do it? What if it turns out you don't like this agent after six months—are you stuck with her for two years?

Thanks to the Writers Guild, you aren't stuck. There is a 90-day clause built in to the contract of every Guild-signatory agent, which states, roughly speaking, that either you or the agent can exercise the right to sever the relationship if the agent hasn't found you above-scale work within a 90-day period. (The term "scale" refers to minimum fees set by the WGA.) Of course, it isn't *mandatory* that you call it quits within that period, and in fact it would be a little unrealistic for a new writer to expect his or her agent to make a sale or find work that quickly; however, it does offer an "escape" for those who feel they need it. (If you are not dealing with a signatory agent, you may want to consider asking for such a clause in your contract.)

Are there agents for scriptwriters who don't write for TV or movies?

Yes, although they are usually the same agents who do handle movie and television writers. Playwrights, for instance, can greatly benefit from an agent. Naturally, there is more action on the East Coast than the West for a playwright, but Hollywood agencies tend to either have a New York office or work closely with a New York agent.

The way for a playwright to get an agent is to invite several to a performance, or even a staged reading, of the play. Not all agents want to represent playwrights, for one reason or another, so be sure to call and ascertain if there is any interest before sending out the invitations. Notice too that it's up to you, the playwright, to get yourself produced at the local level before approaching an agent. That's not the case for television and movie writers.

Interested in writing for animation? There are a limited number of agencies that handle that type of work, and a couple of them who specialize almost exclusively in cartoon writers. The fact is, however, it's not necessary for an animation writer to have an agent. The animation houses and producers are much more accessible than their live-action counterparts, and bring new writers on-board all the time.

Ancillary scriptwriting markets, such as industrials, corporate films or video, marketing, radio, etc. are generally not handled by literary agents. There has been some movement within the Writers Guild to bring educational and informational scriptwriting into the fold in terms of fee schedules and so forth, but it's been a half-hearted effort at best. For the time being, educational and informational scriptwriters remain on their own in terms of finding work and negotiating fees.

Some final advice

Stay informed. There are a number of trade publications and specialty newsletters that should be regular reading for aspiring scriptwriters. *Daily Variety* and *The Hollywood Reporter* are the daily business papers of the entertainment industry. *The Hollywood Scriptwriter* is my newsletter targeted specifically for aspiring and professional scriptwriters, and features agency updates throughout the year, along with an Annual Agency Issue every summer that surveys open agencies. Addresses for these publications appear in Resources near the back of this book.

Know your craft. Invest in some scriptwriting books. *Successful Scriptwriting*, Writer's Digest Books, offers an instructional overview of each type of scriptwriting, and includes a chapter on finding an agent, along with a standard release form you can use when submitting material. Some other books: *Making a Good Script Great*, by Dr. Linda Seger; *How to Sell Your Screenplay*, by Carl Sautter; *Writing Screenplays That Sell*, by Michael Hauge; and of course *Adventures in the Screen Trade*, by William Goldman, which isn't exactly an instructional book but is required reading for all screenwriters.

Be professional. Understand and follow the correct format for whatever type of script you're writing (just about any of the books mentioned will provide you with detailed format specifications). Always include a SASE with any correspondence. Keep phone calls brief and to the point. Send only your best work. Continue to perfect your skills as you search for and after you find an agent. Treat your writing not as a hobby or a dream, but as a chosen career.

Keep the faith. Remember, everyone, even the most successful writers, began their career without an agent. As a top agent once said, "(An agent) is always looking for writing that has a spark, that shows imagination, that has vision . . . and style."

If that's you she's talking about, then keep at it. Persevere. As Jim Cash ("Top Gun," "Dick Tracy") put it in one interview, "There's only one way to succeed: accept failure as a temporary state, however long that state may be, and simply outlast it."

Good luck.

Script Agents:
Nonfee and Fee-charging

If you've written a screenplay, teleplay or stage play and would like help approaching television and film producers or theatrical companies, you may find the agents listed in this section very helpful. While many of the agencies listed in the literary agents' sections of this book also handle scripts, agencies who *primarily* sell scripts make up this section.

As with literary agents, approach a screen agent well-informed. For starters, read Finding and Working with Script Agents, by Kerry Cox on page 144 and check our Resources section on the subject. For a good general discussion of the script markets, you may also want to take a look at the introduction to the scriptwriting section in *Writer's Market*.

Many of the signatories to the Writers Guild of America/West are script agents. You can contact this organization for more information on specific agencies. Agents who are affiliated with this group are not permitted to charge for reading scripts, but they can charge for critiques and other services. The guild also offers a registration service and it's a good thing to register your script with the group before sending it out. Write the Guild for more information on this and on membership (see Resources).

Since different types of scripts require different formats, make sure you know how to present your script. The *Writer's Digest Guide to Manuscript Formats* and *Successful Script Writing* (by Kerry Cox and Jurgen Wolff) are good sources for script formats.

Help with your search

To help you with your search for an agent, we've included a number of special indexes in the back of this book. The Subject Index is divided into sections for fee-charging and nonfee-charging literary agents and script agents. Each of these sections in the index is then divided by nonfiction and fiction subject categories. In general these subjects apply to scripts as well as to books, and script type (television episode, movie-of-the-week, documentary, stage play) is mentioned within the script agent's listing. We've included the Agents and Reps Index as well. Often you will read about an agent, but if that agent is an employee of a large agency, you may not be able to find that person's business number. We've asked agencies to give us the names of agents on their staffs. Then we've listed the names in alphabetical order along with the name of their agency. Find the name of the person you would like to contact and then check the listing for that agency.

Many of the nonfee- and fee-charging literary agents are also interested in scripts and vice versa. If the agency's primary function is selling books, but it is interested in seeing some scripts, we've included them in the Additional Script Agents list at the end of this section.

About the listings

The listings in this section are set up very much like the those in the literary agent sections. We've asked for the breakdown of the type of script each agency handles and have included this information within the listing.

Unlike literary agency listings, we have not separated nonfee-charging and fee-charging agencies. As already noted above WGA signatories are not permitted to charge reading fees, but many agencies do charge for a variety of other services—critiques, consultations, promotion, marketing, etc. Those agencies who charge some type of fee have been indicated with an open box (□) symbol at the beginning of the listing.

You will also notice differences within the heading, Recent Sales. Often scripts are not titled at the time of sale, so we asked for the production company's name. We've found the film industry is very secretive about sales, but you may be able to get a list of clients or other references upon request.

We've ranked the agencies listed in this section according to their openness to submissions. Below is our ranking system:

I Newer agency actively seeking clients.
II Agency seeking both new and established writers.
III Agency prefers to work with established writers, mostly through referrals.
IV Agency handling only certain types of work or work by writers under certain circumstances.
V Agency not currently seeking new clients. (If an agency chose this designation, only the address is given). We have included mention of agencies rated V only to let you know they are not open to new clients at this time. In addition to those ranked V, we have included a few well-known agencies' names who have declined listings. *Unless you have a strong recommendation from someone well-known in the field, our advice is to approach only those agents ranked I-IV.*

AGENCY FOR THE PERFORMING ARTS (II), Suite 1200, 9000 Sunset Blvd., Los Angeles CA 90069. (310)273-0744. Fax: (310)275-9401. Contact: Stuart M. Miller. Estab. 1962. Member of WGA. Represents 50+ clients. Specializes in film and TV rights.
Handles: Movie scripts and TV scripts. Will consider all nonfiction and fiction areas. Query with SASE. Will report in 2-3 weeks on queries.
Terms: Agent receives 10% commission on domestic sales. Offers written contract.
Tips: Obtains new clients through recommendations from others.

‡□ALLIED ARTISTS (II), 811 W. Evergreen, Chicago IL 60622. (312)482-8488. Fax: (312)482-8371. Contact: Coleen Gallagher. Estab. 1984 . Member of SAG/AFTRA. Represents 80 clients. 10% of clients are new/previously unpublished writers. Specializes in "comedy, and character driven scripts." Currently handles: 20% TV scripts; 20% syndicated material; 60% movie scripts.
Handles: Novellas, movie scripts, TV scripts. Will consider these nonfiction areas: government/politics/law; music/dance/theater/film. Will consider these fiction areas: action/adventure; comic; detective/police/crime; erotica; psychic/supernatural; romance (contemporary, gothic, historical, regency); science fiction; sports. Query with outline. Will report in 1 month on queries.
Recent Sales: "Dick Gibson Show," by Peter Amster (Lippitz Productions); "Dumping Ground," by Tom Towles (New Line).
Terms: Agent receives 10% commission on domestic sales; 10% on foreign sales.
Fees: Charges a reading fee "for new writers only." Offers a criticism service "for new writers only." Critiques are written by Coleen Gallagher. 90% of business is derived from commissions on ms sales; 10% is derived from reading or criticism fees.
Tips: Obtains new clients through recommendations from others.

 The double dagger before a listing indicates the listing is new in this edition.

‡ALL-STAR TALENT AGENCY (I), Suite 2, 21416 Chase St., Canoga Park CA 91304. (818)341-4313. Contact: Robert Allred. Estab. 1991. Member of WGA. Represents 2 clients. 100% of clients are new/previously unpublished writers. Specializes in film, TV. Currently handles: 100% TV scripts.
Handles: Novels, movie scripts, stage plays, TV scripts. Will consider these fiction areas: action/adventure; cartoon/comic; contemporary issues; detective/police/crime; family saga; fantasy; historical; humor/satire; mainstream; mystery/suspense; psychic/supernatural; romance (contemporary); science fiction; sports; thriller/espionage; westerns/frontier; "any mainstream film or TV ideas." Query. Will report in 3 weeks on queries; 2 months on mss.
Terms: Agent receives 10% commission on domestic sales; 20% on foreign sales. Offers written contract, binding for 1 year. 100% of business derived from commissions on ms.
Tips: Obtains new clients through recommendations and solicitation. "A professional appearance in script format, dark and large type and simple binding go a long way to create good first impressions in this business; as does a professional business manner."

‡MICHAEL AMATO AGENCY (II), 1650 Broadway, New York NY 10019. (212)247-4456-57. Fax: (212)247-4456. Contact: Susan Tomkins. Estab. 1970. Member of WGA, SAG, AFTRA, Equity. Represents 6 clients. 2% of clients are new/previously unpublished writers. Specializes in television and theater. Currently handles nonfiction books; stage plays. Will handle: nonfiction books, juvenile books, novels, movie scripts, stage plays, TV scripts. Will consider these nonfiction areas: cooking/food/nutrition; current affairs; health/medicine; women's issues/women's studies. Will consider these fiction areas: action/adventure; juvenile; young adult. Query. Will report "within a month" on queries.
Tips: Obtains new clients through recommentaions.

□AMERICAN PLAY CO., INC. (II), Suite 1204, 19 W. 44th St., New York NY 10036. (212)921-0545. Fax: (212)869-4032. President: Sheldon Abenal. Estab. 1889. Subsidiary of Century Play Co. Specializes in novels, plays, screenplays.
Handles: Novels, movie scripts, stage plays. Will consider all nonfiction and fiction areas. Send entire ms, "double space each page." Will report as soon as possible on ms.
Terms: Agent receives 15% commission on domestic sales; 15% on foreign sales.
Fees: Charges $100 reading fee, which includes a 2-3 page critique. Criticism service: $100.
Tips: Obtains new clients through referrals, unsolicited submissions by authors. "Writers should write novels first before screenplays. They need to know what's going on behind the camera. Before they write or attempt a play, they need to understand the stage and sets. Novels need strong plots, characters who are fully developed."

THE MARY BEAL AGENCY (III), 144 North Pass Ave., Burbank CA 91505. (818)846-7812. Estab. 1988. Member of DGA and WGA. Represents 30 clients. 30% of clients are new/previously unpublished writers. Specializes in features and television scripts. Currently handles: 50% movie scripts; 50% TV scripts.
Handles: Nonfiction books, movie scripts, TV scripts. Will consider these nonfiction areas: gay/lesbian issues; government/politics/law; psychology; true crime/investigative. Will consider these fiction areas: detective/police/crime; erotica; feminist; gay/lesbian; literary; mainstream; mystery/suspense; psychic/supernatural; science fiction; thriller/espionage. Query with SASE. Will report in 6 weeks on queries; 3 months on mss.
Terms: Agent receives 10% on domestic sales; 10% on foreign sales. Offers a written contract, binding for 2 years. "Authors supply photocopies. They need to have entertainment attorney when contracts arrive."
Tips: Obtains new clients through referrals mainly. "Be sure that a script is the best it can be before seeking representation."

□ *An open box indicates script agents who charge fees to writers. WGA signatories are not permitted to charge for reading manuscripts, but may charge for critiques or consultations.*

LOIS BERMAN, WRITERS' REPRESENTATIVE (III), 240 W. 44th St., New York NY 10036. (212)575-5114. Contact: Lois Berman or Judy Boals. Estab. 1972. Member of AAR. Represents about 25 clients. Specializes in dramatic writing for stage, film and TV.
Handles: Movie and TV scripts, plays. Query first.
Terms: Agent receives 10% commission.
Tips: Obtains new clients through recommendations from others.

□**THE MARIAN BERZON AGENCY (II)**, 336 E. 17th St., Costa Mesa CA 92627. (818)961-0695. Literary Agent: Mike Ricciardi. Estab. 1979. Member of WGA. "We are also a talent agent and signatory of SAG, AFTRA, Equity and AGVA." 88% of clients are new/previously unpublished writers. Specializes in screenplays of all genres, especially comedy (must be honest), inspirational and thrillers. Currently handles: 4% juvenile books, 2% novels, 1% novellas, 70% movie scripts, 8% stage plays, 10% TV scripts, 5% songs for movies and musical theater (cassettes only). "We now have a Glendale CA office (Suite 110, 1614 Victory Blvd., Glendale CA 90201. (818)548-1560) and will soon have one in NYC."
Handles: Movie scripts, stage plays, TV scripts. Will consider these screenplay areas: action/adventure; contemporary issues; feel good romantic comedies; family saga; fantasy; juvenile comedy/drama; romantic comedy/drama; juvenile; mainstream; mystery/suspense; religious/inspiration; romance (contemporary); thriller/espionage; young adult; screen stories about real people. No slasher or serial killers! Query with bio, small photo, cover letter and one-page summary. SASE with #10 envelope. "Unsolicited scripts will be returned unread C.O.D." Will report in 30 days or sooner on queries. "We will not answer any query without SASE. *Please* inquiry telephone calls only between the hours of 3:00-4:30 p.m. M-F and 9:30-noon Saturday (Pacific Time)."
Recent Sales: "Mr. Park Avenue," by Joan Vincenza (Gerry Wolff Productions); "The Stork Child," (Cinevox—"Neverending Story").
Terms: Agent receives 10% commission on domestic sales; 15% on foreign sales (short fiction and plays 15%; advances 15% on novels). Offers written contract and WGA rider with agreement.
Fees: "Never charges a reading fee. We give a detailed and complete breakdown for free." We charge only for postage, fax, long distance and postal insurance directly related to the client for writers who are not established or members of the guild and only until the writer's first sale. No charges after that." 100% of business derived from commissions on ms sales. We offer some probationary representations to film students who demonstrate outstanding potential, even before their screenplay is finished.
Tips: Obtains new clients through recommendations from others and known producers. "If you really want to be represented, take note of the old saying 'you never get a second chance to make a first impression.' Be sure your queries intrigue us. Forget your ego. Include sufficient SASE and #10 envelope. Write us a personal cover letter. No computer draft or mimeographed correspondence. Write to us like you really want to be considered. Include bio, photo, résumé. Read and absorb *The Complete Guide to Standard Script Format* (parts 1 & 2) by Cole and Haag and Margaret Mehring's *The Screenplay: A Blend of Film Form & Content* before submitting. Screenplays should never be longer than 118 pages. They must be visual and not dialogue heavy. Structure, character development and narrative drive are the most important elements we look for. Screenplay description must be visually and actually alive. Make certain the opening of your screenplay is a 'grabber.' We believe in the new writer and will even spend time and effort by appointment (in person) in our offices in California."

□**BETHEL AGENCY (II)**, Suite 16, 641 W. 59th St., New York NY 10019. (212)664-0455. Contact: Lewis R. Chambers. Estab. 1967. Represents 25+ clients.
Handles: Movie scripts and TV scripts. Will consider these nonfiction areas: agriculture/horticulture; animals; anthropology/archaeology; art/architecure/design; biography/autobiography; business; child guidance/parenting; cooking/food/nutrition; crafts/hobbies; current affairs; ethnic/cultural interests; gay/lesbian issues; government/politics/law; health/medicine; history; interior design/decorating; juvenile nonfiction; language/literature/criticism; military/war; money/finance/economics; music/dance/theater/film; nature/environment; photography; psychology; religious/inspirational; true crime/investigative; science/technology; self-help/personal improvement; sociology; sports; translations; women's issues/women's studies. Will consider these fiction areas: action/adventure; cartoon/comic; confessional; contemporary issues; detective/police/crime; ethnic; family saga; fantasy; feminist; gay; glitz; historical; humor/satire; juvenile; lesbian; literary; mainstream; mystery/suspense; picture book; psychic/supernatural; regional; religious/inspiration; romance (contemporary, gothic, historical, regency); sports; thriller/espionage; westerns/frontier; young adult. Query with SASE and outline plus 1 sample chapter. Will report in 1-2 months on queries.

Terms: Agent receives 15% commission on domestic sales; 20% on foreign sales. Offers written contract, binding for 6 months to 1 year.
Fees: Charges reading fee only to unpublished authors; writer will be contacted on fee amount.
Tips: Obtains new clients through recommendations from others. "Never send original material."

DON BUCHWALD AGENCY (III), 10 E. 44th St., New York NY 10017. (212)867-1070. Contact: Kristin Miller or Michael Traum. Estab. 1977. Member of WGA. Represents 50 literary clients. Talent and literary agency.
Handles: Screenplays, stage plays, TV scripts. Will consider these nonfiction areas: biography/autobiography; current affairs; history; science/technology; sports. Will consider these fiction areas: action/adventure; family saga; mainstream; romance (contemporary, gothic, historical, regency); science fiction; thriller/espionage; westerns/frontier. Query with SASE only.
Tips: Obtains new clients through other authors, agents.

□THE MARSHALL CAMERON AGENCY (II), Rt. 1 Box 125, Lawtey FL 32058. (904)964-7013. Fax: (904)964-6905. Contact: Margo Prescott. Estab. 1986. Member WGA. Specializes in feature films and television scripts and true story presentations for MFTS. Currently handles: 5% nonfiction books; 5% novels; 70% movie scripts; 20% TV scripts. Member agents: Margo Prescott; Ashton Prescott.
Handles: Nonfiction books, juvenile books, novels, movie scripts, TV scripts. Will consider these nonfiction areas: business; health/medicine; juvenile nonfiction; money/finance/economics; true crime/investigative; self-help/personal improvement. Will consider these fiction areas: action/adventure; detective/police/crime; historical; literary; mainstream; mystery/suspense; thriller/espionage. Query. Will report in 1 week on queries; 4-8 weeks on mss.
Terms: Agent receives 10-15% commission on domestic sales; 20% on foreign sales. Offers a written contract, binding for 1 year.
Fees: Charges $150/300 pgs. reading/evaluation for books; no reading fee for screenplays. Charges $85 to review all true story material for TV or film ("maybe higher for extensive material"). Criticism service available for twice the reading fees. Offers overall criticism, some on line criticism. "We recommend changes, usually 3-10 pages depending on length of the material (on request only)." Charges nominal marketing fee which includes postage, phone, fax, Federal Express. 90% of business is derived from commissions on sales; 10% is derived from reading fees or criticism services. Payment of a criticism fee does not ensure representation.
Tips: "Often professionals in film and TV will recommend us to clients. We also actively solicit material."

MARGARET CANATELLA AGENCY (V), P.O. Box 674, Chalmette LA 70044-0674. Agency not currently seeking new clients.

CINEMA TALENT INTERNATIONAL (II), Suite 808, 8033 Sunset Blvd., W. Hollywood CA 90046. (213)656-1937. Contact: George Kriton and George N. Rumanes. Estab. 1976. Represents approximately 23 clients. 3% of clients are new/previously unpublished writers. Currently handles: 1% nonfiction books; 1% novels; 95% movie scripts; 3% TV scripts. Member agents include: George Kriton and George N. Rumanes.
Handles: Nonfiction books, novels, movie scripts, TV scripts. Query with outline/proposal plus 2 sample chapters. Will report in 4-5 weeks on queries; 4-5 weeks on ms.
Terms: Agent receives 10% on domestic sales; 20% on foreign sales. Offers a written contract, binding for 2 years.
Tips: Obtains new clients through recommendations from others.

CIRCLE OF CONFUSION LTD. (II), 131 Country Village Ln., New Hyde Park NY 11040. (212)969-0653. Contact: Rajeev K. Agarwal, Lawrence Mattis. Estab. 1990. Member of WGA. Represents 40 clients. 80% of clients are new/previously unpublished writers. Specializes in screenplays for film and TV. Currently handles: 5% nonfiction books; 5% novels; 10% novellas; 75% movie scripts; 5% TV scripts.
Handles: Nonfiction books, novels, novellas, short story collections, movie scripts, stage plays, TV scripts. Will consider these nonfiction areas: biography/autobiography; business; current affairs; gay/lesbian issues; government/politics/law; health/medicine; history; juvenile nonfiction; true crime/investigative; women's issues/women's studies. Will consider all fiction areas. Send entire ms. Will report in 1 week on queries; 3 weeks on mss.

Terms: Agent receives 10% commission on domestic sales; 10% on foreign sales. Offers a written contract, binding for 1 year.
Tips: Obtains new clients through queries, recommendations and writing contests. "We pitch books, scripts, short stories and plays for film/TV adaptation."

‡**COMEDY INK (II)**, 8070 La Jolla Shores Dr., #243, La Jolla CA 92037. (619)525-7916. Contact: Brian Keliher. Estab. 1986. Member of WGA. Represents 10 clients. 70% of clients are new/previously unpublished writers. Specializes in movie scripts. "Our specialty is comedy, but we also accept dramatic works." Currently handles: 10% nonfiction books; 10% TV scripts; 80% movie scripts.
Handles: Movie scripts. Query or send entire script.
Terms: Agent receives 10% commission on domestic sales. Offers a written contract.
Tips: Obtains new clients at conferences and through recommendations from others. "Remember two important words: patience and persistence. They are not mutually exclusive!"

DISKANT & ASSOCIATES (III), Suite 202, 1033 Gayley Ave., Los Angeles CA 90024. (310)824-3773. Contact: George Diskant. Estab. 1983. Represents 12 clients. Currently handles: 40% nonfiction books; 20% movie scripts; 20% TV scripts. Will consider these nonfiction areas: biography/autobiography; current affairs; history. Will consider these fiction areas: contemporary issues; historical; mystery/suspense; young adult. "Won't accept any unsolicited manuscripts at this time. Telephone query only."
Terms: Agent receives 15% commission on domestic sales.
Tips: "We deal with teleplays and screen plays mostly."

□**EARTH TRACKS AGENCY (I, II)**, Suite 286, 4712 Ave. N, Brooklyn NY 11234. Contact: David Krinsky. Estab. 1990. Member of WGA. Represents 5 clients. 50% of clients are new/previously unpublished writers. Specializes in "movie and TV script sales of original material." Currently handles: 20% novels; 50% movie scripts; 10% stage plays; 20% TV scripts.
Handles: Novels, movie scripts, stage plays, TV scripts ("No Star Trek"), TV movie scripts. Will consider all nonfiction areas. Will consider these fiction areas: action/adventure; cartoon/comic; contemporary issues; detective/police/crime; erotica; humor/satire; romance (contemporary); thriller/espionage; young adult. Query with SASE. Will report in 4-6 weeks on queries; 6-8 weeks on mss ("only if requested").
Terms: Agent receives 10-12% commission on domestic sales; 10-12% on foreign sales. Offers a written contract, binding for 6 months to 2 years.
Fees: "There is no fee if I accept to read a TV/movie script. For plays and books I charge $100 a book or $75 a stage play, nonrefundable. Criticism service: $25 per item (treatment or manuscript) submitted. I personally write the critiques. Critique not provided on scripts. An author *must* provide a *proper* postage (SASE) if author wants material returned. If no SASE enclosed, material is not returned." 90% of business is derived from commissions on ms sales; 10% is derived from reading fees or criticism service. Payment of a criticism fee does not ensure representation.
Tips: Obtains new clients through recommendations and letters of solicitations by mail. "Send a one-page letter describing the material the writer wishes the agency to represent. Do not send anything other than query letter with SASE. Unsolicited script will not be returned. Do not 'hype' the material—just explain exactly what you are selling. If it is a play, do not state 'screen play.' If it is a movie script, do not state 'manuscript,' as that implies a book. Be specific, give description (summary) of material."

FARBER LITERARY AGENCY INC. (II), (formerly Farber & Freeman), 14 E. 75th St., New York NY 10021. (212)861-7075. Contact: Ann Farber. Estab. 1992. Member of WGA. Represents 30 clients. 50% of clients are new/previously unpublished writers. Currently handles: 10% nonfiction books; 60% novels, 30% stage plays.
Handles: Juvenile books, novels, novellas, movie scripts, stage plays. Will consider these fiction areas: action/adventure; contemporary issues; detective/police/crime; historical; humor/satire; juvenile; mainstream; mystery/suspense; contemporary romance; thriller/espionage; young adult. Send outline plus 3 sample chapters. Will report at once on queries; 1 month on mss.
Terms: Offers a written contract, binding for 2 years.
Tips: Obtains new clients through recommendations from others and listings.

‡□**THE FILM & FICTION AGENCY (I)**, Suite 123, 17194 Preston Rd., Dallas TX 75248. (214)380-8392. Contact: Cliff Reed/Nancy De Vaughn. Estab. 1992. Represents 2 clients. 100% of clients are new/previously unpublished writers. Specializes in screenplays and contemporary fiction. Currently han-

dles: 50% novels; 50% movie scripts. Member agents: Cliff Reed (screenplays), Nancy DeVaughn (novels).
Handles: Novels, movie scripts. Will consider these fiction areas: action/adventure; detective/police/crime; humor/satire; mainstream; mystery/suspense; thriller/espionage; westerns/frontier. Query with outline/proposal. Will report in 2 weeks on queries; 4-6 weeks on mss.
Terms: Agent receives 15% commission on domestic sales; 20% on foreign sales. Offers written contract with 30 day cancellation notice.
Fees: Offers criticism service: $55—novels/screenplays to 50,000 words; $75—novels/screenplays to 75,000 words; $125—novels/screenplays to over 75,000 words. Charges $25 log-in charge. Payment of criticism fee does not ensure representation.
Tips: Obtains new clients through recommendation and ads.

ROBERT A FREEDMAN DRAMATIC AGENCY, INC. (II, III), Suite 2310, 1501 Broadway, New York NY 10036. (212)840-5760. President: Robert A. Freedman. Vice President: Selma Luttinger. Estab. 1928. Member of AAR. Prefers to work with established authors; works with a small number of new authors. Specializes in plays, motion picture and television scripts.
Handles: Movie scripts, stage plays and TV scripts. Query. Does not read unsolicited mss. Usually reports in 2 weeks on queries; 3 months on mss.
Terms: Agent receives 10% on dramatic sales; "and, as is customary, 20% on amateur rights." Charges for photocopying manuscripts.
Recent Sales: "We will speak directly with any prospective client concerning sales that are relevant to his/her specific script."

SAMUEL FRENCH, INC. (II, III), 45 W. 25th St., New York NY 10010. (212)206-8990. Editors: William Talbot and Lawrence Harbison. Estab. 1830. Member of AAR. Represents "hundreds" of clients. Prefers to work with published/established authors; works with a small number of new/unpublished authors. Specializes in plays. Currently handles 100% stage plays.
Handles: Stage plays. Query or send entire ms. Replies "immediately" on queries; decision in 2-8 months regarding publication. "Enclose SASE."
Terms: Agent receives usually 10% professional production royalties; 20% amateur production royalties.
Recent Sales: *Mastergate*, by Gelbart.

□**THE GARY-PAUL AGENCY (II)**, 84 Canaan Ct., #17, Stratford CT 06497-4538. (203)336-0257. Contact: Gary Maynard or Chris Conway. Estab. 1990. Member of WGA. Represents 32 clients. 75% of clients are new/previously unpublished writers. Specializes in the promotion of film and television scripts and writer representation (produced and unproduced). Currently handles: 80% movie scripts; 20% TV scripts.
Handles: Movie scripts, TV scripts. Query. Will report in 2 weeks on queries; 6 weeks on mss.
Recent Sales: *Get A Life*, by Patrick Horton (Shapiro Glickenhaus); *Payoff*, by Marcia Womack (Western Films).
Terms: Agent receives 10% commission on domestic sales; 10% on foreign sales. Offers a written contract for one year.
Fees: The cost for each script submitted is $200. "Normally we offer advice at no cost unless the writer is in need of complex advice regarding character, structure and dialogue problems. We can advise on all aspects of screen and television writing. Both Gary Maynard and Chris Conway offer criticism. All writers will provide copies of their scripts including SASE for each submission to producers. There are no other charges." 25% of business is derived from commissions on ms sales; 25% is derived from criticism services. "In all cases, each script submitted finds representation."
Writers' Conferences: NBC Writers Workshop; seminar: Yale University.
Tips: Obtains new clients through advertisements in trade magazines, reference books and published articles "Hollywood Script Writer. If you want help in your writing, ask. This agency will help the writer."

THE GERSH AGENCY (II, III), 232 N. Canyon Dr., Beverly Hills CA 90210. (310)274-6611. Contact: Nancy Nigrosh. Estab. 1962. Less than 10% of clients are new/previously unpublished writers. Special interests: "mainstream—convertible to film and television."

Handles: Movie and television scripts. Send entire ms. Responds to ms in 4 weeks.
Recent Sales: *Hot Flashes*, by Barbara Raskin (Weintraub Entertainment); *Donato & Daughter* (Universal); *Libra* by Don Dellio (A&M).
Terms: Agent's commission: 10% on domestic sales. "We strictly deal in *published* manuscripts in terms of potential film or television sales, on a strictly 10% commission — sometimes split with a New York literary agency or various top agencies."

GRAHAM AGENCY (II), 311 W. 43rd St., New York NY 10036. (212)489-7730. Owner: Earl Graham. Estab. 1971. Represents 35 clients. 35% of clients are new/unpublished writers. Willing to work with new/unpublished writers. Specializes in full-length stage plays and musicals.
Handles: Stage plays and musicals. "We consider on the basis of the letters of inquiry." Writers *must* query before sending any material for consideration. Reports "as soon as possible on queries."
Terms: Agent receives 10% commission on domestic sales; 10% on dramatic sales; and 10% on foreign sales.

□**ALICE HILTON LITERARY AGENCY (II)**, 13131 Welby Way, North Hollywood CA 91606. (818)982-2546. Estab. 1986. Eager to work with new/unpublished writers. "Interested in any quality material, although agent's personal taste runs in the genre of 'Cheers.' 'L.A. Law,' 'American Playhouse,' 'Masterpiece Theatre' and Woody Allen vintage humor."
Handles: Book length mss (fiction and nonfiction), juvenile, movie and television feature length scripts.
Terms: Agent receives 10% commission. Brochure available with SASE. Preliminary phone call appreciated.
Fees: Charges evaluation fee of $2.50/1,000 words. Charges for phone, postage and photocopy expenses.
Recent Sales: *Shadow in a Weary Land*, by Harry Jones (Permanent Press); *Living Foods Survival Manual*, by Boris Isaacson (Tomorrow Now Press).

INTERNATIONAL LEONARDS CORP. (II), 3612 N. Washington Blvd., Indianapolis IN 46205-3534. (317)926-7566. Contact: David Leonards. Estab. 1972. Member of WGA. Currently handles: 50% movie scripts; 50% TV scripts.
Handles: Movie scripts, TV scripts. Will consider these nonfiction areas: anthropology/archaeology; biography/autobiography; business; current/affairs; history; money/finance/economics; music/dance/theater/film; new age/metaphysics; psychology; religious/inspirational; true crime/investigative; science/technology; self-help/personal improvement; sports. Will consider these fiction areas: action/adventure; cartoon/comic; contemporary issues; detective/police/crime; family saga; fantasy; historical; humor/satire; mainstream; mystery/suspense; religious/inspiration; romance (contemporary, gothic, historical, regency); science fiction; sports; thriller/espionage. Query. Will report in 1 month on queries; 6 months on mss.
Terms: Agent receives 10% commission on domestic sales; 10% on foreign sales. Offers a written contract, "WGA standard, which varies."
Tips: Obtains new clients through recommendations and queries.

THE JOYCE P. KETAY AGENCY, 334 W. 89th St., New York NY 10024. (212)799-2398. Contact: Joyce Ketay or Carl Mulert, agents.
Handles: Theater and film scripts. Playwrights and screenwriters only. No novels.

PAUL KOHNER, INC. (IV), 9169 Sunset Blvd., W. Hollywood CA 90069. (310)550-1060. Contact: Gary Salt. Estab. 1938. Member of ATA. Represents 150 clients. 10% of clients are new/previously unpublished writers. Specializes in film and TV rights sales and representation of film and TV writers.
Handles: Nonfiction books, movie scripts, stage plays, TV scripts. Will consider these nonfiction areas: history; military/war; music/dance/theater/film; true crime/investigative. Query with SASE. Will report in 2 weeks on queries.
Recent Sales: Has sold scripts to 20th Century Fox, Warner's, Disney.
Terms: Agent receives 10% commission on domestic sales; 10% on foreign sales. Offers a written contract, binding for 1-3 years. "We charge for copying manuscripts or scripts for submission unless a sufficient quantitiy is supplied by the author. All unsolicited material is automatically returned unread."

□**L. HARRY LEE LITERARY AGENCY (II)**, Box #203, Rocky Point NY 11778. (516)744-1188. Contact: L. Harry Lee. Estab. 1979. Member of WGA, Dramatists Guild. Represents 285 clients. 65% of clients are new/previously unpublished writers. Specializes in motion picture screenplays. "Comedy is our strength, both features and sitcoms, also movie of the week, science fiction, novels and TV. Currently handles 30% novels; 50% movie scripts; 5% stage plays; 15% TV scripts. Member agents: Mary Lee Gaylor (episodic TV, feature films); Charles Rothery (feature films, sitcoms, movie of the week); Katie Polk (features, mini-series, children's TV); Patti Roenbeck (science fiction, fantasy, romance, historical romance); Frank Killeen (action, war stories, American historical, westerns); Hollister Barr (mainstream, feature films, romantic comedies); Ed Van Bomel (sitcoms, movie of the week, mysteries, adventure stories); Colin James (horror, Viet Nam, war stories); Judith Faria (all romance, fantasy, mainstream); Charis Biggis (plays, historical novels, westerns, action/suspense/thriller films); Stacy Parker (love stories, socially significant stories/films, time travel science fiction); Jane Breoge (sitcoms, after-school specials, mini-series, episodic TV); Cami Callirgos (mainstream/contemporary/humor, mystery/suspense); Vito Brenna (action/adventure, romantic comedy, feature films, horror); Anastassia Evereaux (feature films, romantic comedies).
Handles: Novels, movie scripts, stage plays, TV scripts, humor, sitcoms. Will consider these nonfiction areas: history; military/war. Will consider these fiction areas: action/adventure; detective/police/crime; erotica; family saga; fantasy; historical; humor/satire; literary; mainstream; mystery/suspense; romance (contemporary, gothic, historical, regency); science fiction; sports; thriller/espionage; westerns/frontier; young adult. Query "with a short writing or background resume of the writer. A SASE is a must. No dot matrix, we don't read them." Will report in "return mail" on queries; 3-4 weeks on mss. "We notify the writer when to expect a reply."
Recent Sales: *Golden Temptress*, by Patti Roenbeck (Leisure Books); *Outta Australia*, by Anastassia Evereaux and Jim "Big Chair" Colaneri (Lighthorse Productions).
Terms: Agent receives 15% commission on domestic sales; 20% on foreign sales; 10% on screenplays/teleplays and plays. Offers a written contract "by the manuscript which can be broken by mutual consent; the length is as long as the copyright runs."
Fees: Does not charge a reading fee. Criticism service: charges $195 for screenplays; $150 for movie of the week; $95 for TV sitcom; $195 for a mini-series; $1 per page for one-act plays."All of the agents and readers write the carefully thought out critiques, three page checklist, two to four pages of notes, and a manuscript that is written on, plus tip sheets and notes that may prove helpful. It's a thorough service, for which we have received the highest praise." Charges for postage, handling, photocopying per submission, "not a general fee." 90% of business is derived from commissions on ms sales. 10% is derived from criticism services. Payment of a criticism fee does not ensure representation.
Tips: Obtains new clients through recommendations, "but mostly queries." "If interested in agency representation, write a good story with interesting characters and that's hard to do. Learn your form and format. Take courses, workshops. Read *Writer's Digest*; it's your best source of great information."

THE ADELE LEONE AGENCY, INC., (in association with Acton & Dystel) (II), 26 Nantucket Pl., Scarsdale NY 10583. (914)901-2965. Fax: (914)337-0361. Contact: Ralph Leone. Estab. 1978. Represents 50 clients. 20% of clients are new/previously unpublished writers. Specializes in women's fiction, romance (historical, contemporary), horror, science fiction, nonfiction, hard science, self-help, parenting, nutrition. Currently handles: 40% nonfiction books; 60% novels. Member agents: Adele Leone, Ralph Leone, Richard Monaco.
Handles: Nonfiction books, novels. Will consider these nonfiction areas: biography/autobiography; business; child guidance/parenting; cooking/food/nutrition; crafts/hobbies; current affairs; ethnic/cultural interests; gay/lesbian issues; government/politics/law; health/medicine; history; interior design/decorating; language/literature/criticism; military/war; money/finance/economics; music/dance/theater/film; nature/environment; new age/metaphysics; psychology; true crime/investigative; science/technology; self-help/personal improvement; sports; women's issues/women's studies. Will consider these fiction areas: action/adventure; detective/police/crime; family saga; fantasy; glitz; historical; literary; mainstream; mystery/suspense; psychic/supernatural; romance; science fiction; thriller/espionage; westerns/frontier. Query. Will report in 2 weeks on queries.
Terms: Agent receives 15% commission on domestic sales; 15% on foreign sales, "unless foreign agent is used, then 10%." Offers a written contract, binding "no less than 1 year." Charges "only for special services performed at author's request."
Writers' Conferences: Attends RWA Conference; PENN Writers Conference; Harper's Ferry Conference.
Tips: Obtains new clients through recommendations from others, at conferences. "Send simple clear queries and return postage."

HELEN MERRILL LTD. (II), Suite 1 A, 435 W. 23rd St., New York NY 10011. (212)691-5326. Contact: Lourdes Lopez or Helen Merrill. Estab. 1975. Member of AAR. Represents 100 clients. Handles 30% nonfiction books, 70% stage plays.
Handles: Stage plays, fiction, nonfiction. Will consider biographies. Will consider these fiction areas: contemporary issues; literary; mainstream. Query with SASE. Will report in 3 weeks on queries.
Terms: Agent receives 15% on domestic sales. Charges for postage, photocopies.
Tips: Usually obtains new clients through recommendations from others.

MONTGOMERY-WEST LITERARY AGENCY (IV), 7450 Butler Hills Dr., Salt Lake City UT 84121. Contact: Carole Western. Estab. 1989. Member of WGA. Represents 30 clients. 80% of clients are new/previously unpublished writers. Specializes in movie and television scripts and romance novels. Currently handles: 15% novels; 60% movie scripts; 25% TV scripts. Member agents: Carole Western (movie and TV scripts, novels); Nancy Gummery, Linda L. Taylor, consultants and editors.
Handles: Novels, movie scripts, TV scripts. Will consider these fiction areas: action/adventure; detective/police/crime; fantasy; mystery/suspense; psychic/supernatural; romance (contemporary, historical, regency); science fiction; thriller/espionage. Query with outline, 1 sample chapter and SAE. Will report in 6-8 weeks on queries; 8-10 weeks on mss. "We have editing and critiquing branch for reasonable fee."
Terms: Agent receives 15% commission on domestic sales for novels, 10% on movie scripts; 15% on foreign sales for books, 10% for movie scripts.
Writers' Conferences: Attends 3 workshops a year; Writers Guild of America West Conference.
Tips: "Send in only the finest product you can and keep synopses and treatments brief and to the point. Have patience and be aware of the enormous competition in the writing field."

‡PANDA TALENT (II), 3721 Hoen Ave., Santa Rosa CA 95405. (707)576-0711. Fax: (707)544-2765. Contact: Audrey Grace. Estab. 1977. Member of WGA, SAG, Aftra, Equity. Represents 10+ clients. 80% of clients are new/previously unpublished writers. Currently handles: 5% novels; 5% stage plays; 40% TV scripts; 50% movie scripts.
Handles: Movie scripts, TV scripts. Will consider these nonfiction areas: animals; military/war; psychology; true crime/investigative; sports. Will handle these fiction areas: action/adventure; confessional; detective/police/crime; family saga; humor/satire; juvenile; mystery/suspense; sports; thriller/espionage. Query with treatment. Will report in 3 weeks on queries; 2 months on mss.
Terms: Agent receives 10% commission on domestic sales; 10% on foreign sales.

□RAINTREE AGENCY (II), 360 W. 21 St., New York NY 10011. (212)242-2387. Contact: Diane Raintree. Estab. 1977. Represents 6-8 clients. Specializes in novels, TV and film scripts, plays and children's books.
Handles: Will consider all fiction areas. Phone first.
Terms: Agent receives 10% on domestic sales.
Fees: May charge reading fee. "Amount varies from year to year."

STEPHANIE ROGERS AND ASSOCIATES (III), #218, 3855 Lankershim Blvd., Hollywood CA 91604. (818)509-1010. Owner: Stephanie Rogers. Estab. 1980. Represents 24 clients. 20% of clients are new/unproduced writers. Prefers that the writer has been produced (motion pictures or TV), his/her properties optioned or has references. Prefers to work with published/established authors. Specializes in screenplays—dramas (contemporary), action/adventure, romantic comedies and suspense/thrillers for motion pictures and TV. Currently handles 10% novels; 50% movie scripts and 40% TV scripts.
Handles: Novels (only wishes to see those that have been published and can translate to screen) and movie and TV scripts (must be professional in presentation and not over 125 pages). Query. Does not read unsolicited mss. SASE required.

□ *An open box indicates script agents who charge fees to writers. WGA signatories are not permitted to charge for reading manuscripts, but may charge for critiques or consultations.*

Terms: Agent receives 10% commission on domestic sales; 10% on dramatic sales; and 20% on foreign sales. Charges for phone, photocopying and messenger expenses.
Tips: "When writing a query letter, you should give a short bio of your background, a thumbnail sketch (no more than a paragraph) of the material you are looking to market and an explanation of how or where (books, classes or workshops) you studied screenwriting." Include SASE for response.

JACK SCAGNETTI TALENT & LITERARY AGENCY (III), #210, 5330 Lankershim Blvd., N. Hollywood CA 91601. (818)762-3871. Contact: Jack Scagnetti. Estab. 1974. Member of WGA. Represents 40 clients. 50% of clients are new/previously unpublished writers. Specializes in film books with many photographs. Currently handles: 10% nonfiction books; 80% movie scripts; 10% TV scripts.
Handles: Will consider these nonfiction areas: health; military/war; true crime/investigative; self-help/personal improvement; sports. Will consider these fiction areas: mainstream; mystery/suspense; sports; thriller/espionage. Query with outline/proposal. Will report in 1 month on queries; 6-8 weeks on mss.
Terms: Agent receives 10% commission on domestic sales; 15% on foreign sales. Offers a written contract, binding for 6 months-1 year. Charges for postage and photocopies.
Tips: Obtains new clients through "referrals by others and query letters sent to us. Write a good synopsis, short and to the point and include marketing data for the book."

SCRIBE AGENCY (IV), P.O. Box 580393, Houston TX 77258-0393. (713)333-1094. Contact: Marta White or Carl Sinclair. "Please call before sending material." Estab. 1988. Member of WGA. Represents 20 clients. 40% of clients are new/previously unpublished writers. Specializes in book-length literary fiction for adults, motion picture and TV scripts. Currently handles: 40% novels; 40% movie scripts; 20% TV scripts.
Handles: Novels, movie scripts, TV scripts. Does not want to see "horrors/thrillers or other material promoting violence and/or sexual abuse." Will consider these fiction areas: contemporary issues; literary; mainstream. Query with SASE. Will report in 3-4 weeks on queries; 1 month on mss.
Terms: Agent receives 15% commission on domestic sales; 20% on foreign sales. Offers a written contract, binding time is negotiable.
Tips: Obtains new clients through recommendations. "Call, and submit query with SASE first."

KEN SHERMAN & ASSOCIATES (V), 9507 Santa Monica Blvd. Beverly Hills CA 90210. Agency not currently seeking new clients.

ELLEN LIVELY STEELE & ASSOCIATES (III), P.O. Drawer 447, Organ NM 88052. (505)382-5449. Fax: (505)382-9821. Contact: Ellen Lively Steele or Belinda S. Anderson. Estab. 1980. Member of WGA. Represents 20 clients. 60% of clients are new/previously unpublished writers. Specializes in New Age, occult, cookbooks, historical fiction, screenplays, children's. Currently handles: 2% nonfiction books; 1% textbooks; 10% juvenile books; 45% novels; 25% movie scripts; 35% TV scripts; 28% New Age.
Handles: Nonfiction and juvenile books, novels, movie scripts, TV scripts, New Age. Will consider these nonfiction areas: cooking/food/nutrition; history; new age/metaphysics; true crime/investigative; self-help/personal improvement; women's issues/women's studies. Will consider these fiction areas: action/adventure; detective/police/crime; family saga; glitz; historical; humor/satire; juvenile; mainstream; mystery/suspense; picture book; psychic/supernatural; romance (historical); science fiction; thriller/espionage. Query with outline plus 3 sample chapters. Will report in 6 weeks on queries; 2-3 months on ms.
Terms: Agent receives 10% commission on domestic sales; splits % on foreign sales. Offers a written contract, which is binding for 2 years. Charges for postage, fax, copies, phone calls. "Charges no extraordinary expense without written agreement from client. No office expenses. Marketing and editing expenses would fall into above list, usually."
Tips: Obtains new clients through recommendations from other clients, producers and editors, "very few from queries."

H.N. SWANSON INC. (III), 8523 Sunset Blvd., Los Angeles CA 90069. President: N.U. Swanson. Vice-president and Managing Director: Thomas Shanks. Estab. 1934. Member of WGA. Represents 100 clients. 10% of clients are new/previously unpublished writers. Currently handles: 60% novels; 40% movie scripts. Member agents: Annette Van Duren, Adam Fierro, Steven Fisher, Michele Wallerstein, Gail Barrick (in-house development).

Handles: Novels, novellas, movie scripts, TV scripts. Will consider these nonfiction areas: current affairs; sports. Will consider these fiction areas: action/adventure; detective/police/crime; historical; humor/satire; mainstream; mystery/suspense; sports; thriller/espionage. Query. Will report in 5 days on queries; 10 days mss.
Recent Sales: "For the most part, we co-agent with publishing agents, representing the motion picture and television sales of their clients. We do represent the publishing interests of a few clients."
Terms: Agent receives 10% commission on domestic sales; varies on foreign sales. Offers a written contract.
Tips: Obtains new clients through recommendations from others.

□THE TALENT BANK AGENCY (II), 1834 S. Gramercy Place, Los Angeles CA 90019. (213)735-2636. Contact: Douglas J. Nigh. Estab. 1990. Member of WGA. Represents 23 clients. "Seeking established writers: few additional authors are being added now." 99% of clients are new/previously unpublished writers. Currently handles: 73% movie scripts; 2% stage plays; 25% TV scripts.
Handles: Movie scripts, stage plays, TV scripts. Will consider these areas: action/adventure; contemporary issues; detective/police/crime; ethnic; family saga; fantasy; feminist; gay; historical; humor/satire; juvenile; lesbian; mainstream; mystery/suspense; science fiction; thriller/espionage; westerns/frontier. Query. Will report in 2 weeks on queries; 6-8 weeks on mss.
Terms: Agent receives 10% commission on domestic sales. Offers a written contract, binding for 1-2 years.
Fees: Does not charge a reading fee now. Will offer a criticism service at a later date.
Tips: Obtains new clients through recommendations and solicitations. "Be sure your letter of inquiry is grammatical and well-spelled. Avoid arrogance and modesty. Be forthright and business-like; get to your point succinctly. Pitch your work in a two-paragraph format. Treatment depends on length of piece. When submitting a screenplay, be sure it is correctly formatted. Have a "hook" in the first 10 pages or figure no one will read beyond that. Give me a reason to want to continue."

THE TANTLEFF OFFICE (II), Suite 700, 375 Greenwich St,. New York NY 10013. (212)941-3939. President: Jack Tantleff. Agents: John B. Sanlaiannio and Jill Brock. Estab. 1986. Member of WGA and AAR. Represents 50 clients. 20% of clients are new/unpublished writers. Specializes in television, theater and film. Currently handles 15% movie scripts; 70% stage plays; 15% TV scripts. Query with outline.
Terms: Agent receives 10% commission on domestic sales; 10% on dramatic sales; and 10% on foreign sales.

‡□A TOTAL ACTING EXPERIENCE (II), Suite 206, Dept. N.W., 14621 Titus St., Panorama City CA 91402. (818)901-1044. Contact: Dan A. Bellacicco. Estab. 1984. Member of WGA. Represents 30 clients. 50% of clients are new/previously unpublished writers. Specializes in "quality instead of quantity." Currently handles 5% nonfiction books; 5% juvenile books; 10% novels; 5% novellas; 5% short story collections; 50% movie scripts; 5% stage plays; 10% TV scripts; 5% how-to books and videos.
Handles: Films, novels, radio scripts, stage plays, syndicated material and TV scripts. "No heavy violence or drugs. All material must have a harmonious theme and story. Nonfiction books, textbooks, juvenile books, novels, novellas, short story collections, poetry books, movie scripts, stage plays, TV scripts, syndicated material, how-to books and videos. Will consider these nonfiction areas: animals; art/architecture/design; biography/autobiography; business; child guidance/parenting; computers/electronics; cooking/food/nutrition; crafts/hobbies; current affairs; ethnic/cultural interests; gay/lesbian issues; government/politics/law; health/medicine; history; juvenile nonfiction; language/literature/criticism; military/war; money/finance/economics; music/dance/theater/film; nature/environment; new age/metaphysics; photography; psychology; religious/inspirational; true crime/investigative; science/technology; self-help/personal improvement; sociology; sports; translations; women's issues/women's studies; "any well-written work!" Will consider all fiction areas. Query with outline plus 3 sample chapters. Will reports in 3 months on mss. "We will respond *only* if interested, material will *not* be returned."
Terms: Agent receives 10% on domestic sales; 10% on foreign sales. Offers written contract, binding for 2 years or more.
Fees: Offers criticism service (with our clients only at no charge.) 60% of business is derived from commission on ms sales.
Tips: Obtains new clients through mail and conferences. "We seek new sincere, quality writers for long-term relationships. We would love to see film, television, and stage material that remains relevant and provocative twenty years from today; dialogue that is fresh, and unpredictable; and story, theme and characters that are intelligent, enlightening, humorous, witty, creative, inspiring, and, most of all,

entertaining. Please keep in mind quality not quantity. Your character must be well delineated and fully developed with high contrast."

PEREGRINE WHITTLESEY AGENCY (II), 345 E. 80th St., New York NY 10021. (212)838-0153. Fax: (212)734-5176. Contact: Peregrine Whittlesey. Estab. 1986. Represents 20 clients. 60% of clients are new/previously unpublished writers. Specializes in plays and screenplays. Currently handles: 29% movie scripts; 70% stage plays; 1% TV scripts.
Handles: Movie scripts; stage plays; TV scripts. Query first. Will report in 2 weeks on queries; 3 weeks on mss.
Recent Sales: *The Song of Jacob Zulu*, by Tug Yourgrau (The Shubert Organization).
Terms: Agent receives 10% commission on domestic sales; 10% on foreign sales. Offers a written contract, binding for 2 years.
Tips: Obtains new clients through associations with agencies in England, recommendations from others and direct inquiries.

ANN WRIGHT REPRESENTATIVES, INC. (II, III), 2C, 136 E. 56th St., New York NY 10022. (212)832-0110. Head of Literary Department: Dan Wright. Estab. 1963. Member of WGA. Represents 42 clients. 25% of clients are new/unpublished writers. "Writers must be skilled or have superior material for screenplays, stories or novels that can eventually become motion pictures or television properties." Prefers to work with published/established authors; works with a small number of new/unpublished authors. "Eager to work with any author with material that we can effectively market in the motion picture business worldwide." Specializes in themes that make good motion pictures. Currently handles 10% novels; 75% movie scripts; and 15% TV scripts.
Handles: Query with outline – does not read unsolicited mss. Reports in 3 weeks on queries; 2 months on mss. All work must be sent with a SASE to ensure its return.
Terms: Agent receives 10% commission on domestic sales; 10% on dramatic sales; 10% on foreign sales; 20% on packaging. Will critique only works of signed clients. Charges for photocopying expenses.

Additional Script Agents

The following agencies have full listings in other sections of this book. These agencies have indicated they are *primarily* interested in handling book manuscripts, but are also interested in scripts. After reading the listing (you can find the page number in the Listings Index), send them a query to obtain more information on their needs and script manuscript submission policies.

Alden—Literary Service, Farel T.
Allan Agency, Lee
Amsterdam Agency, Marcia
Appleseeds Management
Author Aid Associates
Becker, Maximilian
Brink Literary Agency, The
Brown Ltd., Curtis
Browne Ltd., Pema
Cook Agency, Bruce
Cooper Assoc., Inc., Bill
Dykeman Associates Inc.
Marje Fields-Rita Scott Inc.
Gladden Unlimited
Goldfarb & Associates, Ronald
Grimes Literary Agency, Lew
KC Communications
Keyser Literary Agency
Kroll Agency, Lucy
Law Offices of Robert L.

Fenton PC
Lieberman Agency, The
Literary and Creative Artists Agency
Literary Bridge, The
Literary Representation South
Lyceum Creative Properties, Inc.
Markson Literary Agency, Elaine
Merhige-Merdon Marketing/ Promo Co. Inc., Greg
Morris Agency, William
New Writing Agency
Norma-Lewis Agency, The
Northeast Literary Agency
Northwest Literary Services
Pegasus International, Inc., Literary & Film Agents
PMA Literary and Film Management, Inc.

Puddingstone Literary Agency
Rhodes Literary Agency
Robb Literary Properties, Sherry
Roffman Associates, Richard H.
Roth Literary Agency, The
Russell-Simenauer Literary Agency Inc.
Southern Literary Agency
Wain Agency, Erika
Wald Associates, Inc., Mary Jack
Westchester Literary Agency, Inc.
Wohl Literary Agency, Gary S.
Wright Authors' Representative, Stephen
Writer's Consulting Group

Script Agents/'92-'93 changes

The following agencies appeared in the last (1992) edition of *Guide to Literary Agents & Art/Photo Reps* but are absent from the 1993 edition. These agencies failed to respond to our request for an update of their listing, or were left out for the reasons indicated in parentheses following the agency name.

Brody Agency (unable to contact)
Coconut Grove Talent Agency
International Artists (out of business)

Lake & Douroux Inc. (out of business)
Selected Artists Agency (unable to contact)
Charles Stewart (removed per

request)
Third Millennium Productions
Writers & Artists (unable to contact)

Art/Photo Reps

Finding and Working with Art/Photo Reps

by Barbara Gordon

There seems to be a lack of information as well as a lot of misinformation on the function and role of artists' and photographers' representatives. Whether or not to get a rep is a major career decision, so it's important to understand first what a representative is, what they can and cannot do for you and how they work.

A good definition of a representative is one who is the marketing and selling arm of a talent. First of all, if comparisons are to be made, an artists' and photographers' representative is comparable to a literary agent or talent agent in some respects. A rep does not employ artists and photographers, but acts as their agent in obtaining assignments from advertisers, publishers, corporations and others.

The representative is responsible for packaging the product (art and photography) by getting the portfolio in selling condition. This involves editing of the portfolio as well as advising the talent on what needs to be added to fill in the missing gaps. The representative must then take the product to market. This is done through sales calls and advertising, promotion and public relations channels. To do this effectively a good representative must obviously have a thorough working knowledge of what clients are prospects for the talent's work as well as the knowledge of what advertising and promotion mediums will most effectively reach those clients at the most efficient cost.

On the practical side the representative negotiates the best prices and working conditions for the talent while keeping the talent competitive in the marketplace. The rep must have a knowledge of current market trends, prices and job situations and enough experience to talk knowledgeably about the product he/she is selling and pricing.

In addition to payment received for completing the assignment, the representative will negotiate expenses, usages, terms of payment, deadlines, royalties, licensing and other rights where applicable. The representative will check out the credit worthiness of the new client, do the billing, collecting of invoices, and collecting and paying of sales taxes when necessary. A representative will also develop publicity programs for the talent, handle agency shows and presentations, service current business, open new markets and expand existing markets.

On a personal level a rep should have the health, energy and flexibility to flow with the ups and downs of the freelancing business, as well as enough financing to stay in business during the down times. It goes without saying that a good representative should be honest,

Barbara Gordon *operates Barbara Gordon Associates in New York City, representing both illustrators and photographers. She is a past president of the Society of Photographers and Artists Representatives, has written for both art and photography publications, and recently co-authored (with her husband, Elliott)* How to Sell Your Photographs and Illustrations.

trustworthy and in tune with the talent and their aspirations and believe in the work of the talent they represent.

Talents reps handle, talents they don't

Most representatives primarily handle commercial photographers and artists. A few handle designers, but since designers have a different buying audience than artists and photographers it is not as common. Designers usually have to search longer and harder for a representative.

Commercial reps do not handle fine artists (by fine artists I mean those who are looking for gallery affiliation). If a fine artist has a commercial style and is interested in doing commercial assignments however, a commercial representative may be interested in handling him. Yet there are a few fine art representatives, and interested artists will find them in the Fine Art Reps section in this book.

Commercial reps also do not handle craftspeople primarily because most commercial assignments involve the buying of flat art or photography. Occasionally there is a craftsperson who can make models or do something that applies to the commercial marketplace, but this is a rare situation and craftspeople looking for representation may be better served by a fine art rep or a crafts gallery. Reps, however, often handle photo-retouchers and hair and make-up people, simply because these skills are very compatible with a representative who is handling photographers.

Finding a representative

How does one go about finding a representative? One of the best places to start is to get the names and addresses of people in the field. This directory and the directories of professional organizations are probably the best sources with which to start. I also suggest that a prospective talent ask art directors and art buyers to give them recommendations, since these are the people that the client deals with and obviously you want a representative who clients feel has knowledge and integrity.

With your list in hand send either a promotion sheet or slides of your work to the representative in question, explaining that you are looking for representation. *Never* send original artwork. If you want something returned, send a self-addressed stamped envelope for that purpose. Always label your slides with your name and address just in case the slides become detached from your letter. Indicate "up" and "front" on your slides as well. Most reps ask for 10-15 slides. Plastic slide sleeves are available at most art and photography supply stores.

Since the representative is primarily interested in the salability of your work and must *see* it, this is the best way to approach a prospective representative. Unless a representative specifically requests them, phone calls and résumés are not recommended for first contacting reps since it's the work they are concerned with.

If a representative expresses an interest in you and your work, your next step is to check out the rep. Ask questions. Find out about the talent they currently handle and what type of clients they work with.

Be sure you have a clear understanding of the rep's policies. You might ask a rep:
- Do you handle competitive talents? If yes, do you have a large enough client base to handle talents with similar work?
- Will you share promotion and advertising costs? What is the split?
- What advertising and promotion would you do for my work?

- How long have you been in business?
- How broad is your client base?

You might also want to speak with art directors and buyers in the field about the representative, especially if they deal with the rep on a regular basis:

- Does the rep seem to have heavy talent turnover?
- Does the rep have consistent follow through or does he have an assistant handle the job after the sale is made?
- Is the rep fair, honest, thorough?

One final tip—trust your instincts. If everything checks out and you are getting "bad vibes" from the rep in question anyway, trust those instincts and move on. Conversely, if your instincts are telling you "this is the rep for me," go with those feelings too.

How does a representative work?

The most common arrangement, and the one most sought by talent, is the "exclusive" relationship. In this situation the representative will represent a talent "exclusively." That means the representative will not represent a competing talent. In return for this exclusive arrangement, the representative will get a percentage of the creative fee on all assignments, usually 25% on in-town situations and 30% for out-of town.

Under the exclusive arrangement the talent covers all of his or her own expenses, including portfolio costs (shooting transparencies, prints, laminates, etc.) on the theory that the portfolio is the permanent possession of the talent no matter who represents him/her. The representative covers the cost of running his/her office, making sales calls, etc. On advertising and promotion costs, the talent and representative split them on the same basis as the commission with the representative paying 25-30% of the costs and the talent paying 70-75% of the costs.

Some other representative-talent relationships include representatives who work on a straight salary. This usually occurs with a very large photography or design studio or television production house. Brokering is another situation. A representative represents a large group of competing talents and does not get a percentage on all of the assignments. Because the representative does not get a regular commission on all assignments, the rep will "broker" assignments, taking anywhere from 25-60% per assignment. In this case the representative usually does not pay for any part of the advertising and promotion costs involved.

When we talk about sharing expenses of advertising and promotion, what kinds of advertising and promotion are we referring to? The most common forms of advertising and promotion include: sending direct mail pieces to a specialized list of prospective clients; taking out advertising pages in one of the directories specifically for this purpose; arranging showings of the talent's work; and a variety of public relations efforts such as doing press releases on the talent's accomplishments.

All representatives have a "termination" clause in their contracts allowing them compensation after the talent and representative split. The reasoning behind this is that often it can take a representative years to establish a talent and the representative gets no compensation for this effort. The feeling is the rep is entitled to some part of the talent's compensation after termination based on earlier efforts. The termination compensation is very involved and can range from commissions on assignments for a period of six months or more after termination or sometimes a percentage of the last year's earnings.

As you can gather, the termination and other financial aspects of an agreement between an artist and representative are very complex and all that can be given here are some of the highlights of some of the arrangements. A talent seeking representation should do his/

her own research and confer with several representatives before making a final determination.

Do you really need a representative?

This is a very personal question that needs a very personal, individual answer. However, let me counter with another question. With so many legal and medical books around, does one really need a lawyer or doctor? And the answer is that sometimes all you need is a legal form from a stationery store or a remedy from the health food store, and sometimes you need the real thing.

There are artists and photographers who want to totally control their careers and have the high energy level and determination to promote and sell themselves. They do an excellent job of it without any outside assistance. There are also artists and photographers who are too busy doing assignments to handle the selling and promoting of their works. They want and need representation. Some artists simply like the support and interaction they get from a representative in this isolated world of freelancing.

Practically speaking, there are not enough representatives for the people seeking representation so, initially, many artists and photographers may find they have no choice but to represent themselves. As a working representative myself, I feel it's very good experience for a talent to represent himself sometime in his career. It gives him some insight to his buying audience and some familiarity and appreciation of how a representative functions.

One last word of advice: If you can't get a representative at first, keep trying. Representatives' situations change, and while they may be "booked" up in the beginning of the year, as the months go on they may find they have different needs and will be more receptive to your work at a later time.

For more information on artists' and photographers' reps contact SPAR, the Society of Photographers and Artists Representatives, Suite 1166, 60 E. 42nd St., New York NY 10165. This is a nonprofit organization of photographers' and artists' reps who sponsor educational programs for members and provide members with mailing lists and other educational materials. The group publishes a directory of their members with the types and names of talent they represent.

Commercial Art and Photography Reps

When you make the decision to work with a commercial art (illustration and sometimes design) or photography representative, you must be prepared to invest both time and money in your career. In return, however, a representative can help you earn back this investment many times over. In fact, having someone else act as your business manager and sales staff can give you more time to devote to the creation of your work.

Sound like a good deal? It can be. But getting a rep is a serious career move. In addition to spending money and time getting your portfolio and self-promotion pieces in shape, you must also be ready to approach your career as a business. Your professionalism will mean as much to a rep (and your clients) as your talent.

Taking a professional approach

For the most part a representative will require you to have a well-developed portfolio. Some have specific requirements for uniformity, but others just expect you to include your best work in a neat format. Before approaching a rep, take a good look at your portfolio. Is only your best work included? (Remember your portfolio is only as strong as your weakest piece or image.) Is your work mounted neatly on a page or are your slides labeled and secured in sleeves?

Since your rep may be sending out more than one portfolio at a time, you may have to make copies of many of your pieces (or slides). It's easy to see you will need to spend money—depending on the requirements, you could spend several hundred dollars getting your portfolio ready. Once you have invested this money, however, your portfolio will be the key your rep uses to unlock many doors.

Most reps also require you to provide a direct mail piece or to participate in a group package with other talents the rep handles. This, too, can be a big investment. You may be asked to take out your own ad in one of the creative directories, such as *American Showcase* or *The Creative Black Book*, but in return your work will be seen by hundreds of art directors. One nice little bonus for taking out one of these ads—most of these books provide you with tearsheets of your page which can be used as direct mail pieces. Advertising costs usually are a shared expense. In general, the expense is split on the same proportion as the commission. In other words, most reps receive 25-30% commission and will agree to absorb an equal percentage of advertising costs.

You may be asked to share expenses also, but most reps will absorb the usual office and marketing expenses. Though some reps are now asking for a monthly fee to cover unusual expenses, this does not seem to be a trend.

Most importantly, you must develop a professional attitude. A representative's job is to find you more and better assignments. Yet more assignments mean more deadlines. In this business you must deliver, and on time. Art directors at magazines and ad agencies trust the rep to present to them only those talents who are willing and able to follow through on assignments.

Approaching art or photo reps

Start by approaching a rep with a brief query letter and a direct mail piece, if you have one. If you do not have a flyer or brochure, you will need to send some representation of your work, such as photocopies or (duplicate) slides along with a self-addressed, stamped envelope. Since this can be a costly endeavor, you may want to check the listing or call to make sure the rep is open to queries at this time.

This should go without saying, but never send original work with a query. We hear too many horror stories about originals which have been lost or damaged en route. At a later date (when showing your portfolio) you may be asked to send originals, but this is after the rep has shown strong interest in your work.

When sending slides, be sure to label them. Your name and phone (and/or address) should appear on each slide in case they are separated from your other material. Also label "up" and "front" and any other information you might find helpful.

In your query letter be as brief as possible, but let the rep know a little bit about your background and your career goals. If you already have some established clients, let the rep know who they are and what you have been doing for them. Although most reps prefer an exclusive arrangement, if you have another rep in another part of the country, be sure to mention this too.

Help with your search

To help you with your search for representation, we've included a Geographic Index in the back of the book. It is divided by state and province. There is also an Agents and Reps Index to help you locate individual reps. Often you will read about a rep, but if that rep is an employee of a large agency, you may not be able to find that person's business number. We've asked agencies to give us the names of representatives on their staffs. Then we've listed the names in alphabetical order along with the name of their agency. Find the name of the person you would like to contact and then check the listing for that agency.

Some of the literary agencies and a few of the fine art reps are also interested in commercial illustrators or photographers. This is especially true of agents who deal with children's book publishers. If an agency's *primary* function is selling manuscripts for writers or the work of fine artists, but it's also interested in handling some illustrators or photographers, we've listed them in Additional Commercial Art/Photo Reps at the end of this section.

In addition to examining and contacting the listings in this section, word-of-mouth and referrals are still an important way to find representation. You may also be able to meet a rep at a show or workshop. Artist and photographer organizations provide information on reps to members through newsletters and meetings. For other information on the business of art, see *Artist's Market*; for photographers' organizations and information on the business, see *Photographer's Market* (both by Writer's Digest Books).

For more information on working with art and photo reps, see Barbara Gordon's article, Finding and Working with Art/Photo Reps. See also Resources for a list of other books on the art and photography business.

The Society of Photographers and Artists Representatives (SPAR) is an organization for professional representatives. The group sponsors educational programs for members and also publishes a directory of their membership (including the talent each represents). While some reputable reps do not belong to any organization, SPAR members are required to maintain certain standards and follow a code of ethics. The group has also developed a standard rep-artist agreement. For more information on the group, write to SPAR, Suite 1166, 60 E. 42nd St., New York NY 10165.

About the listings

Many of the representatives listed in this section handle both illustration and photography. Some also handle graphic designers, story board artists, photographer's models and set people. Although most reps like to handle a variety of work, some specialize in fashion or other specific fields.

Many representatives do not charge for additional expenses beyond those incurred in preparing your portfolio and sharing advertising costs. A few, however, require you to pay for special portfolios or other advertising materials. A handful also charge monthly retainers to cover marketing expenses. Where possible, we've indicated these listings with a filled-in box (■) symbol.

We've ranked the agencies listed in this section according to their openness to submissions. Below is our ranking system:

I Newer representative actively seeking clients.

II Representative seeking both new and established artists or photographers.

III Representative prefers to work with established artists or photographers, mostly through referrals.

IV Representative handling only certain types of work or work by artists or photographers under certain circumstances.

V Representative not currently seeking new clients. (If an agency chose this designation, only the address is given.) We have included mention of reps rated V only to let you know they are not open to new clients at this time. *Unless you have a strong recommendation from someone well-known in the field, our advice is to approach only those reps ranked I-IV.*

ARTISTS INTERNATIONAL (II), 7 Dublin Hill Drive, Greenwich CT 06830. (203)869-8010. Fax: (203)869-8274. Contact: Michael Brodie. Commercial illustration representative. Estab. 1971. Represents 25 illustrators. Specializes in children's books. Markets include advertising agencies, corporations/client direct, design firms, editorial/magazines, publishing books.
Handles: Illustration only.
Terms: Agent receives 30% commission. For promotional purposes, talent must provide 2 portfolios. Advertises in *American Showcase*. "We also have our own full-color brochure, 24 pages."
How to Contact: For first contact, send tearsheets, slides, SASE. Will report within 5 days. After initial contact, drop off or mail in appropriate materials for review.
Tips: Obtains new talent through recommendations from others, solicitation, at conferences, etc. "Just send in your book. I will review."

ASCIUTTO ART REPS., INC. (II, IV), 1712 E. Butler Circle, Chandler AZ 85225. (602)899-0600. Fax: (602)899-3636. Contact: Mary Anne Asciutto. Children's illustration representative. Estab. 1980. Member of SPAR, Society of Illustrators. Represents 20 illustrators. Specializes in children's illustration for books, magazines, posters, packaging, etc. Markets include publishing/packaging/advertising.
Handles: Illustration only.
Terms: Agent receives 25% commission. Advertising costs are split: 75% paid by talent; 25% paid by representative. For promotional purposes, talent should provide "prints (color) or originals within an 11 × 14 size format."
How to Contact: Send a direct mail flyer/brochure, tearsheets, photocopies, SASE. Will report within 2 weeks. After initial contact (if requested), send in appropriate materials. Portfolio should include original art on paper, tearsheets, photocopies or color prints of most recent work. If accepted, materials will remain for assembly.

Tips: In obtaining representation "be sure to connect with an agent that handles the kind of accounts you (the artist) *want*."

BARBARA BEIDLER INC. (III), #506, 648 Broadway, New York NY 10012. (212)979-6996. Fax: (212)505-0537. Contact: Barbara Beidler. Commercial illustration and photography representative. Estab. 1986. Represents 1 illustrator, 4 photographers, 3 fashion stylists. Specializes in fashion, home furnishings, life style, portraits. Markets include advertising agencies, catalog agencies, corporations/client direct, design firms, editorial/magazines, publishing/books, sales/promotion firms.
How to Contact: For first contact, send direct mail flyer/brochure. After initial contact, write to schedule an appointment. Portfolio should include tearsheets, slides.
Tips: Obtains new talent through recommendations from others.

BERENDSEN & ASSOCIATES, INC. (III), 2233 Kemper Lane, Cincinnati OH 45206. (513)861-1400. Fax: (513)861-6420. Contact: Bob Berendsen. Commercial illustration, photography, graphic design representative. Estab. 1986. Member of Art Directors Club of Cincinnati AAF (Advertising Club of Cincinnati). Represents 24 illustrators, 4 photographers, 4 designers. Specializes in "high-visibility consumer accounts." Markets include advertising agencies, corporations/client direct, design firms, editorial/magazines, paper products/greeting cards, publishing/books, sales/promotion firms.
Handles: Illustration, photography. "We are always looking for illustrators that can draw people, product and action well. Also we look for styles that are unique."
Terms: Agent receives 25% commission. Charges "mostly for postage but figures not available." Advertising costs are split: 75% paid by the talent; 25% paid by the representative. For promotional purposes, "artist must co-op in our direct mail promotions, and source books are recommended. Portfolios are updated regularly." Advertises in *RSVP, Creative Illustration Book, The Ohio Source Book* and *Advance Magazine.*
How to Contact: For first contact, send query letter, résumé, tearsheets, slides, photographs, photocopies, SASE. Reports back within weeks. After initial contact, drop off or mail in appropriate materials for review. Portfolios should include tearsheets, slides, photographs, photostats, photocopies.
Tips: Obtains new talent "through recommendations from other professionals. Contact Bob Berendsen, president of Berendsen and Associates, Inc. for first meeting."

IVY BERNHARD (III), Suite 401, 270 Lafayette St., New York NY 10012. Contact: Ivy Bernhard. Commercial photography representative. Estab. 1985. Represents 3 photographers. Specializes in fashion stylists. Markets include: advertising agencies, corporations/client direct, design firms, editorial/magazines.
Handles: Photography.
Terms: Agent receives 25% commission. Exclusive area representation required in New York. Advertises in *Creative Black Book.*
How to Contact: Reports back with 1 day. After initial contact, drop off or mail in appropriate materials for review. Portfolio should include tearsheets, photographs.

BERNSTEIN & ANDRIULLI INC. (III), 60 E. 42nd St., New York NY 10165. (212)682-1490. Fax: (212)286-1890. Contact: Sam Bernstein. Commercial illustration and photography representative. Estab. 1975. Member of SPAR. Represents 54 illustrators, 16 photographers. Staff includes Tony Andriulli; Howard Bernstein; Fran Rosenfeld; Judy Miller; Leslie Nosblatt; Molly Birenbaum; Craig Haberman; Natalie Ortiz. Markets include advertising agencies, corporations/client direct, design firms, editorial/magazines, paper products/greeting cards, publishing/books, sales/promotion firms.
Handles: Illustration and photography.
Terms: Agent receives a commission. Exclusive career representation is required. Advertises in *American Showcase, Creative Black Book, The Workbook, New York Gold, Creative Illustration Book.*
How to Contact: For first contact, send query letter, direct mail flyer/brochure, tearsheets, slides, photographs, photocopies. Reports back within 1 week. After initial contact, drop off or mail in appropriate materials for review. Portfolio should include tearsheets, slides, photographs.

‡CAROLYN BRINDLE & PARTNER INC. (II,IV), 203 E. 89th St., New York NY 10128. (212)534-4177. Fax: (212)996-9003. Contact: Carolyn Brindle. Commercial illustration and fine art representative. Estab. 1974. Represents 5 illustrators, 1 fine artist. Specializes in fashion-oriented work. Markets include advertising agencies, corporations/client direct, design firms, editorial/magazines; paper products/greeting cards, publishing/books, corporate and private collections, interior decorators, museums.

Handles: Illustration. Looks for "unusual or new technique."

Terms: Agent receives 25% commission. Exclusive representation is required. Advertising costs are split: 75% paid by talent; 25% paid by representative. For promotional purposes, "we require a well-organized portfolio. We create promotional pieces with the artist that we both feel represents their work." Advertises in *RSVP, Creative Illustration*.

How to Contact: For first contact, send a query letter and direct mail flyer/brochure, tearsheets, photocopies and SASE. Will report within 5 days-1 month, if interested. After initial contact, drop off or mail in appropriate materials for review. Portfolio should include original art, tearsheet, "examples of work that has not been published."

Tips: Usually obtains new talent through "recommendations from others in the fashion field, advertising agency art directors, magazine art directors, illustrators that are friends of artists already represented. If possible, before contacting a representative, look at the advertising annuals, e.g. *Creative Illustration* or *RSVP* and see the kind of work the representative shows. See if your work would fit in with what you see. The promotional pages usually reflect the representative's way of thinking and taste.

‡SAM BRODY, ARTISTS & PHOTOGRAPHERS REPRESENTATIVE (III), 12 E. 46th St., 4th Fl., New York NY 10017. (212)758-0640; (516)482-6422. Fax: (212)697-4518. Contact: Sam Brody. Commercial illustration and photography representative and broker. Estab. 1948. Member of SPAR. Represents 4 illustrators, 3 photographers, 2 designers. Markets include advertising agencies, corporations/client direct, design firms, editorial/magazines, publishing/books, sales/promotion firms.

Handles: Illustration, photography, design, "great film directors."

Terms: Agent receives 25-30% commission. Exclusive area representation is required. Advertising costs are split: 75% paid by the talent; 25% paid by the representative. For promotional purposes, talent must provide 8×10 transparencies (dupes only) and case; plus back-up advertising material, re: cards (reprints—*Black Book*, etc.) and self-promos. Advertises in *Creative Black Book*.

How to Contact: For first contact, send bio, direct mail flyer/brochure, tearsheets. Will report within 3 days or within 1 day if interested. After initial contact, call to schedule an appointment or drop off or mail in appropriate materials for review. Portfolio should include tearsheets, slides, photographs.

Tips: Obtains new talent through recommendations from others, solicitation. In obtaining representation, artist/photographer should "talk to parties he has worked with in the past year."

BROOKE & COMPANY (II), 4323 Bluffview, Dallas TX 75209. (214)352-9192. Fax: (214)350-2101. Contact: Brooke Davis. Commercial illustration and photography representative. Estab. 1988. Represents 10 illustrators, 2 photographers. "Owner has 18 years experience in sales and marketing in the advertising and design fields."

Terms: No information provided.

How to Contact: For first contact, send bio, direct mail flyer/brochure, "sample we can keep on file if possible" and SASE. Will report within 2 weeks. After initial contact, write to schedule an appointment to show a portfolio or drop off or mail in appropriate materials for review. Portfolio should include tearsheets, slides or photographs.

Tips: Obtains new talent through referral or by an interest in a specific style. "Only show your best work. Develop an individual style. Show the type of work that you enjoy doing and want to do more often. Must have a sample to leave with potential clients."

BRUCK AND MOSS ASSOCIATES (IV), 333 E. 49th St,. New York NY 10017. (212)980-8061 or (212)982-6533. Fax: (212)832-8778. Contact: Eileen Moss or Nancy Bruck. Commercial illustration representative. Estab. 1978. Represents 12 illustrators. Markets include advertising agencies, corporations/client direct, design firms, editorial/magazines, publishing/books, sales/promotion firms, direct marketing.

 The double dagger before a listing indicates the listing is new in this edition.

Handles: Illustration.
Terms: Agent receives 30% commission. Exclusive area representation is required. Advertising costs are split: 70% paid by the talent; 30% paid by the representative. For promotional purposes, talent must provide "4×5 transparencies mounted on 7×9 black board. Talent pays for promotional card for the first year and for trade ad." Advertises in *American Showcase*.
How to Contact: For first contact, send tearsheets, "if sending slides, include an SASE." After initial contact, drop off or mail in appropriate materials for review. Portfolios should include tearsheets.
Tips: Obtains new talent through referrals by art directors and art buyers, mailings of promo card, source books, art shows, *American Illustration* and *Print Annual*. "Make sure you have had at least 5 years experience repping yourself. Don't approach a rep on the phone, they are too busy for this. Put them on a mailing list and mail samples. Don't approach a rep who is already repping someone with the same style."

TRICIA BURLINGHAM/ARTIST REPRESENTATION (III), Suite 318, 9538 Brighton Way, Beverly Hills CA 90210. (213)271-3982. Office Manager: Tiffany Bowne. Commercial photography representative. Estab. 1979. Member of APA. Represents 7 photographers, 1 set designer/art director. Markets include advertising agencies, corporations/client direct, design firms, editorial/magazines.
Handles: Photography.
Terms: Agent receives 25-30% commission. Charges for Federal Express, messengers. Exclusive area representation is required. Advertising costs are paid by the talent. For promotional purposes, "we require all artists to provide promotional material with a mailing piece (envelope/tube, etc.) We require at least two portfolios and a shipping case." Advertises in *The Workbook*.
How to Contact: For first contact, send direct mail flyer/brochure. Reports within 3 weeks, only if interested. Portfolio should include tearsheets, slides, photographs, "all promotional material/direct mail pieces."
Tips: Obtains new talent through "recommendations from others and our solicitations and research. All promotional material sent in is viewed by Tricia Burlingham. Please only send nonreturnable items."

‡STAN CARP, INC. (III, IV), 2166 Broadway, New York NY 10024. (212)362-4000. Contact: Stan Carp. Commercial photography representative and director. Estab. 1959. Member of SPAR. Represents 3 photographers. Markets include advertising agencies, corporations/client direct, design firms, editorial/magazines, paper products/greeting cards, publishing/books, sales/promotion firms.
Handles: Photography and "commercial directors."
Terms: Agent receives 25% commission. Exclusive area representation is required. Advertising costs are split: 75% paid by the talent; 25% paid by the representative. Advertises in *Creative Black Book*, *The Workbook*, and other publications.
How to Contact: For first contact, send photographs. Reporting time varies. After initial contact, call to schedule an appointment to show a portfolio, which should include tearsheets, slides and photographs.
Tips: Obtains new talent through recommendations from others.

‡CAROL CHISLOVSKY INC. (II), 853 Broadway, New York NY 10003. (212)677-9100. Fax: (212)353-0954. Contact: Carol Chislovsky. Commercial illustration representative. Estab. 1975. Member of SPAR. Represents 20 illustrators. Markets include advertising agencies, design firms, editorial/magazines, publishing/books.
Handles: Illustration.
Terms: Agent receives 30% commission. Advertising costs are split: 70% paid by the talent; 30% paid by the representative. For promotional purposes, talent must provide direct mail piece. Advertises in *American Showcase*, *Creative Black Book* and sends out a direct mail piece.
How to Contact: For first contact, send direct mail flyer/brochure. Portfolio should include tearsheets, slides, photostats.
Tips: Obtains new talent through solicitation.

WOODY COLEMAN PRESENTS INC. (II), 490 Rockside Rd., Cleveland OH 44131. (216)661-4222. Fax: (216)661-2879. Contact: Woody. Commercial illustration representative. Estab. 1978. Member of Graphic Artists Guild. Represents 26 illustrators. Markets include advertising agencies, corporations/client direct, design firms, editorial/magazines, paper products/greeting cards, publishing/books, sales/promotion firms, public relations firms.

Handles: Illustration.
Terms: Agent receives 25% commission. Advertising costs are split: 75% paid by the talent; 25% paid by the representative. For promotional purposes, talent must provide "all portfolios in 4×5″ transparencies." Advertises in *American Showcase*, *Creative Black Book*, *The Workbook*, other publications.
How to Contact: For first contact, send query letter, tearsheets, slides, SASE. Reports within 7 days, only if interested. Portfolio should include tearsheets, 4×5 transparencies.
Tips: "Solicitations are made directly to our agency. Concentrate on developing eight to ten specific examples of a single style exhibiting work aimed at a particular specialty, such as fantasy, realism, Americana or a particular industry such as food, medical, architecture, transportation, film, etc." Specializes in "quality service based on being the 'world's best listeners.' We know the business, ask good questions and simplify an often confusing process. We are truly representative of being called a 'service' industry."

JAN COLLIER REPRESENTS (III), P.O. Box 470818, San Francisco CA 94147. (415)552-4252. Contact: Jan. Commercial illustration representative. Estab. 1978. Represents 12 illustrators. Markets include advertising agencies, design firms.
Handles: Illustration, photography.
Terms: Agent receives 25% commission. Exclusive area representation is required. Advertising costs are split: 75% paid by the talent; 25% paid by the representative. Advertises in *American Showcase*, *Creative Black Book*, *The Workbook*, *The Creative Illustration Book*.
How to Contact: For first contact, send tearsheets, slides, SASE. Reports within 5 days, only if interested. After initial contact, call to schedule an appointment to show a portfolio. Portfolios should include slides.

DANIELE COLLIGNON (II), 200 W. 15th St., New York NY 10011. (212)243-4209. Contact: Daniele Collignon. Commercial illustration representative. Estab. 1981. Member of SPAR, Graphic Artists Guild, Art Director's Club. Represents 12 illustrators. Markets include advertising agencies, corporations/client direct, design firms, editorial/magazines, publishing/books.
Handles: Illustration.
Terms: Agent receives 30% commission. Exclusive area representation is required. Advertising costs are split: 75% paid by the talent; 25% paid by the representative. For promotional purposes, talent must provide 8×10 transparencies (for portfolio) to be mounted; printed samples; professional pieces. Advertises in *American Showcase*, *Creative Black Book*, *The Workbook*.
How to Contact: For first contact, send direct mail flyer/brochure, tearsheets. Reports within 3-5 days, only if interested. After initial contact, drop off or mail in appropriate materials for review. Portfolio should include tearsheets, transparencies.

JAMES CONRAD & ASSOCIATES (II), 2149 Lyon St., #5, San Francisco CA 94185. (415)921-7140. Contact: James Conrad. Commercial illustration and photography representative. Estab. 1984. Member of SPAR, Society of Illustrators, Graphic Artists Guild. Represents 18 illustrators, 6 photographers. Markets include: advertising agencies, corporate art departments, editorial, graphic designers, paper products/greeting cards, books, poster and calender publishers.
Handles: Illustration, photography.
Terms: Agent receives 25% commission. Exclusive regional or national representation is required. For promotional purposes, talent must provide a portfolio "and participate in promotional programs."
How to Contact: For first contact, send samples.

CREATIVE ARTS OF VENTURA (V), P.O. Box 684, Ventura CA 93002. Representative not currently seeking new talent.

CREATIVE PRODUCTIONS, INC. (III), 7216 E. 99 St., Kansas City MO 64134. (816)761-7314. Contact: Linda Pool. Commercial photography representative. Estab. 1982. Represents 1 illustrator, 2 photographers. Markets include advertising agencies, corporations/client direct, design firms.
Handles: Photography.
Terms: Agent receives 30% commission. Advertising costs are split: 70% paid by the talent; 30% paid by the representative. For promotional purposes, talent must provide transparencies. "I complete promo pieces, but we share the cost." Advertises in *American Showcase*, *The Workbook*.

How to Contact: For first contact, send "sample of his/her favorite piece, what he enjoyed completing." Reports within 2 weeks, only if interested. After initial contact, call to schedule an appointment to show a portfolio.

LINDA DE MORETA REPRESENTS (II), 1839 Ninth St., Alameda CA 94501. (510)769-1421. Fax: (510)521-1674. Contact: Linda de Moreta. Commercial illustration and photography representative; also portfolio and career consultant. Estab. 1988. Represents 4 illustrators, 4 photographers. Markets include advertising agencies; corporations/client direct; design firms; editorial/magazines; paper products/greeting cards; publishing/books; sales/promotion firms.
Handles: Illustration and photography.
Terms: Agent receives 25% commission. Mailing costs are split 75%-25% between talent and representative. Exclusive representation requirements vary. Advertising costs are split: 75% paid by talent; 25% paid by representative. Materials for promotional purposes vary with each artist. Advertises in *The Workbook, The Creative Black Book, Bay Area Creative Sourcebook*.
How to Contact: For first contact, send direct mail flyer/brochure, tearsheets, slides, photocopies, photostats and SASE. "Please do *not* send original art. SASE for any items you wish returned." Will report in 2 weeks. After initial contact, call to schedule an appointment. Portfolios may include tearsheets, photostats, transparencies.
Tips: Obtains new talent through client and artist referrals, primarily, some solicitation. "I look for a personal vision and style of illustration or photography combined with maturity and a willingness to work hard."

DODGE CREATIVE SERVICES INC. (III), 301 N. Water St., Milwaukee WI 53202. (414)271-3388. Fax: (414)347-0493. Contact: Tim Dodge. Commercial illustration, photography and graphic design. Estab. 1982. Represents 15 illustrators, 2 photographers, 6 designers. Specializes in "representation to the Midwest corporate and advertising agency marketplace." Markets include advertising agencies, corporations/client direct, design firms, sales/promotion firms.
Handles: Illustration, photography, design. Looking for "absolutely outstanding and unique work only."
Terms: Agent receives 30% commission. Exclusive area representation is required. Advertising costs are split: 70% paid by the talent; 30% paid by the representative. For promotional purposes, talent must provide "portfolios provided as slides/transparencies (at least 3 complete sets)."
How to Contact: For first contact, send query letter, tearsheets, slides. Reports back within 2 weeks. After initial contact, write to schedule an appointment to show a portfolio. Portfolio should include thumbnails, tearsheets, slides.
Tips: Obtains new talent generally through recommendations and direct inquiries. "Make the presentation meticulous, keep the work focused. Show a desire to build a business and make a commitment."

PAT FORBES INC. (V), 11459 Waterview Cluster, Reston VA 22090-4315. Representative not currently seeking new talent.

(PAT) FOSTER ARTIST REP. (II), 6 E 36 St., New York NY 10016. (212)685-4580. Fax: same. Contact: Pat Foster. Commercial illustration representative. Estab. 1981. Member of Graphic Artists Guild. Represents 10 illustrators. Markets include advertising agencies, corporations/client direct, sales/promotion firms.
Handles: Illustration.
Terms: Agent receives 25% commission. "No additional charge for my services i.e. – shooting, obtaining pix ref/costumes." Advertising costs are split: 75% paid by the talent; 25% paid by the representative. Advertises in *American Showcase*.
How to Contact: For first contact, send direct mail flyer/brochure, tearsheets, slides. After initial contact, call to schedule an appointment or drop off or mail in appropriate materials. Portfolio should include tearsheets, slides, photographs, proofs.
Tips: Obtains new talent through recommendations mostly from associates in the business. "Work must look fresh; good design sense incorporated into illustration."

FRANCISCO COMMUNICATIONS, INC. (II, III), 419 Cynwyd Rd., Bala Cynwyd PA 19004. (215)667-2378. Fax: (215)667-4308. Contact: Carol Francisco. Commercial illustration representative. Estab. 1983. Represents 7 illustrators. Markets include advertising agencies, corporations/client direct.

Handles: Illustration.
Terms: Agent receives 25% commission. Advertising costs are split: 75% paid by the talent; 25% paid by the representative. For promotional purposes, talent must provide "promo samples, originals or same size copies of some samples."
How to Contact: For first contact, send query letter, direct mail flyer/brochure, tearsheets. Reports within 2 weeks only if interested. After initial contact, call to schedule an appointment to show a portfolio. Portfolio should include tearsheets, photographs, photostats, photocopies.

JEAN GARDNER & ASSOCIATES, Suite 108, 444 N. Larchmont Blvd., Los Angeles CA 90004. (213)464-2492. Fax: (213)465-7013. Contact: Jean Gardner. Commercial photography representative. Estab. 1985. Member of APA. Represents 5 photographers. Staff includes Paula Marshall, associate rep. Specializes in photography. Markets include advertising agencies, design firms.
Handles: Photography.
Terms: Agent receives 25% commission. Exclusive representation is required. Advertising costs are paid by the talent. For promotional purposes, talent must provide promos, *Workbook* advertising, a quality portfolio. Advertises in *The Workbook*.
How to Contact: For first contact, send direct mail flyer/brochure. Reports back within 3 weeks. "No appointments."
Tips: Obtains new talent through recommendations from others.

‡STEPHEN GILL (II), 135 E. 55th St., New York NY 10022. (212)832-0800. Fax: (212)832-1122. Contact: Stephen Gill or Anne Gill. Commercial illustration, commercial photography and fine art representative. Estab. 1975. Represents 2 illustrators, 1 photographer and 3 fine artists. Specializes in fashion (conceptual). Markets include corporations/client direct, art publishers, private collections.
Handles: Illustration, photography, fine art, fashion.
Terms: Agent receives 50% commission. "All artists pay for their own promotional materials. A direct mail piece is helpful but not necessary." Advertises in yellow pages.
How to Contact: For first contact, send résumé, direct mail flyer/brochure, slides, SASE, all materials needed to be returned must be accompanied by SASE. Will report within 1 month. After initial contact, drop off or mail in appropriate materials with SASE. Portfolio should include slides with SASE.
Tips: Obtains new clients through recommendations and direct mail. "At this time we need 3-5 fashion illustrators."

MICHAEL GINSBURG & ASSOCIATES, INC. (II, III), 407 Park Ave., South, New York NY 10016. (212)679-8881. Fax: (212)679-2053. Contact: Michael Ginsburg. Commercial photography representative. Estab. 1978. Represents 5 photographers. Specializes in advertising and editorial photographers. Markets include advertising agencies, corporations/client direct, design firms, editorial/magazines, sales/promotion firms.
Handles: Photography.
Terms: Agent receives 25% commission. Charges for messenger costs, Federal Express charges. Exclusive representation is required. Advertising costs are split: 75% paid by the talent; 25% paid by the representative. For promotional purposes, talent must provide a minimum of five portfolios—direct mail pieces two times per year—and at least one sourcebook per year. Advertises in *Creative Black Book* and other publications.
How to Contact: For first contact, send query letter, direct mail flyer/brochure. Reports within 2 weeks, only if interested. After initial contact, call to schedule an appointment to show a portfolio. Portfolio should include tearsheets, slides, photographs.
Tips: Obtains new talent through personal referrals and solicitation.

BARBARA GORDON ASSOCIATES LTD. (II), 165 E. 32nd St., New York NY 10016. (212)686-3514. Contact: Barbara Gordon. Commercial illustration and photography representative. Estab. 1969. Member SPAR, Society of Illustrators, Graphic Artists Guild. Represents 9 illustrators, 1 photographer. "I represent only a small select group of people therefore give a great deal of personal time and attention to the people I represent."
Terms: No information provided.
How to Contact: For first contact, send direct mail flyer/brochure. Reports back within 2 weeks. After initial contact, drop off or mail in appropriate materials for review. Portfolio should include tearsheets, slides, photographs, "if the talent wants materials or promotion piece returned, include SASE."

Tips: Obtains new talent through recommendations from others, solicitation, at conferences, etc. "I have obtained talent from all of the above. I do not care if an artist or photographer has been published or is experienced. I am essentially interested in people with a good, commercial style. Don't send résumés and don't call to give me a verbal description of your work. Send promotion pieces. *Never* send original art. If you want something back, include a SASE. Always label your slides in case they get separated from your cover letter. And always include a phone number where you can be reached."

T.J. GORDON/ARTIST REPRESENTATIVE (II), P.O. Box 4112, Montebello CA 90640. (213)887-8958. Contact: Tami Gordon. Commercial illustration, photography and graphic design representative; also illustration or photography broker. Estab. 1990. Member of SPAR. Represents 1 illustrator, 2 photographers, 1 graphic designer. Markets include advertising agencies, corporations/client direct, design firms, editorial/magazines.
Handles: Illustration, photography, design.
Terms: Agent receives 30% commission. Advertising costs are split: 70% paid by talent; 30% paid by representative (direct mail costs, billable at end of each month). For promotional purposes, talent must provide "a minimum of three pieces to begin a six-month trial period. These pieces will be used as mailers and leave behinds. Portfolio is to be professional and consistent (pieces of the same size, etc.) At the end of the trial period agreement will be made on production of future promotional pieces."
How to Contact: For first contact, send a bio and direct mail flyer/brochure. Will report in 2 weeks, if interested. After initial contact, call to schedule an appointment. Portfolio should include tearsheets.
Tips: Obtains new talent "primarily through recommendations and as the result of artists' solicitations. Have an understanding of what it is you do, do not be afraid to specialize. If you do everything, then you will always conflict with the interests of the representatives' other artists. Find your strongest selling point, vocalize it and make sure that your promos and portfolio show that point."

CAROL GUENZI AGENTS, INC. (II), 609 E. Speer Blvd., #100, Denver CO 80203. (303)733-0128. Contact: Carol Guenzi. Commercial illustration, film and animation representative. Estab. 1984. Member of Denver Advertising Federation and Art Directors Club of Denver. Represents 13 illustrators, 4 photographers, 1 filmaker, 1 animator. Specializes in a "wide selection of talent in all areas of visual communications." Markets include advertising agencies, corporations/client direct, design firms, editorial/magazine.
Handles: Illustration, photography. Looking for "unique style application."
Terms: Agent receives 25% commission. Exclusive area representation is required. Advertising costs are split: 75% paid by talent; 25% paid by the representation. For promotional purposes, talent must provide "promotional material after 6 months, some restrictions on portfolios." Advertises in *American Showcase*, *Creative Black Book*, *The Workbook*, "periodically."
How to Contact: For first contact, send direct mail flyer/brochure. Reports within 2 weeks, only if interested. After initial contact, drop off or mail in appropriate materials for review. Portfolio should include slides, photocopies.
Tips: Obtains new talent through solicitation, art directors' referrals, an active pursuit by individual. "Show your strongest style and have at least twelve samples of that style, before introducing all your capabilities."

PAT HACKETT/ARTIST REPRESENTATIVE (III), Suite 502, 101 Yesler Way, Seattle WA 98104-2552. (206)447-1600. Fax: (206)447-0739. Contact: Pat Hackett. Commercial illustration and photography representative. Estab. 1979. Represents 25 illustrators, 1 photographer. Markets include advertising agencies, corporations/client direct, design firms, editorial/magazines.
Handles: Illustration.
Terms: Agent receives 25-33% commission. Exclusive area representation is required. Advertising costs are split: 75% paid by the talent; 25% paid by the representative. For promotional purposes, talent must provide "standardized portfolio, i.e. all pieces within the book are the same format. Reprints are nice, but not absolutely required." Advertises in *American Showcase*, *Creative Black Book*, *The Workbook*, *Creative Illustration*.

Check the Literary and Script Agents Subject Index to find the agents who indicate an interest in your nonfiction or fiction subject area.

How to Contact: For first contact, send direct mail flyer/brochure. Reports within 1 week, only if interested. After initial contact, drop off or mail in appropriate materials for review. Portfolio should include tearsheets, slides, photographs, photostats, photocopies.
Tips: Obtains new talent through "recommendations and calls/letters from artists moving to the area. We prefer to handle artists who live in the area unless they do something that is not available locally."

HALL & ASSOCIATES (III), 1010 S. Robertson Blvd, #10, Los Angeles CA 90035. (310)652-7322. Fax: (310)652-3835. Contact: Marni Hall. Commercial illustration and photography representative. Estab. 1983. Member of SPAR, APA. Represents 10 illustrators and 5 photographers. Markets include advertising agencies, design firms. Member agent: Christie Deddens (Artist Representative).
Handles: Illustration and photography.
Terms: Agent receives 25-28% commission. Exclusive area representation is required. Advertising costs are paid 100% by talent. For promotional purposes, talent must advertise in "one or two source books a year (double page), provide two direct mail pieces and one specific, specialized mailing. No specific portfolio requirement except that it be easy and light to carry and send out." Advertises in *Creative Black Book*, *The Workbook*.
How to Contact: For first contact, send a direct mail flyer/brochure. Will report in 5 days. After initial contact, drop off or mail in appropriate materials for review. Portfolios should include tearsheets, transparencies, prints (8x10 or larger).
Tips: Obtains new talent through recommendations from others or artists' solicitations. "Don't show work you think should sell but what you enjoy shooting. Only put in tearsheets of great ads, not bad ads even if they are a highly visible client."

‡BARB HAUSER, ANOTHER GIRL REP (V), P.O.Box 421443, San Francisco CA 94142-1443. (415)647-5660. Fax: (415)285-1102. Estab. 1980. Represents 10 illustrators and 1 photographer. Markets include corporations/client direct.
Handles: Illustration (commercial).
Terms: Agent receives 25-30% commission. Exclusive representation in the San Francisco area is required.
How to Contact: For first contact, send direct mail flyer/brochure, tearsheets, slides, photographs, photocopies and SASE. Will report within 3-4 weeks. Call to schedule an appointment. Portfolio should include tearsheets, slides, photographs, photostats, photocopies.

HK PORTFOLIO (III), 666 Greenwich St., New York NY 10014. (212)675-5719. Contact: Harriet Kasak. Commercial illustration representative. Estab. 1986. Member of SPAR. Represents 23 illustrators. Specializes in children's book illustration. Markets include advertising agencies, editorial/magazines, publishing/books.
Handles: Illustration.
Terms: Agent receives 25% commission. Advertising costs are split: 75% paid by the talent; 25% paid by the representative. Advertises in *American Showcase*, *RSVP*.
How to Contact: For first contact, send query letter, direct mail flyer/brochure, tearsheets, slides, photographs, photostats, SASE. Will report within 1 week. After initial contact, drop off or mail in appropriate materials for review. Portfolio should include tearsheets, slides, photographs, photostats, photocopies.
Tips: Obtains new talent through recommendations from others, solicitation, at conferences, etc.

RITA HOLT & ASSOCIATES, INC. (II,III), 920 Main St., Fords NJ 08863 (908)738-5238. Contact: Rita Holt. Commercial photography representative. Estab. 1976. Member of SPAR. Represents 4 photographers. Specializes in automotive and location photography. Markets include advertising agencies, corporations/client direct, design firms, sales/promotion firms.
Handles: Photography, especially automotive.
Terms: Commission taken by agent varies. Charges for all expenses. Advertising costs are paid 100% by talent. For promotional purposes, talent must provide direct mail piece or package and portfolio — "specifics depend on market." Advertises in *Creative Black Book*, *The Workbook* ("depends on the market").
How to Contact: For first contact, send direct mail flyer/brochure, photographs, portfolio with a return Federal Express air bill. Will report only if interested (time varies). After initial contact, drop off or mail in appropriate materials.
Tips: Obtains new talent through recommendations from others. "Sell a rep the same way you would sell a client."

SCOTT HULL ASSOCIATES (III), 68 E. Franklin S., Dayton OH 45459. (513)433-8383. Fax: (513)433-0434. Contact: Scott Hull or Frank Sturges. Commercial illustration representative. Estab. 1981. Represents 20 illustrators.
Terms: No information provided.
How to Contact: Contact by sending slides, tearsheets or appropriate materials for review. Follow up with phone call. Reports back within 2 weeks.
Tips: Obtains new talent through solicitation.

PEGGY KEATING (III, IV), 30 Horatio St., New York NY 10014. (212)691-4654. Contact: Peggy Keating. Commercial illustration representataive. Estab. 1969. Member of Graphic Artists Guild. Represents 7 illustrators. Specializes in fashion illustration (men, women, children and also fashion-related products). Markets include advertising agencies, corporations/client direct, editorial/magazines, sales/promotion firms, "mostly pattern catalog companies and retail."
Handles: "Fashion illustration, but only if top-drawer."
Terms: Agent receives 25% commission. Exclusive area representation is required. For promotional purposes, talent must provide "strong sample material that will provide an excellent portfolio presentation." Advertises by direct mail.
How to Contact: For first contact, send tearsheets, photocopies. Reports back within days only if interested. After initial contact, drop off or mail in appropriate materials for review. Portfolio should include thumbnails, roughs, original art, tearsheets, slides, photographs, photostats, photocopies. "It might include all or one or more of these materials. The selection and design of the material are the important factor."
Tips: Obtains new talent through "recommendations from others, or they contact me directly. The talent must be first-rate. The field has diminished and the competition is fierce. There is no longer the tolerance of not yet mature talent, nor is there a market for mediocrity."

RALPH KERR (II), 239 Chestnut St., Philadelphia PA 19106. (215)592-1359. Fax: (215)592-7988. Contact: Ralph Kerr. Commercial illustration and photography representative. Estab. 1987. Represents 1 photographer. Markets include advertising agencies, corporations/client direct, design firms, editorial/magazines, paper products/greeting cards, publishing/books.
Handles: Illustration, photography.
Terms: Agent receives 20% commission. Exclusive area representation required. Advertising costs are split: 50% paid by the talent; 50% paid by the representative. For promotional purposes, portfolio required. Advertises in *Creative Black Book*.
How to Contact: For first contact, send query letter. Reports within 1 week. After initial contact, call to schedule an appointment. Portfolio should include tearsheets, slides, photographs.

TANIA KIMCIE (III), 10F, 425 W. 23 St., New York NY 10011. (212)242-6367. Fax: (212)691-6501. Contact: Tania. Commercial illustration representative. Estab. 1981. Member of SPAR. Represents 9 illustrators. "We do everything, a lot of design firm, corporate/conceptual work." Markets include advertising agencies, corporations/client direct, design firms, editorial/magazines, publishing books, sales/promotion firms.
Handles: Illustration. Looking for "conceptual/corporate work."
Terms: Agent receives 25% commission if the artist is in town; 30% if the artist is out of town. Splits postage and envelope expense for mailings with artists. Advertising costs are split: 75% paid by the talent; 25% paid by the representative. For promotional purposes, talent "must go into *American Showcase* each year." Advertises in *American Showcase*.
How to Contact: For first contact, send bio, tearsheets, slides. Reports back within months, only if interested. After initial contact, drop off or mail in appropriate materials for review. Portfolio should include tearsheets, slides, photostats.
Tips: Obtains new talent through recommendations from others or "they contact me. Do not call. Send promo material in the mail. Don't waste time with a résumé—let me see the work."

KIRCHOFF/WOHLBERG, ARTISTS REPRESENTATION DIVISION (II), 866 United Nations Plaza, #525, New York NY 10017. (212)644-2020. Fax: (212)223-4387. Director of Operations: John R. Whitman. Estab. 1930s. Member of SPAR, Society of Illustrators, AIGA, Assn. of American Publishers, Book Builders of Boston, New York Bookbinders' Guild. Represents over 50 illustrators. Artist's Represenative: Elizabeth Ford (juvenile and young adult trade book and textbook illustators). Specializes in juvenile and young adult trade books and textbooks. Markets include publishing/books.

Handles: Illustration and photography (juvenile and young adult). Please send all correspondence to the attention of: Elizabeth Ford.

Terms: Agent receives 25% commission. Exclusive representation to book publishers is usually required. Advertising costs paid 100% by the representative ("for all Kirchoff/Wohlberg advertisements only"). "We will make transparencies from portfolio samples; keep some original work on file." Advertises in *American Showcase*, *Art Directors' Index*; *Society of Illustrators Annual*, children's book issue of *Publishers Weekly*.

How to Contact: For first contact, send query letter, "any materials artists feel are appropriate." Will report within 4-6 weeks. "We will contact you for additional materials." Portfolios should include: "whatever artists feel best represents their work. We like to see children's illustration in any style."

BILL AND MAURINE KLIMT (II), 7-U, 15 W. 72nd St., New York NY 10023. (212)799-2231. Contact: Bill or Maurine. Commercial illustration representative. Estab. 1978. Member of Society of Illustrators, Graphic Artists Guild. Represents 14 illustrators. Specializes in paperback covers, young adult, romance, science fiction, mystery, etc. Markets include advertising agencies, corporations/client direct, design firms, editorial/magazines, paper products/greeting cards, publishing/books, sales/promotion firms.

Handles: Illustration.

Terms: Agent receives 25% commission, 30% commission for "out of town if we do shoots. Supplying reference on jobs. The artist is responsible for only their own portfolio. We supply all promotion and mailings other than the publications." Exclusive area representation is required. Advertising costs are split: 75% paid by the talent; 25% paid by the representative. For promotional purposes, talent must provide 4×5 or 8×10 mounted transparencies. Advertises in *American Showcase, RSVP*.

How to Contact: For first contact, send direct mail flyer/brochure, and "any image that doesn't have to be returned unless supplied with self-addressed stamped envelope." Reports back within 5 days. After initial contact, call to schedule an appointment to show a portfolio. Portfolios should include professional, mounted transparencies.

Tips: Obtains new talent through recommendations from others and solicitation.

CLIFF KNECHT–ARTIST REPRESENTATIVE (II, III), 309 Walnut Rd., Pittsburgh PA 15202. (412)761-5666. Fax: (412)261-3712. Contact: Cliff Knecht. Commercial illustration representative. Estab. 1972. Represents 15 illustrators, 1 design firm, 2 fine artists. Markets include advertising agencies, corporations/client direct, design firms, editorial/magazines, paper products/greeting cards, publishing/books, sales/promotion firms.

Handles: Illustration.

Terms: Agent receives 25% commission. Advertising costs are split: 75% paid by the talent; 25% paid by the representative. For promotional purposes, talent must provide a direct mail piece. Advertises in *American Showcase* and *Graphic Artists Guild Directory of Illustration*.

How to Contact: For first contact, send résumé, direct mail flyer/brochure, tearsheets, slides. Reports back within 1 week. After initial contact, call to schedule an appointment to show a portfolio. Portfolio should include original art, tearsheets, slides, photographs.

Tips: Obtains new talent directly or through recommendations from others.

PETER KUEHNEL & ASSOCIATES (III), Suite 2108, 30 E. Huron Plaza, Chicago IL 60611-2717. (312)642-6499. Fax: (312)642-0377. Contact: Peter Kuehnel. Commercial illustration, photography and film representative. Estab. 1984. Member of SPAR. Represents 5 illustrators and 2 photographers. Staff includes Denise Redding. Markets include advertising agencies, corporations/client direct, design firms, editorial/magazines and sales/promotion firms.

Handles: Illustration, photography, film production.

Terms: Agent receives 25% commission. "Any and all expenses billed to artist involved on a 75/25 basis." Exclusive area representation is required. Advertising costs are split 75% paid by talent; 25% paid by representative. Materials talent must provide for promotion vary case by case. Advertises in *Creative Black Book, The Workbook, Chicago Sourcebook*.

How to Contact: For first contact, send query letter, direct mail flyer/brochure, SASE. Will report within 2 weeks. After initial contact, call to schedule an appointment to show portfolio.

Tips: Obtains new talent through "recommendations from buyers, etc." To obtain representation, "work hard, practice, practice, practice."

FRANK & JEFF LAVATY & ASSOCIATES (II), Suite 1014, 509 Madison Ave., New York NY 10022. (212)355-0910. Commercial illustration and fine art representative. Represents 15 illustrators.
Handles: Illustration.
Terms: No information provided.
How to Contact: For first contact, send query letter, direct mail flyer/brochure, tearsheets, slides, SASE. Reports back within 1 week. After initial contact, call to schedule an appointment to show a portfolio. Portfolio should include tearsheets and 8×10 or 4×5 transparencies.
Tips: Obtains new talent through solicitation. "Specialize! Your portfolio must be focused."

PETER & GEORGE LOTT (II), 60 E. 42nd St., New York NY 10165. (212)953-7088. Commercial illustration representative. Estab. 1958. Member of Society of Illustrators, Art Directors Club. Represents 15 illustrators. Markets include advertising agencies, corporations/client direct, design firms, editorial/magazines, publishing/books, sales/promotion firms, "all types fashion and beauty accounts (men's, women's, children's, still life and accessories).
Handles: Illustration. "We are currently looking for romance novel illustrators. As a general rule, we're interested in any kind of saleable commercial art."
Terms: Agent receives 25% commission. Advertises in *American Showcase*, *Creative Black Book*, *The Workbook* and other publications.
How to Contact: For first contact "call to drop off portfolio."
Tips: "Check with us first to make sure it is a convenient time to drop off a portfolio. Then either drop it off or send it with return postage. The format does not matter, as long as it shows what you can do and what you want to do."

COLLEEN MCKAY PHOTOGRAPHY (III), #2, 229 E. 5th St., New York NY 10003. (212)598-0469. Fax: (212)598-0762. Contact: Colleen McKay. Commercial editorial and fine art photography representative. Estab. 1985. Member of SPAR. Represents 4 photographers. Staff includes Cara Sadownick. "Our photographers cover a wide range of work from location, still life, fine art, fashion and beauty." Markets include advertising agencies, design firms, editorial/magazines, stores.
Handles: Commercial and fine art photography.
Terms: Agent receives 25% commission. Exclusive area representation is required. Advertising costs are split: 75% paid by the talent; 25% paid by the representative. "Promotional pieces are very necessary. They must be current. The portfolio should be established already." Advertises in *Creative Black Book*, *Select*, *New York Gold*.
How to Contact: For first contact, send query letter, résumé, bio, direct mail flyer/brochure, tearsheets, slides, photographs. Reports within 2-3 weeks. "I like to respond to everyone but if we're really swamped I may only get a chance to respond to those we're most interested in." Portfolio should include tearsheets, slides, photographs, transparencies (usually for still life).
Tips: Obtains talent through recommendations of other people and solicitations. "I recommend that you look in current resource books and call the representatives that are handling the kind of work that you admire or is similar to your own. Ask these reps for an initial consultation and additional references. Do not be intimidated to approach anyone. Even if they do not take you on a meeting with a good rep can prove to be very fruitful! Never give up! A clear, positive attitude is very important."

MARTHA PRODUCTIONS, INC. (III, IV), 4445 Overland Ave., Culver City CA 90230. (213)204-1771. Fax: (213)204-4598. Contact: Martha Spelman. Commercial illustration and graphic design representative. Estab. 1978. Member of Graphic Artists Guild. Represents 20 photographers, 1 designer (studio). Staff includes Michelle Secof (assignment illustration). Specializes in black-and-white and four-color illustration. Markets include advertising agencies, corporations/client direct, design firms, editorial/magazines, paper products/greeting cards.
Handles: Illustration.
Terms: Agent receives 30% commission. Exclusive area representation is required. Advertising costs are split: 70% paid by the talent; 30% paid by the representative. For promotional purposes, talent must provide "a minimum of 12 images, 3 4×5″ transparencies of each. (We put the transparencies into our own format.) In addition to the transparencies, we require four-color promo/tearsheets and

---

■ *A solid box indicates reps who charge a fee for expenses or who charge special fees in addition to commission and advertising costs.*

participation in the bi-annual Martha Productions brochure." Advertises in *The Workbook, Single Image*.

How to Contact: For first contact, send query letter, direct mail flyer/brochure, tearsheets, slides, SASE (if materials are to be returned). Reports back only if interested. After initial contact, drop off or mail in appropriate materials for review. Portfolio should include tearsheets, slides, photographs, photostats.

Tips: Obtains new talent through recommendations and solicitation.

MATTELSON ASSOCIATES LTD. (II), 37 Cary Road, Great Neck NY 11021. (212)684-2974. Fax: (516)466-5835. Contact: Judy Mattelson. Commercial illustration representative. Estab. 1980. Member of SPAR, Graphic Artists Guild. Represents 2 illustrators. Markets include advertising agencies, corporations/client direct, design firms, editorial/magazines, paper products/greeting cards, publishing/books, sales/promotion firms.

Handles: Illustration.

Terms: Agent receives 25-30% commission. Exclusive area representation is required. Advertising costs are split: 75% paid by talent; 25% paid by representative. For promotional purposes, talent must provide c-prints and tearsheets, custom-made portfolio. Advertises in *American Showcase, Creative Black Book, RSVP, New York Gold*.

How to Contact: For first contact, send direct mail flyer/brochure, tearsheets and SASE. Will report in 2 weeks, if interested. After initial contact, call to schedule an appointment. Portfolio should include tearsheets, c-prints.

Tips: Obtains new talent through "recommendations from others, solicitation. Illustrator should have ability to do consistent, professional-quality work that shows a singular direction and a variety of subject matter. You should have a portfolio that shows the full range of your current abilities. Work should show strong draftsmanship and technical facility. Person should love their work and be willing to put forth great effort in each assignment."

MENDOLA ARTISTS (II), 420 Lexington Ave. Penthouse, New York NY 10170. (212)986-5680. Fax: (212)818-1246. Contact: Tim Mendola. Commercial illustration representative. Estab. 1961. Member of Society of Illustrators, Graphic Artists Guild. Represents 60 or more illustrators, 3 photographers. Markets include advertising agencies, corporations/client direct, design firms, editorial/magazines, sales/promotion firms.

Handles: Illustration. "We work with the top agencies and publishers. The calibre of talent must be in the top 5%."

Terms: Agent receives 25% commission. Artist pays for all shipping not covered by client and 75% of promotion costs. Exclusive area representation is sometimes required. Advertising costs are split: 75% paid by the talent; 25% paid by the representative. For promotional purposes, talent must provide 8×10 transparencies and usually promotion in at least one source book. Advertises in *American Showcase, Creative Black Book, RSVP, The Workbook*.

How to Contact: For first contact, send direct mail flyer/brochure, tearsheets, slides. Reports within 1 week. After initial contact, drop off or mail in appropriate materials for review. Portfolio should include original art, tearsheets, slides, photographs.

FRANK MEO (II, III), 170 Norfolk St., New York NY 10002. (212)353-0907. Fax: (212)673-86979. Contact: Frank Meo. Commercial photography representative. Estab. 1983. Member of SPAR. Represents 2 photographers. Markets include advertising agencies, corporations/client direct, design firms.

Handles: Photography.

Terms: Agent receives 25% commission. Advertising costs are paid by the talent. Advertises in *Creative Black Book*.

How to Contact: For first contact, send query letter, photographs. Will report within 2 days. After initial contact, drop off or mail in appropriate materials for review. Portfolio should include tearsheets, photographs.

Tips: Obtains new talent through recommendations and solicitation.

A IV ranking indicates reps who specialize in a particular type of illustration or photography such as fashion illustration or food photography.

MONTAGANO & ASSOCIATES (II), #1606, 405 N. Wabash, Chicago IL 60611. (312)527-3283. Fax: (312)527-9091. Contact: David Montagano. Commercial illustration photography and television production representative and broker. Estab. 1983. Member of SPAR. Represents 4 illustrators, 2 photographers. Markets include advertising agencies, corporations/client direct, design firms, editorial/magazines, paper products/greeting cards.
Handles: Illustration, photography, design.
Terms: Agent receives 25-30% commission. Advertises in *American Showcase, Sourcebook.*
How to Contact: For first contact, send direct mail flyer/brochure, tearsheets, photographs. Portfolios should include original art, tearsheets, photographs.
Tips: Obtains new talent through recommendations from others.

VICKI MORGAN ASSOCIATES, (III), 194 Third Ave., New York NY 10003. (212)475-0440. Contact: Vicki Morgan. Commercial illustration representative. Estab. 1974. Member of SPAR, Graphic Artists Guild, Society of Illustrators. Represents 12 illustrators. Markets include advertising agencies, corporations/client direct, design firms, editorial/magazines, paper products/greeting cards, publishing/books, sales/promotion firms.
Handles: Illustration. "Fulltime illustrators only."
Terms: Agent receives 25-30% commission. Exclusive area representation is required. Advertising costs are split: 75% paid by the talent; 25% paid by the representative. "We can develop an initial direct mail piece together. We require samples for three duplicate portfolios; the presentation form is flexible." Advertises in *American Showcase.*
How to Contact: For first contact, send any of the following: direct mail flyer/brochure, tearsheets, slides with SASE. "If interested, keeps on file and consults these samples first when considering additional artists. No drop-off policy."
Tips: Obtains new talent through "recommendations from artists I represent and mail solicitation."

PAMELA NEAIL ASSOCIATES (III), 27 Bleecker St., New York NY 10012. (212)673-1600. Fax: (212)673-7687. Contact: Pamela Neail. Commercial illustration representative. Estab. 1983. Member of SPAR, Society of Illustrators. Represents 15 illustrators. Markets include advertising agencies, corporations/client direct, design firms, editorial/magazines, publishing/books, fashion and beauty.
Handles: Illustration.
Terms: Agent receives 25% commission. Exclusive area representation is required. Advertising costs are split: 75% paid by the talent; 25% paid by the representative. Talent must provide established portfolio; "several copies are helpful." Advertises in *American Showcase, Creative Black Book, RSVP, The Workbook.*
How to Contact: For first contact, send query letter, direct mail flyer/brochure, SASE. "We contact only if interested."
Tips: Obtains new talent through recommendations from others.

THE NEIS GROUP (II), 11440 Oak Dr., Shelbyville MI 49344. (616)672-5756. Fax: (616)672-5757. Contact: Judy Neis. Commercial illustration and photography representative. Estab. 1982. Represents 30 illustrators, 7 photographers. Markets include advertising agencies, design firms, editorial/magazines, publishing/books.
Handles: Illustration, photography.
Terms: Agent receives 25% commission. Advertising costs are split: 75% paid by talent; 25% paid by the representative. Advertises in *The American Showcase.*
How to Contact: For first contact, send direct mail flyer/brochure, tearsheets, photographs. Reports within 5 days. After initial contact, drop off or mail in appropriate materials for review. Portfolio should include tearsheets, photographs.
Tips: "I am mostly sought out by the talent. If I pursue, I call and request a portfolio review."

PACIFIC DESIGN STUDIO (II), P.O. Box 1396, Hilo HI 96721. (808)935-6056. Contact: Francine H. Pearson. Commercial illustration and photography representative. Also handles fine art, graphic design and is an illustration or photography broker. Estab. 1980. Represents 6 illustrators, 4 photographers, 2 designers, 12 fine artists (includes 3 sculptors). "This is a small 3-person office." Specializes in "art and design of the Hawaiian Islands; the Big Island in particular." Markets include advertising agencies, editorial/magazines, paper products/greeting cards, t-shirt manufacturers and resorts.

Handles: Illustration, photography, fine art. Looking for "underwater artists, ocean and sea life artists, Pacific Rim artists, Hawaiiana design."
Terms: Agent receives 15-20% commission. Charges for "real costs of freight, etc., which come off the top of a sale." Exclusive area representation is "preferred, but not required." For promotional purposes, "transparencies are required, full-color tearsheet or mailer is preferred; artist must have minimum of 12 pieces for sale."
How to Contact: For first contact, send query letter, résumé, bio, direct mail flyer/brochure, tearsheets, slides, SASE. Reports back within 2 weeks, only if interested, "depending on what is sent for first contact." After initial contact, write to schedule an appointment to show a portfolio or drop off or mail in appropriate materials for review. Portfolios should include original art, slides, photographs, transparencies.
Tips: Obtains new talent through studio visits, recommendations, client reference, architect reference, local news and print media. "Send only your best work and be patient. Good representation requires good timing and creativity as well as client contacts."

JACKIE PAGE (III), 219 E. 69th St., New York NY 10021. (212)772-0346. Commercial photography representative. Estab. 1987. Member of SPAR and Ad Club. Represents 10 photographers. Markets include advertising agencies.
Handles: Photography.
Terms: "Details given at a personal interview." Advertises in *The Workbook*.
How to Contact: For first contact send direct mail flyer/brochure. After initial contact, call to schedule an appointment to show a portfolio. Portfolios should include tearsheets, slides, photographs.
Tips: Obtains new talent through recommendations from others and mailings.

JOANNE PALUHAN (III), 18 McKinley St., Rowayton CT 06853. (203)866-3734 or (212)581-8338. Fax: (203)857-0842. Commercial illustration representative. Estab. 1976. Member of SPAR. Represents 7 illustrators. Markets include advertising agencies, corporations/client direct, design firms, editorial/magazines, sales/promotion firms.
Handles: Illustration.
Terms: Agent receives 30% commission. Exclusive area representation is required. Advertising costs are split: 75% paid by the talent; 25% paid by the representative. For promotional purposes, talent must provide a portfolio and promotional materials. Advertises in *American Showcase*, *Creative Black Book*, *Workbook*, *Graphic Artist Guild Illustration Book*, *Single Image*.
How to Contact: For first contact send direct mail flyer/brochure. Reports within 2 days, only if interested. After initial contact, drop off or mail in appropriate materials for review. Portfolio should include tearsheets, transparencies (4×5 or 8×10) of original art.
Tips: "Talent usually contacts me, follows up with materials that I can keep. If interest is there, I interview. Do not send materials without my consent. Include return packaging with necessary postage. Be courteous and friendly. You are asking someone to give you his or her time and attention for your benefit."

PARALLAX (IV), #5805, 350 Fifth Ave., New York NY 10118. (212)695-0445. Fax: (212)629-5624. Contact: Lylla Demeny. Commercial/editorial photography representative. Estab. 1989. Represents 5 photographers. Specializes in fashion/beauty photography and production; represents hair/make-up also. Markets include advertising agencies, editorial/magazines, catalogs.
Handles: Photography.
Terms: Agent receives 25% commission. Splits costs for messengers and promo pieces. Exclusive area representation is required. Advertising costs are split: 50% paid by the talent; 50% paid by the representative. For promotional purposes, talent must provide promo piece "or one can be designed."
How to Contact: For first contact, send direct mail flyer/brochure. Reports back within 2 weeks. After initial contact, drop off or mail in appropriate materials for review. Portfolios should include original art, tearsheets.

Reps ranked I-IV are actively seeking new talents. Those ranked V or those who prefer not to be listed have been included to inform you they are not currently looking for new talent.

Tips: Obtains new talent through recommendations or from published work.

‡RANDY PATE & ASSOCIATES (III, IV), P.O. Box 2160, Moorpark CA 93021. (805)529-8111. Fax: (805)529-2171. Commercial illustration representative. Estab. 1979. Member of Society of Illustrators, Graphic Artists Guild. Represents 9 illustrators; 2 designers. Specializes in entertainment. Markets include advertising agencies, corporations/client direct, design firms, sales/promotion firms.
Handles: Illustration.
Terms: Agent receives 25% commission. Occasionally charges other fee. "This varies." Exclusive area representation is required. Advertising costs are split: 75% paid by talent; 25% paid by representative. For promotional purposes, talent should provide "a full page in *The Workbook*, and at least 2 portfolios (8 × 10 transparencies or 11 × 14 print/tearsheets preferred)." Advertises in *The Workbook*.
How to Contact: For first contact, send query letter, direct mail flyer/brochure, tearsheets, SASE. Reports back within 2 weeks, only if interested. After initial contact, call to schedule an appointment. Portfolios should include tearsheets and transparencies (4 × 5 or 8 × 10).
Tips: Obtains new talent through recommendations from others.

■PHOTO AGENTS LTD. (III). 24 W. 30th St., #5F, New York NY 10001. Contact: Gary Lerman. Commercial photography representative. Estab. 1973. Member of SPAR. Represents 2-3 photographers. Markets include advertising agencies, corporations/client direct, design firms, editorial/magazines, publishing/books, sales/promotion firms.
Handles: Photography. Looking for specialties in "kids or portraits."
Terms: Agent receives 25-30% commission. Charges other fees which are "defined with talent." Exclusive area representation is required. Advertises in *Creative Black Book*, *Gold Book*.
How to Contact: For first contact, send direct mail flyer/brochure, "follow with call." Reports back within 1 week, only if interested. After initial contact, call to schedule an appointment to show a portfolio. Portfolio should include tearsheets, photographs.
Tips: Obtains new talent through referrals. "Don't rush into representation. Look for a good and lasting relationship!"

MARIA PISCOPO (IV), 2038 Calvert Ave., Costa Mesa CA 92626-3520. (714)556-8133. Fax: (714)556-0899. Contact: Maria Piscopo. Commercial photography representative. Estab. 1978. Member of SPAR, Women in Photography, Society of Illustrative Photographers. Represents 5 photographers. Markets include advertising agencies, design firms.
Handles: Photography. Looking for "unique, unusual styles; handle only established photography."
Terms: Agent receives 25-30% commission. Exclusive area representation is required. Advertising costs are split: 75% paid by the talent; 25% paid by the representative. For promotional purposes, talent must provide one show portfolio, three travelling portfolios, leave-behinds and at least six new promo pieces per year. Advertises in *American Showcase*, *The Workbook*, *New Media*.
How to Contact: For first contact, send query letter, direct mail flyer/brochure, SASE. Reports within 2 weeks, if interested.
Tips: Obtains new talent through personal referral and photo magazine articles. "Be very business-like, organized, professional and follow the above instructions!"

PUBLISHERS' GRAPHICS (II, III, IV), 251 Greenwood Ave., Bethel CT 06801. (203)797-8188. Fax: (203)798-8848. Commercial illustration representative for juvenile markets. Estab. 1970. Member of Graphic Artists Guild, Author's Guild Inc.. Staff includes Paige C. Gillies (President, selects illustrators, develops talent); Susan P. Schwarzchild (sales manager); Diane Carlson (field representative). Specializes in children's book illustration. Markets include design firms, editorial/magazines, paper products/greeting cards, publishing/books, sales/promotion firms.
Handles: Illustration.
Terms: Agent receives 25% commission. Exclusive area representation is required. For promotional purposes, talent must provide original art, proofs and photocopies "to start. The assignments generate most sample/promotional material thereafter unless there is a stylistic change in the work." Advertises in *Literary Market Place*.

> **■ A solid box indicates reps who charge a fee for expenses or who charge special fees in addition to commission and advertising costs.**

How to Contact: For first contact send résumé, photocopies, SASE. Reports back within 6 weeks. After initial contact, "We will contact them. We don't respond to phone inquiries." Portfolios should include original art, tearsheets, photocopies.
Tips: Obtains new talent through "clients recommending our agency to artists. We ask for referrals from our illustrators. We receive submissions by mail."

GERALD & CULLEN RAPP, INC. (III), 108 E. 35th St., New York NY 10016. (212)889-3337. Fax: (212)889-3341. Contact: Amy Shuster. Commercial illustration, photography and graphic design representative. Estab. 1945. Member of SPAR, Society of Illustrators, Graphic Artists Guild. Represents 30 illustrators, 6 photographers, 1 designer. Markets include advertising agencies, corporations/client direct, design firms, editorial/magazines, paper products/greeting cards, publishing/books, sales/promotion firms.
Handles: Illustration, photography.
Terms: Agent receives 25-30% commission. Exclusive area representation is required. Advertising costs are split: 50% paid by the talent; 50% paid by the representative. Advertises in *American Showcase, Creative Black Book, The Workbook*, and *CA, Print, Art Director* magazines. "Conducts active direct mail program, costs split 50-50."
How to Contact: For first contact, send query letter, direct mail flyer/brochure. Reports back within 1 week. After initial contact, call to schedule an appointment to show a portfolio. Portfolio should include tearsheets, slides.
Tips: Obtains new talent through recommendations from others, solicitations.

REDMOND REPRESENTS (III), 7K Misty Wood Circle, Timonium MD 21093. (410)666-1916. Contact: Sharon Redmond. Commercial illustration and photography representative. Estab. 1987. Markets include advertising agencies, corporations/client direct, design firms.
Handles: Illustration, photography.
Terms: Agent receives 30% commission. Exclusive area representation is required. Advertising costs and expenses are split: 50% paid by the talent; 50% paid by the representative. For promotional purposes, talent must provide a small portfolio (easy to Federal Express) and at least 6 direct mail pieces (with fax number included). Advertises in *American Showcase, Creative Black Book*.
How to Contact: For first contact, send photocopies. Will report within 2 weeks. After initial contact, representative will call talent to set an appointment.
Tips: Obtains new talent through recommendations from others, advertisting a "black book," etc. "Even if I'm not taking in new talent, I do want *photocopies* sent of new work. You never know when an ad agency will require a different style of illustration/photography and it's always nice to refer to my files."

KAY REESE & ASSOCIATES, INC. (III), 225 Central Park W., New York NY 10024. (212)799-1133. Fax: (212)533-2509. Photography broker. Estab. 1971. Member of PAI, ASMP. Represents 20 photographers. Specializes in worldwide corporate photojournalism. Markets include corporations/client direct, design firms, sales/promotion firms.
Terms: Agent receives 30% commission (per SPAR). Exclusive area representation is required. Advertising costs are split: 50% paid by the talent; 50% paid by the representative. For promotional purposes, talent must provide portfolios with original material and tearsheets of published work (color and black and white).
How to Contact: For first contact, send query letter only, "please!" Reports within 2 weeks, only if interested. After initial contact, call or write to schedule an appointment to show a portfolio. Portfolio should include tearsheets, slides, photographs.
Tips: Obtains new talent through referrals.

KERRY REILLY: REPS (II), (formerly Trlica/Reilly: Reps), P.O. Box 13025, Charlotte NC 28270. (704)372-6007 or (704)365-6111. Fax: same. Contact: Kerry Reilly. Commercial illustration and photography representative. Estab. 1990. Represents 16 illustrators, 3 photographers. Markets include advertising agencies, corporations/client direct, design firms, editorial/magazines.
Handles: Illustration, photography. Looking for computer graphics, freehand, etc.
Terms: Agent receives 25% commission. Exclusive area representation is required. Advertising costs are split: 75% paid by the talent; 25% paid by the representative. For promotional purposes, talent must provide printed leave-behind samples, at least two pages. Preferred format is 9×12 pages, portfolio work on 4×5 transparencies. Advertises in *American Showcase*.

How to Contact: For first contact, send direct mail flyer/brochure or samples of work. Reports within 2 weeks. After initial contact, call to schedule an appointment to show a portfolio or drop off or mail appropriate materials. Portfolio should include original art, tearsheets, slides, 4×5 transparencies.
Tips: Obtains new talent through recommendations from others. "It's essential to have printed samples—a lot of printed samples."

REPERTOIRE (III), Suite 104-338, 5521 Greenville, Dallas TX 75206. (214)369-6990. Fax: (214)369-6938. Contact: Larry Lynch (photography) or Andrea Lynch (illustration). Commercial illustration and photography representative and broker. Estab. 1974. Member of SPAR. Represents 12 illustrators and 6 photographers. Specializes in "importing specialized talent into the Southwest." Markets include advertising agencies, corporations/client direct, design firms, editorial/magazines.
Handles: Illustration, photography.
Terms: Agent receives 25% commission. Exclusive area representation is required. Advertising costs are split: printing costs are paid by the talent; distribution costs are paid by the representative. Talent must provide promotion, both direct mail and a national directory. Advertises in *The Workbook*.
How to Contact: For first contact, send direct mail flyer/brochure, tearsheets. Will report within 1 month. After initial contact, write to schedule an appointment or drop off or mail appropriate materials for review. Portfolio should include tearsheets, slides, photographs.
Tips: Obtains new talent through referrals, solicitations. "Have something worthwhile to show."

RIDGEWAY ARTISTS REPRESENTATIVE (II), 444 Lentz Ct., Lansing MI 48917. (517)371-3086. Fax: (517)371-5160. Contact: Edwin Bonnen. Commercial illustration and photography representative. Estab. 1985. Member of SPAR. Represents 1 illustrator, 2 photographers. Markets include advertising agencies, corporations/client direct, design firms, editorial/magazines.
Handles: Illustration, photography. "We are primarily looking for individuals who have developed a distinctive style, whether they be a photographer or illustrator. Photographers must have an area they specialize in. We want artists who are pros in the commercial worlds; i.e. working with tight deadlines in sometimes less than ideal situations."
Terms: Agent receives 25% commission in the state of Michigan, 35% out of state. Exclusive area representation is required. Advertising costs are split: 75% paid by the talent; 25% paid by the representative. For promotional purposes, talent "should be prepared to invest at least $1,000 on your portfolio. We will develop a yearly marketing plan that focuses on where you want your career to go. Plan on spending approximately 10-15% of yearly gross receipts on advertising."
How to Contact: For first contact, send query letter, résumé, direct mail flyer/brochure, tearsheets, SASE "if they want material returned." Reports within 2 weeks, only if interested. After initial contact, call to schedule an appointment to show a portfolio. Portfolios should include thumbnails, roughs, original art, slides, photographs. "Send it."
Tips: "We obtain talent primarily through their solicitation of our services." If interested in obtaining representation, "approach all representatives as you would a potential client. Don't waste their time. Have an organized portfolio that shows off your talent and the direction you want to go. Show new material often. Put them on your mailing list. Follow-up, follow-up, follow-up."

ARLENE ROSENBERG (II), 377 W. 11th St., New York NY 10014. (212)675-7983. Fax: (212)691-1318. Contact: Arlene Rosenberg. Commercial photography representative. Estab. 1980. Member of SPAR. Represent 2 photographers. Staff includes Erin Wilheim, assistant. Markets include advertising agencies, design firms, editorial/magazines.
Handles: Photography.
Terms: Agent receives 25% commission. Exclusive area representation is required. Advertising costs are split: 75% paid by the talent; 25% paid by the representative. "Would review with talent" what to provide a portfolio. Advertises in *Creative Black Book*.

The needs of art and photography reps are constantly changing! If you are using this book and it is 1994 or later, buy the newest edition of Guide to Literary Agents and Art/Photo Reps *at your favorite book or art supply store or order directly from Writer's Digest Books.*

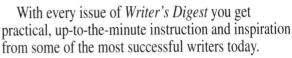

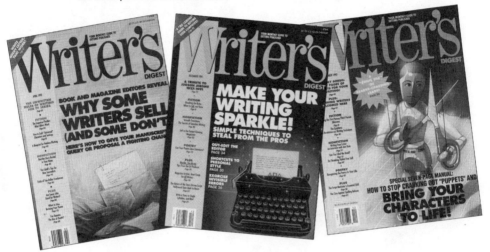

How to Contact: For first contact, send a direct mail flyer/brochure. Will report on queries within days. After initial contact, call to schedule an appointment to show a portfolio. Portfolio should include tearsheets and chromes.
Tips: Obtains new talent through recommendations.

ROSENTHAL REPRESENTS (IV), 3443 Wade St., Los Angeles CA 90066. (213)390-9595. Fax: (213)306-6878. Commercial illustration representative and licensing agent for artists who do advertising, entertainment, action/sports, children's humorous, storyboard, animal, graphic, floral, realistic, impressionistic and game packaging art. Estab. 1979. Member of SPAR, Society of Illustrators, Graphic Artists Guild, Women in Design and Art Directors Club. Represents 100 illustrators, 3 photographers, 2 designers and 5 fine artists. Specializes in game packaging, personalities, licensing, merchandising art and storyboard artists. Markets include advertising agencies, corporations/client direct, paper products/greeting cards, sales/promotion firms, licensees and manufacturers.
Handles: Illustration.
Terms: Agent receives 25-30% as a rep; 40% as a licensing agent. Exclusive area representation is required. Advertising costs are 100% paid by the talent. For promotion purposes, talent must provide 1-2 sets of transparencies (mounted and labeled), 10 sets of slides of your best work (labeled with name on each slide) and 1-3 promos. Advertises in *American Showcase, Creative Black Book* and *The Workbook.*
How to Contact: For first contact, send direct mail flyer/brochure, tearsheets, slides, photocopies, photostats and SASE. Will report within 1 week. After initial contact, call to schedule an appointment to show a portfolio. Portfolios should include tearsheets, slides, photographs and photocopies.
Tips: Obtains new talent through seeing their work in an advertising book or at an award show.

‡S.I. INTERNATIONAL (II), 43 E. 19th St., New York NY 10003. (212)254-4996. Fax: (212)995-0911. Commercial illustration representative. Estab. 1973. Member of SPAR, Graphic Artists Guild. Represents 20 illustrators, 2 photographers. Specializes in license characters; educational publishing and children's illustration; mass market paperbacks. Markets include design firms, publishing/books, sales/promotion firms, licensing firms.
Handles: Illustration (commercial). Looking for artists who have the "ability to do children's illustration and to do license characters."
Terms: Agent receives 25% commission. Advertising costs are split: 75% paid by the talent; 25% paid by representative. "Contact agency for details. Must have mailer." Advertises in *RSVP.*
How to Contact: For first contact send query letter and tearsheets. Will report within 3 weeks. After initial contact, write to schedule an appointment. Portfolio should include tearsheets and slides.

■RICHARD SALZMAN (II, III), 716 Sanchez St., San Francisco CA 94114. (415)285-8267. Fax: (415)285-8268. Contact: Richard Salzman. Commercial illustration representative. Estab. 1982. Member of SPAR, Graphic Artists Guild, AIGA, SFCA, WADC. Represents 14 illustrators. Markets include advertising agencies, corporations/client direct, design firms, editorial/magazines, publishing books.
Handles: Illustration. "We're always looking for visionaries and are also interested in digital art or other 'new' media."
Terms: Agent receives 30% commission. Charges for "portfolios." Talent is required to pay cost of the portfolio (6 copies) created by the representative. Exclusive area representation is required (all of USA). Advertising costs are split: 70% paid by the talent; 30% paid by the representative. "We share promotional costs." Advertises in *American Showcase, The Workbook* and *Creative Illustration Book.*
How to Contact: For first contact, send tearsheets, slides, photocopies. After initial contact, call to schedule an appointment to show a portfolio.
Tips: "We receive 20 to 30 solicitors a week. We sign an average of one new artist a year. Solicit to reps the way you would to a 'client' or art director."

THE SCHUNA GROUP, INC. (V), 700 3rd St., #301, Minneapolis MN 55415. Representative not currently seeking new talent.

FREDA SCOTT, INC. (III), 244 9th St., San Francisco CA 94103. (415)621-2992. Fax: (415)621-5202. Contact: Barry Guillfoil or Freda Scott. Commercial illustration and photography representative. Estab. 1980. Member of SPAR. Represents 7 illustrators, 5 photographers. Markets include advertis-

...ns/client direct, design firms, editorial/magazines, paper products/greeting
...sales/promotion firms.
...hotography.
...25% commission. Advertising costs are split: 75% paid by the talent; 25% paid
...For promotional purposes, talent must provide "promotion piece and ad in a
directory. ... at least 3 portfolios." Advertises in *American Showcase, Creative Black Book,
The Workbook.*
How to Contact: For first contact, send direct mail flyer/brochure, tearsheets, SASE. If you send
transparencies, reports within 1 week, if interested. "You need to make follow up calls." After initial
contact, call to schedule an appointment to show a portfolio or drop off or mail in appropriate materials for review. Portfolio should include tearsheets, photographs, 4×5's or 8×10's.
Tips: Obtains new talent sometimes through recommendations, sometimes solicitation. "If you are
seriously interested in getting repped, keep sending promos—once every 6 months or so. Do it yourself
a year or two until you know what you need a rep to do."

DAVID SCROGGY AGENCY, (III), 2966½ Maple Ct., San Diego CA 92104-4949. (619)544-9571. Contact: David Scroggy. Commercial illustration representative and comic book packages. Estab. 1981.
Represents 7 illustrators. Specializes in illustration only. Markets include advertising agencies, corpo-
rations/client direct, design firms, editorial/magazines, paper products/greeting cards, publishing/
books, comic books.
Handles: Illustration and comic books.
Terms: Agent receives 25% commission. Advertising costs are split: 75% paid by the talent; 25% paid
by the representative. For promotional purposes, talent must provide "samples of professional work
done for clients (i.e., advertising agency, magazine/book publisher, corporation, etc.)." Advertises in
American Showcase, RSVP, San Diego Creative Directory.
How to Contact: For first contact, send query letter, direct mail flyer/brochure, tearsheets. Reports
within 3 weeks. After initial contact, mail in appropriate materials for review. Portfolio should include
tearsheets, photographs.
Tips: "Develop a truly unique and marketable style."

■**SOLDAT & CARDONI, (II),** Suite 1008, 307 N. Michigan, Chicago IL 60601. (312)201-9662. Fax:
(312)236-5752. Contact: Rick Soldat or Pam Cardoni. Commercial illustration and photography representative. Estab. 1990. Member of SPAR. Represents 2 illustrators, 4 photographers. Markets include
advertising agencies, corporations/client direct, design firms, publishing/books, sales/promotion firms.
Handles: Illustration, photography.
Terms: Agent receives 25-30% commission. Charges for postage, shipping, long-distance travel. Exclusive area representation in the Midwest is required. Advertising costs are split: 75% paid by the talent;
25% paid by the representative. For promotional purposes, talent must provide "a promo for direct
mail and other purposes." Advertises in *The Workbook* and *Chicago Talent Sourcebook.*
How to Contact: For first contact, send query letter, tearsheets. Reports within 1 week. After initial
contact, call to schedule an appointment to show a portfolio. Portfolio should include original art,
tearsheets, slides, photographs.
Tips: Obtains new talent through "recommendations from others, talent search, talent calling us
directly."

STUDIO ARTISTS/DON PEPPER (II), 638 S. Van Ness Ave., Los Angeles CA 90005. (213)385-4585.
Fax: (213)381-6763. Contact: Don Pepper. Illustration or photography broker. Estab. 1984. Represents
5 illustrators, 2 designers. Specializes in "full range of styles plus handlettering, layout and design."
Handles: Illustration, design.
Terms: No information provided.
How to Contact: For first contact, send a bio, direct mail flyer/brochure, tearsheets. Will report in
"a few" days, if interested. After initial contact, call to schedule an appointment, drop off or mail in
appropriate materials for review. Portfolio should include "whatever best represents your capabilities."
Tips: Obtains new talent through solicitation.

JOSEPH TRIBELLI DESIGNS, LTD. (II, IV), 254-33 Iowa Rd., Great Neck NY 11020. (516)482-2699.
Contact: Joseph Tribelli. Representative of textile designers only. Estab. 1988. Member of Graphic
Artists Guild. Represents 9 designers. Specializes in textile surface design for apparel (women and
men). "All designs are on paper."

Handles: Textile design for apparel.
Terms: Agent receives 40% commission. Exclusive area representation is required.
How to Contact: "Telephone first." Reports back within 2 weeks. After initial contact, drop off or mail appropriate materials. Portfolio should include original art.
Tips: Obtains new talent through "placing ads, recommendations. I am interested in only textile designers who can paint on paper. Do not apply unless you have a flair for fashion."

URSULA INC., (V), 63 Adrian Ave., Marble Hill (Bronx) NY 10463. Specializing in the European markets.

PHILIP M. VELORIC, ARTIST REPRESENTATIVE (II), 128 Beechtree Dr., Broomall PA 19008. (215)356-0362. Fax: (215)353-7531. Contact: Philip M. Veloric. Commercial illustration representative. Estab. 1963. Member of Art Directors Club of Philadelphia. Represents 22 illustrators. "Most of my business is from textbook publishing, but not all of it." Markets include advertising agencies, design firms, publishing/books, collectibles.
Handles: Illustration. "Artists should be able to do (and have samples to show) all ethnic children (getting ages right; tell a story; develop a character); earth science, life and physical science; some trade books also."
Terms: Agent receives 25% commission. Exclusive area representation is required. Advertising costs are split: 75% paid by the talent; 25% paid by the representative. Advertises in *RSVP*.
How to Contact: For first contact, call. After initial contact, call to schedule an appointment to show a portfolio. Portfolio should include original art, tearsheets, photocopies, laser copies.
Tips: Obtains new talent through recommendations from others.

WARNER & ASSOCIATES (IV), 1425 Belleview Ave., Plainfield NJ 07060. (201)755-7236. Contact: Bob Warner. Commercial illustration and photography representative. Estab. 1986. Represents 4 illustrators, 4 photographers. "My specialized markets are advertising agencies that service pharmaceutical, medical, health-care clients."
Handles: Illustration, photography. Looking for medical illustrators; microscope photographers (photomicrography); science illustrators; special effects photographers.
Terms: Agent receives 25% commission. "Promo pieces and portfolios obviously are needed; who makes up what and at what costs and to whom, varies widely in this business."
How to Contact: For first contact send query letter "or phone me." Reports back within days. Portfolio should include "anything that talent considers good sample material."
Tips: Obtains new talent "by hearsay and recommendations. Also, specialists in my line of work often hear about my work from art directors and they call me."

WARSHAW BLUMENTHAL, INC. (III), 400 E. 56th St., New York NY 10022. (212)867-4225. Fax: (212)867-4154. Contact: Andrea Warshaw. Commercial illustration representative. Estab. 1988. Member of SPAR. Represents 23 illustrators. "We service the ad agencies in offering high-tech storyboard, comp art and animatic art for testing. We also represent a Macintosh computer artist who animates on the system."
Terms: No information provided.
How to Contact: For first contact, send resume, direct mail flyer/brochure, photocopies. Will report within 2 days. After initial contact, call to schedule an appointment or drop off or mail appropriate materials for review. Portfolios should include "finished-looking animatic art and/or a reel."
Tips: Obtains new talent through word of mouth and recommendations.

WASHINGTON-ARTISTS' REPRESENTATIVES (II), Suite 152, 4901 Broadway, San Antonio TX 78209. (512)822-1336. Fax: (512)822-1375. Contact: Dick Washington. Commercial illustration and photography representative. Estab. 1983. Member of CASSA. Represents 10 illustrators, 2 photographers.
Terms: No information provided.
How to Contact: For first contact, send tearsheets. Reports within 2 weeks, only if interested. After initial contact, call to schedule an appointment. Portfolio should include original art, tearsheets, slides.
Tips: Usually obtains, new talent through recommendations and solicitation. "Make sure that you are ready for a real commitment and relationship. It's an important step for an artist, and should be taken seriously. Don't allow an art rep to sign you to an exclusive contract. You will want representation in all the major markets eventually."

ELYSE WEISSBERG (II,III), 299 Pearl St., New York NY 10038. (212)406-2566. Fax: (212)571-7568. Contact: Elyse Weissberg. Commercial photography representative. Estab. 1982. Member of SPAR. Represents 2 photographers. Markets include advertising agencies, corporations/client direct, design firms, editorial/magazines, publishing/books, sales/promotion firms.
Handles: Photography. "I'm not looking for talent now, but I'm always interested in seeing what's out there."
Terms: "Each of my contracts is negotiated separately." No specific promotional requirements. "Some younger talents I have represented did not have stationery when we started together—my only requirement is ambition." Advertises in *American Showcase, Creative Black Book, The Workbook.*
How to Contact: For first contact, send direct mail flyer/brochure. Will report in 1 week, if interested. After initial contact, drop off or mail in appropriate materials for review. Portfolio should include tearsheets, photographs.
Tips: Obtains new talent through recommendations, direct mail. "Don't give up! Someone is always looking for new talent."

SUSAN WELLS & ASSOCIATES, INC. (III), (formerly Susan Wells Associates), 5134 Timber Trail NE, Atlanta GA 30342. (404)255-1430. Fax: (404)255-3449. Contact: Susan Wells. Commercial illustration representative. Estab. 1981. Represents 17 illustrators. Markets include advertising agencies, corporations/client direct, design firms.
Handles: Illustration.
Terms: Agent receives 25% commission. Exclusive area representation is required. Advertising costs are split: 75% paid by talent; 25% paid by representative. For promotional purposes, talent must provide matted 4x5 or 8x10 transparencies for portfolio presentation, 8½x11 promotional piece for direct mail. Advertises in *Creative Illustration Book.*
How to Contact: For first contact, send a query letter and direct mail flyer/brochure, slides and SASE. Will report in 6 weeks, if interested. After initial contact, write to schedule an appointment. Portfolio should include 4x5 or 8x10 transparencies or laminated tearsheets.
Tips: Obtains new talent through "recommendations or direct contact initiated by artist."

WINSTON WEST, LTD. (III, IV), 195 S. Beverly Dr., Beverly Hills CA 90213. (212)275-2858. Fax: (213)275-0917. Contact: Bonnie Winston. Commercial photography representative (fashion/entertainment). Estab. 1986. Represents 8 photographers. Specializes in "editorial fashion and commercial advertising (with an edge)." Markets include advertising agencies, client direct, editorial/magazines.
Handles: Photography.
Terms: Agent receives 25% commission. Charges for courier services. Exclusive area representation is required. Advertising costs are split: 75% paid by the talent; 25% paid by the representative. Advertises by direct mail.
How to Contact: For first contact, send direct mail flyer/brochure, photographs, photocopies, photostats. Reports back within days, only if interested. After initial contact, call to schedule an appointment to show a portfolio. Portfolios should include tearsheets.
Tips: Obtains new talent through "recommendations from the modeling agencies. If you are a new fashion photographer or a photographer that's relocated recently, develop relationships with the modeling agencies in town. They are invaluable sources for client leads and know all the reps."

‡DEBORAH WOLFE LTD., 731 North 24th St., Philadelphia PA 19130. (215)232-6666. Fax: (215)232-6585. Contact: Deborah Wolfe. Commercial illustration representative. Estab. 1978. Represents 25 illustrators. Markets include advertising agencies, corporations/ciient direct, design firms, editorial/magazines, publishing/books.
Handles: Illustration.
Terms: Agent receives 25% commission. Advertises in *American Showcase* and *Creative Black Book.*
How to Contact: For first contact send: direct mail flyer/brochure, tearsheets and slides. Will report within 3 weeks.
Tips: "Artists usually contact us through mail or drop off at our office. If interested, we ask to see more work. (including originals)."

Additional Commercial Art and Photography Reps

The following representatives have full listings in other sections of this book. These reps and agents have indicated they are *primarily* interested in handling book manuscripts or the work of fine artists, but are also interested in illustrators or photographers. After reading the listing (you can find the page number in the Listings Index), send them a query to obtain more information on their needs and artwork or photography submission policies.

Brown Literary Agency, Inc., Andrea
Gusay Literary Agency, The Charlotte

Nathan, Ruth
Norma-Lewis Agency, The
Northwest Literary Services

Rubenstein Literary Agency, Inc., Pesha
Wecksler-Incomco

Commercial Art and Photography Reps/'92-'93 changes

The following representatives appeared in the last (1992) edition of *Guide to Literary Agents & Art Photo Reps* but are absent from the 1993 edition. These reps failed to respond to our request for an update of their listing, or were left out for the reasons indicated in parentheses following the rep name.

Barasa & Associates, Inc. (removed per request)
Noel Becker Associates
Lydia Carriere-Creative Representative (unable to contact)
CVB Creative Resource
Eldridge Corporation (unable to contact)

Rhoni Epstein
Anita Green Inc. (removed per request)
Wendy Hansen (unable to contact)
Gretchen Harris & Associates (removed per request)
Joanne Hedge/Artist Representative

The McCann Company (removed per request)
Trudy Sands & Associates (unable to contact)
Janice Stefanski
Storyboards, Inc. (removed per request)

Fine Art Reps

While much of what we've said about dealing with reps in the intro to the Commercial Art/ Photo Reps section holds true for fine art reps, there are some differences. First of all there are fewer "official" fine art reps. Yet many gallery owners, art consultants, art publishers and art distributors also act as reps for the artists they handle.

Since there are fewer fine art reps, there are also fewer established norms. And fewer norms mean more room for variety in the way reps work. Some promote their talent by presenting portfolios or slide shows to clients; others hold exhibitions; others maintain extensive slide files. It's important to ask a potential rep for as much information about how they work as possible so that you can make the best informed decision.

What do fine art reps do?

Fine art reps promote the work of fine artists, sculptors, craftspeople and fine art photographers to galleries and museums, but they also sell to corporate art collectors, developers, interior designers, art publishers and even some book publishers. They may operate their own gallery as well or they may be in the art publishing or other art-related business.

In general, fine art reps call on clients with your portfolio or other promotional material. Like commercial reps, they may have certain promotional requirements. Most do not advertise in commercial talent books, but they do advertise in art publications—those seen by decorators, gallery owners and collectors.

Although some fine art reps' terms are identical to those of a commercial rep, most take a higher commission and do not charge talent for advertising costs. Most require an exclusive area of representation. In addition to selling the work you've already created, many arrange commission work for you.

Why get a fine art rep?

Reps can help by taking over the sales, marketing and other business aspects of your work so you can devote more time to the creative process. They can handle the recordkeeping, billing and other paper work—keeping track of the money owed you and the particulars of who is considering your work.

Most galleries do an excellent job of promoting and selling work within their immediate areas. Those situated to attract tourists help to "spread the word" about your work across the country, but a rep can broaden your exposure considerably. Depending on the rep, you may find yourself working with clients on a national or even international level.

Reps cultivate contacts. They watch the market carefully and can advise you on trends and prices. They may be able to get you into shows, help get you your own shows or even put on a show for you.

A few considerations

Before approaching a rep, make sure you are ready. That is, you must be willing to make a commitment to your career as an artist. You should have a sizable body of work ready to show and sell. Consider carefully the idea of doing commissioned work—can you do work "on demand" and deliver it on time?

Prepare your portfolio with care. Include slides and other material for promotion. When sending slides, make sure they are labeled individually with your name and address. Also include directions ("up" and "front") on your slides. For finished work, you will need to include a price list with your slides. Make sure your pricing is consistent and logical. One artist suggests pricing by size only. She feels pricing by other, less tangible, considerations puts out signals that you feel some of your work is not as good as your other work. Your rep should be able to advise you on prices or check out your competition at local galleries.

For more information on working with reps see Finding and Working with Art/Photo Reps by Barbara Gordon and the books listed in the Resources section. *Artist's Market* and *Photographer's Market* include more in depth information on the business of art or photography and are a must for your business bookshelf.

Help with your search

To help you with your search for representation, we've included a Geographic Index in the back of the book. It is divided by state and province. The Agents and Representatives Index is provided to help you locate individual reps. Often you will read about a rep, but if that rep is an employee of a large agency, you may not be able to find that person's business number. We've asked agencies to give us the names of representatives on their staffs. Then we've listed the names in alphabetical order along with the name of their agency. Find the name of the person you would like to contact and then check the listing for that agency.

A few of the commercial illustration and photography representatives are also interested in fine artists. This is especially true of reps who work with book publishers. If a rep's *primary* function is selling illustration, but is also interested in handling some fine artists or fine art photographers, we've listed them in Additional Fine Art Reps at the end of this section.

In addition to examining and contacting the listings in this section, word-of-mouth and referrals are still an important way to find representation. You may also be able to meet a rep at a show or workshop. Artist and photographer organizations provide information on reps to members through newsletters and meetings.

About the listings

Most fine art representatives do not charge for additional expenses beyond those incurred in preparing your portfolio. Depending on the arrangement, you may have to help pay for shipping of your work to the rep. A few reps require you to pay for special portfolios or other advertising materials. A handful also charge monthly retainers to cover marketing expenses. Where possible, we've indicated these listings with a filled-in box (■) symbol.

We've ranked the agencies listed in this section according to their openness to submissions. Below is our ranking system:

I Newer representative actively seeking clients.
II Representative seeking both new and established artists or photographers.
III Representative prefers to work with established artists or photographers, mostly through referrals.
IV Representative handling only certain types of work or work by artists or photographers under certain circumstances.
V Representative not currently seeking new clients. (If an agency chose this designation, only the address is given.) We have included mention of reps rated V only to let you know they are not open to new clients at this time. *Unless you have a strong*

recommendation from someone in the field, our advice is to approach only those reps ranked I-IV.

ADMINISTRATIVE ARTS (II), P.O. Box 547935, Orlando FL 32854-7935. (407)578-1266. Contact: Brenda B. Harris. Fine art advisor. Estab. 1983. Registry includes 900 fine artists (includes fine art crafts). Markets include architects, corporate collections, developers, private collections.
Handles: Fine art. "We prefer artists with at least established local and regional credentials as emerging talent."
Terms: "Trade discount requested varies from 15-50% depending on project and medium. Submissions should include: 1) complete résumé; 2) artist's statement or brief profile; 3) slides (with artist's name on each and either slide information or numbered with information attached on separate sheet). 4) slide information: title and date of work, image size, medium, availability, etc.; 5) pricing."
How to Contact: For first contact send query letter, résumé, bio, tearsheets, slides, copies of reviews, etc. and SASE. Reports back within 1-2 weeks. After initial contact, call to schedule an appointment. "Artists usually have sent information prior to an appointment. If art is transportable, original work is shown in a meeting. Art professionals who have accepted artists' information may not be able to meet with the artists immediately. We are often busy getting clients and opening doors for the artist!"
Tips: "Artists are generally referred by their business or art advisor, another art professional, from a university or arts journal that has researched our firm, or are referred by other artists. Make sure that slides are good representations of your work. Always place your name and slide identification on each slide. Understand retail and net pricing structures in the art industry, trends, etc. — and include pricing information. A good impression is made by a well organized, typed résumé. Many artists include concise but very creative cover letters which help introduce the work."

JACK ARNOLD FINE ARTS (II, IV), 5 E. 67 St., New York NY 10021. (212)249-7218. Fax: (212)249-7232. Contact: Jack Arnold. Fine art representative. Estab. 1979. Represents 15 fine artists (includes 1 sculptor). Specializes in contemporary graphics and paintings. Markets include galleries, museums, private collections, corporate collections.
Handles: Looking for contemporary impressionists and realists.
Terms: Agent receives 50% commission. Exclusive area representation is preferred. For promotional purposes, talent must provide color prints or slides.
How to Contact: For first contact send bio, photographs, retail prices, SASE. Reports back within days. After initial contact, drop off or mail in appropriate materials for review. Portfolios should include slides, photographs.
Tips: Obtains new talent through referrals.

ART SOURCE L.A. (II), 1416 Sixth St., Santa Monica CA 90401. (310)917-6688. Fax: (310)917-6685. Contact: Francine Ellman. Fine art representative. Estab. 1980. Member of Architectural Design Council. Represents 10 photographers, 30 fine artists (includes 4 sculptors). Specializes in fine art consulting and curating; creative management, exhibition and design. Markets include architects, corporate collections, developers, public space galleries, interior decorators, museums, private collections, publishing/books, film industry.
Handles: Fine art and fine photography.
Terms: Agent receives commission, amount varies. Exclusive area representation required in some cases. "We request artists or photographers to submit a minimum of five slides/visuals, biography and SASE. Advertises in *Art News, Artscene, Art in America, Blue Book*.
How to Contact: For first contact, send a résumé, bio, slides or photographs and SASE. Will report in 1-2 months. After initial contact, "we will call to schedule an appointment." Portfolio should include original art, slides, photographs.
Tips: Obtains new talent through recommendations, artists' submission and trade shows.

ARTCO INCORPORATED (II, III), 3148 RFD Cuba Rd., Long Grove IL 60047. (708)438-8420. Fax: (708)438-6464. Contact: Sybil Tillman. Fine art representative. Estab. 1970. Member of International Society of Appraisers. Represents 60 fine artists. Specializes in contemporary artists' originals and limited edition graphics. Markets include architects, art publishers, corporate collections, galleries, private collections.

Handles: Fine art.
Terms: "Each commission is determined mutually. For promotional purposes, I would like to see original work or transparencies." Advertises in newspapers, magazine, etc.
How to Contact: For first contact send query letter, résumé, bio, slides, photographs or transparencies. Reports back within 2 weeks. After initial contact, call to schedule an appointment to show a portfolio. Portfolios should include original art, slides, photographs.
Tips: Obtains new talent through recommendations from others, solicitation, at conferences, advertising.

ARTS COUNSEL INC., 116 E. 27th St., 12th Fl., New York NY 10016, (212)725-3806. Fax: (212)779-9589. Contact: Fran Black. Fine art, commercial illustration, commercial photography representative. Estab. 1985. Represents 2 illustrators, 5 photographers, 12 fine artists (includes 4 sculptors). Specializes in marketing, proposal and guide writing, presentation techniques and public relations. Markets include advertising agencies, corporations/client direct, design firms, art publishers, corporate collections, interior decorators, museums, private collections.
Handles: Fine art, illustration, photography. "We are not actively looking, but we will review the work of artists with museum credentials."
Terms: Agent receives 25% commission. Charges 5% for long-distance calls. Advertising costs are split: 75% paid by the talent; 25% paid by the representative. For promotional purposes, talent must provide "promotional materials on hand as well as three to four complete portfolios." Advertises in *Creative Black Book, The Workbook, Graphis*.
How to Contact: For first contact, send query letter, bio, direct mail flyer/brochure. Reports back within 5 days. After initial contact, call to schedule an appointment to show a portfolio. Portfolio should include original art, tearsheets, photographs, laminates.
Tips: Obtains new talent through recommendations from others as well as through select advertising and promotion materials. "Know what you want to achieve in the commercial world. Be open to growth and development while maintaining a distinctive style."

CATHY BAUM & ASSOCIATES, 384 Stevick Dr., Atherton CA 94027. (415)854-5668. Fax: (415)854-8522. Contact: Cathy Baum or Kris Hartman. Art advisory firm. Estab. 1976. Member of National Association for Corporate Art. "Cathy Baum & Associates is a fine arts advisory firm. We do not represent artists, but will work directly with artists, if their work is appropriate for our client's art program. We have slide files on artists in all visual media of the fine arts." Markets include architects, corporate collections, developers, interior designers.
Handles: Fine art media—painting, sculpture, prints, photography.
Terms: Agent receives 20-50% commission. For promotional purposes, talent must provide slides of artwork, prices, biography.
How to Contact: For first contact, send bio, slides, price list. Reports back within 2 weeks. After initial contact, firm will request additional material. Portfolio should include slides.
Tips: Obtains new talent through "contacts in the arts, artists sending slides, galleries, etc."

CORCORAN FINE ARTS LIMITED, INC. (II), (formerly James Corcoran Fine Arts), 2341 Roxboro Rd., Cleveland OH 44106. (216)397-0777. Fax: (216)397-0222. Contact: James Corcoran. Fine art representative. Estab. 1986. Member of NOADA (Northeast Ohio Dealers Association); ISA (International Society of Appraisers). Represents 5 photographers, 11 fine artists (includes 3 sculptors). Staff includes Meghan Wilson (gallery associate); Brian Keough (office administrator); James Corcoran (owner/manager). Specializes in representing high-quality contemporary work. Markets include architects, corporate collections, developers, galleries, interior decorators, museums, private collections.
Handles: Fine art.
Terms: Agent receives 50% commission. Exclusive area representation is required. Advertising costs are "decided case by case."
How to Contact: For first contact send a query letter, résumé, bio, slides, photographs, SASE. Reports back within 1 month. After initial contact, drop off or mail in appropriate materials for review. Portfolio should include slides, photographs.
Tips: Usually obtains new talent by solicitation.

CORPORATE ART ASSOCIATES, LTD. (II), Suite 402, 270 Lafayette St., New York NY 10012. (212)941-9685. Director: James Cavello. Fine art representative. Also handles commercial illustration and photography, graphic design. Art consultant. Estab. 1988. Represents 15 illustrators, 50 photogra-

phers, 20 designers, 2,000 fine artists (includes 40 sculptors). Markets include advertising agencies, corporations/client direct, design firms, editorial/magazines, paper products/greeting cards, publishing/books, sales/promotion firms, architects, art publishers, corporate collections, developers, galleries, interior decorators, private collections.
Handles: Fine art, illustration, photography, design.
Terms: Agent receives 50% commission. Advertising costs are 100% paid by the talent.
How to Contact: For first contact, send query letter, résumé, bio, direct mail flyer/brochure, tearsheets, slides, photographs, photocopies, photostats, SASE. Reports back within days. After initial contact, drop off or mail in appropriate materials for review. Portfolio should include thumbnails, roughs, original art, tearsheets, slides, photographs, photostats, photocopies.
Tips: Obtains new talent through recommendations from others.

FINE ART REPRESENTATIVE (II), 729 Pine Crest, Prospect Heights IL 60070. (708)459-3990. Contact: Nancy Rudino. Fine art representative. Estab. 1977. Represents 45 fine artists. Specializes in "selling to art galleries." Markets include corporate collections, galleries, interior decorators.
Handles: Fine art.
Terms: "We buy for resale." Exclusive area representation is required. For promotional purposes talent must provide slides, color prints, "any visuals." Advertises in *Art News*, *Decor*, *Art Business News*.
How to Contact: For first contact send tearsheets, slides, photographs, SASE. Reports back within 30 days, only if interested. "Don't call us — if interested, we will call you." Portfolio should include slides, photographs.
Tips: Obtains new talent through recommendations from others and word of mouth.

ROBERT GALITZ FINE ART/ACCENT ART (II), 166 Hilltop Ct., Sleepy Hollow IL 60118. (708)426-8842. Fax: (708)426-8846. Contact: Robert Galitz. Fine art representative. Estab. 1985. Represents 100 fine artists (includes 2 sculptors). Specializes in contemporary/abstract corporate art. Markets include architects, corporate collections, galleries, interior decorators, private collections.
Handles: Fine art.
Terms: Agent receives 25-40% commission. For promotional purposes talent must provide "good photos and slides." Advertises in monthly art publications and guides.
How to Contact: For first contact send query letter, slides, photographs. Reports back within 2 weeks. After initial contact, call to schedule an appointment to show a portfolio. Portfolio should include original art.
Tips: Obtains new talent through recommendations from others, solicitation, at conferences. "Be confident, persistent. Never give up or never quit."

ICEBOX, 2401 Central Ave. NE, Minneapolis MN 55418. (612)788-1790. Contact: Howard Christopherson. Fine art representative. Estab. 1988. Represents 4 photographers, 6 fine artists (includes 2 sculptors). Specializes in "thought-provoking art work and photography, predominantly Minnesota artists." Markets include corporate collections, interior decorators, museums, private collections.
Handles: Fine art and fine art photographs. Looking for "new photography and thought-provoking works."
Terms: Agent receives 33-50% commission. Exclusive area representation in Minnesota is required. For promotional purposes, talent must provide slides. Advertises in *Art Paper* and local newspapers and magazines.
How to Contact: For first contact, send résumé, bio, slides, SASE. Reports back within 60 days. After initial contact, drop off or mail in appropriate materials for review. Portfolio should include slides.

INTERNATIONAL ART CONNECTION AND ART CONNECTION PLUS (II), #51, 444 Brickell Ave., Miami FL 33131. (305)371-5137. President: Jane Chambeaux. (between June 15 and November 15, contact Ms. Chambeaux at Museum of the Commanderiè of Unet, 47400, Tonneins, Bordeaux France) "Nonprofit organization dedicated to helping artists." Estab. 1966 in Europe, 1987 in USA. Represents photographers, fine artists and sculptors. "We organize exhibits and promote artists." Markets include galleries, museums, private collectors.
Terms: Not-for-profit service. $25 fee.
How to Contact: For first contact, send résumé, slides, photographs, SASE. Reports back within 4 days. After initial contact, drop off or mail in appropriate materials for review. Portfolios should include original art (or framed), photocopies.

Tips: Obtains new talent through "an ad in *Photo* or *Art Review* and contacts in the museums." If interested in obtaining representation, "make international exhibits in museums."

L.A. ART EXCHANGE (II), 2451 Broadway, Santa Monica CA 90404. (310)828-6866. Fax: (310)828-2643. Contact: Jayne Zehngut. Fine art representative. Estab. 1987. Member of Professional Picture Framers Assoc. Represents 20 fine artists. "We deal with retail, wholesale and corporate accounts." Markets include corporations/client direct design firms, architects, corporate collections, developers, galleries, interior decorators.
Handles: Fine art, photography, design.
Terms: No information provided. Exclusive area representation is "preferred."
How to Contact: For first contact, send résumé, bio, slides, photographs, SASE. Reports back within 1 week. After initial contact, write to schedule an appointment or drop off or mail in appropriate materials for review.
Tips: Obtains new talent through "advertising in *Decor* magazine and *Art Business News* and local newspapers. Primary businesses are custom picture framing; fine art and poster sales; art consulting (corporate and residential)."

NELDA LEE INC. (III), 2610 21st St., Odessa TX 79761. (915)366-8426. Fax: (915)550-2830. Contact: Nelda Lee. Fine art representative. Estab. 1967. Member of American Society of Appraisers, Texas Association of Art Dealers, Appraisers Association of America. Represents 50-60 artists, including 4 sculptors. Markets include corporate collections, developers, galleries, interior decorators, museums, private collections.
Handles: Fine art, illustration.
Terms: Agent receives 40-50% commission. Exclusive area representation is required. Advertising costs are 100% paid by representative. Advertises in *Texas Monthly*, *Southwest Art*, local tv and newspapers.
How to Contact: For first contact, send a query letter and photographs ("include phone number"). Will report within 10 days. After initial contact, call to schedule an appointment. Portfolios should include original art and photographs.
Tips: Obtains new talent through "direct contact from talent. Don't give up. Keep contacting—about every six months to a year. Everbody's needs change."

LESLI ART, INC. (II), Box 6693, Woodland Hills CA 91365. (818)999-9228. Contact: Stan Shevrin. Fine art representative. Estab. 1965. Represents 28 fine artists. Specializes in "artists paintings in oil or acrylic, in the manner of the impressionists. Also represent illustrators whose figurative work can be placed in art galleries."
Terms: Negotiable.
How to Contact: For first contact, send bio, slides, photographs, SASE. Reports back within 2 weeks.
Tips: Obtains new talent through "reviewing portfolios. Artists should show their most current works and state a preference for subject matter and medium."

MADRAZO ARTS (II), 1236 Milan Ave., Coral Gables FL 33134. (305)443-1023. Fax: (305)446-1303. Contact: Mr. Madrazo. Fine art representative. Estab. 1986. Member of Society of Illustrators. Represent 12-13 fine artists (includes 3 sculptors). Specializes in art for hospitality and health care work. Markets include architects, galleries, interior decorators, private collections.
Handles: Fine art and sculpture.
Terms: Agent receives 15-30% commission. Exclusive area representation is required. Advertising costs are split: 50% paid by the talent; 50% paid by the representative. For promotional purposes, talent must provide "visuals, whether photo or slides and curriculum vitae."
How to Contact: For first contact, send query letter, résumé, direct mail flyer/brochure, slides, photographs. Reports back within 10 days. After initial contact, call to schedule an appointment to show a portfolio or write to schedule an appointment. Portfolio should include original art, slides, photographs.
Tips: Obtains new talent through recommendations from others.

■ *A solid box indicates reps who charge a period fee for expenses or who charge special fees in addition to commission and advertising costs.*

MEDIA GALLERY/ENTERPRISES (II), 145 W. 4th Ave., Garnett KS 66032-1313. (913)448-5813. Contact: Robert Cugno. Fine art representative. Estab. 1963. Number of artists and sculptors represented varies. Specializes in clay—contemporary and modern. Markets include galleries, museums, private collections.
Handles: Fine art and clay.
Terms: Agent receives 40-60% commission. For promotional purposes, talent must provide photos and slides.
How to Contact: For first contact send bio, slides, SASE. Reports back within 1-2 weeks. After initial contact, drop off or mail in appropriate materials for review.
Tips: Obtains new talent through recommendations from other artists, collectors, art consultants and gallery directors.

■**PENNAMENITIES (IV)**, R.D. #2, Box 1080, Schuylkill Haven PA 17972. (717)754-7744. Fax: (717)754-7744. Contact: Deborah A. Miller. Fine art representative. Estab. 1988. Member of Summit Arts Fellowship. Represents 20 fine artists. Specializes in "arranging New York City art exhibits." Markets include galleries, private collections.
Handles: Fine art (originals and prints).
Terms: Agent receives 30-50% commission. Charges $350 annual fee which covers correspondence, copies, phone and fax or services involved in setting up NYC exhibit.
How to Contact: For first contact send résumé, bio, slides, price list, SASE required. After initial contact, drop off or mail in appropriate materials for review. Portfolio should include transparencies, photographs and slides.
Tips: "Initial contact is usually made by artist seeking representative's services."

NICKI SHEARER ART SOURCE (II), 6101 Walhonding Rd., Bethesda MD 20816. (301)320-2211. Fax: (301)320-2210. Contact: Nicki Shearer. Fine art representative. Estab. 1979. Represents "many" fine artists (several are sculptors). Specializes in art for hotels, hospitals, other commercial space (law firms, etc.). Markets include architects, corporate collections, developers, interior decorators.
Handles: Fine art. Looking for "lobby art—large wallhangings/sculpture."
Terms: Agent receives 40-50% commission. Exclusive area representation is not required, however "I would like to represent artists who are not represented in this area." Advertising costs are paid by representative. For promotional purposes, talent must provide slides, photographs, résumé, "any other promotional materials" and SASE.
How to Contact: For first contact, send a résumé, bio, direct mail flyer/brochure, 2 or 3 slides, photographs—"call first, if possible." Will report in 1 month, if interested. After initial contact, drop off or mail in appropriate materials for review.
Tips: Obtains new talent through "recommendations from others, museum shows, other exhibits, as well as juried shows."

SIMPATICO ART & STONE (II), 1221 Demaret Ln., Houston TX 77055-6115. (713)467-7123. Contact: Billie Blake Fant. Fine art broker/consultant/exhibitor. Estab. 1973. Specializes in unique fine art, sculpture and Texas domestic stone furniture, carvings architectural elements. Market includes corporate, institutional and residential clients.
Handles: Looking for unique fine art and sculpture not presently represented in Houston, Texas.
Terms: Standard commission. Exclusive area representation required.
How to Contact: For first contact, send query letter, résumé, slides.
Tips: Obtains new talent through travel, publications, exhibits and referrals.

TOLEASE LAUTREC, P.O. Box 8485, Wichita KS 67208. (316)686-2470. Contact: C. Matthew Foley. Fine art, commercial illustration, graphic art representative. Estab. 1984. Member of Societas Artis Illuminatorum/Nepenthe Mundi Society. Represents 3 illustrators, 10 photographers, 5 designers, 36 fine artists (includes 12 sculptors). Specializes in Native American art. Markets includes advertising agencies, corporations/client direct, design firms, editorial/magazines, publishing/books, sales/promotion firms, corporate collections, galleries, interior decorators, museums, private collections, publishing/books. Member agents: Christian DeFauve (painting); Max Alexander (publicist, art agent); Mattphisto Idol (sculpture); Catherine Lynn Foley (marketing director).
Handles: Fine art, illustration, photography. Agent receives 25-40% commission. Exclusive area representation is required. Advertising costs are split: 50% paid by the talent; 50% paid by the representative.

How to Contact: For first contact, send query letter, résumé, bio, direct mail flyer/brochure, tear-sheets, slides, photographs, photocopies, photostats, SASE, "whatever the talent has currently available." Reports back within 2 weeks. Reports back with 1 week, only if interested. After initial contact, write to schedule an appointment to show a portfolio, or drop off or mail in appropriate materials for review. Portfolios should include tearsheets, slides, photographs, photostats, photocopies. "Send no originals."

Tips: Obtains new talent "from many sources. Always on the lookout for exceptional talent."

Fine Art Reps/'92-'93 changes

The following agencies appeared in the last (1992) edition of *Guide to Literary Agents & Art/Photo Reps* but are absent from the 1993 edition. These agencies failed to respond to our request for an update of their listing, or were left out for the reasons indicated in parentheses following the agency name.

Fine Art Associates
Gilmartin Associates (retired)
Palm Fine Art (unable to contact)

Joan Sapiro Art Consultants
Richard R. Storer (unable to contact)
Park Thede Associates

Walkingstick Productions
Elaine Wechsler

Resources

Recommended Books & Publications

For writers and scriptwriters

ADVENTURES IN THE SCREEN TRADE, by William Goldman, published by Warner Books, 666 Fifth Ave., New York NY 10103. An insider's view of screenwriting and the entertainment business.

AGENT & MANAGER, 7th Fl., 650 First Ave., New York NY 10016. Monthly trade magazine for all types of agents and managers. Information on new agents, news and deals.

BEYOND THE BESTSELLER: A LITERARY AGENT TAKES YOU INSIDE PUBLISHING, by Richard Curtis, published by NAL, 375 Hudson St., New York NY 10014. The "inside story" on publishing by a New York agent.

BUSINESS & LEGAL FORMS FOR AUTHORS AND SELF-PUBLISHERS, by Tad Crawford, published by Allworth Press, c/o Writer's Digest Books, 1507 Dana Ave., Cincinnati OH 45207. Forms for all types of agreements and contracts needed in the publishing business.

CHILDREN'S WRITER'S & ILLUSTRATOR'S MARKET, edited by Lisa Carpenter, published by Writer's Digest Books, 1507 Dana Ave., Cincinnati OH 45207. Annual market directory for children's writers and illustrators. Includes information on writing and art business.

THE COMPLETE BOOK OF SCRIPTWRITING, by J. Michael Straczyniski, published by Writer's Digest Books, 1507 Dana Ave., Cincinnati OH 45207. How to write and sell all types of scripts.

THE COMPLETE GUIDE TO STANDARD SCRIPT FORMAT (Parts 1 and 2), by Hillis Cole and Judith Haag, published by CMC Publishing, 11642 Otsego St., N. Hollywood CA 91601. Standard script formats and other information for scriptwriters.

DAILY VARIETY, 5700 Wilshire Blvd., Los Angeles CA 90036. Publication featuring information on the entertainment business, trade oriented.

DRAMATISTS SOURCEBOOK, edited by Angela E. Mitchell and Gilliam Richards, published by Theatre Communications Group, Inc., 355 Lexington Ave., New York NY 10017. Directory listing opportunities for playwrights. Includes agents.

THE GUIDE TO WRITERS CONFERENCES, published by Shaw Associates, Suite 1406, Biltmore Way, Coral Gables FL 33134. Directory of writers' conferences.

HOLLYWOOD REPORTER, Billboard Publications, Inc., 6715 Sunset Blvd., Hollywood CA 90028. Publication covering news and information on the entertainment industry. Includes information on scriptwriters and sales of scripts.

HOLLYWOOD SCRIPTWRITER, #385, 1626 N. Wilcox, Hollywood CA 90028. Newsletter featuring information for scriptwriters. Includes an annual agents issue.

HOW TO PITCH & SELL YOUR TV SCRIPT, by David Silver, published by Writer's Digest Books, 1507 Dana Ave., Cincinnati OH 45207. Information on marketing your television scripts. Includes information on working with script agents.

HOW TO SELL YOUR SCREENPLAY, by Carl Sautter, published by New Chapter Press, Suite 1122, 381 Park Ave. S., New York NY 10016. Tips on selling screenplays.

HOW TO WRITE A BOOK PROPOSAL, by Michael Larsen, published by Writer's Digest Books, 1507 Dana Ave., Cincinnati OH 45207. How to put together a professional-quality book proposal package.

HOW TO WRITE IRRESISTIBLE QUERY LETTERS, by Lisa Collier Cool, published by Writer's Digest Books, 1507 Dana Ave., Cincinnati OH 45207. How to write professional, effective queries.

THE INSIDER'S GUIDE TO BOOK EDITORS & PUBLISHERS, by Jeff Herman, published by Prima Publishing & Communications, Box 1260, Rocklin CA 95677-1260. An inside look at the publishing industry. Includes information on agents.

LITERARY AGENTS: A WRITER'S GUIDE, by Debby Mayer, published by Poets & Writer's, 72 Spring St.,

New York NY 10012. Directory of literary agents. Includes articles on working with agents. Published every five years.

LITERARY AGENTS: HOW TO GET AND WORK WITH THE RIGHT ONE FOR YOU, *by Michael Larsen, published by Paragon House, 90 Fifth Ave., New York NY 10011. How to approach and work with an agent.*

LITERARY MARKET PLACE (LMP), *R.R. Bowker Company, 121 Chanlon Road, New Providence NJ 07974. Book publishing industry directory. In addition to publishing companies, includes a list of literary agents and a list of art representatives.*

MAKING A GOOD SCRIPT GREAT, *by Dr. Linda Seger, published by Samuel French Trade, 7623 Sunset Blvd., Hollywood CA 90046. Information on improving your script.*

MANUSCRIPT SUBMISSION, *by Scott Edelstein, published by Writer's Digest Books, 1507 Dana Ave., Cincinnati OH 45207. How to prepare submissions for publishers and agents, especially for the fiction writer.*

NOVEL & SHORT STORY WRITER'S MARKET, *edited by Robin Gee, published by Writer's Digest Books, 1507 Dana Ave., Cincinnati OH 45207. Annual market directory for fiction writers. Includes information on the writing business, organizations and conferences for fiction writers.*

POETS AND WRITERS, *72 Spring St., New York NY 10012. Magazine for writers. Includes interviews and articles of interest to poets and literary writers. Poets and Writers also publishes several books and directories for writers.*

PROFESSIONAL WRITER'S GUIDE, *revised and expanded edition, edited by Donald Bower and James Lee Young, National Writers Press, Suite 620 S. Havana, Aurora CO 80012. The basics of starting and building a writing career.*

PUBLISHERS WEEKLY, *205 W. 42nd St., New York NY 10017. Weekly magazine covering industry trends and news in the book publishing industry. Contains announcements of new agencies.*

PUBLISHING NEWS, *Hanson Publishing Group, Box 4949, Stamford CT 06907-0949. Bimonthly newsmagazine of the publishing industry.*

SUCCESSFUL SCRIPTWRITING, *by Jurgen Wolff and Kerry Cox, published by Writer's Digest Books, 1507 Dana Ave., Cincinnati OH 45207. Includes information on the movie and television business, as well as tips on marketing and selling scripts.*

THEATRE DIRECTORY, *Theatre Communications Group, Inc., 355 Lexington Ave., New York NY 10017. Directory listing theaters in the U.S.*

THE TV SCRIPTWRITER'S HANDBOOK, *by Alfred Brenner, published by Writer's Digest Books, 1507 Dana Ave., Cincinnati OH 45207. Includes all aspects of writing for television including marketing scripts.*

THE WRITER, *120 Boylston St., Boston MA 02116. Magazine for writers. Includes articles on technique and writing issues.*

WRITER'S DIGEST, *1507 Dana Ave., Cincinnati OH 45207. Monthly magazine for writers. Includes technique, lifestyle, business and market information.*

THE WRITER'S DIGEST GUIDE TO MANUSCRIPT FORMATS, *by Dian Dincin Buchman and Seli Groves, published by Writer's Digest Books, 1507 Dana Ave., Cincinnati OH 45207. Models for all types of manuscript formats including query and cover letters to editors, publishers and agents.*

WRITER'S ESSENTIAL DESK REFERENCE, *edited by Glenda Tennant Neff, published by Writer's Digest Books, 1507 Dana Ave., Cincinnati OH 45207. Reference guide for writers including business, tax and legal information for both U.S. and Canadian writers.*

A WRITER'S GUIDE TO CONTRACT NEGOTIATIONS, *by Richard Balkin, published by Writer's Digest Books, 1507 Dana Ave., Cincinnati OH 45207. Written by an agent, this is an insider's view of book contract negotiations.*

THE WRITER'S LEGAL COMPANION, *by Brad Bunnin and Peter Beren, published by Addison Wesley, Jacob Way, Reading MA 01867. Legal guide for writers. Bunnin is a publishing-industry lawyer.*

WRITER'S MARKET, *edited by Mark Kissling, published by Writer's Digest Books, 1507 Dana Ave., Cincinnati OH 45207. Annual market directory for writers and scriptwriters. Includes information on the writing business.*

WRITING SCRIPTS THAT SELL, *by Michael Hauge, published by McGraw-Hill, 1221 Ave. of the Americas, New York NY 10020. Technique information for scriptwriters.*

For artists and photographers

ADVERTISING AGE, *740 Rush St., Chicago IL 60611-2590. Weekly advertising and marketing tabloid.*

ADWEEK, *A/S/M Communications, Inc., 49 E. 21st St., New York NY 10010. Weekly advertising and marketing magazine.*

AMERICAN ARTIST, *P.O. Box 1944, Marion OH 43306-2044. Magazine featuring instructional articles, profiles and technique information for artists.*

AMERICAN PHOTO, *43rd Fl., 1633 Broadway, New York NY 10019. Monthly magazine emphasizing the craft and philosophy of photography.*

AMERICAN SHOWCASE, *14th Fl., 915 Broadway, New York NY 10010., Annual talent sourcebook featuring illustrators, photographers and designers.*

ART DIRECTION, *6th Fl., 10 E. 39th St., New York NY 10016-0199. Monthly magazine featuring art directors' views on advertising and photography.*

ART IN AMERICA, *575 Broadway, New York NY 10012. Features in-depth articles on art issues, news and reviews. August issue includes an annual guide to artists, galleries and museums.*

THE ARTIST'S FRIENDLY LEGAL GUIDE, *by Floyd Conner, Peter Karlan, Jean Perwin & David M. Spatt, published by North Light Books, 1507 Dana Ave., Cincinnati OH 45207. Tips on taxes and legal matters by tax experts and lawyers familiar with the art business.*

THE ARTIST'S MAGAZINE, *1507 Dana Ave., Cincinnati OH 45207. Monthly art magazine featuring how-to technique and business information for artists.*

ARTIST'S MARKET, *edited by Lauri Miller, published by Writer's Digest Books, 1507 Dana Ave., Cincinnati OH 45207. Annual markets directory for artists. Includes art business information.*

ASMP BULLETIN, *monthly newsletter of American Society of Magazine Photographers, 419 Park Ave. South, New York NY 10016. Subscription comes with membership in ASMP.*

BUSINESS AND LEGAL FORMS FOR FINE ARTISTS, *by Tad Crawford, published by Allworth Press, % North Light Books, 1507 Dana Ave., Cincinnati OH 45207. Forms for agreements and other contracts for fine artists.*

BUSINESS AND LEGAL FORMS FOR ILLUSTRATORS, *by Tad Crawford, published by Allworth Press, c/o North Light Books, 1507 Dana Ave., Cincinnati OH 45207. Forms for agreements and contracts for illustrators.*

CHICAGO CREATIVE DIRECTORY, *Suite 810, 333 N. Michigan Ave., Chicago IL 60610. Annual talent sourcebook featuring illustrators and designers in the Chicago area.*

CHICAGO MIDWEST FLASH, *Alexander Communications, Suite 203, 212 W. Superior, Chicago IL 60610. Quarterly magazine including articles and news on graphic art and advertising in the Midwest.*

COMMUNICATIONS ARTS, *410 Sherman Ave., Box 10300, Palo Alto CA 94303. Magazine covering design, illustration and photography. Published 8 times a year.*

CREATIVE BLACK BOOK, *3rd Fl., 115 Fifth Ave., New York NY 10003. Annual talent sourcebook featuring illustrators, photographers and designers.*

CREATIVE SOURCE, *Wilcord Publications Ltd., Suite 110, 511 King St. West, Toronto, Ontario M5V 2Z4. Annual talent sourcebook featuring illustrators and designers in Canada.*

DECOR, *Commerce Publications, 408 Olive St., St. Louis MO 63102. Monthly magazine covering trends in art publishing, home accessories and framing.*

THE DESIGNER'S COMMONSENSE BUSINESS BOOK, *by Barbara Ganim, published by North Light Books, 1507 Dana Ave., Cincinnati OH 45207. Includes information on business matters for graphic designers.*

DIRECTORY OF FINE ART REPRESENTATIVES, *edited by Constance Franklin, published by Directors Guild Publishers & The Consultant Press. DGP address: 13284 Rices Crossing Road, P.O. Box 369, Renaissance CA 95962. Directory listing fine art reps and corporate art collectors.*

EDITOR & PUBLISHER, *The Editor & Publisher Co., Inc., 11 W. 19th St., New York NY 10011. Weekly magazine covering latest developments in journalism and newspaper production.*

THE FINE ARTIST'S GUIDE TO SHOWING & SELLING YOUR WORK, *by Sally Prince Davis, published by North Light Books, 1507 Dana Ave., Cincinnati OH 45207. Information on developing a marketing plan for fine artists.*

FOLIO, *Box 4949, Stamford CT 06907-0949. Monthly magazine featuring trends in magazine circulation, production and editorial.*

GETTING STARTED AS A FREELANCE ILLUSTRATOR OR DESIGNER, *by Michael Fleishman, published by North Light Books, 1507 Dana Ave., Cincinnati OH 45207. Book presenting information on promotion, portfolios and markets open to freelancers.*

THE GRAPHIC ARTIST'S GUIDE TO MARKETING & SELF-PROMOTION, *by Sally Prince Davis, published by North Light Books, 1507 Dana Ave., Cincinnati OH 45207. Contains information on marketing and promotion for graphic artists and designers.*

GRAPHIS, *Graphis U.S. Inc., 141 Lexington Ave., New York NY 10016. Bimonthly international journal of the graphic design industry.*

GUILFOYLE REPORT, *% AG Editions, 142 Bank St., New York NY 10014. Quarterly market tips newsletter for nature and stock photographers.*

HOW, *1507 Dana Ave., Cincinnati OH 45207. Bimonthly magazine featuring trends in graphic design and illustration.*

HOW TO SELL YOUR PHOTOGRAPHS AND ILLUSTRATIONS, *by Elliott and Barbara Gordon, published by Allworth Press, % North Light Books, 1507 Dana Ave., Cincinnati OH 45207. Business-building*

*tips from commercial reps Elliott and Barbara Gordon. Contains information on working with art/
photo reps.*
HUMOR & CARTOON MARKETS, *edited by Bob Staake, published by Writer's Digest Books, 1507 Dana
Ave., Cincinnati OH 45207. Annual directory of markets for humor writers and cartoonists. Includes
business information for writers and artists (cartoonists).*
INTERIOR DESIGN, *249 W. 17th St., New York NY 10011. Monthly magazine featuring industry news and
trends in furnishing and interior design.*
LEGAL GUIDE FOR THE VISUAL ARTIST, *by Tad Crawford, published by Allworth Press, c/o North Light
Books, 1507 Dana Ave., Cincinnati OH 45207. Guide to art law covering copyright and contracts.*
MAGAZINE DESIGN AND PRODUCTION, *Suite 106, 8340 Mission Road, Prairie Village KS 66206.
Monthly magazine with information on all aspects of magazine design and production.*
NEW YORK GOLD, *10 E. 21st St., New York NY 10010. Annual talent sourcebook featuring photographers.*
THE PERFECT PORTFOLIO, *by Henrietta Brackman, published by Amphoto Books, c/o Watson Guptill
Publishing, 1515 Broadway, New York NY 10036. Information on how to develop and improve your
photography portfolio.*
PHOTO DISTRICT NEWS, *49 East 21st St., New York NY 10010. Monthly trade magazine for the photogra-
phy industry.*
PHOTO/DESIGN, *1515 Broadway, New York NY 10036. Monthly magazine emphasizing photography in
the advertising/design fields.*
THE PHOTOGRAPHER'S BUSINESS & LEGAL HANDBOOK, *by Leonard Duboff, published by Images
Press, c/o Writer's Digest Books, 1507 Dana Ave., Cincinnati OH 45207. A guide to copyright, trade-
marks, libel law and other legal concerns for photographers.*
PHOTOGRAPHER'S GUIDE TO MARKETING AND SELF-PROMOTION, *by Maria Piscopo, published
by Writer's Digest Books, 1507 Dana Ave., Cincinnati OH 45207. Information on marketing and promo-
tion for photographers. Includes information on photographers' reps.*
PHOTOGRAPHER'S MARKET, *edited by Sam Marshall, published by Writer's Digest Books, 1507 Dana
Ave., Cincinnati OH 45207. Annual market directory for photographers. Includes photography business
information.*
PHOTOGRAPHING YOUR ART WORK, *by Russell Hart, published by North Light Books, published by
Writer's Digest Books, 1507 Dana Ave., Cincinnati OH 45207. How to photograph all types of artwork
to create the best slides for your portfolio.*
THE PROFESSIONAL DESIGNER'S GUIDE TO MARKETING YOUR WORK, *by Mary Yeung, published
by North Light Books, 1507 Dana Ave., Cincinnati OH 45207. Tips on marketing for graphic designers.
Includes information on finding a rep.*
PROMO, *by Rose DeNeve, published by North Light Books, 1507 Dana Ave., Cincinnati OH 45207. A
collection of outstanding promo pieces that have worked for illustrators and graphic designers.*
RSVP, *Box 314, Brooklyn NY 11205. Annual talent sourcebook featuring illustrators and designers.*
STEP-BY-STEP GRAPHICS, *Dynamic Graphics, Inc., 6000 N. Forest Park Drive, Peoria IL 61614-3597.
Bimonthly magazine featuring instruction for graphic design and illustration projects.*
U&lc, *Upper and Lower Case, 2 Hammarskjold Plaza, New York NY 10017. Newspaper format quarterly
featuring news and information for the graphic artist.*
THE ULTIMATE PORTFOLIO, *by Martha Metzdorf, published by North Light Books, 1507 Dana Ave.,
Cincinnati OH 45207. A showcase of some of the best and most successful portfolios by illustrators and
graphic designers.*
WOMEN'S WEAR DAILY, *Fairchild Publications, 7 West 34th St., New York NY 10001. Tabloid (Monday
through Friday) focusing on women's and children's apparel.*
THE WORK BOOK, *Scott & Daughters Publishing, Suite A, 940 N. Highland Ave., Los Angeles CA 90038.
Annual talent sourcebook listing illustrators, photographers and designers primarily in the Los Angeles
area.*

Professional Organizations

Organizations for agents and reps

ASSOCIATION OF AUTHORS' REPRESENTATIVES (AAR), *merger of Independent Literary Agents Association (ILAA) and Society of Authors' Representatives (SAR), 10 Astor Pl., 3rd Fl., New York NY 10003. A list of member agents is available for SASE with 52 cents for postage.*
SOCIETY OF PHOTOGRAPHERS' AND ARTISTS' AGENTS (SPAR), *Suite 1166, 60 E. 42nd St., New York NY 10165. A membership directory is available for about $35 (check for current price).*

Organizations for writers, artists and photographers

The following professional organizations for writers, artists and photographers publish newsletters and hold conferences and meetings in which they often share information on agents or reps.

ADVERTISING PHOTOGRAPHERS OF AMERICA (APA), *Room 601, 27 W. 20th St., New York NY 10011.*
AMERICAN INSTITUTE OF GRAPHIC ARTS (AIGA), *1059 Third Ave., New York NY 10021. (212)752-0813.*
AMERICAN SOCIETY OF JOURNALISTS & AUTHORS, *Suite 302, 1501 Broadway, New York NY 10036. (212)997-0947.*
AMERICAN SOCIETY OF MAGAZINE PHOTOGRAPHERS (ASMP), *Suite 1407, 419 Park Ave. S., New York NY 10016.*
AMERICAN SOCIETY OF PHOTOGRAPHERS (ASP), *Box 52900, Tulsa OK 74152.*
THE AUTHORS GUILD INC., *330 W. 42nd St., New York NY 10036. (212)563-5904.*
GRAPHIC ARTIST GUILD, *8th Fl., 11 W. 20th St., New York NY 10011. (212)463-7730.*
INTERNATIONAL ASSOCIATION OF CRIME WRITERS (North American branch), *JAF Box 1500, New York NY 10116. (212)757-3915.*
THE INTERNATIONAL WOMEN'S WRITING GUILD, *P.O. Box 810, Gracie Station, New York NY 10028. (212)737-7536. Provides a literary agents list to members. Also holds "Meet the Agents and Editors" sessions for members twice a year (April and October).*
MYSTERY WRITERS OF AMERICA (MWA), *6th Fl., 17 E. 47th St., New York NY 10017.*
NATIONAL WRITERS CLUB, *Suite 424, 1450 S. Havana, Aurora CO 80012. (303)751-7844. In addition to agent referrals, also operates an agency for members.*
NATIONAL WRITERS UNION, *Suite 203, 873 Broadway, New York NY 10003-1209. A trade union, this organization has an agent data base available to members.*
PROFESSIONAL PHOTOGRAPHERS OF AMERICA, INC. (PPA), *1090 Executive Way, Des Plaines IL 60018. (708)299-8161.*
ROMANCE WRITERS OF AMERICA (RWA), *13700 Veterans Memorial Dr., #315, Houston TX 77014. (713)440-6885. Publishes an annual agent's list, available for $8.50.*
SOCIETY OF CHILDREN'S BOOK WRITERS (SCBW), *P.O. Box 66296, Mar Vista Station, Los Angeles CA 90066. (818)342-2849. Provides a literary agents list to members.*
WRITERS GUILD OF AMERICA (WGA)—EAST, *555 W. 57th St., New York NY 10019. (212)767-7800. Provides a list of WGA signatory agents for $1.33 and SASE. Signatories are required to follow certain standards and a code of ethics.*
WRITERS GUILD OF AMERICA (WGA)—WEST, *8955 Beverly Blvd., West Hollywood CA 90048. (310)550-1000. Provides a list of WGA signatory agents for $1 and SASE, addressed to the Agency Department. Signatories are required to follow certain standards and a code of ethics.*

Glossary

Advance. A sum of money that a publisher pays a writer prior to publication of a book. It is usually paid in installments, such as one-half upon signing the contract; one-half upon delivery of the complete and satisfactory manuscript. The advance is paid against the royalty money that will be earned by the book. Agents take their percentage off the top of the advance as well as from the royalties earned.

Advertising costs. Costs incurred by placing advertisements in newspapers or magazines, purchasing pages in industry talent books, promoting a show or exhibition, creation and mailing of direct mail or other promo pieces, list rental, slide copying—anything that promotes the work of the talent and may lead to sales.

Auction. Publishers sometimes bid for the acquisition of a book manuscript that has excellent sales prospects. The bids are for the amount of the author's advance, guaranteed dollar amounts, advertising and promotional expenses, royalty percentage, etc.

Backlist. A publisher's list of its books that were not published during the current season, but which are still in print.

Bio. Brief (usually one page) background information about an artist, writer or photographer. Includes work and educational experience.

Boilerplate. A standardized publishing contract. "Our standard contract" usually means the boilerplate without changes. Most authors and agents make many changes on the boilerplate before accepting the contract.

Book. When used in commercial art circles, it refers to a portfolio. See *portfolio*.

Book proposal. See *proposal*.

Broker. A situation in which a rep handles only some of the work of an artist or photographer or in which the rep sells just what the talent has brought to them to sell. A percentage is taken from each sale. The rep is not handling the talent's career, only certain work.

Business-size envelope. Also known as a #10 envelope, it is the standard-size envelope used in most business situations.

Category fiction. A term used to include all various types of fiction. See *genre*.

Cibachrome. Trademark for a full-color positive print made from a transparency.

Client. When referring to a literary or script agent "client" is used to mean the writer whose work the agent is handling, but when referring to art or photography representation, "client" refers to the art/photo buyer. The word "talent" is used to refer to the artist or photographer whose work is handled by the rep.

Client direct. Sales directly to a corporate client instead of to a middle person such as a developer, architect or interior decorator.

Clips. Writing samples, usually from newspapers or magazines, of your published work.

Coffee table book. A heavily illustrated, oversized book, suitable for display on a coffee table.

Collaterals. Accompanying or auxiliary pieces, such as brochures, especially used in advertising. Samples of these may be included in a portfolio.

Commercial novel. A novel designed to appeal to a broad audience. It often falls into a category or genre such as western, romance, mystery and science fiction. See also *genre*.

Concept. A statement that summarizes a screenplay or teleplay—before the outline or treatment is written.

Contemporary. Material dealing with popular current trends, themes or topics.

Contributor's copies. Copies of the author's book sent to the author. Often the number of contributor's copies is negotiated in the publishing contract.

Copyediting. Editing of a manuscript for writing style, grammar, punctuation and factual accuracy. Some agents offer this service.

Cover letter. A brief descriptive letter sent along with a complete manuscript submitted to an agent or publisher.

C-print. Any enlargement printed from a negative. Any enlargement from a transparency is called an R-print.

Creative sourcebook. Also known as creative or talent directory. An annual book sent to art directors and others who buy the work of illustrators or photographers. Each page is an advertisement for the work of a talent or a group of talents and includes a representation of their style and contact information. Pages may be purchased by the rep or talent.

Critiquing service. A service offered by some agents in which writers pay a fee for comments on the salability or other qualities of their manuscript. Sometimes the critique includes suggestions on how to improve the work. Fees vary, as do the quality of the critiques.

Demo. A sample reel of film or sample videocassette which includes excerpts of a filmmaker's or videographer's production of work for clients.

Direct mail package. Sales or promotional material that is distributed by mail. Usually consists of an outer envelope, a cover letter, brochure or flyer, SASE or postpaid reply card.

Direct mail piece. A flyer or brochure used in advertising the work of an artist, designer or photographer. The piece usually includes more than one image or one striking image that best shows the artist's or photographer's style.

Division. An unincorporated branch of a company (e.g., Penguin Books, a division of Viking, Penguin, Inc.)

Docudrama. A fictional film rendition of recent newsmaking events or people.

Editing service. A service offered by some agents in which writers pay a fee—either lump sum or a per-page fee—to have the agent edit their manuscript. The quality and extent of the editing varies from agent to agent.

Electronic submission. A submission made by modem or computer disk. For permission and information on how to make an electronic submission, talk to your agent or publisher.

El-hi. Elementary to high school. A term used in textbook publishing to indicate reading or interest level.

Evaluation fees. Fees an agent may charge to evaluate material. The extent and quality of this evaluation varies, but comments usually concern the salability of the manuscript.

Exclusive. Offering a manuscript, usually for a set period of time, to just one agent and guaranteeing that agent is the only one looking at the manuscript.

Exclusive area representation. Requirement that an artist's or photographer's work be handled by only one rep within a given area.

Floor bid. If a publisher is very interested in a manuscript he may offer to enter a floor bid when the book goes to auction. The publisher sits out of the auction, but agrees to take the book by topping the highest bid by an agreed-upon percentage (usually 10 percent).

Foreign rights agent. An agent who handles selling the rights to a country other than that of the first book agent. Usually an additional percentage (about 5 percent) will be added on to the first book agent's commission to cover the foreign rights agent.

Galleys. The first typeset version of a manuscript that has not yet been divided into pages.

Genre. Refers to either a general classification of writing such as a novel, poem or short story or to the categories within those classifications, such as problem novels or sonnets. Genre fiction is a term that covers various types of commercial novels such as mystery, romance, western or science fiction.

Ghosting or ghost writing. When a writer puts into literary form the words, ideas or knowledge of another person under that person's name it is called ghostwriting. Some agents offer this service. Others will pair ghostwriters with celebrities or experts.

Glossy. A black and white photograph with a shiny surface as opposed to one with a non-shiny matte finish.

Imprint. The name applied to a publisher's specific line of books (e.g. Aerie books, an imprint of Tor Books.)

IRC. International Reply Coupons; purchased at a post office to enclose with material sent outside your country to cover the cost of return postage. The recipient can turn in the coupons for stamps in their own country.

Leave-behinds. Promotional or direct mail flyers, brochures or other information about a talent designed to be left with a prospective buyer.

Letter-quality submission. A computer printout that looks like a typewritten manuscript.

Mainstream fiction. Fiction on subjects or trends that transcend popular novel categories such as mystery or romance. Using conventional methods, this kind of fiction tells stories about people and their conflicts.

Marketing fee. Fee charged by some agents to cover marketing expenses. It may be used to cover postage, telephone calls, faxes, photocopying or any other expense incurred in marketing a manuscript.

Mass market paperbacks. Softcover book, usually around 4 × 7, on a popular subject directed at a general audience and sold in groceries and drugstores as well as bookstores.

MFTS. Made for TV series. A series developed for television also known as episodics, usually used when referring to a dramatic series.

Middle reader. The general classification of books written for readers 9-11 years old.

Midlist. Those titles on a publisher's list expected to have limited sales. Midlist books are mainstream, not literary, scholarly or genre, and are usually written by new or unknown writers.

Mini-series. A limited dramatic series written for television, often based on a popular novel.

MOW. Movie of the week. A movie script written especially for television, usually seven acts with time for commercial breaks. Topics are often contemporary, sometimes controversial, fictional accounts. Also known as a made-for-TV-movie.

Multiple submission. The practice of submitting copies of the same manuscript to several agents or publishers at the same time. Also called simultaneous submissions.

Net receipts. One method of royalty payment based on the amount of money a book publisher receives on the sale of the book after the booksellers' discounts, special sales discounts and returned copies.

Novelization. A novel created from the script of a popular movie, usually called a movie "tie-in" and published in paperback.

Novella. A short novel or long short story, usually 7,000 to 15,000 words. Also called a novelette.

Option Clause. A publishing contract clause giving a publisher the right to publish an author's next book.

Outline. A summary of a book's contents in five to 15 double-spaced pages; often in the form of chapter headings with a descriptive sentence or two under each one to show the scope of the book. A screenplay's or teleplay's outline is a scene-by-scene narrative description of the story (10-15 pages for a ½-hour teleplay; 15-25 pages for 1-hour; 25-40 pages for 90 minutes and 40-60 pages for a 2-hour feature film or teleplay).

Over-the-transom. Slang for the path of an unsolicited manuscript into the slush pile.

Photostats. Black-and-white copies produced by an inexpensive photographic process using paper negatives; only line values are held with accuracy. Also called a stat.

Picture book. A type of book aimed at the preschool to 8-year-old that tells the story primarily or entirely with artwork. Agents and reps interested in selling to publishers of these books often handle both artists and writers.

PMT. Photomechanical transfer, photostat produced without a negative, somewhat like the Polaroid process.

Portfolio. A group of photographs or artwork samples (slides, originals, tearsheets, photocopies) assembled to demonstrate an artist's or photographer's style and abilities, often presented to clients.

Profit and Loss Profile (P&L). A publishers estimate of the profitability of a particular book. P&Ls help publishers decide whether or not to publish a book and how much to offer as an advance.

Promotional piece. Also called promo piece. Material designed to promote an artist's or photographer's work. Usually more expensively produced and elaborate than a direct-mail or leave-behind piece, a promo piece can be colorful, include special printing techniques or folds.

Proofreading. Close reading and correction of a manuscript's typographical errors. A few agents offer this service for a fee.

Proofs. A typeset version of a manuscript used for correcting errors and making changes, often a photocopy of the galleys.

Proposal. An offer to an editor or publisher to write a specific work, usually a package consisting of an outline and sample chapters.

Prospectus. A preliminary, written description of a book, usually one page in length.

Query. A letter written to an agent, rep, or a potential market, to elicit interest in a writer's, artist's or photographer's work.

Release. A statement that your idea is original, has never been sold to anyone else and that you are selling negotiated rights to the idea upon payment.

Remainders. Leftover copies of an out-of-print or slow-selling book, which can be purchased from the publisher at a reduced rate. Depending on the author's contract, a reduced royalty or no royalty is paid on remaindered books.

Reporting time. The time it takes the agent or rep to get back to you on your query or submission.

Roughs. Preliminary sketches or drawings.

Royalties. A percentage of the retail price paid to the author for each copy of the book that is sold. Agents take their percentage from the royalties earned as well as from the advance.

SASE. Self-addressed, stamped envelope. This or a self-addressed, stamped postcard should be included with all your correspondence with reps or agents.

Scholarly books. Books written for an academic or research audience. These are usually heavily researched, technical and often contain terms used only within a specific field.

Screenplay. Script for a film intended to be shown in movie theaters.

Script. Broad term covering teleplay, screenplay or stage play. Sometimes used as a shortened version of the word "manuscript" when referring to books.

Simultaneous submission. Sending the same manuscript to several agents or publishers at the same time. Simultaneous query letters are common, but simultaneous submissions are unacceptable to many agents or publishers. See also *multiple submission*.

Sitcom. Situation comedy. Episodic comedy script for a television series. Term comes from the characters dealing with various situations with humorous results.

Slides. Usually called transparencies; positive color slides.

Slush pile. A stack of unsolicited submissions in the office of an editor, agent or publisher.

Standard commission. The commission an agent or rep earns on the sales of a manuscript, illustration or photograph. For literary agents, this commission percentage (usually between 10 and 20 percent) is taken from the advance and royalties paid to the writer. For script agents, the commission is taken from script sales; if handling plays, agents take a percentage from the box office proceeds. For art and photo reps the commission (usually 25 to 30 percent) is taken from sales.

Stock photo agency. A business that maintains a large collection of photos which it makes available to clients such as advertising agencies and periodicals. These agencies (not listed in this book) take a percentage from work sold for the photographer. Unlike photo reps, these agencies do not handle the careers of individual photographers, but sell the work of various photographers to clients looking for specific images. Stock agency listings may be found in *Photographer's Market*.

Storyboards. Series of panels which illustrates a progressive sequence or graphics and story copy for a TV commercial, film or filmstrip. Serves as a guide for an eventual finished product. Some artists specialize in doing storyboard work.

Subagent. An agent who handles certain subsidiary rights. This agent usually works in conjunction with the agent who has handled the book rights and the percentage paid the book agent is increased to cover paying the subagent.

Subsidiary. An incorporated branch of a company or conglomerate (e.g. Alfred Knopf, Inc., is a subsidiary of Random House, Inc.)

Subsidiary rights. All rights other than book publishing rights included in a book publishing contract, such as paperback rights, bookclub rights, movie rights. Part of an agent's job is to negotiate those rights and advise you on which to sell and which to keep.

Synopsis. A brief summary of a story, novel or play. As a part of a book proposal, it is a comprehensive summary condensed in a page or page and a half, single-spaced. See also *outline*.

Talent. When used in commercial art circles, talent refers to the artist or photographer. See *client*.

Tearsheet. Published samples of your work, usually pages torn from a magazine.

Textbook. Book to be used in a classroom situation—may be on the elementary, high school or college level.

Thumbnail. A rough layout in miniature, usually used in reference to a book or other large project.

Trade book. Either a hard cover or soft cover book; subject matter frequently concerns a special interest for a general audience; sold mainly in bookstores.

Trade paperback. A softbound volume, usually around 5 × 8, published and designed for the general public, available mainly in bookstores.

Transparencies. Positive color slides; not color prints.

Treatment. Synopsis of a television or film script (40-60 pages for a 2-hour feature film or teleplay).

Unsolicited manuscript. An unrequested manuscript sent to an editor, agent or publisher. A cold submission of an entire manuscript.

Young adult. The general classification of books written for readers age 12-18.

Young reader. Books written for readers 5-8 years old. Unlike picture books, artwork only supports the text.

Indexes

Subject Index

The following subject index is divided intononfiction and fiction subject categories for each of three sections—Nonfee-charging Literary Agents, Fee-charging Literary Agents and Script Agents. To find an agent who is interested in the type of manuscript you've written, see the appropriate sections under subject headings that best describe your work. Check the Listings Index for the page number of the agent's listing. Agents who said they were open to most nonfiction or fiction subjects appear in the "Open" heading.

Nonfee charging agents/Fiction

Action/Adventure. A.M.C. Literary Agency; Acton, Dystel, Leone & Jaffe, Inc.; Allan Agency, Lee; Amsterdam Agency, Marcia; Appleseeds Management; Barrett Literary Agency, Helen; Brandt & Brandt Literary Agents Inc.; Carvainis Agency, Inc., Maria; Curtis Associates, Inc., Richard; Diamant, The Writer's Workshop, Inc., Anita; Diamond Literary Agency, Inc.; Dijkstra Literary Agency, Sandra; Doyen Literary Services, Inc.; Ducas, Robert; Dupree/Miller and Associates Inc. Literary; Ellenberg Literary Agency, Ethan; Fields-Rita Scott Inc., Marje; Garon-Brooke Assoc. Inc., Jay; Gotler Metropolitan Talent Agency, Joel; Greenburger Associates, Stanford J.; Hawkins & Associates, Inc., John; Jarvis & Co., Inc., Sharon; Klinger, Inc., Harvey; Lampack Agency, Inc., Peter; Lantz-Joy Harris Literary Agency, The Robert; Lincoln Literary Agency, Ray; Literary Bridge, The; Literary Group, The; Love Literary Agency, Nancy; Lyceum Creative Properties, Inc.; Merhige-Merdon Marketing/Promo Co. Inc., Greg; Naggar Literary Agency, Jean V.; Parks Agency, The Richard; Pelter, Rodney; Perkins Associates, L.; Picard Literary Agent, Alison J.; Schmidt Literary Agency, Harold; Siegel Literary Agency, Bobbe; Wald Associates, Inc., Mary Jack; Weiner Literary Agency, Cherry; Westchester Literary Agency, Inc.; Zeckendorf Assoc. Inc., Susan

Cartoon/comic. Axelrod Agency, The; Dupree/Miller and Associates Inc. Literary; Ellenberg Literary Agency, Ethan; Hawkins & Associates, Inc., John; Lampack Agency, Inc., Peter; Lantz-Joy Harris Literary Agency, The Robert; Lyceum Creative Properties, Inc.; Merhige-Merdon Marketing/Promo Co. Inc., Greg; Miller Associates, Roberta D.; Pelter, Rodney; Perkins Associates, L.; Rubenstein Literary Agency, Inc., Pesha; Van Der Leun & Associates

Confessional. Barrett Literary Agency, Helen; Fields-Rita Scott Inc., Marje; Lantz-Joy Harris Literary Agency, The Robert; Literary Bridge, The; Merhige-Merdon Marketing/Promo Co. Inc., Greg; Naggar Literary Agency, Jean V.; Pelter, Rodney

Contemporary issues. Acton, Dystel, Leone & Jaffe, Inc.; Agents Inc. for Medical and Mental Health Professionals; Barrett Literary Agency, Helen; Bartczak Associates Inc., Gene; Boates Literary Agency, Reid; Bova Literary Agency, The Barbara; Brandt Agency, The Joan; Brandt & Brandt Literary Agents Inc.; Cantrell-Colas Inc., Literary Agency; de la Haba Agency Inc., The Lois; Diamant, The Writer's Workshop, Inc., Anita; Diamond Literary Agency, Inc.; Dijkstra Literary Agency, Sandra; Doyen Literary Services, Inc.; Ducas, Robert; Dupree/Miller and Associates Inc. Literary; Fogelman Publishing Interests Inc.; Garon-Brooke Assoc. Inc., Jay; Gotler Metropolitan Talent Agency, Joel, Joel; Greenburger Associates, Stanford J.; Hawkins & Associates, Inc., John; Kouts, Lieary Agent, Barbara S.; Kroll Literary Agency, Edite; Lampack Agency, Inc., Peter; Lantz-Joy Harris Literary Agency, The Robert; Lasbury Literary Agency, M. Sue; Lincoln Literary Agency, Ray; Literary Bridge, The; Los Angeles Literary Associates; Love Literary Agency, Nancy; Lyceum Creative Properties, Inc.; McGrath, Helen; Marmur Associates Ltd., Mildred; Miller Associates, Roberta D.; Naggar Literary Agency, Jean V.; Noetzli Literary Agency, Regula; Parks Agency, The Richard; Pelter, Rodney; Picard Literary Agent, Alison J.; Quicksilver Books-Literary Agents; Raymond, Literary Agent, Charlotte Cecil; Rees Literary Agency, Helen; Riverside Literary Agency; Rose Literary Agency; Roth Literary Agency, The; Schmidt Literary Agency, Harold; Seligman, Literary Agent, Lynn; Shepard Agency, The; Siegel Literary Agency, Bobbe; Singer Literary Agency Inc., Evelyn; Spitzer Literary Agency, Philip G.; Stauffer Associates, Nancy; Stern Literary Agency, Gloria; Van Der Leun & Associates; Wald Associates, Inc., Mary Jack; Watkins Loomis Agency, Inc.; Weiner Literary Agency, Cherry; Weingel-Fidel Agency, The; Westchester Literary Agency, Inc.; Zeckendorf Assoc. Inc., Susan

Detective/police/crime. A.M.C. Literary Agency; Acton, Dystel, Leone & Jaffe, Inc.; Agency Chicago; Allan Agency, Lee; Allen, Literary Agency, James; Appleseeds Management; Axelrod Agency, The; Bach Literary Agency, Julian; Barrett Literary Agency, Helen; Boates Literary Agency, Reid; Brandt Agency, The Joan; Brandt & Brandt Literary Agents Inc.; Cantrell-Colas Inc., Literary Agency; Carvainis Agency, Inc., Maria; Clark Literary Agency, SJ; Cohen, Inc. Literary Agency, Ruth; Collin Literary Agent, Frances; Curtis Associates, Inc., Richard; Diamant, The Writer's Workshop, Inc., Anita; Diamond Literary Agency, Inc.; Dijkstra Literary Agency, Sandra; Doyen Literary Services, Inc.; Ducas, Robert; Dupree/Miller and Associates Inc. Literary; Ellenberg Literary Agency, Ethan; Fields-Rita Scott Inc., Marje; Garon-Brooke Assoc. Inc., Jay; Gotler Metropolitan Talent Agency, Joel; Greenburger Associates, Stanford J.; Hawkins & Associates, Inc., John; Hull House Literary Agency; J de S Associates Inc.; Jarvis & Co., Inc., Sharon; Kidde, Hoyt & Picard; Klinger, Inc., Harvey; Lampack Agency, Inc., Peter; Lantz-Joy Harris Literary Agency, The Robert; Lasbury Literary Agency, M. Sue; Lincoln Literary Agency, Ray; Literary Bridge, The; Literary Group, The; Love Literary Agency, Nancy; Lyceum Creative Properties, Inc.; McGrath, Helen; Marmur Associates Ltd., Mildred; Merhige-Merdon Marketing/Promo Co. Inc., Greg; Miller Associates, Roberta D.; Multimedia Product Development, Inc.; Noetzli Literary Agency, Regula; Parks Agency, The Richard; Pelter, Rodney; Perkins Associates, L.; Picard Literary Agent, Alison J.; Rees Literary Agency, Helen; Riverside Literary Agency; Rubenstein Literary Agency, Inc., Pesha; Schmidt Literary Agency, Harold; Seligman,.. Literary Agent, Lynn; Siegel Literary Agency, Bobbe; Singer Literary Agency Inc., Evelyn; Spitzer Literary Agency, Philip G.; Steele & Co., Ltd., Lyle; Stern Literary Agency, Gloria; Wald Associates, Inc., Mary Jack; Weiner Literary Agency, Cherry; Weingel-Fidel Agency, The; Westchester Literary Agency, Inc.; Wieser & Wieser, Inc.; Zeckendorf Assoc. Inc., Susan

Erotica. Agency Chicago; Brandt & Brandt Literary Agents Inc.; Diamond Literary Agency, Inc.; Lantz-Joy Harris Literary Agency, The Robert; Lyceum Creative Properties, Inc.; Pelter, Rodney; Spatt, Esq., David M.; Acton, Dystel, Leone & Jaffe, Inc.

Ethnic. Brandt & Brandt Literary Agents Inc.; Cantrell-Colas Inc., Literary Agency; Cohen, Inc. Literary Agency, Ruth; Collin Literary Agent, Frances; Crown International Literature and Arts Agency, Bonnie R.; Diamond Literary Agency, Inc.; Dijkstra Literary Agency, Sandra; Doyen Literary Services, Inc.; Gotler Metropolitan Talent Agency, Joel; Greenburger Associates, Stanford J.; Hawkins & Associates, Inc., John; Lantz-Joy Harris Literary Agency, The Robert; Lincoln Literary Agency, Ray; Love Literary Agency, Nancy; Lyceum Creative Properties, Inc.; Merhige-Merdon Marketing/Promo Co. Inc., Greg; Naggar Literary Agency, Jean V.; Noetzli Literary Agency, Regula; Pelter, Rodney; Perkins Associates, L.; Picard Literary Agent, Alison J.; Raymond, Literary Agent, Charlotte Cecil; Riverside Literary Agency; Rose Literary Agency; Roth Literary Agency, The; Schmidt Literary Agency, Harold; Seligman, Literary Agent, Lynn; Stern Literary Agency, Gloria; Van Der Leun & Associates; Wald Associates, Inc., Mary Jack; Zeckendorf Assoc. Inc., Susan

Experimental. Agency Chicago; Brandt & Brandt Literary Agents Inc.; Cantrell-Colas Inc., Literary Agency; de la Haba Agency Inc., The Lois; Diamant, The Writer's Workshop, Inc., Anita; Doyen Literary Services, Inc.; Hawkins & Associates, Inc., John; Lantz-Joy Harris Literary Agency, The Robert; Lyceum Creative Properties, Inc.; Pelter, Rodney; Stern Literary Agency, Gloria; Wald Associates, Inc., Mary Jack

Family saga. Acton, Dystel, Leone & Jaffe, Inc.; Axelrod Agency, The; Barrett Literary Agency, Helen; Boates Literary Agency, Reid; Brandt & Brandt Literary Agents Inc.; Cantrell-Colas Inc., Literary Agency; Cohen, Inc. Literary Agency, Ruth; Collin Literary Agent, Frances; Crown International Literature and Arts Agency, Bonnie R.; Curtis Associates, Inc., Richard; Diamant, The Writer's Workshop, Inc., Anita; Diamond Literary Agency, Inc.; Doyen Literary Services, Inc.; Ellenberg Literary Agency, Ethan; Fields-Rita Scott Inc., Marje; Garon-Brooke Assoc. Inc., Jay; Gotler Metropolitan Talent Agency, Joel; Greenburger Associates, Stanford J.; Hawkins & Associates, Inc., John; KC Communications; Klinger, Inc., Harvey; Kouts, Liteary Agent, Barbara S.; Lampack Agency, Inc., Peter; Lantz-Joy Harris Literary Agency, The Robert; Literary Bridge, The; McGrath, Helen; Marmur Associates Ltd., Mildred; Merhige-Merdon Marketing/Promo Co. Inc., Greg; Naggar Literary Agency, Jean V.; Noetzli Literary Agency, Regula; Parks Agency, The Richard; Pelter, Rodney; Rees Literary Agency, Helen; Roth Literary Agency, The; Schmidt Literary Agency, Harold; Shepard Agency, The; Siegel Literary Agency, Bobbe; Steele & Co., Ltd., Lyle; Wald Associates, Inc., Mary Jack; Weiner Literary Agency, Cherry; Westchester Literary Agency, Inc.; Wieser & Wieser, Inc.; Zeckendorf Assoc. Inc., Susan

Fantasy. Allan Agency, Lee; Allen, Literary Agency, James; Appleseeds Management; Butler, Art and Literary Agent, Jane; Carvainis Agency, Inc., Maria; Collin Literary Agent, Frances; Curtis Associates, Inc., Richard; Dijkstra Literary Agency, Sandra; Doyen Literary Services, Inc.; Ellenberg Literary Agency, Ethan; Embers Literary Agency; Garon-Brooke Assoc. Inc., Jay; Gotler Metropolitan Talent Agency, Joel, Joel; Jarvis & Co., Inc., Sharon; Lincoln Literary Agency, Ray; Literary Bridge, The; Lyceum Creative Properties, Inc.; Naggar Literary Agency, Jean V.; Riverside Literary Agency; Seligman, Literary Agent, Lynn; Siegel Literary Agency, Bobbe; Smith, Literary Agent, Valerie; Spatt, Esq., David M.; Stern Literary Agency, Gloria; Wald Associates, Inc., Mary Jack; Weiner Literary Agency, Cherry; Westchester Literary Agency, Inc.

Feminist. Bach Literary Agency, Julian; Brandt & Brandt Literary Agents Inc.; Cantrell-Colas Inc., Literary Agency; Curtis Associates, Inc., Richard; Diamant, The Writer's Workshop, Inc., Anita; Diamond

Literary Agency, Inc.; Dijkstra Literary Agency, Sandra; Ducas, Robert; Dupree/Miller and Associates Inc. Literary; Greenburger Associates, Stanford J.; Hawkins & Associates, Inc., John; Kidde, Hoyt & Picard; Kouts, Liteary Agent, Barbara S.; Kroll Literary Agency, Edite; Lantz-Joy Harris Literary Agency, The Robert; Lincoln Literary Agency, Ray; Literary Bridge, The; Lyceum Creative Properties, Inc.; Marmur Associates Ltd., Mildred; Merhige-Merdon Marketing/Promo Co. Inc., Greg; Naggar Literary Agency, Jean V.; Noetzli Literary Agency, Regula; Pelter, Rodney; Picard Literary Agent, Alison J.; Rees Literary Agency, Helen; Riverside Literary Agency; Rose Literary Agency; Roth Literary Agency, The; Schaffner Agency, Inc.; Schmidt Literary Agency, Harold; Seligman, Literary Agent, Lynn; Siegel Literary Agency, Bobbe; Stern Literary Agency, Gloria; Wald Associates, Inc., Mary Jack

Gay. Brandt & Brandt Literary Agents Inc.; Diamant, The Writer's Workshop, Inc., Anita; Ducas, Robert; Dupree/Miller and Associates Inc. Literary; Fields-Rita Scott Inc., Marje; Garon-Brooke Assoc. Inc., Jay; Greenburger Associates, Stanford J.; Hawkins & Associates, Inc., John; Kidde, Hoyt & Picard; Lantz-Joy Harris Literary Agency, The Robert; Lincoln Literary Agency, Ray; Lyceum Creative Properties, Inc.; Naggar Literary Agency, Jean V.; Parks Agency, The Richard; Picard Literary Agent, Alison J.; Raymond, Literary Agent, Charlotte Cecil; Rose Literary Agency; Steele & Co., Ltd., Lyle; Wald Associates, Inc., Mary Jack

Glitz. Acton, Dystel, Leone & Jaffe, Inc.; Amsterdam Agency, Marcia; Carvainis Agency, Inc., Maria; Diamond Literary Agency, Inc.; Dijkstra Literary Agency, Sandra; Doyen Literary Services, Inc.; Dupree/Miller and Associates Inc. Literary; Ellenberg Literary Agency, Ethan; Garon-Brooke Assoc. Inc., Jay; Greenburger Associates, Stanford J.; Hawkins & Associates, Inc., John; Jarvis & Co., Inc., Sharon; Klinger, Inc., Harvey; Lampack Agency, Inc., Peter; Lantz-Joy Harris Literary Agency, The Robert; Literary Bridge, The; Multimedia Product Development, Inc.; Naggar Literary Agency, Jean V.; Parks Agency, The Richard; Pelter, Rodney; Picard Literary Agent, Alison J.; Rees Literary Agency, Helen; Riverside Literary Agency; Rubenstein Literary Agency, Inc., Pesha; Schmidt Literary Agency, Harold; Siegel Literary Agency, Bobbe; Teal Literary Agency, Patricia; Wald Associates, Inc., Mary Jack; Weiner Literary Agency, Cherry; Zeckendorf Assoc. Inc., Susan

Historical. Acton, Dystel, Leone & Jaffe, Inc.; Allan Agency, Lee; Allen, Literary Agency, James; Amsterdam Agency, Marcia; Appleseeds Management; Axelrod Agency, The; Barrett Literary Agency, Helen; Butler, Art and Literary Agent, Jane; Cantrell-Colas Inc., Literary Agency; Carvainis Agency, Inc., Maria; Cohen, Inc. Literary Agency, Ruth; Collin Literary Agent, Frances; Crown International Literature and Arts Agency, Bonnie R.; Curtis Associates, Inc., Richard; Davie Literary Agency, Elaine; de la Haba Agency Inc., The Lois; Diamant, The Writer's Workshop, Inc., Anita; Diamond Literary Agency, Inc.; Dijkstra Literary Agency, Sandra; Doyen Literary Services, Inc.; Ducas, Robert; Dupree/Miller and Associates Inc. Literary; Ellenberg Literary Agency, Ethan; Elmo Agency Inc., Ann; Fields-Rita Scott Inc., Marje; Fogelman Publishing Interests Inc.; Garon-Brooke Assoc. Inc., Jay; Gotler Metropolitan Talent Agency, Joel; Greenburger Associates, Stanford J.; Hawkins & Associates, Inc., John; J de S Associates Inc.; Jarvis & Co., Inc., Sharon; KC Communications; Kouts, Liteary Agent, Barbara S.; Lampack Agency, Inc., Peter; Lantz-Joy Harris Literary Agency, The Robert; Lincoln Literary Agency, Ray; Literary Bridge, The; Lyceum Creative Properties, Inc.; Multimedia Product Development, Inc.; Naggar Literary Agency, Jean V.; Noetzli Literary Agency, Regula; Parks Agency, The Richard; Pelter, Rodney; Picard Literary Agent, Alison J.; Rees Literary Agency, Helen; Roth Literary Agency, The; Rubenstein Literary Agency, Inc., Pesha; Seligman, Literary Agent, Lynn; Shepard Agency, The; Siegel Literary Agency, Bobbe; Singer Literary Agency Inc., Evelyn; Steele & Co., Ltd., Lyle; Van Der Leun & Associates; Wald Associates, Inc., Mary Jack; Wecksler-Incomco; Weiner Literary Agency, Cherry; Westchester Literary Agency, Inc.; Zeckendorf Assoc. Inc., Susan

Humor/satire. Agency Chicago; Ajlouny Agency, The Joseph S.; Allan Agency, Lee; Amsterdam Agency, Marcia; Appleseeds Management; Brandt & Brandt Literary Agents Inc.; Cantrell-Colas Inc., Literary Agency; Carvainis Agency, Inc., Maria; Diamond Literary Agency, Inc.; Dijkstra Literary Agency, Sandra; Doyen Literary Services, Inc.; Ducas, Robert; Dupree/Miller and Associates Inc. Literary; Ellenberg Literary Agency, Ethan; Gotler Metropolitan Talent Agency, Joel; Greenburger Associates, Stanford J.; Hawkins & Associates, Inc., John; Kidde, Hoyt & Picard; Lantz-Joy Harris Literary Agency, The Robert; Lincoln Literary Agency, Ray; Literary Bridge, The; Literary Group, The; Lyceum Creative Properties, Inc.; Merhige-Merdon Marketing/Promo Co. Inc., Greg; Miller Associates, Roberta D.; Noetzli Literary Agency, Regula; Pelter, Rodney; Picard Literary Agent, Alison J.; Rees Literary Agency, Helen; Rose Literary Agency; Roth Literary Agency, The; Seligman, Literary Agent, Lynn; Shepard Agency, The; Wald Associates, Inc., Mary Jack; Westchester Literary Agency, Inc.; Wohl Literary Agency, Gary S.

Juvenile. Allan Agency, Lee; Bartczak Associates Inc., Gene; Brown Literary Agency, Inc., Andrea; Butler, Art and Literary Agent, Jane; Carvainis Agency, Inc., Maria; Clark Literary Agency, SJ; Cohen, Inc. Literary Agency, Ruth; de la Haba Agency Inc., The Lois; Diamant, The Writer's Workshop, Inc., Anita; Dijkstra Literary Agency, Sandra; Doyen Literary Services, Inc.; Elek Associates, Peter; Ellenberg Literary Agency, Ethan; Embers Literary Agency; Gotham Art & Literary Agency Inc.; Greenburger Associates, Stanford J.; Hawkins & Associates, Inc., John; J de S Associates Inc.; Kouts, Liteary Agent, Barbara S.; Lincoln Literary Agency, Ray; Lyceum Creative Properties, Inc.; Maccoby Literary Agency, Gina; Markowitz Literary Agency, Barbara; Marmur Associates Ltd., Mildred; Merhige-Merdon Marketing/Promo Co. Inc.,

Greg; MGA Agency Inc.; Naggar Literary Agency, Jean V.; Norma-Lewis Agency, The; Picard Literary Agent, Alison J.; Rubenstein Literary Agency, Inc., Pesha; Seymour Agency, The; Spatt, Esq., David M.; Wald Associates, Inc., Mary Jack; Westchester Literary Agency, Inc.

Lesbian. Brandt & Brandt Literary Agents Inc.; Ducas, Robert; Greenburger Associates, Stanford J.; Hawkins & Associates, Inc., John; Kidde, Hoyt & Picard; Lantz-Joy Harris Literary Agency, The Robert; Lincoln Literary Agency, Ray; Lyceum Creative Properties, Inc.; Naggar Literary Agency, Jean V.; Parks Agency, The Richard; Pelter, Rodney; Picard Literary Agent, Alison J.; Raymond, Literary Agent, Charlotte Cecil; Riverside Literary Agency; Schmidt Literary Agency, Harold; Steele & Co., Ltd., Lyle

Literary. Acton, Dystel, Leone & Jaffe, Inc.; Agents Inc. for Medical and Mental Health Professionals; Allan Agency, Lee; Axelrod Agency, The; Bach Literary Agency, Julian; Borchardt Inc., Georges; Brandt Agency, The Joan; Brandt & Brandt Literary Agents Inc.; Cantrell-Colas Inc., Literary Agency; Carvainis Agency, Inc., Maria; Cohen, Inc. Literary Agency, Ruth; Cole And Lubenow: Books; Collin Literary Agent, Frances; Congdon Associates, Inc., Don; Crown International Literature and Arts Agency, Bonnie R.; Darhansoff & Verrill Literary Agents; de la Haba Agency Inc., The Lois; Diamant, The Writer's Workshop, Inc., Anita; Dijkstra Literary Agency, Sandra; Ducas, Robert; Dupree/Miller and Associates Inc. Literary; Ellenberg Literary Agency, Ethan; Ellison Inc., Nicholas; Embers Literary Agency; Fallon Literary Agency, The; Fields-Rita Scott Inc., Marje; Fuhrman Literary Agency, Candice; Garon-Brooke Assoc. Inc., Jay; Gotham Art & Literary Agency Inc.; Gotler Metropolitan Talent Agency, Joel; Greenburger Associates, Stanford J.; Gregory Associates, Maia; Hawkins & Associates, Inc., John; Herner Rights Agency, Susan; Hull House Literary Agency; J de S Associates Inc.; KC Communications; Kidde, Hoyt & Picard; Klinger, Inc., Harvey; Kouts, Literary Agent, Barbara S.; Kroll Literary Agency, Edite; Lampack Agency, Inc., Peter; Lantz-Joy Harris Literary Agency, The Robert; Lasbury Literary Agency, M. Sue; Levine Literary Agency, Inc., Ellen; Lincoln Literary Agency, Ray; Love Literary Agency, Nancy; Maccoby Literary Agency, Gina; McGrath, Helen; Mann Agency, Carol; Marmur Associates Ltd., Mildred; Merhige-Merdon Marketing/ Promo Co. Inc., Greg; Miller Associates, Roberta D.; Naggar Literary Agency, Jean V.; Noetzli Literary Agency, Regula; Parks Agency, The Richard; Paton Literary Agency, Kathi J.; Pelter, Rodney; Perkins Associates, L.; Picard Literary Agent, Alison J.; Quicksilver Books-Literary Agents; Raymond, Literary Agent, Charlotte Cecil; Riverside Literary Agency; Rose Literary Agency; Roth Literary Agency, The; Schaffner Agency, Inc.; Schmidt Literary Agency, Harold; Seligman, Literary Agent, Lynn; Shepard Agency, The; Siegel Literary Agency, Bobbe; Smith, Literary Agent, Valerie; Snell Literary Agency, Michael; Spitzer Literary Agency, Philip G.; Stauffer Associates, Nancy; Steele & Co., Ltd., Lyle; Stern Literary Agency, Gloria; Van Der Leun & Associates; Wald Associates, Inc., Mary Jack; Watkins Loomis Agency, Inc.; Wecksler-Incomco; Weingel-Fidel Agency, The; Westchester Literary Agency, Inc.; Wieser & Wieser, Inc.; Wieser & Wieser, Inc.; Writers' Productions; Writers' Representatives, Inc.; Zeckendorf Assoc. Inc., Susan

Mainstream. Acton, Dystel, Leone & Jaffe, Inc.; Allan Agency, Lee; Allen, Literary Agency, James; Amsterdam Agency, Marcia; Appleseeds Management; Axelrod Agency, The; Bach Literary Agency, Julian; Barrett Literary Agency, Helen; Boates Literary Agency, Reid; Bova Literary Agency, The Barbara; Brandt Agency, The Joan; Brandt & Brandt Literary Agents Inc.; Cantrell-Colas Inc., Literary Agency; Carvainis Agency, Inc., Maria; Cleaver Inc., Diane; Cohen, Inc. Literary Agency, Ruth; Collin Literary Agent, Frances; Columbia Literary Associates, Inc.; Curtis Associates, Inc., Richard; de la Haba Agency Inc., The Lois; Diamant, The Writer's Workshop, Inc., Anita; Diamond Literary Agency, Inc.; Dijkstra Literary Agency, Sandra; Doyen Literary Services, Inc.; Ducas, Robert; Dupree/Miller and Associates Inc. Literary; Eisenberg Literary Agency, Vicki; Ellenberg Literary Agency, Ethan; Ellison Inc., Nicholas; Embers Literary Agency; Fallon Literary Agency, The; Fields-Rita Scott Inc., Marje; Fogelman Publishing Interests Inc.; Fuhrman Literary Agency, Candice; Garon-Brooke Assoc. Inc., Jay; Gartenberg, Literary Agent, Max; Goodman Literary Agency, Irene; Gotham Art & Literary Agency Inc.; Gotler Metropolitan Talent Agency, Joel; Greenburger Associates, Stanford J.; Hawkins & Associates, Inc., John; Herner Rights Agency, Susan; Hull House Literary Agency; International Publisher Associates Inc.; J de S Associates Inc.; Jarvis & Co., Inc., Sharon; KC Communications; Kidde, Hoyt & Picard; Klinger, Inc., Harvey; Kouts, Literary Agent, Barbara S.; Kroll Literary Agency, Edite; Lantz-Joy Harris Literary Agency, The Robert; Lasbury Literary Agency, M. Sue; Levant & Wales, Literary Agency, Inc.; Lincoln Literary Agency, Ray; Lipkind Agency, Wendy; Literary Bridge, The; Los Angeles Literary Associates; Love Literary Agency, Nancy; Lowenstein Associates, Inc.; Lyceum Creative Properties, Inc.; Maccoby Literary Agency, Gina; McGrath, Helen; Marmur Associates Ltd., Mildred; Merhige-Merdon Marketing/Promo Co. Inc., Greg; Miller Associates, Roberta D.; Multimedia Product Development, Inc.; Naggar Literary Agency, Jean V.; Noetzli Literary Agency, Regula; Parks Agency, The Richard; Paton Literary Agency, Kathi J.; Pelter, Rodney; Perkins Associates, L.; Picard Literary Agent, Alison J.; Quicksilver Books-Literary Agents; Raymond, Literary Agent, Charlotte Cecil; Rees Literary Agency, Helen; Riverside Literary Agency; Roth Literary Agency, The; Schmidt Literary Agency, Harold; Seligman, Literary Agent, Lynn; Siegel Literary Agency, Bobbe; Smith, Literary Agent, Valerie; Spitzer Literary Agency, Philip G.; Stauffer Associates, Nancy; Sterling Lord Literistic, Inc.; Stern Literary Agency, Gloria; Teal Literary Agency, Patricia; Van Der Leun & Associates; Wald Associates, Inc., Mary Jack; Ware Literary Agency, John A.; Watkins Loomis Agency, Inc.; Weiner Literary Agency, Cherry; Weingel-Fidel

Agency, The; Westchester Literary Agency, Inc.; Wieser & Wieser, Inc.; Wreschner, Authors' Representative, Ruth; Zeckendorf Assoc. Inc., Susan

Mystery/suspense. A.M.C. Literary Agency; Acton, Dystel, Leone & Jaffe, Inc.; Allan Agency, Lee; Allen, Literary Agency, James; Amsterdam Agency, Marcia; Appleseeds Management; Axelrod Agency, The; Barrett Literary Agency, Helen; Boates Literary Agency, Reid; Bova Literary Agency, The Barbara; Brandt Agency, The Joan; Brandt & Brandt Literary Agents Inc.; Butler, Art and Literary Agent, Jane; Cantrell-Colas Inc., Literary Agency; Carvainis Agency, Inc., Maria; Clark Literary Agency, SJ; Cleaver Inc., Diane; Cohen, Inc. Literary Agency, Ruth; Collin Literary Agent, Frances; Columbia Literary Associates, Inc.; Curtis Associates, Inc., Richard; Davie Literary Agency, Elaine; de la Haba Agency Inc., The Lois; Diamant, The Writer's Workshop, Inc., Anita; Diamond Literary Agency, Inc.; Dijkstra Literary Agency, Sandra; Doyen Literary Services, Inc.; Ducas, Robert; Dupree/Miller and Associates Inc. Literary; Eisenberg Literary Agency, Vicki; Ellenberg Literary Agency, Ethan; Embers Literary Agency; Fallon Literary Agency, The; Fields-Rita Scott Inc., Marje; Garon-Brooke Assoc. Inc., Jay; Gartenberg, Literary Agent, Max; Goodman Literary Agency, Irene; Gotler Metropolitan Talent Agency, Joel; Greenburger Associates, Stanford J.; Hawkins & Associates, Inc., John; Herner Rights Agency, Susan; Hull House Literary Agency; J de S Associates Inc.; Jarvis & Co., Inc., Sharon; KC Communications; Kidde, Hoyt & Picard; Klinger, Inc., Harvey; Kouts, Liteary Agent, Barbara S.; Kroll Literary Agency, Edite; Lampack Agency, Inc., Peter; Lantz-Joy Harris Literary Agency, The Robert; Lasbury Literary Agency, M. Sue; Lincoln Literary Agency, Ray; Lipkind Agency, Wendy; Literary Bridge, The; Literary Group, The; Love Literary Agency, Nancy; Lyceum Creative Properties, Inc.; Maccoby Literary Agency, Gina; McGrath, Helen; Marmur Associates Ltd., Mildred; Merhige-Merdon Marketing/Promo Co. Inc., Greg; MGA Agency Inc.; Multimedia Product Development, Inc.; Naggar Literary Agency, Jean V.; Noetzli Literary Agency, Regula; Parks Agency, The Richard; Pelter, Rodney; Perkins Associates, L.; Picard Literary Agent, Alison J.; Rees Literary Agency, Helen; Riverside Literary Agency; Rosenthal Literary Agency, Jean; Roth Literary Agency, The; Rubenstein Literary Agency, Inc., Pesha; Schmidt Literary Agency, Harold; Seligman, Literary Agent, Lynn; Siegel Literary Agency, Bobbe; Singer Literary Agency Inc., Evelyn; Snell Literary Agency, Michael; Spitzer Literary Agency, Philip G.; Steele & Co., Ltd., Lyle; Stern Literary Agency, Gloria; Teal Literary Agency, Patricia; Wald Associates, Inc., Mary Jack; Ware Literary Agency, John A.; Watkins Loomis Agency, Inc.; Weiner Literary Agency, Cherry; Weingel-Fidel Agency, The; Westchester Literary Agency, Inc.; Wieser & Wieser, Inc.; Wohl Literary Agency, Gary S.; Wreschner, Authors' Representative, Ruth; Zeckendorf Assoc. Inc., Susan

Open to all fiction categories. Allen Literary Agency, Linda; Barrett Books Inc., Loretta; Brown Ltd., Curtis; Cohen Literary Agency Ltd., Hy; Collier Associates; Congdon Associates, Inc., Don; Curtis Bruce Agency, The; Elek Associates, Peter; Goldfarb & Associates, Ronald; Goodman Associates; Gusay Literary Agency, The Charlotte; Hamilburg Agency, The Mitchell J.; Kirchoff/Wohlberg, Inc., Authors' Representation Division; Larsen/Elizabeth Pomada Literary Agents, Michael; Maccampbell Inc., Donald; Martell Agency, The; Ober Associates, Harold; Rock Literary Agency; Writers House

Picture book. Axelrod Agency, The; Brown Literary Agency, Inc., Andrea; Brown Literary Agency, Inc., Andrea; de la Haba Agency Inc., The Lois; Dijkstra Literary Agency, Sandra; Doyen Literary Services, Inc.; Elek Associates, Peter; Ellenberg Literary Agency, Ethan; Embers Literary Agency; Greenburger Associates, Stanford J.; Hawkins & Associates, Inc., John; Kouts, Liteary Agent, Barbara S.; Kroll Literary Agency, Edite; Lantz-Joy Harris Literary Agency, The Robert; Lyceum Creative Properties, Inc.; Merhige-Merdon Marketing/Promo Co. Inc., Greg; MGA Agency Inc.; Naggar Literary Agency, Jean V.; Norma-Lewis Agency, The; Rubenstein Literary Agency, Inc., Pesha; Wald Associates, Inc., Mary Jack

Psychic/supernatural. A.M.C. Literary Agency; Allan Agency, Lee; Appleseeds Management; Cantrell-Colas Inc., Literary Agency; Clark Literary Agency, SJ; Cohen, Inc. Literary Agency, Ruth; Collin Literary Agent, Frances; de la Haba Agency Inc., The Lois; Diamant, The Writer's Workshop, Inc., Anita; Dijkstra Literary Agency, Sandra; Doyen Literary Services, Inc.; Dupree/Miller and Associates Inc. Literary; Greenburger Associates, Stanford J.; Hawkins & Associates, Inc., John; Jarvis & Co., Inc., Sharon; Lantz-Joy Harris Literary Agency, The Robert; Lincoln Literary Agency, Ray; Literary Bridge, The; Lyceum Creative Properties, Inc.; McGrath, Helen; Merhige-Merdon Marketing/Promo Co. Inc., Greg; Naggar Literary Agency, Jean V.; Noetzli Literary Agency, Regula; Parks Agency, The Richard; Pelter, Rodney; Perkins Associates, L.; Picard Literary Agent, Alison J.; Riverside Literary Agency; Schmidt Literary Agency, Harold; Siegel Literary Agency, Bobbe; Spatt, Esq., David M.; Steele & Co., Ltd., Lyle; Wald Associates, Inc., Mary Jack; Weiner Literary Agency, Cherry

Regional. Agency Chicago; Brandt & Brandt Literary Agents Inc.; Collin Literary Agent, Frances; Diamond Literary Agency, Inc.; Greenburger Associates, Stanford J.; Hawkins & Associates, Inc., John; Lantz-Joy Harris Literary Agency, The Robert; Lincoln Literary Agency, Ray; Merhige-Merdon Marketing/Promo Co. Inc., Greg; Naggar Literary Agency, Jean V.; Pelter, Rodney; Raymond, Literary Agent, Charlotte Cecil; Shepard Agency, The

Religious/inspiration. Bach Literary Agency, Julian; Diamant, The Writer's Workshop, Inc., Anita; Embers Literary Agency; Hawkins & Associates, Inc., John; Lantz-Joy Harris Literary Agency, The Robert; Merhige-Merdon Marketing/Promo Co. Inc., Greg; Pelter, Rodney; Westchester Literary Agency, Inc.

Romance. Acton, Dystel, Leone & Jaffe, Inc.; Allan Agency, Lee; Allen, Literary Agency, James; Amsterdam Agency, Marcia; Axelrod Agency, The; Barrett Literary Agency, Helen; Brandt & Brandt Literary Agents Inc.; Carvainis Agency, Inc., Maria; Cohen, Inc. Literary Agency, Ruth; Collin Literary Agent, Frances; Columbia Literary Associates, Inc.; Curtis Associates, Inc., Richard; Davie Literary Agency, Elaine; Diamant, The Writer's Workshop, Inc., Anita; Diamond Literary Agency, Inc.; Dijkstra Literary Agency, Sandra; Doyen Literary Services, Inc.; Dupree/Miller and Associates Inc. Literary; Ellenberg Literary Agency, Ethan; Elmo Agency Inc., Ann; Embers Literary Agency; Fallon Literary Agency, The; Fields-Rita Scott Inc., Marje; Fogelman Publishing Interests Inc.; Garon-Brooke Assoc. Inc., Jay; Goodman Literary Agency, Irene; Herner Rights Agency, Susan; Jarvis & Co., Inc., Sharon; KC Communications; Kidde, Hoyt & Picard; Klinger, Inc., Harvey; Kouts, Liteary Agent, Barbara S.; Lantz-Joy Harris Literary Agency, The Robert; Lincoln Literary Agency, Ray; Literary Bridge, The; Lowenstein Associates, Inc.; Lyceum Creative Properties, Inc.; Merhige-Merdon Marketing/Promo Co. Inc., Greg; MGA Agency Inc.; Multimedia Product Development, Inc.; Picard Literary Agent, Alison J.; Rubenstein Literary Agency, Inc., Pesha; Seymour Agency, The; Siegel Literary Agency, Bobbe; Stern Literary Agency, Gloria; Teal Literary Agency, Patricia; Wald Associates, Inc., Mary Jack; Wallace Literary Agency, Bess; Weiner Literary Agency, Cherry; Wieser & Wieser, Inc.; Wohl Literary Agency, Gary S.; Zeckendorf Assoc. Inc., Susan

Science fiction. Allan Agency, Lee; Allen, Literary Agency, James; Amsterdam Agency, Marcia; Appleseeds Management; Brandt & Brandt Literary Agents Inc.; Butler, Art and Literary Agent, Jane; Cantrell-Colas Inc., Literary Agency; Cole And Lubenow: Books; Collin Literary Agent, Frances; Curtis Associates, Inc., Richard; de la Haba Agency Inc., The Lois; Dijkstra Literary Agency, Sandra; Doyen Literary Services, Inc.; Dupree/Miller and Associates Inc. Literary; Ellenberg Literary Agency, Ethan; Embers Literary Agency; Garon-Brooke Assoc. Inc., Jay; Gotler Metropolitan Talent Agency, Joel; Hawkins & Associates, Inc., John; Herner Rights Agency, Susan; Jarvis & Co., Inc., Sharon; Lincoln Literary Agency, Ray; Literary Bridge, The; Lyceum Creative Properties, Inc.; McGrath, Helen; MGA Agency Inc.; Naggar Literary Agency, Jean V.; Protter Literary Agent, Susan Ann; Rees Literary Agency, Helen; Riverside Literary Agency; Siegel Literary Agency, Bobbe; Smith, Literary Agent, Valerie; Spatt, Esq., David M.; Wald Associates, Inc., Mary Jack; Watkins Loomis Agency, Inc.; Weiner Literary Agency, Cherry

Sports. Acton, Dystel, Leone & Jaffe, Inc.; Brandt & Brandt Literary Agents Inc.; de la Haba Agency Inc., The Lois; Dijkstra Literary Agency, Sandra; Ducas, Robert; Dupree/Miller and Associates Inc. Literary; Ellenberg Literary Agency, Ethan; Fields-Rita Scott Inc., Marje; Greenburger Associates, Stanford J.; Hawkins & Associates, Inc., John; Lantz-Joy Harris Literary Agency, The Robert; Lincoln Literary Agency, Ray; Literary Bridge, The; Literary Group, The; McGrath, Helen; Merhige-Merdon Marketing/Promo Co. Inc., Greg; Noetzli Literary Agency, Regula; Pelter, Rodney; Picard Literary Agent, Alison J.; Rees Literary Agency, Helen; Shepard Agency, The; Spitzer Literary Agency, Philip G.; Wald Associates, Inc., Mary Jack; Wohl Literary Agency, Gary S.

Thriller/espionage. A.M.C. Literary Agency; Acton, Dystel, Leone & Jaffe, Inc.; Allan Agency, Lee; Amsterdam Agency, Marcia; Appleseeds Management; Axelrod Agency, The; Barrett Literary Agency, Helen; Boates Literary Agency, Reid; Brandt Agency, The Joan; Brandt & Brandt Literary Agents Inc.; Cantrell-Colas Inc., Literary Agency; Carvainis Agency, Inc., Maria; Clark Literary Agency, SJ; Cleaver Inc., Diane; Columbia Literary Associates, Inc.; Curtis Associates, Inc., Richard; Darhansoff & Verrill Literary Agents; de la Haba Agency Inc., The Lois; Diamant, The Writer's Workshop, Inc., Anita; Diamond Literary Agency, Inc.; Dijkstra Literary Agency, Sandra; Doyen Literary Services, Inc.; Ducas, Robert; Dupree/Miller and Associates Inc. Literary; Ellenberg Literary Agency, Ethan; Fields-Rita Scott Inc., Marje; Gotler Metropolitan Talent Agency, Joel; Greenburger Associates, Stanford J.; Hawkins & Associates, Inc., John; Herner Rights Agency, Susan; Jarvis & Co., Inc., Sharon; Kidde, Hoyt & Picard; Klinger, Inc., Harvey; Lampack Agency, Inc., Peter; Lantz-Joy Harris Literary Agency, The Robert; Levine Literary Agency, Inc., Ellen; Lincoln Literary Agency, Ray; Literary Bridge, The; Literary Group, The; Los Angeles Literary Associates; Love Literary Agency, Nancy; Lyceum Creative Properties, Inc.; Maccoby Literary Agency, Gina; McGrath, Helen; Marmur Associates Ltd., Mildred; Merhige-Merdon Marketing/Promo Co. Inc., Greg; Multimedia Product Development, Inc.; Naggar Literary Agency, Jean V.; Noetzli Literary Agency, Regula; Parks Agency, The Richard; Pelter, Rodney; Perkins Associates, L.; Picard Literary Agent, Alison J.; Protter Literary Agent, Susan Ann; Raymond, Literary Agent, Charlotte Cecil; Rees Literary Agency, Helen; Riverside Literary Agency; Rose Literary Agency; Roth Literary Agency, The; Schmidt Literary Agency, Harold; Shepard Agency, The; Siegel Literary Agency, Bobbe; Singer Literary Agency Inc., Evelyn; Snell Literary Agency, Michael; Steele & Co., Ltd., Lyle; Stern Literary Agency, Gloria; Wald Associates, Inc., Mary Jack; Ware Literary Agency, John A.; Wecksler-Incomco; Weiner Literary Agency, Cherry; Weingel-Fidel Agency, The; Westchester Literary Agency, Inc.; Wieser & Wieser, Inc.; Zeckendorf Assoc. Inc., Susan

Westerns/frontier. Allan Agency, Lee; Amsterdam Agency, Marcia; Brandt & Brandt Literary Agents Inc.; Carvainis Agency, Inc., Maria; Curtis Associates, Inc., Richard; Davie Literary Agency, Elaine; de la Haba Agency Inc., The Lois; Diamant, The Writer's Workshop, Inc., Anita; Doyen Literary Services, Inc.; Ducas, Robert; Dupree/Miller and Associates Inc. Literary; Ellenberg Literary Agency, Ethan; Embers Literary Agency; Fields-Rita Scott Inc., Marje; Hawkins & Associates, Inc., John; J de S Associates Inc.;

Literary Bridge, The; Lyceum Creative Properties, Inc.; McGrath, Helen; Merhige-Merdon Marketing/ Promo Co. Inc., Greg; Multimedia Product Development, Inc.; Parks Agency, The Richard; Pelter, Rodney; Picard Literary Agent, Alison J.; Schmidt Literary Agency, Harold; Wald Associates, Inc., Mary Jack; Weiner Literary Agency, Cherry; Westchester Literary Agency, Inc.

Young adult. Allan Agency, Lee; Amsterdam Agency, Marcia; Brandt & Brandt Literary Agents Inc.; Brown Literary Agency, Inc., Andrea; Butler, Art and Literary Agent, Jane; Cantrell-Colas Inc., Literary Agency; Carvainis Agency, Inc., Maria; Clark Literary Agency, SJ; Cohen, Inc. Literary Agency, Ruth; de la Haba Agency Inc., The Lois; Diamant, The Writer's Workshop, Inc., Anita; Dijkstra Literary Agency, Sandra; Doyen Literary Services, Inc.; Ellenberg Literary Agency, Ethan; Embers Literary Agency; Fields-Rita Scott Inc., Marje; J de S Associates Inc.; Kouts, Liteary Agent, Barbara S.; Lantz-Joy Harris Literary Agency, The Robert; Lincoln Literary Agency, Ray; Literary Bridge, The; Maccoby Literary Agency, Gina; Merhige-Merdon Marketing/Promo Co. Inc., Greg; MGA Agency Inc.; Miller Associates, Roberta D.; Naggar Literary Agency, Jean V.; Parks Agency, The Richard; Picard Literary Agent, Alison J.; Raymond, Literary Agent, Charlotte Cecil; Rubenstein Literary Agency, Inc., Pesha; Seymour Agency, The; Smith, Literary Agent, Valerie; Stern Literary Agency, Gloria; Wald Associates, Inc., Mary Jack; Westchester Literary Agency, Inc.

Nonfee charging agents/Nonfiction

Agriculture/horticulture. de la Haba Agency Inc., The Lois; Dijkstra Literary Agency, Sandra; Gartenberg, Literary Agent, Max; Hawkins & Associates, Inc., John; Jarvis & Co., Inc., Sharon; Lincoln Literary Agency, Ray; Parks Agency, The Richard; Roth Literary Agency, The; Shepard Agency, The; Wallace Literary Agency, Bess

Animals. Acton, Dystel, Leone & Jaffe, Inc.; Agency Chicago; Balkin Agency, Inc.; Boates Literary Agency, Reid; Brandt & Brandt Literary Agents Inc.; Brown Literary Agency, Inc., Andrea; Cole And Lubenow: Books; Crown International Literature and Arts Agency, Bonnie R.; de la Haba Agency Inc., The Lois; Diamant, The Writer's Workshop, Inc., Anita; Diamond Literary Agency, Inc.; Ducas, Robert; Fuhrman Literary Agency, Candice; Gartenberg, Literary Agent, Max; Hawkins & Associates, Inc., John; Kidde, Hoyt & Picard; Lincoln Literary Agency, Ray; Literary Bridge, The; Literary Group, The; Merhige-Merdon Marketing/Promo Co. Inc., Greg; Noetzli Literary Agency, Regula; Parks Agency, The Richard; Riverside Literary Agency; Rosenthal Literary Agency, Jean; Shepard Agency, The; Wallace Literary Agency, Bess; Writers House

Anthropology. Bach Literary Agency, Julian; Balkin Agency, Inc.; Barrett Literary Agency, Helen; Boates Literary Agency, Reid; Borchardt Inc., Georges; Brandt & Brandt Literary Agents Inc.; Cantrell-Colas Inc., Literary Agency; Collin Literary Agent, Frances; Darhansoff & Verrill Literary Agents; de la Haba Agency Inc., The Lois; Dijkstra Literary Agency, Sandra; Educational Design Services, Inc.; Fuhrman Literary Agency, Candice; Hawkins & Associates, Inc., John; Hull House Literary Agency; Ketz Agency, Louise B.; Lincoln Literary Agency, Ray; Literary Bridge, The; Lyceum Creative Properties, Inc.; Mann Agency, Carol; Noetzli Literary Agency, Regula; Parks Agency, The Richard; Peter Associates, Inc., James; Quicksilver Books-Literary Agents; Rose Literary Agency; Rosenthal Literary Agency, Jean; Schmidt Literary Agency, Harold; Seligman, Literary Agent, Lynn; Siegel Literary Agency, Bobbe; Singer Literary Agency Inc., Evelyn; Steele & Co., Ltd., Lyle; Stern Literary Agency, Gloria; Wallace Literary Agency, Bess; Ware Literary Agency, John A.; Wecksler-Incomco; Weingel-Fidel Agency, The

Art/architecture/design. Agency Chicago; Axelrod Agency, The; Boates Literary Agency, Reid; Brandt & Brandt Literary Agents Inc.; Cantrell-Colas Inc., Literary Agency; Cole And Lubenow: Books; de la Haba Agency Inc., The Lois; Diamant, The Writer's Workshop, Inc., Anita; Dijkstra Literary Agency, Sandra; Fuhrman Literary Agency, Candice; Gartenberg, Literary Agent, Max; Gregory Associates, Maia; Hawkins & Associates, Inc., John; Hull House Literary Agency; Lincoln Literary Agency, Ray; Lyceum Creative Properties, Inc.; Mann Agency, Carol; Merhige-Merdon Marketing/Promo Co. Inc., Greg; Miller Associates, Roberta D.; Nathan, Ruth; Parks Agency, The Richard; Perkins Associates, L.; Peter Associates, Inc., James; Picard Literary Agent, Alison J.; Rose Literary Agency; Rosenthal Literary Agency, Jean; Schmidt Literary Agency, Harold; Seligman, Literary Agent, Lynn; Stern Literary Agency, Gloria; Watkins Loomis Agency, Inc.; Wecksler-Incomco; Weingel-Fidel Agency, The; Writers House; Zeckendorf Assoc. Inc., Susan

Biography/autobiography. A.M.C. Literary Agency; Acton, Dystel, Leone & Jaffe, Inc.; Ajlouny Agency, The Joseph S.; Allan Agency, Lee; Andrews & Associates Inc., Bart; Appleseeds Management; Bach Literary Agency, Julian; Balkin Agency, Inc.; Barrett Literary Agency, Helen; Bartczak Associates Inc., Gene; Boates Literary Agency, Reid; Borchardt Inc., Georges; Brandt & Brandt Literary Agents Inc.; Cantrell-Colas Inc., Literary Agency; Carvainis Agency, Inc., Maria; Clausen Associates, Connie; Cole And Lubenow: Books; Collin Literary Agent, Frances; Curtis Associates, Inc., Richard; Curtis Bruce Agency, The; Darhansoff & Verrill Literary Agents; de la Haba Agency Inc., The Lois; Diamant, The Writer's Workshop, Inc., Anita; Diamond Literary Agency, Inc.; Dijkstra Literary Agency, Sandra; Ducas, Robert;

Ellenberg Literary Agency, Ethan; Fallon Literary Agency, The; Fields-Rita Scott Inc., Marje; Fogelman Publishing Interests Inc.; Fuhrman Literary Agency, Candice; Garon-Brooke Assoc. Inc., Jay; Gartenberg, Literary Agent, Max; Gotler Metropolitan Talent Agency, Joel; Hawkins & Associates, Inc., John; Holub & Associates; Hull House Literary Agency; J de S Associates Inc.; Jarvis & Co., Inc., Sharon; KC Communications; Ketz Agency, Louise B.; Kidde, Hoyt & Picard; Klinger, Inc., Harvey; Kouts, Literary Agent, Barbara S.; Lampack Agency, Inc., Peter; Levine Literary Agency, Inc., Ellen; Lincoln Literary Agency, Ray; Lipkind Agency, Wendy; Literary and Creative Artists Agency; Literary Bridge, The; Literary Group, The; Los Angeles Literary Associates; Love Literary Agency, Nancy; Lyceum Creative Properties, Inc.; Maccoby Literary Agency, Gina; McGrath, Helen; Mann Agency, Carol; Marmur Associates Ltd., Mildred; Merhige-Merdon Marketing/Promo Co. Inc., Greg; Miller Associates, Roberta D.; Multimedia Product Development, Inc.; Naggar Literary Agency, Jean V.; Nathan, Ruth; New England Publishing Associates, Inc.; Noetzli Literary Agency, Regula; Parks Agency, The Richard; Peter Associates, Inc., James; Picard Literary Agent, Alison J.; Protter Literary Agent, Susan Ann; Quicksilver Books-Literary Agents; Raymond, Literary Agent, Charlotte Cecil; Rees Literary Agency, Helen; Riverside Literary Agency; Rose Literary Agency; Rosenthal Literary Agency, Jean; Roth Literary Agency, The; Schaffner Agency, Inc.; Schmidt Literary Agency, Harold; Seligman, Literary Agent, Lynn; Shepard Agency, The; Siegel Literary Agency, Bobbe; Singer Literary Agency Inc., Evelyn; Spitzer Literary Agency, Philip G.; Stauffer Associates, Nancy; Steele & Co., Ltd., Lyle; Stern Literary Agency, Gloria; Teal Literary Agency, Patricia; Wald Associates, Inc., Mary Jack; Ware Literary Agency, John A.; Wecksler-Incomco; Weingel-Fidel Agency, The; Westchester Literary Agency, Inc.; Writers House; Zeckendorf Assoc. Inc., Susan

Business. Acton, Dystel, Leone & Jaffe, Inc.; Allan Agency, Lee; Appleseeds Management; Axelrod Agency, The; Bach Literary Agency, Julian; Boates Literary Agency, Reid; Brandt & Brandt Literary Agents Inc.; Carvainis Agency, Inc., Maria; Clausen Associates, Connie; Cole And Lubenow: Books; Collin Literary Agent, Frances; Columbia Literary Associates, Inc.; Curtis Associates, Inc., Richard; Diamant, The Writer's Workshop, Inc., Anita; Diamond Literary Agency, Inc.; Dijkstra Literary Agency, Sandra; Ducas, Robert; Educational Design Services, Inc.; Ellenberg Literary Agency, Ethan; Fogelman Publishing Interests Inc.; Fuhrman Literary Agency, Candice; Hawkins & Associates, Inc., John; Hull House Literary Agency; J de S Associates Inc.; Jarvis & Co., Inc., Sharon; Jones Literary Agency, Lloyd; Ketz Agency, Louise B.; Kouts, Literary Agent, Barbara S.; Lampack Agency, Inc., Peter; Lasbury Literary Agency, M. Sue; Levant & Wales, Literary Agency, Inc.; Lincoln Literary Agency, Ray; Literary and Creative Artists Agency; Literary Bridge, The; Literary Group, The; Los Angeles Literary Associates; Love Literary Agency, Nancy; Lyceum Creative Properties, Inc.; McGrath, Helen; Mann Agency, Carol; Marmur Associates Ltd., Mildred; Multimedia Product Development, Inc.; Naggar Literary Agency, Jean V.; New England Publishing Associates, Inc.; Odenwald Connection, The; Parks Agency, The Richard; Paton Literary Agency, Kathi J.; Peter Associates, Inc., James; Picard Literary Agent, Alison J.; Quicksilver Books-Literary Agents; Rees Literary Agency, Helen; Riverside Literary Agency; Rock Literary Agency; Rose Literary Agency; Roth Literary Agency, The; Schmidt Literary Agency, Harold; Seligman, Literary Agent, Lynn; Shepard Agency, The; Singer Literary Agency Inc., Evelyn; Spitzer Literary Agency, Philip G.; Steele & Co., Ltd., Lyle; Stern Literary Agency, Gloria; Wecksler-Incomco; Westchester Literary Agency, Inc.; Wieser & Wieser, Inc.; Wohl Literary Agency, Gary S.; Writers House; Zeckendorf Assoc. Inc., Susan

Child guidance/parenting. A.M.C. Literary Agency; Acton, Dystel, Leone & Jaffe, Inc.; Agents Inc. for Medical and Mental Health Professionals; Allan Agency, Lee; Balkin Agency, Inc.; Boates Literary Agency, Reid; Brandt & Brandt Literary Agents Inc.; Cantrell-Colas Inc., Literary Agency; Cole And Lubenow: Books; Columbia Literary Associates, Inc.; Curtis Associates, Inc., Richard; Curtis Bruce Agency, The; Diamant, The Writer's Workshop, Inc., Anita; Diamond Literary Agency, Inc.; Dijkstra Literary Agency, Sandra; Educational Design Services, Inc.; Ellenberg Literary Agency, Ethan; Fogelman Publishing Interests Inc.; Fuhrman Literary Agency, Candice; Garon-Brooke Assoc. Inc., Jay; Gartenberg, Literary Agent, Max; Hawkins & Associates, Inc., John; Kouts, Literary Agent, Barbara S.; Lincoln Literary Agency, Ray; Literary Group, The; Love Literary Agency, Nancy; Lyceum Creative Properties, Inc.; Mann Agency, Carol; Merhige-Merdon Marketing/Promo Co. Inc., Greg; Naggar Literary Agency, Jean V.; New England Publishing Associates, Inc.; Noetzli Literary Agency, Regula; Parks Agency, The Richard; Peter Associates, Inc., James; Picard Literary Agent, Alison J.; Quicksilver Books-Literary Agents; Raymond, Literary Agent, Charlotte Cecil; Riverside Literary Agency; Rose Literary Agency; Rosenthal Literary Agency, Jean; Roth Literary Agency, The; Seligman, Literary Agent, Lynn; Shepard Agency, The; Siegel Literary Agency, Bobbe; Singer Literary Agency Inc., Evelyn; Steele & Co., Ltd., Lyle; Stern Literary Agency, Gloria; Teal Literary Agency, Patricia; Westchester Literary Agency, Inc.; Writers House; Zeckendorf Assoc. Inc., Susan

Computers/electronics. Allan Agency, Lee; Axelrod Agency, The; Diamond Literary Agency, Inc.; Lyceum Creative Properties, Inc.; Moore Literary Agency; Shepard Agency, The; Singer Literary Agency Inc., Evelyn

Cooking/food/nutrition. Acton, Dystel, Leone & Jaffe, Inc.; Agents Inc. for Medical and Mental Health Professionals; Allan Agency, Lee; Bach Literary Agency, Julian; Brandt & Brandt Literary Agents

Inc.; Cantrell-Colas Inc., Literary Agency; Clausen Associates, Connie; Cole And Lubenow: Books; Columbia Literary Associates, Inc.; Diamant, The Writer's Workshop, Inc., Anita; Diamond Literary Agency, Inc.; Dijkstra Literary Agency, Sandra; Ellenberg Literary Agency, Ethan; Elmo Agency Inc., Ann; Fields-Rita Scott Inc., Marje; Fogelman Publishing Interests Inc.; Fuhrman Literary Agency, Candice; Hawkins & Associates, Inc., John; Klinger, Inc., Harvey; Lincoln Literary Agency, Ray; Literary and Creative Artists Agency; Love Literary Agency, Nancy; Lyceum Creative Properties, Inc.; Marmur Associates Ltd., Mildred; Merhige-Merdon Marketing/Promo Co. Inc., Greg; Multimedia Product Development, Inc.; Naggar Literary Agency, Jean V.; Parks Agency, The Richard; Picard Literary Agent, Alison J.; Quicksilver Books-Literary Agents; Riverside Literary Agency; Rose Literary Agency; Roth Literary Agency, The; Seligman, Literary Agent, Lynn; Shepard Agency, The; Siegel Literary Agency, Bobbe; Steele & Co., Ltd., Lyle; Stern Literary Agency, Gloria; Wieser & Wieser, Inc.; Wohl Literary Agency, Gary S.; Writers House

Crafts/hobbies. Brandt & Brandt Literary Agents Inc.; Diamant, The Writer's Workshop, Inc., Anita; Diamond Literary Agency, Inc.; Ellenberg Literary Agency, Ethan; Fuhrman Literary Agency, Candice; Hawkins & Associates, Inc., John; Jarvis & Co., Inc., Sharon; Lincoln Literary Agency, Ray; Parks Agency, The Richard; Peter Associates, Inc., James; Shepard Agency, The; Wohl Literary Agency, Gary S.

Current Affairs. A.M.C. Literary Agency; Acton, Dystel, Leone & Jaffe, Inc.; Allan Agency, Lee; Bach Literary Agency, Julian; Balkin Agency, Inc.; Barrett Literary Agency, Helen; Boates Literary Agency, Reid; Borchardt Inc., Georges; Brandt & Brandt Literary Agents Inc.; Cantrell-Colas Inc., Literary Agency; Carvainis Agency, Inc., Maria; Clausen Associates, Connie; Cole And Lubenow: Books; Darhansoff & Verrill Literary Agents; Diamant, The Writer's Workshop, Inc., Anita; Diamond Literary Agency, Inc.; Dijkstra Literary Agency, Sandra; Ducas, Robert; Educational Design Services, Inc.; Ellenberg Literary Agency, Ethan; Fogelman Publishing Interests Inc.; Fuhrman Literary Agency, Candice; Gartenberg, Literary Agent, Max; Hawkins & Associates, Inc., John; Hull House Literary Agency; J de S Associates Inc.; Jones Literary Agency, Lloyd; Ketz Agency, Louise B.; Kouts, Liteary Agent, Barbara S.; Kroll Literary Agency, Edite; Lampack Agency, Inc., Peter; Lasbury Literary Agency, M. Sue; Levine Literary Agency, Inc., Ellen; Lincoln Literary Agency, Ray; Lipkind Agency, Wendy; Literary Group, The; Love Literary Agency, Nancy; Lyceum Creative Properties, Inc.; Maccoby Literary Agency, Gina; McGrath, Helen; Mann Agency, Carol; Marmur Associates Ltd., Mildred; Miller Associates, Roberta D.; Multimedia Product Development, Inc.; Naggar Literary Agency, Jean V.; Noetzli Literary Agency, Regula; Odenwald Connection, The; Parks Agency, The Richard; Perkins Associates, L.; Peter Associates, Inc., James; Picard Literary Agent, Alison J.; Raymond, Literary Agent, Charlotte Cecil; Rees Literary Agency, Helen; Rose Literary Agency; Roth Literary Agency, The; Schmidt Literary Agency, Harold; Seligman, Literary Agent, Lynn; Shepard Agency, The; Singer Literary Agency Inc., Evelyn; Spitzer Literary Agency, Philip G.; Stauffer Associates, Nancy; Steele & Co., Ltd., Lyle; Stern Literary Agency, Gloria; Wald Associates, Inc., Mary Jack; Wallace Literary Agency, Bess; Ware Literary Agency, John A.; Wecksler-Incomco; Wieser & Wieser, Inc.

Ethnic/cultural interests. Acton, Dystel, Leone & Jaffe, Inc.; Agency Chicago; Boates Literary Agency, Reid; Brandt & Brandt Literary Agents Inc.; Cantrell-Colas Inc., Literary Agency; Clausen Associates, Connie; Cohen, Inc. Literary Agency, Ruth; Crown International Literature and Arts Agency, Bonnie R.; Diamond Literary Agency, Inc.; Dijkstra Literary Agency, Sandra; Educational Design Services, Inc.; Fuhrman Literary Agency, Candice; Hawkins & Associates, Inc., John; Hull House Literary Agency; J de S Associates Inc.; Jones Literary Agency, Lloyd; Kouts, Liteary Agent, Barbara S.; Lincoln Literary Agency, Ray; Love Literary Agency, Nancy; Lyceum Creative Properties, Inc.; Maccoby Literary Agency, Gina; Mann Agency, Carol; Marmur Associates Ltd., Mildred; Merhige-Merdon Marketing/Promo Co. Inc., Greg; Miller Associates, Roberta D.; Noetzli Literary Agency, Regula; Parks Agency, The Richard; Perkins Associates, L.; Peter Associates, Inc., James; Picard Literary Agent, Alison J.; Raymond, Literary Agent, Charlotte Cecil; Rees Literary Agency, Helen; Rose Literary Agency; Roth Literary Agency, The; Schaffner Agency, Inc.; Schmidt Literary Agency, Harold; Seligman, Literary Agent, Lynn; Siegel Literary Agency, Bobbe; Spitzer Literary Agency, Philip G.; Stauffer Associates, Nancy; Steele & Co., Ltd., Lyle; Stern Literary Agency, Gloria; Wald Associates, Inc., Mary Jack

Gay/Lesbian issues. Acton, Dystel, Leone & Jaffe, Inc.; Brandt & Brandt Literary Agents Inc.; Clausen Associates, Connie; Ducas, Robert; Fields-Rita Scott Inc., Marje; Garon-Brooke Assoc. Inc., Jay; Hawkins & Associates, Inc., John; Kidde, Hoyt & Picard; Lincoln Literary Agency, Ray; Literary Group, The; Lyceum Creative Properties, Inc.; Naggar Literary Agency, Jean V.; Parks Agency, The Richard; Picard Literary Agent, Alison J.; Raymond, Literary Agent, Charlotte Cecil; Riverside Literary Agency; Rose Literary Agency; Schmidt Literary Agency, Harold; Steele & Co., Ltd., Lyle

Government/politics/law. Acton, Dystel, Leone & Jaffe, Inc.; Allan Agency, Lee; Axelrod Agency, The; Bach Literary Agency, Julian; Barrett Literary Agency, Helen; Black Literary Agency, Inc., David; Boates Literary Agency, Reid; Brandt & Brandt Literary Agents Inc.; Cantrell-Colas Inc., Literary Agency; Carvainis Agency, Inc., Maria; Cole And Lubenow: Books; Diamant, The Writer's Workshop, Inc., Anita; Dijkstra Literary Agency, Sandra; Ducas, Robert; Educational Design Services, Inc.; Ellenberg Literary Agency, Ethan; Fogelman Publishing Interests Inc.; Hawkins & Associates, Inc., John; Hull House Literary

Agency; J de S Associates Inc.; Lampack Agency, Inc., Peter; Lasbury Literary Agency, M. Sue; Lincoln Literary Agency, Ray; Literary and Creative Artists Agency; Literary Bridge, The; Love Literary Agency, Nancy; Lyceum Creative Properties, Inc.; Mann Agency, Carol; Marmur Associates Ltd., Mildred; Naggar Literary Agency, Jean V.; New England Publishing Associates, Inc.; Parks Agency, The Richard; Peter Associates, Inc., James; Picard Literary Agent, Alison J.; Rees Literary Agency, Helen; Rose Literary Agency; Roth Literary Agency, The; Schmidt Literary Agency, Harold; Seligman, Literary Agent, Lynn; Shepard Agency, The; Singer Literary Agency Inc., Evelyn; Spitzer Literary Agency, Philip G.; Steele & Co., Ltd., Lyle; Stern Literary Agency, Gloria; Wallace Literary Agency, Bess; Westchester Literary Agency, Inc.

Health/medicine. Acton, Dystel, Leone & Jaffe, Inc.; Agents Inc. for Medical and Mental Health Professionals; Ajlouny Agency, The Joseph S.; Allan Agency, Lee; Appleseeds Management; Axelrod Agency, The; Balkin Agency, Inc.; Boates Literary Agency, Reid; Brandt & Brandt Literary Agents Inc.; Cantrell-Colas Inc., Literary Agency; Carvainis Agency, Inc., Maria; Clausen Associates, Connie; Collin Literary Agent, Frances; Columbia Literary Associates, Inc.; Darhansoff & Verrill Literary Agents; de la Haba Agency Inc., The Lois; Diamant, The Writer's Workshop, Inc., Anita; Diamond Literary Agency, Inc.; Dijkstra Literary Agency, Sandra; Ducas, Robert; Ellenberg Literary Agency, Ethan; Fallon Literary Agency, The; Fields-Rita Scott Inc., Marje; Fuhrman Literary Agency, Candice; Garon-Brooke Assoc. Inc., Jay; Gartenberg, Literary Agent, Max; Hawkins & Associates, Inc., John; J de S Associates Inc.; Jarvis & Co., Inc., Sharon; Jones Literary Agency, Lloyd; Klinger, Inc., Harvey; Kouts, Literary Agent, Barbara S.; Lampack Agency, Inc., Peter; Lasbury Literary Agency, M. Sue; Levant & Wales, Literary Agency, Inc.; Lincoln Literary Agency, Ray; Lipkind Agency, Wendy; Literary and Creative Artists Agency; Literary Bridge, The; Literary Group, The; Love Literary Agency, Nancy; Lowenstein Associates, Inc.; McGrath, Helen; Mann Agency, Carol; Marmur Associates Ltd., Mildred; Multimedia Product Development, Inc.; Naggar Literary Agency, Jean V.; New England Publishing Associates, Inc.; Noetzli Literary Agency, Regula; Parks Agency, The Richard; Peter Associates, Inc., James; Picard Literary Agent, Alison J.; Protter Literary Agent, Susan Ann; Quicksilver Books-Literary Agents; Raymond, Literary Agent, Charlotte Cecil; Rees Literary Agency, Helen; Riverside Literary Agency; Rock Literary Agency; Rose Literary Agency; Rosenthal Literary Agency, Jean; Roth Literary Agency, The; Schmidt Literary Agency, Harold; Seligman, Literary Agent, Lynn; Shepard Agency, The; Siegel Literary Agency, Bobbe; Singer Literary Agency Inc., Evelyn; Spitzer Literary Agency, Philip G.; Steele & Co., Ltd., Lyle; Stern Literary Agency, Gloria; Teal Literary Agency, Patricia; Wald Associates, Inc., Mary Jack; Ware Literary Agency, John A.; Weingel-Fidel Agency, The; Wieser & Wieser, Inc.; Writers House; Zeckendorf Assoc. Inc., Susan

History. A.M.C. Literary Agency; Acton, Dystel, Leone & Jaffe, Inc.; Ajlouny Agency, The Joseph S.; Allan Agency, Lee; Axelrod Agency, The; Bach Literary Agency, Julian; Balkin Agency, Inc.; Barrett Literary Agency, Helen; Boates Literary Agency, Reid; Borchardt Inc., Georges; Brandt & Brandt Literary Agents Inc.; Cantrell-Colas Inc., Literary Agency; Carvainis Agency, Inc., Maria; Cole And Lubenow: Books; Collin Literary Agent, Frances; Curtis Associates, Inc., Richard; Darhansoff & Verrill Literary Agents; de la Haba Agency Inc., The Lois; Diamant, The Writer's Workshop, Inc., Anita; Diamond Literary Agency, Inc.; Dijkstra Literary Agency, Sandra; Ducas, Robert; Educational Design Services, Inc.; Ellenberg Literary Agency, Ethan; Fallon Literary Agency, The; Fuhrman Literary Agency, Candice; Garon-Brooke Assoc. Inc., Jay; Gartenberg, Literary Agent, Max; Gotler Metropolitan Talent Agency, Joel; Gregory Associates, Maia; Hawkins & Associates, Inc., John; Hull House Literary Agency; J de S Associates Inc.; KC Communications; Ketz Agency, Louise B.; Kouts, Literary Agent, Barbara S.; Lampack Agency, Inc., Peter; Lasbury Literary Agency, M. Sue; Lincoln Literary Agency, Ray; Lipkind Agency, Wendy; Literary Bridge, The; Literary Group, The; Los Angeles Literary Associates; Love Literary Agency, Nancy; Lyceum Creative Properties, Inc.; McGrath, Helen; Mann Agency, Carol; Marmur Associates Ltd., Mildred; Naggar Literary Agency, Jean V.; New England Publishing Associates, Inc.; Noetzli Literary Agency, Regula; Parks Agency, The Richard; Peter Associates, Inc., James; Picard Literary Agent, Alison J.; Raymond, Literary Agent, Charlotte Cecil; Rees Literary Agency, Helen; Riverside Literary Agency; Rose Literary Agency; Rosenthal Literary Agency, Jean; Roth Literary Agency, The; Schmidt Literary Agency, Harold; Seligman, Literary Agent, Lynn; Shepard Agency, The; Siegel Literary Agency, Bobbe; Spitzer Literary Agency, Philip G.; Steele & Co., Ltd., Lyle; Stern Literary Agency, Gloria; Wald Associates, Inc., Mary Jack; Wallace Literary Agency, Bess; Ware Literary Agency, John A.; Watkins Loomis Agency, Inc.; Wecksler-Incomco; Westchester Literary Agency, Inc.; Wieser & Wieser, Inc.; Writers House; Zeckendorf Assoc. Inc., Susan

Interior design/decorating. Barrett Literary Agency, Helen; Brandt & Brandt Literary Agents Inc.; Fuhrman Literary Agency, Candice; Hawkins & Associates, Inc., John; Lincoln Literary Agency, Ray; Mann Agency, Carol; Naggar Literary Agency, Jean V.; Peter Associates, Inc., James; Picard Literary Agent, Alison J.; Seligman, Literary Agent, Lynn; Shepard Agency, The; Writers House

Juvenile nonfiction. Allan Agency, Lee; Bartczak Associates Inc., Gene; Brandt & Brandt Literary Agents Inc.; Brown Literary Agency, Inc., Andrea; Cantrell-Colas Inc., Literary Agency; Cohen, Inc. Literary Agency, Ruth; de la Haba Agency Inc., The Lois; Diamant, The Writer's Workshop, Inc., Anita; Educational Design Services, Inc.; Elek Associates, Peter; Ellenberg Literary Agency, Ethan; Elmo Agency Inc., Ann;

GET TOMORROW'S INFORMATION AT LAST YEAR'S PRICE

The most current information vital to your career!

You already know an agent or rep can be the key to successfully selling your work. And you don't want to waste your time or money sending your work to the wrong address. By ordering each new edition of *Guide to Literary Agents and Art/Photo Reps*, you'll stay up to date on all the changes in this industry. And if you order the 1994 edition now, you can reserve your copy — and pay the old price for the new edition.

Make sure you have the most current marketing information available by ordering *1994 Guide to Literary Agents & Art/Photo Reps* today. All you have to do is complete the attached post card and return it with your payment or charge card information. Order now, and there's one thing that won't change from your 1993 edition - the price! That's right, we'll send you the 1994 edition for just $18.95. *1994 Guide to Literary Agents & Art/Photo Reps* will be published and ready for shipment in February 1994.

So, out with the old...In with the new *1994 Guide to Literary Agents & Art/Photo Reps*. Order the new edition today!

(See other side for more books to help sell your work)

- -

To order, drop this postpaid card in the mail.   Offer expires August 1, 1994

☐ **Yes!** I want the most current edition of *Guide to Literary Agents & Art/Photo Reps*. Please send me the 1994 edition at the 1993 price -- $18.95.* (NOTE: *The 1994 Edition* will be ready for shipment in February 1994.) #10363
Also send me the following books NOW:

____(#10272) *1993 Writer's Market* $26.95*
____(#10306) *1993 Novel & Short Story Writer's Market* $19.95*
____(#10307) *1993 Children's Writer's & Illustrator's Market* $18.95*
____(#10274) *1993 Artist's Market* $22.95*
____(#10273) *1993 Photographer's Market* $22.95*

> *Plus postage & handling: $3.00 for one book, $1.00 for each additional book. Ohio residents add 5½% sales tax.

Credit Card Orders Call Toll-Free 1-800-289-0963

☐ Payment enclosed (Slip this card and payment into an envelope)
☐ Please charge my: ☐ Visa ☐ MasterCard

Account # _____Exp._____Signature _____

Name _____ Phone (_____) _____

Address _____

City _____ State_____ Zip _____

30-DAY MONEY BACK GUARANTEE

Writer's Digest Books
1507 Dana Avenue
Cincinnati, OH 45207

6341

THESE BUYERS WANT TO PURCHASE YOUR WORK!

1993 WRITER'S MARKET
edited by Mark Garvey
This new edition contains up-to-date information on 4,000 buyers of freelance materials, as well as listings of workshops, contests and awards. Helpful articles and interviews with top professionals make this the source for your marketing efforts.
1056 pages/$26.95/hardcover

1993 Novel & Short Story Writer's Market
edited by Robin Gee
This exclusive market guide for novel and short story writers includes complete information on 1,900 fiction publishers, coupled with helpful articles and interviews with notable fiction writers.
624 pages/$19.95/paperback

1993 Children's Writer's & Illustrator's Market
edited by Lisa Carpenter
The two key aspects of children's publishing are brought together in this handy volume, offering hundreds of outlets for your work, along with professional guidance from those who have already succeeded in this lucrative field.
256 pages/$18.95/paperback

1993 Artist's Market
edited by Lauri Miller
You'll find 2,500 buyers of all types of art in this indispensable directory. Handy geographical indexes are included, in addition to articles and interviews with successful professionals.
608 pages/$22.95/hardcover

1993 Photographer's Market
edited by Mike Willins
The most comprehensive book of its kind, this directory contains 2,500 up-to-date listings of U.S. and international buyers of freelance photos, coupled with advice from top professionals in the field.
608 pages/$22.95/hardcover

Use the coupon on the other side to order these books today!

Hawkins & Associates, Inc., John; Jones Literary Agency, Lloyd; Kouts, Liteary Agent, Barbara S.; Lincoln Literary Agency, Ray; Literary Bridge, The; Lyceum Creative Properties, Inc.; Maccoby Literary Agency, Gina; Markowitz Literary Agency, Barbara; Marmur Associates Ltd., Mildred; Merhige-Merdon Marketing/Promo Co. Inc., Greg; Naggar Literary Agency, Jean V.; Norma-Lewis Agency, The; Parks Agency, The Richard; Picard Literary Agent, Alison J.; Raymond, Literary Agent, Charlotte Cecil; Rosenthal Literary Agency, Jean; Rubenstein Literary Agency, Inc., Pesha; Shepard Agency, The; Singer Literary Agency Inc., Evelyn; Wald Associates, Inc., Mary Jack; Wallace Literary Agency, Bess; Westchester Literary Agency, Inc.; Writers House

Language/literature/criticism. Ajlouny Agency, The Joseph S.; Bach Literary Agency, Julian; Balkin Agency, Inc.; Boates Literary Agency, Reid; Brandt & Brandt Literary Agents Inc.; Cantrell-Colas Inc., Literary Agency; Cole And Lubenow: Books; Darhansoff & Verrill Literary Agents; Educational Design Services, Inc.; Fallon Literary Agency, The; Fuhrman Literary Agency, Candice; Gregory Associates, Maia; Hawkins & Associates, Inc., John; Lincoln Literary Agency, Ray; Lyceum Creative Properties, Inc.; Miller Associates, Roberta D.; New England Publishing Associates, Inc.; Parks Agency, The Richard; Quicksilver Books-Literary Agents; Riverside Literary Agency; Rose Literary Agency; Roth Literary Agency, The; Schmidt Literary Agency, Harold; Seligman, Literary Agent, Lynn; Shepard Agency, The; Siegel Literary Agency, Bobbe; Stauffer Associates, Nancy; Stern Literary Agency, Gloria; Wald Associates, Inc., Mary Jack; Westchester Literary Agency, Inc.

Military/war. A.M.C. Literary Agency; Acton, Dystel, Leone & Jaffe, Inc.; Allan Agency, Lee; Bach Literary Agency, Julian; Brandt & Brandt Literary Agents Inc.; Cantrell-Colas Inc., Literary Agency; Carvainis Agency, Inc., Maria; Curtis Associates, Inc., Richard; Diamond Literary Agency, Inc.; Dijkstra Literary Agency, Sandra; Ducas, Robert; Educational Design Services, Inc.; Ellenberg Literary Agency, Ethan; Garon-Brooke Assoc. Inc., Jay; Gartenberg, Literary Agent, Max; Hawkins & Associates, Inc., John; Hull House Literary Agency; J de S Associates Inc.; Jarvis & Co., Inc., Sharon; Ketz Agency, Louise B.; McGrath, Helen; Marmur Associates Ltd., Mildred; Merhige-Merdon Marketing/Promo Co. Inc., Greg; New England Publishing Associates, Inc.; Parks Agency, The Richard; Peter Associates, Inc., James; Picard Literary Agent, Alison J.; Riverside Literary Agency; Rose Literary Agency; Schmidt Literary Agency, Harold; Spitzer Literary Agency, Philip G.; Wald Associates, Inc., Mary Jack; Wallace Literary Agency, Bess; Westchester Literary Agency, Inc.; Writers House

Money/finance/economics. Acton, Dystel, Leone & Jaffe, Inc.; Allan Agency, Lee; Appleseeds Management; Axelrod Agency, The; Brandt & Brandt Literary Agents Inc.; Cantrell-Colas Inc., Literary Agency; Carvainis Agency, Inc., Maria; Clausen Associates, Connie; Cole And Lubenow: Books; Curtis Associates, Inc., Richard; Diamant, The Writer's Workshop, Inc., Anita; Diamond Literary Agency, Inc.; Dijkstra Literary Agency, Sandra; Ducas, Robert; Educational Design Services, Inc.; Ellenberg Literary Agency, Ethan; Fogelman Publishing Interests Inc.; Fuhrman Literary Agency, Candice; Gartenberg, Literary Agent, Max; Hawkins & Associates, Inc., John; Hull House Literary Agency; Jarvis & Co., Inc., Sharon; Jones Literary Agency, Lloyd; Ketz Agency, Louise B.; Lampack Agency, Inc., Peter; Lasbury Literary Agency, M. Sue; Lincoln Literary Agency, Ray; Literary Bridge, The; Los Angeles Literary Associates; Love Literary Agency, Nancy; Mann Agency, Carol; Marmur Associates Ltd., Mildred; Multimedia Product Development, Inc.; Naggar Literary Agency, Jean V.; New England Publishing Associates, Inc.; Noetzli Literary Agency, Regula; Parks Agency, The Richard; Peter Associates, Inc., James; Raymond, Literary Agent, Charlotte Cecil; Riverside Literary Agency; Rock Literary Agency; Rose Literary Agency; Schmidt Literary Agency, Harold; Seligman, Literary Agent, Lynn; Shepard Agency, The; Singer Literary Agency Inc., Evelyn; Steele & Co., Ltd., Lyle; Stern Literary Agency, Gloria; Wald Associates, Inc., Mary Jack; Wieser & Wieser, Inc.; Writers House

Music/dance/theater/film. Acton, Dystel, Leone & Jaffe, Inc.; Agency Chicago; Allan Agency, Lee; Andrews & Associates Inc., Bart; Appleseeds Management; Axelrod Agency, The; Bach Literary Agency, Julian; Balkin Agency, Inc.; Brandt & Brandt Literary Agents Inc.; Clausen Associates, Connie; Cole And Lubenow: Books; Curtis Associates, Inc., Richard; Diamond Literary Agency, Inc.; Dijkstra Literary Agency, Sandra; Fuhrman Literary Agency, Candice; Garon-Brooke Assoc. Inc., Jay; Gartenberg, Literary Agent, Max; Gotler Metropolitan Talent Agency, Joel; Gregory Associates, Maia; Hawkins & Associates, Inc., John; Hull House Literary Agency; KC Communications; Kouts, Liteary Agent, Barbara S.; Lincoln Literary Agency, Ray; Literary Group, The; Lyceum Creative Properties, Inc.; Maccoby Literary Agency, Gina; Marmur Associates Ltd., Mildred; Merhige-Merdon Marketing/Promo Co. Inc., Greg; Naggar Literary Agency, Jean V.; Nathan, Ruth; Parks Agency, The Richard; Perkins Associates, L.; Picard Literary Agent, Alison J.; Riverside Literary Agency; Rose Literary Agency; Roth Literary Agency, The; Schmidt Literary Agency, Harold; Seligman, Literary Agent, Lynn; Shepard Agency, The; Siegel Literary Agency, Bobbe; Spitzer Literary Agency, Philip G.; Stauffer Associates, Nancy; Wald Associates, Inc., Mary Jack; Wecksler-Incomco; Weingel-Fidel Agency, The; Westchester Literary Agency, Inc.; Writers House; Zeckendorf Assoc. Inc., Susan

Nature/environment. Acton, Dystel, Leone & Jaffe, Inc.; Allan Agency, Lee; Axelrod Agency, The;

Bach Literary Agency, Julian; Balkin Agency, Inc.; Boates Literary Agency, Reid; Brandt & Brandt Literary Agents Inc.; Cantrell-Colas Inc., Literary Agency; Clausen Associates, Connie; Cole And Lubenow: Books; Collin Literary Agent, Frances; Crown International Literature and Arts Agency, Bonnie R.; Darhansoff & Verrill Literary Agents; Diamant, The Writer's Workshop, Inc., Anita; Diamond Literary Agency, Inc.; Dijkstra Literary Agency, Sandra; Ducas, Robert; Ellenberg Literary Agency, Ethan; Fuhrman Literary Agency, Candice; Gartenberg, Literary Agent, Max; Hawkins & Associates, Inc., John; Jarvis & Co., Inc., Sharon; Kouts, Liteary Agent, Barbara S.; Lasbury Literary Agency, M. Sue; Levant & Wales, Literary Agency, Inc.; Lincoln Literary Agency, Ray; Literary Bridge, The; Literary Group, The; Love Literary Agency, Nancy; Lyceum Creative Properties, Inc.; Marmur Associates Ltd., Mildred; Multimedia Product Development, Inc.; New England Publishing Associates, Inc.; Noetzli Literary Agency, Regula; Parks Agency, The Richard; Picard Literary Agent, Alison J.; Quicksilver Books-Literary Agents; Raymond, Literary Agent, Charlotte Cecil; Riverside Literary Agency; Roth Literary Agency, The; Rubenstein Literary Agency, Inc., Pesha; Schaffner Agency, Inc.; Schmidt Literary Agency, Harold; Seligman, Literary Agent, Lynn; Shepard Agency, The; Siegel Literary Agency, Bobbe; Spitzer Literary Agency, Philip G.; Stauffer Associates, Nancy; Steele & Co., Ltd., Lyle; Wald Associates, Inc., Mary Jack; Wecksler-Incomco; Westchester Literary Agency, Inc.; Wieser & Wieser, Inc.; Writers House

New age/metaphysics. Bach Literary Agency, Julian; Cantrell-Colas Inc., Literary Agency; Clark Literary Agency, SJ; Diamant, The Writer's Workshop, Inc., Anita; Dijkstra Literary Agency, Sandra; Ellenberg Literary Agency, Ethan; Fuhrman Literary Agency, Candice; Hawkins & Associates, Inc., John; J de S Associates Inc.; Jarvis & Co., Inc., Sharon; Literary and Creative Artists Agency; Literary Bridge, The; Lyceum Creative Properties, Inc.; Naggar Literary Agency, Jean V.; Noetzli Literary Agency, Regula; Picard Literary Agent, Alison J.; Quicksilver Books-Literary Agents; Rees Literary Agency, Helen; Riverside Literary Agency; Schmidt Literary Agency, Harold; Steele & Co., Ltd., Lyle

Open to all nonfiction categories. Allen Literary Agency, Linda; Barrett Books Inc., Loretta; Brown Ltd., Curtis; Bykofsky Associates, Sheree; Cleaver Inc., Diane; Cohen Literary Agency Ltd., Hy; Collier Associates; Congdon Associates, Inc., Don; Doyen Literary Services, Inc.; Dupree/Miller and Associates Inc. Literary; Eisenberg Literary Agency, Vicki; Ellison Inc., Nicholas; Goldfarb & Associates, Ronald; Goodman Associates; Gotham Art & Literary Agency Inc.; Greenburger Associates, Stanford J.; Gusay Literary Agency, The Charlotte; Hamilburg Agency, The Mitchell J.; Herman Agency, Inc., The Jeff; International Publisher Associates Inc.; Kirchoff/Wohlberg, Inc., Authors' Representation Division; Larsen/Elizabeth Pomada Literary Agents, Michael; Martell Agency, The; MGA Agency Inc.; Ober Associates, Harold; Pelter, Rodney; Snell Literary Agency, Michael; Writers' Productions

Photography. Diamond Literary Agency, Inc.; Hawkins & Associates, Inc., John; KC Communications; Kidde, Hoyt & Picard; Merhige-Merdon Marketing/Promo Co. Inc., Greg; Roth Literary Agency, The; Wald Associates, Inc., Mary Jack; Wecksler-Incomco; Westchester Literary Agency, Inc.

Psychology. Acton, Dystel, Leone & Jaffe, Inc.; Agents Inc. for Medical and Mental Health Professionals; Allan Agency, Lee; Appleseeds Management; Bach Literary Agency, Julian; Boates Literary Agency, Reid; Brandt & Brandt Literary Agents Inc.; Cantrell-Colas Inc., Literary Agency; Carvainis Agency, Inc., Maria; Clausen Associates, Connie; Cole And Lubenow: Books; Diamant, The Writer's Workshop, Inc., Anita; Diamond Literary Agency, Inc.; Dijkstra Literary Agency, Sandra; Ellenberg Literary Agency, Ethan; Fallon Literary Agency, The; Fuhrman Literary Agency, Candice; Garon-Brooke Assoc. Inc., Jay; Gartenberg, Literary Agent, Max; Hawkins & Associates, Inc., John; Jarvis & Co., Inc., Sharon; Jones Literary Agency, Lloyd; Kidde, Hoyt & Picard; Klinger, Inc., Harvey; Kouts, Liteary Agent, Barbara S.; Lasbury Literary Agency, M. Sue; Levant & Wales, Literary Agency, Inc.; Lincoln Literary Agency, Ray; Literary Bridge, The; Literary Group, The; Love Literary Agency, Nancy; Lyceum Creative Properties, Inc.; McGrath, Helen; Mann Agency, Carol; Naggar Literary Agency, Jean V.; New England Publishing Associates, Inc.; Noetzli Literary Agency, Regula; Parks Agency, The Richard; Peter Associates, Inc., James; Picard Literary Agent, Alison J.; Protter Literary Agent, Susan Ann; Quicksilver Books-Literary Agents; Raymond, Literary Agent, Charlotte Cecil; Rees Literary Agency, Helen; Riverside Literary Agency; Rose Literary Agency; Roth Literary Agency, The; Schmidt Literary Agency, Harold; Seligman, Literary Agent, Lynn; Shepard Agency, The; Siegel Literary Agency, Bobbe; Spitzer Literary Agency, Philip G.; Steele & Co., Ltd., Lyle; Stern Literary Agency, Gloria; Teal Literary Agency, Patricia; Wallace Literary Agency, Bess; Ware Literary Agency, John A.; Weingel-Fidel Agency, The; Westchester Literary Agency, Inc.; Wieser & Wieser, Inc.; Writers House; Zeckendorf Assoc. Inc., Susan

Religious/inspirational. Brandenburgh & Associates Literary Agency; Cole And Lubenow: Books; Curtis Bruce Agency, The; Diamant, The Writer's Workshop, Inc., Anita; Diamond Literary Agency, Inc.; Donlan, Thomas C.; Fuhrman Literary Agency, Candice; Gregory Associates, Maia; Holub & Associates; Kidde, Hoyt & Picard; Marmur Associates Ltd., Mildred; Naggar Literary Agency, Jean V.; Quicksilver Books-Literary Agents; Rees Literary Agency, Helen; Shepard Agency, The; Siegel Literary Agency, Bobbe; Westchester Literary Agency, Inc.

Science/technology. Acton, Dystel, Leone & Jaffe, Inc.; Agents Inc. for Medical and Mental Health

Professionals; Allan Agency, Lee; Axelrod Agency, The; Balkin Agency, Inc.; Boates Literary Agency, Reid; Bova Literary Agency, The Barbara; Brandt & Brandt Literary Agents Inc.; Brown Literary Agency, Inc., Andrea; Cantrell-Colas Inc., Literary Agency; Cole And Lubenow: Books; Curtis Associates, Inc., Richard; Darhansoff & Verrill Literary Agents; de la Haba Agency Inc., The Lois; Diamant, The Writer's Workshop, Inc., Anita; Diamond Literary Agency, Inc.; Dijkstra Literary Agency, Sandra; Ducas, Robert; Educational Design Services, Inc.; Fuhrman Literary Agency, Candice; Gartenberg, Literary Agent, Max; Hawkins & Associates, Inc., John; Jarvis & Co., Inc., Sharon; Ketz Agency, Louise B.; Klinger, Inc., Harvey; Lasbury Literary Agency, M. Sue; Levant & Wales, Literary Agency, Inc.; Levine Literary Agency, Inc., Ellen; Lincoln Literary Agency, Ray; Lipkind Agency, Wendy; Love Literary Agency, Nancy; Lowenstein Associates, Inc.; Marmur Associates Ltd., Mildred; Multimedia Product Development, Inc.; New England Publishing Associates, Inc.; Noetzli Literary Agency, Regula; Parks Agency, The Richard; Picard Literary Agent, Alison J.; Protter Literary Agent, Susan Ann; Rees Literary Agency, Helen; Riverside Literary Agency; Rose Literary Agency; Schmidt Literary Agency, Harold; Seligman, Literary Agent, Lynn; Singer Literary Agency Inc., Evelyn; Steele & Co., Ltd., Lyle; Stern Literary Agency, Gloria; Wald Associates, Inc., Mary Jack; Ware Literary Agency, John A.; Watkins Loomis Agency, Inc.; Weingel-Fidel Agency, The; Writers House; Zeckendorf Assoc. Inc., Susan

Self-help/personal improvement. Acton, Dystel, Leone & Jaffe, Inc.; Agents Inc. for Medical and Mental Health Professionals; Ajlouny Agency, The Joseph S.; Allan Agency, Lee; Appleseeds Management; Bach Literary Agency, Julian; Barrett Literary Agency, Helen; Boates Literary Agency, Reid; Brandt & Brandt Literary Agents Inc.; Cantrell-Colas Inc., Literary Agency; Clausen Associates, Connie; Cole And Lubenow: Books; Columbia Literary Associates, Inc.; Curtis Associates, Inc., Richard; Curtis Bruce Agency, The; Davie Literary Agency, Elaine; Diamant, The Writer's Workshop, Inc., Anita; Diamond Literary Agency, Inc.; Dijkstra Literary Agency, Sandra; Ellenberg Literary Agency, Ethan; Fallon Literary Agency, The; Fields-Rita Scott Inc., Marje; Fogelman Publishing Interests Inc.; Fuhrman Literary Agency, Candice; Garon-Brooke Assoc. Inc., Jay; Gartenberg, Literary Agent, Max; Hawkins & Associates, Inc., John; J de S Associates Inc.; Jarvis & Co., Inc., Sharon; Jones Literary Agency, Lloyd; Kidde, Hoyt & Picard; Klinger, Inc., Harvey; Kouts, Liteary Agent, Barbara S.; Lasbury Literary Agency, M. Sue; Lincoln Literary Agency, Ray; Literary and Creative Artists Agency; Literary Bridge, The; Literary Group, The; Los Angeles Literary Associates; Love Literary Agency, Nancy; McGrath, Helen; Mann Agency, Carol; Merhige-Merdon Marketing/Promo Co. Inc., Greg; Naggar Literary Agency, Jean V.; New England Publishing Associates, Inc.; Noetzli Literary Agency, Regula; Odenwald Connection, The; Parks Agency, The Richard; Peter Associates, Inc., James; Picard Literary Agent, Alison J.; Quicksilver Books-Literary Agents; Rees Literary Agency, Helen; Riverside Literary Agency; Rose Literary Agency; Roth Literary Agency, The; Schmidt Literary Agency, Harold; Seligman, Literary Agent, Lynn; Shepard Agency, The; Siegel Literary Agency, Bobbe; Singer Literary Agency Inc., Evelyn; Stauffer Associates, Nancy; Steele & Co., Ltd., Lyle; Stern Literary Agency, Gloria; Teal Literary Agency, Patricia; Weiner Literary Agency, Cherry; Westchester Literary Agency, Inc.; Writers House

Sociology. Agents Inc. for Medical and Mental Health Professionals; Ajlouny Agency, The Joseph S.; Balkin Agency, Inc.; Brandt & Brandt Literary Agents Inc.; Cantrell-Colas Inc., Literary Agency; Diamond Literary Agency, Inc.; Dijkstra Literary Agency, Sandra; Educational Design Services, Inc.; Hawkins & Associates, Inc., John; Hull House Literary Agency; J de S Associates Inc.; Lasbury Literary Agency, M. Sue; Lincoln Literary Agency, Ray; Lipkind Agency, Wendy; Literary Group, The; Love Literary Agency, Nancy; Lyceum Creative Properties, Inc.; Mann Agency, Carol; Merhige-Merdon Marketing/Promo Co. Inc., Greg; Naggar Literary Agency, Jean V.; New England Publishing Associates, Inc.; Noetzli Literary Agency, Regula; Parks Agency, The Richard; Paton Literary Agency, Kathi J.; Raymond, Literary Agent, Charlotte Cecil; Rees Literary Agency, Helen; Rose Literary Agency; Roth Literary Agency, The; Schmidt Literary Agency, Harold; Seligman, Literary Agent, Lynn; Shepard Agency, The; Spitzer Literary Agency, Philip G.; Stauffer Associates, Nancy; Steele & Co., Ltd., Lyle; Stern Literary Agency, Gloria; Wald Associates, Inc., Mary Jack; Weiner Literary Agency, Cherry; Weingel-Fidel Agency, The; Zeckendorf Assoc. Inc., Susan

Sports. Acton, Dystel, Leone & Jaffe, Inc.; Agency Chicago; Agents Inc. for Medical and Mental Health Professionals; Allan Agency, Lee; Bach Literary Agency, Julian; Black Literary Agency, Inc., David; Boates Literary Agency, Reid; Brandt & Brandt Literary Agents Inc.; Cole And Lubenow: Books; Curtis Associates, Inc., Richard; Diamant, The Writer's Workshop, Inc., Anita; Dijkstra Literary Agency, Sandra; Ducas, Robert; Ellenberg Literary Agency, Ethan; Fields-Rita Scott Inc., Marje; Fuhrman Literary Agency, Candice; Gartenberg, Literary Agent, Max; Hawkins & Associates, Inc., John; J de S Associates Inc.; Jones Literary Agency, Lloyd; Ketz Agency, Louise B.; Klinger, Inc., Harvey; Lincoln Literary Agency, Ray; Literary Bridge, The; Literary Group, The; McGrath, Helen; Marmur Associates Ltd., Mildred; Merhige-Merdon Marketing/Promo Co. Inc., Greg; Noetzli Literary Agency, Regula; Paton Literary Agency, Kathi J.; Picard Literary Agent, Alison J.; Rees Literary Agency, Helen; Rose Literary Agency; Shepard Agency, The; Siegel Literary Agency, Bobbe; Spitzer Literary Agency, Philip G.; Stauffer Associates, Nancy; Steele & Co., Ltd., Lyle; Stern Literary Agency, Gloria; Wald Associates, Inc., Mary Jack; Ware Literary Agency, John A.; Wohl Literary Agency, Gary S.

Translations. Balkin Agency, Inc.; Crown International Literature and Arts Agency, Bonnie R.; Dijkstra Literary Agency, Sandra; Donlan, Thomas C.; J de S Associates Inc.; Lyceum Creative Properties, Inc.; Raymond, Literary Agent, Charlotte Cecil; Rubenstein Literary Agency, Inc., Pesha; Schmidt Literary Agency, Harold; Seligman, Literary Agent, Lynn; Stauffer Associates, Nancy; Wald Associates, Inc., Mary Jack; Watkins Loomis Agency, Inc.; Wieser & Wieser, Inc.

True crime/investigative. A.M.C. Literary Agency; Acton, Dystel, Leone & Jaffe, Inc.; Allan Agency, Lee; Appleseeds Management; Bach Literary Agency, Julian; Balkin Agency, Inc.; Barrett Literary Agency, Helen; Boates Literary Agency, Reid; Brandt & Brandt Literary Agents Inc.; Cantrell-Colas Inc., Literary Agency; Carvainis Agency, Inc., Maria; Clausen Associates, Connie; Cohen, Inc. Literary Agency, Ruth; Collin Literary Agent, Frances; Curtis Associates, Inc., Richard; Davie Literary Agency, Elaine; Diamant, The Writer's Workshop, Inc., Anita; Diamond Literary Agency, Inc.; Dijkstra Literary Agency, Sandra; Ducas, Robert; Fields-Rita Scott Inc., Marje; Fogelman Publishing Interests Inc.; Fuhrman Literary Agency, Candice; Garon-Brooke Assoc. Inc., Jay; Gartenberg, Literary Agent, Max; Gotler Metropolitan Talent Agency, Joel; Hawkins & Associates, Inc., John; Hull House Literary Agency; Jarvis & Co., Inc., Sharon; Jones Literary Agency, Lloyd; Ketz Agency, Louise B.; Klinger, Inc., Harvey; Lampack Agency, Inc., Peter; Lasbury Literary Agency, M. Sue; Literary Bridge, The; Literary Group, The; Love Literary Agency, Nancy; Lyceum Creative Properties, Inc.; Mann Agency, Carol; Marmur Associates Ltd., Mildred; Merhige-Merdon Marketing/Promo Co. Inc., Greg; Multimedia Product Development, Inc.; Naggar Literary Agency, Jean V.; New England Publishing Associates, Inc.; Noetzli Literary Agency, Regula; Parks Agency, The Richard; Picard Literary Agent, Alison J.; Quicksilver Books-Literary Agents; Raymond, Literary Agent, Charlotte Cecil; Rees Literary Agency, Helen; Riverside Literary Agency; Rose Literary Agency; Roth Literary Agency, The; Rubenstein Literary Agency, Inc., Pesha; Schmidt Literary Agency, Harold; Seligman, Literary Agent, Lynn; Siegel Literary Agency, Bobbe; Spitzer Literary Agency, Philip G.; Steele & Co., Ltd., Lyle; Stern Literary Agency, Gloria; Teal Literary Agency, Patricia; Wald Associates, Inc., Mary Jack; Wallace Literary Agency, Bess; Ware Literary Agency, John A.; Weingel-Fidel Agency, The; Westchester Literary Agency, Inc.; Wieser & Wieser, Inc.; Writers House; Zeckendorf Assoc. Inc., Susan

Women's issues/women's studies. A.M.C. Literary Agency; Acton, Dystel, Leone & Jaffe, Inc.; Bach Literary Agency, Julian; Barrett Literary Agency, Helen; Bartczak Associates Inc., Gene; Boates Literary Agency, Reid; Borchardt Inc., Georges; Brandt & Brandt Literary Agents Inc.; Cantrell-Colas Inc., Literary Agency; Carvainis Agency, Inc., Maria; Clausen Associates, Connie; Cohen, Inc. Literary Agency, Ruth; Crown International Literature and Arts Agency, Bonnie R.; Davie Literary Agency, Elaine; Diamant, The Writer's Workshop, Inc., Anita; Diamond Literary Agency, Inc.; Dijkstra Literary Agency, Sandra; Educational Design Services, Inc.; Elmo Agency Inc., Ann; Fallon Literary Agency, The; Fogelman Publishing Interests Inc.; Fuhrman Literary Agency, Candice; Gartenberg, Literary Agent, Max; Hawkins & Associates, Inc., John; Jones Literary Agency, Lloyd; Kidde, Hoyt & Picard; Klinger, Inc., Harvey; Kouts, Liteary Agent, Barbara S.; Kroll Literary Agency, Edite; Lasbury Literary Agency, M. Sue; Levine Literary Agency, Inc., Ellen; Lincoln Literary Agency, Ray; Literary Bridge, The; Literary Group, The; Love Literary Agency, Nancy; Maccoby Literary Agency, Gina; McGrath, Helen; Mann Agency, Carol; Marmur Associates Ltd., Mildred; Merhige-Merdon Marketing/Promo Co. Inc., Greg; Naggar Literary Agency, Jean V.; New England Publishing Associates, Inc.; Noetzli Literary Agency, Regula; Parks Agency, The Richard; Paton Literary Agency, Kathi J.; Picard Literary Agent, Alison J.; Raymond, Literary Agent, Charlotte Cecil; Rees Literary Agency, Helen; Riverside Literary Agency; Rose Literary Agency; Roth Literary Agency, The; Schmidt Literary Agency, Harold; Seligman, Literary Agent, Lynn; Shepard Agency, The; Siegel Literary Agency, Bobbe; Stauffer Associates, Nancy; Stern Literary Agency, Gloria; Teal Literary Agency, Patricia; Weingel-Fidel Agency, The; Writers House; Zeckendorf Assoc. Inc., Susan

Fee-charging agents/Fiction

Action/Adventure. Ahearn Agency, Inc., The; Alden—Literary Service, Farel T.; Anthony Agency, Joseph; Argonaut Literary Agency; Authors' Literary Agency; Authors' Marketing Services Ltd.; Brady Literary Management; Browne Ltd., Pema; Chadd-Stevens Literary Agency; Cook Agency, Bruce; Creative Concepts Literary Agency; Dorese Agency Ltd.; Fishbein Ltd., Frieda; Flaherty, Literary Agent, Joyce A.; Flannery White and Stone; ForthWrite Literary Agency; Gladden Unlimited; Hamilton's Literary Agency, Andrew; Independent Publishing Agency; Iorio, Esq., Gary F.; Kaltman Literary Agency, Larry; Kellock & Associates Ltd., J.; Kern Literary Agency, Natasha; Keyser Literary Agency; Lighthouse Literary Agency; Marshall Agency, The Evan; Nelson Literary Agency & Lecture Bureau, BK; Northwest Literary Services; Olesha Agency, Andrea; Panettieri Agency, The; Pegasus International, Inc., Literary & Film Agents; Peterson Associates Literary Agency; Pine Associates, Inc, Arthur; PMA Literary and Film Management, Inc.; Shoestring Press; Southern Literary Agency; Southern Writers; Steinberg Literary Agency, Michael; Wallerstein Agency, The Gerry B.; Waterside Productions, Inc.; West Coast Literary Associates; Wilshire Literary Agency, The

Cartoon/comic. Colby: Literary Agency; Cook Agency, Bruce; Hamilton's Literary Agency, Andrew; Independent Publishing Agency; Lighthouse Literary Agency; Singer Media Corporation

Confessional. Ackerman Literary services; Anthony Agency, Joseph; Argonaut Literary Agency; Author Author Literary Agency; Hamilton's Literary Agency, Andrew; Independent Publishing Agency; Kaltman Literary Agency, Larry; Northwest Literary Services; Pegasus International, Inc., Literary & Film Agents; Strong, Marianne; Zelasky Literary Agency, Tom

Contemporary issues. Ahearn Agency, Inc., The; Argonaut Literary Agency; Author Author Literary Agency; Authors' Literary Agency; Brady Literary Management; Browne Ltd., Pema; Chester, Literary Agency, Linda; Connor Literary Agency; Creative Concepts Literary Agency; Dorese Agency Ltd.; Fishbein Ltd., Frieda; Flaherty, Literary Agent, Joyce A.; Flannery White and Stone; Hamilton's Literary Agency, Andrew; Independent Publishing Agency; Iorio, Esq., Gary F.; Kaltman Literary Agency, Larry; Kellock & Associates Ltd., J.; Keyser Literary Agency; Law Offices of Robert L. Fenton PC; Lighthouse Literary Agency; Marshall Agency, The Evan; Nelson Literary Agency & Lecture Bureau, BK; Northwest Literary Services; Olesha Agency, Andrea; Pegasus International, Inc., Literary & Film Agents; Sebastian Literary Agency; Southern Writers; State of the Art Ltd.; Steinberg Literary Agency, Michael; Tiger Moon Enterprises; Wallerstein Agency, The Gerry B.; Waterside Productions, Inc.; West Coast Literary Associates; Zelasky Literary Agency, Tom

Detective/police/crime. Ackerman Literary Services; Ahearn Agency, Inc., The; Alden—Literary Service, Farel T.; Anthony Agency, Joseph; Argonaut Literary Agency; Author Author Literary Agency; Authors' Literary Agency; Authors' Marketing Services Ltd.; Brady Literary Management; Browne Ltd., Pema; Colby: Literary Agency; Creative Concepts Literary Agency; Dorese Agency Ltd.; Fishbein Ltd., Frieda; Flaherty, Literary Agent, Joyce A.; Hamilton's Literary Agency, Andrew; Handaris, Literary Agency, Marisa; Independent Publishing Agency; Iorio, Esq., Gary F.; Kaltman Literary Agency, Larry; Kellock & Associates Ltd., J.; Law Offices of Robert L. Fenton PC; Lighthouse Literary Agency; Marshall Agency, The Evan; Northwest Literary Services; Oceanic Press; Panettieri Agency, The; Pegasus International, Inc., Literary & Film Agents; Pine Associates, Inc, Arthur; Sebastian Literary Agency; Singer Media Corporation; Southern Literary Agency; Southern Writers; Steinberg Literary Agency, Michael; Strong, Marianne; Toomey Associates, Jeanne; Wallerstein Agency, The Gerry B.; Waterside Productions, Inc.; Watt & Associates, Sandra; West Coast Literary Associates; Wilshire Literary Agency, The; Zelasky Literary Agency, Tom

Erotica. Anthony Agency, Joseph; Author Author Literary Agency; Chadd-Stevens Literary Agency; Hamilton's Literary Agency, Andrew; Independent Publishing Agency; Iorio, Esq., Gary F.; Kaltman Literary Agency, Larry; Northwest Literary Services; Oceanic Press; Pegasus International, Inc., Literary & Film Agents; Peterson Associates Literary Agency; Singer Media Corporation; Steinberg Literary Agency, Michael

Ethnic. Ahearn Agency, Inc., The; Chester, Literary Agency, Linda; Connor Literary Agency; Dorese Agency Ltd.; Flannery White and Stone; Hamilton's Literary Agency, Andrew; Independent Publishing Agency; Kaltman Literary Agency, Larry; Kellock & Associates Ltd., J.; Keyser Literary Agency; Lighthouse Literary Agency; Northwest Literary Services; Olesha Agency, Andrea; Pegasus International, Inc., Literary & Film Agents; Sebastian Literary Agency

Experimental. Chadd-Stevens Literary Agency; Flannery White and Stone; Independent Publishing Agency; Iorio, Esq., Gary F.; Kellock & Associates Ltd., J.; Keyser Literary Agency; Lighthouse Literary Agency; Northwest Literary Services; Oceanic Press; Olesha Agency, Andrea; Pegasus International, Inc., Literary & Film Agents; West Coast Literary Associates

Family Saga. Ackerman Literary Services; Ahearn Agency, Inc., The; Alden—Literary Service, Farel T.; Brady Literary Management; Cook Agency, Bruce; Creative Concepts Literary Agency; Dorese Agency Ltd.; Fishbein Ltd., Frieda; Flaherty, Literary Agent, Joyce A.; Flannery White and Stone; ForthWrite Literary Agency; Hamilton's Literary Agency, Andrew; Kellock & Associates Ltd., J.; Lighthouse Literary Agency; Marcil Literary Agency, The Denise; Marshall Agency, The Evan; Nelson Literary Agency & Lecture Bureau, BK; Northwest Literary Services; Oceanic Press; Olesha Agency, Andrea; Panettieri Agency, The; Sebastian Literary Agency; Southern Writers; Strong, Marianne; Tiger Moon Enterprises; Wallerstein Agency, The Gerry B.; Zelasky Literary Agency, Tom

Fantasy. Ahearn Agency, Inc., The; Alden—Literary Service, Farel T.; Anthony Agency, Joseph; Chadd-Stevens Literary Agency; Cook Agency, Bruce; Fishbein Ltd., Frieda; Gladden Unlimited; Independent Publishing Agency; Iorio, Esq., Gary F.; Kellock & Associates Ltd., J.; Northwest Literary Services; Olesha Agency, Andrea; Pegasus International, Inc., Literary & Film Agents; Peterson Associates Literary Agency; Singer Media Corporation; Southern Writers

Feminist. Ahearn Agency, Inc., The; Author Author Literary Agency; Browne Ltd., Pema; Chester, Literary Agency, Linda; Dorese Agency Ltd.; Fishbein Ltd., Frieda; Flaherty, Literary Agent, Joyce A.; Flannery White and Stone; Independent Publishing Agency; Kellock & Associates Ltd., J.; Keyser Literary Agency; Lighthouse Literary Agency; Nelson Literary Agency & Lecture Bureau, BK; Northwest Literary

Services; Olesha Agency, Andrea; PMA Literary and Film Management, Inc.; Southern Writers; State of the Art Ltd.; Zelasky Literary Agency, Tom

Gay. Ahearn Agency, Inc., The; Author Author Literary Agency; Dorese Agency Ltd.; Flannery White and Stone; Hamilton's Literary Agency, Andrew; Olesha Agency, Andrea; Sebastian Literary Agency; Southern Writers

Glitz. Ackerman Literary Services; Ahearn Agency, Inc., The; Brady Literary Management; Browne Ltd., Pema; Connor Literary Agency; Creative Concepts Literary Agency; Dorese Agency Ltd.; JLM Literary Agents; Kellock & Associates Ltd., J.; Law Offices of Robert L. Fenton PC; Marshall Agency, The Evan; Olesha Agency, Andrea; Panettieri Agency, The; Robb Literary Properties, Sherry; Singer Media Corporation; Southern Writers; Wallerstein Agency, The Gerry B.; Waterside Productions, Inc.; Watt & Associates, Sandra

Historical. Ackerman Literary Services; Ahearn Agency, Inc., The; Alden—Literary Service, Farel T.; Argonaut Literary Agency; Brady Literary Management; Browne Ltd., Pema; Cook Agency, Bruce; Creative Concepts Literary Agency; Dorese Agency Ltd.; Fishbein Ltd., Frieda; Flaherty, Literary Agent, Joyce A.; Flannery White and Stone; ForthWrite Literary Agency; Handaris, Literary Agency, Marisa; Independent Publishing Agency; Iorio, Esq., Gary F.; Kellock & Associates Ltd., J.; Kern Literary Agency, Natasha; Keyser Literary Agency; Lee Shore Agency; Lighthouse Literary Agency; Marcil Literary Agency, The Denise; Marshall Agency, The Evan; Northwest Literary Services; Panettieri Agency, The; Pegasus International, Inc., Literary & Film Agents; Sebastian Literary Agency; Southern Writers; Tiger Moon Enterprises; Wallerstein Agency, The Gerry B.; West Coast Literary Associates; Zelasky Literary Agency, Tom

Humor/satire. Ahearn Agency, Inc., The; Alden—Literary Service, Farel T.; Argonaut Literary Agency; Browne Ltd., Pema; Colby: Literary Agency; Connor Literary Agency; Cook Agency, Bruce; Fishbein Ltd., Frieda; Flannery White and Stone; Hamilton's Literary Agency, Andrew; Independent Publishing Agency; Kaltman Literary Agency, Larry; Kellock & Associates Ltd., J.; Keyser Literary Agency; Law Offices of Robert L. Fenton PC; Lighthouse Literary Agency; Northwest Literary Services; Olesha Agency, Andrea; Pegasus International, Inc., Literary & Film Agents; Peterson Associates Literary Agency; Southern Literary Agency; Southern Writers; Wallerstein Agency, The Gerry B.

Juvenile. Ahearn Agency, Inc., The; Alden—Literary Service, Farel T.; Author Author Literary Agency; Browne Ltd., Pema; Catalog Literary Agency, The; Cook Agency, Bruce; Flannery White and Stone; ForthWrite Literary Agency; Hamersfield Agency, The; Hamilton's Literary Agency, Andrew; Independent Publishing Agency; Kellock & Associates Ltd., J.; Lighthouse Literary Agency; March Media Inc.; Northwest Literary Services; Olesha Agency, Andrea; Panettieri Agency, The; Pegasus International, Inc., Literary & Film Agents; Popkin, Julie; Southern Writers; Zelasky Literary Agency, Tom

Lesbian. Ahearn Agency, Inc., The; Author Author Literary Agency; Dorese Agency Ltd.; Flannery White and Stone; Hamilton's Literary Agency, Andrew; Olesha Agency, Andrea; Southern Writers

Literary. Ahearn Agency, Inc., The; Author Author Literary Agency; Authors' Literary Agency; Brady Literary Management; Browne Ltd., Pema; Chester, Literary Agency, Linda; Connor Literary Agency; Cook Agency, Bruce; Creative Concepts Literary Agency; Dorese Agency Ltd.; Flaherty, Literary Agent, Joyce A.; Flannery White and Stone; ForthWrite Literary Agency; Independent Publishing Agency; Iorio, Esq., Gary F.; Kaltman Literary Agency, Larry; Kellock & Associates Ltd., J.; Keyser Literary Agency; Lighthouse Literary Agency; Nelson Literary Agency & Lecture Bureau, BK; Northwest Literary Services; Olesha Agency, Andrea; Pegasus International, Inc., Literary & Film Agents; Pine Associates, Inc, Arthur; Popkin, Julie; Robb Literary Properties, Sherry; Sebastian Literary Agency; Shoestring Press; Tiger Moon Enterprises; Wallerstein Agency, The Gerry B.; Waterside Productions, Inc.; West Coast Literary Associates; Wilshire Literary Agency, The; Zelasky Literary Agency, Tom

Mainstream. Ackerman Literary Services; Ahearn Agency, Inc., The; Alden—Literary Service, Farel T.; Author Author Literary Agency; Authors' Literary Agency; Brady Literary Management; Browne Ltd., Pema; Catalog Literary Agency, The; Chester, Literary Agency, Linda; Creative Concepts Literary Agency; Dorese Agency Ltd.; Fishbein Ltd., Frieda; Flaherty, Literary Agent, Joyce A.; Flannery White and Stone; ForthWrite Literary Agency; Gladden Unlimited; Independent Publishing Agency; Iorio, Esq., Gary F.; Kaltman Literary Agency, Larry; Kellock & Associates Ltd., J.; Kern Literary Agency, Natasha; Keyser Literary Agency; Lee Shore Agency; Lighthouse Literary Agency; Marshall Agency, The Evan; Nelson Literary Agency & Lecture Bureau, BK; Northwest Literary Services; Oceanic Press; Olesha Agency, Andrea; Panettieri Agency, The; Pegasus International, Inc., Literary & Film Agents; Peterson Associates Literary Agency; Popkin, Julie; Robb Literary Properties, Sherry; Sebastian Literary Agency; Southern Literary Agency; Southern Writers; Steinberg Literary Agency, Michael; Wallerstein Agency, The Gerry B.; Waterside Productions, Inc.; Watt & Associates, Sandra; West Coast Literary Associates; Wilshire Literary Agency, The; Zelasky Literary Agency, Tom

Mystery/suspense. Ackerman Literary Services; Ahearn Agency, Inc., The; Alden—Literary Service,

Farel T.; Anthony Agency, Joseph; Argonaut Literary Agency; Author Author Literary Agency; Authors' Literary Agency; Authors' Marketing Services Ltd.; Brady Literary Management; Browne Ltd., Pema; Chadd-Stevens Literary Agency; Chester, Literary Agency, Linda; Colby: Literary Agency; Connor Literary Agency; Cook Agency, Bruce; Creative Concepts Literary Agency; Dorese Agency Ltd.; Fishbein Ltd., Frieda; Flaherty, Literary Agent, Joyce A.; Flannery White and Stone; ForthWrite Literary Agency; Hamilton's Literary Agency, Andrew; Handaris, Literary Agency, Marisa; Independent Publishing Agency; Iorio, Esq., Gary F.; JLM Literary Agents; Kaltman Literary Agency, Larry; Kellock & Associates Ltd., J.; Kern Literary Agency, Natasha; Law Offices of Robert L. Fenton PC; Lee Shore Agency; Lighthouse Literary Agency; Marshall Agency, The Evan; Nelson Literary Agency & Lecture Bureau, BK; Northwest Literary Services; Oceanic Press; Oceanic Press Service; Olesha Agency, Andrea; Panettieri Agency, The; Pegasus International, Inc., Literary & Film Agents; PMA Literary and Film Management, Inc.; Popkin, Julie; Porcelain, Sidney E.; Robb Literary Properties, Sherry; Sebastian Literary Agency; Singer Media Corporation; Southern Literary Agency; Southern Writers; State of the Art Ltd.; Steinberg Literary Agency, Michael; Wallerstein Agency, The Gerry B.; Waterside Productions, Inc.; Watt & Associates, Sandra; West Coast Literary Associates; Wilshire Literary Agency, The; Zelasky Literary Agency, Tom

Open to all fiction categories. Author Aid Associates; Bernstein Literary Agency, Meredith; Brink Literary Agency, The; Follendore Literary Agency, Joan; Glenmark Literary Agency; Goodkind, Larney; Jenks Agency, Carolyn; Literary Representation South; Morgan Literary Agency, Inc., David H.; New Writing Agency; Northeast Literary Agency; Sullivan Associates, Mark

Picture book. Alden—Literary Service, Farel T.; Brady Literary Management; Browne Ltd., Pema; Connor Literary Agency; Flannery White and Stone; ForthWrite Literary Agency; Independent Publishing Agency; Kellock & Associates Ltd., J.; Lighthouse Literary Agency; Northwest Literary Services; Pegasus International, Inc., Literary & Film Agents; Singer Media Corporation

Psychic/supernatural. Ackerman Literary Services; Ahearn Agency, Inc., The; Alden—Literary Service, Farel T.; Anthony Agency, Joseph; Author Author Literary Agency; Authors' Literary Agency; Brady Literary Management; Browne Ltd., Pema; Chadd-Stevens Literary Agency; Dorese Agency Ltd.; Flaherty, Literary Agent, Joyce A.; Flannery White and Stone; Hamilton's Literary Agency, Andrew; Independent Publishing Agency; JLM Literary Agents; Keyser Literary Agency; Marshall Agency, The Evan; Northwest Literary Services; Oceanic Press; Olesha Agency, Andrea; Panettieri Agency, The; Pegasus International, Inc., Literary & Film Agents; Peterson Associates Literary Agency; Singer Media Corporation; Southern Writers; Tiger Moon Enterprises; Toomey Associates, Jeanne

Regional. Ahearn Agency, Inc., The; Cook Agency, Bruce; Dorese Agency Ltd.; Flannery White and Stone; Keyser Literary Agency; Lighthouse Literary Agency; Olesha Agency, Andrea; Pegasus International, Inc., Literary & Film Agents; Southern Writers; Tiger Moon Enterprises; West Coast Literary Associates

Religious/inspiration. Browne Ltd., Pema; Cook Agency, Bruce; Creative Concepts Literary Agency; Hamilton's Literary Agency, Andrew; Keyser Literary Agency; Northwest Literary Services; Olesha Agency, Andrea; Shoestring Press; Southern Writers; Tiger Moon Enterprises

Romance. Ackerman Literary Services; Ahearn Agency, Inc., The; Anthony Agency, Joseph; Author Author Literary Agency; Authors' Marketing Services Ltd.; Browne Ltd., Pema; Creative Concepts Literary Agency; Fishbein Ltd., Frieda; Flaherty, Literary Agent, Joyce A.; Flannery White and Stone; ForthWrite Literary Agency; Hamilton's Literary Agency, Andrew; Handaris, Literary Agency, Marisa; JLM Literary Agents; Kaltman Literary Agency, Larry; Kellock & Associates Ltd., J.; Kern Literary Agency, Natasha; Keyser Literary Agency; Law Offices of Robert L. Fenton PC; Lee Shore Agency; Marcil Literary Agency, The Denise; Marshall Agency, The Evan; Nelson Literary Agency & Lecture Bureau, BK; Northwest Literary Services; Oceanic Press; Oceanic Press Service; Panettieri Agency, The; Pegasus International, Inc., Literary & Film Agents; Popkin, Julie; Singer Media Corporation; Southern Writers; Strong, Marianne; Wallerstein Agency, The Gerry B.; Waterside Productions, Inc.; West Coast Literary Associates; Zelasky Literary Agency, Tom

Science fiction. Ahearn Agency, Inc., The; Anthony Agency, Joseph; Author Author Literary Agency; Browne Ltd., Pema; Cook Agency, Bruce; Creative Concepts Literary Agency; Fishbein Ltd., Frieda; Flannery White and Stone; Gladden Unlimited; Iorio, Esq., Gary F.; Kellock & Associates Ltd., J.; Keyser Literary Agency; Law Offices of Robert L. Fenton PC; Lighthouse Literary Agency; Northwest Literary Services; Oceanic Press; Olesha Agency, Andrea; Pegasus International, Inc., Literary & Film Agents; Peterson Associates Literary Agency; Popkin, Julie; Shoestring Press; Singer Media Corporation; Southern Writers; State of the Art Ltd.; Steinberg Literary Agency, Michael; West Coast Literary Associates; Zelasky Literary Agency, Tom

Sports. Argonaut Literary Agency; Colby: Literary Agency; Connor Literary Agency; Dorese Agency Ltd.; Flaherty, Literary Agent, Joyce A.; Hamilton's Literary Agency, Andrew; Iorio, Esq., Gary F.; Kaltman Literary Agency, Larry; Kellock & Associates Ltd., J.; Law Offices of Robert L. Fenton PC; Lighthouse

Literary Agency; Nelson Literary Agency & Lecture Bureau, BK; Northwest Literary Services; Oceanic Press; Pegasus International, Inc., Literary & Film Agents

Thriller/espionage. Ackerman Literary Services; Ahearn Agency, Inc., The; Anthony Agency, Joseph; Argonaut Literary Agency; Author Author Literary Agency; Authors' Literary Agency; Authors' Marketing Services Ltd.; Brady Literary Management; Browne Ltd., Pema; Colby: Literary Agency; Cook Agency, Bruce; Creative Concepts Literary Agency; Fishbein Ltd., Frieda; Flaherty, Literary Agent, Joyce A.; Flannery White and Stone; Gladden Unlimited; Hamilton's Literary Agency, Andrew; Independent Publishing Agency; Iorio, Esq., Gary F.; Kaltman Literary Agency, Larry; Kellock & Associates Ltd., J.; Kern Literary Agency, Natasha; Law Offices of Robert L. Fenton PC; Lighthouse Literary Agency; Marshall Agency, The Evan; Nelson Literary Agency & Lecture Bureau, BK; Northwest Literary Services; Oceanic Press; Panettieri Agency, The; Pegasus International, Inc., Literary & Film Agents; Peterson Associates Literary Agency; Pine Associates, Inc, Arthur; PMA Literary and Film Management, Inc.; Sebastian Literary Agency; Shoestring Press; Singer Media Corporation; Southern Literary Agency; Southern Writers; Steinberg Literary Agency, Michael; Strong, Marianne; Toomey Associates, Jeanne; Wallerstein Agency, The Gerry B.; Waterside Productions, Inc.; Watt & Associates, Sandra; West Coast Literary Associates; Zelasky Literary Agency, Tom

Westerns/frontier. Ahearn Agency, Inc., The; Argonaut Literary Agency; Brady Literary Management; Colby: Literary Agency; Flannery White and Stone; Hamilton's Literary Agency, Andrew; Handaris, Literary Agency, Marisa; Iorio, Esq., Gary F.; Kellock & Associates Ltd., J.; Kern Literary Agency, Natasha; Keyser Literary Agency; Law Offices of Robert L. Fenton PC; Lee Shore Agency; Lighthouse Literary Agency; Northwest Literary Services; Oceanic Press; Pegasus International, Inc., Literary & Film Agents; Sebastian Literary Agency; Shoestring Press; Singer Media Corporation; Southern Writers; Wallerstein Agency, The Gerry B.; West Coast Literary Associates; Zelasky Literary Agency, Tom

Young adult. Anthony Agency, Joseph; Author Author Literary Agency; Authors' Literary Agency; Brady Literary Management; Browne Ltd., Pema; Chadd-Stevens Literary Agency; Cook Agency, Bruce; Creative Concepts Literary Agency; Dorese Agency Ltd.; Fishbein Ltd., Frieda; Flannery White and Stone; ForthWrite Literary Agency; Hamilton's Literary Agency, Andrew; Independent Publishing Agency; Kaltman Literary Agency, Larry; Kellock & Associates Ltd., J.; Kern Literary Agency, Natasha; Lighthouse Literary Agency; Northwest Literary Services; Oceanic Press; Olesha Agency, Andrea; Panettieri Agency, The; Pegasus International, Inc., Literary & Film Agents; Singer Media Corporation; Southern Writers; Wallerstein Agency, The Gerry B.; Zelasky Literary Agency, Tom

Fee-charging agents/Nonfiction

Agriculture/horticulture. Catalog Literary Agency, The; Creative Concepts Literary Agency; ForthWrite Literary Agency; Lighthouse Literary Agency; Northwest Literary Services; Toomey Associates, Jeanne; Urstadt Inc. Writers and Artists Agency, Susan P.

Animals. Ahearn Agency, Inc., The; Alden—Literary Service, Farel T.; Author Aid Associates; Brady Literary Management; Creative Concepts Literary Agency; Fishbein Ltd., Frieda; Flaherty, Literary Agent, Joyce A.; ForthWrite Literary Agency; Hamilton's Literary Agency, Andrew; Kellock & Associates Ltd., J.; Lighthouse Literary Agency; Nelson Literary Agency & Lecture Bureau, BK; Northwest Literary Services; Pegasus International, Inc., Literary & Film Agents; Toomey Associates, Jeanne; Urstadt Inc. Writers and Artists Agency, Susan P.; Watt & Associates, Sandra

Anthropology. Author Aid Associates; Brink Literary Agency, The; Browne Ltd., Pema; ForthWrite Literary Agency; Independent Publishing Agency; Kellock & Associates Ltd., J.; Lighthouse Literary Agency; Nelson Literary Agency & Lecture Bureau, BK; Pegasus International, Inc., Literary & Film Agents; Peterson Associates Literary Agency; Sebastian Literary Agency; Southern Literary Agency; Sullivan Associates, Mark; Toomey Associates, Jeanne; Urstadt Inc. Writers and Artists Agency, Susan P.; Waterside Productions, Inc.; Watt & Associates, Sandra

Art/architecture/design. Browne Ltd., Pema; Chester, Literary Agency, Linda; Dorese Agency Ltd.; ForthWrite Literary Agency; Independent Publishing Agency; Kellock & Associates Ltd., J.; Lighthouse Literary Agency; Marcil Literary Agency, The Denise; Northwest Literary Services; Pegasus International, Inc., Literary & Film Agents; Popkin, Julie; Sebastian Literary Agency; State of the Art Ltd.; Toomey Associates, Jeanne; Urstadt Inc. Writers and Artists Agency, Susan P.; Waterside Productions, Inc.

Biography/autobiography. Ahearn Agency, Inc., The; Argonaut Literary Agency; Author Aid Associates; Author Author Literary Agency; Authors' Literary Agency; Authors' Marketing Services Ltd.; Brady Literary Management; Browne Ltd., Pema; Chester, Literary Agency, Linda; Cook Agency, Bruce; Creative Concepts Literary Agency; Dorese Agency Ltd.; Fishbein Ltd., Frieda; Flaherty, Literary Agent, Joyce A.; ForthWrite Literary Agency; Gladden Unlimited; Hamilton's Literary Agency, Andrew; Heacock Literary Agency, Inc.; Independent Publishing Agency; Iorio, Esq., Gary F.; JLM Literary Agents; Kellock

& Associates Ltd., J.; Kern Literary Agency, Natasha; Keyser Literary Agency; Law Offices of Robert L. Fenton PC; Lighthouse Literary Agency; Marshall Agency, The Evan; Nelson Literary Agency & Lecture Bureau, BK; Northwest Literary Services; Oceanic Press; Oceanic Press Service; Pegasus International, Inc., Literary & Film Agents; PMA Literary and Film Management, Inc.; Robb Literary Properties, Sherry; Sebastian Literary Agency; Shoestring Press; Singer Media Corporation; Southern Literary Agency; Southern Writers; Steinberg Literary Agency, Michael; Sullivan Associates, Mark; Toomey Associates, Jeanne; Urstadt Inc. Writers and Artists Agency, Susan P.; Waterside Productions, Inc.; West Coast Literary Associates; Zelasky Literary Agency, Tom

Business. Ahearn Agency, Inc., The; Author Author Literary Agency; Authors' Literary Agency; Authors' Marketing Services Ltd.; Browne Ltd., Pema; Catalog Literary Agency, The; Chester, Literary Agency, Linda; Cook Agency, Bruce; Creative Concepts Literary Agency; Dorese Agency Ltd.; Flaherty, Literary Agent, Joyce A.; Flannery White and Stone; ForthWrite Literary Agency; Gladden Unlimited; Hamilton's Literary Agency, Andrew; Heacock Literary Agency, Inc.; Independent Publishing Agency; Iorio, Esq., Gary F.; Kellock & Associates Ltd., J.; Kern Literary Agency, Natasha; Law Offices of Robert L. Fenton PC; Lighthouse Literary Agency; Marcil Literary Agency, The Denise; Marshall Agency, The Evan; Nelson Literary Agency & Lecture Bureau, BK; Oceanic Press; Pegasus International, Inc., Literary & Film Agents; Peterson Associates Literary Agency; Pine Associates, Inc, Arthur; Sebastian Literary Agency; Singer Media Corporation; Southern Literary Agency; Southern Writers; Steinberg Literary Agency, Michael; Sullivan Associates, Mark; Urstadt Inc. Writers and Artists Agency, Susan P.; Waterside Productions, Inc.; Writer's Consulting Group

Child guidance/parenting. Ahearn Agency, Inc., The; Author Aid Associates; Author Author Literary Agency; Authors' Literary Agency; Authors' Marketing Services Ltd.; Brady Literary Management; Browne Ltd., Pema; Catalog Literary Agency, The; Chester, Literary Agency, Linda; Connor Literary Agency; Cook Agency, Bruce; Creative Concepts Literary Agency; Dorese Agency Ltd.; Flaherty, Literary Agent, Joyce A.; Flannery White and Stone; ForthWrite Literary Agency; Hamilton's Literary Agency, Andrew; Heacock Literary Agency, Inc.; Independent Publishing Agency; Kellock & Associates Ltd., J.; Kern Literary Agency, Natasha; Law Offices of Robert L. Fenton PC; Lighthouse Literary Agency; Marcil Literary Agency, The Denise; Marshall Agency, The Evan; Nelson Literary Agency & Lecture Bureau, BK; Northwest Literary Services; Oceanic Press; Panettieri Agency, The; Pegasus International, Inc., Literary & Film Agents; Sebastian Literary Agency; Singer Media Corporation; Southern Literary Agency; Southern Writers; Steinberg Literary Agency, Michael; Urstadt Inc. Writers and Artists Agency, Susan P.; Waterside Productions, Inc.

Computers/electronics. Authors' Literary Agency; Catalog Literary Agency, The; Creative Concepts Literary Agency; Lighthouse Literary Agency; Nelson Literary Agency & Lecture Bureau, BK; Oceanic Press; Pegasus International, Inc., Literary & Film Agents; Sebastian Literary Agency; Singer Media Corporation; Steinberg Literary Agency, Michael; Waterside Productions, Inc.

Cooking/food/nutrition. Authors' Literary Agency; Browne Ltd., Pema; Connor Literary Agency; Cook Agency, Bruce; Creative Concepts Literary Agency; Dorese Agency Ltd.; Fishbein Ltd., Frieda; Flaherty, Literary Agent, Joyce A.; ForthWrite Literary Agency; Hamilton's Literary Agency, Andrew; Independent Publishing Agency; Kellock & Associates Ltd., J.; Kern Literary Agency, Natasha; Lighthouse Literary Agency; Marcil Literary Agency, The Denise; Marshall Agency, The Evan; Nelson Literary Agency & Lecture Bureau, BK; Northwest Literary Services; Olesha Agency, Andrea; Pegasus International, Inc., Literary & Film Agents; Sullivan Associates, Mark; Tiger Moon Enterprises; Urstadt Inc. Writers and Artists Agency, Susan P.

Crafts/hobbies. Ackerman Literary Services; Catalog Literary Agency, The; Connor Literary Agency; Creative Concepts Literary Agency; Dorese Agency Ltd.; Flaherty, Literary Agent, Joyce A.; ForthWrite Literary Agency; Heacock Literary Agency, Inc.; Independent Publishing Agency; Lighthouse Literary Agency; Nelson Literary Agency & Lecture Bureau, BK; Northwest Literary Services; Pegasus International, Inc., Literary & Film Agents; Sullivan Associates, Mark; Tiger Moon Enterprises; Urstadt Inc. Writers and Artists Agency, Susan P.

Current Affairs. Ahearn Agency, Inc., The; Argonaut Literary Agency; Author Aid Associates; Authors' Literary Agency; Authors' Marketing Services Ltd.; Brady Literary Management; Chester, Literary Agency, Linda; Connor Literary Agency; Creative Concepts Literary Agency; Dorese Agency Ltd.; Fishbein Ltd., Frieda; Flannery White and Stone; Hamilton's Literary Agency, Andrew; Independent Publishing Agency; JLM Literary Agents; Kellock & Associates Ltd., J.; Kern Literary Agency, Natasha; Keyser Literary Agency; Law Offices of Robert L. Fenton PC; Lighthouse Literary Agency; Marshall Agency, The Evan; Nelson Literary Agency & Lecture Bureau, BK; Pegasus International, Inc., Literary & Film Agents; Pine Associates, Inc, Arthur; Sebastian Literary Agency; Southern Writers; Steinberg Literary Agency, Michael; Strong, Marianne; Sullivan Associates, Mark; Urstadt Inc. Writers and Artists Agency, Susan P.; West Coast Literary Associates; Zelasky Literary Agency, Tom

Ethnic/cultural interests. Ahearn Agency, Inc., The; Author Aid Associates; Connor Literary

Agency; Creative Concepts Literary Agency; Flannery White and Stone; Hamilton's Literary Agency, Andrew; Independent Publishing Agency; Keyser Literary Agency; Lighthouse Literary Agency; Olesha Agency, Andrea; Pegasus International, Inc., Literary & Film Agents; Sebastian Literary Agency; Steinberg Literary Agency, Michael; Waterside Productions, Inc.; West Coast Literary Associates

Gay/Lesbian issues. Ahearn Agency, Inc., The; Author Aid Associates; Author Author Literary Agency; Dorese Agency Ltd.; Flannery White and Stone; Hamilton's Literary Agency, Andrew; Olesha Agency, Andrea; Southern Writers

Government/politics/law. Author Aid Associates; Authors' Literary Agency; Brady Literary Management; Browne Ltd., Pema; Creative Concepts Literary Agency; Dorese Agency Ltd.; Flannery White and Stone; Hamilton's Literary Agency, Andrew; Independent Publishing Agency; Iorio, Esq., Gary F.; Kellock & Associates Ltd., J.; Keyser Literary Agency; Law Offices of Robert L. Fenton PC; Marshall Agency, The Evan; Pegasus International, Inc., Literary & Film Agents; Sebastian Literary Agency; Shoestring Press; Steinberg Literary Agency, Michael; Toomey Associates, Jeanne; West Coast Literary Associates; Zelasky Literary Agency, Tom

Health/medicine. Ahearn Agency, Inc., The; Anthony Agency, Joseph; Author Aid Associates; Authors' Literary Agency; Browne Ltd., Pema; Catalog Literary Agency, The; Chester, Literary Agency, Linda; Connor Literary Agency; Cook Agency, Bruce; Creative Concepts Literary Agency; Dorese Agency Ltd.; Flaherty, Literary Agent, Joyce A.; Flannery White and Stone; ForthWrite Literary Agency; Hamilton's Literary Agency, Andrew; Heacock Literary Agency, Inc.; Kaltman Literary Agency, Larry; Kellock & Associates Ltd., J.; Kern Literary Agency, Natasha; Lee Shore Agency; Lighthouse Literary Agency; Marcil Literary Agency, The Denise; Marshall Agency, The Evan; Nelson Literary Agency & Lecture Bureau, BK; Northwest Literary Services; Oceanic Press; Panettieri Agency, The; Pegasus International, Inc., Literary & Film Agents; Sebastian Literary Agency; Singer Media Corporation; Southern Literary Agency; Southern Writers; Sullivan Associates, Mark; Tiger Moon Enterprises; Urstadt Inc. Writers and Artists Agency, Susan P.; Waterside Productions, Inc.; Writer's Consulting Group

History. Ahearn Agency, Inc., The; Alden—Literary Service, Farel T.; Argonaut Literary Agency; Author Aid Associates; Authors' Literary Agency; Brady Literary Management; Chester, Literary Agency, Linda; Cook Agency, Bruce; Dorese Agency Ltd.; Flaherty, Literary Agent, Joyce A.; ForthWrite Literary Agency; Hamilton's Literary Agency, Andrew; Independent Publishing Agency; Iorio, Esq., Gary F.; Kellock & Associates Ltd., J.; Keyser Literary Agency; Lighthouse Literary Agency; Marshall Agency, The Evan; Northwest Literary Services; Pegasus International, Inc., Literary & Film Agents; PMA Literary and Film Management, Inc.; Popkin, Julie; Sebastian Literary Agency; Shoestring Press; Southern Literary Agency; Southern Writers; Steinberg Literary Agency, Michael; Tiger Moon Enterprises; Toomey Associates, Jeanne; West Coast Literary Associates

Interior design/decorating. Authors' Literary Agency; Creative Concepts Literary Agency; Dorese Agency Ltd.; ForthWrite Literary Agency; Lighthouse Literary Agency; Marcil Literary Agency, The Denise; Marshall Agency, The Evan; Olesha Agency, Andrea; Strong, Marianne; Sullivan Associates, Mark; Toomey Associates, Jeanne; Urstadt Inc. Writers and Artists Agency, Susan P.

Juvenile nonfiction. Ahearn Agency, Inc., The; Alden—Literary Service, Farel T.; Author Aid Associates; Author Author Literary Agency; Authors' Literary Agency; Brady Literary Management; Browne Ltd., Pema; Catalog Literary Agency, The; Cook Agency, Bruce; Creative Concepts Literary Agency; Fishbein Ltd., Frieda; Flannery White and Stone; ForthWrite Literary Agency; Hamersfield Agency, The; Hamilton's Literary Agency, Andrew; Heacock Literary Agency, Inc.; Independent Publishing Agency; Kellock & Associates Ltd., J.; Lighthouse Literary Agency; March Media Inc.; Northwest Literary Services; Pegasus International, Inc., Literary & Film Agents; Southern Writers; Tiger Moon Enterprises; Zelasky Literary Agency, Tom

Language/literature/criticism. Author Aid Associates; Author Author Literary Agency; Cook Agency, Bruce; Creative Concepts Literary Agency; Dorese Agency Ltd.; Independent Publishing Agency; Kellock & Associates Ltd., J.; Keyser Literary Agency; Northwest Literary Services; Olesha Agency, Andrea; Sullivan Associates, Mark; West Coast Literary Associates

Military/war. Anthony Agency, Joseph; Argonaut Literary Agency; Author Aid Associates; Authors' Literary Agency; Authors' Marketing Services Ltd.; Brady Literary Management; Browne Ltd., Pema; Creative Concepts Literary Agency; Dorese Agency Ltd.; Fishbein Ltd., Frieda; Flaherty, Literary Agent, Joyce A.; Independent Publishing Agency; Iorio, Esq., Gary F.; Law Offices of Robert L. Fenton PC; Lighthouse Literary Agency; Nelson Literary Agency & Lecture Bureau, BK; Pegasus International, Inc., Literary & Film Agents; Sebastian Literary Agency; Shoestring Press; Sullivan Associates, Mark; Tiger Moon Enterprises; Urstadt Inc. Writers and Artists Agency, Susan P.; Zelasky Literary Agency, Tom

Money/finance/economics. Argonaut Literary Agency; Authors' Literary Agency; Catalog Literary Agency, The; Chester, Literary Agency, Linda; Connor Literary Agency; Creative Concepts Literary

Agency; Dorese Agency Ltd.; Flaherty, Literary Agent, Joyce A.; Flannery White and Stone; ForthWrite Literary Agency; Hamilton's Literary Agency, Andrew; Independent Publishing Agency; Iorio, Esq., Gary F.; JLM Literary Agents; Kellock & Associates Ltd., J.; Law Offices of Robert L. Fenton PC; Lighthouse Literary Agency; Marcil Literary Agency, The Denise; Marshall Agency, The Evan; Nelson Literary Agency & Lecture Bureau, BK; Oceanic Press; Pegasus International, Inc., Literary & Film Agents; Pine Associates, Inc, Arthur; Sebastian Literary Agency; Singer Media Corporation; Southern Literary Agency; Southern Writers; Steinberg Literary Agency, Michael; Strong, Marianne; Sullivan Associates, Mark; Tiger Moon Enterprises; Toomey Associates, Jeanne; Urstadt Inc. Writers and Artists Agency, Susan P.; Waterside Productions, Inc.

Music/dance/theater/film. Ahearn Agency, Inc., The; Author Aid Associates; Authors' Literary Agency; Brady Literary Management; Chester, Literary Agency, Linda; Cook Agency, Bruce; Dorese Agency Ltd.; Flannery White and Stone; ForthWrite Literary Agency; Hamilton's Literary Agency, Andrew; Independent Publishing Agency; Kellock & Associates Ltd., J.; Law Offices of Robert L. Fenton PC; Lighthouse Literary Agency; Marshall Agency, The Evan; Nelson Literary Agency & Lecture Bureau, BK; Northwest Literary Services; Oceanic Press; Olesha Agency, Andrea; Southern Writers; Sullivan Associates, Mark; Tiger Moon Enterprises; Urstadt Inc. Writers and Artists Agency, Susan P.; Waterside Productions, Inc.; West Coast Literary Associates

Nature/environment. Author Aid Associates; Authors' Literary Agency; Brady Literary Management; Browne Ltd., Pema; Catalog Literary Agency, The; Chester, Literary Agency, Linda; Creative Concepts Literary Agency; Fishbein Ltd., Frieda; Flaherty, Literary Agent, Joyce A.; Flannery White and Stone; ForthWrite Literary Agency; Independent Publishing Agency; JLM Literary Agents; Kellock & Associates Ltd., J.; Lighthouse Literary Agency; Marcil Literary Agency, The Denise; Nelson Literary Agency & Lecture Bureau, BK; Northwest Literary Services; Olesha Agency, Andrea; Pegasus International, Inc., Literary & Film Agents; Sebastian Literary Agency; Steinberg Literary Agency, Michael; Sullivan Associates, Mark; Tiger Moon Enterprises; Toomey Associates, Jeanne; Urstadt Inc. Writers and Artists Agency, Susan P.; Waterside Productions, Inc.; West Coast Literary Associates

New age/metaphysics. Alden—Literary Service, Farel T.; Author Aid Associates; Author Author Literary Agency; Browne Ltd., Pema; Dorese Agency Ltd.; Heacock Literary Agency, Inc.; Kellock & Associates Ltd., J.; Keyser Literary Agency; Lee Shore Agency; Marshall Agency, The Evan; New Age World Services; Northwest Literary Services; Oceanic Press; Pegasus International, Inc., Literary & Film Agents; Peterson Associates Literary Agency; Shoestring Press; State of the Art Ltd.; Sullivan Associates, Mark; Tiger Moon Enterprises; Waterside Productions, Inc.; Watt & Associates, Sandra

Open to all nonfiction categories. Bernstein Literary Agency, Meredith; Follendore Literary Agency, Joan; Glenmark Literary Agency; Goodkind, Larney; Jenks Agency, Carolyn; Literary Representation South; Morgan Literary Agency, Inc., David H.; New Writing Agency; Northeast Literary Agency; Wallerstein Agency, The Gerry B.

Photography. Author Aid Associates; Connor Literary Agency; Dorese Agency Ltd.; ForthWrite Literary Agency; Hamersfield Agency, The; Independent Publishing Agency; Lighthouse Literary Agency; Northwest Literary Services; Pegasus International, Inc., Literary & Film Agents; Sullivan Associates, Mark; Urstadt Inc. Writers and Artists Agency, Susan P.

Psychology. Anthony Agency, Joseph; Author Aid Associates; Author Author Literary Agency; Brady Literary Management; Browne Ltd., Pema; Catalog Literary Agency, The; Chester, Literary Agency, Linda; Cook Agency, Bruce; Creative Concepts Literary Agency; Dorese Agency Ltd.; Flaherty, Literary Agent, Joyce A.; Flannery White and Stone; ForthWrite Literary Agency; Hamilton's Literary Agency, Andrew; Heacock Literary Agency, Inc.; Independent Publishing Agency; JLM Literary Agents; Kern Literary Agency, Natasha; Keyser Literary Agency; Lighthouse Literary Agency; Marcil Literary Agency, The Denise; Marshall Agency, The Evan; Nelson Literary Agency & Lecture Bureau, BK; Oceanic Press; Panettieri Agency, The; Pegasus International, Inc., Literary & Film Agents; Peterson Associates Literary Agency; Pine Associates, Inc, Arthur; Sebastian Literary Agency; Singer Media Corporation; Southern Literary Agency; Southern Writers; Steinberg Literary Agency, Michael; Sullivan Associates, Mark; Waterside Productions, Inc.; West Coast Literary Associates

Religious/inspirational. Author Aid Associates; Author Author Literary Agency; Browne Ltd., Pema; Cook Agency, Bruce; ForthWrite Literary Agency; Hamilton's Literary Agency, Andrew; Independent Publishing Agency; JLM Literary Agents; Keyser Literary Agency; Law Offices of Robert L. Fenton PC; Nelson Literary Agency & Lecture Bureau, BK; Pegasus International, Inc., Literary & Film Agents; Shoestring Press; Southern Writers; Sullivan Associates, Mark; Tiger Moon Enterprises

Science/technology. Anthony Agency, Joseph; Author Aid Associates; Browne Ltd., Pema; Catalog Literary Agency, The; Creative Concepts Literary Agency; ForthWrite Literary Agency; Heacock Literary Agency, Inc.; Independent Publishing Agency; Kaltman Literary Agency, Larry; Kern Literary Agency, Natasha; Keyser Literary Agency; Nelson Literary Agency & Lecture Bureau, BK; Oceanic Press; Pegasus International, Inc., Literary & Film Agents; Peterson Associates Literary Agency; PMA Literary and Film Management, Inc.; Sebastian Literary Agency; Shoestring Press; Sullivan Associates, Mark

Self-help/personal improvement. Ahearn Agency, Inc., The; Alden—Literary Service, Farel T.; Anthony Agency, Joseph; Author Aid Associates; Author Author Literary Agency; Authors' Literary Agency; Brady Literary Management; Browne Ltd., Pema; Catalog Literary Agency, The; Connor Literary Agency; Cook Agency, Bruce; Creative Concepts Literary Agency; Dorese Agency Ltd.; Fishbein Ltd., Frieda; Flaherty, Literary Agent, Joyce A.; Flannery White and Stone; ForthWrite Literary Agency; Gladden Unlimited; Hamilton's Literary Agency, Andrew; Independent Publishing Agency; JLM Literary Agents; Kaltman Literary Agency, Larry; Kellock & Associates Ltd., J.; Kern Literary Agency, Natasha; Law Offices of Robert L. Fenton PC; Lee Shore Agency; Lighthouse Literary Agency; Marcil Literary Agency, The Denise; Marshall Agency, The Evan; Nelson Literary Agency & Lecture Bureau, BK; Northwest Literary Services; Oceanic Press; Olesha Agency, Andrea; Panettieri Agency, The; Pegasus International, Inc., Literary & Film Agents; Peterson Associates Literary Agency; Popkin, Julie; Sebastian Literary Agency; Singer Media Corporation; Southern Literary Agency; Southern Writers; State of the Art Ltd.; Steinberg Literary Agency, Michael; Tiger Moon Enterprises; Urstadt Inc. Writers and Artists Agency, Susan P.; Watt & Associates, Sandra; Zelasky Literary Agency, Tom

Sociology. Author Author Literary Agency; Brink Literary Agency, The; Cook Agency, Bruce; Creative Concepts Literary Agency; Dorese Agency Ltd.; Flannery White and Stone; ForthWrite Literary Agency; Hamilton's Literary Agency, Andrew; Independent Publishing Agency; Iorio, Esq., Gary F.; JLM Literary Agents; Keyser Literary Agency; Nelson Literary Agency & Lecture Bureau, BK; Pegasus International, Inc., Literary & Film Agents; Sebastian Literary Agency; Waterside Productions, Inc.

Sports. Argonaut Literary Agency; Author Aid Associates; Browne Ltd., Pema; Connor Literary Agency; Dorese Agency Ltd.; Flaherty, Literary Agent, Joyce A.; Flannery White and Stone; Hamilton's Literary Agency, Andrew; Heacock Literary Agency, Inc.; Independent Publishing Agency; Iorio, Esq., Gary F.; Kaltman Literary Agency, Larry; Kellock & Associates Ltd., J.; Law Offices of Robert L. Fenton PC; Lighthouse Literary Agency; Nelson Literary Agency & Lecture Bureau, BK; Northwest Literary Services; Oceanic Press; Pegasus International, Inc., Literary & Film Agents; Sebastian Literary Agency; Sullivan Associates, Mark; Taylor Literary Agency, Dawson; Urstadt Inc. Writers and Artists Agency, Susan P.; Waterside Productions, Inc.; Watt & Associates, Sandra

Translations. Author Aid Associates; Hamersfield Agency, The; Northwest Literary Services; Pegasus International, Inc., Literary & Film Agents; Singer Media Corporation

True crime/investigative. Ackerman Literary Services; Ahearn Agency, Inc., The; Alden—Literary Service, Farel T.; Anthony Agency, Joseph; Argonaut Literary Agency; Author Aid Associates; Author Author Literary Agency; Authors' Literary Agency; Authors' Marketing Services Ltd.; Brady Literary Management; Browne Ltd., Pema; Chester, Literary Agency, Linda; Connor Literary Agency; Dorese Agency Ltd.; Fishbein Ltd., Frieda; Flaherty, Literary Agent, Joyce A.; Hamilton's Literary Agency, Andrew; Independent Publishing Agency; Iorio, Esq., Gary F.; JLM Literary Agents; Kellock & Associates Ltd., J.; Law Offices of Robert L. Fenton PC; Marcil Literary Agency, The Denise; Marshall Agency, The Evan; Nelson Literary Agency & Lecture Bureau, BK; Northwest Literary Services; Oceanic Press; Panettieri Agency, The; Pegasus International, Inc., Literary & Film Agents; PMA Literary and Film Management, Inc.; Robb Literary Properties, Sherry; Sebastian Literary Agency; Singer Media Corporation; Southern Writers; Strong, Marianne; Toomey Associates, Jeanne; Waterside Productions, Inc.; Watt & Associates, Sandra; West Coast Literary Associates; Zelasky Literary Agency, Tom

Women's issues/women's studies. Ahearn Agency, Inc., The; Author Aid Associates; Author Author Literary Agency; Authors' Literary Agency; Brady Literary Management; Browne Ltd., Pema; Catalog Literary Agency, The; Chester, Literary Agency, Linda; Creative Concepts Literary Agency; Dorese Agency Ltd.; Fishbein Ltd., Frieda; Flaherty, Literary Agent, Joyce A.; Flannery White and Stone; ForthWrite Literary Agency; Hamilton's Literary Agency, Andrew; Heacock Literary Agency, Inc.; Independent Publishing Agency; JLM Literary Agents; Kellock & Associates Ltd., J.; Kern Literary Agency, Natasha; Keyser Literary Agency; Law Offices of Robert L. Fenton PC; Lighthouse Literary Agency; Marcil Literary Agency, The Denise; Nelson Literary Agency & Lecture Bureau, BK; Northwest Literary Services; Oceanic Press; Olesha Agency, Andrea; Panettieri Agency, The; Sebastian Literary Agency; Singer Media Corporation; Southern Writers; State of the Art Ltd.; Waterside Productions, Inc.; Watt & Associates, Sandra; West Coast Literary Associates; Writer's Consulting Group; Zelasky Literary Agency, Tom

Script agents/Fiction

Action/Adventure. Allied Artists; All-Star Talent Agency; Amato Agency, Michael; Berzon Agency, The Marian; Bethel Agency; Buchwald Agency, Don; Cameron Agency, The Marshall; Earth Tracks Agency;

Farber Literary Agency Inc.; Film And Fiction Agency, The; International Leonards Corp.; Lee Literary Agency, L. Harry; Leone Agency, Inc., The Adele; Montgomery-West Literary Agency; Panda Talent; Rogers and Associates, Stephanie; Steele & Associates, Ellen Lively; Swanson Inc., H.N.; Talent Bank Agency, The

Cartoon/comic. Allied Artists; All-Star Talent Agency; Bethel Agency; Earth Tracks Agency; International Leonards Corp.

Confessional. Bethel Agency; Panda Talent

Contemporary issues. All-Star Talent Agency; Berzon Agency, The Marian; Bethel Agency; Diskant & Associates; Earth Tracks Agency; Farber Literary Agency Inc.; International Leonards Corp.; Merrill Ltd., Helen; Rogers and Associates, Stephanie; Scribe Agency; Talent Bank Agency, The

Detective/police/crime. Allied Artists; All-Star Talent Agency; Beal Agency, The Mary; Berzon Agency, The Marian; Bethel Agency; Cameron Agency, The Marshall; Earth Tracks Agency; Farber Literary Agency Inc.; Film And Fiction Agency, The; International Leonards Corp.; Lee Literary Agency, L. Harry; Leone Agency, Inc., The Adele; Montgomery-West Literary Agency; Panda Talent; Steele & Associates, Ellen Lively; Swanson Inc., H.N.; Talent Bank Agency, The

Erotica. Allied Artists; Beal Agency, The Mary; Earth Tracks Agency; Lee Literary Agency, L. Harry

Ethnic. Bethel Agency; Talent Bank Agency, The

Family saga. All-Star Talent Agency; Berzon Agency, The Marian; Bethel Agency; Buchwald Agency, Don; International Leonards Corp.; Lee Literary Agency, L. Harry; Panda Talent; Steele & Associates, Ellen Lively; Talent Bank Agency, The

Fantasy. All-Star Talent Agency; Berzon Agency, The Marian; Bethel Agency; International Leonards Corp.; Lee Literary Agency, L. Harry; Leone Agency, Inc., The Adele; Montgomery-West Literary Agency; Talent Bank Agency, The

Feminist. Beal Agency, The Mary; Bethel Agency; Talent Bank Agency, The

Gay. Beal Agency, The Mary; Bethel Agency; Talent Bank Agency, The

Glitz. Bethel Agency; Leone Agency, Inc., The Adele; Steele & Associates, Ellen Lively

Historical. Bethel Agency; Cameron Agency, The Marshall; Diskant & Associates; Farber Literary Agency Inc.; International Leonards Corp.; Lee Literary Agency, L. Harry; Leone Agency, Inc., The Adele; Steele & Associates, Ellen Lively; Swanson Inc., H.N.; Talent Bank Agency, The

Humor/satire. All-Star Talent Agency; Bethel Agency; Earth Tracks Agency; Farber Literary Agency Inc.; Film And Fiction Agency, The; International Leonards Corp.; Lee Literary Agency, L. Harry; Panda Talent; Steele & Associates, Ellen Lively; Swanson Inc., H.N.; Talent Bank Agency, The

Juvenile. Amato Agency, Michael; Berzon Agency, The Marian; Farber Literary Agency Inc.; Panda Talent; Steele & Associates, Ellen Lively; Talent Bank Agency, The

Lesbian. Beal Agency, The Mary; Bethel Agency

Literary. Beal Agency, The Mary; Bethel Agency; Cameron Agency, The Marshall; Lee Literary Agency, L. Harry; Leone Agency, Inc., The Adele; Merrill Ltd., Helen; Scribe Agency

Mainstream. All-Star Talent Agency; Beal Agency, The Mary; Berzon Agency, The Marian; Bethel Agency; Buchwald Agency, Don; Cameron Agency, The Marshall; Farber Literary Agency Inc.; Film And Fiction Agency, The; International Leonards Corp.; Lee Literary Agency, L. Harry; Leone Agency, Inc., The Adele; Merrill Ltd., Helen; Scagnetti Talent & Literary Agency, Jack; Scribe Agency; Steele & Associates, Ellen Lively; Swanson Inc., H.N.; Talent Bank Agency, The

Mystery/suspense. All-Star Talent Agency; Beal Agency, The Mary; Berzon Agency, The Marian; Bethel Agency; Cameron Agency, The Marshall; Diskant & Associates; Farber Literary Agency Inc.; Film And Fiction Agency, The; International Leonards Corp.; Lee Literary Agency, L. Harry; Leone Agency, Inc., The Adele; Montgomery-West Literary Agency; Panda Talent; Scagnetti Talent & Literary Agency, Jack; Steele & Associates, Ellen Lively; Swanson Inc., H.N.; Talent Bank Agency, The

Open to all fiction categories. Agency for the Performing Arts; American Play Co., Inc.; Circle of Confusion Ltd.; Raintree Agency; Total Acting Experience, A

Picture book. Bethel Agency; Steele & Associates, Ellen Lively; Talent Bank Agency, The

Psychic/supernatural. Allied Artists; All-Star Talent Agency; Beal Agency, The Mary; Bethel Agency; Leone Agency, Inc., The Adele; Montgomery-West Literary Agency; Steele & Associates, Ellen Lively

Regional. Bethel Agency; International Leonards Corp.

Religious/inspiration. Berzon Agency, The Marian; Bethel Agency

Romance. Allied Artists; All-Star Talent Agency; Berzon Agency, The Marian; Bethel Agency; Buchwald Agency, Don; Earth Tracks Agency; Farber Literary Agency Inc.; International Leonards Corp.; Lee Literary Agency, L. Harry; Leone Agency, Inc., The Adele; Montgomery-West Literary Agency; Rogers and Associates, Stephanie; Steele & Associates, Ellen Lively

Science fiction. Allied Artists; All-Star Talent Agency; Beal Agency, The Mary; Buchwald Agency, Don; International Leonards Corp.; Lee Literary Agency, L. Harry; Leone Agency, Inc., The Adele; Montgomery-West Literary Agency; Steele & Associates, Ellen Lively; Talent Bank Agency, The

Sports. Allied Artists; All-Star Talent Agency; Bethel Agency; International Leonards Corp.; Lee Literary Agency, L. Harry; Panda Talent; Scagnetti Talent & Literary Agency, Jack; Swanson Inc., H.N.

Thriller/espionage. All-Star Talent Agency; Beal Agency, The Mary; Berzon Agency, The Marian; Bethel Agency; Buchwald Agency, Don; Cameron Agency, The Marshall; Earth Tracks Agency; Farber Literary Agency Inc.; Film And Fiction Agency, The; International Leonards Corp.; Lee Literary Agency, L. Harry; Leone Agency, Inc., The Adele; Montgomery-West Literary Agency; Panda Talent; Rogers and Associates, Stephanie; Scagnetti Talent & Literary Agency, Jack; Steele & Associates, Ellen Lively; Swanson Inc., H.N.; Talent Bank Agency, The

Westerns/frontier. All-Star Talent Agency; Bethel Agency; Buchwald Agency, Don; Film And Fiction Agency, The; Lee Literary Agency, L. Harry; Leone Agency, Inc., The Adele; Talent Bank Agency, The

Young adult. Amato Agency, Michael; Berzon Agency, The Marian; Bethel Agency; Diskant & Associates; Earth Tracks Agency; Farber Literary Agency Inc.; Lee Literary Agency, L. Harry

Script agents/Nonfiction

Agriculture/horticulture. Bethel Agency

Animals. Bethel Agency; Panda Talent

Anthropology. Bethel Agency; International Leonards Corp.

Art/architecture/design. Bethel Agency

Biography/autobiography. Bethel Agency; Buchwald Agency, Don; Circle of Confusion Ltd.; Diskant & Associates; International Leonards Corp.; Leone Agency, Inc., The Adele; Merrill Ltd., Helen

Business. Bethel Agency; Cameron Agency, The Marshall; Circle of Confusion Ltd.; International Leonards Corp.; Leone Agency, Inc., The Adele

Child guidance/parenting. Bethel Agency; Leone Agency, Inc., The Adele

Cooking/food/nutrition. Amato Agency, Michael; Bethel Agency; Leone Agency, Inc., The Adele; Steele & Associates, Ellen Lively

Crafts/hobbies. Bethel Agency; Leone Agency, Inc., The Adele

Current Affairs. Amato Agency, Michael; Bethel Agency; Buchwald Agency, Don; Circle of Confusion Ltd.; Diskant & Associates; International Leonards Corp.; Leone Agency, Inc., The Adele; Swanson Inc., H.N.

Ethnic/cultural interests. Bethel Agency; Leone Agency, Inc., The Adele

Gay/Lesbian issues. Beal Agency, The Mary; Bethel Agency; Circle of Confusion Ltd.; Leone Agency, Inc., The Adele

Government/politics/law. Allied Artists; Beal Agency, The Mary; Bethel Agency; Circle of Confusion Ltd.; Leone Agency, Inc., The Adele

Health/medicine. Amato Agency, Michael; Bethel Agency; Cameron Agency, The Marshall; Circle of Confusion Ltd.; Leone Agency, Inc., The Adele; Raintree Agency; Scagnetti Talent & Literary Agency, Jack

History. Bethel Agency; Buchwald Agency, Don; Circle of Confusion Ltd.; Diskant & Associates; International Leonards Corp.; Kohner, Inc., Paul; Lee Literary Agency, L. Harry; Leone Agency, Inc., The Adele; Steele & Associates, Ellen Lively

Interior design/decorating. Bethel Agency; Leone Agency, Inc., The Adele; Bethel Agency; Cameron Agency, The Marshall; Circle of Confusion Ltd.

Language/literature/criticism. Bethel Agency; Leone Agency, Inc., The Adele

Military/war. Bethel Agency; Kohner, Inc., Paul; Lee Literary Agency, L. Harry; Leone Agency, Inc., The Adele; Panda Talent; Scagnetti Talent & Literary Agency, Jack

Money/finance/economics. Bethel Agency; Cameron Agency, The Marshall; International Leonards Corp.; Leone Agency, Inc., The Adele

Music/dance/theater/film. Allied Artists; Bethel Agency; International Leonards Corp.; Kohner, Inc., Paul; Leone Agency, Inc., The Adele

Nature/environment. Bethel Agency; Leone Agency, Inc., The Adele; Raintree Agency

New age/metaphysics. International Leonards Corp.; Leone Agency, Inc., The Adele; Steele & Associates, Ellen Lively

Open to all nonfiction categories. Agency for the Performing Arts; American Play Co., Inc.; Earth Tracks Agency; Total Acting Experience, A

Photography. Bethel Agency

Npsychology. Beal Agency, The Mary; Bethel Agency; International Leonards Corp.; Leone Agency, Inc., The Adele; Panda Talent

Religious/inspirational. Bethel Agency; International Leonards Corp.

Science/technology. Bethel Agency; Buchwald Agency, Don; International Leonards Corp.; Leone Agency, Inc., The Adele

Self-help/personal improvement. Bethel Agency; Cameron Agency, The Marshall; International Leonards Corp.; Leone Agency, Inc., The Adele; Scagnetti Talent & Literary Agency, Jack; Steele & Associates, Ellen Lively

Sociology. Bethel Agency; Raintree Agency

Sports. Bethel Agency; Buchwald Agency, Don; International Leonards Corp.; Leone Agency, Inc., The Adele; Panda Talent; Scagnetti Talent & Literary Agency, Jack; Swanson Inc., H.N.

Translations. Bethel Agency

True crime/investigative. Beal Agency, The Mary; Bethel Agency; Cameron Agency, The Marshall; Circle of Confusion Ltd.; International Leonards Corp.; Kohner, Inc., Paul; Panda Talent; Scagnetti Talent & Literary Agency, Jack; Steele & Associates, Ellen Lively

Women's issues/women's studies. Amato Agency, Michael; Bethel Agency; Circle of Confusion Ltd.; Leone Agency, Inc., The Adele; Raintree Agency; Steele & Associates, Ellen Lively

Commercial Art/Photo and Fine Art Reps Geographic Index

All art/photo and fine art reps are listed together in this index by state. Some talents have just one rep to handle all their work, but many talents choose to have more than one rep covering different sections of the country.

Arizona
Asciutto Art Reps., Inc.

California
Art Source L.A.
Baum & Associates, Cathy
Burlingham/Artist Representation, Tricia
Collier Represents, Jan
Conrad & Associates, James
De Moreta Represents, Linda
Gardner & Associates, Jean
Gordon/Artist Representative, T.J.
Hall & Associates
Hauser, Another Girl Rep, Barb
L.A. Art Exchange
Lesli Art, Inc.
Martha Productions, Inc.
Piscopo, Maria
Rosenthal Represents
Salzman, Richard
Scott, Inc., Freda
Scroggy Agency, David
Studio Artists/Don Pepper
Winston West, Ltd.

Colorado
Guenzi Agents, Inc., Carol

Connecticut
Artists International
HK Portfolio
Paluhan, Joanne
Publishers' Graphics

Florida
Administrative Arts
International Art Connection and Art Connection Plus
Madrazo Arts

Georgia
Wells & Associates, Inc., Susan

Hawaii
Pacific Design Studio

Illinois
Artco Incorporated

Fine Art Representative
Galitz Fine Art/Accent Art, Robert
Kuehnel & Associates, Peter
Montagano & Associates
Soldat & Cardoni

Kansas
Media Gallery/Enterprises
ToLease Lautrec

Maryland
Redmond Represents
Shearer Art Source, Nicki

Michigan
Neis Group, The
Ridgeway Artists Representative

Minnesota
Icebox

Missouri
Creative Productions, Inc.

New Jersey
Holt & Associates, Inc., Rita
Warner & Associates

New York
Arnold Fine Arts, Jack
Arts Counsel Inc.
Beidler Inc., Barbara
Bernhard, Ivy
Bernstein & Andriulli Inc.
Brindle & Partner Inc., Carolyn
Brody, Artists and Photographers Representative, Sam
Bruck And Moss Associates
Carp, Inc., Stan
Chislovsky Inc., Carol
Collignon, Daniele
Corporate Art Associates, Ltd.
Foster Artist Rep., (Pat)
Ginsburg & Associates, Inc., Michael
Gordon Associates Ltd., Barbara
Keating, Peggy
Kimcie, Tania

Agents and Reps Index

This index of agent and rep names was created to help you locate agents or reps even when you do not know for which agency they work. You may have read or heard about a particular representative, but do not know how to contact them. Agent and rep names are listed with their agencies' names. Check the Listing Index for the page number of the agency listed.

A

Abenal, Sheldon (American Play Co., Inc.)
Ackerman, Sharon (Ackerman Literary Services)
Agarwal, Rajeev K. (Circle of Confusion Ltd.)
Ahearn, Pamela G. (The Ahearn Agency, Inc.)
Ajlouny, Joe (The Joseph S. Aljouny Agency)
Alden, Farel T. (Farel T. Alden-Literary Service)
Alexander, Max (Tolease Lautrec)
Allen, Linda (Linda Allen Literary Agency)
Allred, Robert (All-Star Talent Agency)
Amparan, Joann (Wecksler-Incomco)
Amsterdam, Marcia (Marcia Amsterdam Agency)
Andrews, Bart (Bart Andrews & Associates)
Andriulli, Tony (Bernstein & Andriulli Inc.)
Anthony, Joseph (Joseph Anthony Agency)
Aragi, Nicole (Watkins Loomis Agency, Inc.)
Arnold, Jack (Jack Arnold Fine Arts)
Asciutto, Mary Anne (Asciutto Art Reps., Inc.)
Atwell, Carol (Diamond Literary Agency, Inc.)

B

Bach, Julian (Julian Bach Literary Agency)
Baldi, Malaga (Malaga Baldi Literary Agency)
Balkin, R. (Balkin Agency, Inc.)
Barmeier, Jim (Writer's Consulting Group)
Barnes, Morgan (Loretta Barrett Books Inc.)
Barr, Hollister (L. Harry Lee Literary Agency)
Barr, Mary (Sierra Literary Agency)
Barrett, Helen (Helen Barrett Literary Agency)
Barrett, Loretta A. (Loretta Barrett Books Inc.)
Barrick, Gail (H.N. Swanson Inc.)
Bartczak, Sue (Gene Bartczak Associates Inc.)
Barvin, Jude (The Brink Literary Agency)
Batra, Sunita (Dupree/Miller and Associates Inc. Literary)
Baum, Cathy (Cathy Baum & Associates)
Becker, Maximillian (Maximillian Becker)
Beidler, Barbara (Barbara Beidler Inc.)
Beisch, Karin (Elaine Markson Literary Agency)
Bellacicco, Dan A. (A Total Acting Experience)
Benson, John (BK Nelson Literary Agency & Lecture Bureau)
Berendsen, Bob (Berendsen & Associates, Inc.)
Berkower, Amy (Writers House)
Berman, Lois (Lois Berman, Writers' Representative)
Bernard, Alec (Puddingstone Literary Agency)
Bernhard, Ivy (Ivy Bernhard)
Bernstein, Howard (Bernstein & Andriulli Inc.)

Bernstein, Meredith (Meredith Bernstein Literary Agency)
Bernstein, Sam (Bernstein & Andriulli Inc.)
Berry, Henry (Independent Publishing Agency)
Berstein, Roger (The Lieberman Agency)
Biggis, Charis (L. Harry Lee Literary Agency)
Birenbaum, Molly (Bernstein & Andriulli Inc.)
Black, Fran (Arts Counsel Inc.)
Blake, Laura J. (Curtis Brown Ltd.)
Blanton, Sandra (Peter Lampack Agency, Inc.)
Boals, Judy (Lois Berman, Writers' Representative)
Boates, Reid (Reid Boates Literary Agency)
Bobke, C.J. (Lee Allan Agency)
Bohannon, Kendall (Flannery, White and Stone)
Bonnen, Edwin (Ridgeway Artists Representative)
Bonnett, Carol (MGA Agency Inc.)
Bowne, Tiffany (Tricia Burlingham/Artist Representation)
Brandenburgh, Don (Brandenburgh & Associates Literary Agency)
Brandt, Carl (Brandt & Brandt Literary Agents)
Brandt, Joan (The Joan Brandt Agency)
Branson, Richard (The Lieberman Agency)
Brenna, Vito (L. Harry Lee Literary Agency)
Breoge, Jane (L. Harry Lee Literary Agency)
Brindle, Carolyn (Carolyn Brindle & Partner)
Brock, Jill (The Tantleff Office)
Brod, A.T. (Ruth Hagy Brod Literary Agency)
Brodie, Michael (Artists International)
Brody, Sam (Sam Brody, Artists & Photographers Representative)
Brophy, Phillipa (Sterling Lord Literistic, Inc.)
Broussard, Michael (Dupree/Miller and Associates Inc. Literary)
Brown, Andrea (Andrea Brown Literary Agency, Inc.)
Brown, Marie (Marie Brown Associates Inc.)
Brown, William C. (Qcorp Literary Agency)
Browne, Jane Jordan (Multimedia Product Development, Inc.)
Browne, Pema (Pema Browne Ltd.)
Browne, Perry (Pema Browne Ltd.)
Bruck, Nancy (Bruck and Moss Associates)
Brutto, Patrick Lo (Meredith Bernstein Literary Agency)
Burke, Anna Mae (A & R Burke Corporation)
Burke, Janet (Alison J. Picard Literary Agent)
Burke, Robert (A & R Burke Corporation)

F

Fallon, Eileen (The Fallon Literary Agency)
Fant, Billie Blake (Simpatico Art & Stone)
Farber, Ann (Farber Literary Agency Inc.)
Faria, Judith (L. Harry Lee Literary Agency)
Fastenberg, Amy (Connie Clausen Associates)
Feldman, Leigh (Darhansoff & Verrill Literary Agents)
Fenton, Robert L. (Law Offices of Robert L. Fenton PC)
Fidel, Loretta (The Weingel-Fidel Agency)
Fierro, Adam (H.N. Swanson Inc.)
Finch, Diana (Ellen Levine Literary Agency)
Fishbein, Janice (Frieda Fishbein Ltd.)
Fisher, Steven (H.N. Swanson Inc.)
FitzGerald, Robert (Flannery, White and Stone)
Flaherty, John (Joyce A. Flaherty, Literary Agent)
Flaherty, Joyce (Joyce A. Flaherty, Literary Agent)
Fleenor, Bruce (State of the Art Ltd.)
Fogelman, Evan (Fogelman Publishing Interests)
Foiles, S. James (Appleseeds Management)
Foley, C. Matthew (Tolease Lautrec)
Foley, Catherine Lynn (Tolease Lautrec)
Follendore, Joan (Joan Follendore Literary Agency)
Fortunato, Lena (Joseph Anthony Agency)
Foster, Pat (Pat Foster Artist Rep.)
Fox, Laurie (Linda Chester Literary Agency)
Francisco, Carol (Francisco Communications)
Freedman, Robert A. (Robert A. Freedman Dramatic Agency, Inc.)
Friedman, Sharon (John Hawkins & Associates)
Friedrich, Molly (Aaron M. Priest Literary Agency)
Frohbieter-Mueller, Jo (Printed Tree, Inc.)
Fruchter, Lev (David Black Literary Agency)
Fuhrman, Candice (Candice Fuhrman Literary Agency)

G

Galitz, Robert (Robert Galitz Fine Art/Accent Art)
Gallagher, Coleen (Allied Artists)
Gardner, Anthony (Peter Lampack Agency)
Gardner, Jean (Jean Gardner & Associates)
Garon, Jay (Jay Garon-Brooke Assoc. Inc.)
Gartenberg, Max (Max Gartenberg, Literary Agent)
Gaylor, Mary Lee (L. Harry Lee Literary Agency)
Geriale, Jodi (Ackerman Literary Services)
Gershel, Larry (Wieser & Wieser, Inc.)
Getty, Mary P. (The Lieberman Agency)
Gill, Anne (Stephen Gill)
Gill, Stephen (Stephen Gill)
Gillies, Paige C. (Publishers' Graphics)
Ginsberg, Peter L. (Curtis Brown Ltd.)
Ginsberg, Susan (Writers House)
Ginsburg, Michael (Michael Ginsburg & Associates, Inc.)
Gladden, Carolan (Gladden Unlimited)
Gladstone, Bill (Waterside Productions, Inc.)
Glasser, Carla (The Betsy Nolan Literary Agency)

Golden, Winifred (Margaret McBride Literary Agency)
Goldfarb, Ronald (Ronald Goldfarb & Associates)
Goodkind, Larney (Larney Goodkind)
Goodman, Elise Simon (Goodman Associates)
Goodman, Irene (Irene Goodman Literary Agency)
Gordon, Barbara (Barbara Gordon Associates)
Gordon, Charlotte (Charlotte Gordon Agency)
Gordon, Tami (T.J. Gordon/Artist Representative)
Gores, Martha R. (The Authors and Artists Resource Center/Tarc Literary Agency)
Gotler, Joel (Joel Gotler Metropolitan Talent Agency)
Grace, Audrey (Panda Talent)
Graham, Earl (Graham Agency)
Graybill, Nina (Ronald Goldfarb & Associates)
Gregory, Maia (Maia Gregory Associates)
Griffin, Emilie (Southern Writers)
Grimes, Lew (Lew Grimes Literary Agency)
Gross, Shelley (Literary/Business Associates)
Grossman, Elizabeth (Sterling Lord Literistic)
Guenzi, Carol (Carol Guenzi Agents, Inc.)
Guillfoil, Barry (Freda Scott, Inc.)
Gummery, Nancy (Montgomery-West Literary Agency)
Gusay, Charlotte (The Charlotte Gusay Literary Agency)

H

Haberman, Craig (Bernstein & Andriulli Inc.)
Hackett, Pat (Pat Hackett/Artist Representative)
Halff, Ms. Lee B. (The Blake Group Literary Agency)
Hall, Marni (Hall & Associates)
Hamilburg, Michael (The Michael J. Hamilburg Agency)
Hamilton, Andrew (Andrew Hamilton's Literary Agency)
Hamlin, Faith (Stanford J. Greenburger Associates)
Han, Katherine (Singer Media Corporation)
Handaris, Marisa (Marisa Handaris, Literary Agency)
Hanke, Mellie (Marisa Handaris, Literary Agency)
Hanna, Frances (Acacia House Publishing Services Ltd.)
Harbison, Lawrence (Samuel French, Inc.)
Harding, Alexandra (Georges Borchardt Inc.)
Harper, Laurie (Sebastian Literary Agency)
Harriet, Sydney H. (Agents Inc. for Medical and Mental Health Professionals)
Harris, Brenda B. (Administrative Arts)
Harris, Joy (The Robert Lantz-Joy Harris Literary Agency)
Harrison, Lesley (MGA Agency Inc.)
Hartley, Glen (Writers' Representatives, Inc.)
Hartman, Kris (Cathy Baum & Associates)
Hawkins, John (John Hawkins & Associates)
Hayes, Linda (Columbia Literary Associates)
Heacock, Jim (Heacock Literary Agency)
Heacock, Rosalie (Heacock Literary Agency)
Heifetz, Merrillee (Writers House)
Henshaw, Richard (Richard Curtis Associates)

Herman, Jeffrey H. (The Jeff Herman Agency)
Herner, Susan (Susan Herner Rights Agency)
Hill, Chris (Lee Allan Agency)
Hochman, Gail (Brandt & Brandt Literary Agents Inc.)
Hoffman, Larry (Authors' Marketing Services)
Hogenson, Barbara (Lucy Kroll Agency)
Holt, Rita (Rita Holt & Associates, Inc.)
Holtje, Bert (James Peter Associates, Inc.)
Holub, William (Holub & Associates)
Hopkins, Christine (Ackerman Literary Services)
Hotchkiss, Jody (Sterling Lord Literistic, Inc.)
Hull, David Stewart (Hull House Literary Agency)
Hull, Scott (Scott Hull Associates)

I
Idol, Mattphisto (Tolease Lautrec)
Iorio, Gary (Gary F. Iorio, Esq.)

J
Jacobson, Emilie (Curtis Brown Ltd.)
James, Colin (L. Harry Lee Literary Agency)
Jarvis, Sharon (Sharon Jarvis & Co., Inc.)
Jasso, Caspar (Lyceum Creative Properties)
Jenks, Carolyn (Carolyn Jenks Agency)
Jenson, Kathryn (Columbia Literary Associates)
Johnson, Jan (Sebastian Literary Agency)
Jones, Lloyd (Lloyd Jones Literary Agency)
Jordan, L.F. (Chadd-Stevens Literary Agency)

K
Kaltman, Larry (Larry Kaltman Literary Agency)
Kangas, Sandra (Lighthouse Literary Agency)
Kaplan, Elizabeth (Sterling Lord Literistic, Inc.)
Kasak, Harriet (HK Portfolio)
Kaufman, Joshua (Ronald Goldfarb & Associates)
Keating, Peggy (Peggy Keating)
Keliher, Brian (Comedy Ink)
Kellock, Joanne (J. Kellock & Associates Ltd.)
Kennedy, Terry (Tiger Moon Enterprises)
Keppler, Jim (Lyle Steele & Co., Ltd.)
Kern, Natasha (Natasha Kern Literary Agency)
Kerr, Ralph (Ralph Kerr)
Ketay, Joyce P. (The Joyce P. Ketay Agency)
Ketz, Louise B. (Louise B. Ketz Agency)
Keyser, Grace R. (Keyser Literary Agency)
Keyser, John O. (Keyser Literary Agency)
Kidde, Katharine (Kidde, Hoyt & Picard)
Killeen, Frank (L. Harry Lee Literary Agency)
Kimcie, Tania (Tania Kimcie)
Klein, Cindy (Georges Borchardt Inc.)
Klimt, Bill (Bill and Maurine Klimt)
Klimt, Maurine (Bill and Maurine Klimt)
Klinger, Harvey (Harvey Klinger, Inc.)
Knappman, Edward W. (New England Publishing Associates, Inc.)
Knappman, Elizabeth Frost (New England Publishing Associates, Inc.)
Knecht, Cliff (Cliff Knecht-Artist Representative)
Knickerbocker, Andrea (Lee Allan Agency)
Knightstep, L.J. (Joan Follendore Literary Agency)
Knowlton, Perry (Curtis Brown Ltd.)

Knowlton, Timothy (Curtis Brown Ltd.)
Knowlton, Virginia (Curtis Brown Ltd.)
Kouts, Barbara (Barbara S. Kouts, Literary Agent)
Kramer, Sidney B. (Mews Books Ltd.)
Krichevsky, Stuart (Sterling Lord Literistic, Inc.)
Krinsky, David (Earth Tracks Agency)
Kriton, George (Cinema Talent International)
Kroll, Edite (Edite Kroll Literary Agency)
Kuehnel, Peter (Peter Kuehnel & Associates)
Kurman, B. (Rights Unlimited)
Kurz, Norman (Lowenstein Associates, Inc.)

L
Lampack, Peter (Peter Lampack Agency, Inc.)
Lande, Trish (Julian Bach Literary Agency)
Lange, Heide (Stanford J. Greenburger Associates)
Larsen, Mike (Michael Larsen/Elizabeth Pomada Literary Agents)
Lasbury, Sue (M. Sue Lasbury Literary Agency)
Laughren, Brent (Northwest Literary Services)
Lee, Helen J. (Oceanic Press, Singer Media Corporation)
Lee, L. Harry (L. Harry Lee Literary Agency)
Lee, Lettie (Ann Elmo Agency Inc.)
Lee, Nelda (Nelda Lee Inc.)
Lehr, Donald (The Betsy Nolan Literary Agency)
Leonards, David (International Leonards Corp.)
Leone, Adele (The Adele Leone Agency, Inc.)
Leone, Ralph (The Adele Leone Agency, Inc.)
Lerman, Gary (Photo Agents Ltd.)
Levant, Dan (Levant & Wales, Literary Agency)
Levine, Ellen (Ellen Levine Literary Agency)
Levine, Victor A. (Northeast Literary Agency)
Liebert, Norma (The Norma-Lewis Agency)
Lincoln, Mrs. Ray (Ray Lincoln Literary Agency)
Linder, Bertram (Educational Design Services)
Lipkind, Wendy (Wendy Lipkind Agency)
Liss, Laurie (Aaron M. Priest Literary Agency)
Lloyd, Lem (Mary Jack Wald Associates, Inc.)
Lockwood, Hal (Penmarin Books)
Lopez, Lourdes (Helen Merrill Ltd.)
Lord, Sterling (Sterling Lord Literistic, Inc.)
Love, Nancy (Nancy Love Literary Agency)
Lovitz, Gene (Pegasus International, Inc., Literary & Film Agents)
Lowenstein, Barbara (Lowenstein Associates)
Lubenow, Jerry (Cole and Lubenow: Books)
Lundgren, Curtis H.C. (The Curtis Bruce Agency)
Luttinger, Selma (Robert A. Freedman Dramatic Agency, Inc.)
Lynch, Andrea (Repertoire)
Lynch, Larry (Repertoire)
Lynch, Richard (New Writing Agency)

M
McCarthy, Cheryl (Greg Merhige-Merdon Marketing/Promo Co. Inc.)
McCleary, Carol (The Wilshire Literary Agency)
McClusky, Neil G. (Westchester Literary Agency, Inc.)
Maccoby, Gina (Gina Maccoby Literary

Agency)
McDonald, Lisa (The Joseph S. Aljouny Agency)
McDonough, Richard P. (Richard P. McDonough, Literary Agency)
McGrath, Helen (Helen McGrath)
McKay, Colleen (Colleen McKay Photography)
Mackey, Elizabeth (The Robbins Office, Inc.)
McKnight, Linda (MGA Agency Inc.)
Madrazo, Mr. (Madrazo Arts)
Mann, Carol (Carol Mann Agency)
Marcil, Denise (The Denise Marcil Literary Agency)
Markowitz, Barbara (Barbara Markowitz Literary Agency)
Marlowe, Marilyn (Curtis Brown Ltd.)
Marmur, Mildred (Mildred Marmur Associates)
Marshall, Evan (The Evan Marshall Agency)
Martell, Alice Fried (The Martell Agency)
Matson, Peter (Sterling Lord Literistic, Inc.)
Mattelson, Judy (Mattelson Associates Ltd.)
Matthias, Lee (Lee Allan Agency)
Mattis, Lawrence (Circle of Confusion Ltd.)
Maynard, Gary (The Gary-Paul Agency)
Mazmamian, Joan (Helen Rees Literary Agency)
Meade, Sam (New Writing Agency)
Mendola, Tim (Mendola Artists)
Meo, Frank (Frank Meo)
Merhige, Greg (Greg Merhige-Merdon Marketing/Promo Co. Inc.)
Merrill, Helen (Helen Merrill Ltd.)
Meth, David L. (Writers' Productions)
Michael, Douglas (Frieda Fishbein Ltd.)
Miller, Deborah A. (Pennamenities)
Miller, Jan (Dupree/Miller and Associates Inc. Literary)
Miller, Judy (Bernstein & Andriulli Inc.)
Miller, Kenni (Embers Literary Agency)
Miller, Kristin (Don Buchwald Agency)
Miller, Mark James (Tiger Moon Enterprises)
Miller, Peter (PMA Literary and Film Management, Inc.)
Miller, Roberta D. (Roberta D. Miller Associates)
Miller, Stuart M. (Agency for the Performing Arts)
Monaco, Richard (The Adele Leone Agency, Inc.)
Montagano, David (Montagano & Associates)
Moore, Claudette (Moore Literary Agency)
Moran, Maureen (Donald MacCampbell Inc.)
Morgan, David (David H. Morgan Literary Agency, Inc.)
Morgan, Katherine (David H. Morgan Literary Agency, Inc.)
Morgan, Vicki (Vicki Morgan Associates)
Morling, Carole (Pegasus International, Inc., Literary & Film Agents)
Mortimer, Lydia (Hull House Literary Agency)
Moss, Eileen (Bruck and Moss Associates)
Mulert, Carl (The Joyce P. Ketay Agency)

N
Nadell, Bonnie (Frederick Hill Associates)
Naggar, Jean V. (Jean V. Naggar Literary Agency)
Nalaer, Barbara (Singer Media Corporation)

Neail, Pamela (Pamela Neail Associates)
Neis, Judy (The Neis Group)
Nellis, Muriel (Literary and Creative Artists Agency)
Nelson, Bonita (BK Nelson Literary Agency & Lecture Bureau)
Nichols, K.C. (KC Communications)
Nichols, Rhonda (KC Communications)
Nigh, Douglas J. (The Talent Bank Agency)
Nigrosh, Nancy (The Gersh Agency)
Noetzli, Regula (Regula Noetzli Literary Agency)
Nolan, Betsy (The Betsy Nolan Literary Agency)
Nosblatt, Leslie (Bernstein & Andriulli Inc.)

O
Odenwald, Sylvia (The Odenwald Connection)
Olesha, Andrea (Andrea Olesha)
Olm, Sandrine (Lucianne S. Goldberg Literary Agents, Inc.)
Orrmont, Arthur (Author Aid Associates)
Ortiz, Natalie (Bernstein & Andriulli Inc.)
Osborne, Geoff (Lyceum Creative Properties)
Otte, Jane H. (The Otte Company)
Otte, L. David (The Otte Company)

P
Painter, John (Penmarin Books)
Panettieri, Eugenia (The Panettieri Agency)
Pantel, Elena (The Joseph S. Aljouny Agency)
Parker, Stacy (L. Harry Lee Literary Agency)
Parks, Richard (The Richard Parks Agency)
Paton, Kathi (Kathi J. Paton Literary Agency)
Pearson, Francine H. (Pacific Design Studio)
Pell, William (William Pell Agency)
Pelter, Rodney (Rodney Pelter)
Pepper, Don (Studio Artists/Don Pepper)
Perkins, Lori (L. Perkins Associates)
Perkins, M. (Acton, Dystel, Leone, & Jaffee)
Peterson, Lawrence (Peterson Associates Literary Agency)
Picard, Alison (Alison J. Picard Literary Agent)
Pinkston, Jim (Sherry Robb Literary Properties)
Piscopo, Maria (Maria Piscopo)
Plunkett, Paul (The Martell Agency)
Polk, Katie (L. Harry Lee Literary Agency)
Pollak, Fran (Mews Books Ltd.)
Pomada, Elizabeth (Michael Larsen/Elizabeth Pomada Literary Agents)
Pool, Linda (Creative Productions, Inc.)
Porcelain, Sidney (Sidney E. Porcelain)
Powers, Jennifer (Schaffner Agency, Inc.)
Prescott, Ashton (The Marshall Cameron Agency)
Prescott, Margo (The Marshall Cameron Agency)
Priest, Aaron (Aaron M. Priest Literary Agency)
Protter, Susan (Susan Ann Protter Literary Agent)
Pryor, Roberta (Roberta Pryor, Inc.)
Pugarelli, Fred C. (Rhodes Literary Agency)
Pugarelli, Ms. Angela (Rhodes Literary Agency)
Pulitzer-Voges, Elizabeth (Kirchoff/Wohlberg, Inc., Authors' Representation Division)

R
Radley-Regan, D. (D. Radley-Regan & Associates)

Sturges, Frank (Scott Hull Associates)
Sullivan, Mark (Mark Sullivan Associates)
Suter, Anne Elisabeth (Gotham Art & Literary Agency Inc.)
Sutton, Sheree (Lloyd Jones Literary Agency)
Swanson, N.U. (H.N. Swanson Inc.)
Sweeney, Emma (Curtis Brown Ltd.)

T
Talbot, William (Samuel French, Inc.)
Tantleff, Jack (The Tantleff Office)
Targ, Roslyn (Roslyn Targ Literary Agency)
Taylor, Clyde (Curtis Brown Ltd.)
Taylor, Dawson (Dawson Taylor Literary Agency)
Taylor, Jess (Curtis Brown Ltd.)
Taylor, Linda L. (Montgomery-West Literary Agency)
Teal, Patricia (Patricia Teal Literary Agency)
Terry, Roger (Executive Excellence)
Thomas, Geri (Elaine Markson Literary Agency)
Tillman, Sybil (Artco Incorporated)
Tomkins, Susan (Michael Amato Agency)
Toomey, Jeanne (Jeanne Toomey Associates)
Tornetta, Phyllis (Phyllis Tornetta Agency)
Traum, Michael (Don Buchwald Agency)
Travis, Susan (Margaret McBride Literary Agency)
Tribelli, Joseph (Joseph Tribelli Designs, Ltd.)
Trupin, James (Jet Literary Associates, Inc.)

U
Uchitel, Sandra (Joan Follendore Literary Agency)
Urstadt, Susan (Susan P. Urstadt Inc. Writers and Artists Agency)

V
Van Bomel, Ed (L. Harry Lee Literary Agency)
Van Duren, Annette (H.N. Swanson Inc.)
Van der Leun, Patricia (Van der Leun & Associates)
Vandertuin, Victoria (New Age World Services)
Veloric, Philip M. (Philip M. Veloric, Artist Representative)
Verrill, Charles (Darhansoff & Verrill Literary Agents)
Vesel, Beth (Stanford J. Greenburger Associates)

W
Wagner, Matthew (Waterside Productions, Inc.)
Wain, Erika (Erika Wain Agency)
Wales, Elizabeth (Levant & Wales, Literary Agency, Inc.)
Wallace, Bess D. (Bess Wallace Literary Agency)
Wallerstein, Michele (H.N. Swanson Inc.)

Wallerstein, Ms. Gerry B. (The Gerry B. Wallerstein Agency)
Walters, Maureen (Curtis Brown Ltd.)
Ward, Julia (The Bank Street Literary Agency)
Ware, John (John A. Ware Literary Agency)
Warner, Bob (Warner & Associates)
Warshaw, Andrea (Warshaw Blumenthal, Inc.)
Washington, Dick (Washington-Artists' Representatives)
Wasserman, Harriet (Harriet Wasserman Literary Agency)
Watt, Sandra (Sandra Watt & Associates)
Wecksler, Sally (Wecksler-Incomco)
Weimann, Frank (The Literary Group)
Weiner, Cherry (Cherry Weiner Literary Agency)
Weissberg, Elyse (Elyse Weissberg)
Wells, Susan (Susan Wells & Associates, Inc.)
Westberg, Phyllis (Harold Ober Associates)
Western, Carole (Montgomery-West Literary Agency)
Weyr, Rhoda A. (Rhoda Weyr Agency)
Whelan, Elisabeth (Roberta D. Miller Associates)
White, Marta (Scribe Agency)
Whitman, John R. (Kirchoff/Wohlberg)
Whittlesey, Peregrine (Peregrine Whittlesey Agency)
Wieser, George (Wieser & Wieser, Inc.)
Wieser, Olga (Wieser & Wieser, Inc.)
Wilheim, Erin (Arlene Rosenberg)
Williamson, Dean (Dupree/Miller and Associates Inc. Literary)
Wilson, Etta (March Media Inc.)
Winston, Bonnie (Winston West, Ltd.)
Winston, Joan (Sharon Jarvis & Co. Inc.)
Wittes, Naomi (Mildred Marmur Associates)
Wofford, Sally (Elaine Markson Literary Agency)
Wolfe, Deborah (Deborah Wolfe Ltd.)
Wreschner, Ruth (Ruth Wreschner, Authors' Representative)
Wright, Dan (Ann Wright Representatives, Inc.)
Wright, Stephen (Stephen Wright Authors' Representative)

Y
Yost, Nancy (Lowenstein Associates, Inc.)
Young, Elizabeth (Bruce Cook Agency)
Yuen, Sue (Susan Herner Rights Agency)

Z
Zabel, Bruce W. (The Curtis Bruce Agency)
Zeckendorf, Susan (Susan Zeckendorf Assoc.)
Zehngut, Jayne (L.A. Art Exchange)
Zelasky, Tom (Tom Zelasky Literary Agency)
Zhorne, Wendy L. (Forthwrite Literary Agency)
Ziemska, Elizabeth (Nicholas Ellison, Inc.)
Zuckerman, Albert (Writers House)

Listing Index

Other Books of Interest

General Writing Books
   Beginning Writer's Answer Book, edited by Kirk Polking (paper) $13.95
   Dare to Be a Great Writer, by Leonard Bishop (paper) $14.95
   Discovering the Writer Within, by Bruce Ballenger & Barry Lane $17.95
   Freeing Your Creativity, by Marshall Cook $17.95
   Getting the Words Right: How to Rewrite, Edit and Revise, by Theodore A. Rees Cheney (paper) $12.95
   How to Write a Book Proposal, by Michael Larsen (paper) $11.95
   How to Write Fast While Writing Well, by David Fryxell $17.95
   How to Write with the Skill of a Master and the Genius of a Child, by Marshall J. Cook $18.95
   Knowing Where to Look: The Ultimate Guide to Research, by Lois Horowitz (paper) $18.95
   Make Your Words Work, by Gary Provost $17.95
   On Being a Writer, edited by Bill Strickland (paper) $16.95
   Pinckert's Practical Grammar, by Robert C. Pinckert (paper) $11.95
   12 Keys to Writing Books That Sell, by Kathleen Krull (paper) $12.95
   The 28 Biggest Writing Blunders, by William Noble $12.95
   The 29 Most Common Writing Mistakes & How to Avoid Them, by Judy Delton (paper) $9.95
   The Wordwatcher's Guide to Good Writing & Grammar, by Morton S. Freeman (paper) $15.95
   Word Processing Secrets for Writers, by Michael A. Banks & Ansen Dibell (paper) $14.95
   The Writer's Book of Checklists, by Scott Edelstein $16.95
   The Writer's Digest Guide to Manuscript Formats, by Buchman & Groves $18.95
   The Writer's Essential Desk Reference, edited by Glenda Neff $19.95
Nonfiction Writing
   The Complete Guide to Writing Biographies, by Ted Schwarz $6.99
   Creative Conversations: The Writer's Guide to Conducting Interviews, by Michael Schumacher $16.95
   How to Do Leaflets, Newsletters, & Newspapers, by Nancy Brigham (paper) $14.95
   How to Write Irresistible Query Letters, by Lisa Collier Cool (paper) $10.95
   The Writer's Digest Handbook of Magazine Article Writing, edited by Jean M. Fredette (paper) $11.95
Fiction Writing
   The Art & Craft of Novel Writing, by Oakley Hall $17.95
   Characters & Viewpoint, by Orson Scott Card $13.95
   The Complete Guide to Writing Fiction, by Barnaby Conrad $18.95
   Creating Characters: How to Build Story People, by Dwight V. Swain $16.95
   Creating Short Fiction, by Damon Knight (paper) $10.95
   Dialogue, by Lewis Turco $13.95
   The Fiction Writer's Silent Partner, by Martin Roth $19.95
   Get That Novel Started! (And Keep Going 'Til You Finish), by Donna Levin $17.95
   Handbook of Short Story Writing: Vol. I, by Dickson and Smythe (paper) $12.95
   Handbook of Short Story Writing: Vol. II, edited by Jean Fredette (paper) $12.95
   How to Write & Sell Your First Novel, by Collier & Leighton (paper) $12.95
   Manuscript Submission, by Scott Edelstein $13.95

Mastering Fiction Writing, by Kit Reed $18.95

Plot, by Ansen Dibell $13.95

Practical Tips for Writing Popular Fiction, by Robyn Carr $17.95

Spider Spin Me a Web: Lawrence Block on Writing Fiction, by Lawrence Block $16.95

Theme & Strategy, by Ronald B. Tobias $13.95

The 38 Most Common Writing Mistakes, by Jack M. Bickham $12.95

Writer's Digest Handbook of Novel Writing, $18.95

Writing the Novel: From Plot to Print, by Lawrence Block (paper) $11.95

Special Interest Writing Books

Armed & Dangerous: A Writer's Guide to Weapons, by Michael Newton (paper) $14.95

Cause of Death: A Writer's Guide to Death, Murder & Forensic Medicine, by Keith D. Wilson, M.D. $15.95

The Children's Picture Book: How to Write It, How to Sell It, by Ellen E.M. Roberts (paper) $19.95

Children's Writer's Word Book, by Alijandra Mogliner $19.95

Comedy Writing Secrets, by Mel Helitzer (paper) $15.95

The Complete Book of Feature Writing, by Leonard Witt $18.95

Creating Poetry, by John Drury $18.95

Deadly Doses: A Writer's Guide to Poisons, by Serita Deborah Stevens with Anne Klarner (paper) $16.95

Editing Your Newsletter, by Mark Beach (paper) $18.50

Families Writing, by Peter Stillman (paper) $12.95

A Guide to Travel Writing & Photography, by Ann & Carl Purcell (paper) $22.95

Hillary Waugh's Guide to Mysteries & Mystery Writing, by Hillary Waugh $19.95

How to Pitch & Sell Your TV Script, by David Silver $17.95

How to Write & Sell Greeting Cards, Bumper Stickers, T-Shirts and Other Fun Stuff, by Molly Wigand (paper) 15.95

How to Write & Sell True Crime, by Gary Provost $17.95

How to Write Horror Fiction, by William F. Nolan $15.95

How to Write Mysteries, by Shannon OCork $13.95

How to Write Romances, by Phyllis Taylor Pianka $15.95

How to Write Science Fiction & Fantasy, by Orson Scott Card $13.95

How to Write Tales of Horror, Fantasy & Science Fiction, edited by J.N. Williamson (paper) $12.95

How to Write the Story of Your Life, by Frank P. Thomas (paper) $11.95

How to Write Western Novels, by Matt Braun $1.00

The Magazine Article: How To Think It, Plan It, Write It, by Peter Jacobi $17.95

Mystery Writer's Handbook, by The Mystery Writers of America (paper) $11.95

Powerful Business Writing, by Tom McKeown $12.95

Scene of the Crime: A Writer's Guide to Crime-Scene Investigation, by Anne Wingate, Ph.D. $15.95

Successful Scriptwriting, by Jurgen Wolff & Kerry Cox (paper) $14.95

The Writer's Complete Crime Reference Book, by Martin Roth $19.95

The Writer's Guide to Conquering the Magazine Market, by Connie Emerson $17.95

Writing for Children & Teenagers, 3rd Edition, by Lee Wyndham & Arnold Madison (paper) $12.95

Writing Mysteries: A Handbook by the Mystery Writers of America, Edited by Sue Grafton, $18.95

Writing the Modern Mystery, by Barbara Norville (paper) $12.95

The Writing Business

A Beginner's Guide to Getting Published, edited by Kirk Polking (paper) $11.95

Business & Legal Forms for Authors & Self-Publishers, by Tad Crawford (paper) $4.99

The Complete Guide to Self-Publishing, by Tom & Marilyn Ross (paper) $16.95

How to Write with a Collaborator, by Hal Bennett with Michael Larsen $1.00

This Business of Writing, by Gregg Levoy $19.95

Writer's Guide to Self-Promotion & Publicity, by Elane Feldman $16.95

A Writer's Guide to Contract Negotiations, by Richard Balkin (paper) $4.25

Writing A to Z, edited by Kirk Polking $24.95

To order directly from the publisher, include $3.00 postage and handling for 1 book and $1.00 for each additional book. Allow 30 days for delivery.

Writer's Digest Books, 1507 Dana Avenue, Cincinnati, Ohio 45207
Credit card orders call TOLL-FREE 1-800-289-0963

Stock is limited on some titles; prices subject to change without notice.

Write to this same address for information on *Writer's Digest* magazine, *Story* magazine, Writer's Digest Book Club, Writer's Digest School, and Writer's Digest Criticism Service.